EVEN NOW

TWO BOOKS IN ONE

EVER AFTER

Other Life-Changing Fiction™ by Karen Kingsbury

9/11 Series

One Tuesday Morning
Beyond Tuesday Morning
Every Now and Then

Lost Love Series

Even Now
Ever After

Above the Line Series

Above the Line: Take One
Above the Line: Take Two
Above the Line: Take Three
Above the Line: Take Four (summer 2010)

Stand-Alone Titles

Oceans Apart
Between Sundays
This Side of Heaven
When Joy Came to Stay
On Every Side
Divine
Like Dandelion Dust
Where Yesterday Lives
Shades of Blue
Unlocked (Fall 2010)

Redemption Series

Redemption
Remember
Return
Rejoice
Reunion

Firstborn Series

Fame
Forgiven
Found
Family
Forever

Sunrise Series

Sunrise
Summer
Someday
Sunset

Red Glove Series

Gideon's Gift
Maggie's Miracle
Sarah's Song
Hannah's Hope

Forever Faithful Series

Waiting for Morning
Moment of Weakness
Halfway to Forever

Women of Faith Fiction Series

A Time to Dance
A Time to Embrace

Cody Gunner Series

A Thousand Tomorrows
Just Beyond the Clouds

Children's Titles

Let Me Hold You Longer
Let's Go on a Mommy Date
We Believe in Christmas
Let's Have a Daddy Day

Miracle Collections

A Treasury of Christmas Miracles
A Treasury of Miracles for Women
A Treasury of Miracles for Teens
A Treasury of Miracles for Friends
A Treasury of Adoption Miracles

Gift Books

Stay Close Little Girl
Be Safe Little Boy
Forever Young: Ten Gifts of Faith for the Graduate

www.KarenKingsbury.com

KAREN KINGSBURY

NEW YORK TIMES BESTSELLING AUTHOR

EVEN NOW

TWO BOOKS IN ONE

EVER AFTER

ZONDERVAN.com/
AUTHORTRACKER
follow your favorite authors

ZONDERVAN

Even Now/Ever After

Even Now

This title is also available as a Zondervan ebook.
Visit www.zondervan.com/ebooks.

This title is also available in a Zondervan audio edition.
Visit www.zondervan.fm.

Ever After

This title is also available as a Zondervan ebook.
Visit www.zondervan.com/ebooks.

This title is also available in a Zondervan audio edition.
Visit www.zondervan.fm.

Requests for information should be addressed to:

Zondervan, *Grand Rapids, Michigan 49530*

ISBN 978-0-310-33092-9

Published in association with the literary agency of Alive Communications, Inc., 7680 Goddard Street, Suite 200, Colorado Springs, CO 80920. www.alivecommunications.com

Cover Design: Michelle Lenger / Kirk DuPonce, Dog Eared Design
Cover photography: iStockphoto.com
Interior design: Michelle Espinoza

Printed in the United States of America

---

10 11 12 13 /DCI/ 22 21 20 19 18 17 16 15 14 13 12 11 10 9 8 7 6 5 4 3 2 1

EVEN NOW

Dedicated to . . .

Donald, my best friend, my prince charming. The years have flown past, and I'm amazed that we're into our eighteenth year of marriage. I remember our honeymoon and how you'd look at me every few hours and say, "It took so long to get here; I can't believe we're finally married!" That'll teach us to hurry time. With you, Donald, the dance is a beautiful one, sometimes slow, sometimes tapped out at a frantic pace. But I wish the music would go on forever, because every day is better than the last. Can you feel it? How we're entering this new phase of life with teenagers? Stay close by and keep praying! I think we're going to need each other more in the coming years than ever. I love being your wife.

Kelsey, my precious daughter. I had a sudden disconnect the other day when I took you to get your driver's permit. I glanced at the little girl beside me, half-expecting to see a ponytailed sixth grader. Because this is supposed to go on forever, right? The part where I drive you places and we hold deep, meaningful conversations about your friendships and your faith? But instead, there you sat, a willowy young woman with the future shining in your eyes. Has anyone ever been more excited to get behind the wheel of a car? Hmmm. Every minute matters, honey. I'm grateful for the relationship we've shared—and the one that will take us into this next stage of your life. Don't ever forget you're a one-in-a-million girl, Kels. I love you. Shine for Jesus!

Tyler, my oldest son. This has been an amazing year for you, my Broadway boy! A lead part in a professional local theater company? I stand back in awe at how God has brought you from that precocious kindergartner walking around the house in an Annie wig singing "Tomorrow" at the top of your lungs, to the self-possessed young man, serious about shaping your voice and your acting skills so that you can be an even brighter light for the Lord. Your song is still the soundtrack of our lives, Ty. I love you. Keep singing for Him!

Sean, my smiley boy. Everyone who sees you or gets to know you says the same thing: "That kid is always so happy!" You've been home more than four years now, but it feels like you've been here since the beginning. I love your smile and your energy, the way you listen at devotions every morning. You've blossomed in so many ways. God has big plans for you, Sean. Keep trying your best and reaching for the stars! I love you, honey.

Josh, my soccer star. When it comes to picking teams, everyone wants you, and you're the first to explain the reason: "God made me an athlete." The same is true for your brothers, but I have a feeling Jesus will use your athleticism in a very special way. I marvel at your confidence, the easy way you have of excelling in everything from art to keeping your room clean. But the reason I'm most glad you're on *our* team is because of your desire to please the Lord. Everyone else might be asleep, but there you are, a flashlight under the covers, reading your Bible. Keep your determination, Josh. I love you. Keep first place for God and all the rest will come.

EJ, my determined chosen child. Long ago, God could've led us to any of a million little boys who needed a family. But He chose you, and we quickly did the same. You are living proof of how love and determination, boundaries and praise can change someone for Jesus. You have no quit in you, EJ, and I stand in awe at that. I love when you think no one's watching and suddenly you launch into a silly song or dance. My heart delights in knowing that your talents are more than running faster than anyone at school. You make us laugh, and one day I pray God uses you to bring a smile to the faces of many people. I love you. Keep smiling when no one's looking.

Austin, my miracle boy. You will always be my little Isaac, the child we were given and then nearly lost. But sweet boy, you are simply growing up too fast, coming to me more often than before with sweatpants that hit above your ankle. I thank God that you're still a towhead, still adorable with that toothless grin of yours. Yesterday I found a dinosaur on my bathroom floor and I realized you'd been in there an hour earlier. I went to move it, but then I stopped myself and let it stay. My days of dinosaurs on the bathroom floor are numbered. I love watching you run and gun on the basketball court, love hearing the other coaches ask, "Hey, that blond kid who's a head taller than the other boys, is he really in first grade?" I'm so proud of your hustle and the way you listen to your daddy. He's the best coach of all, honey. Now and in the years to come—whether the sport is basketball, baseball, or walking with God. I'm so glad you're healthy and strong. I love you.

And to God Almighty, who has—for now—blessed me with these.

ACKNOWLEDGMENTS

No book comes together without the help of many people. A thanks to my great friends at Zondervan Publishing, including my greatest supporters: Bruce Ryskamp, Doug Lockhart, Sue Brower, Chris Ornsdorff, Karen Campbell, my friends in England, and everyone who has helped make my place at Zondervan so enjoyable. These books are touching and changing lives, and you play a significant part in that. I'm honored to be working with you. A special thanks to my amazing editor, Karen Ball. You continue to challenge me and help me bring glory to God with the gift He's given me. Don't ever stop!

A big thank you to my agent, Rick Christian, president of Alive Communications. I am more amazed as every day passes at your integrity, your talent, and your commitment to getting my Life-Changing Fiction™ out to people all over the world. You are a strong man of God, Rick. You care for my career as if you are personally responsible for the souls God touches through these books. Thank you for looking out for my spiritual growth, my personal time, and my relationships with my husband and kids. I couldn't do this without you.

As always, my book writing depends on the help of my husband and kids, who are so good about eating tuna sandwiches and quesadillas when I'm on deadline. Thanks for understanding the sometimes-crazy life I lead and for always being my greatest support.

Thanks to my friends and family—especially my once-in-awhile assistants, Susan Kane and Tricia Kingsbury, and all of you who continue to surround me with love and prayers and support. I couldn't write without you lifting me to the Lord and covering my work and my family in prayer.

A very special thanks to my mother and assistant, Anne Kingsbury, for having a great sensitivity and love for my readers. Your personal touch is so precious to me—thank you with all my heart. In the same light, thanks to my father, Ted Kingsbury, who remains my biggest supporter. You believed in me way, way back—proof that parents must always encourage the dreams of their child.

Thanks also to my office assistant, Katie Johnson, who stepped in this year and helped me more than I could've imagined. I pray that you will be a part of this ministry for years to come. Also to Nicole Chapman for filling in on days when the tasks were overwhelming, and Katy Head and Tim Head for your assistance in some of the practical aspects of my working day.

And a thank you to God Almighty, the greatest author of all—the Author of Life. The gift is yours. I pray I might have the incredible opportunity and responsibility to use it for You all the days of my life.

EVEN NOW

Prologue

Christmas

It was time.

Emily Anderson had waited all her life for this moment.

The box on the floor in front of her held the hope of a lifetime ... *her* lifetime. Inside could be a window, a glimpse, a pathway to the past, to a time still littered with question marks. But what if it wasn't? What if it was nothing?

For a moment Emily could only sit, stone still, and stare at it. Doubts gathered around her like summer storm clouds. This was her last chance. If the box held only high school mementoes, framed photographs, and old stuffed animals, then she'd know she'd reached her final dead end.

And barring a miracle, her search for her parents would be over.

She laid her hands on the dusty cardboard top and traced her fingers across the words. *Lauren's Things.* The box would be nearly nineteen years old now.

A lump stuck in her throat and she swallowed, forcing it down. "Mom ..." she stared at her mother's name. "Did you leave me a trail?" She closed her eyes and hugged the box. "Please, God, let there be something here."

Downstairs her grandparents were fixing dinner. They'd given her this time. Her tender old papa had found the worn box in the garage stashed away in a cobwebbed corner with a dozen other forgotten cartons. He had known how much it would mean to her, how long she'd been waiting for a breakthrough like this.

"Emily, honey," he'd told her when she came home from college that day. "This belonged to your mother." He held the box in his hands. As tall as she was, she still felt tiny next to him. He had to look around the brown edges of the box to see her. "I'll take it to your room. You'll need some time."

Indeed.

She opened her eyes and stared at the box, hard and long, drilling imaginary holes through the flimsy cardboard. As if maybe she could see inside before she tore into it and found out for sure. Panic tap-danced around her, and she grabbed two quick breaths. What if she went through the whole thing and found no clues at all? Two more breaths. *Come on, Emily. Exhale.* She tightened her middle, pursed her lips, and blew out. *God, get me through this. There has to be something.*

How many times had she prayed for a clue or a sign? A trail that would lead her to her parents, even for a day? Then she could ask them why they'd left and how come they never cared to find out what happened to their little girl?

Emotion flooded her, tightening her throat, closing her eyes. Memories rushed back like forgotten classmates—hateful ones, who used to laugh when you weren't picked at recess.

Suddenly she was in kindergarten again, at the Mother's Day luncheon. She and the other boys and girls had made place mats with bright green handprints and pretty painted flowers coming from the top of every finger. They sang a song, and Emily could hear their young, off-key voices booming out, "Thanks for all you do … Mommy, I love you!"

As with everything around Mother's Day, Emily directed the words to her grandma.

Even back then, she'd known. She was the only kindergartner without a mother. The only one whose mommy left when she was just a few weeks old. Now she watched her kindergarten self as the memory of what happened next played back, every painful detail intact …

"Grandma," she asked, "where is my mommy? Do you know?"

Her grandmother got sort of nervous. "No, sweetie. Papa and I tried to find her but, well, we haven't had any luck."

Emily had felt suddenly lost. Like the day she was at the park and couldn't find her papa. Then an idea came to her. She smoothed her fancy dress and swung her legs, setting her patent-leather shoes in motion. "Maybe *I* could find her!"

"Honey." Her grandma patted her hair. "I don't think she wants to be found."

And that was that.

Emily drew a shuddering breath, relieved that the memory was over. But on its heels came another. The time she was thirteen and all of eighth grade was getting "the talk."

"I feel funny talking about girl stuff in school," she told one of her friends at lunch that day. "Seems like it should be private."

"So talk to your mom." The friend smiled. "Moms are great for that."

The emptiness and loss were so terrible, Emily felt like there was an actual hole in her heart, a hole so thorough she bet her friend could see straight through her. That afternoon, Emily went home and made a promise.

Someday, I'm going to find my parents. No matter what.

Emily brushed a hand across her face, as though she could free her mind from the haunting thoughts. She opened her eyes and stared at the box.

Eventually her grandparents got Internet access. After that there were days of typing in her mother's name—L-a-u-r-e-n A-n-d-e-r-s-o-n—and searching through lists of schoolteachers and scientists and track stars, but never—not in all the thousand entries that popped up, making her breathless with possibility—did she find her mother. Same with her dad. She'd spent hopeless afternoons looking for him any way she could imagine.

And now, at eighteen, she was no closer to finding them than when she first started. What she wanted—what she'd *always* wanted—was the truth. Because the sketchy details she knew made up barely a handful of dots. Nowhere near enough to connect.

Cobwebs stuck to the top of the box, and Emily brushed them off. She let her hands rest on the old, worn carton, wondering. Could it be? Did this box hold the secrets—secrets that would answer the questions that had haunted Emily all her life?

Why did her mother leave? Where was she? Why hadn't she been in touch since she ran away? Had her parents ever connected again?

She gripped the top of the box. Maybe ... maybe she was about to discover enough pieces to put together a trail.

And maybe the trail would lead her to the story.

She couldn't wait another minute as she opened the side flaps. It was really happening; she was about to see her mother's things, touch them and read them and breathe them in. Her heart beat so hard and fast she wondered if her grandparents could hear it downstairs.

She peered inside. The first few items were framed photographs of her parents. Emily reached in, lifting them with careful fingers. Beneath them were yearbooks and folded handwritten letters. Emily's heart jumped. Hours of exploration stretched before her. As she pulled out the contents of the box, she lay each item on her bed, staring at it even as she reached for the next item.

Did the letters hold declarations of love from her dad to her mom, maybe words that explained the feelings they had for each other or their plans for after their baby was born? She would read them later. For now she had to keep digging, because she had to make it through the entire box, just in case.

In case the answers lay somewhere near the bottom.

She reached back into the carton and pulled out another layer of pictures and photo albums, and two-thirds of the way down, a tattered stuffed bear. Only after the bear was removed did she see something that caused her loud, demanding heart to jerk to a silent halt.

Journals. Eight ... maybe ten of them. And beneath those, what looked like notebooks, dozens of notebooks.

Emily rifled through the carton, collecting the journals and placing them on the bed next to the photos, yearbooks, and letters. Then she pulled out the first notebook and opened it. The pages were a little warped and yellowed, filled with page after page of narrative and dialogue. Emily scanned the text and caught her breath.

She'd found it. A missing piece.

Her mother was a writer! She set that notebook on the bedspread and reached for another. This one was thicker, and on the front someone—her mother probably—had written, "*Lauren loves Shane.*" Emily stared at the words and felt the sting of tears in her eyes. Her hands trembled and she ran her thumb over the words.

She slid further back on the bed, until she was leaning against the wall. She propped a pillow behind her and settled in. The clues she'd been hunting for all her life had to be here, buried somewhere between the paper covers of these spiral-bound notebooks. In the stories her mother had written, the stories she'd left behind.

Tales of her parents' love. Maybe the story of their loss. And perhaps even the reason why they'd gone away and left their baby to live without them.

Biting her lip, Emily turned the page.

And then, carefully so as not to miss a single detail, she began to read.

ONE

March 12, 1988

The death of a friendship was usually slow and insidious, like the wearing away of a hillside after years of too much rain. A handful of misunderstandings, a season of miscommunication, the passing of time, and where once stood two women with a dozen years of memories and tears and conversation and laughter—where once stood two women closer than sisters—now stood two strangers.

But Angela Anderson had no time to consider those things, no warning that such a death was about to occur. Because her friendship with Sheila Galanter died a sudden death the afternoon of March 12, 1988, in the time it took Angela to say a single sentence:

"Lauren wants to keep the baby."

That was it. The look on Sheila's face said it all.

Angela's teenage daughter, Lauren, had been in love with Sheila's son, Shane, since the kids were ten years old. Both families were Chicago upper crust with healthy six-figure incomes, known in all the right circles across the city, prominent members at the most elite clubs. Their husbands owned a bank together, and by all estimates the kids' futures were figured out.

On afternoons when Angela and Sheila bared their hearts, snickering about the pompous women they knew, planning trips to London, and complaining about the five pounds they'd gained over the holidays, they sometimes dreamed about their children's future. The engagement that would likely come after college, the ring, and, of course, the wedding.

Then, to leave room for the kids to make up their own minds, they'd laugh about how silly they were and let the dreams pass. But as the years wore on, Shane grew smitten with Lauren, and there seemed more truth than silliness to the possibility. When the kids started their junior year in high school, Shane had—between baseball games—started referring to the impending wedding.

"After I marry your daughter," he'd tell Angela and her husband, Bill, "the four of us can vacation in Mexico." Or he'd look at his own parents and say, "Where should we have the reception?"

Shane's pretentious statements made Lauren blush and kept the adults amused, but secretly every one of them believed it would happen. That one day, sometime after the kids finished university—probably at Wheaton College—after Shane found his place at the family-owned First Chicago Trust, he and Lauren would marry. And the four of them—Angela and Bill, and Sheila and Samuel—would finish their years not only the best of friends and business partners, but family. Family in every sense of the word.

The bombshell came the day before Christmas.

Lauren and Shane called a meeting after dinner. The talk was held at the Galanter house, and Sheila slipped a frozen pie in the oven for the occasion. Whatever the occasion might be.

Lauren looked thin and pale, her light blonde hair almost white against her black cable-knit sweater. "Shane and I . . ." Her mouth hung open and she stared at her tennis shoes. "We have something to tell you."

Shane sat next to her, holding her hand. Their knuckles were tight, their posture tense. Only then did Angela sense that whatever was coming couldn't possibly be good. Shane slipped his arm around Lauren, shielding her. He was tall and dark and rugged looking, a product of his Greek heritage. Lauren seemed even more fair than usual next to him.

"What Lauren's trying to say is—" Shane ran his tongue along his lower lip; his voice trembled—"she's pregnant. It was an accident, but it ..." He looked straight at his father. "It was an accident."

Angela would never forget the silence that cloaked the room. She wanted to reach for Bill's hand, but she didn't dare move, couldn't consider drawing a breath or trying to process the news. It was impossible. Shane and Lauren were good kids, kids who spent less time together than they did practicing their sports—Lauren her sprinting and Shane his pitching and throwing and hitting. They were raised in the church! Maybe they weren't regular churchgoers, but the kids went to youth group every Wednesday, right? Wasn't that supposed to count for something?

Across from the adults, Shane pulled Lauren close and whispered something near her ear. Their faces were masked in fear and shame.

As the first bit of air seeped through Angela's teeth, she glanced at her friend. Sheila sat at an unnatural tilt, frozen. Next to her, Samuel dug his elbows into his knees and hung his head. But it was the look on Sheila's face that caused a ripple of offense in Angela's heart. Sheila was staring at Lauren, her eyes angry and intense, like two lasers drilling into Lauren's being.

It wasn't a look of shock or horror or sorrow. Rather it was a look of blame.

Sheila was the first to speak. "Well—" she stood and smoothed the wrinkles in her dress slacks—"when is the ... baby due?"

Shane blinked. "Uh ..." He looked at Lauren. "Mid-July, right?"

"Yes." She tried to sit a little straighter, but she looked sick to her stomach. She crossed her arms over her midsection and leaned into Shane once more.

Angela wanted to go to her, take her in her arms, and rock away the hurt, like she used to when Lauren was little and came home sad after a hard day. But this was so much bigger. And with everyone watching, going to Lauren would only look like she approved of the situation somehow. *Honey.* Angela gripped the seat of the chair and stayed put, her eyes on Lauren. *Honey, I'm so sorry.*

Again Sheila took the initiative. "Certainly you're much too young to have a baby." She looked at her husband, Samuel, but his eyes were still aimed at the floor. Sheila turned her attention back to Lauren. "You'll be giving the baby up for adoption, is that right?"

Angela wanted to cut in. Why was Sheila acting so harsh? She didn't need to presume anything at this point. Angela held her breath. Shock must be having its way with her friend. That had to be it. Shock was having its way with all of them. How could anyone discuss adoption when they were still absorbing the idea of a baby?

Bill cleared his throat. "Let's not be hasty, Sheila." His tone was gentle, though Angela heard the weight of disappointment in his words. "This is hard for all of us. We need to hear the kids out."

"Actually—" Shane looked from Bill back to his parents—"Lauren and I . . . well, we want to keep the baby. We'll still finish high school, and I'll go to college the way I'd planned." He licked his lips, but his words sounded like they were stuck to the roof of his mouth. "It won't be easy." He looked at Lauren and smoothed his hand over her hair. "But we know we can make it. We're sure."

The anger that sparked in Sheila's eyes next was something new, something Angela had never seen before. Her friend paced to the window, stopped and spun around, all her focus on Shane. "That's the most insane thing I've ever heard."

Angela's head was spinning. All around her people were making sweeping statements, statements that would change the course of their lives forever. Lauren was pregnant halfway through her junior year in high school? She was about to become a mother at just seventeen? How irresponsible and sneaky the kids had been, and how little Shane had cared for Lauren's virtue. As if that wasn't enough shock, Sheila already had the baby signed off and sent to another family. What about Shane's desire to raise the baby and still attend college in a year?

None of it made sense, and in the end—after very little discussion—they could only agree on one thing: any decision on the matter would have to wait. Finally as the group stood, and an uncomfortable silence fell around them, Angela took Bill's hand and went to Lauren. This was her little girl, her only child.

Angela searched her daughter's face. All her dreams for Lauren were gone now, too far gone to salvage. Angela wanted to shake Lauren, scold her for compromising everything she held to be true, scream at her for being a party to the disaster at hand. The news was the worst Angela had ever dreamed possible.

But as bad as it was, it had to be worse for Lauren.

Surrounded by a silence that had gone from uncomfortable to awkward, Angela finally held out her arms and let Lauren come to her. It was Lauren's life that would change the most now, so what option was there but to embrace her and give her the love and support she needed? After a few seconds, Bill put his arms around both of them and joined their tight circle. Angela wasn't sure how long they stayed close like that, but finally they parted and the three of them left.

It took less than a week for Angela and Bill to reluctantly agree that Sheila—though hasty—was probably right. The best choice was for the kids to give up the baby. That way some of high school could be salvaged, and college would still lie ahead. They pulled Lauren aside on New Year's Eve and shared their thoughts.

"We'd like to help you find an adoption agency." Angela put her hand on her daughter's shoulder. "It'd be the best thing for everyone, especially the baby."

Lauren jerked away. "It isn't up to you." Her wide eyes darted from Angela to Bill. "It's not up to Shane's parents, either." Her hand was on her abdomen, as if she were protecting her unborn baby from a life she had little control over. "Shane has a plan. He'll still go to college."

"It won't work, Lauren." Bill crossed his arms, the lines on his forehead deeper than before. He'd spent a lifetime adoring their daughter. Now his eyes made it clear he was hurting, buried beneath the burden of the trouble she was in. "You're too young to raise a child. Where would you live?"

Angela forced herself to remain calm. "Besides, you're a bright girl. You're cheating yourself and your baby if you decide to raise a child now. You should be thinking of college, not how to change diapers."

"I'm a writer, Mother." She strained with every word, her cheeks red. "I don't need school for that."

"Yes, you do." Angela looked at Bill. "Tell her."

"Your mom's right." He put his arm around Lauren's shoulder. "Honey, the timing is wrong. Think of the baby."

Lauren pulled away from him and ran to her room. Her crying filled the house all that week, bringing a somber end to Christmas break. On Sunday, Lauren called Shane and the two talked for hours. When she came out of her room, her eyes were swollen from crying. Angela and Bill tried to talk to her, but she had only a few words for them. "We won't do it." She sniffed and ran her fingers beneath her eyes. "We won't give up our baby."

The discussion wore on every day for weeks after that, though Angela and Bill avoided telling Sheila and Samuel about the kids' decision. School started again, and Lauren and Shane managed to keep their news a secret from their peers. At least three times a week, Sheila Galanter called and gave what felt like an ultimatum: "Talk some sense into her, Angela. I don't want these kids to lose everything over one mistake."

Angela should've seen the signs those first few months of the new year, should've realized what was coming. Sheila's clipped tone whenever she called, the absence of dinner invitations and shared weekend evenings. Most of all, the way things changed between the men. For a decade, investors had come to Bill and Samuel with offers to buy their bank. Once in a while the men would talk about selling and investing the profits in something new, maybe moving their families to the suburbs. But they never seriously considered the idea.

Not until after Lauren and Shane's announcement.

When an offer on the bank came in late January, the four of them decided to sell and move on. Though they talked about heading to the Chicago suburbs, by March the Galanters had a different plan.

"We're moving to Los Angeles."

Angela stared from her friend to Samuel, speechless. They'd stopped by unexpectedly, saying they had something to tell Angela and Bill. Just Angela and Bill.

Not the kids.

"We have other investments there. I know it's a long ways away, but we'll still see each other." Sheila's smile looked forced. "And this way the kids can have a break from each other."

Angela and Bill agonized long hours about telling Lauren, but in the end they kept the news to themselves. The move was still months off, and there was no point fueling the intensity of the kids' feelings for each other. As the Galanters' secret plans quickly came together, Sheila continued her phone calls to Angela. "She's your daughter. Talk some sense into her. These kids don't need that sort of responsibility. Not yet." On another phone call she pushed it further. "Maybe you should tell Lauren we're thinking of moving. Maybe that would change her mind."

Angela was appalled. "You mean blackmail her? Tell her you'll stay if she gives up the baby?"

"I'm just saying it might make a difference. We need an answer, Angela. Tell us what she's going to do."

The entire situation felt like it was attached to one of those odd-shaped bouncy balls, ricocheting out of control. Twice more Angela talked with Lauren about her intentions, but her daughter never wavered.

She and Shane wanted to keep their baby. As soon as they were out of high school, they would marry and start their lives together.

Finally Angela couldn't put Sheila off another day. On March 12, Angela asked her friend over so she could break the news. She served coffee and cream, and they took their places in the Andersons' familiar sunroom.

Angela wasted no time getting to the point. "Lauren wants to keep the baby." She folded her hands in her lap. They were sitting on white wicker furniture, the sun streaming through the window. Bill was at the new bank in Wheaton, an hour out of Chicago, getting things set up. Lauren was at school.

"That's ridiculous." Sheila brushed her hand through the air, erasing Angela's statement. "She's too young to know what she wants."

"Sheila, listen—" Angela searched her friend's eyes—"I can't change her mind. I won't."

At that, Sheila's expression hardened, and her cheeks grew red. "Of course you can, Angela. You're her mother. She's a minor. She'll do whatever you tell her to do."

"You're serious, aren't you?"

"Dead serious." Sheila's voice raised a notch.

"You think I can force my daughter to give away her baby?" Angela squinted at the woman sitting next to her. When had Sheila become so heartless? "She may be a minor, but the baby is *hers.* I can't make this decision for her."

"Of course you can." Sheila set her coffee cup down and slid to the edge of the sofa. Even as her voice fell, her sharp tone sliced through the growing tension. "*My* son has a future. He isn't going to stay here while his pregnant girlfriend has a baby." A fine layer of perspiration broke out across her brow. "Absolutely not."

"His pregnant girlfriend?" Angela laughed, but without a trace of humor. "Is that all Lauren is now? Shane's pregnant girlfriend? Shane had a little something to do with it too."

"Shane's a teenage boy." Sheila spat the words. "If a girl makes herself available, what teenage boy wouldn't take advantage of her?"

A chill passed over Angela. "Listen to you." She stood and looked down at the woman she'd considered her friend. Had she ever really known her? "This is *Lauren* you're talking about."

"No." Sheila raised her hand. Her fingers were shaking. "This is my son's future we're talking about." She sat back a few inches and the lines in her forehead eased. "Be sensible, Angela. The last thing these kids need is more time together. We're both moving the first week of June. Shane's coming with us. That's final." Her hesitation was cool, indifferent.

Angela felt like she'd been kicked in the gut. How had Angela been so wrong about the woman, trusting her all these years? "We've been friends for a long time, Sheila."

"And my son's future will go on far longer." Sheila's tone lightened some. "I'm sorry, Angela. This isn't your fault, it's just—" she narrowed her eyes, intent—"the kids need to be apart."

Her words put their friendship on the firing line. Angela was angry at Sheila's tone and her accusation that Lauren's pregnancy made Shane a victim and Lauren the villain. But suddenly there was more, and Angela was able to look ahead.

In that moment she could stare hard down the road and see what her daughter's life would be like with Sheila Galanter as a mother-in-law.

It would be a life doomed to guilt and shame and never being good enough. The past would forever be brought out and examined, commented on with a series of tongue clucks and disdainful looks in Lauren's direction. The idea made Angela's heart hurt. She would never wish that for her daughter. How *dare* Sheila take that attitude about Lauren, as if Shane were the only one affected by what had happened?

"Okay." Angela straightened in the chair and leveled her gaze at Sheila. "I agree."

Sheila sat all the way back, the fight suddenly gone. "You do?"

"Yes. Completely."

Sheila's voice was almost a whisper. "What about the baby?"

Angela knew the answer as well as she knew her own name. Lauren was going to keep the child. She and Bill would do whatever they could to help Lauren be successful as a single mom. For however long Lauren needed them.

She cleared her throat. "We'll talk to Lauren again. I think you're right. We can convince her about this. Especially if Shane's gone from her life."

Of course, it was a lie. Lauren wouldn't give up her baby. But saying the false words came easily now that she too was ready to cut ties with the Galanters. Angela didn't blink. "That'll be best for everyone."

Relief flooded Sheila's features. "Yes. I'd hate to have a grandchild on the other side of the country and not know about it."

Angela wanted to stand up and shout at the woman. *You* already *have a grandchild growing inside my daughter! You're so blind and vain and empty you'd do anything to protect your son's reputation. Even this.* Instead she stood and motioned to the door. "She'll give the baby up. Don't worry about it." She crossed her arms and took a step toward the backyard. "Now, if you'll excuse me, I have things to do. As you said, there's no point pretending about our friendship."

Sheila looked almost as if she might apologize for making such a statement, but the look passed. She stood, collected her purse and car keys, and headed for the entryway. When Angela heard the door shut it was like gunfire, and something deep inside her heart took its last breath, shuddered, and died. Angela knew exactly what it was.

Her friendship with Sheila Galanter.

Two

Something was wrong with their parents.

Lauren was sitting in Shane's Camry, just outside her parents' house, and she could feel it. Almost like a force, something bigger than the two of them or their families or anything they'd ever come up against. A steady snow had been falling on the windshield for half an hour and now they couldn't see out. It was a picture of their lives, really. Living life on the inside, with no way to see out, no way for anyone else to see in.

Shane gripped the steering wheel with both hands and looked straight ahead at the white nothingness. They'd known each other as far back as they could remember, and Shane was always the first one in a room to smile or tell a joke. But in the last few months he'd grown quiet and anxious, trapped and searching for a way out. "Maybe— " he looked at her, looked straight to her soul— "we should drive off and never look back."

"Maybe." She turned and leaned against the passenger door.

They were supposed to see a movie that night, but instead they drove around town, scared and silent. No one at school knew she was pregnant, but they would soon. She was four months along now. Already she could barely button her jeans. Reality was closing in on them like a vice grip.

A year ago she'd seen a movie with her dad where the main character was trapped in a hallway with no doors and no windows. Scary music pounded from the big screen as the walls began closing in, closer and closer, leaving the guy no way to escape, no way out. Just when it looked like he'd be crushed, he spotted a trap door and got out with his life.

That's the way it was with her and Shane now. The walls were closing in—but there was no trap door. No way of escape in sight.

They never meant to sleep together, but it happened. Not once, but a few times. Only a few times. Lauren stared at her hands. Her fingers were trembling. Proof that she was falling apart a little more every day. She'd fought so hard to get a little freedom from her parents. To get them to trust her. Getting them to let her go alone with Shane to youth group had been a major deal. But finally they gave in. Let her have some freedom.

Maybe too much.

Over the summer, their parents started letting them hang out together in their bedrooms with the doors closed. At first Lauren was thrilled. But now ... She shook her head. What did they think was going on in there? Especially in the past year, since Shane had his own car and didn't take her home until hours after his parents were asleep.

"We trust you," her mother said once. "As long as you're with Shane."

Lauren felt a wave of disgust well up inside her. Why would that make things safe between them? Knowing someone as long as she'd known Shane made it *more* dangerous, not less. They were so comfortable together that giving in, going all the way, seemed like nothing more than an extension of kissing. Until it was over.

The first time, when they were finished and they got dressed, they both were scared to death. "God'll punish us for sure," Lauren told him.

Shane hadn't argued. They skipped youth group that week-—and the next too. After that it was easier not to go, not to look in the faces of their leaders and lie about how well they were doing or how they were praying or reading their Bibles.

The punishment came, all right. A positive pregnancy test six weeks later. Since then everything changed between her and Shane.

Everything but this one fact: they loved each other. And it wasn't just a kid thing. They loved with a realness and a longing that consumed them. Yeah, they'd messed up and they were sorry. One of the youth group leaders knew about their situation, and the guy had met with them and their families a few times to pray and ask for God's wisdom.

But the punishment remained. She was seventeen and pregnant, and her parents' friendship with Shane's parents seemed to have all but disappeared. Their fathers were even breaking up their business relationship. Where would they work once they sold the bank?

Lauren had a hard time breathing whenever she thought about it. She studied Shane again.

His jaw was set, his eyes distant. He hit the steering wheel with his right hand. "I *hate* this." He let his head fall back against the seat. "Something's going on, but not one of them is talking."

"Tell me about the bank again." Lauren's stomach hurt. She leaned over and studied his profile.

Shane closed his eyes. "I heard my dad on the phone. He said something about the sale of the bank, how it would close in a few weeks and then he could make the investment. Some new investment."

Panic made her squirm. "If they're selling the bank, why haven't my parents told me? That's the part I don't get."

For a long time he was quiet, then he turned and let his hands fall from the steering wheel. "Lauren …" His expression softened. "There's more." He took hold of her fingers, sheltering them with his own. His eyes told her more than his words ever could, that he loved her, that he wanted to make this work but he was just a kid and he didn't know how. He ran his thumbs along the edge of her hands.

"What?" Her word was barely loud enough to hear. The inside of her throat was so dry she couldn't swallow right. It was hard to believe there was more, that something else could be wrong.

He hung his head for a moment and then looked her straight in the eyes. "I think we're moving." Fear took over his expression and he blinked it back.

"Moving?" She shook her head slowly, not wanting the word to sink in, not wanting anything to do with it.

"In that same phone call." He swallowed hard. "My dad said something about going to Los Angeles in June, when school was out."

"*LA?*" She grew still, and from somewhere deep inside her she felt the faintest fluttering. "Why … why would they do that?"

His expression was intense, more serious than she'd ever seen it. "I think they're trying to keep us apart." He released her hands and shoved his fingers through his hair. "I don't know what to do, Lauren. I won't let them tear us apart, even if I have to live on the streets, I won't let them."

Her heart raced and her breathing grew shallow. It wasn't real, was it? His family wouldn't move him across the country a little more than a month before their baby was due, would they? "In June?" She gulped, trying to find her voice. "They might move to LA in June?"

He searched her eyes. "I'm sure your parents know. They all know. We're the only ones they aren't telling." His eyes grew watery, and he gritted his teeth. "They can't do this. We need to know their plans so we can fight against them, okay?"

Fight against her parents? When they'd finally accepted the fact that she was keeping her baby? If they didn't have her parents or his parents, who would they have? Who would support them? She wanted to ask Shane, but she bit her lip instead. Her hand came up to his face and she touched his cheek with her fingertips. "I'll find out what I can."

He gave a quick nod and looked at the snow-covered windshield again. His eyes were still serious, as if he were searching through a list of options trying to find one that made sense. Finally he looked at her and gave a sad shake of his head. "I can't believe this."

"Me either." She looked at her watch. It was midnight, time for her to get inside. She leaned close to him and kissed him, slow and tender. They hadn't shared more than an occasional kiss since they found out she was pregnant. Almost as if they'd found a way back to how things had been before Shane had a car, back when holding hands and sharing a once-in-a-while kiss was the extent of their physical relationship.

"Lauren." His eyes had a sweet intensity. "Promise me nothing will change, no matter what they try to do to us."

She needed to get inside, but he still held tight to her hands. Her heart melted and she slid closer, slipping her arms around his neck. "I love you, Shane. I'll never love anyone else."

"I want to be older." He pulled back, his eyes wide and intense. "I wanna wake up tomorrow and be twenty-five, with a college degree and a job and a ring in my hand."

A ring? "A wedding ring?"

"Yes." He framed her face with his hands. "I want to marry you. I always have. This is *our* situation, our problem. But we need to figure it out, even if we *are* young." He was breathing hard, almost frantic with hopelessness. "I'm not letting you go." He kissed her again. "I love you, Lauren. I don't care how old I am; I'll never love anyone like this. Never."

"I love you too, Shane. You won't have to let go. I promise." She spoke the words straight to his heart and when she was sure she'd start crying if she didn't leave, she opened the door and stepped out into the snow. She waved once more as she turned and took light, careful steps up the walkway.

Inside, she leaned against the front door and waited until she heard his car drive away. The worse things got, the more she loved him, the more certain she was that somehow they could handle the days ahead. If only their parents would give them the chance.

Her father's voice came from the den down the hall and she followed the sound. What was he saying? Something about the bank? She slowed her pace. He mustn't have heard her come in. She tiptoed to the edge of the door so she could hear better.

"How far is it from here?" It was her mother's voice. She must've been filing papers, because a rustling sound made it hard to understand her.

"Only about an hour. The town's great, wonderful schools. Lauren can have the baby this summer and start her senior year fresh, no baggage."

"I'm not sure." Her mother sounded skeptical. "If she keeps the baby, we'll have more than prom and college applications to deal with."

"If she does or if she doesn't, I want her to have a fresh start. You know how it'll be around here, Angela. She'll always be the good girl who went and got pregnant with the school's baseball jock."

Anger surged into her veins, but Lauren didn't move. They might have more to say, and she didn't want to miss it.

"Come on, Bill." Kindness filled her mother's tone. "Shane's more than the school's baseball jock."

"I know that." Her father's words were fast and frustrated, like hail in a summer thunderstorm. "But right now the two of them need to be apart. That's what's best for them."

"And Sheila and Samuel found something in LA?"

"Definitely." For the first time in the exchange, her father's voice relaxed some. "They'll be gone by mid-June." He paused. "I never realized how hard it is to work with Samuel Galanter. The man's a control freak, and so's his wife."

"They used to be our friends." Her mother's voice was soft, defeated. "It's like we didn't know them."

"In a few months, we won't." His words sounded pinched. "The nerve of that kid to take advantage of my little girl. We'll see how much time he gets with her once they move to California."

Lauren had heard enough. She burst through the doorway, hands on her hips. "Don't you listen for the door?"

Both her parents opened their mouths, shock written in their expressions. "Lauren!" Her mother was on her feet. She tried a smile, but it died long before it hit her eyes. "No … we didn't hear you come in."

"Obviously." She paced in front of them, looking from her mother to her father and back again. "So you're part of this … this moving to California thing?" Her face was hot.

"We're not part of it." Her mother was at her side, touching her shoulder. "We wouldn't have anything to do with another family moving away, honey."

"But that's it, isn't it?" Her voice was louder than before. She glared at her father. "You and Mr. Galanter sold your bank, and now you're going your own ways. And if that breaks up me and Shane then so be it, right?"

"The Galanters might be moving, yes." Her mother's voice was calm, and that was bad. The more upset her mom got, the calmer her voice. "That plays a factor in what we're doing, obviously. We're selling the bank, so—"

"*Right!*" She was shouting now. "That's what I mean. How come Shane had to tell me? Why didn't I hear anything before this?"

"Watch your tone, young lady." Her father stood and walked closer, his finger pointed at her. "We've been conducting business in this family for years without consulting you. You might be seventeen and pregnant, but that doesn't mean you're an adult, and it certainly doesn't mean you'll be privy to everything your mother and I do."

His tone wounded her, hurt her to the depths of her soul. Shane was right. The sale of the bank, the idea of both families moving, all of it was part of a giant plan to tear them apart. She closed the distance between them and took his hand in hers. "Why, Daddy? Why are you doing this to us?"

He pursed his lips and looked away. When his eyes found her again, they were softer. "There is no *us* when it comes to you and Shane. You're kids, nothing more than children. We're going to save you from yourself, Lauren." His voice was thick. "I love you too much to do anything else."

Her world rocked hard to one side, tilted in a way that made her wonder if it would ever be right side up again. She glanced at her mother, her ally, but she received nothing back. Her mom wouldn't even look at her. One small step at a time, Lauren backed up. Her heart was beating so hard she figured they could hear it across the room. "You won't win this!" Her voice was loud again—loud and shrill.

"You will not talk to us that way, Lauren." Her father's gentleness from a moment earlier was gone. "Go to your room and think about your actions. This is no way for a daughter of mine to act."

She shook her head, stunned. Nothing was making sense, not his words or his expression or his tone of voice. It all ran together and she dropped her voice to little more than a whisper. "You won't win." Wetness filled her eyes, blurred her vision. She couldn't make out the details of her father's face through her tears, but she stared at him anyway. "I love him, Daddy. Selling the bank, moving away ..." Her throat was too swollen to talk.

"Honey." Again his expression eased. "You don't know what love is."

An ache filled her chest and she could no longer draw a breath. Not with the two of them so close, knowing full well that they'd done this, planned against her and Shane this way. Her tone was still quiet, thick with the pain that coursed through her. "No matter what you and his parents do, the two of us will be together. You can't live our lives for us."

She turned and ran to her room. She was about to throw herself onto the bed, when she remembered the baby. The precious little baby. It wasn't his fault or her fault, but here they were. She sat down on the bed and stretched out on her side. With both hands on her middle, she let the tears come.

All she wanted was to love Shane. How had things gotten so crazy, so mixed up? So she and Shane were young. So what? Did that mean they didn't have a right to try to make this work, to figure out a way to raise their child and find a life together? She looked around her room at the pretty furniture and luxury bedspread.

Her parents had more money than they knew what to do with—and so did Shane's—but somehow they'd all missed out on how to *love.* The more she thought about their houses and their cars, the lifestyles they lived, the angrier she got. If they were poor or even average, the way most of her friends were, then this problem wouldn't be nearly as big. Her pregnancy would be a disappointment to them, sure, but she'd stay home and raise her baby, and Shane would visit as often as he could. Then, when they graduated from high school, they'd get married and everything would work out fine.

It was the money—the power and prestige that came with it. *That's* why they were stuck in this situation. Then for the first time an idea came to her, a crazy, wild idea. She had five thousand dollars in a private account, money she could access if she needed it for clothes or a milk shake. What if she and Shane ran away together? What if they took the money and set out on their own? That could work, couldn't it?

But even as the idea took root, it died. She couldn't run away with Shane. Not when she was expecting a baby. She needed medical care *and* her parents' help if she was going to learn how to be a mother. Still, the thought wouldn't quite go away. And as she lay there, as she stared at the ceiling and thought about Shane and their uncertain future, the movie scene came to mind again. The man in the hallway with the walls closing in, the trap door that had allowed him to escape.

That was them, wasn't it? Exactly like their situation. As she fell asleep she thought about the place they were stuck in, and how the walls were closing in on their plans and their time together. There had to be a way out, didn't there? She could wait until her baby was born and take her money then, right? The thought came to life again and the slightest bit of peace filled her heart.

Yes, the walls were closing in. But maybe—just maybe-—their prison might have a trap door too.

Three

Shane Galanter felt like he was drowning.

His mind was stuck on something that happened a few summers back, a terrifying memory that actually fit his life now. He'd been sailing with some friends on Lake Michigan, and the guys took turns diving off the sailboat and swimming fifty yards out and back. Someone had a stopwatch, so it became a competition. One swimmer would best another's time by a few seconds, and everyone would try it again.

Shane was on his third swim out from the sailboat when a strong wind came up. It hit him just about the time his energy ran out. And suddenly there he was — a mile from shore, fifty yards out from the sailboat, paddling toward the vessel and not making any headway at all.

"Help!"

But his shout was lost on the wind. His friends had their backs to him, all but the guy holding the stopwatch. And even he wasn't watching.

Shane kicked harder and harder, but didn't get any closer to the boat. About that time, a wave hit him in the face, and he sucked in a mouthful of water. That's when he realized what was happening. He was starting to drown, right in plain sight of his friends. He was taking in water and sinking a little more every few seconds, spending all his energy and not making any progress.

Suddenly one of his friends stood up and pointed at him. "Hey! Galanter's in trouble!"

Another wave hit him and he swallowed a mouthful of water. The guys adjusted the sails and four of them started paddling. In a few minutes they reached him and pulled him into the boat.

He still remembered how he felt. Remembered swallowing the water, feeling his strength leave him, knowing he wasn't going to make it.

Just like now.

He was in over his head, but this time with no boat or shore or help in sight. One thing was sure, though. If he was going to drown, he wanted to know the details. Every single one of them. When he got home from baseball practice, he searched out his father and found him in his home office on the second floor. Shane walked in and closed the door behind him, just as his father looked up from a stack of papers. He had a pencil tucked behind his ear and a smile on his face.

"How was practice?"

Shane stared at him, stunned. "How was practice?" He gave a bitter laugh. "My girlfriend's pregnant and my parents are having some kind of midlife crisis, and you ask me how was *practice?*" He removed his baseball cap and smoothed his hand over his hair. "Distracting, okay, Dad? How's that for an honest answer?"

His father turned his chair in his direction and crossed one leg over the other. "Okay, Shane." He pointed to the leather sofa next to his desk. "Sit down. Looks like you want to talk."

"Not really." The anger was a part of him at this point. It was there when he woke up and when he lay back down. "I *have* to talk. There's a difference."

"Okay." His father gave a thoughtful nod. "Why don't you tell me what's on your mind?"

Shane sat on the edge of the sofa and dug his elbows into his knees. His eyes locked on his father's. "Why don't *you* tell me about California?"

Surprise filled his father's features. No question he'd caught the man off guard. His dad took a moment to recover, then frowned that practiced sort of frown. The one Shane so often saw him use with his mother when things didn't go his way. "We have investments there, son. You know that."

"We've lived here twelve years and never once have you talked seriously about moving to California." Shane kept his voice controlled. It wouldn't get him anywhere to lose his temper, even if his blood was boiling.

"You're a child, son." His dad squinted, stopping just short of being condescending. "We don't talk to you about everything."

Shane's heart slammed against his chest. "So it's true? We're moving to Los Angeles?"

For a moment his father hesitated, as if maybe he might deny it or try to buy a little more time. But finally he exhaled hard and gave a slow nod. "Yes." He brought his lips together and nodded slower this time. "In June."

"We can't!" Shane was on his feet, ready to kick something. "Dad, that's a month before the baby comes."

"In my day that would've made June the perfect time to move." The moment his dad's harsh words were out, regret shone in his eyes. He opened his mouth and closed it again. Then he pressed his fist to his forehead and looked at Shane. "I'm sorry. That came out wrong."

Shane sat back against the sofa. "It came out just how you meant it to come out. You're moving so I won't stay with Lauren."

"That's not it." His dad sounded tired, discouraged. "We've been talking about selling the bank for awhile, and a good offer came in." He tossed his hands up. "It was time. What else can I say?"

"Why California, Dad?" Shane uttered a sad chuckle. "Why not move to the suburbs, like Lauren's family? You could invest here, couldn't you?"

"We already have investments in California." His father stood and walked to his bookcase. He took a framed photograph from the top shelf and stared at it—Shane's first-grade baseball photo. He turned and met Shane's eyes again. "This is not how your mother and I pictured your life, son. Expecting a baby before your senior year in high school. Can you understand that?" He put the picture back on the shelf. "We only want the best for you. You and Lauren and the baby. All of you."

"Okay." Shane was on his feet again. His blood was hotter than before, and he was breathing harder. "Help me understand how tearing us apart is good for anyone."

When his dad didn't say anything, Shane turned and stormed out of the office. He had to find Lauren, had to reach her and tell her the truth. His parents were moving him to California; they had to find some way to keep him here, close to her. Maybe if he asked her to marry him now, maybe that would do it. Then they could be together through their senior years, he could go to college and one day he could become a pilot, as he'd always dreamed.

He didn't have much. His car, any money he had—it all belonged to his father. Except his birthday money, maybe four hundred dollars saved up in a box under his bed. He jogged to his room, pulled out the box, and grabbed the handful of bills. A quick count told him it wasn't quite that much, but it was enough.

Their parents couldn't separate them if they were engaged, could they? His parents or hers, *some*one would have to come to their senses and let the two of them stay together. That way they could share the early days with the baby, and when they graduated they could have a wedding.

His mother was shopping, so it was just him and his father at home. Shane stuffed the money in his wallet and shoved his wallet in the pocket of his jeans. Then he tore down the stairs, jumped in his car, and drove to the mall. They always had deals on rings at the mall, didn't they? He knew her ring size, because a few months before she got pregnant they were seeing a movie at the mall and before the show started they stopped in at a jewelry store. It was all pretend and silliness, but he remembered her size. Six. The lady had said Lauren had beautiful, slender fingers. He parked and ran inside. The first jewelry store he saw, he walked straight in and up to the sales clerk.

"I need a ring." He was out of breath. The money felt like a million dollars in his pocket.

"Very well." The woman was older, with soft wrinkles across her cheeks and forehead. "Is this a promise ring, young man?"

He was about to tell her no, that this was an engagement ring. But before the words would come, he realized how they would sound. Ridiculous, that's how. He was just seventeen, and most people told him his baby face made him look younger than that. He met the woman's eyes. "Uh, yes. Yeah. A promise ring." He managed a nervous smile. "Anything like that?"

The woman stood and led him to a section in the glass cabinet with smaller rings. Some of them had white little stones on them, and others had pink or blue. A few had what looked like diamonds. He lifted his eyes to the woman. "I want something real."

"Okay." She smiled again. "A diamond, then?"

"Yes." Definitely a diamond. He'd loved Lauren Anderson since he was in fourth grade. She made him feel things he'd never felt before. She was fun and witty and his best friend of all. Nothing less than a diamond.

"Very well, have you thought of what size stone?" She folded her hands and tilted her head to the side. "Diamonds come in many sizes. Full carat, half, quarter, and so on."

Shane's eyes lit up. "Let's try the full carat." His mother had something like that. A full carat would make a nice ring for Lauren.

"All righty then." She opened the case from behind and pulled out a velvet pad with eight rings stuck into separate sections. Each one glistened and shot colors across the glass counter. "They start at fifteen hundred dollars."

He felt suddenly ill. The smell of mall popcorn and cinnamon buns filled the air, making him queasy. He looked at the woman and gave a tight shake of his head. "Not that big." His shoulders fell a little. "I have three hundred and eighty dollars."

"Well." The woman returned the tray of brilliant rings back to the counter. "We have something in that range. It'll be a circle of maybe some crusted diamond chips. Something totaling about a quarter carat."

The rings she brought out this time were much smaller, without the shimmer. He tried not to frown at them, but he couldn't help it. "Hmm." Then he had an idea. Excitement rang out in his voice in a way he couldn't stop. "Can you engrave them?"

"Definitely. It'll be an extra twenty dollars." She looked over her shoulder at an older man sitting behind a glass partition. "You're in luck. My husband does all the engraving. He can get it done in a few minutes, if you have time to wait."

"Perfect." His palms were sweaty. He rubbed them on his jeans. "I'll wait right here."

She helped him pick out a size six ring that would work with his budget, even with the cost of engraving. The ring was small. The diamonds made a crusty little heart at the center and the band was white gold. But it was pretty, and it would serve the purpose.

While he waited he thought of the talks he'd heard at youth group since he and Lauren had slept together. Just the day before there'd been one. Lauren wasn't there—her parents didn't let her go anymore. But the message hit him straight in the heart. One of the youth pastors had taken two sheets of construction paper, one red, one blue.

"These represent you and your girlfriend." He held them up and looked around the room. Then he took a bottle of white glue and drizzled it over the back side of one of the pieces of paper. He pressed the two pieces of paper together, back to back. "This is what happens when you and your girlfriend have sex."

He set the glued-together papers down on his podium and spent twenty minutes talking about the body, how God had asked His people to set aside their bodies as temples for the Holy Spirit, and how sexual immorality was never right for God's people.

"Basically ..." The guy smiled. Shane really liked him. He was younger than the main ministers and he talked like one of the guys. "Basically sex is a great thing. But it's only great because God thought it up, and it's only great when the people having sex are married. Because that was God's plan from the beginning." He grew more serious. "Any other sex is sin because God says so. And He says so for our own good. Sex outside of marriage hurts us. It always will, whether we think so or not."

He walked back to the podium and picked up the two glued-together pieces of paper. Then he took hold of the corners of each sheet and slowly pulled them apart so that the fronts of the paper faced the kids in the audience. "See?" He kept pulling until they were completely separated again. "Looks okay on the outside. That's why so many of you think, 'No big deal. I have sex with my girlfriend, so what? We aren't hurting anyone.' "

The room was silent, the kids staring at the two pieces of paper. It felt like everyone in the room knew what was coming. The pastor turned the pieces of paper over. The red piece was gooey and ripped up, with small sections of blue stuck to it. On the blue piece, small bits of red clung in sections. Both pieces were an ugly mess.

"See." He held the sheets of paper up a little higher. "God tells us to wait until marriage because sex outside marriage hurts us. Sometimes it hurts in a way everyone can see. And other times it hurts in ways only God and us ever know about. The bottom line is this: sex outside marriage will scar us, and we will never, ever be the same again."

The man's words faded from Shane's memory. He blinked and spotted a group of kids his age walking past the jewelry store. They were from another high school, the rivals a few miles east. Two of the girls and three of the guys wore letterman jackets. All of them looked happy and carefree.

He wanted to shout at them, "Don't do it! Don't be alone together, don't take chances, don't do things your way! The Bible's right about sex!" But he only watched them walk off, laughing and teasing and enjoying high school life the way it was meant to be enjoyed.

Shane turned and faced the older couple working over his ring. Why hadn't he listened? What made him and Lauren think they could beat the odds or get away with something that was so wrong? The bench he was sitting on was cold and uncomfortable, the same way he felt inside. He stood and wandered out into the mall. If only there was a way to go back, to tell God they were sorry and they needed a second chance ...

Not that he didn't want the baby. He did. He wanted the baby and Lauren and the life they'd have together. But he wished like crazy they'd listened to God. He stared up through a glass window in the roof of the mall. *God ... we need you so bad. Please ...* He glanced back at the store, at the couple working on his ring. *Please let this work out.*

A verse came to mind, one that the youth group leader wore once in a while on a T-shirt. It was written in big pink letters on a funky pale green background and it said, "I know the plans I have for you."

He hadn't been in church all that much—his parents were never very good at making Sunday service—but he knew the verse anyway. It was a favorite among the kids because it talked about the very thing they all worried about—tomorrow. "'For I know the plans I have for you,' declares the Lord, 'plans to prosper you and not to harm you, plans to give you hope and a future.'" It was from Jeremiah 29:11.

He sighed, and it rattled all the way to his knees. Just then, the old woman gave him a little wave and a nod that told him the ring was ready. He went to the counter and studied it. The words he'd asked them to engrave were the words that summed up how he felt about this season in their lives.

Even now.

Even now, when Lauren was seventeen and pregnant, when their future and the future of their baby hung in the balance, he loved her. He loved her the way he always had, with a singleness and a focus. Even now, because no matter when she would see the ring or read the inscription on the inside of the band, it would be true. Even now, when they were struggling; even now, when they were not sure how to get from today to tomorrow. Even now . . . he loved her.

No, they hadn't done things right. But he would stand by her. He would stand by her as long as the sun came up in the morning, as long as spring followed winter. He paid for the ring, and the woman slipped it in a little velvet gray box.

"I think your girlfriend will love it," the woman was saying.

In the background, her husband gave him a wink. "Young love is so precious."

Shane bit his lip. If they only knew. He thanked them, tucked the bag tight into his coat pocket, and left the mall. Since he was in sixth grade he'd wondered what it would be like to ask Lauren Anderson to marry him. He'd planned to take her to a beautiful mountaintop or a sandy beach overlooking the ocean. He'd get down on one knee and tell her how his life wouldn't be complete unless she was his wife.

But there was no time for anything like that now.

It was mid-April, and his parents wanted to move him to Los Angeles in two months. He needed to set his plans in motion now, to find a way to keep them together. He was the man, after all. It was his job to take care of her and the baby, and he certainly couldn't do that from three thousand miles away.

He drove to her house and knocked on her door. That was something new also. He used to give a quick knock and walk straight in. But these days he felt ... not quite welcome. Lauren's mother looked out a side window and he heard her yell for Lauren. After a few minutes she came to the door, her eyes wide.

"I didn't know you were coming." Her sweatshirt was oversized, pulled down around her jeans.

The idea of her pregnancy starting to show sent a wave of fear over him. More proof that he really was drowning. He glanced at the window, but her mother was no longer standing there. "Hi."

"Hi." She stepped out onto the porch and crossed her arms. Her eyes were sad—the way they usually were lately—but a smile tugged at the corners of her lips. "I felt the baby move today."

"You did?" A sense of wonder filled his heart, and it bubbled with life and awe and overwhelming love all at once. He wasn't sure what to say. This should've been something they celebrated under the same roof, ten years from now, when they were married and old enough to have children the way they'd planned. Still, the life within her was *their* child. Too young or not, that baby was growing bigger every day. He reached out and touched his fingers to her stomach. It felt hard and just a little rounder than before. His eyes lifted and he looked straight at her. "What did it feel like?"

"Like butterfly wings." She giggled. "I think it's a girl, Shane." She shrugged with one shoulder, and suddenly she looked like the sweet, silly girl he'd fallen for so many years ago. "I can picture her fingers tickling the inside of my stomach. That's what it felt like."

"Wow." He crossed his arms again and shook his head. "I can't imagine."

"You're the first person I've told." She lowered her chin, her eyes big and a little shy. "I wish you could feel it. It's the most amazing thing."

"Me too." He shifted his weight and stuck his hand in the pocket. The one where the ring box lay deep inside. It was too cold to go for a walk, and inside her house had too much tension. They weren't ready to go out on a date, but an urgency pressed in on him. If he didn't ask her now, another day would slip by—another day when they wouldn't have a plan or a way to stay together even if his family moved to Mars.

He coughed once and raised his shoulders up near his neck. "It's cold out here."

"Yeah." She didn't invite him in. Another bad sign. "Wanna talk in your car?"

It was the perfect idea. "Definitely." He grinned at her, but stopped short of kissing her. Her mother might be somewhere, watching.

The sun was fading, and the snow that had melted in the late afternoon had grown icy and slippery. They took careful steps to his car and climbed into the front seat, him behind the wheel and her next to him. When they were inside, her smile faded. "Is it something else? Something about our parents?"

"No, nothing like that." Shane felt a lump in his throat. Until Lauren's pregnancy, he couldn't remember ever crying. But in the past few months he'd felt tears in his eyes several times. This was one of them. "Lauren ..." How was he supposed to do this? It wasn't anything like he'd always dreamed it would be. Still, he couldn't have meant it any more if he'd flown a banner from the top of the Empire State Building.

She had a funny look on her face, almost a smile but not quite. "What is it, Shane?"

He gulped. Then he pulled the small gray velvet box from his pocket and held it out to her. Her eyebrows lifted, and she looked from the box to him and then back to the box. He opened the lid and showed her the ring inside. His voice cracked as he asked her the question, the emotion leaking in between every word. "Marry me, Lauren. Not today or tomorrow. But as soon as we can, okay? I'll still go to college and I can become a pilot." He released a nervous laugh. "I always wanted to fly, remember?"

"Shane!" She was staring at the ring. She put her fingers over her mouth. Then she reached for it and stopped short. "Do you wanna take it out? So you can put it on my finger?"

He laughed, and it sounded nervous even to him. This wasn't going exactly the way he'd planned. His eyes met hers. "Does that mean you're saying yes?"

"Oh." She gasped and gave a little giggle. "Sorry." Her eyes grew suddenly serious and she sat up straighter, smoothing the wrinkles in her sweatshirt. "Yes, Shane. I'll marry you."

"Good." He smiled, laughing a little now, too. He took the ring from the box and dropped it. "Oops."

The ring bounced on his emergency brake handle and slid down under the seat. "I think I can get it." She eased her hand down the crack next to the seat and felt around for a few seconds. "Hmm. Do you have a flashlight?"

Shane was trying to hold back, but he couldn't. Not for another minute. The laughter came slowly at first, in quiet bursts. When she saw that he'd given into the humor of the moment, she laughed too. Pretty soon they were both laughing hard, their heads back against the seats. "You know something?" Shane caught a breath and wiped at his eyes.

"What?" She was still giggling. Her words didn't come easily.

"This is how it'll be if we're married." He laughed again. "Lots of mistakes."

"But we'll—" she drew a long breath and her laughter faded--"we'll learn together. That's what'll make it work."

"That and something we should've had from the beginning." He was calmer now, the laughter gone from his voice. "God in the middle of everything."

"Yes." A shadow fell over her face. "You think He forgives us? I mean, you think He's done punishing us?"

"I don't know if this was a punishment, Lauren." He put his left hand on the steering wheel and cocked his head in her direction. "You getting pregnant, that was a consequence. Okay, maybe it was a punishment too. But it was something that happened because we invited it to happen."

"You mean—" her expression took on a hopeful look—"you think God still cares about us? After what we did?"

"Yes, I think He still cares. Listen to what I heard yesterday."

For the next half hour he told her about it, about the blue paper and the red paper and how they looked after they'd been glued together. Then he told her the rest of the pastor's message. The point was clear. Yes, they might mess up. Some of them in that room had probably already messed up, he told them. The point was to take those mistakes to God, tell Him you were sorry, and then move on in His strength and light, along His path. "See—" he took her hands in his—"we have to find that ring because I want to marry you, Lauren. Then we'll be one again and, well, our backsides won't look so messed up."

"Okay." She giggled again, but she didn't say much about his story. Shane understood. She was bound to feel guilty, and that meant she didn't feel close to God. Not that she ever really had. They were just getting close to Him when this happened. He swallowed back the desire to say anything else. She would feel close to God eventually. If they were married, he was sure about that.

Because with every day he felt surer he couldn't get by without the Lord.

"I'll try once more." She eased her fingers down along the side of the seat and felt around for half a minute. Her eyes lit up then, and she pulled the ring out and held it in the air. "Here you go." She looked at it, then at him. "It's beautiful. Now you can put it on."

"Read it first." He pointed. "There, on the inside."

She held it in the glow of the streetlights. "'Even now'?" She looked at him. Then she held up the ring and read it again. As she did, an understanding came into her eyes. She hesitated some more, and as she looked at him this time, she blinked back tears. "Even now, we have this, right? What we've always had together?"

"Yes. I love you, Lauren Anderson. Even now, when everything in life feels crazy. I love you no matter what."

He took the ring from her, and as he slipped it on her finger, they were both smiling. It was a good sign, a glimpse of hope that maybe they would find their way together and work things out. Maybe one of their sets of parents would let them marry after high school and offer them a room. And yes, their start would be rough. There would be goofs and laughs and awkward moments, for sure. But they would have each other.

The ring—even with its small bits of crusted diamonds-—shimmered in the fading light and Shane took her hand, running his thumb over the white gold. For the briefest moment, it wasn't an engagement ring at all, but the tiniest, most miniature, life preserver. Something to cling to so that just for a moment he could keep his head above water. So the drowning feeling would go away and he could know that God did indeed love them and forgive them. That together they had a future and a hope waiting for them.

Even now.

FOUR

Angela Anderson was beyond worried.

The kids had talked about wedding plans every day for a month now, and nothing was changing their minds. Clearly they had a plan to convince both sets of parents, and they'd started with her and Bill.

"We want to get married." Shane stood straight and tall, Lauren beside him, when they broke the news. "We're engaged. We need to be together." He hesitated. "If my parents move away, I'd like to ask if I could live here, in the spare bedroom, until I turn eighteen this fall." He swallowed hard. "Then we can get married."

Bill took a deep breath and lit into the kid. "First of all, you're *not* engaged, and you're *not*— "

"Yes, we are, Daddy!" Lauren stepped forward and held up her left hand. It was the first time they'd seen the ring, and both Angela and Bill were silent for a moment. "We're engaged, and we have to be together. Shane's right."

"Do not interrupt me, young lady!" Bill continued his tirade. "You're not engaged because you're too young. You're not going to live together and you're not going to get married the summer before your senior year in high school." He lowered his voice. "None of this is going to work. You need to understand that before another day goes by."

The argument raged, and Angela could feel her heart breaking. Her husband's expression was beyond angry, but she could see his fear. He'd confided to her that he was afraid he was losing Lauren.

"We used to be so ... so close." He stared out their bedroom window. "Sometimes I wonder if I've lost her for good."

Now his words haunted her, even as he fought with their daughter. And the pain didn't stop there. Shane's face was marked with disappointment, and a gut-wrenching despair filled Lauren's eyes. Their daughter wanted this as badly as Shane did, that much was clear. So what about that? Were she and Bill doing the right thing by forcing their daughter and the boy she loved to part? By giving them no way to make it work?

Finally Shane and Lauren left, but Lauren tried again twice more that week. With each conversation, Angela's doubt grew, and over the next month it caused a quiet crack in her facade of certainty. Shane tried his parents too, and of course they wanted nothing to do with the plan. No way on earth Lauren was moving with *them*, out west. And so, without the help of either set of parents, the kids really didn't have a choice.

Shane didn't have a car of his own or money or a place to stay. For a week or so he talked about quitting school and taking a job at the greasy chicken joint down the street. Then, according to Lauren, his father helped him do the math, showing him that even if he worked sixty hours a week he couldn't afford an apartment, a car, and food. Let alone support a wife and a baby. No, the kids didn't have a chance of staying together without help.

But that wasn't the only issue that kept the weeks through mid-May tense and painful. Sheila called every few days. Whereas in the past they would make small talk and find things to smile and laugh about, now the conversations were about one thing only.

"So—" Sheila's tone seemed harder with each call—"has she decided to give the baby up for adoption? That's what she needs to do, Angela. You said it was going to happen. You can force her hand in this, you know."

Angela released a heavy breath and explained, yet again, that the decision had to be Lauren's and Shane's. Of course she'd recommended that the kids give the baby up. That would seem the most logical, kindest thing for everyone involved. "But you're missing something here," she finally told Sheila.

"What's that?"

"Our kids love each other. They have for a very long time."

Sheila made a sound that suggested she couldn't have disagreed more. "They don't know what love is."

You don't know what love is. That was the phrase being bandied about among all the adults. Even Angela wanted to go with that. It was neat and tidy and gave them a reason to control the kids, figure things out for them. They didn't know what love was.

But what if they were wrong?

That fear stuck like a thorn in her conscience, and no matter how she tried to work past it or look around it, she couldn't dislodge it. By mid-May, Lauren was seven months pregnant and showing. Angela wanted her daughter to quit school so the kids wouldn't talk. Lauren explained that the kids would talk anyway, and she was right. By then everyone in their circle knew she was pregnant.

What made it more painful for Angela was the loss of Sheila's friendship. The woman had been like a sister, the one she'd shared her deepest insecurities with, her greatest joys and fears. Now Sheila grew less considerate, more accusing of Lauren and even Angela, and finally Angela made a decision. She had to spare her daughter a lifetime of being hated by Shane's family. The two were going to be apart—that much was already decided. The relationship they shared was all but over. Now it was up to Angela to keep Lauren from desiring a place in a family where the parents wanted nothing to do with her. She knew what she had to do next, and it was for Lauren's own good. Because she loved her.

On Saturday afternoon that week, Angela invited Sheila over, and the two of them sat down in the sunroom again. She studied the other woman, choosing her words with care. "Sheila, I know what you're hoping. You're hoping Bill and I were able to talk Lauren into giving the baby up for adoption."

"Yes." Sheila folded her hands in her lap. She was careful not to look too long into Angela's eyes. "It's craziness for a girl her age to keep a baby, Angela. We've been over all this." She paused. "So ... is that why you called me here?"

"No." Angela took a slow breath and steadied herself. She had thought this through for days and now she believed it was all they had, the only chance of moving forward. "It's about the kids, about our moves coming up next month."

"Our moves?" Sheila looked up and for a fraction of a moment, the old Sheila shone through. The one who was kind and open-minded, the one who would listen and offer support no matter the subject. Every subject except this one.

"Yes." Angela poured them each a cup of coffee. She took a sip of hers and sat it back down again. Bill was out supervising a work crew doing maintenance on some trees near the new bank building in Wheaton. Lauren was up in her room writing, something she did more than ever. Angela closed her eyes and willed herself to move forward with the plan. "I think we should wait at least a month before exchanging phone numbers. After we move, I mean."

Sheila made a face, but gradually the lines in her face eased. "What'll we tell the kids? That we don't want them to talk?"

"No, nothing like that." She lowered her voice. The last thing she wanted was for Lauren to hear her. "We can blame it on the phone company. It can take weeks to set up phone service. That way it'll give Lauren a chance to have the baby and think things through without the pressure of talking to Shane every day, trying to do things as if they were still a couple."

Sheila's arms relaxed to her sides and her face looked almost pleasant. "I like it." She looked at Angela, her eyes imploring her to understand. "I'm glad you're helping me on this. I mean friendship aside, we have to care about our kids. They're too young to be together this way."

"You're right." Angela wasn't so certain, but this was all she and Sheila had left now, a series of actions and reactions, a practice in going through the motions. "Let's see if we can keep them apart for a month, month and a half."

"So when we get to LA—and Shane *is* coming with us to LA, regardless of what he thinks—I give you our new number, but you don't give it to Lauren until forty-five days later. You call me with your new number, but I don't give it to Shane for the same period. Something like that?"

"Exactly."

"I like it a lot. It's a good plan."

"It is. I feel the same as you. They need time apart." The lie made Angela wince. Lauren and Shane would disown them for life if they could hear this conversation. This meeting wasn't about making Sheila happy or believing that the kids were better off staying away from each other. It was about protecting Lauren from the hostility that Shane's family held toward her. For that, she would lie even if it meant hurting Lauren in the short term. She looked at Sheila. "It's only for a month, maybe six weeks. After that they can catch up and we'll see what happens."

Sheila was already on her feet. "Very well." She looked at her watch. "I can't stay. I have a church dinner tonight." Her eyes met Angela's one last time. She stopped short of flashing that phony smile Angela had seen too often in the past months. Instead she let the corners of her mouth raise just a little. "This isn't easy for any of us, Angela." She paused. "Please let us know if you get anywhere with Lauren. There are so many wonderful families waiting to adopt children. It would be a great sacrifice if Lauren would consider it."

Angela wanted to spit at her. A great sacrifice for Lauren? Yes, and a great victory for Sheila. Angela took a few steps toward the door and held it open wide so Sheila wouldn't stay longer than necessary. Then, since she was on a roll, she told yet another lie. "I was right about adoption, Sheila. Lauren's leaning more toward it every day."

"She is?" Sheila's eyes sparked to life, the same way they did when Bloomingdale's announced a storewide sale.

Angela felt sick to her stomach. She bit her lip and nodded. "Yes. I'm almost positive."

Sheila left, spouting platitudes and half smiles, making comments about things being meant to be and life working out for the best and how every change was like another season meant to be savored and how nothing stays the same anyway.

The silence after Sheila left gave Angela her first peaceful moment all morning. She sat down on the sofa, leaned back, and closed her eyes. She'd done it. She'd convinced Sheila to stay out of her life, out of her daughter's life. At least for a month or more. That meant Lauren could have her baby in peace, without constant phone calls and directives from Sheila about why the baby should be given up and when.

As she sat there, everything about the morning meeting felt right except one thing, the same thing that had troubled Angela for much of the past month: What if the kids' love didn't fade away? What if Sheila and all the adults were wrong? What if age didn't determine whether or not a person could truly understand what love was and whether it was real?

Angela folded her arms and gripped her sides. They were teenagers; of course they would move on. They'd be heartbroken for a season. But they'd get past their grief and given a month or so of separation, they might reevaluate and decide it was better to take time away from each other. In fact, if that happened, Lauren might indeed decide to give her baby up for adoption. And yes, everyone would win in the process.

She blinked her eyes open, stood, and padded her way up to Lauren's bedroom. She did a light knock on the door.

"Come in." Lauren sounded tired and distracted. Shane had baseball all that day, so she'd spent most of the afternoon in her room writing.

"What're you working on?" Angela sat on the edge of her daughter's bed. The memory of her conversation with Sheila burned in her mind. She felt like a traitor.

"A short story." She held up a blue notebook. "I have lots of them."

"What's this one about?"

"A little girl named Emily. She's a princess in a faraway land, where everyone else is a rabbit or a bear or a fox. She goes all her life not knowing where to find her prince until she meets a special woman on the other side of the mountains."

"Hmm." Angela nodded. "I love your imagination."

"Even without a college degree?" She smiled at her mother. The ring Shane gave her was still on her finger, the two of them still believing that somehow one set of parents would give in and let them stay in the same house for the next six months. As Shane had pointed out the week before, they could even get married *now* with their parents' permission. Not that anyone was about to grant that.

Angela stayed silent for awhile and Lauren wrote a few more lines. Then she closed the notebook and looked at her mother. "Why was Mrs. Galanter here?"

Guilt poked pins at Angela and she forced a smile. "We were talking about their move. They haven't decided on a house in California yet."

"Shane's meeting with his dad today. They might let him stay with one of his friends on the baseball team." She smiled, content. No question about it. Lauren really believed it would work out and the two of them wouldn't be separated.

Angela remembered Sheila's tone. *Shane is coming with us, regardless of what he thinks.* She cleared her throat and tried to smile at her daughter. "I'm not sure about that, honey."

"I am." She set her notebook down beside her bed and sat cross-legged near her pillow. "God'll work something out."

"God, huh?" Angela felt a curious twist in her heart. She was the parent, after all. Talk about God at a time like this should've been coming from her and Bill. And it would one day, when they weren't as busy, when they were out in the suburbs in Wheaton and life was simpler. Then they would go to church every weekend and figure out how to get more God into their every day.

Lauren looked out the window, her eyes gently pensive. "If we'd spent more time talking about God last summer, you know, putting Him first, then maybe we wouldn't have made so many mistakes."

They were quiet for a bit, and outside a light rain started to fall. Finally Angela found the words she was looking for. "Tell me how you feel about Shane." Her voice was soft, not threatening the way so many of their conversations had been since the first of the year. "How do you really feel?"

Lauren wrinkled her nose, and her eyebrows lowered in a soft V. "You already know how I feel, Mom."

"I know what you say. But that's what you're supposed to say. You're pregnant. Of course you're supposed to say you love him. But what does that really mean to you?"

Lauren exhaled slowly and looked out the window again. "It means that no matter what happens, even if they take him from me, a part of me will always stay with him." She looked at her mother. "A part of him will always stay with me." Her hands had been tucked beneath her knees, but now she held out her left hand. "I'll wear his ring forever, Mother." She smiled. "Shane Galanter loves me like no one else ever will. He stands up for me when no one else does, and he believes in me when I don't believe in myself." A laugh sounded low in her throat. "Everyone thinks we're too young to know what love is. But I look at the way you and Daddy and the Galanters are, the way your friendship has died because of this, and you know what I think?"

Angela's throat was thick, her emotions choking her. "What?"

"Being old hasn't helped you know what love is, either."

She didn't want to cry, not with Lauren watching. But the tears came anyway, and since she couldn't speak, she leaned in and hugged her daughter. Hugged her for a long time. As she left her room a few minutes later, the doubt she had about what they were doing to their children was no longer a single small thorn poking at her conscience.

It was a full-size dagger.

☙

Lauren couldn't wait for Shane to show up at her house that night. She hadn't told her parents he was coming, and now it was after eleven o'clock and her mom and dad were in bed. Lauren sat by the window watching the rain. It had been a light sprinkle all day, but now the drops were harder, heavier.

Still, the roads were clear. Shane should be there any time.

In her lap was the story she was working on, the latest one. Ever since she could hold a pencil she'd been writing stories—-especially when her heart was full of unresolved emotions. She stared at the notebook in her hands and flipped back to the beginning of the story, reading the first page: *Even Now—the Story of Us* by Lauren Gibbs.

A smile tugged at her lips. *Lauren Gibbs* was the name she always used when she wrote. A long time ago she'd read the name in a book and something about it—the way it fit the character or the strength of it—stayed with her.

The day she'd found it she ran up to her dad, struggling to reign in her enthusiasm. "Dad ... this is the perfect name."

He was reading the newspaper. The pages crackled in his hands as he bent it in half and lowered it so he could see her. "What's that?"

"The name in this book." She held it up. "It's perfect."

Slowly he began to open the paper again. His eyes darted from the article to her and back again. "Good, honey."

"Dad!" She huffed at him. "You're not listening."

"What?" The paper fell a few inches, and he looked at her. "Of course I am. You like the book you're reading."

"No!" Another huffy breath. "I like the character name in the book."

He blinked. "Character name?"

"Yes. *Lauren Gibbs*." She smiled big again. "Isn't that the greatest name?"

Her dad chuckled a few times. "I think Lauren Anderson is pretty enough."

Lauren stuffed the memory. Her father didn't need to see anything special in the name. She made good on her word. Using it on her short stories was a way to leave herself behind. In her mind, Lauren Gibbs wasn't a seventeen-year-old high school student. She was worldly and wise, with years of education and a fascination with international affairs. She traveled the world and met interesting people from a dozen different cultures.

That was the perspective she wrote from, as if she, like her fictitious alter ego, actually lived such a life.

Her eyes traveled down the page. The first line of the story read: "She watched him from her quiet place at the dinner table. She would remember this day for the rest of time—the day she fell in love with Shane Galanter."

She heard a car in the distance and shut the cover. Once in a while she shared her stories with Shane, but not this time. They had too much else to work through. She set the notebook down and looked out the window again. This was the big chance they'd been waiting for. His father had told him they could talk about the possibility of him living with one of the baseball players for the next year. That would work perfectly. It meant his parents would be out of the picture. The way his mother treated her lately, it would be nice to have some distance between them. Headlights rounded the corner and she squinted into the dark night. It was him. He pulled his Camry up in front of her house and cut the engine. She watched him get out of the car, watched the way his shoulders slumped forward a little, the way his steps were slow.

She sat up a little straighter and a thought hit her, one she had resisted for the past month. What if his dad hadn't given him permission? What if they were insisting Shane move with them? They wouldn't do that, would they? Not when she was wearing his ring. Not when they were engaged to be married.

He was almost to the door, but she reached it first, opening it and motioning for him to be quiet as he stepped inside. Once the door was closed she leaned against it and searched his eyes. "He's going to let you, right?"

"Lauren." He looked down, and in that instant the answer was as clear as the Chicago skyline in August. When he lifted his eyes to hers, they were shiny wet. "He wants me to come to LA for my senior year. Just until I'm finished school. Then he'll do everything he can to help us."

The room felt wobbly, and she wouldn't have been surprised to see the ceiling fall down around their ankles. "You … you're leaving? In a month?"

"What else can I do?" A hint of anger colored his tone. "I have nothing, Lauren. No car, no job, no education, not even a lousy twenty dollar bill." He pulled her close. After awhile he leaned back and looked at her again. The sorrow in his eyes was so raw it hurt. "My mom says you're thinking about giving up the baby?"

She shook her head, frustrated. "Never, Shane. Never once." Her hands came in tight around his waist and she held him. "Why does she keep saying that?"

"It's not just her." His voice was kind, gentle. "Your mom said the same thing."

"*What?*" She took a step back and shook her head. "Is that what you want?"

"Of course not." He reached for her hands, but she kept her distance. "It's just ... for the next year, nothing's up to us."

She turned her back to him and stared out the window. A trembling started in her arms and moved to her hands. If Shane was leaving, then maybe she *should* give up the baby. How would she raise it without his support? Her parents had promised their help, but clearly they didn't approve. The trembling moved down her legs to her knees, and suddenly her entire body was shaking.

He came up and slipped his arms around her, resting his hands on her swollen belly. "I want this baby, Lauren. I wish it were coming ten years from now, but I still want it." He eased her around so that she was facing him. "Don't ever think I don't."

"You're really leaving?"

"I won't give up. I'll keep looking for a way, pushing my dad and trying to make this work somehow until the last minute." He took her hands in his. "I promise."

"I know, but—" her teeth were chattering now—"but if it doesn't work out, then we only have a month left together."

"They can take me out of Chicago, but they can't take me out of your life. So we finish up school, Lauren. Then we'll be together. My dad promised."

She wanted to scream or cry or grab him and run as far away as they could get. But they were stuck. The walls closing in a little more every day. She felt the baby move, and it made her eyes fill with tears. "Find a way, Shane." A sob broke free and she buried her face in his shoulder. "Please. I can't do this without you."

He held her, whispering promises that he'd try, that maybe there was something they hadn't thought about. But in the end, as he drove away that night, she was convinced that she wasn't the only one who knew the truth about their situation. He knew it too.

Never mind about love. Good-byes were a month away.

FIVE

The days passed like so many minutes, each one colored with a different set of new and frightening emotions.

Some afternoons Lauren drove to the lake with Shane, and they'd walk along the shore talking about forever. They barely noticed the strange looks they drew from people who passed by. With her straight blonde hair, she looked younger than her seventeen years. Whispers came with the territory.

Neither of them cared. They were too caught up in their own world to mind what anyone thought. Even their parents.

"I'm talking to one of my teachers about renting a room," Shane told her one sunny afternoon as they sat side by side on the beach. "You know her. Mrs. Tilp."

"Mrs. Tilp, the calculus teacher?" Lauren squinted into the sun. Her abdomen was tight, the baby pressing against her.

"Yeah, she and her husband have an extra room. I heard her talking about it to another teacher. I asked if I could rent it, you know. Through next year. We could get married in the fall and live there together with the baby."

The possibility sounded doubtful. "Did you tell her it would be you? Or you and me and the baby?"

"Me for now." He adjusted his baseball cap. "I thought I'd ask about the two of you after she says yes."

A day later, Shane had the answer. The teacher didn't want a student boarder. Especially not a minor. Shane's next attempt was a neighbor three doors down, a retired man who lived by himself.

While the possibilities dwindled one at a time, Lauren refused to believe it wouldn't somehow work out. At night, when Shane's school day was over, the two of them were almost always together. They felt uncomfortable in either of their homes, so Shane would pick her up and they'd park someplace to talk.

"What about names?" Shane asked her one night. They'd discussed a few, but hadn't decided anything. "We need a plan, just in case."

"In case?" Lauren searched his eyes, and instantly she understood. "You mean if they take you to California?"

He pressed his lips together and nodded. His eyes fell to her belly and then rose again. "I have one."

This was wonderful, sitting alone with him, pretending they were like any other normal couple about to be parents. She leaned back against the car door and grinned at him. "For a boy or a girl?"

"Girl."

"Okay, what?" The baby moved inside her, and she set her hands over the area. "Here." She took his hand and laid it on her belly. "You haven't felt this yet."

"Really?" His touch was light as they waited. The baby kicked again, and Shane's face lit up. "Wow … That was amazing." He put both hands on her now and caressed the place where the baby lay. Then he leaned in and whispered, "Hey, little one, I felt that. You've got a strong kick."

The baby moved again, and the happiness in Lauren was so great she wondered if she was glowing. This was Shane's first contact with their baby. It made everything about her pregnancy feel normal and real and wonderful. The way it was supposed to feel.

Shane ran his hand over her middle once more and then he leaned back against his door and grinned. "Here it is—Emily." His eyes shone. "What do you think?"

"I like it." She pictured her daughter—it was a daughter, she was sure of it—dressed in pink and lace and bearing the sweet, feminine name. Justine or Tabitha had been on her list, something a little modern. But it touched her that Shane had chosen a name. "I didn't know you were thinking about baby names."

"I can't think of anything else." He gave a weak chuckle. "School's barely holding my attention because I'm dreaming about you and the baby, when it'll be born and whether ..." His smile faded. "Whether we'll be together when it happens."

She ignored that last part. If their parents would let them, she was sure Shane would make the best father ever. Another time when they were together she asked, "What about for a boy?"

"I'm not sure." He made a curious face. "Maybe Josh or Jared. Something like that."

The discussions always felt the same to Lauren. Like they were playing house in the shadow of an impending tidal wave. Still, the normalcy of talking about names made the days bearable. Especially when each one drew them closer to his parents' moving date.

With a week left, the call Lauren had expected all along finally came.

"I have to go." Shane sounded like he'd been crying. "I'll finish school in California and then I'll come find you. Whatever it takes. We'll figure something out from there."

Even then she wasn't ready to give up. All week she tried to talk sense into her parents. "Do something, please!" She took hold of her mother's hand, her father's shoulder. "We love each other; we don't want to be apart. Please, help us."

Her parents listened and once in a while offered some show of sadness on her behalf. But they never once offered a way out. Lauren cornered her mother in the kitchen one day near the end of that week. "Call the Galanters. Have them over. Tell them we can't do this living so far apart. Please, Mother."

"Lauren, things are different. The Galanters have made it clear they want no part of our family."

It was like the shrinking hallway. No doors. No windows. No way out.

Finally it was Sunday night. Shane and his family were leaving the next morning, and he was on his way over to say good-bye. Lauren headed outside to meet him.

"Stay in, honey," her mother called from the kitchen. "We want to say good-bye, too."

"No, you don't. You couldn't care less if he leaves." Lauren's tone was sharp. Things between her and her parents had never been worse. If they didn't want to help keep Shane around, then what good were they? Everyone was against them. She slammed the door behind her, walked to the end of the sidewalk and waited.

She wore a faded oversized yellow T-shirt and her father's navy running shorts. Her middle was gigantic, so big it scared her, and even though the air was heavy and hot, she began to shiver. How had things gotten so crazy? Why hadn't they listened to their youth group pastor before, back when they still had time to finish high school like any other kids?

The moon was full that night, casting light through the trees and spraying shadows around the place where she stood. She heard a car in the distance and she squinted at the headlights coming closer. It was him. She knew the sound of his car. When he stopped and climbed out, she knew for sure. He'd been crying. He still was. He shoved his hands in his pockets, walked around the front of his car, and came to her.

"Lauren ..." He pulled her into his arms and tried to hug her. But her abdomen was so large that the moment was awkward, and he drew back. "I only have ten minutes. My dad wants the movers to hook the car up to the moving truck."

She searched his face. "What if we give the baby up, would that make them stay?"

"No." He ran his fingers along her brow and into her hairline near her temple. "We've been over this." Question marks danced in his eyes. "Do you want to give the baby up?"

"Of course not." She sniffed and a pounding filled her chest. "But I can't have the baby on my own, without you. My parents aren't on my side, Shane." She took a step back. "I don't know what to do."

He felt her hand, moved his thumb across the surface of her engagement ring. "Remember what it says."

She blinked, trying to see him more clearly. "Yes."

"Even now, Lauren. When everything's falling apart I still love you. I still want to marry you."

The minutes counted down, and finally they were left with only a lingering, desperate hug and a flurry of promises. "I'll call." Shane eased himself from her and started toward his car.

"I'll be waiting." She took a step closer.

"The year'll go fast." He stopped a few feet from his door. "I'll visit, I promise."

"We'll meet you there as soon as you graduate."

"I know." He narrowed his eyes, seeing past her fear and uncertainty. His cheeks were wet. "You gotta keep that promise."

Another step closer. "I'll tell you as soon as I go into labor."

He was about to get into his car, but for a moment he did nothing but keep his eyes on hers. She understood what he was doing. These few seconds would have to last for her too. Then, in a voice quieter than before, he said, "I'll never love anyone like I love you, Lauren. Never."

She massaged her throat and swallowed hard, willing the words to come. "Me neither, not as long as I live."

There was nothing left to say. He climbed into his car and drove away. Only then did she notice the pains in her belly. Not sharp pains, nothing serious. Just an aching sensation.

As if even the baby inside her was grieving.

Angela tried not to watch, but she couldn't help it.

She sat in the dark living room, staring out the window as Lauren and Shane said good-bye, as they hugged and wept, and finally as he drove away and Lauren dropped to the grass, her head in her hands. That's when it came over Angela—a suffocating guilt.

"Baby, it'll be okay." She put her fingers against the cool glass, her voice a whisper. "We'll get through this."

She was still sitting there when Bill walked up and put his hand on her shoulder.

"They'll be all right." His voice was low, confident. He hadn't once allowed for any other possibility.

Angela understood. Lauren was so precious to Bill. His protective instinct toward her was intense. This was his way of keeping her from what he believed to be a painful decision. If she and Shane stayed together, she'd keep the baby for sure—even if that wasn't the best decision. If that happened, she'd never get the chance to really grow up, to experience her senior year in high school or her college days after that. Even more, if she married Shane she'd be stuck with in-laws who no longer liked her.

Bill had no doubts at all. Separating Lauren and Shane was the best decision for everyone. Angela wanted to feel the same way, but she was too busy trying to grab a single breath. She put her hand over her husband's. "What if they're not?" She turned and looked at him, and her heart pounded out a strange rhythm. "What if they're not all right? Maybe we're wrong, Bill. This is all our doing, us and the Galanters."

He frowned and looked out the window at their daughter. "They're only kids. They don't know what's right for them." He lifted his chin a little. "I think we all know the best thing for the baby is for Lauren to give it up."

Angela felt the stirrings of anger. "We've been through this. She wants to keep it, you know that."

"But with Shane gone ..." He shrugged. "With him out of the picture, I think she'll change her mind." He straightened and gave her shoulder a final squeeze. "I hope so."

Then he turned and went back to the living room. She heard the television click on, and after that, the sound of an announcer talking about the Reds and the White Sox and who was in the lineup that night.

Angela watched him go and a soft cry escaped her. She shook her head. No matter how sincere his motives, could he really be a party to breaking the kids up and never have a single doubt? Between them and the Galanters, they had manipulated their kids' futures in every way possible. They had more than a decade of history together, yet the four of them had willingly stood by as their friendship died. Then they'd agreed to keep their new forwarding phone numbers a secret. At least for a month. All so that maybe Lauren would change her mind and give the baby up for adoption. Angela looked out at Lauren and even through the dark night she could see the obvious. Lauren was sobbing, crying alone on the damp early summer grass with no one to comfort her. A chill ran down Angela's spine and she shuddered. The thought wouldn't leave her alone, wouldn't allow her a minute's peace. It was the same thought she'd had all week, all month. Yes, in some twisted way they were all trying to do what was best for the kids.

But what in all of heaven would happen if they were wrong?

ꕥ

Shane couldn't see for the tears.

He was the best player on his baseball team, a kid no one dared cross in the locker room or anywhere else. But in the past month he felt his life falling apart one day at a time. And there was nothing he could do about it. A red light ahead brought him to a stop. He pressed his fists against his eyes and rubbed. They wouldn't have the last word, no, not if he could help it. They could take him away from Chicago, away from Lauren and the baby and all he wanted for their future. But they couldn't change the way he felt about her.

All his life he had pictured himself growing up to be a businessman, an investor like his father; a man who would earn his pilot's license and fly to important meetings. But in the past month that had changed. He had a new outlook on his parents and their world and all they stood for. Somewhere along the way the money had become them, who they were. It was no longer an asset to be used as a tool. The wealth they'd accumulated defined them.

It was their wealth that wouldn't allow for an only son of the Galanter family to be a father the summer before his senior year. That's what the move was about, no matter what they told him. If they could rush him across the country and enroll him in a new school where no one knew him, then life could go on pretty much the way it always had. No worries, no cares, and a future as good as gold.

As if by taking him from Lauren, the truth would somehow disappear.

Instead, the truth had become clearer than ever. The life he would lead one day would never be the life his parents led. He would find meaning and value in something other than money, and he would find it with Lauren and their baby, their children. He remembered the feeling of the baby moving beneath his hands. The child growing inside Lauren was his, and he would spend a lifetime figuring out how to be a daddy.

The light turned green and he pulled into the intersection. His eyes were dry now, the tears gone. In their place was a resolve strong enough to last a lifetime. Because the truth he could see so clearly was this: he really wouldn't love anyone the way he loved Lauren Anderson. One day, as soon as he could make it happen, they would find each other once more. He would add a white gold band to the ring he'd already given her.

And then they'd never be apart again.

Six

Lauren's determination grew with every tear she cried. She and Shane would be together again, sooner than later. The day after Shane left, he called her from a pay phone in Oklahoma somewhere. Static played between his words, but she made out most of what he said.

"My mom told me we won't have a phone at first." He sounded far away, nervous, and rushed for time. "We're at a gas station. They're filling up the car, so I don't have long."

Lauren was confused. "You won't have a phone?" Why was everything starting to feel like a conspiracy against them? "Everyone has a phone, Shane. How come?"

"My parents said it takes time. Something about where our house is. I guess the whole neighborhood's new and phone service could take a few weeks."

Panic welled up in her. "We're moving this Friday." She ran her hand along her forehead and tried to concentrate. "We'll have a new number too. How am I supposed to get it to you if you don't have a phone?"

"My mom's going to talk to your mom. I'm not sure, but maybe through your dad's work or something." His voice was calmer now, but she could hear a car engine in the background. "I called because I want you to remember something, Lauren. If I don't call, I'll be thinking of you. That'll never change. We'll figure out the phone number thing even if it takes a few weeks."

She felt herself relax. "Okay. If our moms have it worked out."

"They do. They have to." He paused. "I gotta go, but how are you feeling?"

"Good. The baby's heartbeat is strong."

"You ... you haven't changed your mind about anything, have you?"

Why did he keep asking her? She clenched her teeth. "I told you. I've made up my mind, okay?"

"Okay. Hey ... I have to go. I love you, Lauren. I'll call as soon as I can."

"I love you too."

They hung up and that was the last she heard from him. Now she and her family were completely moved into their new house in the suburbs of Wheaton, a full hour out of the city. They had a new phone number, and once they were unpacked she approached her mother. "How's Shane supposed to get our new number?"

"I'm waiting for his mother to contact us, honey. She'll give it to us when their phone service gets connected."

"Okay, but how will she reach us when our number's new too?" She had two weeks until her due date, and she was uncomfortable most of the time. "I need to talk to him, Mom."

"Oh." Her mother didn't blink. "The phone company has a forwarding service, sweetheart. Anyone can call our old number and get the new one for the next three months."

Light dawned in her heart. A forwarding service? "Really?" She hadn't thought of that. "So he'll call any day."

"Exactly." Her mother smiled.

Three more days passed after that, making it two weeks since she'd heard from Shane. Her back ached and she took a walk down their winding drive to the mailbox. Where was he and what was he doing? Were they unpacked and getting used to their new neighborhood? And what part of Los Angeles had they settled in? Was it a suburb or near the city, and why hadn't she asked before?

She wandered inside. Her dad was at the new bank, the one near Town Square, and her mother was in the den with an interior decorator, going through a sampling of window coverings. She went to the kitchen, sat at the desk chair, and stared at the telephone. Why wouldn't it ring? No one would go this long without phone service, would they?

But that had to be it, that the phones simply weren't connected. Because Shane would've called the minute he had a chance. She tapped the phone with her finger. As she did, her abdomen tightened, and stayed that way for half a minute. False contractions. She'd been having them for a few days now. She breathed out a few quick times in a row, and tried to remember their last conversation.

What had he said? That he would call as soon as he could, right? She let that play in her mind for a moment. Why hadn't he found another pay phone by now? He could've gone with his parents to the market or the gas station or anyplace in Los Angeles. Pay phones were everywhere. He could call her old number and get the forwarding message, right? But then why hadn't he called yet?

She ran her finger along the receiver. Maybe the information on the forwarding service was wrong, maybe they were a digit or two off, and he couldn't figure out her new number. An idea came upon her slowly, in fits and starts. She could call their old number, couldn't she? Then she could hear the recording for herself, make sure it gave the right new number. Why hadn't she thought of that sooner?

Her mother's lighthearted laughter sounded in the background. Most of her time had been spent with the decorator lately, and her father was practically never home. Board meetings with the new trustees, an intensive program of learning the operations systems, and meeting the employees.

So maybe it was up to her to figure out how to reach Shane.

She picked up the receiver and dialed her old number. A one and the area code, and the seven digits that had been as familiar to her as her first name. As soon as the numbers were all in, she waited for the ringing. But it never came. Instead a strange tone sounded in her ear, and a mechanical voice said, "The number you've reached has been disconnected. No new number is available."

What? No new number is ... Gradually, like the slow collapse of a line of dominoes, the floor began to fall away beneath her. She gripped the receiver. The recording was still playing. "—you've reached has been disconnected. No new—"

Her mother had lied to her. There was no other explanation. They'd disconnected the old number, the one Shane knew, and they'd intentionally left no new number. The reason was as shocking as it was obvious. Her parents didn't want her talking to him. They'd moved her to the suburbs, and now they were preventing phone contact.

Lauren was on her feet. She slammed the receiver down. "Mother!" Her voice boomed across the house. "I need to talk to you!"

In the other room, her mother's laugh stopped short. "Lauren ... I'm busy. Can't it wait?"

She stormed through the kitchen, down the hall, and into the den. The decorator was watching, eyes wide. Lauren glared at her mother. "I need to talk to you right now." Her tone was angry and just barely controlled. She stepped back into the hall and headed for the kitchen. Then she spun around and waited.

Her mother whispered something to the decorator Lauren couldn't make out, then she slipped into the hallway and locked eyes with Lauren. Her mother should've been angry. After all, Lauren had interrupted her in the middle of a business meeting, with a tone of voice that would never have been acceptable in the past.

But as her mother walked toward her, her eyes didn't hold a bit of anger. They held concern and anxiety and fear. Most of all, fear. Her mom waited until they were inches apart, then she folded her arms. "Are you in labor?"

"Do I *look* like I'm in labor?" She snapped the words. Her voice was still a little too loud, but she didn't care. "This isn't about me, Mother. It's about you." She pointed to the telephone on the desk behind her. "I called our phone number, our old one."

Her mother looked at the phone and then back at her. The fear in her eyes grew. "And?"

"Oh, don't act surprised." She wanted to scream. It was all she could do to keep her tone somewhat controlled. "You know exactly what I'm about to say."

"Lauren, watch how you talk to me."

"You don't sound very convincing." She studied her mother's eyes. Who was this woman standing in front of her? All her life her mother had been her friend, her ally. The first one to listen and lend a bit of advice when her girlfriends ganged up against her at different times during her school years, or when a certain teacher gave her a hard time. But ever since she got pregnant, her mother had worked against her at every turn. Her mother and father, and Shane's parents, too.

Her mother shifted her weight. "Maybe you could tell me what you're talking about."

Lauren let out a small scream. "Don't *do* this! You know what I'm talking about. Stop lying to me!" She clenched her fists. "You didn't leave a forwarding number on our old phone. If Shane tried to call me since we moved, he would've gotten nothing, no new number, no clue how to reach me."

"What?" Her mother walked around her to the phone. She picked up the receiver, dialed a series of numbers, and held it to her ear. After several beats, she looked at Lauren and set the phone back down. "No forwarding number."

"Yeah, and you knew that." Her anger was growing with every few words. As she spoke, another wave of tightness seized at her middle. She winced and pointed at her mother. "You lied to me."

"I didn't, Lauren. I promise." Shock filled her voice, and she was suddenly indignant as the implication took root. "I told your father to put the new number on when he disconnected the ..." Her voice trailed off and she turned slowly to the phone. "I told him ..."

The tightness was worse now, stronger than it had been all day. "You're saying Dad did this, that you had nothing to do with it?" How could she trust her? How could she believe either of them? "What does it matter? The two of you are determined to tear us apart. I should've run off with Shane." She was yelling now, the truth settling in around her heart.

Her mother shook her head, her voice softer than before. "I swear to you, Lauren, I didn't do this." She picked up the receiver again. This time she punched in fewer numbers. After a moment she said, "Yes, this is Mrs. Anderson. I need to talk with my husband, please."

Lauren had heard enough. What did it matter whose fault it was? One of her parents had kept their new number off the recording so they could separate her from Shane. With her head spinning, she ran upstairs to her room.

Only then did the first real pain grab her. It ripped across her middle and dropped her to the edge of her bed. She bent in half, trying to survive it. When it passed, she eased herself onto the mattress and set her head on the pillow. It was too soon for the baby, but the pain that had just hit her sure felt like the real thing.

She stared at the ceiling, red hot anger flooding her veins. How could her parents have done this? They'd betrayed her, and now how would she get hold of Shane? In the distance she could hear some of what her mother was saying.

"But I thought you'd leave the number, Bill. Lauren's very upset about this and now she thinks I did it on purpose and— "

Another cramping pain hit, hard and sure. She rolled onto her side and drew her knees to her middle. Every breath was a struggle until finally the hurt let up. That's when she knew for sure. These were contractions, and if they were coming this close, she might be in labor.

"Mother!" She shouted as loud as she could. Her mom was at her side in a few minutes.

"Lauren, your father meant to leave the message, but—"

"I'm in labor." She panted, trying to catch her breath. "It hurts so bad." Another pain hit, and she yelled out loud. From downstairs she could hear the decorator gathering her things and shouting a good-bye. There was the sound of the front door shutting behind her, just as the contraction let up.

"We need to get you in." Her mother helped her to her feet, made a few phone calls, and in thirty minutes they were at the local hospital. The plan had been to have the baby in Chicago, at the hospital they were familiar with. But they had no time, and the staff at the local Central DuPage worked quickly to get her into a delivery room.

"She's been in labor for quite some time," the doctor told them. "The baby'll be here within the hour."

Lauren was scared and angry and worn out. She could barely breathe as one wave of pain after another rocked her. She tried to concentrate on the doctor's words. What had he said? Within the hour? How was that possible? Her due date wasn't for two weeks, and until she figured out about her parents' lie, she'd felt fine. Now she was breathless, the pain radiating up through her chest and around to her back. She couldn't begin to sort through her emotions. Shane was completely out of touch, and she would be a mother in an hour. All that, and the fact that her parents weren't on her side.

Her mother touched her elbow. "I'll stay here, honey. Your father's on his way."

Lauren moaned. She wanted to tell her mother to leave. If she really cared she'd help her find a way to reach Shane. But the next contraction was already on her, and she couldn't talk. A memory flashed through her mind. She and her mother at a baby shower for a neighbor. Lauren had been maybe thirteen years old.

"What if I don't know how to have a baby, I mean when it's my turn?" She'd turned to her mother, genuinely anxious about the idea.

Her mother had squeezed her hand. "I'll be there for you, Lauren. I'll tell you what to expect, and I'll help you through it. You'll be just fine."

That's how their relationship was before she got pregnant. Now, here she was, going through the very thing that had frightened her. Yes, her mother was with her, but not really. Their relationship was strained and tense, as if the woman beside her wasn't her mom at all, but someone who only looked like her.

"Are you okay?" Her mother pulled a chair up next to her. She crossed her legs and leaned closer, concern written in the lines of her forehead. "Do you need anything?"

"Yes." Lauren was between contractions. She ran her tongue over her lip and locked eyes with her mother. "Shane."

Her mother didn't ask again.

The doctor's prediction proved to be right on. Exactly fifty minutes after arriving at the hospital, with only a mild amount of medication for the pain, Lauren gave birth to a six-pound, three-ounce baby girl. The moment the doctor held the baby up, tears flooded Lauren's eyes. This was her *daughter*, her child. A part of her and of Shane. She covered her mouth and shook her head, amazed. "She's ... she's perfect."

The doctor smiled, and in the next chair, her mother was crying too. For some reason Lauren was bothered by her mother's tears. Was she crying because this wasn't how things were supposed to go, or because she was too young to be a grandmother? It was an instant that would never come again—the birth of her first child. It was a time when her mother's emotion should've been joy, not pain.

For Lauren, of course, the tears were joyous, but they were also filled with sorrow. This was her daughter, a fair-skinned beauty who would forever be a part of her, a part of her life. But Shane should've been here, beside her, seeing their daughter for the first time. How long would it be before he knew about her, before his parents would let him fly back to Chicago to see their little girl?

That night, her parents took turns holding the baby and spouting the types of things first-time grandparents were supposed to say. "She has Lauren's chin ... she's perfect." Or, "Look at those blue eyes!" Her mother was no longer crying. Instead, by the time they were ready to head home, her parents were upbeat, promising to return in the morning.

No one said a word about adoption.

When they left, Lauren held her daughter close against her chest. As terrible as it was that her parents had been trying to keep her from Shane, at least they weren't going to force her to give her daughter up. She studied her little girl's face. "Hi, sweetie. Mommy's here."

The baby squirmed a little, her eyes never veering from Lauren's. "You need me, don't you, little one?"

The precious child in her arms trusted her with her entire being. Lauren had no idea what she was doing, no clue where they would go or how they would find Shane again. But they would find him. They would go to him as soon as they could. She owed Shane that much.

By the end of that first night, she'd given the baby a name: Emily.

Now she would press her parents to do everything in their power to help her find Shane. Then they could figure something out so that they could be a family sooner than later. Little Emily needed her daddy too. In the glow and marvel of those early hours of being a mother, Lauren would've walked barefoot to California with Emily in her arms if it meant finding Shane. If her parents weren't going to help, she would find him on her own. She stared at her ring and brought it to her face, brushing it against her cheek.

Whatever it took for the three of them to be together. The way they should've been now.

The way they would be forever.

SEVEN

Lauren was determined: she was going to find Shane.

Every day that passed, her resolve grew stronger. She would find him, and she would do it soon. The baby was four weeks old by the time she felt strong enough to take the subject to her parents. It was after eight o'clock on a Monday night the first week of August. Lauren had rocked Emily to sleep and tucked her into her crib. Now she padded down the carpeted hallway toward her parents' den. They often spent time there after dinner. The room had a full-size patio door that led to a covered porch. It was one of the nicest spots in the house.

She was almost to the door when she heard her father's voice. He sounded stern, frustrated. Lauren stopped and listened.

"I don't *want* his contact information, don't you see that, Angela?" He uttered a harsh chuckle. "In fact, this is just how I want it. Our daughter doesn't need any ties to that family, that woman."

"It's both of them." Her mother's voice was tired, the way she often sounded since the move. "Sheila doesn't want her son dragged down by Lauren, but Samuel's right there with her. Believe me, the idea of tearing these kids apart comes from both of them."

"Okay, fine. Exactly." His tone was louder than before. "So why should I take calls from the kid? So he called the bank, so what?"

"Bill." Her mother's voice was slower, more calm. "Listen to yourself. This is Shane we're talking about, honey. He was practically part of the family for all those years, remember?" She sighed loud enough that Lauren could hear it in the hallway. "I mean the kid calls the bank looking for you, looking for some way to reach Lauren, and you have your secretary tell him he's got the wrong bank? Is that fair?"

Lauren's knees felt weak. She felt the room begin to spin, and she braced herself against the wall. Shane had called the bank, her father's new bank? And he'd been told he had the wrong place? So what would he think next? Did he even know what Chicago suburb they'd settled in or what neighborhood? She squeezed her eyes shut and forced herself to listen.

"Of course it's fair, Angela. The things Sheila and Samuel said about our daughter, the way they treated her ... Lauren's my child, Angela. I don't want her around people who don't like her. If she's away from Shane, she'll be away from his parents."

Her mother was quiet for a moment, and Lauren wondered if she was crying. Finally she said, "How did it all turn so bad? They were our friends. Our best friends."

"I've learned something." Her father sounded matter-of-fact. "Playing cards together, vacationing together, doesn't always mean you know people." His voice grew wistful. "I thought I knew Sheila and Sam. But you watched how they handled this. The only thing that mattered was Shane. They would've burned down our house if it meant protecting their boy from his responsibility."

There was silence for a moment. Lauren's entire body shook and she felt sick to her stomach. This was the sign she'd been looking for, the proof that her parents really and truly had conspired against her and Shane. Now she would leave this house, walk out of their lives without looking back, and one day, when she and Shane were settled, she would consider being a part of this family again. But not until then. She was about to burst into the room, but she waited in case there was more.

There was.

After another few seconds, her mother said, "So what did he say? I mean, did he leave a message?"

"He told my secretary his name was Shane Galanter, and he was looking for Bill Anderson." A long sigh came from her father. "I'd already told her that if anyone named Galanter called, she was to say they had the wrong bank. No one there by my name."

Her mother groaned. "The kids miss each other, Bill. What if we're wrong?"

"We're protecting Lauren." Her father was curt, adamant. "It's for her own good, because I love her. Besides, she'll never find out."

"Yes, I will." Lauren stepped into the room, still holding onto the door frame to keep her balance. Her head pounded, and she could barely feel her feet. She stared from her mother to her father, her eyes wide, unblinking. "I heard it all, Daddy. Shane called you at work and you had some ... some woman tell him he had the wrong bank." She wanted to scream at him, shout at both of them that they couldn't do this. But it was already done. All that was left inside her was an eerie sort of iciness, an anxiety that defied expression.

"Lauren—" Her father was on his feet. His mouth hung open for a few seconds. But he rebounded quickly. "The two of you need time away from each other. The Galanters and we agreed. It's important, so the two of you can figure out what you want from here."

"We already *know* what we want." She was imploding, her voice fading with every few words. "You and Mom don't have any idea what I want." She pressed her hand to her chest. "What Shane and I want. We need to be together."

"Okay." Her father looked across the room.

As if on cue, her mother turned to Lauren. "We'll help you find him, honey. It won't be hard. Your father has ways." She paused. "It's like your dad said. We all felt it would be best if we gave the two of you some time apart. If you could've heard the things Mrs. Galanter said about you, honey ..."

"I don't care about her. I care about Shane." Her voice was getting louder, and she brought it back down again. "All you've done is tear us apart."

"We were trying to help you."

"The phone connection thing, the made-up forwarding information, and now this—Shane calls the bank and gets a lie." She laughed, but it came out low and sad. "Thanks for the help, Mom." She looked at her father. "You too, Dad." She turned to walk out, but her mother was on her feet, crossing the room and coming toward her.

"Where are you going?"

Lauren was done sharing information with her parents. "My room." She looked at her mother over her shoulder. "I have nothing left to say."

Her parents must've felt the same way, because they didn't speak another word as she walked away. Not until she was in the hallway did she hear her mother's voice. "I'm sorry, Lauren. We ... we never meant to hurt you."

She stopped and closed her eyes for a few seconds, holding back the sudden rush of tears that stung at her eyes. "I know." She blinked and looked back at them one last time. "I know."

As she made her way through the house and up the stairs to her room, she was certain her mother was telling the truth. In some strange, twisted way the things she and her father had done to keep her and Shane apart really were acted out with the thought that it would be best for her.

But some part of their consciences must've known it was wrong. She sat on the edge of her bed and looked across the room at Emily's crib. The baby stirred and gave a small sneeze.

Lauren stood and went to her. "Hey, little one, you okay? Mommy's here." She leaned out and touched her forehead. It was warm, but that might've been from the blankets or the sticky summer night. Lauren frowned and adjusted the layers so the baby had less over her body.

The most amazing thing about being a new mother was the intensity of the love she felt for her daughter. She would've done anything for little Emily, and come tomorrow she would prove it. She soothed her hand over Emily's forehead again. She wasn't that warm, after all. "Everything's going to be okay."

She should've been furious with her parents, devastated by their betrayal, fighting mad about everything that had happened to Shane and her. Instead, as she stared at her daughter, she felt a surging sense of freedom. She and Emily would be fine on their own.

She leaned over the crib and kissed her daughter on the cheek. Then she went to the top drawer in her nightstand and pulled out the envelope just inside. It held five thousand dollars, money she'd taken from her personal account that afternoon. Since her money was still at the bank in the city, she'd found a local branch first. Her mother thought she was running to the grocery store with Emily, but she stopped at the bank on her way home. It was her money, gifts she'd gotten over the years, money she'd earned babysitting. Some of it was from her parents, but only when it was given as a birthday or Christmas present or for getting A's on her report card.

Now it felt like a million dollars in her hands. With that kind of cash she could take Emily to Los Angeles, find someplace to live, and start searching for Shane. She would try the local banks, places where his father might work. Then once school started again, she would try every high school in Los Angeles if she had to. Her parents would get over her decision. She'd done the unforgivable. By getting pregnant she and Shane had cast a shadow of shame on their families too long and dark and wide to ever step out of. The only way she'd live in the light of happiness and freedom again was by finding Shane.

As she fell asleep, she heard Emily sneeze twice more. Nothing to worry about. Just a small case of the sniffles, probably something all little babies dealt with in the first few months of life. And if she came down with a real full-blown cold, they could stop at any supermarket along the way to California and find something to help her.

The next morning Lauren's father left early, without saying good-bye. Her mother checked in and reported that she was spending the day with the interior decorator.

"We're accessorizing today. Looking at a few of the local boutiques." Her mother gave her a tentative smile. "You're not still upset about your father's situation at the bank, are you?" She paused, the corners of her lips locked in an upward lift. "You and Shane will connect one of these days real soon. We'll help you."

"How, Mom?" She had Emily cradled in her arms. Her suitcases were packed and in the closet. "I don't have his phone number, and he doesn't have mine." She narrowed her eyes. "Where exactly does he live? Do you know that?"

Her mother's shoulders lowered a little. "Los Angeles. That's all they told me."

"Okay, what about his dad's business? He had investments in LA, so what are they? *Where* are they?"

"Gas stations, I think. And a small airport, maybe." She bit her lip. "At least I think so."

"You see?" She made a sound that was part laugh, part moan. "Why say we'll connect soon? Shane found Daddy's bank, which is pretty good with nothing to go on, don't you think?"

Her eyes fell to the floor, but she nodded. "Yes. Yes, it was."

"So he found it, and then someone tells him it's not the right bank. No one there by the name of Bill Anderson." She kept her voice calm so it wouldn't wake Emily. "What makes you think I'll be able to find Shane now?"

A pair of robins sang from a tree outside her window. Her mother looked up and gave the slightest shrug. "I've been asking myself the same thing all night." She hugged her arms tight around her waist. "Honestly, Lauren, I don't know. I have to believe he'll find you, but I don't know how."

"Maybe if our phone number was listed." She hated the sarcasm in her voice. It made her feel ugly and jaded, like a world of distance lay between her and her mom.

"Lauren—" her mother sighed—"you know we can't list our number, not with your dad's involvement at the bank. We've never been listed, and neither have the Galanters."

It was all she needed to hear. She had to go to Shane. Whether he was in California or on the moon, she had to find him. She held Emily closer. "I love you, Mother, and I always will." Her voice cracked. "But I can't believe what you and Daddy have done to me."

Her mom came to her then and placed her arms around Lauren and Emily, holding them tight. When she drew back, she looked deep into her eyes, "I love you too, honey. I'm sorry. Really."

She turned and walked away. When Lauren heard the front door close behind her, she stood and set Emily down in her crib. With her heart in her throat, she added a few more items to each suitcase. All of Emily's clothes, and more than enough for herself.

As she left the room, a suitcase in each hand, she stopped and looked back. She scanned the room, taking in her box of short stories and photo albums, her yearbooks and souvenirs from a childhood that ended far too quickly. She could always come back for those things once she found Shane.

The only memento she packed was a framed photograph of her and Shane, something she would set next to her bed so that wherever the next place was she called home, she would be driven every day to find him.

Only then would she send for the rest of her things.

She packed the car with the suitcases, then came back for Emily. She left a note in Emily's crib that said simply, "Gone to meet Shane. I'll call when I find him. Love, Lauren."

By four that afternoon they were three hundred miles out of Wheaton. Everything ahead of her looked bright and promising. The sky was clear, the map on the seat beside her had the route marked out perfectly. A woman at the local auto club had helped her with the best possible freeways and stopping points. She would get to California in six days and after that she'd find Shane and they could be together. Only one thing caused her even an inkling of doubt.

In the backseat, Emily was still sneezing.

EIGHT

Something tragic had happened.

By six o'clock that night, Angela Anderson was sure of it. She called Bill at the bank and struggled to keep the panic from her voice. "Have you seen Lauren?"

"Lauren?" His tone told her he was busy. "Of course not. She's home with the baby. You know that."

"She's not here, Bill. I think she's gone."

"If she's not there, then of course she's gone." His impatience grated on her. "Honey, I'm in a meeting. She's probably at the store, and she'll be back in a few minutes."

"What if... what if she's gone?"

"Gone where?"

"Gone *gone*. I think she left, maybe to find Shane." Angela's voice was controlled, but only barely. "She didn't leave a note, not one that I could find. I looked in her room, everywhere."

He uttered an exaggerated sigh. "She's out shopping."

"I thought of that, but Bill, I've been home for an hour. She wouldn't be gone this long." She hesitated. "I have a bad feeling."

"All right, well listen." There was kindness in his voice now. "Why don't you check her room again and see what you can find. This is Lauren we're talking about, honey. She wouldn't do anything crazy."

A sense of peace washed over her. Bill was right. Lauren was grounded. Before getting pregnant, she'd been a standout student, a kid who always told them where she was; one who preferred staying home and playing Scrabble and Hearts with her parents and Shane rather than hitting a high school party.

Of course she wouldn't just take Emily and leave.

Still, just to be sure, she needed to check her room one more time. She hurried up the stairs, a sick feeling in her heart. She pulled Lauren's door open and scanned the bed. This time she saw something she hadn't before. Lauren's photo of herself and Shane, which always sat on her bedside table, was gone. Angela looked at the crib again. The bedding was gone too. The first time she'd checked Lauren's room she'd assumed the baby's sheets and blankets were being washed. Her heart beat hard in her throat. What if the bedding was missing for another reason? She moved in closer, her steps slow and fearful.

On the mattress lay a piece of paper, something else she hadn't seen her first time up.

Angela's heart screamed at her to leave the room, run back downstairs and convince herself that Lauren and Emily were only at the store, that they hadn't gone farther away than that. But the note demanded her attention. She forced her feet to take her to the edge of the crib, and then without drawing another breath she lifted the note and read it.

Gone to meet Shane. I'll call when I find him. Love, Lauren.

A burning sensation flooded her veins, a mix of adrenaline and fear all wrapped up in a shock that wouldn't let her believe her own eyes. "No ..." Even as she spoke, she read the words again, then one more time. "No, Lauren. *No!*" Her hand shook so hard she could barely make out the words.

What was Lauren thinking? She and Emily wouldn't last on a trip across the country by themselves. Lauren had never driven more than an hour or two at any one time. She was only seventeen! How would she know which freeways to take or how to make it from Chicago to Los Angeles?

Angela wasn't sure whom to call first. The note clutched in her hand, she raced down the stairs. Bill. He had to know before anyone else. She had to dial his number three times before getting it right. She had him on the line in less than a minute.

"So—" Angela heard the nervous tension in his voice—"is she home?"

Angela dropped to the nearest chair and grabbed a handful of her hair. *Think! Say something.* She squeezed the receiver and found her voice. "She's gone. She and Emily. I found a note."

"A note?" She had his attention now. She heard a door shut in the background. "What did it say?"

"She's gone to California to find Shane. She'll call when she gets hold of him."

He made a disbelieving sound. "That's ridiculous, Angela. She's just a child. She doesn't have any idea how to drive across the country."

"Or how to care for little Emily."

"I'll be right home. You call the police, and tell them what happened." He was in a hurry now, anxious to fix the problem. "And pray, Angela. I can't have anything happen to her." A catch sounded in his voice. "I can't have it."

She told him she'd do her best, then she hung up and called the local police office. "Our daughter ran away. We need your help."

"Okay, hold on." He connected her to another officer.

"I'm Officer Rayson. Your daughter ran away?"

"Yes." Angela put her hand against her chest. Her heart was racing so fast she could barely feel the beat. "Just today."

"Okay, let's start with her age." His voice held compassion, but still she had the sense this was a routine call for him.

"She's seventeen. She … she just had a baby."

The officer hesitated. "A baby? Is the baby with her?"

"Yes. She's four weeks old. My daughter packed a few suitcases, best I can tell, and the two of them set off today. Probably this morning."

"Ma'am, you're asking me to make a report on a seventeen-year-old runaway with a newborn baby?"

"Yes." Angela clenched her fists. The man wasn't going to help her. She forced her next words. "Is ... is that a problem?"

"Sort of." The sound of rustling papers came across the phone line. "Ma'am, she's almost an adult, and since she has a four-week-old baby, we can assume she left on her own without any foul play, is that right?"

"Definitely. She left a note." Angela gripped the counter in front of her and stared at the piece of paper. "She said she was going to California to find the baby's father."

"Okay, then." Resignation rang in his tone. "If she doesn't call in a few weeks, let us know. Maybe we can get someone in California on the case."

"*What?*" It was a shriek. "Sir, we need your help! She's only seventeen. She hasn't had a driver's license for a full year yet!"

"I'm afraid we look at things a little differently." He waited a beat. "She may not be an adult, but because of the baby we see her as one. At that age, they have a pretty good idea of what they want. It's a family issue."

"What about—" She gave a series of light taps to her forehead. *Think, Angela. Come on.* "What about a missing person's report. Couldn't I file one of those even if she's almost an adult?"

"You can file one on a person of any age, ma'am. But they need to be missing for twenty-four hours." He sounded doubtful. "I have to be honest with you, though. We can't put manpower behind every missing person's report."

She couldn't make sense of what was happening. The room felt like it was shaking beneath her feet, and all the colors seemed to melt together. The police couldn't help her? What good was a police force, then? Her daughter was gone, headed one of a dozen different ways toward California. Los Angeles. But LA was a huge city, gigantic. How would Lauren find Shane?

More important, how would she and Bill find their daughter?

Bill came home while she was still sitting there, still poring through the yellow pages looking for someone who could help. She contacted three private investigators, but all of them said it was too soon to do anything. Lauren would be driving for the next week. If she wanted to call, she would. If not, there wasn't much any of them could do. She would need to arrive in Los Angeles and set up residency before they could be of much help.

Bill walked in, set his things on the kitchen counter, and put his hand on her shoulder. "Are the police on their way?"

She looked at him, and for just a moment hatred gripped her. He had done this to them. He and the Galanters. She'd gone along with it because they were convincing. They made her believe the kids really would be better off apart. But hadn't she doubted the decision all along? Watching the two of them say good-bye that night in the city, hadn't she known this could happen?

She blinked, letting the rage go. She could hate him later. Right now they had to find Lauren and Emily. "The police aren't going to help." She explained the situation. "I've tried a few private investigators, but they all say it's too soon."

He hesitated, but only for a handful of seconds. "Then we have no choice." He turned and went to the kitchen cupboard. It was his routine when he came home from work, and now he went ahead with it as if this were nothing more serious than a traffic ticket. He took a glass and filled it with ice water. "We'll have to wait till she gets there." He sipped the water. "I'm sure she'll call."

"Bill!" She stood, slamming the chair back in against the counter. "Do you *hear* yourself? Your daughter has run away. She's taken her newborn daughter, our grandchild, and you—" she gestured at him—"calmly pour a glass of water and tell me she'll call?" She was trembling, her voice loud and shrill. "I can't believe who you've become. Sometimes I think I hate you for what you've done to her."

The water was still in his hand, but he set it down. His eyes found hers and a layer of remorse colored his expression. "Angela, calm down." He went to her, but as he tried to touch her shoulder, she jerked away.

"Don't *touch* me." She pushed her finger at his chest. "I didn't want this, Bill. We pushed her out, don't you see that?" Tears flooded her eyes and her throat felt scratchy. "All that mattered to any of you, to any of us, was how things looked. The kids needed to be apart, but why? So we could pretend this never happened, so we could pretend Lauren didn't get pregnant and everything was perfectly normal, right?"

"Lower your voice, please." Though his tone was kind, Angela knew he still didn't understand what she was feeling. "Everything will work out. You'll see."

"No, it won't. We let this happen, and now … now we might never see her again."

She spun away from him and hurried around the corner to their bedroom. How had life become so crazy? And where were Lauren and Emily? She wasn't sure she could survive without them. Suddenly she realized her daughter held a piece of her heart, the part that understood life and the purpose and meaning of getting up in the morning. And now that Lauren was gone, that part of Angela was dead.

The part capable of loving.

Even loving the man she had married.

❧

Emily was sick. There was no denying that now. They'd been on the road for two full days, and the baby was burning up. Lauren drove aimlessly through the streets of Oklahoma City trying to decide what to do. She'd already stopped at a drugstore and bought pain reliever, something to lower Emily's fever. That was half an hour ago, and it seemed to be working, but her baby still sounded terrible. She was sneezing and coughing and now she was wheezing every time she breathed in.

A rush of fear and desperation worked its way through Lauren's veins. Where should she take Emily? She had money, enough to see a doctor, but then what? Would they put the baby in the hospital? Would they find out that Lauren was a seventeen-year-old runaway? And what then? Maybe she would lose her daughter forever.

In the backseat, Emily started to cry, and the sound of it made her wheezing worse.

"Okay, honey, it's okay. Mommy's here."

The words hung in the small, stuffy car and mocked her. Mommy was here? So what? She didn't have a clue how to be a mother, otherwise her baby wouldn't be sick. She was about to get back on the freeway, head for the next town, when she spotted a sign that read, Hospital.

She sped up and pulled into the parking lot. The least she could do was get someone to look at Emily. That shouldn't raise too many flags. She parked and lifted the car seat from the back. Once inside the emergency area, she stood there, shaking, mouth dry. Other people were waiting in the lobby, and most of them turned and looked at her. Could they tell she was on the run? Was it obvious? And what about the people who worked there? What would she say? How would she explain her situation, other than by telling the truth?

A blonde woman behind the counter smiled at her. "Can I help you?"

"Yes." She looked at Emily and back at the woman. "My baby's sick."

The woman handed Lauren a clipboard and a pen. "Fill out the information sheet, and we'll get your baby seen as soon as we have an empty room."

"Okay."

The form asked a dozen questions, some of which she couldn't answer. Address, for instance. And phone number. She also left blank the part about emergency contact information and next of kin. But she filled in Emily's birth date and the fact that they didn't have insurance. Then she signed the form and turned it in. They were called back five minutes later. The woman from the front office led her to a room. "Wait here. Dr. West will be in to see you in just a moment."

"Thank you." Lauren sat on a chair in the corner and slid Emily's car seat close to her feet. She felt her daughter's forehead and a shudder passed through her. The baby was hotter than before. There was a knock at the door.

"Yes?" Lauren gulped. What if they called the police or sent her back home? What if they could tell she was running?

The door opened and a pretty black woman walked in. "I'm Dr. West." She held her hand out to Lauren. "Let's take a look at your baby. Why don't you get her undressed, everything except her diaper."

Lauren lifted Emily from her car seat and laid her on the cold examination table. She started to cry, and as Lauren undressed her, she noticed that her baby's face was red. "I think she has a cold."

When Emily's hot body had nothing on but her diaper, the doctor held a stethoscope to her chest. She moved it three times before looking up, her face knit in concern. "Her lungs sound pretty full. Do you live nearby?"

"Is it a cold?"

"I'm not sure." The woman gave her a slight frown. "Where did you say you lived? We might have to admit her. I'd like to see her get an X-ray."

Panic coursed through Lauren. She put her hand on Emily's head and patted her hair. "I'm not from around here. I'm . . . I'm moving to California." She looked at her daughter. "The two of us are moving there."

The doctor waited until Lauren looked back up at her. Then she made a thoughtful sort of sound. "I tell you what. Wait here for a minute." She gave a last quick look at Emily and then she left the room.

Lauren couldn't draw a deep breath. Where was the woman going? Was she calling the police or maybe a social services department? Maybe she was doing a check on her name, and by now her parents would've called and reported her missing. That would bring the police for sure. Emily was crying, squirming on the table. Lauren studied her, the look in her eyes. She didn't look that sick. And with the pain reliever and maybe a cough syrup, they should be okay until she got help. There was only one place where she could turn now, and it would feel like utter defeat. But her medical insurance, her support system, everything was in Chicago. She had no choice but to go back.

Then, when Emily was well, they could head for California once more.

"It's all right, sweetie." She cooed at Emily as she slipped the baby's tiny arms into her little sleeper. After four weeks it no longer felt awkward dressing her, but here she felt anxious, like she was doing everything wrong. When her baby was dressed, Lauren picked her up and cradled her close, bouncing her slightly so that she would settle down.

After a minute Emily was quieter, her crying only in small bursts. Lauren checked the clock on the wall. No wonder her baby was upset. It had been four hours since she'd eaten; she was probably starving. The idea brought a memory back to her. She'd been maybe eleven years old, home with the flu, but she came downstairs and found her mother in the kitchen.

"I'm hungry, Mama. Can I eat something, please?"

"That's a great sign." Her mother pulled her close and stroked the back of her head. "Little girls get their appetite back when they're feeling better."

Her mother's words faded from her mind. Hunger meant that children weren't that sick, right? That was what her mother had told her that day. She sat down and adjusted her shirt so she could nurse her daughter. Sure enough. Emily was starving. She made precious little sounds as she ate.

Maybe that's all this was. A little cold, a fever, and a lot of hunger. She'd driven a long way that day. They probably should've stopped sooner.

The doctor walked in then. She was holding the form Lauren had filled out. "Lauren." Her voice was tender. "I see you've listed no emergency contact and no next of kin."

"No." She looked at Emily. The baby was much happier now, content to be eating. Her eyes lifted to the doctor's. "No, we don't have family at this point. We're making a new life for ourselves out in California."

"Okay." She leaned against the examining table and took a slow breath. "But you're a minor, is that right?"

Lauren searched her mind for the right answer. She hadn't written her age on the form, so how did the doctor know? Had the woman contacted the police or found out that she'd been reported missing? Lauren gulped and just as she was about to shake her head and deny anything of the sort, she felt herself nodding. "Yes. I'm ... seventeen. I'll be eighteen before Christmas."

"You know what I think?"

"What?" Lauren held Emily a little closer.

"I think you need help, Lauren. We have social workers here in Oklahoma City who can help you if we admit Emily. They can find somewhere for you to stay while your daughter's being treated."

Lauren shook her head and looked at her daughter. "Actually, I think she's doing much better. She's eating." She lifted her eyes to the doctor again. "I think maybe she was just hungry."

"I'm worried she could have pneumonia." The doctor winced. "I can't be sure without an X-ray, but I'm concerned."

"What happens if a social worker helps me? I mean, what happens next?" She hated the thought. It meant that there was a possibility someone would take Emily from her. That's what agencies did to mothers like her, right? Mothers too young to know how to care for a baby?

"We'd have to cross those bridges when we reached them." The doctor frowned again, but Lauren didn't sense any anger from her. Just a compassion she hadn't felt from either of her parents. "Everyone would do their best to keep you and Emily together. I'm sure about that. I think we'd want to run a missing persons check. Just to see if you've been reported missing."

A missing persons check? Lauren felt herself closing down. That wasn't going to happen. The police would come and they'd make sure Emily was admitted to the hospital, then they'd take Lauren to the station and call her parents. Social workers would get involved, and when Emily was better they wouldn't consider giving her back to a seventeen-year-old runaway. Then Lauren would be shipped back to her parents. She might never see her daughter again.

She had to buy time. "Okay." Lauren licked her lips. "Well, first I need to get some things from the car. Then we can talk about it, okay?"

"All right." The doctor straightened and felt Emily's head. "She doesn't feel as warm as before."

She wasn't as warm! That was a good sign — a sign that Lauren could take Emily and race back home and still get her the care she needed without risking the possibility that social services or the police would get involved. Lauren slipped her daughter back into her car seat and thanked the doctor. "I'll be right back."

Dr. West turned a different direction as they left the examination room. Lauren wanted to race out the door. She only had a few minutes to get away without being noticed. But she wouldn't leave without paying. She took two twenty-dollar bills from her purse and set them on the counter since no one was behind the desk at that moment. Without looking back, she hurried out the door.

She drove as fast as she could and was on the freeway before she looked over her shoulder. When she did, Emily was sleeping. Then, for the first time since she'd left home, Lauren thought about God. In the days after she got pregnant, Shane had talked all the time about faith and the Lord and His plans for them. Lauren never quite understood how God could want anything to do with them.

Still, she'd told Him she was sorry for messing up, sorry for sleeping with Shane when this whole mess could've been avoided if they'd only done things the right way. She was forgiven, at least that's what the youth group leaders had told her. It was what Shane said too. But still she'd felt like a failure, a disappointment. If God was her heavenly Father, then she would be the last one He'd want to hear from.

But there, with Emily sick and a thousand miles between her and the help she needed, Lauren couldn't do anything but cry out for help.

"Lord, I'm here again," she whispered the words out loud. "Help me, please! I'll drive fast, I won't stop for food, just gas. But please get me home so Emily can get help. Don't let her die, God." Suddenly she realized there were tears on her cheeks. What was she doing, turning around from Oklahoma City and heading back to Chicago? She should never have left home in the first place. She should've let her mother take care of Emily. That way she could've gone after Shane on her own, without risking any harm to her daughter.

"God, I'm the worst mother of all. But you're our Father. For both of us. Please get us home safely, and please, please let Emily be okay."

She wanted an answer, a loud shout maybe from the dashboard speakers, something that would tell her everything was going to be all right. Instead, she felt only a sense of urgency. As if maybe God Himself was telling her that Emily was sicker than any of them knew. She pressed her foot on the gas pedal and picked up another ten miles per hour.

Then just as quickly she eased up. She couldn't get pulled over for speeding. That wouldn't do either of them any good. "God, help me!"

Daughter, my peace I give you ... I am with you always.

The answer might not have come across the stereo speakers, but it resonated in her heart. *I am with you always.* What a wonderful thought. Lauren could feel her heart begin to respond to this truth. She wasn't alone, driving into the dusk and facing fifteen hours of freeway time before she could get help for Emily. She was driving with God right next to her. God Himself.

She leaned back in the seat and relaxed her grip on the steering wheel. He would see her home safely, and He'd help Emily get better. It was all going to be okay. The peace that felt nothing short of divine stayed with her for the next twenty-four hours. It was on the last stretch that everything began falling apart again.

Emily cried all the time and nothing made her feel better. She was burning up and with every breath her little chest rose higher than before. Lauren pulled over at a rest stop and slid into the backseat. She leaned up and locked the doors. It was pitch dark, and there was a group of shady-looking people standing near the water fountain. The stop would have to be a short one. She unbuckled Emily from her seat and felt her fear double. Her daughter's body was still burning up. "Are you hungry, little one?"

Emily's wheezing was worse, but it wasn't until she refused to eat that Lauren felt truly terrified.

Come on, God ... I need you. Make her eat, please ...

She held her daughter tight, tried to help her nurse, but nothing worked. Emily was too sick. Lauren gave her a small dose of cough syrup and another spoon of pain reliever. But still she cried for most of the last five hours of the drive. By the end of that time she sounded so sick, Lauren could barely focus on the road.

All along she'd been blaming herself for being a bad mother, for having no experience, for thinking she could take a newborn on a road trip across the country. But in those final hours, her anger shifted toward her parents. This wasn't her fault, it was theirs. They intentionally separated her from Shane. If he hadn't gone away, she would never have packed up a car and taken Emily on the road.

The whole situation was her parents' fault. Theirs and the Galanters. The people who were supposed to love her and Shane the most had almost destroyed them. Her very own parents had betrayed her by allowing the Galanters to leave without any forwarding information. The reason was obvious now. Shane's parents and hers never had any intention of staying in touch. They'd been willing to sacrifice their friendship for the sake of keeping up appearances.

Lauren's stomach hurt as the reality sank in.

Appearances. That's what it came down to. Shane could have his life without the responsibility of being a teenage father. And with Shane gone, then just maybe she would give up the baby and she too could carry on into her senior year without a care in the world. If things had gone according to her parents' plan, Emily would be safe in the arms of some adoptive family by now.

Lauren gritted her teeth and shifted her lower jaw from one side of her mouth to the other. Were they right? Should she have given little Emily up for adoption? Was that the answer in all of this? She shuddered at the thought of saying good-bye. It wasn't possible; she loved Emily with everything in her.

No, she would take her home, get the help she needed from her parents, and then she would leave them and never look back.

Because they would never accept her for who she was, never accept Emily. Her life and the life of her daughter would always feel like second-best to her parents. And she couldn't have that attitude coloring Emily's life. No, they wouldn't stay. They would get help, get Emily better again, and then they would leave.

And this time they would never, ever come back.

NINE

Angela was sitting alone in the dark, her head in her hands, when a car pulled into the driveway. Her heart leaped into her throat and she raced for the door in time to see Lauren get out of the car.

"Mother! I need your help!"

Angela wasn't sure what to do first. The reality was just hitting her. There was Lauren standing in the driveway, when only a minute earlier it seemed they might never see her again. But her tone snapped Angela out of her shock. She stepped out onto the walkway, ran to her daughter, and embraced her. When Lauren remained stiff, unresponsive, Angela drew back and took hold of her daughter's forearms. That's when she saw it. Intense anger and fear, all mixed together, burned in her daughter's eyes.

"Lauren ..." The fear was hers now. She brought her hand to her daughter's face. "What is it?"

"She's sick." Lauren jerked away. She opened the back door and unbuckled Emily from her car seat.

As Lauren lifted the baby, Angela grabbed a sharp breath. The baby was limp, her face red and blotchy. Angela took a step closer. "How long has she been like this?"

Lauren cradled Emily against her chest. "I don't know." Her face was pale and drawn. She looked as if she hadn't slept in days. "We need to get her to the hospital."

The hospital? Angela's head was spinning. It was just after eleven o'clock at night. "Let me go get your father. He's asleep already and he should—"

"No!" Lauren was wide-eyed. She looked crazed, like maybe she was having a nervous breakdown. "I don't want him coming with us." She held Emily out toward Angela. "Take her, tell me how sick she is."

Angela took the baby in her arms and immediately felt the heat. The child was burning up. Worse, her eyes were open but she was indeed unresponsive. "Is she half asleep?"

"No." Lauren was breathing fast, wiping her palms on her shorts and pacing a few steps in either direction. "She's been like this for a few hours. She won't eat."

Angela held her head near the baby's chest. She was having a terrible time trying to breathe. Angela felt the blood drain from her face. Emily wasn't only sick. She was deathly sick. "Okay—" she nodded toward Lauren's car—"let's get her back in her car seat. She needs a doctor. I'll drive."

They made the trip in silence, Lauren in the backseat with Emily. Angela wanted to ask where Lauren had gone and why she hadn't gotten help in one of the cities she'd passed through along the way. But it was too late for any of that. All that mattered now was Emily.

"Sweetie, it's okay," Lauren cooed at her daughter, but Angela could hear the tears in her voice, hear the way her hushed sobs broke her statements into short bursts of words. "Mommy's here, honey."

When they reached the emergency room entrance at the hospital, Angela directed Lauren to take Emily inside. She parked the car and when she ran in to join them a nurse was taking the baby from Lauren and rushing her through a set of double doors.

"Lauren ..." Angela stopped, not sure what to do.

Lauren looked over her shoulder. "Follow us!"

They gathered in an examination room just inside the double doors. In seconds, a doctor joined them and began undressing the baby. It took him less than a minute to look up from her, his expression grim. "She has pneumonia. We need to start treatment right away. We'll put her on an IV antibiotic and give her immediate breathing treatments."

He rattled off a series of orders to a few attendants and nurses standing by. When everyone was in action—with one nurse putting an IV in Emily's arm, and another preparing a machine with a miniature face mask—the doctor motioned for the two of them to follow him.

In the hallway outside Emily's room, he directed them to a quiet alcove. Then he held his clipboard to his chest and looked first at Angela, then at Lauren. "I have to be honest with you." His expression was deeply troubled. "She should've come in much sooner. I'm afraid her chances aren't good."

Lauren began to fall, slowly at first and then her knees buckled beneath her. Angela hurried to catch her, but she was out cold.

"We need some help!" The doctor snapped his finger and a pair of nurses jumped into action. "Smelling salts; let's hurry."

Angela was on her knees, her daughter's head in her lap. Everything was falling apart, and there was nothing she could do to stop it. Emily might not make it? Was that the next terrible thing that would happen? And then what? How would they ever have a restored relationship with Lauren after this? She wanted to pray, but she was out of practice. Besides, they hadn't exactly asked God about what to do when it came to Shane and Lauren. Why ask Him now? He had probably washed His hands of them a long time ago.

The nurses were at Lauren's side now, waving smelling salts beneath her nose. In a few seconds she came to, but she looked deathly white. Her eyes were glazed over, and Angela could only imagine all she'd been through. She must've turned back to Chicago when she realized Emily was so sick. She probably drove straight through, terrified that she wouldn't get back home in time.

Lauren was fully awake now. She sat up and rubbed her eyes. A frantic look came across her face and she stared at the doctor. "Where is she?"

"Your daughter's in the room across the hall, Miss Anderson. We're doing everything we can."

"What was that part you said? Before ... before I fell?" Lauren didn't look even a little familiar. The fear in her eyes made her look like a crazy person. "Something about my little girl and her chances."

The doctor sighed and helped the nurses get Lauren back to her feet. Then he looked straight into Lauren's eyes. "She's getting everything she needs, but I'm not sure it'll be enough."

"Meaning what?" Lauren's words were fast and hard. "Tell me what that means."

The doctor looked to the nurses and then to Lauren. "Your daughter's very, very sick, Miss Anderson." He pursed his lips and gave a slight shake of his head. "She won't make it without a miracle."

"Lauren ..." Angela moved to take hold of her daughter's arm, but she pulled away.

"Leave me alone." Her anger lasted only a moment. When she turned back toward the doctor there was no trace of it. "Can I sit in the room with her? I ... I won't be in the way?"

"Yes." He nodded toward the door. "You can be with her the entire time."

Angela looked at the doctor. "Can I stay too?"

"No!" Lauren held out her hand in a stop-sign fashion. Her eyes were ablaze with anger. "I don't want you in there. This is—" She looked at the doctor. "Excuse us, please."

"Certainly." The doctor cast Angela a quick look as if to ask if Lauren was all right. Angela gave him a slight nod. Everything wasn't okay, of course, but the two of them could work through it. "I'll be coming in often to check on her and give you updates." He hesitated. "I'm sorry."

When he was gone, Lauren's eyes blazed. "I don't want you in the room with us." Her words were a hiss, and Angela took a step back. She'd never seen Lauren act like this, never.

"Honey, I think I should stay."

"Mother, listen to me." The confusion and craziness seemed to fade, and she looked more lucid than she had since she'd pulled in the driveway. She pointed at the door of Emily's room. "My baby's dying in there because you lied to me, you lied to me and you pushed me and Shane apart, and you left me no choice but to go after him." Her voice was a study in controlled fury. "So I'm going in there to sit with her, and I don't want you anywhere near me. Or her. Understand?"

A shiver passed down Angela's spine. "I'm sorry, Lauren. I never meant for this to—"

Lauren wasn't listening. She opened the door, stepped inside the room, and shut it behind her. Only then did Angela turn and walk back to the waiting room. She would stay until Lauren was willing to talk to her again. As she sat there, she was too stunned to cry, too shocked to do anything but go over what had just happened. She'd wondered what the repercussions might be if they separated the kids, if it all didn't go the way they'd planned. She'd doubted Lauren and Shane would be okay, as the others asserted. Agonized over what would happen if they all were wrong.

Well, now Angela knew.

And the worst was yet to come.

☙

Lauren didn't move from her chair for the next six hours. She slid it up against Emily's little bed and watched as one person or another came in to work on her. She watched them monitor Emily and place a plastic mask over her face to help her breathe, and she watched the medicine drip into her daughter's veins.

The whole time she begged God for one thing: that He might find it in His heart to let Emily live.

Through two o'clock and three in the morning, things still seemed horribly grim. The doctor checked on her and shook his head. "I'm not sure she'll make it, Miss Anderson. Babies this sick usually don't go home."

In between his visits, she looked at Emily, afraid to touch her. Once in a while she'd put her fingers against her daughter's forehead and run them down her tiny arm. "I'm sorry, Emily. Mommy's sorry."

Most of the night her eyes were dry. She was too scared to cry, too worried that she might lose a minute of praying and willing life back into her little girl.

Then, at four o'clock, the doctor came in with the best news of the night, the best news of the past two days. "Her white count is better. It looks like she's responding to the antibiotics."

"Really?" Lauren didn't usually say much when the doctor came in. She was too afraid of the answers. But this time she felt a surge of hope so great she couldn't keep quiet. "You mean she might pull out of it?"

"I can't say." He studied Emily, placing his stethoscope to her chest and listening. When he straightened, he looked at Lauren. "I hear an improvement. I'm amazed, really. If things continue in this direction, she might get better quickly. Once babies make a turn for the better they can be eating in twelve hours." He paused and lowered his brow. "But don't get too excited, Miss Anderson. Your baby is still very sick."

When the doctor left, Lauren felt an absolute certainty. Emily was going to pull through! God had heard her cry and He'd reached down from heaven and given them a miracle. She thought about what the doctor said. Emily could be awake and wanting food in twelve hours. If that were true, she'd need to be rested enough to take care of her. Especially because she didn't want to spend any more time than necessary in Chicago.

She considered her options. What she really needed was sleep. She could take the car and go home, get eight hours of sleep, and then come back. If she stayed at the hospital it wouldn't help Emily, and if she didn't get sleep she'd be no use at all to her daughter. But first she needed to talk to her mother. Lauren wasn't any less angry, but she needed to tell her that Emily was doing better. She deserved to know at least that much.

Emily's breathing sounded better, much better. Lauren hesitated. She hated leaving, hated being apart from her daughter for even a few hours. But she had no choice, not if she was going to be well enough to care for Emily when she woke up. Lauren stood and leaned over her baby. "Keep fighting, Emily." She kissed her daughter's feathery soft cheek. "I love you, sweetheart. I'll be here in the morning."

With one last look at Emily, she left the room and went to the waiting area. Her mother was awake, sitting in a chair at the far end of the room. Their eyes met, and Lauren moved toward her, refusing further eye contact until the last moment.

"Emily's doing better. The doctor says he can't believe it." She sat down in a chair opposite her mother. "I want to be strong for her when she wakes up. I thought I'd go home and get some sleep."

Her mother nodded. "I'll stay here."

Lauren hadn't considered that. She figured her mother would go home, since she might need sleep too. "Are you sure?"

"Yes. I'm fine. I'll go in and sit with her while you're gone."

For a moment Lauren considered telling her mother she was sorry about the scene earlier. But things between them were still a twisted ball of knots. It would take months to unravel all the hurt and resentment. For now she stood and her mother did the same. And even though it went against everything she felt, Lauren hugged her.

It was a short hug, but it was a start.

She drove home, slipped in through the front door, and crawled up the stairs. She was asleep before her head hit the pillow. By the time she woke up, it was two in the afternoon, and the house was silent. She sat straight up and looked at the crib.

Where was Emily?

It took her a few minutes to remember that she'd come home not quite halfway to Los Angeles, and that Emily was sick. And then it all rushed back.

She jumped from the bed. She needed to know how Emily was more than she needed her next breath. She called information and got the number for the hospital, and a minute later she was talking to a nurse.

"Hi." Lauren swallowed. The fear from the night before was back. "My little girl is a patient there. I need to check on her."

"What's her name?" The woman seemed kind, not rushed the way nurses sometimes seemed.

"Emily Anderson."

"Okay, let me check. I'll be right back."

Please, God … please.

The seconds passed like hours, and finally the woman came back. "I'm sorry, you're the baby's mother?"

Lauren's heart tripped over itself. "Yes, I need to know … how is she?"

"Well … I don't know how to tell you this, but she's gone. Just a few hours ago. I'm sorry someone didn't call you and—"

The woman's words grew too dim to hear. Gone? Emily, her baby girl, was gone? Lauren dropped her head in her hand, and the phone slid down her cheek. She could hear the woman speaking, but it didn't matter, it didn't make a bit of difference. Her baby was gone. Just a few hours ago … a few hours ago.

God ... God where were You?

She was the worst mother ever.

Her feet and hands and heart felt numb, and she eased off the bed to her knees. *I begged you, God. You let us down. My baby is dead and I wasn't even there to hold her or tell her it would be okay. You knew ... You* had *to know it was going to happen and You didn't make me stay there ...*

She gripped the edge of the bed and strained for a single breath, but it wouldn't come. The room was spinning, tilting hard to one side. In the distance a tinny voice was saying, "If you'd like to make a call, please hang up and try again ... If you'd like to make a call ..."

God, why? Why didn't You let her live? She was everything I had, all that mattered. Her tears came then, delayed only by the shock racking her being. Waves of tears shook her, tearing at her soul. Emily was gone, and Shane never even had a chance to meet her. *Is that fair to him, Lord? He wanted to be a father and now he'll never even know her!* She squeezed her eyes shut and remembered a few months back, when she was pregnant and sitting beside Shane in his car. He'd put his hand on her belly and felt Emily kick. The wonder and awe on his face ...

He would've made the most wonderful father, but now ...

Now he would never have the chance.

Everyone had failed her. Her parents and Shane's parents. And now even God. "Will the punishment never end?" She whispered the words, but as she did the anger came back fast and furious and her voice rose. "Will it never end?" She pounded the bed and opened her eyes, staring out the window. "How could You let her die, God? Why did You take her from me? She never ... never even got to live."

She sobbed out her anger, her grief, letting her forehead fall against the bed. "Emily ... baby girl ..." The fight left her, and all she could do was picture her precious daughter, the way she'd looked in the hospital bed. The doctor said she was doing better, right? So what went wrong? The tears came harder now, and Lauren wondered if they'd fill the room and drown her. "Emily ... baby, Mommy's sorry." Her words were muffled, spoken into a bunched up section of blankets. "I should've stayed with you, sweetheart." She gasped for whatever air she could get. "Emily ... I love you, baby. I'm sorry."

It took time, but finally her tears slowed. As they did she was left with an emptiness that knew no bounds, a hollow place that was chilling cold and pitch dark. She could still hear chatter coming from the phone, but she blocked it out. There was only one person she wanted now, one who could hold her and make sense of the nightmare that her life had become.

Shane Galanter.

She wanted him now more than ever before. Lauren stood, slowly and carefully, because the room was still spinning. After a minute she found her balance, drew a slow breath, and walked out of her room. No need to stop and look around, to think of the memories she was leaving behind. Memories of her little girl would live forever in her heart, a single bright light in a place that would be dark until she found Shane.

Emily was gone, and with her every hope for the life the two of them could've lived with Shane. But Shane was still out there. Somewhere. As she drove out of the suburbs toward the freeway, she passed the hospital and thought about going inside. She could at least hold her baby one more time. Certainly her body would still be there. Or maybe not. Maybe they'd already taken her to the morgue. Yes, that would be it. There was no way she could go into the hospital now.

She had a handful of photographs and a month full of memories of Emily Sue Anderson. She was too late even to see her daughter's lifeless body, and beyond that, to see her mother. Not when all of this—every bit of it—could've been prevented if only their parents hadn't separated them.

She and Shane should've been together, at home with Emily in their arms. Gripped with emotion, Lauren pulled off the road and stared at the hospital. She wouldn't forget her last day with Emily. Watching her breathe, and believing with everything in her that God was going to give them a miracle.

Her lips pressed tight together.

But You didn't do that, did You? You summed up my abilities as a mother, and You chose to take Emily home with You. I'll never forgive You for that, God. Not ever.

She cradled her empty arms against her chest and imagined the feel of Emily against her, warm and alive and fully dependent on her. "I let you down, baby… Mommy's sorry." The tears in her heart became sobs, and Lauren let her head fall against the steering wheel. "Emily … if I could hold you one more time." But she couldn't, because everyone had worked against her and Shane. Even God. What good was it that Emily was in heaven? *Didn't You have enough babies up there? Did you have to take mine*? As angry and scared and empty as she felt, even that one truth—that Emily was in a better place—meant nothing to her.

Not when all she wanted was one more chance to hold her daughter.

She blinked until she could see. Then she pulled the car onto the road and headed toward the first freeway onramp. She was finished with Chicago, with her parents, with their God… with every piece of her past. She would find Shane. They'd make a way to be together. Then later, when they were married and more stable, they could return to Chicago and talk to her parents. They could see about mending ties. Nothing would ever be the same again, but she could always go back home. Always pick up her things.

But she could never have her little Emily again.

Grief filled every breath as she pulled out of town and headed for her new life in Los Angeles. The drive would take six full days, and on the third day she sold her sports car to a dealer in Texas. She used that money to pay cash for another car, a sensible four-door sedan with low mileage.

Not only was the new car more economical, but her parents couldn't trace her license plate. They wouldn't expect her to have a new car, and by the time she registered it in California, she'd think of some way to keep her parents from knowing about it.

By her fifth day on the road, she began to worry about money. She had forty-five hundred dollars left, but it was going fast. Before she could look for Shane she had to have a plan, a place to live, a job.

She settled in a town called Northridge, and on her second day there she drove to the California State University, located in the center of the town. On a bulletin board she found three sets of girls looking for a roommate. One sounded more serious than the others, and the rent was only a couple hundred dollars a month. Perfect for her budget.

She made the call, and by that afternoon she had a place to stay and roommates who seemed nice enough. One of them asked about her age, but she brushed off the comment.

"I look young. Everyone always says so." She smiled, though it felt foreign on her lips. A smile hadn't touched her face since she left Chicago, since she drove away from the place where her daughter had died. But she wouldn't share any of that, not with strangers. Not with anyone except Shane.

One of them, a petite Chinese-American girl, raised a curious eyebrow. "Are you a student at Cal State Northridge?"

"Not yet." Lauren swung her purse over her shoulder. "I need to earn money this semester."

"What was your name again?" A tall, thin brunette leaned against the wall. Her eyes sparkled, and Lauren guessed that a lifetime ago if she'd met the girl, the two might've become friends.

"Lauren."

"Got a last name?"

The cool facade cracked down the middle, but just for a minute. She smoothed her hand over her button-down blouse and grinned. "Sorry. Lauren Gibbs."

"Lauren Gibbs?" The Chinese-American girl made a curious face. "I've seen that somewhere before."

Lauren shrugged. "It's a common name." She kept her breathing even, unwilling to give herself away. "What about you?"

Their names were Kathy, Song, and Debbie. They talked about the campus and classes, and then they all fell silent. Kathy, the girl who seemed most in charge, held out her hand. "Welcome. The first rent is due when you move your stuff in."

"Would now work?" Lauren took out her wallet and pulled out two hundred dollars.

They all laughed, and Lauren went back out to the car for her things. She ached inside. So this was her life now. Lies and making do and pretending she was someone she wasn't. The pain she carried buried deep within her. She blinked tears away.

So be it.

All that mattered was surviving long enough to find Shane.

Her room was small and she shared it with Song. It took thirty minutes to unpack and get her area set up. She placed the photo of Shane and her on the windowsill. The pictures of Emily she would keep in the drawer. She'd buy a photo album, so she could look at them often.

The next day she found a job waiting tables at Marie Callender's, a restaurant across the street from her apartment. On the application, she wrote Lauren Gibbs, and all her contact information came from the new life she'd started the day before.

By then, she had a plan. When she got her first paycheck, she'd get identification and a driver's license with her new name. It was possible. Especially since she didn't have a Social Security card yet. One of the girls at the restaurant had given her some information, a way to start the process. Once she had her new identity firmly in place, she'd register her car and get on with life.

There was a community college not far from Northridge. She would contact the school and take her GED. Then she'd enroll in classes on that campus for the first two years. After that she'd transfer to Cal State Northridge and earn a degree in journalism. Life would be the way it should have been. At least on the surface.

That afternoon Lauren went back to the apartment and found the single phone on a desk in the living room. She grabbed a pad of paper from the counter and a pen from the drawer. August was too soon for school to be in progress, but by now Shane would be enrolled somewhere. Office staff started earlier than teachers, didn't they? She tapped the pad of paper with her pen. A phone book sat not far away, and she reached for it. A section in the front had the names and numbers of all the local high schools. She started at the beginning

Canoga Park High School.

She picked up the phone and dialed the number.

"Canoga Park High School."

"Yes, hello." She did her best to sound old. After all she'd been through it wasn't a stretch. "I need to verify that our son's enrolled for the coming semester."

"Very well. Is he a new student?"

It was working! Lauren swallowed hard. "Yes. We just moved here from Chicago."

"Okay, let me get the list of incoming students." She hesitated. "What was the name?"

She closed her eyes and pictured him, his dark hair and damp eyes, the way he'd looked that last day when he told her good-bye. The woman was waiting. "Shane Galanter."

"Shane Galanter." The woman repeated his name slowly, and the rustling of papers sounded in the background. "Nope. He's not registered yet. Would you like me to start the paperwork?"

Lauren opened her eyes and wrote a tiny NO next to the name Canoga Park. "That's okay." She uttered a polite laugh. "I'll talk with my husband. We'll come in later this week. Thank you."

Next on the list was Taft High School.

By three o'clock she'd tried every school in the San Fernando Valley. Shane wasn't enrolled at any of them. But that was okay. She had a room and a job and a plan for the future. And she had a new identity. Lauren Anderson was no more. Her death date was the same as her daughter's. She died the moment the nurse told her that Emily was gone. From that moment on, Lauren had no family, no daughter, no desire to do anything but move on and fulfill her single goal in life: to find Shane. She would look as often as she had a chance, every day, every hour.

Even if it took the rest of her life.

TEN

Shane couldn't think of anything but Lauren.

They'd been tricked, that much was obvious. The whole phone number thing didn't make sense unless it was intentional. At least on the part of Lauren's parents. He'd brought it up to his parents a handful of times, and they always seemed surprised. His mother looked confused the first time he told her about the recording on Lauren's old phone number. "We thought they were leaving a forwarding number. Angela told me they were leaving it on the recording."

"So why didn't they?" Shane was ready to get in his car and go back to Chicago. Except the car wasn't his, and his parents wouldn't let him take it farther than the mall. He fought his frustration as he looked at his mother, trying to figure out the situation. "What do you think happened?"

"Truthfully?" Pained sorrow filled his mother's face. "I think maybe they wanted to be rid of us ... rid of you, Shane."

"Why?" He was on his feet. "They know how much Lauren and I want to be together. I can't call her without a phone number." He thought for a minute. "Do they know ours?"

His mother frowned. "I don't see how they could. We're in a new development, and getting our phone service in took a while. You know that." She took hold of his hand. "It feels like they wanted to cut ties, son. I'm sorry."

Time wore on and he watched the calendar. When it came time for Lauren's due date, he waited until he had the house to himself, which happened every afternoon. His father was always at his new mortgage office, and his mother spent her afternoons there helping set it up. So every afternoon Shane worked through a list of hospitals within a hundred-mile radius around the city of Chicago.

"My girlfriend's having a baby," he told the receptionist at the first hospital on his list. "I need to know if you've admitted her."

"Sir, I'm afraid we can't give patient information out to anyone except next of kin."

He felt the frustration build. "You mean if I were her husband you'd tell me if she was there?"

"Exactly."

He didn't have to be told twice. He called the next hospital on his list. "My wife's having a baby. I need to know if you've admitted her."

"Her name?"

He felt a surge of hope. "Lauren Anderson."

The sound of typing filled the phone line. "No, sir. No one here by that name."

Then he'd go to the next hospital on the list. When he was finished, he'd hide the list where his parents wouldn't find it. Not that they'd stop him from trying to find her. But they weren't happy about the pregnancy, and he had the sense it would be better to keep his phone calling to himself.

Each day, after his parents were gone, he'd pull the list from his hiding spot under his bed and start again at the beginning. Lauren's due date was mid-July, and he made the phone calls until the end of the month. Then he began to panic. What if something had happened to the baby, or what if Lauren left the area or decided to give the baby up?

There were nights he couldn't sleep because his mind wouldn't stop thinking of ways to find her. She was in the Chicago suburbs somewhere. He tried calling directory assistance, but none of the

Bill Andersons listed outside the city were the right one. That's when he hit on the idea of calling the banks. There were dozens in the suburbs around Chicago, but he had plenty of time.

He made another list and started at the beginning.

"Hi, a friend of mine recently bought a bank in your area. I'm trying to find him. Could you tell me if Bill Anderson is the new owner there?"

"Bill Anderson?"

"Yes. It was only a few months ago."

"No, we've had the same owner for ten years."

The answers were mostly the same. Only a few times did people give him a little bit of possibility. Once he called a bank outside Wheaton and started the conversation the same way:

"A friend of mine bought a bank in your area. Could you tell me if Bill Anderson bought your bank recently?"

"Yes. Could I get your name please?"

Yes? Shane was so excited he stood up and paced across the empty kitchen. "My name's Shane. Shane Galanter."

"Just a minute please." The woman put him on hold and after a short time she came back. "I'm sorry, that's not the name of our owner."

"But you told me yes, you just said that, remember?" Shane pushed his fingers through his hair and rested his forearms on his knees. "Please, check again."

"Sir, I'm very busy. I don't keep track of the bank owners. Can I help you in any other way? Would you like to open an account?"

Shane slammed the phone in the cradle. He tried that bank three more times, but he never again had the strange response he'd gotten that first time.

At the end of another week the bank list turned up nothing, and that made Shane wonder. Maybe Lauren's father had chosen a different investment, the way his father had. A mortgage company or an insurance office, something new. The possibilities were endless, and that meant another dead end.

He tried the few friends Lauren still had, but none of them had her new contact information. Besides, most of them had faded away by the time summer came. Teenage girls didn't spend time with one of their own who was seven months pregnant.

More time passed, and now it was late August and school was starting in a week. Shane was going crazy trying to find her. She would have the baby now, and that meant she'd made her decision. Either she was learning how to be a mother with their baby at her side, or she had given the baby up.

One night that week he was quiet at dinner, and his father asked him about it. "You okay, Shane?"

"I can't stop thinking about her."

His father took a bite of his chicken. "Who?"

"*Who?*" He looked from his father to his mother. "Are you serious?"

"Honey, he's talking about Lauren, of course." His mother passed a bowl of mashed potatoes across the table. She looked his way. "Have you tried her old number again? Maybe they've left a forwarding number by now."

"I try it every day." He raked his fork through his green beans and pushed his chair back from the table. "I can't find her. I hate this."

"I'll tell you what, son. You get through this next year of school, and if she hasn't turned up by then, we'll go looking for her."

By the end of the year? Shane stared at him. Did he really think that was a possibility? That the two of them wouldn't find each other for a whole year? What about the baby? He was a father; he certainly had the right to spend time with his child, to meet him or her.

That night he turned in early. Baseball was done for the summer, and he still had a few days before school started. He opened his closet and pulled out a box he kept near the back. Then he shut his bedroom door, carried the box to his bed, and gently lifted the first thing from the top. It was a framed photo that Lauren had given him at the end of their fifth-grade year. The two of them had just finished a track meet, and they had their arms locked around each others' necks. In the background, he could see her parents, talking to some of the other adults. His mother had taken the picture. He could hear her voice still.

"You two are darling together."

"Mom, come on." He hadn't been into girls back then. Lauren was his friend. "Take the picture."

When she finally snapped it, Lauren grabbed her water bottle and sprayed him. The move took him by surprise. He grabbed his and chased her, but she was fast and she had a head start. They ran, and as he caught up to her he tore the lid from his bottle. He doused her before she could get away, and they both wound up lying on the grass, side by side, soaking wet and laughing hard.

He looked at the picture now. It was faded, and their faces looked so young. Like that moment had happened to a different couple of kids altogether. He reached back into the box and the next thing he brought out was a handmade card, something Lauren had made him for his thirteenth birthday.

On the outside she'd drawn stick figures of the two of them on opposite sides of a football stadium. It reminded him of his parents and hers sitting at a high school football game, talking and laughing and watching the action on the field. He and Lauren had walked down behind the bleachers and there—in the shadows of the stadium—they shared their first kiss.

"Don't tell anyone ever, okay?" Lauren's cheeks were red. She could hardly wait to get back up to the bleachers.

"I won't. We can stay on opposite sides of the stadium, okay?" He grinned at her. "That way no one will ever guess."

"Okay. Let's do that."

He looked at the card now. It was lightly yellowed from the years that had passed. The stick figures couldn't have been farther apart. On the inside she'd written, "How's life on your side of the bleachers?"

He ran his fingers over the cover of the card and slipped it back into the box.

How had everything gone so wrong? They were the couple their friends liked to hold up as the perfect pair. Their families were best friends, they both had a determination to stay away from the pitfalls other couples fell to—either by spending too much time together or by getting too physical. It was that last summer, that's what did them in. When he looked back, it made sense that they'd fallen. They were alone so much of the time, and by then they were almost too comfortable with each other.

He looked back into the box. It was half full of cards and letters. He reached in and pulled out one that was folded into a small square. Carefully so he wouldn't rip the paper, he opened it and found the beginning. "Shane, we were studying zoo animals and Miss Erickson assigned me to work on the monkey. Which made me think of you. Remember the monkey? I never laughed so hard in all my life. Love you lots and lots, Lauren."

The monkey. A chuckle sounded low in his throat. He and Lauren had gone to the zoo with their sixth grade science class. He'd been caught talking to her, and the teacher forced him to give a speech on monkeys to the class.

Again the memory dimmed, and he reached for another folded note. This one had a picture Lauren had drawn. It was a fighter jet with a little man sitting in the cockpit. She'd drawn an arrow to the figure and scrawled the words, "You're gonna fly one day! When you go, take me with you."

The evening wore on that way with one special picture or letter after another. In the end, he packed everything back in the box and slipped it back into his closet. Wherever she was, he needed her. And he was certain she needed him. She was his best friend, the girl at the center of all his good memories of growing up.

He stared out the window into the dark. *God, You know where she is and what she's doing. I have to find her. Please, God. I don't know what else to do.*

The answer came clear and quick. *Follow me, son, follow me.*

The words took him by surprise. He hadn't been to youth group or read a Bible since he moved to Los Angeles. What he had done, though, was pray. And prayer felt more and more natural. Okay, so he'd follow Jesus. But what did that mean when it came to Lauren? When he told her he wouldn't ever love anyone the way he loved her, he'd been telling the truth. He needed her like water, like air.

He would pray for her and he would look for her until he found her. As long as he lived he would look. And one day—he believed without a single doubt—he'd find her. And then they could go through the box of memories together and laugh at all the funny times they'd shared.

The stick figures and the stadium, and especially the drawing of the fighter jet. All of that and a baby too. He could hardly wait.

ELEVEN

Bill Anderson was in his office doing something he'd done every waking hour since Lauren left.

Talking to God.

He braced his elbows on his desk and covered his face with his hands. *I'm back, God. I need to talk to you again about Lauren.* His throat grew thick, and he held his breath to ward off the wave of sorrow. All he ever meant to do was love her. She was his precious girl, his only child. His daughter. Of course he wanted a bright future for her. Before Lauren's pregnancy, if that future had included Shane, then wonderful. Everyone would win. But once a baby was involved ...

Everything changed.

Bill forced himself to exhale. When he first learned about his daughter's pregnancy, he was crushed. How he hated that his little girl would have to grow up too fast. But he didn't embrace the idea of keeping her from Shane until he saw the shallow, biting reaction from the Galanters. Anger stirred in him again at the thought, and he shifted in his chair. How dare Sheila and Samuel make his daughter out to be nothing more than a cheap tramp! And that's exactly how they treated her at the end. The more he thought about Lauren having the Galanters as in-laws, the more he felt angry and sick. She deserved so much more than that. But now, somehow everything had backfired.

God, I'm sorry. I took matters into my own hands, and now, well, I'm desperate. He made his hands into fists and pressed them against his eyes. He hadn't let Angela see him cry much, but the tears were there. Any time he thought about Lauren. Every few minutes he had an overwhelming desire to get in the car and drive after her, search the highways and byways from Chicago to California until he found her, until he could hold her in his arms and tell her how sorry he was.

I only meant to love her, Lord. Forgive me for not listening to her, for thinking I had all the answers. Give me a second chance with her, please. She's all alone out there, and she needs us. She needs us more than she knows. Thank you, God. He straightened and lowered his hands to his desk. He still had work to do that day, not the kind that used to keep his attention. But phone calls and meetings with a private investigator, someone who might help him find his daughter.

He pulled a list close and noticed that his hands were trembling. He missed her so much it was a physical pain, an ache slicing right through him. It was there when he woke up and when he turned off the lights each night. Where was she and what was she doing? How was she getting by without their help?

He let out a shaky sigh. His prayer was right on. Wherever she was, his little girl needed him, the way she always had. But now he understood something he hadn't before.

How desperately he needed her too.

❧

The truth was beginning to sink in.

Lauren was gone from their lives and she wasn't coming back. Three months had passed, and none of their efforts had made a bit of difference. Angela finished cleaning the kitchen and put the kettle on. Tea was always good at this time of the morning, something to give her day a sense of normalcy. As if she wasn't dying a little more every day.

Bill was home because it was Monday, the day he'd dedicated to finding Lauren.

"The business can do without me one day a week," he'd told her. "I can't stop looking. Not ever."

The kettle began to rattle, the water inside halfway to boiling. She leaned back and surveyed her kitchen. It was bright and airy, the sort of kitchen in the sort of home she and Bill had always dreamed of having. But the dream never materialized, because always it had included Lauren. She should've been there, enjoying her upstairs bedroom, excited about her senior year in high school.

Her loss was a constant ache for both of them, the way it would be until they found her. She crossed her arms and heard Bill coming in from the other room. "Making tea?"

"Yes." She smiled at him as he walked through the doorway. "Want some?"

"Sure." He took up his position opposite her, the kitchen island between them. "I have an appointment with another investigator. He wants more information, anything we can remember about her past. Things that might be significant."

Angela took another mug from the cupboard and gave him a sad smile. "Shane Galanter." She shrugged one shoulder. "That's the most significant thing, right?"

He slumped a little. "Right." He blinked and his eyes looked wet. "Pastor Paul's coming over again tonight. There's three more to the Bible study we're doing."

Bible studies and meetings with pastors, all of it was so new to them. Why hadn't they found the richness of faith before, back when they were still living the perfect dream life, before Shane and Lauren fell to temptation and life turned upside down? How different things might've been if she and Bill had made faith more important to their daughter. To themselves.

The kettle began to whistle, low and steady. She flipped the burner off and poured the tea. "I love meeting with him. Everything he's showing us, it's just what we need."

Bill bit his lip. "It's what we needed years ago." He took his tea, moved around the kitchen island and kissed her tenderly. "I'm sorry, Angela. I'll tell you every day until we find her. It's my fault she left." He pulled back a few inches. "You asked me to think it through, and I didn't do it. I thought ... I thought I was protecting her, loving her."

"I know." She lifted her eyes to her husband. "We have to keep praying."

"And searching." He took the tea and headed back toward the doorway and the den around the corner. "I have a few phone calls to make before I meet with the PI. I'm guessing by now she's enrolled in college somewhere. The PI wanted me to make a list of the schools she might've been interested in."

"Okay." She watched him go. First it had been a search on Lauren's license plate, and then a search of the hotels she might've stayed in along the way. Next it was hotels in California, and now they were moving on to colleges.

It all felt so futile.

The only bit of searching that had turned up anything at all was the license plate check. According to the information found by the first investigator, Lauren had sold her car in New Mexico. Clearly she must've used the money to buy a new car, but that's where the trail died off. Angela picked up her tea and remembered back, the way she always did at this time of the day. There had been no warnings, no sign that her daughter was about to bolt. Lauren had spent the night at Emily's side, and when she left at four-thirty that morning, it was with the promise that she'd come back after she got some sleep.

Angela closed her eyes and drifted back to that day, the way it had played out hour after hour. By midafternoon she was concerned about Lauren and where she might've gone. She called home, but there was no answer. Finally around six o'clock, Bill called her.

"I'm coming down." He hesitated. "How's Lauren doing?"

Alarm rang through her heart and mind. "Lauren's at home." She pressed the receiver to her ear so she could hear above the commotion in the waiting room.

"No, she isn't." His voice held instant alarm. "I thought she was there."

"Have you checked her room?"

"No, I just thought... give me a minute, I'll check." He wasn't gone long. When he returned, his voice was more strained than before. "She's not here. It looks like she slept in her bed, but she's gone. Maybe she's on her way there."

Back then, Angela was still furious with her husband, still barely able to talk to him without feeling hateful toward him for what he'd done by breaking up Shane and Lauren. Even if it had been done with love as the motive. When he suggested that Lauren might be on her way to the hospital, Angela didn't push the issue; she only hurried the phone call and agreed that it would be wise for him to come. Maybe he was right, she'd told herself. Lauren was on her way back; that had to be it. She wouldn't simply leave town—and Emily—without some sort of explanation, would she? Not when she hadn't given them any warning. But after another thirty minutes, she had a certainty equaled only by the pain inside her.

Lauren was gone.

Again Angela called the police, and she was given the same answer: wait twenty-four hours and file a missing persons report. She was frantic at the thought of Lauren back on the road, setting out to find Shane, especially when she was so upset. After an hour Angela went to the nurse's station and questioned everyone on staff, trying to figure out if Lauren had called. By all accounts, she hadn't talked to any of them since she left the hospital that morning.

Angela's only clue came when she talked to the woman manning the desk in the pediatric unit.

"Have you asked anyone in labor and delivery? Sometimes our calls get mixed up."

She thanked the woman and hurried to the other side of the floor where labor and delivery was housed. The woman at the desk was pleasant, but distracted.

"Can I help you?" She had a novel in her hand, and she seemed anxious to get back to her reading.

"Yes." Angela gripped the edge of the counter. "My daughter is supposed to be here. I'm trying to figure out if she called."

"What's her name?"

"Lauren Anderson. She would've called looking for her infant daughter, Emily."

A light dawned in the woman's eyes, and just as quickly a sheepishness. "You know, something that happened earlier this afternoon's starting to make sense." She nodded. "She might've called."

"What ... what makes you think so?" Angela wanted to run around the counter and shake the woman. The information wasn't coming nearly fast enough.

"Well—" the nurse closed her book and sat up straighter—"I took a call from a woman looking for an Emily Anderson." She cringed. "I thought she must've been one of our new moms. See, we had a newborn named Emma Henderson who had gone home a few hours earlier."

The pieces swirled in Angela's head. She pressed her fingers to her temples and stared at the woman. "I'm not seeing the connection."

"Sorry." A nervous laugh sounded from her throat. "I think she asked about Emily, and I told her she was gone. That she'd been gone for a few hours." The woman sifted through a pile of papers. "After she hung up, I realized we were maybe talking about different babies. Emily Anderson, Emma Henderson. You know, pretty close."

Angela wanted to scream. "That's it? Did she say anything else?"

"Actually ..." The nurse's smile faded. "She sounded a little distracted. She never actually said good-bye, just sort of hung up on me."

Angela's heart sank to her knees. "Great."

"The woman who called, she's your daughter?" The nurse seemed sorry, but she was already picking up the novel again, positioning herself to dig into the next chapter.

"Yes." She took a few steps backward and shook her head. "Don't worry about it."

"Yeah, I mean it was an honest mistake." She gave her a weak smile. "Sorry if it caused any confusion."

Any confusion? Angela could barely make her feet move as she left the labor and delivery area and returned to the pediatric wing. She found a seat in a quiet part of the waiting room and covered her face with her hands. The details were shaky, but they were easy to string together. If Lauren had called and asked about Emily, and if she'd been told that the baby was gone, that she'd been gone for a few hours, then Lauren might've figured—

She could never quite finish the thought. Not then and not now.

Her tea wasn't steaming like before, so she picked it up and cradled her hands around the warm mug. In the days since then it was easier to believe that Lauren had run for other reasons. That she had convinced herself she needed to find Shane before she could be a mother, and that she wasn't able to handle the responsibility at this time in her life.

The alternative was terrifying.

A soft little cry drifted down the stairs, and Angela looked at the clock. Almost eleven, right on schedule. Her days were nothing if not directed by a routine since Lauren had left. It was a good thing, really. The busyness of her day kept her sane, and gave her a reason to hang on.

She set down her tea and headed upstairs. With each step the memory of that awful day returned. Bill had arrived at the hospital minutes after her conversation with the labor and delivery nurse, and after he realized that Lauren was gone again, he dropped to one of the waiting room chairs, and for the first time since she'd known him, he wept. The sobs that came from him that day told her that he was not the hard, dominating person she was beginning to think him. He was a father who had sought the best for his only child, his daughter. But everything he'd done in the past six months had backfired, and now he was as overcome by grief as she.

They filed the missing person's report the next day, but it did no good. The first police officer they'd talked to was right. No one on the force was going to spend man-hours searching for a seventeen-year-old runaway, a girl driving a nearly new sports car and headed for California.

But something happened in the days that followed. Though Angela and Bill came no closer to finding Lauren, they did come closer to each other. They dropped to their knees near the side of Lauren's bed and did something they'd never done together before. They prayed. Since then, though they carried the pain of Lauren's loss with them, they had a strength and a hope that was unexplainable, unearthly.

The cry from the upstairs room grew louder.

"Coming, honey." Angela hurried her pace. She rounded the corner into the room that should've belonged to Lauren. The baby had kicked off her light blanket, her arms and legs flailing as her cry turned lusty. "Emily, shh. It's okay."

She swept the baby up in her arms and cuddled her close against her chest. Lauren was missing so much. Her baby was changing with every passing week, losing that newborn look and getting more of her own personality and facial expressions.

"Shh, sweetheart. It's okay." She held her close and carried her downstairs, cooing at her the whole way. "Grandma'll heat up your bottle, okay?"

Emily settled down, her eyes big and blue as they looked straight at her. She made a soft sound, and Angela had the sense—as she'd had before—that this little girl would be a fighter, a child of determination. Already she knew what she wanted and when, and she wasn't about to go unnoticed.

Angela warmed the bottle and took Emily to a rocking chair in the living room. They were just seated when Bill came up and stood behind them, his hand on Angela's shoulder.

"She's beautiful."

"Yes."

"Can you see it?" He leaned down and brushed his fingers over Emily's forehead, down the side of her cheek. "The way she looks like her parents."

"I can." Tears stung at Angela's eyes, but she blinked them away. She'd already cried enough tears for a lifetime. Emily needed her now, and she needed her happy and full of energy. "I think she's going to have dark hair like Shane."

"And Lauren's blue eyes."

"Mmm-hmm." She smiled at the baby, but inside her heart was breaking. "Sometimes I'm not sure which hurts more. Missing Lauren, or seeing her every day in Emily's eyes."

Bill didn't say anything. After a few minutes he leaned closer and kissed Emily on the head. Then he straightened and gave Angela a side hug. "I'll let you know how it goes with the PI."

"Okay." She put her hand over his and squeezed. "I'll be praying."

He left through the door to the garage, and she listened as he started his car and pulled away. Private investigators and phone calls and desperate threads of possibility. That's all they had to go on now, all they could draw from if they wanted to find their daughter.

She ran her thumb along Emily's cheek.

The thing was, Lauren had been crazy for her daughter, completely taken with her. Yes, she wanted to find Shane, and no, her trip west with Emily hadn't gone well. But she wouldn't have walked out of the hospital that day without saying good-bye. She would've at least explained that she needed to find Shane, and that she wanted to hand responsibility to Emily over. For a short time, anyway.

Since she hadn't done that, Angela could only imagine the absolute worst.

Lauren believed Emily was dead. From the way she'd acted when Emily was sick, Angela was terrified that Lauren blamed Bill and her for the baby's death. She probably blamed herself, also. And God. With no baby to bid good-bye, and no desire to talk to her parents, she would've been five hundred miles out of town by midnight.

Grief and guilt settled like a cement blanket on her shoulders. Now that she'd allowed herself to admit that scenario, now that she could give herself permission to believe that was why Lauren had left, it made horrible, perfect sense.

When Bill returned a few hours later, she told him her theory so he could share it with the private investigator. The possibility was enough to make her heart race whenever she thought of it. Because nothing was sadder than the thought of Lauren living on her own, believing her daughter was dead, when in reality she was growing up a little more every day. They would spare no expense; stop at nothing to find Lauren. And one day they would get the call or the clue they were looking for, the information that would bring Lauren and Emily back together again. Angela believed that with all her heart.

Even if they had to spend a lifetime searching.

TWELVE

Eighteen years later

Wheaton College was everything Emily Anderson hoped it would be.

The only downside was that it kept her in Illinois, when everything in her wanted to be in Los Angeles. There, or anywhere on the coast of Southern California. Especially this time of year. It was Friday afternoon, and Christmas break was looming.

She stretched her elbow out along her desk and rested her face in her hand. Her feature story on the women's soccer coach was due at five o'clock, but she couldn't focus. Three other journalism students were hanging out at the newspaper office that afternoon, but they were working on a project, so they didn't pay her any attention. The outline for her feature was spread out on the desk in front of her. She glanced at it and tried to be interested. Footsteps sounded from behind, and her professor pulled up a chair beside her.

"Hi, Emily." Ms. Parker was young and likeable. Emily hadn't ever heard anyone say anything bad about her. "How's the story coming?"

She sat up and gave her teacher a weak smile. "Not so good." She looked at the clock. "I still have a few hours."

Ms. Parker found the outline on the desk. "You have your points down."

"Yes." Her heart wasn't into it; that was the problem. She met Ms. Parker's eyes. "Did you always love writing?"

"Not always." She laughed. "Most of my students are the other way around, though. For me, when I was in high school I thought I wanted to be a math teacher. It wasn't until college that I knew I wanted to write."

"Hmm." Emily looked at her notes, not really seeing them. Her eyes lifted to the teacher's again. "Did your mom like to write?"

Ms. Parker angled her head. "Yeah, I guess she did. I never really made the connection." She folded her arms and leaned them on the desk. "She kept a journal and wrote poetry, that sort of thing. Maybe that's where I get it."

Emily nodded. "Maybe."

"Did your mother like writing?" The question was an innocent one. Ms. Parker didn't know Emily well enough to understand the territory she was treading.

Emily forced a smile. "I've never met my mother." She made sure she sounded upbeat. She hated people feeling sorry for her. "My grandma told me she spent time in her room, maybe writing, maybe reading. She isn't sure."

"Oh." Ms. Parker was quiet for a moment. "Well, I bet she was a writer."

"Yeah, maybe."

The instructor tapped lightly on the notes. "You're one of the best soccer players this school has ever had, Emily. A feature on the coach should be easy for you."

"I know." She drew in a long breath and grinned at the woman. The message was clear. Whatever was distracting her, the story had to be written. "I'll get on it."

"Okay." Her smile was compassionate. "Maybe you and your grandma can talk about your mom later tonight." She raised an eyebrow. "When the story's written and put to bed."

Emily made a silly face and nodded, then she took her notes to the computer and in half an hour she had the story finished. Ms. Parker was right. The soccer coach was a burly Nigerian man named Wolf, and if anyone understood him, she did. The man was demanding, but he'd improved her game by miles. If she were more committed, she could make a run at the national team. But competing in college was enough, because she wanted to spend at least some of her time thinking about her future. A future writing for a newspaper in Los Angeles. That's all she'd ever wanted. Talent or no, soccer wasn't her passion. Writing held that spot. It always had.

Writing and her faith in Christ.

From the time she was a little girl her grandma had told her simply, "Your mother and father loved you very much, but they weren't ready to be parents."

The answer sounded sad and empty, but Grandma followed it up with this explanation. "God will always be your daddy, Emily. He'll be there for you wherever you are, wherever you go. He'll never leave you."

Her words proved true year after year, and now Emily considered God more than her father. She considered Him her best friend. He was her life giver, her soul maker, her redeemer. He brought her the greatest gifts—joy and love and forgiveness when she messed up. And He brought her peace. But He couldn't quite fill the emptiness in her heart, in the hidden places where she wondered every day *why.* Why did her mom and dad leave? Why didn't they ever come back for her? She'd met kids without parents and often they were rebellious or angry or distant. Not her. She had a wonderful life. Grandparents who loved her, a beautiful home, and a bright future.

But the emptiness was always there.

Sometimes it made her step back and wonder. Especially when the sky was full of snow clouds and California felt a world away and her heart simply wouldn't leave the past alone. What were her parents like? What sort of people had they become? She focused her attention on the computer screen once more and repositioned her hands over the keyboard. The feature was easy, once she gave it some thought. Wolf had escaped captivity from an underground political group in Nigeria and made it to the United States with just the clothes on his back. He earned a soccer tryout at UCLA and two years later he was on the men's national team. Wheaton College was lucky to have him, and she had quotes from the school's athletic director saying as much.

When she finished the story, she sent it to the editor's desk and stretched her feet out. She was going to spend Christmas break at her grandparents' house, but they weren't expecting her until five-thirty. For now she could surf the Internet, look for something to take her mind off the conversation she'd had with Ms. Parker.

And off her mother.

One headline proclaimed an outbreak of violence had flared up in Iraq. Four U.S. soldiers had been killed when their car hit a roadside bomb, and more troops were being sent over. She scanned the details and tried to imagine life in a war-torn country, a place where bombs and death and violence were commonplace. God is a God of peace, so she didn't understand war or whether the United States should be involved. But she knew this: lots of her friends were fighting in Afghanistan and Iraq, and she supported them with everything she was. Still it was easier not to think about it, not to sort through the whys and how comes. *I don't really understand it, God.*

She typed another Web address into the search line, and in a matter of seconds she was looking at the soccer team's standings. Wheaton was at the top. Unless someone got injured or one of the other teams had an unexplainable surge, Emily was pretty sure her team would stay in first. Wolf had done a great job recruiting over the past few years. For the most part the team was older. Emily was the only freshman.

The room was quieter than before. Two of the three students had gone home, and the other was working at one of the computer stations. She clicked her tongue against the roof of her mouth. Then she typed in *writing* and *genetic.* After a brief pause, the computer screen showed a list that was thousands of websites long. The first one asked this question: "How much of who we are is a result of our parents?" She clicked it, and an article appeared.

"Some things are explainable by science, but some things simply can't be figured out. One such phenomenon that defies scientific understanding is the truth that talent and interests are often passed on from one generation to another. For instance, a person with a talent for writing might well have a child with a similar talent ..."

The article was dry, poorly written, and made up of unbroken small print. She closed it down and stared at the *welcome* screen. She needed to get going. Her grandma hated when she drove home in the snow, and a storm was forecast for that night. She was about to push her chair back, but she couldn't resist. Her hands found the keyboard again. Every few days she checked, the way she had always done. Because mothers didn't just disappear, did they? Her grandmother had told her the story, at least the basics of it. Emily was sick in the hospital and her mother was given bad information—information that might've convinced her Emily was dead. Probably frightened and confused, maybe devastated over the loss of her little girl, her mother had most likely left for California to find Emily's father. Whatever had driven her, she'd left without saying good-bye. To anyone.

In a familiar rush of letters, she typed, *L-a-u-r-e-n A-n-d-e-r-s-o-n*, and hit the search button. Another list of websites appeared, but a quick scan of the first page told her there was nothing new. The number of sites was the same as last time. Every one of them was a site she'd already checked.

Next she tried her dad's name: *S-h-a-n-e G-a-l-e-n-t-e-r.* But the same thing was true; nothing had been added on the Web under his name, either.

"What are you looking for?" Ms. Parker came up behind her.

Emily shut down the list and closed out of the Internet. She turned wide eyes to her teacher. "Something for another feature. I want to do a comparison of culture and expenses between college life in Chicago and Los Angeles."

She gave a nod of her head. "Sounds interesting. You might need more of a local angle, a stronger hook." She looked at her watch. "But for tonight, how about getting home. Snow's coming soon. I want to lock up."

Emily was out of the chair and gathering her things before Ms. Parker walked away. She didn't grab a full breath until she was outside in the car. Why did it matter so much that she found her mom and dad? They had moved on with their lives, and apparently never looked back. She would follow their lead.

Still …

Where had this deep longing come from, to leave the Midwest and live in Southern California? She knew the answer, of course. Knew the region held more draw than sunshine and strong newspapers. It was the place her grandparents always talked about, the place where they thought her mom and dad lived.

Snow began falling, and the clouds overhead grew dark and threatening. Emily didn't mind. She was only twenty minutes from home. A storm didn't frighten her. Funny, how peace was so much a part of how she was raised. Her grandparents explained early on that life wouldn't always go the way she wanted it to. But still she could have peace if she understood that God was in control, that He was there for her no matter what was happening around her.

That's why it was strange when—once in a while—she would come home and find her grandparents huddled together at the dining room table, deep in conversation. At times like that, they looked anything but peaceful. It happened again just a week ago, when she came home. As she walked through the door, her grandparents stopped whatever conversation they were having. She still remembered the strange way they'd acted that day.

"Emily." Her grandma stood up, came to her, and hugged her. "We weren't expecting you until later."

"Journalism let out early." She drew back and set her purse and books on the kitchen table. "Did I interrupt anything?"

"No." Her grandpa was a successful businessman; even now when he was pushing sixty years old, he was a sharp dresser, a man known throughout Wheaton for his power and influence. But with her he'd always had a soft side. He held out his hand to her and she went to him, taking hold of it.

She bent down and kissed him on the cheek. "It's quiet in here." She gave him a hesitant smile. "You sure you weren't talking about something private?"

For the quickest instant, her grandparents looked at each other, as if to question whether they should go into detail about whatever they'd been discussing. But her grandfather only cleared his throat and gave the dining room table a light slap with his open palm. "Dinner. That's what we're talking about. What we can fix for our young college student, home for the weekend."

Their explanations didn't fool her. They never did. She could only guess that they were talking about the one thing they never brought up in her presence: the search for their daughter, Emily's mother. Emily knew they were still looking for her. Every now and then Emily would bring in the mail and see a bill from a private investigator, or a return letter from a congressman's office in California. But their only conversation about Emily's mother was centered on the happier times, the days when she was growing up.

"Your mother colored just like that, with eighteen shades of green in a single tree," her grandma told her when she was little. And as she grew older, "Your mother had a bicycle like that one, shiny red with streamers flying from the handlebars."

From everything she could determine, her grandparents had been on close terms with their daughter. That's why it didn't make sense that her mother would leave in the weeks after she was born. There were so many missing pieces, there always had been. Through the years she had asked her grandparents whenever she felt driven to understand the past better.

Of course, sometimes she dealt with the loneliness all by herself. Too many nights to count she would smile at her grandparents as they kissed her good night and prayed with her. But when they left her room, she would roll onto her side and stare at the open door, wishing just once that her mom would walk through it. She had a picture in her mind of what her mother would look like, the way her eyes would light up when she saw Emily, the tender smile she'd have. Sometimes her imagination would be so vivid she'd actually imagine her mother walking through the door, taking a seat on the edge of her bed, and smoothing her hair.

"I love you, Emily. I always have," she'd say.

But when her imagination let up even for an instant, the image disappeared.

There were other times—times at the park with her grandparents, when she saw a young couple with their children, and for a moment she'd pretend the couple was her parents. She'd think what it would be like to run up to them and take their hands and hug them.

"Emily," her father might say. "We've been looking all our lives for you. Now you're finally where you belong."

The older she got, the less she pretended that way, but still she kept a picture in her mind, the way her parents might look now. Sometimes she encountered something that it seemed only a mom or a dad could help her with. On those days she'd wait until it was time for bed, then hold quiet, one-sided conversations with them. Usually her hushed whispers turned into prayers, requests spoken to God, begging Him to bring them back, to reconnect them somehow.

"I know my mom was young," Emily once told her grandparents when she was seventeen. "But why didn't she check to see if I was alive? She wanted to find my dad, right?"

"Right." Her grandmother was folding laundry. She set a towel down on the sofa beside her and looked up at Emily. "But honey, don't think she had any doubts. I really think she thought you were dead."

"Yeah." Emily folded her arms across her middle, warding off the hurt inside. "But wouldn't she have stayed just in case? In case I was still alive?"

"I don't know." Her grandma sounded sad and tired. "She was desperate to find your father. She wanted to find him more than she wanted anything."

"Anything?" The answer stabbed through her soul. "Even me?"

Her grandmother reached out and took careful hold of her hand. "Not you, sweetheart. She wanted you. That's why I'm sure she must've had incorrect information about you."

Emily thought for a minute. "Well ... maybe we should go to California and find her."

"We've tried." Grandma smiled, but her eyes stayed flat. "Believe me, Emily, we've done everything we know to do. The only way we're going to find your mother again is if God gives us a miracle."

Now Emily stared at the road ahead of her. The snow was heavier than before. Two miles and she'd be home, ready to sleep in her own bed and cuddle up with her grandparents for a couple of movie nights. She didn't have a boyfriend, and most of her friends were spending Christmas break with their families. Emily was glad for the time that lay ahead. With soccer practice every day, her first semester of college was tougher than she'd expected, and she and her grandparents hadn't had much time together.

She took the exit leading to her house and thought again about what her grandmother had said two years ago. It would take a miracle. Fine. She gripped the steering wheel. If it took a miracle, then that's what she'd keep praying for. Because more often lately she couldn't get through a day without thinking of her mom and dad and what had happened to them. Had her mother found him? If so, did they marry and start a new family? Was it possible she had brothers or sisters out west? And if her mom and dad hadn't found each other, were they happy?

And then there was the hardest truth of all. The truth that threatened to tear at the center of everything peaceful about her life and faith and future. The truth that always brought the sting of tears to her eyes. If her grandma was right then there was no point wondering about when she might come back or what type of life she was living.

If her mother thought she was dead, then by now the truth was painfully clear.

She wasn't coming back. Not ever.

Thirteen

Angela had been looking forward to this day since the semester started. She'd decorated the house and opened the seasonal storage boxes so the ornaments were ready to go on the tree. The red felt Advent calendar hung on the wall, all the numbered hand-sewn ornaments ready to be placed on it—even those that should've been up by now.

This would be a very special Christmas. Special and sad, for reasons they didn't want to tell Emily. Not just yet. The news would mar the season, and Angela didn't want that. She wanted one last Christmas celebrated the special way they'd celebrated it every year since Emily was a little girl. Bill had his favorite Mitch Miller CD in the player and a kettle of hot cinnamon apple cider was simmering on the stove. Time enough for sad announcements and changes later.

For now, all they needed was Emily.

She heard the front door open and the cheerful voice of her granddaughter rang through the house. Her delightful, precious granddaughter. "Hi! I'm home."

"Emily!" She gave the garland a last nudge and hurried toward the front door. When she rounded the corner, her granddaughter flew into her arms before she could take another step.

"It's so good to be home!" She circled her arms around Angela and kissed her cheek. "I finished my finals." She pulled back and grinned. "I even finished my feature on the soccer coach."

Angela looped her arm through Emily's and led her into the kitchen. "How do you think you did?"

"Good." She raised her brow a bit. "I guess the first semester is always hard, but I think my grades'll be up there. A's and B's for the most part." She winced. "Maybe a C in biology and Algebra II."

"That's okay." She smiled. "With your sports and your work at the school paper, I think a few C's are to be expected. First semester of high school was hard too, remember?"

"*Do* I." She gave her a dizzying look as she took a seat on one of the bar stools and leaned her elbows on the counter. "In ninth grade I wasn't sure if I'd make it to graduation."

"Your gold tassel took a few of your teachers by surprise." Angela chuckled as she reached into the cupboard and pulled out three mugs. "But not us, honey. We knew you could do it."

She looked around. "Where's Papa?"

"Upstairs." Angela was careful to keep her expression steady. "He's been a little tired lately. He thought he'd get a short nap before dinner." She handed Emily a mug of steaming cider. "Here. Be careful, it's hot."

"Thanks." She held it in both hands and breathed it in. "This is so great." Her eyes took in the adjacent family room, where Angela had most of the decorations up. "All I did was walk through the door and already it feels like Christmas." She took a small sip of her cider. "Is Papa okay?"

"He'll feel better later. That reminds me!" Angela could feel her eyes light up. "He's taken the next two weeks off. He's never done that around the holidays."

"Two weeks?" Emily set her cup down. "That's great!"

"I know." She gave a sideways shake of her head. "The board told him it was time he took a break. He'll be off through New Year's Day." She didn't add that he might be home even longer. Again, that could come later.

They shared their drinks, humming along to Mitch Miller when the conversation slowed. Angela checked the oven and the meatloaf and baked potatoes she had inside. "Dinner'll be ready in half an hour."

"Perfect." Emily drank the last of her cider. "I'm going to freshen up. I'll be back down in a little bit." She flashed a quick smile and took light running steps around the corner into the entryway. She left behind a trail of her things—her duffel bag and backpack and purse. But that was Emily. Loving and friendly, but not the neatest person. Much the way Lauren had been when she was—

No. Angela promised herself that this Christmas—with the news about Bill—she wouldn't spend countless hours thinking about Lauren. It was simply more than she could bear. Still ... with Emily back home it was impossible not to think about the daughter she'd lost, the one who was always only a sad thought away. She checked the dishwasher. The dishes were clean. Time to unload. She put away a row of glasses and then her mind started to drift. How different she was with Emily compared to her days of raising Lauren. With Lauren, everything needed to be perfect. An A minus in algebra meant a brief lecture on the importance of pulling grades up and the necessity of going for the best possible mark. A few scattered items on her bedroom floor, and Angela would've cut out her phone privileges for an entire week.

It was petty and ridiculous how she'd treated Lauren, and all for appearances. So they'd look like the perfect family. Nice house, powerful job, an orderly, intelligent, high-achieving daughter. Just the way she and Bill had always known their lives would play out. But of course, all their plans backfired when they lost Lauren.

Things were entirely different with Emily.

She and Bill prayed with their granddaughter and took her to church. They talked and went on walks around their Wheaton neighborhood and laughed at old movies. Back when Lauren expressed an interest in dance, Angela and Bill signed her up for four classes.

"She's good, she has natural rhythm," Bill said after her first lesson. "We need to be serious about this, help her reach the top. She might be a prima ballerina one day."

Lauren was five at the time.

When Emily showed an interest in soccer, Angela and Bill signed her up, bought her a pink soccer bag, and cheered at her games. Win or lose, they took her out for lunch afterward and didn't talk about the sport again until her next practice session. In the process, she developed a love for the game that went beyond anything Lauren had felt for dance or piano or debate team—the things they'd pushed her toward.

Angela finished her drink and set the cup in the dishwasher. Their attitude toward Emily was different in other ways too. They understood now how fragile life could be. Never had they dreamed they'd go nineteen years without seeing Lauren. If Emily had come home with hair dyed green or a piercing through her eyebrow or a desire for drugs, if she'd come home pregnant by a boy she loved more than life itself, Angela and Bill would never have manipulated her life, the way they did with Lauren. They would've held on to her until love brought her back around again.

Angela shook her head. What irony! The mistakes they'd made with Lauren had taught them how to truly parent. And those lessons allowed Emily the best possible life. Lauren's little girl was grounded in her faith, she had a deep love for the Lord and for Bill and her. She'd never done anything more rebellious than stay on the phone too long once in a while on a school night. Angela drew a deep breath. Emily's future seemed good as gold. She would become a writer—one of the best—and she would go into the world bright and beautiful and sure of herself.

Lauren would've been so proud of her.

She heard the sound of Emily bounding down the stairs. "No soccer practice for two weeks! Isn't that great?"

"Longer than that, right? The season's over." The CD had stopped playing, so she drifted into the family room and started Alabama's *Christmas*, another of Bill's favorites.

"College soccer's a little different." Emily made a face. "We'll be conditioning again, doing scrimmages as soon as the field thaws out. Until then we'll be in the weight room."

The music started, filling the air with the gentle sounds of Christmas, Christmas the way they'd lived it and celebrated it since moving to Wheaton. "How's tomorrow sound for getting the tree?"

"At the farm?" Emily's voice held an excitement reserved for the season. But as she made her way back to the kitchen counter and sat back on the bar stool, she looked distracted.

"As always." Angela followed her and took the spot next to her. "Rain, snow, or sun. You know your papa."

"The cutting is the best part." She brought her hands to her face. "My fingers always smell like pinesap for a week."

"You know what I love?"

"What?" Emily gripped the stool's arms and swung her feet.

"Watching you and your grandfather pick a tree. I think we're twelve years running finding the absolute most interesting tree on the lot."

Emily giggled. "Interesting?"

"Definitely." Angela laughed out loud. "Remember last year? You wanted a tree that would reach the ceiling, but the tall ones were scraggly on top."

"Right." She tipped her head back, her eyes dancing. "That's because a Christmas tree doesn't have to be perfect."

"No, it doesn't." Angela smiled. Neither did people. That was something else she'd learned this second time around.

Their laughter died down and Emily drummed her fingers lightly on the counter, a familiar and comfortable action. It was her sign that she had something deep to talk about. Angela waited.

Finally Emily drew a long breath and their eyes met. "Grandma, can we talk about my mom? I wanna know more about her."

Angela steadied herself. Emily had asked this sort of question before, and always she'd been content with basic answers. But Angela had known that one day Emily would want more. She put her hand over her granddaughter's. "What would you like to know?"

"Well . . ." Emily squinted, as if trying to sort through which questions were most important. "You've looked for her, right?"

"Yes." Angela felt a heaviness in her heart. How many hours and conversations and phone calls had they made? As technology advanced, they'd used the Internet, sometimes every day. "Yes, we've looked."

"Okay, but how did she just disappear? I mean, she thought I was dead, but then what? She just drove out of town?"

"It seems that way." Angela ordered herself to stay unemotional. Emily needed her to be calm; she couldn't give in to nineteen years of sorrow. "She was exhausted and frantic. The two of you had just driven back from halfway across the country, and you were very, very sick."

Emily looked like she was trying to imagine how her mother must've felt, scared and tired and then convinced that her baby was dead. "But you think she went to California, right?"

"We have our theories." Her hand was still covering Emily's. She gave it a soft squeeze. "She might not have made it to California, for one."

Emily nodded. "I've thought about that. She might be dead."

"Yes. Or maybe she changed her name. If that's what happened we could look forever and not find her. In my heart I believe she's alive and out there somewhere."

"Me too." Emily looked out the kitchen window.

From the side, her profile was so like Shane's, a mirror of his striking Greek features. Between that and the fact that she had Lauren's eyes, Angela had a constant reminder of the kids they'd lost.

"I was thinking today whether she ever found my dad and whether they got together or not."

Angela doubted that. "Anything's possible."

"So the last time you saw her was at the hospital, right? When I was sick?"

"Yes. She was overwhelmed, honey."

"I was wondering today," Emily looked at her again, "whether she was a writer or not."

"We've talked about that."

"But I wish I knew for sure."

"Wait..." Angela straightened. "I just remembered something."

A few days earlier Bill had found a box of Lauren's things in the storage section of the garage. Until then, they'd assumed Lauren had taken all her personal belongings with her. But since they'd just moved to Wheaton at the time of Emily's birth, apparently Lauren's box had been shoved with a dozen others into a corner they'd designated for records and tax documents.

Bill was cleaning out there when he found it and called to her. "Angela, come quick."

She hurried to the garage and over to his side. "What is it?"

"Look at this." He was standing next to a big cardboard carton with Lauren's name scribbled on the side. The sight of her daughter's handwriting brought pangs of both joy and sorrow. They lifted the lid, and inside were what looked like old yearbooks, photo albums, and journals. Everything sentimental that had ever mattered to Lauren. She looked at Bill. "I thought... I figured she took this stuff with her."

"Imagine what the private investigators could've done with this if they'd had it back when she first left."

They brought the box inside and took it up to what had been Lauren's room. It was a home office now, a sterile room with a sofa sleeper along one wall. The only trace that it once belonged to Lauren was a photo of her that sat on the desk. That afternoon they spread the contents of the box out and looked at it. Halfway through, though, they stopped and packed it back up. "I can't do this without Emily," Bill said. "There's nothing in here that would help us find Lauren now." He dabbed at his eyes. "Emily deserves to see it first."

Angela agreed, though she thought Bill's reluctance to look through the box had at least as much to do with the fact that it was too painful to sort through. But since Emily was coming home for Christmas, they agreed to wait. It was one more reason she'd been looking forward to the holidays. But in the rush of seeing her and sitting with her, she'd forgotten about the oversized box until just now.

"Grandma, what is it?"

Angela slid down from the bar stool and motioned to her. "Follow me."

They went into the hallway and Angela pointed to the carton in the corner. "We found that a few days ago." She walked closer and put her hand on the edge of the box. "Everything in here belonged to your mother. I'm not sure it'd help us find her now. But ... we thought it would help you know her a little better."

Emily stared at the carton, her eyes wide and unblinking. When she looked up, tears shimmered on her cheeks. "Do you ... know what's in it?"

"Some." Angela put her arm around Emily's shoulders. "Yearbooks, photo albums, journals. That sort of thing. Everything that was special to your mother."

A framed photo sat near the top of the box, and Emily reached for it. The image was a picture of Lauren and Shane, taken before a formal dance their freshman year of high school. Emily had seen photos of her parents before, but nothing from a professional photographer. She held it up, studying it. "Look at their eyes."

Angela removed her arm from Emily's shoulders and leaned in closer, staring at their faces. That's when she saw it, saw it clearer than she ever had when the kids had been a part of her life. "Yes. I see."

"Grandma, they were so in love." Emily pressed the photo to her chest. Her eyes were damp, but her smile lit up her expression. "It makes me feel so good to know they loved each other."

Regret wrapped itself around her, squeezing her chest and making it hard to draw a breath. Why hadn't she seen the depth of their feelings for each other back when Lauren and Shane wanted so badly to be together? How different would their lives be if she'd recognized it then? She swallowed her sorrow and gave Emily a partial smile. "That's why we wanted you to have these things, to look through them while you were home." Angela sniffed. Watching Emily cradle the framed picture gave her a flashback, and she saw Lauren, cradling Emily as a baby. The memory was gone as quickly as it had come, but the sadness lingered. Angela had a feeling that not everything Emily would find in the box would leave her feeling happy and whole.

Still it was her right to look through it.

In the background, they heard Bill getting out of bed and heading into the bathroom. "Dinner'll be ready in a few minutes." She looked at the box. "Papa will help you get it up to your room. You can look through it later."

Emily bit her lip. "I can't wait." She kept the photo tight against her heart. "Grandma, can I ask you something else?"

"Yes, honey. Whatever you want."

"My parents didn't have God in their lives, did they? Not God and not peace." She held the photo out enough to see it.

Angela felt the regrets again, as heavy as they'd been in the days and weeks after Lauren left. "No, Em. They didn't have either."

"Do you think they have that now?"

Angela had asked herself the question a hundred times every year. Was Lauren happy and at peace, had she found the faith that had been missing in her childhood? A sad sigh eased up from the deepest corners of her soul. She shook her head. "I don't think so, honey."

Emily looked at the picture again. "It was because of me, right? She got pregnant and everything fell apart."

Angela worked the muscles in her jaw. Emily was right, more so than she knew. There was no way around the truth. "It felt like a tragedy at the time. You understand that, right?"

"Yes." Emily looked up, her expression far wiser than her eighteen years. She pursed her lips and let her eyes find the faces of her parents once more. "But if my birth tore them apart, then maybe I'm the only one who can bring them back together again."

"Hmm." Angela wanted to warn her not to think that way. If two decades of private investigators and elected officials couldn't find her, what could Emily possibly do to find either of them? Instead she gave a slow nod and framed Emily's face with her hand. "I'm praying for a miracle, Emily. You are too. It's certainly worth a try."

Emily set the photo back down, and the two of them greeted Bill in the hallway.

"Papa! It's so good to see you." Emily threw her arms around his neck and held on tight. "I miss you so much!"

A lump formed in Angela's throat because she knew what Bill was feeling, how precious this Christmas would be with Emily. But it wasn't time for sorrow now. Bill tousled Em's hair and looked her up and down. "Looks like that soccer coach has you down to skin and bones."

"Ah, it's not that bad." She linked arms with him, and the three of them went to the kitchen and worked on dinner. When they were seated at the table, Emily said the prayer. "Jesus, you have me home this Christmas for a reason. I sense that so strongly." Emily squeezed her grandparents' hands. "Thank you for letting my papa find the box of my mom's things. I pray that somewhere inside we'll find a miracle." Her voice was clear, as genuine as a summer sunset. "So that I can meet my mom and dad and help them find the peace that might be missing from their lives. In Jesus' name, amen."

As she finished the prayer, the strangest thing happened in Angela's heart. She felt a surge of hope, the kind she hadn't felt since the first year of Lauren's disappearance. As if maybe God was telling her something very important. That they were indeed standing on the brink of a miracle.

And Emily would have everything to do with it.

FOURTEEN

War didn't take a break for Christmas. This was Lauren Gibbs's third Christmas season on the war-torn fields of Afghanistan and Iraq, and still it amazed her. The opposing sides would set up roadside bombs, aerial attacks, and raids on insurgent headquarters right through December 25. As if the birth of Christ didn't matter at all.

Not that it affected her one way or the other. Christ's birth didn't mean anything to her. It was four days before Christmas, and she didn't feel anything different—no special magic or joy or desire to marvel at a decorated evergreen tree.

She had her memories. That was enough.

As a correspondent for *Time* magazine, her duty was in Afghanistan. Her assignment was complex. First and foremost, she was responsible for reporting the trends of the war before the competition figured them out. In addition, she looked for daily stories, word pictures, snapshots of a war-torn life. She was also responsible for feature stories and predictions on when the white flags would wave and the American troops would head home.

Her job meant everything to her. She was thirty-six, single, and unattached. Her life in the Middle East was comfortable, an apartment in an eight-story building near the border, a place where dozens of journalists stayed. A few of them had spent years there, the way she had. Her days in the States were so few that she'd sold her condo a year ago. For now she needed to be here. It was almost a calling.

"Hey, Gibbs. Wait up."

She turned and walking toward her was Jeff Scanlon, a *Time* photographer. The two had spent more time together in the past three years than most married couples. But they'd only let their friendship cross lines a few times. Scanlon was interested. His rugged good looks had gotten any girl he wanted in his younger years. Now, at forty, he seemed interested only in spending his days with her.

She was fine with that. He was good company, and he shared her views of peace at all cost. But she didn't want a relationship, not when it meant revealing layers she'd spent a lifetime hiding. Layers that felt like they belonged to someone else altogether.

"Hey." She smiled. It was a beautiful day, clear blue skies and eighty degrees. It could be LA but for the broken buildings and starving people lining the narrow streets. "I wanna get out to that orphanage. The one ten miles from here."

They kept walking, heading for the apartment building. Scanlon had a room there too. "Maybe I can get a photo-essay out of it."

"Perfect." Her pace was fast, the way she liked it. "My story'll be a little longer than usual."

"They always are when kids are involved." He heaved his camera bag higher up on his shoulder and gave her a lopsided grin. "Ever notice that?"

She hesitated. "Yeah, I guess so."

They reached the entrance to the building. A frail-looking woman sat huddled near the door. Next to her were three children, their arms and legs bone thin. The woman didn't say a word, but she held out a cracked ceramic bowl.

Lauren stopped and rifled through her pocket. She pulled out a handful of coins and set them in the container. Scanlon stood nearby while she stooped down and gave a gentle touch to each child's forehead. One of them was a little girl, and her eyes made Lauren's breath catch in her throat. Something about them made her look almost like …

No, she wouldn't go there. Not now. Not with Scanlon standing next to her. She blinked and looked back at the mother. In a language that was becoming more familiar to her than English, she said, "I want peace as you do. May I buy you food?"

The woman's eyes widened. She was new to the journalists' building. Most of the street people were regulars and knew to expect help from Lauren. The woman put her arms around her children, clearly protective as she locked eyes with Lauren. "Yes." She spoke with a shame and disbelief that was common among the Afghans. Years of repression had caused most women to fear speaking at all, let alone to an American stranger. The woman lifted her chin a little. "That would be more than I could ask."

"Very well." Lauren nodded to Scanlon. "It's early still. Let's meet down here in half an hour."

"Okay." They went through the doors together. A café on the first floor was operational now that Western journalists were always passing through the lobby. At the entrance, Scanlon waved. "I'll meet you here."

She nodded and turned her attention to a young girl working behind the café counter. Service was slow, but she paid for four rice bowls and four juice drinks. Then she took them outside and handed them to the children's mother. It was important that the woman be the one to give the food to her own children. It was one small way of giving her back some of her dignity.

"Thank you." There were tears in the woman's eyes. "All Americans, I thank you."

Lauren smiled, but gritted her teeth. Not all Americans. Some Americans still believed they were doing everyone a service by fighting in Afghanistan and Iraq. But whatever slim reason the president might've had for starting the war, it was long past. It was time to call the war off and send over humanitarian help. If *she* were the one in charge, peace in this part of the world would be easy. But it was peace in her own life that was impossible to figure out.

She flipped her straight blonde hair over her shoulder and nodded at the woman. Then she turned back, went through the entrance, and walked past the elevator. Her room was on the seventh floor, and she always took the stairs. She could lie in foxholes next to soldiers, taking notes and working on a story while missiles exploded all around her. But she couldn't ride an elevator to save her life. The idea of stepping inside one was enough to make her heart race. Just the thought of them made her feel trapped, like she was suffocating.

She headed into the stairwell and started up.

The little Afghani girl's face flashed in her mind. What was it about her? Those eyes maybe, dark striking eyes, like Shane's. The sort of eyes Emily might've had. Of course, if she'd lived, she wouldn't be a little girl now. She'd be a young woman. For a moment Lauren stopped and closed her eyes, her hand tight around the railing.

It hurt so much spending time with children, knowing that her daughter would be alive if she'd been a better mother. If she hadn't taken chances with her baby's life. She opened her eyes and kept walking. As much as it hurt, she'd rather spend time with Afghani children than with any of the adults she'd met. Children reminded her that no matter how frozen her heart felt, no matter how driven she was to be the best, most hard-hitting reporter at *Time*, somewhere inside she was still seventeen years old, driving from Chicago to Los Angeles, grieving the loss of her little Emily. How different her life might've been if her daughter had lived.

Stop it! She'd given herself that same order so many times. Not that it made much difference. She breathed in and closed her eyes for a moment. *How come I can still smell her, still feel her in my arms?*

Enough. Lauren opened her eyes and picked up her pace. Scanlon would be down early, the way he always was. After a few minutes she reached her floor. The stairs were good for her.

They helped her stay in shape, a crucial factor if she was going to continue reporting from active areas of the war theater. And she *would* continue, as long as she believed her articles might have even the smallest influence on bringing the war to an end.

She reached room 722, slipped her card in the slot above the door handle, and pushed her way inside. She changed from her heavy khaki pants to a pair of shorts. The day promised to get hotter and spending time at the orphanage would mean she didn't need extra clothing. There would be no slamming herself into the sand or hiding in craggy bluffs while a battle played out before her eyes.

Most Americans figured the war in Afghanistan was over. But there were uprisings of insurgents all the time, and an entire contingency of U.S. troops were still battling them on a daily basis. The problem wasn't the insurgents, of course. Countries like Afghanistan would always have radical insurgents and terrorist groups. The problem was the innocent people harmed along the way. No wonder the country had so many orphans.

She sat on the edge of her bed and caught her breath. Her chest hurt and she leaned back on her elbows. The stairs must've done it, right? That's why she felt so tight. But even as the thought tried to take root, she let it go. It was a lie. The walk up hadn't made her chest ache. It was the little girl. The child's eyes burned in her mind, taking her back the way orphans' faces often took her back. Back to that terrible day, when she left the life she'd known ...

She'd driven away from the hospital and headed for California, determined never to come home again. Her plan had been straightforward. She would live in LA until she found Shane. Three or four months, if it took that long. Then the two of them could find a way to stay together and, when things were stable, they'd go back to Chicago and have a proper burial for Emily. Give their baby the funeral service she deserved.

Much had gone just the way she'd planned. With a place to live, a car, and a job, she had no trouble getting her new ID and her residency established. School came easily, also. She passed the GED without studying at all, and the community college was more than happy to have her. Only one thing hadn't gone according to schedule.

She never found Shane.

As the months turned into years, she thought about going home. She could walk up to the front door and tell her parents she needed their help to find him. By then, maybe they would've known a way to reach Shane. She would hug them and hold them and tell them she forgave them for what they'd done. At least she'd have a family again, even if she never found Shane.

But she couldn't do it. She kept telling herself she needed to find him first. That way she could go home and make a clean start, without the need to hold anything against her parents.

The memories stirred dusty emotions in her soul, making her throat thick. She grabbed a water bottle from the half-full case on the nightstand next to her bed. There wasn't one thing she hadn't done to find Shane Galanter. She called high schools and eventually colleges. She searched out his last name, and three times she had help from one of her university professors, a man who specialized in investigative reporting.

"He must be living under his parents' corporation name," the guy finally concluded. "His parents could've called their California business just about anything. All the assets would be listed under that name."

The question she never asked, the thing that didn't make sense, was why Shane would do such a thing? Didn't he realize she couldn't find him if he lived that way? Of course, by changing *her* name she might've kept him away without meaning to. She'd done it to hide from her parents, not from Shane. Regardless, she kept looking. Every week she thought of something else, but each idea fizzled, turning up no sign of him. Sometimes she thought she'd go crazy looking. Back when every tall, dark-haired, Greek-looking man caused her heart to skip a beat. Back when she would race across a street and into a store or office building chasing after someone with Shane's build, his look.

"Excuse me," she'd shout at the man. "Are you— "

He'd turn and she'd be looking at a complete stranger—who clearly thought she was crazy.

"I'm ... I'm sorry. I thought you were someone else."

It happened again and again. A different street, different store, different tall, dark man. Sometimes she got close enough to touch his arm or his shoulder before realizing it wasn't Shane.

"I'm sorry." She would back away, her face hot. "I thought you were someone else."

She didn't give up until the ten-year anniversary of Emily's death. On that day she took off Shane's ring and put it in a small, square cardboard jewelry box with the pictures she'd kept: one of the two of them, their arms around each other, and the other of Emily. Before she closed the lid she read the words on the ring, words Shane had engraved for her alone.

Even now.

They were still true that dark day. In some ways they always would be. She loved Shane, even now. Even when he was dead to her, when she had moved a million miles beyond the days of loving him.

As time wore on, she no longer lived under a different name. She *became* Lauren Gibbs. A single woman, alone in a world that had turned upside down overnight. If Shane had tried to find her, he wouldn't have had a clue to look for her under that name. No one would've. Even so, she didn't change her name back. She didn't want to be Lauren Anderson again. That Lauren had been trapped by her circumstances and forced into a series of actions that cost her the two people she loved most.

No, Lauren Anderson was as dead as her baby daughter.

Lauren sat up straighter and took a long swig of the water. It was room temperature, as usual. She swallowed some more and then lowered the bottle back to her lap. A wind had picked up outside, kicking dust into the atmosphere and dulling the blue morning sky. What were her parents doing these days? They would be nearing retirement age, probably traveling and talking about the old days. In the beginning they probably looked for her, but after awhile it would've become obvious that she didn't want to be found. Not then, and not now. Except . . .

Except once in a while, when a cool wind kicked up in the middle of December and she could still feel how it was, sitting around a Christmas tree with her parents and Shane's parents and Shane. She stared out the hotel window, but instead of the wind-beaten sky, she saw a scene from two decades ago, heard the laughter, felt the warmth of shared love.

What would happen if she went back now?

She blinked, and the memory swirled into nothingness, like dust in the desert wind. It didn't matter what would happen, because she couldn't go back. She didn't know the way if she wanted to. Her throat still hurt, and her eyes grew moist. She coughed. *Get a grip, Lauren.*

"Come on, Gibbs. You're tougher than this." She pressed her hands to her eyes and inhaled sharply. "A story's waiting."

She grabbed her backpack and double-checked to see that her lip balm was still inside. Then she snatched a bag of American lollipops from one of her dresser drawers. Lollipops were in high demand at orphanages. It gave her a way to connect with the kids. With that she was out the door and headed down the stairs.

Normally with a story pending, she could shake off any memories of the past. But today it wasn't so easy. Was it Christmas making things so difficult? Whatever it was, times like this she had to wonder which battle affected her more. The one that still raged in parts of Afghanistan.

Or the one deep in her heart.

FIFTEEN

Shane Galanter had been putting off the engagement party for nearly a month. But when Ellen suggested December 23, he knew he'd run out of excuses. Even the Top Gun flight school where he worked as an instructor was closed down that Friday and the following week. Fighter pilots needed a Christmas break, same as anyone.

Maybe even more so.

The engagement party was at the Marriott in Reno. Ellen had worked with his mother to pull it together. Eighty people in one of the hotel's smaller banquet rooms. Shane left his car with a valet and squinted up at the building. It wasn't true that it never rained in the desert states. That afternoon was fifty degrees with drizzle. Another reason he hated spending a Friday night in a room packed with people.

"Here, sir." A blond surfer kid handed him a claim check.

"Thanks." He stuffed it into his pocket and faced the hotel entrance.

He wanted to marry Ellen. It wasn't that. But throwing a party to announce their engagement seemed a little outdated. He was thirty-six, after all, and Ellen was twenty-seven. People their age were supposed to have a quiet ceremony and get on with their lives.

He sucked in a quick breath and slipped his hands in his pocket. The party was more his mother's idea than anything. His parents loved Ellen, the way they hadn't loved any of his previous girlfriends. He maneuvered himself through the lobby to the bank of elevators. Not that he'd had many girlfriends.

None that ever really mattered until now.

Ellen Randolph, the daughter of Congressman Terry Randolph, was a Christian connected to the most powerful Republican circles in the country. Shane met her two years earlier at a congressional award dinner. He was receiving an honor for being one of the top fighter pilots in Operation Enduring Freedom. She was working for her father, and he noticed her a minute after entering the room.

Halfway through the night, Shane saw one of the veteran flight instructors talking with her and her father. The man was one of Shane's most respected mentors, so he made his way to the small cluster of people and managed to get an introduction.

He and Ellen had been inseparable ever since.

He stopped at the front desk and waited until one of the attendants looked his way. "Yes, I'm trying to find the Galanter banquet room."

The girl blushed as she looked at him. She was a heavy redhead with pale blue eyes. "The engagement party, right?"

Shane smiled. "That's the one."

"Let's see." She checked a list taped to the desk. "You're in the Hillside Room. It's on the tenth floor, right turn off the elevator." She batted her lashes at him. "You by yourself?"

He gave her a half grin. "I'm the guy getting married."

"Oh." Her cheeks darkened. "Lucky girl."

"I guess." He gave her a nod and headed for the elevator. It had taken him longer to get ready than he'd expected. He'd wrapped things up at the air base early that afternoon and made good time getting back to his home in La Costa. But he'd lost time after he got dressed. He was looking for a certain set of cuff links when he spotted the picture. Her picture.

The one Lauren gave him before he moved.

Seeing her face stopped him cold. He took hold of the photo and found his way to the recliner in the corner of his bedroom.

For half an hour he held it, looking at her, studying the way her eyes seemed to look straight at him. He'd never really stopped looking for her. But over time it seemed ridiculous to keep trying so hard. He was through officer's training and naval flight school before his father sat him down and put it to him as kindly as he could. "Son, you need to let her go. She doesn't want to be found or you would've come across her by now."

"I'm not looking." His answer was quick, but it wasn't the truth.

"You are. All of life is out there waiting for you." His dad was sitting across from him in the apartment he was renting at the time. He leaned closer, his expression intense. "Somewhere out there is a woman who will love you and make you happy. If that woman was Lauren Anderson, you'd know."

He didn't want to admit it, but his father's argument made sense. He'd done everything but go door-to-door throughout all of Illinois looking for her. Still, he hated the lack of closure. The last thing he'd told Lauren Anderson was that he'd love her forever. No matter what. Nothing had happened to change that, except the obvious. She'd vanished from his life without a trace, without a single trail to follow.

And yet, here he was, on the night of his engagement party, staring at Lauren's picture and wondering what had happened. When his family first made the move, and it seemed only a matter of days before they could talk to each other, he had believed everything would work out after his senior year. But as months wore on without any way to contact her, he began to suspect his parents.

"You must know how to reach them," he'd say every few days. "Just tell me the number. It's my life. I have to live it the way I want to. And I want Lauren."

But his parents always denied having any of her family's information. "A few weeks separation was all we agreed to," his mother would tell him. "When Angela Anderson calls with their phone number, you'll be the first person to have it."

Shane shook off the memories and looked at his watch. The party was starting in five minutes, and Ellen had asked him to be there half an hour early. He stepped into the elevator and pushed the button for the tenth floor. Four floors up, the lift stopped and a family of five stepped inside. They wore bathing suits and had towels draped around their shoulders.

"Headed for the pool." The man raised one eyebrow as if to say it wasn't his idea.

"Sounds like fun."

"What about you?" The guy surveyed him. "Christmas shindig?"

"Engagement party." Shane leaned against the elevator wall. "Mine."

"Hey—" the man reached out and shook his hand—-"congratulations."

"Thanks." He smiled at the guy. His wife was busy helping one of the kids with his shoes.

On the eighth floor the family got off. Shane watched them go, and a sudden stab of envy pierced him. He shook it off. What on earth did he have to be envious about? Just as the door was closing, a blonde woman walked past, headed in the same direction as the family. Probably another swimmer...

But Shane hesitated, staring. Almost without thinking, he hit the "door open" button. There was something familiar about her. Something he didn't quite understand—not until she looked over her shoulder.

Shane's breath screeched to a halt.

Lauren!

The girl was the mirror image of Lauren! He let go of the button, intending to step out, but the doors started to close. He slid his hand between them, stopping them. But by the time the doors opened again, she was gone. He checked his watch and frowned. This was crazy. He was already late. Still ... He couldn't leave without knowing.

It was a long shot, but it was possible. Maybe she'd located him through his rank and file, or found him with the help of a private investigator. How many Shane Galanters could possibly live in the Reno, Nevada, area? Maybe she was staying at the hotel. His heart thudded hard against his chest as he darted off the elevator and jogged down the carpeted hallway. A fitness center and a spa were on opposite sides of the corridor. The pool was at the very end, and since she'd been wearing flip-flops he guessed that was the most likely place to find her.

He passed a few kids on his way, and when he reached the pool door, he flung it open. He hurried inside and scanned the deck area. It took seconds to spot her. She was sitting next to a small-framed older man, watching a couple of older teenage boys in the pool. Was one of them his son? The child he'd never met? Shane clearly wasn't dressed for the pool, and because he'd rushed into the deck area, he suddenly had everyone's attention.

Including hers.

Now that she was looking at him square on, he could see the obvious. It wasn't Lauren. He gave a sheepish nod in her direction, then backed away. He was on the elevator again in less than a minute, his heart still racing. What had he been *thinking?* His days of searching for Lauren were over. He had Ellen now. He wasn't supposed to still be seeing his childhood love behind the sunglasses of every blonde in Nevada.

But for a moment, he'd been overwhelmed by the idea that the woman *was* Lauren—and that could mean one of the teenage boys was his. His very own son. He made a fist and banged it twice against the elevator wall. *Insanity, Galanter. Pure insanity.* He gave up on the idea of having kids years ago. Somewhere out there he had a child, one that was probably being raised by a kind adoptive family. Hadn't he decided that was enough?

He caught his breath and let his arms fall back at his sides. Cold feet, that's all this was. He was marrying a lovely, intelligent girl, someone who would make a wonderful wife. She was articulate and excited about the politics he was passionate for. She didn't want children, either.

That suited him fine. Children would only remind him every day of what he could've had—should've had—with Lauren.

He stepped off the elevator, straightened his suit jacket, and followed the signs to the Hillside Room. Half the guests were already there, mingling around the perimeter of the room. Before he had time to look for her, Ellen was at his side. She wore a conservative blue floor-length evening gown, one that subtly emphasized her figure and complimented her eyes.

"Hi." She eased herself into his arms and smiled at him. Her expression was soft and sexy, her attention his completely. She brought her lips to his and kissed him. It was a kiss slow enough to stir him, but brief enough to keep up the polished look of propriety that was important to both of them. She pulled back a few inches and searched his gaze. Her tone was low and teasing. "Glad you could make it."

"Me too." He refused to think about the blonde at the pool. "You look wonderful. Sorry I'm late."

"It's okay." She flashed him a grin, stepped back and fell in beside him, her arm around his waist. "Come see your mother. She's looking for you."

They crossed the room to a bank of windows on the other side. The view from the tenth floor was stunning. Even under gray skies, the mountains that stretched along the horizon looked spectacular. His mother was by herself, leaning on a handrail and staring out at the view. Ellen kissed his cheek this time. "I'm going to greet some of the guests."

"Okay." He smiled at her as he turned toward his mom.

Her dress was simple and elegant. She looked ten years younger than her age as she glanced at him over her shoulder. He would've expected her to be bubbly and ecstatic that night. It was what she'd always wanted, that he'd marry a girl like Ellen. Instead her expression was shadowed with what looked like doubt and fear.

"Mom, you okay?" He hugged her, and then leaned on the railing next to her. He gave a low chuckle. "You're supposed to be right there with Ellen, remember? The belles of the ball."

She set her chin and looked back out the window. "This is Ellen's party, not mine."

He hesitated. "Hey ..." He slung his arm over her shoulders and gave her a light squeeze. Whatever was eating at her, it wasn't going away. "I was just kidding."

"I know." She sighed and stood a little straighter. "I'm sorry." Her eyes narrowed, but she kept her gaze straight ahead. "I can't get something out of my head."

"What?" Shane had no idea where she was headed with this. He removed his arm from her shoulders and turned just enough to see her face. His tone was still light. "Don't tell me you changed your mind about having an engagement party."

"No, Shane." She looked at him. "It's more serious than that." Lines webbed out from the corners of her eyes. More lines than usual. "I need to know something."

"Okay." He let the humor fade from the moment. "Shoot."

She looked around the room, as if she wanted to make sure only the two of them could hear what she was about to say. Then her eyes locked on his. "Are you *settling* for Ellen, son? I need to know."

A strange sensation worked its way through his gut, something he couldn't identify. Lauren's face came to mind again, but only for an instant. He made a sound that was more exasperation than shock. "Of course not. What would make you ask that?"

She'd always been good at reading him. Whenever she looked deep into his soul, he knew better than to hide the truth from her. And she was looking at him that way now. "Shane, the last thing I want you to do is marry someone because you think your father and I like her. That's not the case, is it?"

"Mother." He raised a single eyebrow. "No offense, but you're giving yourself a lot of credit here." There was a small wall that went two feet up toward the window. Shane put his foot on the low sill and leaned toward his knee. "Ellen's perfect for me. Of course I'm not settling for her. I could've stayed single forever if I hadn't met her."

"Because of Lauren, you mean." Her eyes softened. "Right?"

Hearing her name brought the familiar ache. "Lauren's out of my life."

She watched him, studying him. "Don't lie to me, Shane. Please."

"Mom, listen to you!" Her words were like a slap in the face. "I'm not lying."

"Shane, you loved that girl." She looked back at the view of the distant mountains. "I woke up this morning scared to death that you didn't wind up with her because of something we did. Something her parents did. I just don't want you to marry Ellen if you're still in love with Lauren."

He was about to refute her again, but he couldn't. He let the pretense fall from his eyes. "The truth is," his voice was low, "Lauren's gone forever. I've moved on. That's why I was able to fall in love with Ellen."

She frowned. "You're sure? I don't want you doing this if you're not sure."

"Mother." This time he laughed out loud. "This is ridiculous. Really." He reached for her hand. "Come, enjoy my engagement party with me."

They caught up with Ellen, and his mother stayed with his father and a few of their business associates. He and Ellen made the rounds, visiting with one cluster of their friends after another. Shane focused on matters at hand, refusing to give any real thought to his mother's concerns.

An hour into the party, Ellen's father stepped up to a podium at the center of the room. He tapped the microphone, and when he was satisfied with the sound level, he welcomed everyone.

"The occasion is certainly a wonderful one." He flashed a smile at the crowd, the smile that had earned him a large percentage of the votes in the most recent election. "I want to go on record saying I couldn't be happier about my daughter's choice for her future husband."

A polite round of applause followed.

Shane took hold of Ellen's hand and squeezed it.

Her father went on. "I think it's clear to everyone that Shane Galanter has political potential for the GOP." He found Ellen in the crowd and nodded at her. "I know my daughter thinks so."

Laughter bubbled up around the room.

"He might be a Top Gun instructor today, but the Nevada Senate needs someone like Shane, and one day not too far from now I can see him living in the governor's mansion."

This time a few hoots rippled through the crowd. Shane looked at his feet. What was Ellen's father doing? No one had ever said anything about a political rally. He clenched his jaw. The fact that Ellen's father viewed him as a bright spot on the Republican Party's future road map was clear enough. The point didn't need to be made here, as they announced their engagement.

Besides, Shane hadn't decided anything yet.

He was completely supportive of the party's platform, yes. But he enjoyed flying fighter jets, loved getting into the cockpit with a young gun and showing him the ropes. America relied heavily on her fighter pilots. Maybe teaching the next generation was enough of a contribution.

Her father was saying, "Please help me welcome Ellen and Shane." He stepped back and began the loudest applause yet.

Next to Shane, Ellen beamed. She tugged on his hand. "Come on."

"I'm with you." He took the lead, his head high as he nodded at friends along the way. When they reached the podium, he put his arm around Ellen and dismissed his concerns. This wasn't the time for doubts. He smiled big at the group before him. "Ellen and I will be getting married Saturday, May 20." He directed his grin at her, and then back to the audience. "We wanted you to be the first to know."

The group was warmed up now. They whistled and hollered and called for a toast. By then most of the people in attendance had glasses of champagne. Someone ran a few glasses up to Shane and Ellen, and at the same time her father returned to the microphone.

"To Shane and Ellen. May their influence and power grow even stronger because of their relationship, and may this be a season of love and laughter as they plan their wedding day."

Shane had thought driving over to the hotel that a prayer might be a good idea. He and Ellen both had a strong faith, and since they'd talked about getting even more serious about their relationships with God, the engagement party seemed a good place for a group of people to pray for them. But somehow in a room full of people sipping champagne and celebrating the possibility of another Republican hero in their midst, prayer didn't seem appropriate. Maybe later ... Before everyone left. Maybe he'd close the night that way.

Ellen's father asked the crowd to return to their discussions and make sure they took a plate of food from the table at the back of the room. The next hour passed in a blur of conversations, nearly every one of which had to do with politics.

"Shane, you'd be perfect for the Senate," people told him time and again. "You'd have my vote, that's for sure."

Not until the party was over and he and Ellen were outside waiting for his car, did she turn to him and take playful hold of his jacket lapels. "What'd you think of Daddy's speech?"

Shane studied her. "His talk? The one he gave before he introduced us?"

"Yes." She bounced a few times, her voice giggly. "It was perfect, don't you think?"

He blinked. Was she saying what he thought she was saying? "What? It was set up?"

She squealed. "Of course it was set up, silly. Nothing a politician says is accidental."

For a moment he stared at her. Then he looked out at the lights along the ridge of mountains and uttered a single laugh. "Was *that* the point of the party?" His eyes found hers again. "A chance for your dad to introduce me as the newest political hopeful?"

Her expression fell and she settled back on her heels. "That's what you want, isn't it?"

"Maybe." He stared at her, then he paced a few steps away. When he turned to face her, his smile was a show of disbelief. "I mean, I haven't signed my campaign contract yet, have I?"

"Shane." Her voice held a reprimand. "Come back here. You're making a scene."

He closed the gap between them and spoke a few inches from her face. "We wouldn't want that, would we?" His tone was just short of rude. "What would your *father* think?"

"Listen." She pointed a finger at his chest. "That speech wasn't my father's idea. It was mine."

"Yours?" Shane wanted to laugh out loud. "You asked your dad to say that without talking to me?"

"I *have* talked to you." She lifted her chin, her composure back in place. "For two years I've talked to you. Every time it comes up you tell me it's your dream, running on the Republican ticket."

Anger rippled through his veins. "I'm excited about the party, that's why." He hissed the words. "And yeah, maybe I'd like to run some day." He crossed his arms. "That doesn't mean I need your dad making an announcement at my engagement party."

"He was trying to help." For the first time since the conversation began, she sounded hurt. "We both were."

Guilt washed over him. Why was he fighting with her? The talk was over, done. What had it hurt that her father was proud of him? The man was as honest a politician as he'd ever known, a leader respected around the country for his values and integrity. Most men would've been thrilled with the sort of speech he'd given that night.

He sighed long and hard. "Ellen." He put his hands on her shoulders. "I'm sorry." He pulled her into a hug. "I guess it just took me by surprise."

She responded to his touch and melted against him. "It's okay." Her cheek pressed against his chest, then she lifted her eyes to him. "You do want it, don't you? A chance to run for office one day?"

The right answer was yes. But standing there in the dark, his arms around her, with the damp December air thick around them, he wasn't sure. "It sounds interesting," he whispered against her dark hair. "I'll have to think more seriously about it."

"Okay. That's all I'm asking." She gave him a squeeze and then stepped back. The valet was pulling up with his car. "I guess I always pictured myself married to a politician like my dad."

They fell silent as they climbed inside. It took half an hour to reach her place, and when he dropped her off he smiled. "Tell your dad thanks for tonight. I'm sure someday I'll be begging him to talk to groups on my behalf."

Her smile lit up her eyes. "You will, Shane. And who knows how far God will let you go with it."

They said good-bye, and Shane drove home. He kept the radio off. The quiet suited his mood better, with all the bits of conversations playing in his mind. Most important were the expectations Ellen and her father had for him. He knew all along they were there, but tonight they'd felt like a noose around his neck. As if his thoughts about the future no longer really mattered. He would be a politician because he stood for all the right things, and because his party needed him. After tonight how could he look at it any other way?

But other memories played in his mind as he pulled into his driveway. His mother and her sudden outpouring of guilt and doubt, for one. Most of the past two years she'd done nothing but gush about Ellen Randolph, the same way his father did.

"A girl like that will suit you well for a lifetime," his father had told him. "We couldn't be happier for you, son."

So what had happened that would make his mother doubt his decision to marry her? And how had she known exactly what had been messing with his mind all day long? He rubbed the back of his neck as he climbed out of his car and went inside. Every now and then, Ellen joined him at his house for a movie or a late dinner. They had agreed to save their physical intimacy for after they were married. Because of that, neither of them thought it was smart to spend too much time alone. Tonight he was glad for the privacy. His thoughts left him feeling like he'd been going Mach five for two hours straight. He went to his room, changed into a pair of sweats and a T-shirt, and dropped into his recliner.

Everything in him wanted to go to his dresser drawer and find Lauren's picture again, let her memory keep him company and help him sort through the strange events of the night. He closed his eyes. *Come on, Shane, get a grip. God, keep me focused.* Lauren Anderson was gone. He couldn't make one more decision with her in mind because she didn't exist. Period.

He willed himself to relax, to let his back muscles unwind against the chair. Something had been missing from the night, but he couldn't think of what it was. He tightened his grip on the chair arms, and then it hit him. He'd forgotten to pray. There they were, a couple of supposedly strong faith, and they'd done a toast—but not a prayer. He frowned and pinched the bridge of his nose with his thumb and forefinger. He didn't even like champagne.

Minutes passed and he still couldn't unwind. Maybe his first instinct had been a good one. He should've avoided an engagement party altogether. That way he wouldn't be thinking about giving up the career he maybe still loved and marrying a girl he maybe only liked.

And he certainly wouldn't be spending the day before Christmas Eve thinking about teenage sons and willowy blondes and the life he could've had. Would have had.

If only he'd found Lauren.

SIXTEEN

The defender saw Emily coming across the field and she raced toward the wall to stop the pass. She reacted with a quickness that surprised even her. Breathing hard, she drew the ball back, dribbled it through another two defenders, then powered it into the net just as the buzzer sounded.

It was her third score of the morning. A hat trick!

She congratulated her former high school teammates. "It might be the day before Christmas, but it's never a bad time for a game," one of them shouted as she waved. "Tell your grandparents thanks for coming out. They've always been our best fans."

Emily saluted the gang, threw a towel around the back of her neck, and grabbed her gear bag. Her grandparents had a full day lined up for them. Last-minute shopping and an early Christmas Eve service. Playing soccer on Christmas Eve morning was a last-minute plan, but it came together just fine.

A group of girls she'd played with through high school were home for Christmas break. Since the current high school soccer team was always looking for a challenge, they put together a scrimmage at the indoor arena. Emily's squad included three college players. They beat the high schoolers, 8–2.

She found her grandparents sitting in the bleachers on the other side of the Plexiglas wall. "Well," she panted, "what did you think?"

Her grandpa was slow getting up. He looked pale and thinner than usual. Emily studied him. Or maybe it was only his new navy Christmas sweater making him look that way. His eyes sparkled in her direction. "I think I love watching you play." He walked toward her and held out his hand. "You're poetry in motion out there, sweetheart."

"Sorry it had to be on Christmas Eve." She fell in beside him, but glanced back at her grandma. "I know you have lots to do today."

"It's okay." Grandma caught up with them. "It makes me miss the days when you were in high school." She smiled at the two of them. "We had four or five games a week."

"Special times, for sure." Her grandpa patted her shoulder. "I'm gonna hate it when you play your last game."

"That won't be for awhile." Her grandparents had been to all her home games that college season and a few on the road. "You still have three more years to put up with my schedule."

They fell into a comfortable quiet as they made their way to the car. Emily needed to shower, so she stayed home while her grandparents shopped. The afternoon flew by and the Christmas Eve service was beautiful. The pastor talked about looking for God's fingerprints.

"Miracles still happen today," he told them. "God in the flesh? The king of Kings lying in a humble manger?" He smiled at them and held his hands out. "What about you? A healed marriage? A healthy family? A job you love?" He paused, his voice expectant. "Every one of us has been witness to a whole host of miracles. But what will it be this Christmas? Lift that thing to God and let the Lord of all creation meet you near the manger. Let Him have a chance to work a miracle in your life once again."

The choir sang a haunting version of "O Holy Night." In the midst of it, Emily bowed her head and closed her eyes. *God, You know what I need, You know the miracle I'm asking for.*

Daughter, I'm with you.

The familiar peace ran through her veins, softening her heart and soul to the presence of the Holy Spirit. Martha, the pianist, was finishing the song and leading into another, the song they always finished with every Christmas Eve service, "Silent Night." Emily opened her eyes as she let the words fill her. Especially the last part. "Sleep in heavenly peace ... sleep in heavenly peace."

Back at home, Emily and her grandparents sat around the Christmas tree and opened one present—their Christmas Eve tradition. Emily's gift was a new pair of pajamas, same as every Christmas Eve. She giggled and held them up. They were fuzzy and warm, perfect for the coming winter.

Her grandparents opened one gift from each other. Both packages held new pairs of socks. When they'd cleaned up the wrapping paper and exchanged hugs and conversation, Emily bid them good night. "I want lots of energy for tomorrow."

"Emily." Her grandma lifted her brow and wagged a finger at her. "You won't be sleeping. You want to go through the box, right?"

She winced and gave a little nod. "Is that okay?" Emily couldn't wait to spend time alone with her mother's photos and yearbooks. She touched her grandma's elbow. "Maybe I'll find something we can look at tomorrow."

Her grandma's smile was genuine. "That'd be fine, honey. Take your time. Christmas morning can start as late as you'd like."

Before she went to bed, they stood near the tree and held hands. Her grandpa led them in prayer.

"This Christmas is a special one, God. We can all feel it. Please help us find the miracle near the manger this year. The one the pastor referred to." He hesitated, his voice thick. "I think we could really use one. We love you, Lord. In Christ's name."

Emily kissed them both and went up to her room. With the door shut behind her, she pulled the box close to her bed again, sat down on the edge, and began taking things from inside. The framed photo—the one she'd already seen—she set gently near the wall to make room for everything else in the box. Next was a photo album. She picked it up and opened it on her lap. It smelled musty from being in the garage all those years.

"Wow, Mom." She ran her finger under each of the first photos, beneath which her mother had written a caption. "Look how much you cared."

The pictures started when her mom was in middle school. There were several shots of her with her girlfriends, and Emily studied her mother closely. If her mother's eyes were any indication, she was happy, popular with her friends.

Her light blonde hair hung straight and halfway down her back through most of those early years. Toward the center of the album, her hair got a little shorter, and a boy started appearing in the pictures with her. A smile tugged at Emily's lips. The boy was her father—he had to be. He had the same dark hair and eyes she saw every morning in the mirror. But he was skinny and about an inch shorter than her mother.

Even so, there was no denying how they felt about each other. It was palpable throughout the photo album. Even back then nothing could've kept them apart. "Look at you, Dad." She laid her hand on his picture. "The other guys are hanging out together somewhere, but there's you. Right next to Mom."

The captions grew even more precious toward the back of the book. There was a picture with her dad handing her mother a dandelion. Her mom had written, "Shane is the most romantic guy in eighth grade. Even if I am allergic to dandelions."

On the very last page, she found something that made her gasp. The entire sheet was a letter her dad wrote to her mom. Her mother must've hidden the letter there, because the page was stuck at the back, where most people might not look.

Dear Lauren, I don't think people are supposed to feel this way in eighth grade. All our friends are doing stupid stuff, having their friends ask a girl out for them. You know, that kind of thing. But I feel like I could marry you tomorrow. I'm not even kidding.

Emily put her fingers to her lips. "Dad ... you were so smitten."

I don't know if I wanna graduate because that means going to high school. And high school means more people to deal with. All the senior guys will fall over each other to get to know you. Anyway, that's all right, 'cause I'm never going to leave you. Not ever. Love you, Lauren. Yours, Shane.

Yours, Shane?

Emily cooed. "You guys were so cute." Her parents were adorable as kids. How could this have been in the garage all those years when she would've given anything to know some of these details? She closed the album and set it aside. The next few items in the box were framed photographs. One showed her parents dressed in sports gear, only it looked like her mother was the football player and her father was a cheerleader. She squinted at the picture. Yes, a cheerleader with eye makeup.

Emily giggled, but she kept her voice hushed. The rest of the lights in the house were off now, and she didn't want to wake her grandparents. She looked at the picture again. What were her parents doing? She spotted something in the background. A carved pumpkin sitting on the porch. Of course, the outfits were costumes. Her parents had probably been invited to a Halloween party.

But even more noticeable than the uniforms was the now-familiar look in their eyes. Like they were born to be together. She set the pictures aside and pulled out a journal. Her fingers trembled as she set the photo album down. It was time to read one of her journals. Emily took hold of the nearest one. She'd waited all of her life for whatever lay between the covers—the short stories and journal entries her grandma had mentioned—because then she'd have the answer she'd been looking for. The answer about whether her mother had a passion for writing, the way she did.

She held the journal, fingering the cover. These pages held an inside look at her mother's heart. Something she'd wanted for as far back as she could remember. Emily frowned, wishing she didn't feel so ... guilty. Journals were private. She'd kept a little pink diary in second grade, then later on, a full-size journal. Page after page of stories and personal reflections and letters to the Lord. No one had ever read any of them.

Until now.

Emily bit her lip and balanced the journal on her lap, then she exhaled and opened the cover. As she did, her guilt faded. Of course she could read her mother's journals. They might well offer the only chance to get to know her.

The first entry was dated spring 1985.

Shane and I talked about love. Real love. We both think it's weird that our parents don't understand how we feel about each other. They act like we're a couple of kids who have no clue what love is. But here's what I've learned when I'm with Shane. Real love waits in the snow on your front porch so you can walk to school together in the fifth grade. It brings you a chocolate bar when you fall and finish last in the seventh grade Olympics.

Real love whispers something in the middle of algebra about your pink fingernail polish so that you don't forget how to smile when you're doing math, and it saves a seat for you in the lunchroom every Friday through high school. Even when the other baseball players think you're stupid. Real love has time to listen to your hopes and dreams when your parents are too busy with the PTA or the auxiliary club or the business they run at the local bank.

Real love stays up late on a Saturday making chocolate chip cookies together, flicking flour at you and getting eggshells in the batter and making sure you'll remember that night the rest of your life. And real love thinks you're pretty even when your hair is pulled back in a ponytail and you don't stand perfectly straight. Real love is what I have with Shane. I just wanted to say so.

Emily blinked, suddenly aware of tears on her cheeks. She was overwhelmed with the enormity of the find. But more than that, she was struck breathless by her parents' feelings for each other. She wanted to read the entry again, but she was driven to turn the page, to capture another glimpse of her mother's life as a teenager.

What she found as she traveled the pages was a love that she hadn't known about before, a love between her parents that was both triumphant and tragic. Triumphant because it was the picture of how love was supposed to be: patient and kind, trusting and hopeful. Never mind their ages, her mom and dad had known about love. But tragic, because it hadn't lasted, because they'd lost each other, and as far as any of them knew, they'd never found each other again.

The last entries in her mother's journal must've been written after her dad left for California. One in particular caught Emily's attention.

I'm so mad at my parents. I hate them. They told me they'd leave a forwarding message when they disconnected our old phone service. It should've told anyone who called the house what our new number was. That way Shane could reach me and then he could give me his number.

But now they're telling me the recording isn't working yet. The worst part is this feeling I have that my mom and dad lied to me. Maybe, because shouldn't it be working by now?

My baby's due in a few weeks and I'm convinced Shane's parents and my parents don't want us together anymore. The thing that makes me most afraid is that if they really do feel that way, I think they could keep us apart. How would I know where to get his phone number? How would he know where to get mine? I can only pray that somehow, someway he finds me soon. I can't stand being without him.

"Mom." It was as though Emily were sitting across from her mother. She looked out her window at the dark, snowy sky. "Did you ever find him again? Did Dad ever call you?"

She ached for the loss her parents suffered. For the first time she considered the possibility that maybe her grandparents had played some role in separating her parents. The idea seemed crazy, but why else wouldn't they help figure out the phone number situation in the weeks before her birth?

She looked at the clock and she felt a slow smile creep up her cheeks. It was after midnight, which meant it was Christmas. A quiet, silent Christmas morning, and already—even with the sadness of all her parents had lost—she could see one very obvious miracle in her mind, lying near the manger. The miracle of her parents' love, a love that shone as bright as the star of Bethlehem. And in the glow of that light, she begged God for an even bigger miracle.

That she would be used not only to find her parents, but to bring them back together again.

Seventeen

The meeting Angela had been dreading was about to take place.

She and Bill woke earlier than usual and made Emily her favorite breakfast: cinnamon French toast with scrambled eggs. She came down groggy and smiling, her pink padded slippers scuffling along the floor. "Hey." She gave Bill a hug first and then crossed the kitchen to hug Angela. "You guys are so sweet. Christmas never ends around here."

The words pierced Angela's heart. It would end soon enough. In about an hour, she guessed. Emily was chattering on about what a wonderful Christmas day it had been and how much she liked her new sweaters and her cute purse.

Her chatter was like music. If only they could hold on to that innocence, that joy.

"You were up late again." Angela studied Emily. "Are you finding what you wanted to know?"

"I am." She lowered her chin, her look a mix of gratitude and apology. "You can join me any time, Grandma. But thanks for letting me see it all first." Her eyes shone. "I feel like I actually know Mom now." Her smile faded some. "At least the way she was as a teenager."

"Yes." Angela's throat ached. This was too much. All the memories of Lauren, the terrible awareness of what was coming ... She didn't want to cry, not yet. "Yes, your mother was quite something back then. Never rebellious or sarcastic, the way so many teenagers are today." She leaned over and kissed Emily's cheek. "She was a lot like you in that way."

"Well, I need a little background music." Bill stood and slipped his Mitch Miller CD back into the player. A few seconds passed, and then the sweet refrains of "White Christmas" filled the room. "I always say Christmas songs should play till January 1." He did a little soft-shoe shuffle on the living room carpet. Then he smiled at the two of them. "That's what I'm talking about."

Emily giggled and waltzed her way into the living room, where she took her grandpa's hand and let him twirl her between the sofa and the television. Their voices mingled, a sound that was glorious, and not because either of them could sing on key. Angela watched them, mesmerized, fighting the sorrow struggling to overtake her.

Precious moments like this needed to be savored, because if the doctors were right their time together would end all too soon. But oh, if only they could go on this way another ten years. And how she wished Bill had danced like that with Lauren. What if he'd been more concerned with making memories than protecting her from Shane's parents?

Angela needed to flip the last batch of French toast, but she couldn't draw herself away from the picture they made. Bill and Emily, waltzing around the room, knocking into a bookcase and stepping on each others' toes. Their singing eventually dissolved to giggles, and before the song ended, they were doubled over, laughing hard at themselves.

They each worked their way to a standing position. With their arms around each others' shoulders, they danced back into the kitchen. Angela pointed to the cupboard, ignoring the way her stomach hurt. "We're ready for the plates."

Breakfast was more of the same, smiles and laughter and shared memories of Christmases long past. All the while, Angela gave Bill anxious glances. If only they could avoid what was coming, if they could just continue to breeze through the day, enjoying the light of Emily's presence. But that just wasn't an option.

When the dishes were cleared, Angela made three cups of coffee, passed them out, and directed her attention to her granddaughter. "We need to talk, Emily." She looked at Bill. "Let's go sit in the living room."

Emily's expression was blank. She looked from Angela to Bill and back again. "Is something wrong?"

"Yes." It was time to get to the heart of the matter. "Something is wrong, honey." She led the way into the living room. "Come sit down."

Bill took his usual seat, the recliner closest to the television. His cheeks were still full of color from the dance and the laughter. Angela felt a surge of hope. He hadn't looked this well in months. Emily moved slowly, probably because she was caught off guard at the possibility that anything could be wrong.

Angela sat on one end of the tweed sofa and Emily took the other, fidgeting, her eyebrows knit together. All that athletic energy made her struggle with sitting still. That was always the case, but it was especially difficult when something serious was at hand.

"Okay." Emily's tone was a mix of hurt and fear. "So what's wrong? And how come you didn't say anything until now?"

"I'm going to let your papa tell you." Angela swallowed the lump in her throat. She folded her hands and bit her lip, unable to say another word without losing control.

Emily slid to the edge of the sofa, her eyes locked on Bill's. "What, Papa? Tell me."

"Well, honey." Bill coughed and his chin quivered. He shaded his eyes with his hands but only for a few seconds. "See … I have cancer." His eyes welled up, but he managed a sad, crooked sort of smile. "Doc says I've got about two months."

Emily was on her feet. The color drained from her face and she began to shake. "Two *months?*" She took a few steps in his direction, stopped, and took a step toward the front door. Another stop, and a step toward the sofa again. She looked like she wasn't sure if she should run out the door and scream or run to her grandpa and hold him tight. Finally she looked over her shoulder at Angela. "Two months? How long … how long have you known about this?"

"The doctors have been running tests for a few weeks." Angela blinked back the tears, but it didn't help. Her voice cracked all the same. "They told us the Thursday before you came home. It's all through his body, honey. It's very aggressive."

Emily went to Bill and stood near his chair, her hand on his shoulder. "But, Papa, you look so good. You—" she gestured toward the CD player—"you can sing and dance and laugh." Her eyes found Angela again. "Maybe there's been a mistake."

Angela understood the hope in her granddaughter's voice. Hadn't she felt the same way when the doctors told them the results of the tests? But like the doctors, she had to be honest. "There's no mistake. From the first test they told us this was possible."

Emily shook her head. "What about surgery? What about chemo or radiation or something. I mean—" she shot an anxious look at Angela—"we can't just take a death sentence and not fight it, right?"

"Honey, MRIs don't lie. We had the tests read by three doctors. The reports came in Thursday and Friday, but we wanted to wait until after Christmas to tell you." Her eyes met her husband's. "That was your papa's wish."

He reached for Emily's hand, and she leaned down, hugging him even as the tears broke free. "No, Papa, no. I still need you."

His arms closed around her. "I still need you, too, honey."

That was all Angela could take. She covered her face with her hands and wept. And across the room she could hear Bill and Emily weeping too. From somewhere in the midst of her pain, Angela heard her granddaughter mumble something about God being in control, and miracles, and how quickly everything would have to come together now. And her sweet Bill was saying something about strength and prayer and feeling healthy enough to fight the cancer. Angela wasn't getting all of it, but she understood why. She couldn't hear it over the loudest sound of all.

The sound of her breaking heart.

❧

It was some horrible nightmare. It had to be.

Even after she finished helping her grandma with the dishes, and after her grandparents had gone to their room for an early nap, Emily still couldn't believe it.

Papa had cancer? Okay, he looked a little pale and maybe thinner than usual. But that could be a good thing, couldn't it? Maybe the doctors were wrong. Everyone's MRI couldn't possibly be the same. Maybe her grandpa had the sort of blood and bones that tricked machinery like the MRI. She went to her room, sat on her bed cross-legged, and tried to concentrate. Suppose the news was true and her grandpa had only a few months to live. If that was the case, she couldn't wait another day. She couldn't take her time sorting through the box her mother left behind.

They were in a race now. And time wasn't going to win.

The miracle she was praying for wasn't just to find her mom and eventually her dad, but to help her mom make peace with her grandparents. Which meant if it didn't happen in the next few months, it might not happen at all.

She pressed her hands against the sides of her head, shutting out everything but the problem at hand. The cardboard box sat near the end of her bed. It held hours and hours of fascinating, heart-wrenching mementos, but did it really hold any clues to finding her mother or father? It was still only the day after

Christmas, so nothing official would be open yet, which meant she had no way to make phone calls that might offer a clue to her mother's whereabouts.

So be it. She'd use this day to get through the box. Just in case something vital lay hidden. She'd already gone through a third of the contents. Most of it she'd stacked along the far wall, out of the way so nothing would be bumped or kicked or stepped on. Now she lifted another photo album from the box and scanned it. She could come back and savor it later.

Two more smaller photo albums were next, and then she found another journal. Again she skimmed, though anything her mother had written had far more potential for holding a clue of some sort. Maybe mention of a favorite place where she and Emily's dad wanted to live when they were older, or something she'd always wanted to do, a place where she wanted to work. Anything that would shine a light on a trail, no matter how narrow that trail might be.

"Come on, Mom, show me something."

More framed photos and a stack of yearbooks were next. It was all Emily could do to pass over them, to place them in another stack by her wall until later. But the minute she removed the last yearbook, she felt her mouth fall open. A slight gasp escaped her as she reached into the bottom of the carton.

Notebooks.

One after another. Emily's heart raced. These had to be the notebooks her grandma had told her about. The journals held no short stories, so maybe they were here in the notebooks. The ones her mother was always writing in.

A chill ran down Emily's back as she lifted the stack of them—maybe twenty in all—and placed them on her bed. They wouldn't be journals. Her mother seemed to like journaling in hardback books with lined paper and pretty covers. These were simple, ordinary spiral notebooks. She opened the first one and scanned the front page. Half of it was taken up by oversized handwritten letters that read:

The Greatest Walk
by Lauren Gibbs

Emily frowned and ran her thumb over the words. It was indeed a short story, but who was Lauren Gibbs? If her mother wrote these stories, then why had she used a different last name? Whose last name was it, anyway? She let her eyes move down the page to the beginning of the story.

A sidewalk can be many things to many people. But for Rudy Johnson, in the summer of 1985, the sidewalk was his path to freedom ...

Emily flipped the pages, one at a time. The story went on for half the notebook. She turned back to the beginning and studied the title page again. Lauren Gibbs? Had a cousin or a friend of her mother's written the story? Emily's eyes narrowed. The story was written by hand, so all she had to do was compare handwriting styles.

She jumped to her feet and grabbed one of her mother's journals from the floor. In a rush she opened the journal, laying it side by side with the notebook. She compared the printing styles, then the cursive. Both had *y*'s that dropped low on the line and *i*'s with tiny circles where the dot should be. It didn't take a detective to see that the writing was from the same person. No question about it. Her mother wrote the short story.

So where did Lauren *Gibbs* come from?

Emily checked the back of the notebook for more stories, details, anything. It was empty, so she set it to the side and opened the second notebook. The title area on the first page read:

A Summer Sunset
by Lauren Gibbs

Emily's heart began to pound. Whatever it was with *Gibbs*, her mother hadn't merely pretended to be someone else for a single story. She sifted through the entire stack, checking the first page of each notebook. When she was finished, there were goose bumps on her arms.

Every single one was written by Lauren Gibbs.

She swallowed hard and straightened the stack. The name was worth asking about, at least. She was about to stand up and go find her grandparents when something else caught her attention. On the front of one of the notebooks, her mom had scribbled this:

Lauren Anderson loves Shane Galanter.

Only something looked different about it. Emily stared at the sentence for nearly three minutes before it finally hit her. She had always spelled her father's name *Galenter.* She'd never asked her grandparents, not when their conversations about the past were almost entirely taken up by questions about her mother. Somewhere along the years she must've seen her dad's name scribbled somewhere and assumed she was reading an *e* where an *a* should've been.

A fountain of possibility welled within her. She raced to her door, flung it open—and hesitated. It was just past three and the house was quiet. She tiptoed down the stairs and peeked into her grandparents' room. They were both on the bed, still sleeping. She could ask them about the spelling later. She zipped back up the stairs and went into the office, the room that used to belong to her mother.

She flicked on the computer, pulled out the chair, and sat down. "Hurry," she ordered it. "Warm up, already." Her eyes stayed glued to the screen while she massaged her calves. They were still sore from the soccer game the other day, a reminder that she needed to get out and jog. But she couldn't think clearly about anything—not even breathing—until she at least ran a check.

She'd have to ask her grandma about the Lauren Gibbs thing. Maybe there was a family member who had that name, or a friend out in California. It was the best clue in the entire box, and even then it might be nothing. But her father's name? That was huge. Now that she knew the right spelling, she couldn't wait to Google it.

The computer was up and ready. Next she signed onto the Internet and waited. Her grandparents had a blazing fast connection, and she was online in seconds. She found the search line and took a deep breath. "Okay, here goes." Her father's name was familiar to her, because she'd typed it into a search engine hundreds of times, easily, before she finally gave up. But now ...

Once more she typed in S-h-a-n-e G-a-l-e-n-t-e-r, just in case she'd missed something all these years.

The results came up instantly and there in the top corner it said ...

Her mouth hung open. How come she hadn't seen it before? At the top of the page it read, "Did you mean: *Shane Galanter*?"

She exhaled hard and exaggerated. "Yes. I meant that, okay?" She clicked the link beneath the correct spelling of his name. Another list came up and Emily felt her heart in her throat. Somewhere in this list of possibilities might lie the information that would lead her to her father. She scanned the few lines of details for the first four websites. Shane Galanter wasn't exactly a common name, but still there were a few hundred entries. The first one was for a Shane Galanter, president of a pest control company.

"Pest control?" Emily wrinkled her nose. "You wouldn't be doing pest control, would you, Dad?" She clicked the link and a home page covered with spiders filled the screen. Once every few seconds a cockroach scurried across the page. Emily shuddered. Bugs were the worst. But where was a picture of this Shane Galanter who owned the company?

She scanned the page and near the top she saw a link that said "Contact Me."

"Okay, I will." She clicked the words and another page popped up. This one had the smiling face of a black man. Next to the photo it said, "Shane Galanter has what you need for pest control!"

Emily blew at a piece of her dark hair. "One down."

She hit the back button and returned to the list of websites. One was a playwright, with a photo of a white-haired man in his seventies. Emily returned to the list once more. "Two down."

The next Shane Galanter ran track at Azusa Pacific University. Just for fun, she clicked the link and found his picture. "Hmm." She raised an eyebrow at the online photo. "You're cute, but you're not my dad."

The fourth website had the words *Top Gun flight instructor* next to Shane Galanter. Emily angled her head. "Interesting ..." She clicked the link, but this time there was no photograph. The page was a listing of personnel at a naval air base outside Reno, Nevada. She clicked the link and read a few paragraphs. In the late 1990s, the Top Gun fighter pilot training academy moved to Nevada, but it was still called Top Gun. Like the old 1980s movie.

Was her dad an instructor for fighter pilots? Her grandma had said he came from a wealthy family, a family involved in banking and investments. Papa said Shane's parents had plans for him to be a businessman. Most likely that's what he had become. She grabbed a pad of paper and scribbled down the information.

She went back to the list of search results again and found a few more possibilities. One Shane Galanter managed a grocery store in Utah, and another served as president of the Boys and

Girls Club in Portland, Oregon. She wrote down the details for both, and for one more: a Shane Galanter selling insurance in Riverside, California.

"Perfect!" She stared at her list of details. "One in California!"

The hope inside her doubled. It was Sunday, and with so few Shane Galanters, she could start making phone calls in the morning. Her dad was thirty-six, just like her mom. And she could describe him over the phone or fax a photo if she had to. She looked out the window at the setting sun. Morning couldn't come fast enough.

From downstairs, she heard her grandparents up and moving around. She was on her feet instantly, racing out the room and headed for them. "Grandma! Papa!" Her stocking feet slipped and she nearly lost her balance as she rounded the corner into the kitchen. Adrenaline poured through her body, leaving her out of breath by the time she anchored herself at the kitchen counter and looked from one of them to the other. "I found something."

"You did?" Her grandma was putting a tray of leftover turkey into the oven. Even cold, the smell filled the kitchen. "What'd you find?"

Emily ran her tongue over her lips. Her throat was dry. She looked at her grandpa and then shifted her eyes to her grandma again. "What do you know about the name Lauren Gibbs?"

Her grandma frowned, and her grandpa's expression went slack. He spoke first. "Never heard of her."

Emily's hope leaked from her soul like air from a punctured tire. "Never?"

"Me neither." Her grandma pulled a serving fork from the drawer in the island and set it on the counter. "Where'd you see that, sweetheart? Was it something your mother wrote about?"

She pulled out one of the bar stools and sat down. "It was the name she wrote all her short stories under." Emily used her hands to show the size of the stack of notebooks she'd looked through. "Mom had tons of short stories, Grandma." She looked at her grandpa. "Every one of them has a title and under that it says, 'By Lauren Gibbs.'"

"Lauren Gibbs?" Her grandma stopped moving and wrinkled her nose. "Why in the world would she do that?"

"Wait a minute." At the other side of the kitchen, her grandpa leaned against the refrigerator and waved a finger in the air. He looked at the two of them, one at a time. "Angie, you remember that book Lauren read when she was, I don't know, maybe twelve or thirteen?"

Her grandma released a single baffled laugh. "Honey, I didn't keep track of the books Lauren read. Besides—" she took a stack of plates from the cupboard—"that was twenty-three years ago."

"I know, but I remember her telling me about it. At least ... I think I do." He squeezed his eyes shut, as if he was trying to take himself back to that time, to remember every detail. When he blinked open, his eyes were brighter. "Yes, I remember exactly. It was one of her favorites. Every few nights she'd come find me and read a chapter out loud." He looked at his wife. "Remember? One of the characters in that book was Lauren Gibbs."

"Really?" Emily felt the thrill of discovery course through her again. She crossed the kitchen and pulled a series of salads and side dishes out of the fridge. There were six in all, and she set them on the counter opposite the oven.

"It doesn't sound even a little familiar." Her grandma slid the green bean casserole into the microwave. She wiped her hands on her apron and turned to her husband. "Did Lauren say something about it?"

"Yes." He punctuated the air in front of him. "I remember now. She told me she loved the name Lauren Gibbs. She liked something about the character, I guess. I remember her saying something about being that way when she grew up."

"So what was the book, Papa?" Emily went to him, her eyes wide as she searched his. "Maybe that'd give us another clue."

He squinted at nothing in particular and waited for several seconds. Then he shook his head and looked at her. "I can't remember."

Emily didn't care. At least it was something to go on. Then there was her father's name, the way it was supposed to be spelled. Over dinner she told them about the Shane Galanters detailed on the website.

"A flight instructor?" Her grandma set her fork down. "What was the other one?"

"An insurance guy from California."

"I'd put money on the insurance guy, if it's either of them." Papa looked tired. His words lacked the energy they'd held even half an hour earlier. "Samuel Galanter's son wouldn't have joined the navy. Not with the business plans that man had for his son."

"I'd have to agree." Her grandmother gave Emily a guarded smile. "But sweetheart, you need to be realistic. There's no reason Shane's name has to be on the Internet. You know that, right?"

"Yes." Emily looked at her nearly full plate. She was far too excited to think about eating. Her eyes found her grandma's again. "It's a long shot." She smiled. "But that's what a miracle is, right?"

"Right." Her grandma's expression softened. "I guess maybe it's time I believed in long shots too."

That night, after they'd watched a movie and talked a little bit more about her papa's cancer, Emily turned in early. She lay in her bed staring at the ceiling, willing the clock to speed past the hours so she could start checking out the Shane Galanters on her list. But that wasn't what filled her mind. She couldn't stop thinking about her mother and the book she'd told Papa about, and how she'd been crazy about the name Lauren Gibbs. Crazy enough to use it as her pen name for every one of her short stories.

"God—" she turned onto her side so she could see out the window—"there has to be something in that box besides a bunch of short stories, doesn't there? Can you help me find what I need? Please?" She thought about her grandpa and the battle that had just begun. "I don't have much time, Lord."

Usually when she talked to God, a peace filled her from the inside out. That was true this time, also, but there was something else. An urging grew within her … as if she'd stumbled onto something important.

Now all she had to figure out was what, exactly, it was.

Eighteen

The orphanage story turned out to be more than a sentimental feature.

On Lauren's first visit to the badly damaged building, where a hundred children were housed, she assumed the story was obvious. Capture a detailed look at the children orphaned by war, make it heartfelt, and get it in before her Friday deadline. The feature part of the story had gone as anticipated, and the staff at the New York office was thrilled with the piece.

"This story would make a right-winger do an about-face," her editor told her. "It's a five-hanky read for sure."

That would've been enough, especially combined with the amazing photo-essay Scanlon pulled together during their day with the children. But during lunch, one of the workers carrying a water pitcher came up and whispered something in her ear.

"Some of the babies are American."

Then the worker looked around, her eyes darting about as if she could be in danger for what she'd just said. "They were fathered by American soldiers."

Lauren wanted to react, but she kept cool. She smiled and pointed to her sandwich and nodded, as if the woman's comment had something to do with the food on her plate. Then she whispered, "I'll meet you outside in five minutes."

The woman refilled Lauren's water, nodded, then moved on down the line. At the right time, Lauren excused herself from the table and found Scanlon. "I'll be right back."

"Where're you going?" He looked nervous. For the past eighteen months he'd taken on the unspoken role of bodyguard for her. She was an easy American target because of her pale blonde hair and her involvement in every facet of life in Afghanistan. Her editors had warned her about being alone, since Westerners were still often the focus of kidnappings for ransom or political favors.

"I'll be fine." She nodded to the courtyard outside the orphanage. "One of the workers needs to talk to me."

Scanlon arched a brow, then shifted from one foot to the other and adjusted his camera. "I'll be here if you need me."

"Okay." She squeezed his shoulder and gave him a quick grin. Then she worked her way through the main room, stopping to chat with three children. When she reached the door, she stretched and drew a deep breath. She looked around—no one seemed to be watching her. Once outside, she spotted the worker near a broken brick wall. The wind was howling, and the woman had a veil over her nose and mouth. She still had the water pitcher in her hand, and Lauren realized she was standing near a leaky tap. Lauren went to her, glancing over her shoulder to make sure they were alone.

"This big," the woman said in broken English. "Your people say Americans here help us." She nodded. "Some yes. Some no. Some sleep with our women and make babies." She pointed back to the orphanage. "American babies have no place here. No one wants them."

Lauren was horrified. Why hadn't the idea occurred to her before? There were thousands of U.S. soldiers in Afghanistan, most of them men. Of course some of them must be having their way with the local women. They probably figured it was one way to spend a weekend. No doubt some of the women were willing parties to that sort of carousing. But until now it hadn't occurred to her that those women might've gotten pregnant.

"Why not keep the babies?" She looked again at the doorway. No one was watching them.

The woman's eyes grew horrified and she shook her head. "No babies when no husband. Not okay."

Right. Women in Afghanistan might be out from beneath the veil, but there were still social codes they had to live by. Being single and pregnant was probably akin to leprosy in biblical times. Another gust of silty air blew across the courtyard, and Lauren shielded her face. When it passed she squinted at the woman. "How do they get their babies here? And what happens to the babies next?"

"There is more." The woman looked around and took a step closer. "I meet you here two weeks. Two weeks. Then I tell rest of story."

The two weeks had passed quickly. A flare-up of violence near the hill country took her and Scanlon away from the apartment for three days after Christmas. Twice they were close enough to the action that she wondered about her sanity. Journalists liked to think of themselves as invincible, mere spectators to the sport of war. But that wasn't true. Lauren was well aware that a number of reporters had lost their lives since the war began more than two years ago.

Now it was January 5, and she and Scanlon caught a ride back to the orphanage. So far she hadn't reported on the situation. She wanted all the details before she wrote it for the magazine. If it played out the way she thought it might, the story could wind up on the cover. American soldiers leaving a generation of orphans behind? It'd be the top story for a month.

The road to the orphanage was dotted with potholes, and she and Scanlon bounced along in the backseat. It was another sunny day, dry and windy the way it had been for the past month. The air was cooler than last time she and Scanlon made the trip out, but not by much. The two of them still wore shorts and tank tops. Next to her, Scanlon looked out the window and exhaled hard. "I have a funny feeling about this story."

"Me too." She picked up her worn shoulder bag and sifted through it. For stories like this she needed more than paper. She had a tape recorder and a supply of fresh tapes and batteries. She looked at Scanlon. "I have the feeling it'll be the biggest story to come out of Afghanistan in a year."

He shook his head and narrowed his eyes, seeing past her into the barren hillsides beyond the narrow roadway. "Not that sort of feeling." His eyes found hers. "Why couldn't she give you the story when you were there the first time?" He nodded toward the road ahead. "We have to get another driver, make the hour-long trip a second time." He paused and looked at the road ahead of them. "Seems weird to me."

"Scanlon, you worry too much." Lauren scrounged in her bag again and pulled out a bottle of sunscreen. A pair of flies was buzzing around the back window and she waved them off. "The woman was scared to death. Another five minutes with me and she would've fainted from fear."

"Okay." He put his arm up along the back of the seat and leaned against the door. "I still feel funny."

"Well you can feel funny all day long." She patted his knee. "Just get pictures of those fair-skinned babies in the back room."

"Did you see them? I mean, do you know where they are?"

"Of course not." She rubbed lotion onto her right leg and worked it down to her ankle. "That's part of why we're going back. The woman has more information, and then I'm going to convince her to let me have a look."

"Good luck." His eyes danced and he shook his head. "The woman's scared to talk to you and you think she'll give you a tour of the back room?" He nodded. "If we get that far, don't worry. I'll get a hundred pictures." His smile faded. "Just be careful, Lauren."

"Always." They didn't talk for the rest of the ride. Lauren could hardly wait to get inside, not just to talk with the worker, but because she wanted to see the children. She had several favorites already, kids who had bonded with her the last time she was there. Her bag held another supply of lollipops. If Scanlon didn't mind, she'd stay into the afternoon visiting with them.

When they pulled into the long driveway that led to the isolated building, they paid their driver and climbed out. He had nowhere to go, he told them. No other jobs. He pulled his car next to a scraggly tree and rolled down the windows. "I ready when you are."

"Thank you." Lauren smiled at him and tapped her watch. "Could be many hours."

"Okay." He put his hands together and held them along the side of his face. "I sleep here."

"Good." Lauren nodded at him, and she and Scanlon headed inside. The kids were playing in the courtyard and scattered throughout the main room. If today was like the other day, they would have lunch in fifteen minutes or so.

They were inside for less than a minute when a man approached them. He hadn't been around the other day. "Hello, I'm Feni." His accent was slight, his English strong. "You're here to do a story on our orphans, yes?"

"Yes." Lauren stepped forward. She wasn't about to tell him that she had a private meeting with one of the workers. "People want to know about the children, how the war has hurt them."

"Very good." He smiled. "I am the director of the orphanage. You may find me in the office if you have something to know." He turned his hand palm up and spread it out toward the children on the floor. "Our children are very kind, very hopeful. Please ... let me know if you need anything."

A gust of wind shook the windows. Lauren held her hand out to Feni. "Thank you. I'll come find you if we have questions."

The man nodded at Scanlon, turned, and walked back to the office. As he left, a chill passed over Lauren's arms. "Why wasn't he here last time?"

"I told you." Scanlon moved closer to her so their arms were touching. "I have a funny feeling about this. Remember what the army's media man told us. Never make an appointment with a local, unless it's in plain sight of everyone. Even then we're supposed to watch our backs."

"Right." She wiped her palms on her shorts and ordered herself not to feel frightened. "This is different, though. The woman was a worker, Scanlon." She gave him a confident look. "Really."

At that moment, a little girl came running up. She had hair halfway down her back, and Lauren recognized her from the other day. She'd been something of a shadow around Lauren through most of her last visit. The girl was adorable, not much older than seven, with one of her front teeth missing.

The girl stopped a foot from her and did a little bow. "Hello, Miss."

"Hello." Lauren smiled at her, looking into her eyes. She held out her hand and the girl took it, squeezing her fingers. "Senia, right?"

"Yes." The girl's eyes danced.

"How are you, Senia?" Lauren kept her smile in place, but felt the grief rise again in her heart. She had missed so much by losing Emily. So very much. But the grief was for more than the loss of her daughter. It was also because her job made it impossible to even consider adopting a girl like Senia.

The child was grinning bigger than before. "I fine." She peered into Lauren's bag. Then she lifted her eyebrows halfway up her forehead. "Sweets, Miss? Sweets, please?" She held out her hand. "Please, Miss."

The children knew very little English, but they took pride in using it. They could've spoken their native tongue, and Lauren would've understood it. Especially in the simple words and phrases the children used. But clearly they wanted to impress her, and so for the most part they spoke English.

Lauren smiled at the girl. "Okay." She pointed to the table already set with lunch plates. "After lunch."

The girl looked at the table and immediately she understood. She nodded and her eyes got shy. "Miss, you pretty."

Next to her, Scanlon had his camera out. He was snapping pictures of the girl, her earnest expression, the way she looked up with adoring eyes at the Americans. "You brought your playing cards, right?" He gave her a light nudge with his knee. "Get 'em out and sit on the floor. You'll be surrounded before you can shuffle the deck."

It was a good idea.

Lauren opened her bag and took out her pack of cards. Then she held them up so the little girl could see them, and she dropped slowly to the floor. "See," she told the girl. "We play a game."

Scanlon stepped back and sure enough, a dozen kids were seated around her in no time, all of them with eyebrows raised at the cards in Lauren's hands. She gave the first boy on her right a four of clubs. "Four," she told him. Then she held up four fingers and counted them down. "One, two, three, four."

A light dawned in the boy's eyes. He bounced a little and took the card, rattling off something about numbers and a game to the girl next to him. The other children held out their hands and waited as she gave each of them a card and explained what it meant. They were still holding their cards when the workers filed out of the kitchen and into the dining area.

"Here—" Lauren held out the card box and slipped the rest of the cards inside. The kids followed her example. "Later." She winked at Senia. "When we have sweets."

The kids spotted the lunch servers, and they jumped to their feet, scrambling to their places at the table.

"Where's the informant?" Scanlon kept his voice low so only she could hear it.

Lauren searched the faces of the women. "She's not there."

"See." The workers walked slowly toward the lunch table. "Something funny's going on."

The lunch women spotted Lauren and Scanlon, and they smiled and waved. There were six long tables squeezed into the room, and each seated twenty children. Lauren was amazed at how quickly the workers slapped sandwiches on the table and poured water for the children. She stopped a few feet away, while Scanlon switched discs in his digital camera.

All along Lauren figured this was the time when she'd meet the woman. They'd spoken during lunch before and they'd been uninterrupted because the kids were preoccupied. But where was she? And was it just Scanlon making her nervous, or did she feel the same thing he did? An uneasiness that somehow, something about the meeting wasn't right?

Feni, the man in the office, stepped out during lunch and watched the children for a minute or two. Then he looked in her direction and gave a little wave. She did the same, and he disappeared back into the room. She looked past him and saw a desk and a phone, not much else.

"That Feni guy makes me nervous." Scanlon had his camera open. He was checking one of the settings. "He seems shady."

Lauren bit her lip. "Maybe he doesn't like Americans hanging out at his orphanage."

"Maybe."

The children were just finishing lunch, and Scanlon was saying something about the workers, how they seemed distracted, when Lauren caught the glimpse of a woman walking across the courtyard toward the front door. She held her breath; it was her informant. She stood in the doorway, and their eyes locked.

"Hey." Lauren leaned close to Scanlon, a smile playing on her lips so she wouldn't catch the attention of any of the adults in the room. "She's here. I'll be right back."

"I'll come too." He slipped his camera into his bag and started in beside her.

"No." She gave him a look that left no room for negotiation. "She wanted me by myself."

He pursed his lips and made a frustrated sound. "All right." He looked around her toward the front door. "Don't go far."

"I won't."

This time as she left the building, she could hear the children calling after her. She looked back over her shoulder and saw Scanlon running interference, gathering them and telling them that she would be right back inside. Lauren picked up her pace.

They didn't have much time. She stepped into the courtyard and was met by yet another gust of gritty wind. Shading her eyes, she looked around, but the woman wasn't there. "Hello?" She took another ten steps and scanned the yard. There were several nooks and small areas near half-standing walls, but the woman was nowhere.

Unease slithered up her spine, and she half-expected to see Feni step out from behind one of the broken walls. She owned a gun, but she didn't carry it with her. If Feni had something planned, she couldn't offer much resistance. She was about to turn around and go back inside, when she heard the sound of children's voices behind her.

"Miss!" It was Senia, leading another little girl and two boys out into the courtyard. "Miss, sweets? Please?"

Lauren was about to tell them no, that the sweets had to be eaten inside and that they needed to go back and wait for her, when an explosion of bullets rang out across the patio. In a blur that took a fraction of a second, she turned toward the sound and saw three figures cloaked in black, each with a machine gun aimed in their direction.

"Stop!" She held out her hand toward them, then spun to look at the children. Two of the kids lay spread out on the ground, their white shirts spattered with blood, a dark pool fanning out beneath them. "*No!*" She was about to run toward them when another round of bullets rang through the air.

A burning sensation ripped through her shoulder and knocked her onto the hot cement. She'd been hit, and even though she kicked her legs and tried to find her way to a sitting position, she couldn't do it, couldn't move. All at once a series of voices began shouting at each other, and she looked toward the desert sand at the place where the gunmen were still standing. They waved their guns and started toward her, and she understood. She was the one they wanted. In the blur of pain and confusion she realized what was happening. Scanlon was right. It was a setup. The story probably held no more truth than half the other crazy lures that had been tossed her way.

Usually she was smart enough to avoid meeting with unnamed informants who promised a shocking truth. But this time it had involved kids ... babies. She felt herself losing consciousness and she fought to keep her eyes open. The men were coming closer, and she wanted to scream. But that would only make them open fire on her. Instead she lay unmoving. Maybe they would think they'd killed her.

And maybe they had. Her shoulder was on fire, and she felt something warm and wet beneath her. Spots danced before her eyes, and she willed herself not to let go, not to give into the darkness that pulled at her. *No*, she ordered herself. *Not yet!* The children needed her. They were hit, two of them, right?

She inched herself backward, toward them. But as she did, Feni ran out from behind a door across the courtyard, and in a rush of bullets, he shot and laid out the first of the three gunmen. At the same time, bullets came from a window in the orphanage and before the gunmen could react, all three were on the ground.

Feni ran closer and sprayed another round of bullets at them. When he seemed sure they weren't going to move again, he raced to her. She heard Scanlon's voice from behind her at the same time.

"Lauren!" He was at her side, turning her over. "We have to get help." He looked at Feni, who was just reaching them. "Call for help, please!"

She moved her good arm and took hold of Scanlon's ankle. "The children ..."

"The women are helping them." He gulped. His face was pale and lined with worry. "Don't move, Lauren. Help's coming."

"It's ... just my shoulder." She winced. Her words were sticking together, and she felt faint again. "I'm ... okay."

A woman ran up to them with a roll of bandaging. She handed it to Scanlon and he worked fast, pressing it hard against her upper arm. The pain was like white-hot lightning hitting her again and again. It roused her up and brought her back to the moment.

"We need to stop the bleeding."

"The children, Scanlon." She waited until he had her shoulder wrapped tight, then she sat up. Nausea built in her, but she shook it off. Scanlon tried to stop her, but she jerked away from him. Crawling on her knees, she covered the three feet that separated her from the cluster of women. "Please! Let me ... let me see."

"Move, please," Scanlon took the lead and helped clear a path to the kids at the center of the circle.

Lauren pushed her way closer until she could see them clearly. One of them was a little boy, moaning and moving his head from side to side. He lay on the ground and Lauren looked at the place where the women were working. The child's kneecap had been blown off his leg.

She brought the back of her hand to her mouth, but she stopped herself from getting sick. What about the other child? Two women were kneeling beside her and only then did Lauren notice that they were weeping. Weeping and wailing and stroking the child's hair. Lauren still couldn't quite make her out, so she crept a little closer and then ...

"No! No, not her!" The words that came from her were almost silent, spoken with what remained of her strength. Senia, the little girl with the missing front tooth. "Oh, please!"

Scanlon dropped down beside her. "Lauren, come on. They're taking care of her."

One of the women let her head drop back. She clenched her fists and shook them at the sky. "Why? Why her?"

Lauren reached out, but she had no more strength, no way to reach the little girl. "Scanlon, is she dead? Tell me if she's dead."

"Lauren—" he put his hand on her shoulder—"let's move. They need room to work."

The wailing from the women grew louder, and others joined them. The only woman missing was the informant, the one who must've gotten away once the shooting began. The one who had set her up. She looked up one last time. The little girl's eyes were open and unblinking. One of the weeping women near her shut first one of Senia's lids, then the other.

Scanlon brought his head close to hers. "She's gone, Lauren. Let it go. Come on."

She wanted to run to the child and hold her in her arms. They hadn't had time for sweets. That's all the girl wanted. A lollipop. A lollipop and a chance to hold her hand the way she'd done the last time Lauren was there. The spots were back, and she let her forehead rest on the ground. It wasn't too late, was it? The sweets were still in her bag. Maybe if she found one she could give it to Senia and everything would be—

The spots connected, and Lauren felt herself falling, as if she were being dropped from a thirty-story building and there was no way to stop. Something warm and salty was coming from her mouth, but she couldn't move her head, couldn't open her eyes. *Help me ...* But the words died long before they reached her lips.

She felt the heat from the patio radiating through her arms and legs, and then a dizzying sensation. She was dying. She must've been shot in the chest, not the shoulder. Her heart was spilling out everything within it, the ocean of sorrow, the desire to bring peace to these people, and her will to live. All of it was leaving her.

"Lauren, stay with me!" Scanlon sounded a hundred miles away. His voice was tinny and distant, and she couldn't figure out where it was coming from. He was saying something else, but his voice faded more and more.

And then there was nothing.

Nothing but hot, burning pain, utter sorrow, and darkness.

NINETEEN

Shane was finishing up a final briefing with a student fighter pilot. The guy was twenty-four, educated, and had a promising future at the Top Gun academy. He'd been through enough training that he knew what he was doing. But this would be his first solo flight, and Shane couldn't leave anything to chance.

Shane held a checklist in his hands. "Bail-out procedure."

"Bail out." The young man's words were clear and clipped. He stood at attention throughout the short examination, his flight suit perfect, his helmet tucked beneath his arm. Then, as Shane took notes, the guy rattled off a perfect description of the circumstances and situations when a bail out was necessary, and followed it up with a detailed account of the procedure.

"Good." Shane placed a check next to the words *bail out* on the form. They went through three more terms, and then Shane looked at the pilot. "You ready?"

"Sir, yes, sir."

"Okay, call sign Doogie." Shane grinned. "Let's see you fly." He shook the pilot's hand, spun around, and headed for the tower. For the next half hour he was in constant communication with the pilot as he practiced routine flight maneuvers. Finally-—right on time—he requested permission to land.

"Roger that, Doogie. Bring 'er in." Another instructor was watching from over Shane's shoulder. Shane held up his hand and the two gave each other a high five. He pressed the radio button one more time. "I can see why they recommended you for Top Gun, Doogie. You're gonna be a good one."

"Thank you, sir."

Shane had some more paperwork and another fifteen minutes with the pilot. Then it was time for lunch. He strutted across the flight deck and wiped the sweat off his brow. The cloudiness of a few weeks ago was gone, and the sun was hotter than usual for January.

He went to the cafeteria, bought himself a chicken Caesar salad, and took a table by himself on the outdoor patio, the one that overlooked the runway. It was loud outside, but Shane didn't mind. Every landing and takeoff still shot adrenaline through him, and made him long to be in the cockpit. He bowed his head and thanked the Lord for his food.

Then he adjusted his sunglasses and stared into the vast blue. There was nothing like taking an F–15 out over Nevada and looping up across New Mexico and down along the coast of California all in less than thirty minutes. That kind of power never left a guy. He leaned forward and anchored his elbows on the glass-top table.

What was it about flying lately? His job as flight instructor had always been rewarding, but these days he couldn't wait to come in and work with the young pilots. Part of his job was to stay adept at the cockpit himself, but since his engagement party he'd been putting in twice the required hours in the sky. As if he couldn't get enough sky time.

He was about to take another bite of his salad when he felt his phone vibrating in his pants pocket. With the noise on the flight deck he'd miss every call if he didn't have it set to vibrate. He pulled the phone out and squinted at the small Caller ID window. Ellen. He waited for the surge of excitement to hit him, but it never came.

He tapped the receive button. "Hey, how's my girl?" He set his fork down and pushed his chair back, giving himself room to cross one of his ankles over his knee.

"Hi." She was talking loud, and he heard a chorus of voices in the background. "I'm in D.C., and you won't believe it!"

D.C.? Had he known she was going there? He massaged his brow with his fingertips. "You're in D.C.?"

She did a frustrated breath. "Yes, Shane. I told you Wednesday I was coming to D.C. for the weekend." Her tone lightened some. "Daddy had some friends he wanted me to meet."

"Oh." Shane let his hands drop back to his lap. He had no memory of her telling him about the trip. Not that it mattered. She flew to Washington, D.C., at least once a month. He removed his sunglasses and checked them for scratches. There were none. "Okay, what's up?"

"I took the red-eye, so I got here in time for some meetings." Excitement made her voice shrill. "A lot of the big guys from the party were here, and Daddy put in a plug for you."

"He did?" Shane slipped the glasses on again and watched a pair of F–16s coming in for a landing. He released a single laugh, but it didn't sound amused, even to him. "I thought we talked about this, Ellen. I'm not running for office."

"I know, but that doesn't matter." She was undaunted, her voice louder still. "Sorry about the noise. The meeting just broke up. Daddy explained it to the group. He told them that by the time you were on a ballot, he wanted everyone to know who you were."

A small thrill ran through Shane. "Everyone?"

"Yes." She paused for effect. "Even the president, Shane. The whole party's excited."

"That's amazing." He tried to imagine Ellen's father getting the big hitters in the Republican Party excited about his future son-in-law. It was a heady picture. "Tell him thanks for me."

"He wants you to come with me next month. Everyone wants to get to know you."

"Sounds good." Another plane was taking off from a different runway. Shane imagined himself behind the controls. He blinked and gripped the arms of his chair. "I'll have to see about getting off."

Ellen giggled. "If the president of the United States wants to meet you, I think the navy might be willing to give you a few days."

"True." He squirmed in his seat and uncrossed his legs. "Hey, listen. Lunch is almost over, I better go."

"Okay, me too." She made a squealing sound. "I'm so excited for you, Shane. For both of us."

"Right. Thanks. Tell your dad I said hi."

The conversation was over before Shane realized that he hadn't told her he loved her. Of course, they didn't say it all the time—mostly only when they were alone or kissing good-bye after an evening together. Even then it felt almost businesslike. He slipped his phone back into his uniform pocket.

If he really wanted to be a politician, if he wanted the chance to represent the people on the Republican ticket, he should've felt like flying across the flight deck without any plane at all. This was the chance most aspiring political leaders only dreamed about. Perfect connections, a groundswell of favorable opinion, the support of leaders—all the way to the president.

Shane picked up his fork and took another bite of his salad. He *should* be excited. He and Ellen had talked more about the idea in the days since the engagement party, and he had to admit the possibility was enticing. The country was ready for someone with his moral fiber, she'd told him. Everyone was saying so.

He poked at his salad. The lettuce had wilted during his phone call, but he was too hungry to care. He chewed another bite and thought about the plan he and Ellen had devised. He would work another year as flight instructor, through the days of their May wedding and their honeymoon to Jamaica. Then as the year drew to a close, he would line himself up for position on a ballot. His parents and Ellen's father would bankroll them for the next year while he built a following in Nevada.

"After that," her father told him the last time they were together, "there'll be no stopping you, my boy."

It sounded wonderful. Who wouldn't be excited about that sort of plan? Still ... Shane stared into the blue. None of it felt like his plan. Before meeting Ellen, he'd been content to be an instructor at Top Gun. No, not content. That wasn't how he felt. He was living his dream. Yes, the idea of running on the Republican ticket sounded good, but not nearly as good as teaching young guys to be hotshot fighter pilots.

A warm breeze blew over him. *God, everything is happening so fast. I feel like I've lost me.*

He waited for some kind of response, a sign of God's guidance. But today there was nothing like that, no sense of understanding, no quiet inner whispers of reassurance. Shane watched yet another jet leave the runway and lift into the sky above Reno.

Okay, God, I know You're there. Even when I don't feel You. Give me wisdom, please. Just a little wisdom to help me know what to do next.

Still no answer resonated within him. He returned to his salad and suddenly, as it had done every day since his engagement party, Lauren Anderson's face came to mind. He had prayed about that too. He was getting married. It was time to let Lauren go forever. He looked at his salad, and her image faded. The chicken was lukewarm, but it tasted all right. As he ate he thought about his prayer. Wisdom was exactly what he needed. Direction about what to do next, something that would help him understand why he was uncertain about a future that only a few months ago had felt bright and exciting. Yes, wisdom was exactly what he needed.

So he didn't make a decision he'd spend a lifetime regretting.

TWENTY

Emily was pretty sure her father was an instructor at the navy's Top Gun training facility. The problem was, she couldn't prove it. She had his birth date, his physical description, and his name. But three times she'd contacted the academy, and all three times she'd come away with no information. The last time she'd called was Friday, two days ago, and her conversation was particularly frustrating.

"Hi." She tried to make herself sound older than her eighteen years. "I'm doing a story on your flight instruction program." She held her breath.

"You'll have to talk to the public information office, ma'am." The guy connected her call to the right department.

Emily didn't mind. This had happened each of the other two times she'd called. She waited until someone picked up the call. "Media relations, Private Walton here."

"Yes, hello." She paused, so she wouldn't seem desperate. "I'm a freelance writer working on a feature story about flight instructors."

"How can I help you?" The woman was pleasant, but her tone said she was in a hurry.

"Actually, I'd like to set up an interview with one specific flight instructor. Shane Galanter."

"Officer Galanter's a busy man. Maybe I can fax you over a list of frequently asked questions and their answers."

"I already have that." She gave a polite laugh. "It's important for the story that I have a chance to meet face-to-face with one of the pilots. I've researched the instructors, and I'd really like to interview Officer Galanter."

"Tell you what, why don't you fax me a list of questions, and I'll see if Officer Galanter can get the answers to you sometime next week." She sounded suddenly distracted. "Anything else?"

"You know," Emily could feel the call slipping away, "maybe you could help me figure something out. I've met Officer Galanter one other time, and I want to make sure we're talking about the same man. He has dark hair, dark eyes, and he's tall, right? Thirty-six years old?"

The woman hesitated. "Ma'am, we do not give out that type of information on our flight instructors, or on anyone else. I'm afraid I can't help you with this particular story." She hung up before Emily could say another word.

Now it was Sunday afternoon, and her frustration was growing by the hour. She'd called the insurance company in Riverside, California. It hadn't taken five minutes to figure out that the fifty-eight-year-old redhead who ran the office wasn't the Shane Galanter she was looking for. The others had been easy to rule out also, so that left two choices. Either her father was an instructor at the Top Gun school, or he wasn't listed anywhere on the Internet.

She sat on her bed surrounded by her mother's journals and short-story notebooks. Her grandparents were at the store, but they wouldn't be gone long. Her grandpa had very little energy these days, and he looked far worse than he had at Christmastime.

"I don't understand," she told her grandma one day the week before. "I never knew cancer could be fast like this."

"It is sometimes." Her grandma was teary-eyed again. She dabbed at her cheek. "He doesn't have long, Emily. We're both so glad you can be home."

Emily shuddered at the memory. Thank heaven she didn't have to be back to school until the sixth of February. Some of the kids took short, one-unit classes in January, but Emily decided to stay home. Her grandparents needed her. Besides, she had to find her parents. Absolutely *had* to find them. Her grandpa's quick deterioration told her that much. First thing Monday she was going to do what she should've done a week ago. She would call the Top Gun academy and leave a straightforward message. *Please have Shane Galanter contact Emily Anderson in Wheaton, Illinois.* Then she would give her phone number and keep praying.

With that decided she stared at her mother's notebooks and journals, scattered on the bed around her, and willed herself to see something she had missed. She opened one of the journals and read several entries. Each one was another window to the girl her mother had been. But none of them had anything she could go on, nothing that would lead her to wherever her mother was living now. She stood and went to the window. A foot of snow covered the ground, and all of life looked the way the search for her mother felt: freezing and dormant. "God ..." She looked into the thick gray sky and tried to imagine the Lord looking down on her. "You know where she is. So show me how to find her, okay? I'm running out of time, Lord. Please ..."

She was quiet, her nose against the cold glass window. Then, in the smallest inner voice, a Scripture began to play in her mind.

I am the Alpha and the Omega, the Beginning and the End ... I am that I am.

The verse was from Revelation, and it righted her world in a heartbeat. God was everything. He was Lord and Savior, Alpha and Omega. What did she have to worry about? A sense of awe came over her. God had more names than she could imagine, more names than—

Like a bolt of lightning, it hit her.

What if her mother had used more than one name too? Everyone assumed she'd changed her name, otherwise the private investigators hired by her grandparents would've found something by now. She darted back to her bed and grabbed the first spiral notebook she could reach. As fast as her fingers could move, she opened the cover and stared at the title page.

A Summer's Day
by Lauren Gibbs

Maybe her mother was using the name Lauren Gibbs! Emily stared at it, then she smacked her knee. Of *course!* Why hadn't she thought of that sooner? Once her grandpa told her the name came from a fictional character, she assumed there was no point searching it on the Internet. The most she would find would be a novel her mom liked to read as a young teenager. But now …

She dropped the notebook and sprinted down the hallway to the office. The computer was on and connected to the Internet in no time.

"God—" she whispered His name, her fingers trembling—"You gave me this. I can feel it." She centered her hands over the keyboard, typed in the name, and hit enter. She couldn't breathe while the machine worked, and then in a flash a list of entries appeared.

Emily stared and began reading them out loud. "*Time* magazine correspondent Lauren Gibbs has been stationed in Afghanistan since—"

Emily's heart raced. *Time* magazine correspondent? Her eyes flew to the next entry. "'Children of War'—a profile on the orphans of Operation Enduring Freedom, by Lauren Gibbs, *Time* magazine correspondent. Photos by …"

One after another she read the entries in the list of hits and by the time she reached the end of the page, she was shaking all the way to her toes. Every entry mentioned Lauren Gibbs as a *Time* magazine reporter. Emily pressed her palm against her forehead, pushing her bangs back, the way she did when a soccer game got too intense. "Okay, God, walk me through this."

Just because Lauren Gibbs wrote for *Time* magazine didn't mean Emily had found her mother. She went back to the search line and typed, "Lauren Gibbs *Time* magazine profile."

The results were just as quick as before. The first link said simply "a profile of Lauren Gibbs, *Time* magazine correspondent." Again Emily held her breath as she clicked the link. And there, instantly, was a photo that took up a fourth of the screen. The woman was blonde and pretty in a plain sort of way. She wore khaki clothing, and in the background were what looked like army tents. More than that, though, was the look on her face. A haunting look that revealed everything and nothing all at the same time. A look Emily had seen more often than she cared to admit.

In photographs of herself.

"Dear God ..." Tears filled Emily's eyes, and she reached out, brushing the image with the tips of her fingers. It was her mother, she was absolutely sure. After a lifetime of looking, she'd found the woman who had walked out of her life when she was just an infant. She had no doubts, none at all. Because in more ways than one, looking at the woman's image was like looking at her own.

She brought her hands back to the keyboard and scanned the profile, gobbling up every small detail, all the pieces that had been missing for so long. Lauren Gibbs was based in Los Angeles, but she'd lived in the Middle East for most of the past three years. She was thirty-six years old with a master's degree in journalism from University of Southern California. She interned with the *Los Angeles Times*, and took a position at *Time* magazine a few years later, when she was just twenty-six.

Emily read the last part out loud again. "Lauren Gibbs has won numerous awards for her gutsy reporting throughout the war in Afghanistan and Iraq. She is credited with helping bring humanitarian assistance to the Middle East and with helping to open a number of orphanages throughout the region. She is single and has no children."

What? Emily sat back, hard. The last line screamed at her, hurting her as much as if she'd been slapped. The single part was sad, but not surprising. Her mother went to Los Angeles to find the love of her life, and her search apparently turned up nothing. But …

No children?

"Is that what you tell people, Mom?" Fresh tears slid down her cheeks, and she didn't bother to wipe them away. The information was a lie, and it made her mad. Lauren Gibbs—Lauren *Anderson*—did too have a child. She had a daughter. Even if she thought her daughter was dead, she had a child.

Emily stared at her mother's image, trying to see past the hurt in her eyes. Other people might think the look was stone cold, the way people would expect a hardened journalist to look. But Emily recognized the look. It was the way she, herself, looked when she let circumstances get to her. When going through a tough day without a mom and a dad was more than she could handle, when she saw her teammates scan the sideline and wave to parents and the reminder hit her again. Her parents hadn't seen her play a single game.

Again she touched the image, tracing her mother's cheek, her chin. "Was it that easy to let me go? To tell yourself I never existed?" Her tears became sobs, and she drew back from the computer, hanging her head and giving way to a lifetime of sadness and doubt and question marks.

After a few minutes, she heard someone at the door behind her. "Emily?" It was her grandma's voice, and it was filled with alarm. "What on earth—"

Emily sat up and looked over her shoulder. Between sobs she said, "I found her. I found my mom."

Her grandma looked like she might drop from shock. Her face went pale, and she sat on the arm of the sofa, her eyes glued to the computer screen. "How did you—"

Emily dragged her fists over her eyes and found a trace of control. "Her ... her name's Lauren Gibbs."

"Lauren Gibbs." Her grandma was on her feet, moving trance-like across the office toward the computer screen. The closer she got the more grief-stricken her face became. She reached toward the image on the screen and a cry left her. "Lauren ... my baby." She brought her hand to her mouth and shook her head. Again she reached out, as tears flooded her eyes. "My girl."

Emily couldn't stop the sobs. All her life living with her grand-parents, they talked about her mother only a handful of times. It was as if they wanted to give her the most normal life possible, and that meant they couldn't raise her in an environment of sor-row and regret. But now—watching her grandmother—she knew the truth.

The woman had grieved the loss of her daughter every day of her life. Emily watched her back up a few steps and sit on the other arm of the sofa, the one closest to the screen. Then she dropped her face into her hands and wept, praying out loud as her emotion allowed. "God, You found her for us. Thank you ... thank you. My baby girl ... my Lauren."

Emily went to wrap her arms around her. In every way, her grandmother had been a mother to her, but they both paid the price for being without the woman on the computer screen. Now, their tears were for too many reasons to count. They were for every one of Emily's missed birthdays and lost milestones, for all her school years and teenage years and soccer tourna-ments when she had privately ached for her mother. And they were tears of relief. Because they'd found her. Finally.

Emily sniffed and grabbed three quick breaths. "It's the mir-acle we prayed for."

Her grandma uncovered her face and looked at the computer screen again. Beneath her eyes, her mascara had left dark smudges, and her cheeks were red and blotchy. But Emily had never seen her look more joyful. Grandma grabbed two tissues from the office desk and handed one of them to her. They both blew their noses and wiped their eyes some more.

"I still can't believe it." Grandma slumped forward and her eyes found Emily's. "I can't believe we didn't think of it a few weeks ago."

"Me neither." Emily sniffed, but she felt a grin tugging at the corners of her mouth. "I was standing at the window in my room and I begged God to show me the next clue. You know what He did?"

"What?" Her grandma reached out and the two of them joined hands.

"He reminded me of His names, all His marvelous names." She made a sound that was more laugh than cry. "All of a sudden, it was so obvious. God has dozens of names, and some people have multiple names too."

Her grandmother looked drained, as if she wouldn't have had the energy to stand if she needed to. "What do we do next?"

Emily released her grandma's hands and sat in the computer chair again. She slid it forward and looked once more at the profile next to her mother's picture. At the bottom was the thing she was looking for. A link that read, "Contact Lauren Gibbs." Emily's breath caught in her throat, and she shook her head. It was too much, but she wasn't going to stop now.

She clicked the link and an e-mail template opened up. In the top line was her mother's e-mail address: *Lauren.Gibbs@Time Magazine.com*. Her hands were still shaky, but she tabbed down to the subject line and typed, "From Emily." Then she moved the cursor to the text area and drew a deep breath. She'd had a lifetime to think about what to say next. Her fingers began to move across the keyboard, and the words came without any effort at all.

> Hi, my name is Emily Anderson, and I'm eighteen years old.

She exhaled and looked at her grandmother. "I can't believe I'm doing this."

Her grandmother looked breathless, dazed. "Keep typing."

"Okay." Emily looked back at the screen.

> I believe that you might be my mother. I've looked for you since I was old enough to know how to do it. I live with my grandparents—Bill and Angela Anderson. They've looked for you too. But just today I thought about looking under the name Lauren Gibbs, because that's the name my mother used when she was young and wrote short stories. I found that out a few weeks ago.
>
> I did a search on the Internet, and I found your profile. Please, could you write back and let me know if I have the right person. This is very important to me, obviously. Sincerely, Emily Anderson.

She lifted her hands from the keyboard and scanned the note once more. There were a million more things she wanted to say, but she had to make contact first. Once her mother read the e-mail, they could talk about all the other details. Why she'd changed her name and what she'd been doing for the past nineteen years and whether she'd ever come close to finding Shane Galanter.

She exhaled hard. "That'll have to do for now."

Her grandmother made an approving sound. "Send it, honey. Please."

Emily moved the cursor over the send button and clicked it. In an instant, the e-mail was gone. Emily stared at the screen and thought for a moment. They still had some logistical problems to work through. If her mother was overseas in Afghanistan, then maybe she wouldn't see the e-mail right away. Soldiers could get e-mail. Emily knew because she kept in touch with a few guys from high school who were serving overseas. Certainly the same would be true for reporters. Unless she had a different business e-mail address, one that her editors could use for her. The one on the website might only be for readers, and because of that maybe she only checked it when she was stateside.

Emily turned to her grandma and pushed her fears back down. "We need to pray."

"Yes." They held hands. "Let's do that."

Emily closed her eyes and for a few seconds she was too overwhelmed to speak. After a few moments she found her voice. "Dearest Lord, thank You." She giggled and it became a sharp breath. "*Thank You* doesn't even come close. The miracle we asked for is at hand, God, so please … let my mother read the e-mail soon. And direct her to respond to me so we can arrange a meeting." She paused, her heart full. "I'm doing what You ask, Lord. I'm praying, expecting you to help us. Thanks in advance, God. In Your name, amen."

When she opened her eyes, her grandma pointed at the screen. "Print me a copy, will you, honey?"

Emily grinned and gave her grandma a quick hug. "Definitely." When the picture was finished printing, Emily picked it up and handed it over. Then she printed another copy for herself.

"Your papa's resting downstairs. He's had so much bad news the past few weeks." Grandma looked at the single page. "Let's go give him the best news ever, news he's waited eighteen years to hear."

❧

Angela felt weak as she took the stairs, arm in arm with Emily.

Her heart was exploding with a dozen brilliant colors, because this was the day she never really believed would come. They'd found Lauren! After all the private detectives and investigators and phone calls to elected officials, they'd found her the simplest way of all. With information that had been sitting for nearly twenty years a dozen yards away in the garage. They went into the family room and found Bill in his chair, his eyes closed.

"Bill." She held out the piece of paper. Emily stayed back as Angela approached him.

He opened his eyes and a slow smile filled his face. He held out his hand toward her. "Hi, love." He looked past her. "Emily, how are you?"

"Good, Papa." She managed a teary smile.

Angela moved closer to him. "Sweetheart, I have something to show you." Her voice was shaky. She wouldn't last long before breaking. She held out the piece of paper. "Emily found Lauren."

Bill sat up straighter in his chair, but his smile faded. He took the paper and looked at it, his expression frozen. "What ... how did you ...?" He sat there, still, searching the information on the page, and then his chin began to tremble.

From the corner of her eye, Angela saw Emily move into the room and sit on the edge of the sofa. It was hard to remember to breathe. She wrapped her arms around her husband's neck. "God answered our prayers, Bill. He did."

Her eyes stung again as she watched him close his eyes and pinch the bridge of his nose. He shook his head, as if to say he couldn't accept the idea that they'd actually found her. Angela straightened and let him have this moment. It was impossible for any of them to really believe she'd been found. All the searching had culminated in this amazing moment.

And God had allowed it when Bill had only weeks to live. Angela's heart felt lighter than it had since Lauren left.

Finally Bill lowered his hand and looked at her. "Why didn't we try that sooner?"

She pressed her finger to his lips and gave a soft shake of her head. "That isn't important. She's found, Bill. We can only move forward."

"But all the lost days and years." His voice was gravelly, the tears still stuck in his throat. He turned his eyes back to her picture. "Look at her, Angie. She looks so much like you."

Angela touched the image, willing away the days until they might see her in person, hold her ... "She's all grown up."

"A reporter for *Time* magazine." His voice held a new level of concern. "Not married, no children."

"No children?" Angela's heart missed a beat. She hadn't read every word of the profile yet. Now her conscience felt like it was being ripped apart. "It says that?"

"Here." He pointed to that part of the write-up.

She read it, and the suspicions she'd had since the day Lauren left became realities in as much time as it took her to draw breath. If Lauren wasn't married, then she hadn't found Shane. And if she was telling people she had no children, then she had believed that Emily was dead. Wherever she was, she must still believe it.

Angela looked at Emily and her voice seized up again. "Your mother really does think you're dead, honey."

A lifetime of sorrow flooded Emily's eyes. And in that instant, Angela's grief was so great it nearly knocked her to the floor.

☙

Emily listened to her grandmother. The anger was gone. Her mother wouldn't mention a dead daughter in a professional bio. Of course not. Now the freedom in her heart was more than she could take in. Freedom and a deep sadness for her mother, who had gone her entire adult life not knowing that she had a daughter growing up in the suburbs of Chicago. No wonder she'd wound up alone and working in Afghanistan and Iraq. Her mother's passion for writing had taken her to magazine work, but Emily couldn't help but feel that her loneliness made her look the way she did. Empty, haunted, so very sad ...

"Grandma ..." She stood and went to her. They fell together in an embrace that needed no words, and Emily leaned back, searching her grandmother's eyes. "I hurt for her. She's been so lonely all these years."

Lonely the same way *she* was, but Emily didn't say that. She'd always kept her emptiness to herself, and now her tears told the story, that she'd missed her mother every day since she was old enough to understand that she was missing.

"I'm sorry, Emily." Her grandma brushed her hair off her forehead. "The two of you never should've been apart."

From a few feet away, Papa held out his hand. "Come here, Em."

Emily released her grandma and went to him. "Papa ..."

"If we would've loved our girl better, if we would've handled her situation differently, then maybe—"

"No, Papa." Emily bent down and kissed his cheek. The loss of so many years together was enormous for all of them. "We can't go back." She sucked in a few fast breaths. "Just pray that she'll write back."

The evening was slow and deep, filled with stories from the past and shared memories of Emily's life, moments her mother had missed along the way. Despite her sorrow and loss, by the time they turned in that night, Emily had never felt happier in all her life. Maybe it was because the photo of her mother did something even her faith hadn't done before. It took away the emptiness inside her. The only thing that marred the moment was watching her papa take slow steps to his bedroom. He was getting sicker; the plans would have to come together soon.

When Emily woke the next morning, she was intent on checking her e-mail and then leaving a message for Shane Galanter at the Top Gun naval air training facility. She was about to run to the office when she heard her grandma finishing a phone call.

"Yes, Doctor. Yes, I understand." Silence. "I'll tell him. Yes, we know. Thank you." The phone call must've ended, because Grandma directed her next words to her husband. "They got your latest tests results." She had fear in her voice. "It's worse than they thought."

Emily sat up in bed and blinked the sleep from her eyes. Worse than they thought? She felt a burst of sheer terror, and she headed straight for the office. Her mother's e-mail couldn't come soon enough. Never mind whatever hurt feelings might've stood between her mother and her grandparents before. If her mother was going to have peace, she needed to know the entire story. That her daughter was alive and her parents were sorry—and that her father was dying. Yes, Emily needed to connect with her mother.

Before they all ran out of time.

Twenty-One

Her recovery was happening faster than the doctor expected. The gritty wind that blew across the Afghanistan desert rattled the windows of Lauren's apartment, and made it impossible to sleep. She sat up in bed and surveyed the bandages on her arm. At least she was out of the hospital. That place was terrible, filled with victims of war and people desperate for healing and hope. She could still hear their wailings, mothers called in to identify young sons, soldiers who might've been on the right or the wrong side. Lauren winced as she felt near her wound. Sides didn't matter to a mother.

Lauren closed her eyes, recalling one grief-stricken woman. Her son had been in the next room, but he hadn't survived the night. The next morning the mother stood at his bedside, screaming his name, shouting at the heavens that she wanted him back, *had* to have him back.

All Lauren could think about was her own family. The way she'd felt when Emily died; the way her parents must feel now. If they were still alive, it would've been nearly twenty years since they'd had any idea even where to find her. How had they handled all that time alone together? Had they, too, shared moments of wailing and ranting at the heavens?

She sighed and opened her eyes. It was the first cloudy day in a month, and it fit her mood. Her mind drifted back to the day at the orphanage. Feni had gotten wind that an ambush might take place against visiting Westerners. That's why he was in the office that morning, armed and ready in case she and Scanlon were the intended targets.

An American army captain filled her in on the other details at the hospital.

The woman wasn't an orphanage worker at all. She'd blended in with the others, pretending to be a volunteer. Orphanages were always shorthanded, so no one would've questioned her motives. The only uncertain thing was how she'd known Lauren and Scanlon were coming in that first day, but the army had its theory on that too.

The driver of the car on that first visit must've been connected with the group. He could easily have called and tipped them off. Lauren and Scanlon talked openly about their plans for a story and their concerns about the orphanage.

"This is a bad group, Miss Gibbs," the captain told her. "They run a terrorist training camp, an operation we're trying to shut down. We've had some success, but they're spread out. We haven't found them all."

"Why'd they want me?" She was numb to the pain by then, six hours on a medication that barely allowed her to stay awake. A surgeon removed two bullets from beneath her shoulder. The wounds were deep and dangerous, but her joint hadn't been affected. They expected her to heal completely.

The captain thought about her question. "You represent America." He raised an eyebrow, as if he didn't agree with that assessment. "At least, that's the way *they* see it. They probably wanted to wound you. Take you captive. Most journalists and photographers aren't armed, and Feni rarely works out of the orphanage." He shrugged. "They weren't expecting retaliation."

She looked away. "They weren't expecting to kill children, either."

"Maybe, maybe not." He was a big man, his hair cropped short against his square face. "When kids die, Americans always get the blame. They might've shot at the children on purpose."

Lauren blinked away the memory of the conversation and winced as she tried to move her arm. All this time she had sympathized with the insurgents. Yes, they were violent and sometimes behaved in a crazed manner. But this was their homeland. Didn't they have a right to want Americans to stay out? Even if they desired a type of government Americans didn't agree with, should it concern the U.S.? Was democracy the only valid form of leadership?

But now...

Now she didn't know what to think. People had a right to form their own government, but if that government was ruthless and brutal, then what? If she had to do it over again, she would've thrown herself in front of the children to keep them from being hit. She would've gladly taken the bullets intended for them if it meant saving their lives. And wasn't that all the U.S. troops were doing, really? Bad people had taken over the Middle East, and innocent people were living in fear, oppressed, and sometimes killed. If Lauren wouldn't stand by and watch that sort of behavior take place, then how could she expect the U.S. to do so?

She shuddered and gave a quick shake of her head. The medicine was making her loopy. There had to be another answer, something better than fighting and bombings and war. Solutions could be worked out at bargaining tables or in courtrooms, couldn't they? The entire mess gave her a headache. The political picture was more complicated than she first thought, that much was certain. But what mattered was this: Because she and Scanlon had gone back to the orphanage, little Senia was dead. A girl whose eyes were bright enough to light up the room. Now she was gone.

Lauren hated crying. She feared that sort of emotion almost as much as she feared elevators. Giving in to sorrow would be like driving a freightliner through the dam in her heart. The emotion of nearly twenty years would become a flood that would drown her. But in the days since she'd been released from the hospital, she could barely last an hour without feeling tears on her cheeks.

She would've adopted little Senia if she'd had the chance.

How could she know that the woman was working for the insurgents, or that the whole story had been concocted? The army captain told her that a thorough check had been done. "We have birth records for every child in that orphanage." His eyes blazed. "Not a child there has a single drop of American blood."

Lauren had hung her head then, not sure what to say.

The captain wasn't finished. "I'm surprised you didn't go with the story before the second meeting." The sarcasm in his laugh cut at her. "Can you imagine the headlines? Orphanages overflowing with the children of American soldiers?"

Her eyes met his. "I didn't have enough information. Of course I wouldn't have written the story before I had the facts."

The captain only raised his eyebrow at her again. "Okay. Whatever." His look was utter disgust. "Maybe we should talk about something else."

"We don't have to talk at all." She'd hated the way he treated her. As though she were the enemy.

"Look, ma'am, I've been assigned to guard you as long as you're in this hospital." He shifted to the front of his chair. "Fine with me if you don't wanna talk."

By the time Scanlon came to take her home, Lauren had no doubt about the army's viewpoint of her reporting. The captain picked apart ten of her top stories from the last two years. She had untrustworthy sources and a strong bias, he told her. She wasn't there to find the truth, but to make the U.S. armed forces the enemy.

The last thing he said before he left would stay with Lauren for the rest of her days: "You think the military's all gung ho for war, that we're a bunch of bullies coming over here and flexing our muscles." He pointed at her, and his voice grew low and intense. "Let me tell you something, lady. We want peace as much as you do. Maybe more." He thumbed himself in the chest.

"Because *we're* layin' our lives down for it." He took a few steps back. "Don't forget that."

She turned away, not willing to respond or bid him goodbye. But his speech affected her more than she'd been willing to admit. Now it was Wednesday, and she'd been home for two days. Scanlon was in often, making sure she had water and meals and whatever else she needed.

It was time for more pain medication. She took the bottle from beside her bed and brought it close. Her fingers on her left arm worked fine, as long as she didn't move her arm. She tapped a single pill into her palm. Then she used the water bottle lying on the pillow next to her to wash it down.

Once the pills were back on the nightstand, she lifted her arm again and let it fall quickly to her side. The pain was still intense. An army nurse was coming by three times a day to change the dressing and administer a shot of antibiotics. But one day soon her arm would heal. Her heart? Well, that was another matter.

She swung her feet over the edge of the bed and stared at the room around her. Life was happening outside her apartment building. Life and conflict and heartache, all translating into stories that needed to be written. That she needed to write. She hoped to be off bed rest by the end of the week.

Her eyes followed a familiar trail around the room, but this time they landed on her computer. She could at least check e-mail. That wasn't much removed from bed rest, was it? She took a deep breath. Why hadn't she thought of that sooner? She could've been researching and checking in with her editors instead of staring at the walls all day from her spot on the lumpy bed.

She stood and steadied herself for a few seconds. Amazing how weak she'd become after just five days of inactivity. She shuffled across the room and fell, exhausted, onto the hard-framed chair in front of her computer. The thud of her heart made her feel light-headed and dizzy. She turned on the computer and waited.

There was a knock on her door. "Lauren, you in there?"

It was Scanlon. She'd given him a key to her apartment a long time ago. She cleared her throat. "Come on in."

He opened the door and gave her a hesitant look. In his arms was a case of water bottles. "Aren't you supposed to be in bed?"

"They told me to rest." She gave him a wry look and faced the computer screen. "How 'bout *you* lie on the bed, and I'll sit here."

He set the case of water on a table in her makeshift kitchen, at the other side of the room. Lauren watched him. His face was tanned, his hair cut short the way he liked it. He was nice looking, in his own way.

She could tell he didn't have the desire to fight with her. He shrugged. "Okay." He went to her bed and flopped down. "I am kinda tired."

She laughed, but her energy was waning fast. "Don't get too comfortable. I won't be here long."

"Still weak?" He sat up, his legs straight in front of him. "Is that normal?"

"Yeah." She wiped her hand over her damp forehead. "I felt this way once when I had the flu for a week, back when I was a teenager."

"In Chicago?" He put his hand behind his head and leaned against the wall above her tiny headboard. "Remember, Lauren? You already told me about Chicago."

"I was drunk." She signed onto the Internet and waited for the connection. "That doesn't count."

"Okay, but I still know." The tenderness in his voice was evidence that he cared deeply for her. "Everyone has a past. You wouldn't be living here if that wasn't the case."

She let his comment pass. She was connected to her server, and she found the little mailbox icon at the top of her home page. The number on top of the box read 68. Sixty-eight new e-mails.

Even looking at them felt overwhelming. Especially now, when she could feel her strength ebbing with every minute.

"Forget the e-mail. Come here." From the corner of her eye she saw Scanlon move to one side of the bed. "There, you have room now. I'll keep my hands to myself. Promise."

"Not yet." She tried to draw a full breath, but she was too shaky. She felt this way one other time since she'd been living in the Middle East, when the area store ran out of food and she drank coffee for three days straight. Still, if she didn't fight it, how was she going to get stronger?

Summoning her energy, she clicked her in-box, and scanned the list of e-mails. Most were from other staff members who'd learned of her injury. The subjects read, "Get better!" and "Close call!" and "Time to come home, friend!" A few were from her editor, with subject lines that said, "Say the word," or "Maybe it's time."

She was halfway down the page when she stopped cold. Her heart thudded faster and harder. The subject line read simply: "From Emily." Lauren blinked and read it a second time. What sort of strange timing was this, anyway? She'd been lying in bed thinking about peace and how she and her family had never found any, and here was a letter from a reader named—of all things—Emily.

A soft laugh left her, and from off to her side she saw Scanlon open his eyes. "What's so funny?"

"Nothing." She gave a shake of her head and brushed off his question. Her eyes were still locked onto the e-mail from Emily. Okay, so what did this Emily want? Lauren hadn't planned to actually open any of the e-mails. Not when her body was wilting badly. But "From Emily"? She could hardly resist. She clicked the link and the letter came up.

Hi, my name is Emily Anderson, and I'm eighteen years old—

Lauren couldn't catch her breath, couldn't force her lungs to draw even half a mouthful of air. She closed her eyes and gripped the desktop in front of her.

"Hey, Lauren." Scanlon's voice was more urgent. "You okay? Maybe you need to lie down."

She waved him off, but she opened her eyes. Again she tried the e-mail, but she couldn't get past that first line. Emily Anderson? Eighteen? Was this some sort of trick? Her Emily would've been eighteen. Eighteen years, six months, and twenty-one days. She pursed her lips and forced the air from her lungs. The effort gave her just enough room to take in a small breath. Her injured arm felt numb, and her right hand trembled so hard she could barely scroll down and read the rest.

> I believe that you might be my mother.

Lauren felt the room collapse around her. Felt everything begin to spin. What *was* this? And who would've written it? Her daughter was dead, so a letter like this had to be a prank. She willed herself to stay steady long enough to finish reading.

> I've looked for you since I was old enough to know how to do it. I live with my grandparents—Bill and Angela Anderson. They've looked for you too. But just today I thought about looking under the name Lauren Gibbs, because that's the name my mother used when she was young and wrote short stories. I found that out a few weeks ago.
>
> I did a search on the Internet, and I found your profile. Please, could you write back and let me know if I have the right person. This is very important to me, obviously. Sincerely, Emily Anderson.

Lauren couldn't exhale. She read the letter again, and a third time, and all she could do was gasp little breaths. Scanlon was up now, hurrying to her side.

"You're blacking out, Lauren, come on." He eased her up and over to the bed. Then he lowered her to the mattress and rushed to the bathroom. When he came back he put a cool cloth on her head. "You're white as a sheet."

She still couldn't breathe right. Scanlon was asking her something, but she couldn't make out his words. All she could think about was the e-mail. It was a hoax, right? It had to be a hoax. But then the past came trampling into the room, screaming at her. Emily was alive? Could it really have been from her? And if so ... if so ...

Her heart raced along at triple speed. No way her baby had lived, no way. She hadn't walked away from a living child and left her parents to raise her. It was impossible. What had the nurse said? Her baby was gone, right? Gone for a few hours by the time Lauren had called. Gone meant dead, didn't it? Three more times she tried to breathe, but the air wouldn't come. Not until she exhaled, and she couldn't do that no matter how hard she tried.

She grabbed her friend's arm and gasped. "Scanlon ... get me ... a bag." She was hyperventilating. Her head told her she'd be fine, even if she passed out. A person couldn't die from hyperventilation. But right now she didn't want to battle herself, she wanted to battle the past. The giant, monstrous past. And she couldn't face it for a second until she could breathe.

Scanlon tore across the room, rifled through her kitchen drawers, and finally found a brown paper sack, the kind they used when they needed to pack an overnight meal. He raced it to her and held it to her mouth.

"Breathe, Lauren. Come on." He was genuinely worried, and in the rush of all that was dawning on her, she realized one more thing. Scanlon loved her.

She couldn't sort through that thought any more than she could understand the e-mail she'd just read. Instead she focused all her attention on breathing into the bag. Eventually she felt each breath last a little longer, felt her rib cage relax so she could finally exhale. Only then did she dare move the bag and take the smallest drink of fresh air.

She was drenched with sweat, and she felt weaker than she had all day. But still she struggled to sit up, desperate for a glance at the computer screen. When she was fully sitting, she saw it was still there. An e-mail with the shape and form of the one she'd read a few minutes ago.

Next to her, Scanlon wiped the wet cloth tenderly over her forehead. "What in the world was all that about?"

She sat up straighter on the bed. Then she brushed away the wet cloth and looked him straight in the eyes. "Can you do me a favor?"

"Anything." He searched her face, ready to jump.

With her elbow she motioned toward the computer screen. "Could you answer that girl's letter?" She hesitated. "Don't read it, just hit reply, okay?"

"Sure." He let his eyes linger on her, doubt flashing in his expression. "For a person who couldn't breathe a minute ago, you're pretty demanding."

Another out breath. "I know." She leaned forward and dug her elbows into her thighs. "Can you do this, Scanlon? Please?"

"Okay, okay." He went to the computer and sat down. "Don't get crazy on me again."

He clicked the reply link and a blank screen appeared. "Shoot."

"Give me a second." She willed herself to think clearly. What if it wasn't a hoax or a mistake? What if her daughter was really alive and living in Wheaton, Illinois? Maybe in the same house her parents had moved to when she was pregnant? She squeezed her eyes shut and refused to think about anything but the e-mail. "Okay, write this." She paused. "Emily, call me as soon as you can. Here's my number with the country code. Dial it just like this." She was winded again, so she stopped and breathed. "Put the number next, okay?"

He was still typing. "I figured." After a few more key strokes his hands fell silent. "Send it?"

"Yes. Thanks, Scanlon." It wasn't the time to write anything flowery at the end. Because whoever she was, she couldn't be her Emily. The daughter she'd brought into the world. Her Emily was dead.

Scanlon was up and moving back to the bed. She shifted so he could sit beside her, but as he did he met her eyes and held them. "Wanna tell me about it?"

"No." She didn't want to, but she had no choice. Suddenly in all the world, Scanlon felt like her only ally, her only friend. And since the past was threatening to swallow her alive, she had no option but to cut it wide open and let it spill out. She put her hand over Scanlon's, her voice softer than before. "I didn't tell you everything about Chicago."

"Why am I not surprised?" He wove his fingers between hers, his expression softer. "I'm listening."

She nodded, and slowly at first, the story came out. How she'd been so in love with Shane Galanter, and her desperate belief that after he left, she had to find him. She told him about leaving for California and being terrified when little Emily got sick, and she explained how she'd taken her daughter to the clinic, but left when she thought for sure the police would come and take Emily away.

"What happened then?" Scanlon still had his fingers laced between hers. "Did you make it back?"

"I did." She told him how she'd rushed home and begged her mother for help, even though the two of them hadn't been speaking before she left. "We raced to the hospital." Her eyes fell and she shook her head. "It took the doctor ten minutes to tell us he didn't think Emily would survive. In fact, he said it would take a miracle."

Scanlon listened, his eyes full of compassion.

She told him how she'd sat by Emily all night, and how around four in the morning her little girl had taken a turn for the better. "An hour after that, I wasn't sure I'd survive without sleep." She shrugged. "I don't know, I was seventeen and scared out of my mind. I hadn't slept in two days. I wasn't thinking straight or I would've found a bed in the hospital somewhere."

"Your mom was still there, right?"

"Right. She offered to stay. So I went home and fell asleep for ten hours—much longer than I planned. When I woke up I called the hospital and someone connected me to a nurse." Her heart pounded at the memory. She let go of Scanlon's hand and pressed her fingers into her temples. "The woman told me Emily was gone. That she'd been gone for a few hours."

"She died?"

Lauren let her hands fall to her sides. "That's what I thought." She nodded toward the computer. "Until just now, that's what I always thought. I had one baby, and I did everything wrong, so she died."

Scanlon groaned. He slipped his arm around her and pulled her to him. She let her head fall against his shoulder. "The e-mail—it was from an Emily Anderson, who says she's eighteen." She sat up and searched her friend's eyes. "She says she's living with Bill and Angela Anderson in Wheaton and that she thinks I'm her—"

Her cell phone sprang to life, ringing and moving about as it vibrated on the table next to the medicine bottle. She felt her lungs seizing up again, but she willed them to stay calm. Scanlon handed her the phone and she flipped it open.

"Hello?"

"Is this ... is this Lauren Gibbs?" The voice was young and tender, a voice that sounded like her own, like she'd sounded before everything had gone so terribly wrong.

She breathed out. "Yes." Her head was spinning. "Who's this?"

"This is Emily Anderson." The girl waited a moment. "My mother's been missing for ... for eighteen years, and I thought maybe you might be— "

"Emily." The girl's name felt wonderful on her lips. She tried to remember to be guarded, to doubt whether the caller was really her daughter. A journalist never trusts people without checking facts. "Is ... this really you?"

"Yes." Emily started to cry. "Are you— "

This wasn't happening; it couldn't be happening. Lauren gripped Scanlon's arm. She felt a searing white-hot pain in her heart, like the pain that pierced her arm a week ago. As if she was being shot square in the middle. She squeezed her eyes shut and pressed the phone to her ear. "They told me you were dead."

"I know." The girl was crying harder now. "Grandma told me. She thought that's what happened."

Lauren leaned on Scanlon, determined to keep breathing, slow and steady. The phone call was too important to lose. "I never would've left, never! Not if I'd known. I— " Emotions choked her words. She swallowed, searching for a way to sum up a lifetime of feelings. "I thought about you every day, Emily. I still do."

"Me too." Tears filled the girl's voice, but her words rang with a joy that seemed boundless. "Mom, did you ever find him?"

Lauren's tears came then.

She called me Mom ... I have a daughter! Aching sobs welled up in her. *Emily was alive!* She forced herself to think about Emily's question. "Shane?"

"Yes. Did you ever find him?"

The ache in her heart doubled. She had spent a lifetime missing Emily, but she had missed Shane Galanter too. He was the reason she left Chicago, after all. How long had she looked for him and waited for him, when all along her daughter had been growing up without her? If only she hadn't been so stubborn.

She could've gone home and made peace with her parents, and she would've found more than a mended relationship.

She would've found her daughter.

"No, Emily." She pressed her finger against her upper lip and fought to keep control. "No, I never found him."

"I'm sorry." Her voice was thick again. "You loved him very much, didn't you?"

"I did." A few rebel sobs escaped, but she swallowed the rest. "I always told myself I'd go home again once I found him."

"But you never found him, so you never came home."

"No."

They fell quiet. Next to her Scanlon rubbed her good arm, lending whatever support he could. She would've given anything to reach through the phone lines and hold her daughter. "I have so many questions."

Emily laughed. "Me too."

"Listen to you." She clung to the sound of her daughter's laughter, a sound that was like water to her barren soul. "I used to laugh like that when ... before ..."

"Before you got pregnant." The laughter faded from her voice. "I was talking to God the other day, and I told Him I knew what had happened. You got pregnant and everything went bad from there." There was no self-pity in her voice. "One event tore everyone apart, didn't it?"

Regret came upon her like a monsoon. "It did."

"So I asked God if one event tore everyone apart, maybe He could use me to bring everyone back together."

Usually, when Lauren heard someone talk about God, she was repulsed—probably because she usually heard such talk from politicians. But now ... Emily's sincerity—her *daughter's* sincerity—rang across the phone lines. When Lauren didn't say anything, her daughter continued.

"The thing is, Mom, you need to come home quick." She sounded serious. Scared and serious.

It was the first time Lauren considered the possibility that her daughter might not be well. She stiffened, gripping the phone tighter than before. "Are you ... is everything okay?"

"No." She sighed, and her voice filled with fresh tears. "Papa's got cancer. He ... he doesn't have long."

Papa? Who was ...? Understanding dawned. Her father. Was that what Emily called him? Papa? She had a flashback, an image of her daddy swinging her in his arms when she was six or seven years old. Senia's age. She swallowed another wave of sorrow. "My father?"

"Yes." She waited a beat. "I don't know what happened between the three of you, but Grandma and Papa, they're wonderful. They have such a strong faith." She took a quick breath. "I need you, Mom. I've waited all my life for this. But now you have to come fast."

Her new reality was taking shape quicker than she could make sense of it. Her parents were wonderful? That wasn't such a surprise, was it? They'd been wonderful all her life until they forced her to separate from Shane. And something else consumed her. Emily wasn't only alive, but she wanted Shane and her to connect. What had she said? That she'd waited all her life for this? It was more than Lauren could take in. She shielded her eyes and leaned her head against her hand. How much had she missed over the years? She'd never planned to leave her parents forever, had she? Not even after what they'd done to keep her and Shane apart.

It was just that one year blended into the next, and pretty soon the road home was so overgrown with blame and hurt she couldn't find her way back. Wasn't even sure she wanted to. But now her daddy was dying. "Do they want me there? With my dad so sick?"

Emily laughed again, and it sounded like a release. As if she'd been holding her breath waiting for the answer. "*Yes*, they want you to come home. Please, Mom. Come as fast as you can, okay?"

Lauren straightened. She had vacation time, but she needed a medical release before she could fly home. That, and the debriefing day at the magazine office. "I can be there a week from Saturday. Will that work?"

"Yes! Oh yes!" Again her daughter's voice sang with hope and promise. "Here, write this down."

Lauren motioned to Scanlon that she needed him to take a note. He grabbed the pad of paper and pen on the nightstand and waited, ready. Lauren held the receiver tight. "Okay, go ahead."

Emily rattled off several phone numbers, one for home and one for her cell. Lauren repeated every digit, watching to make sure Scanlon wrote it correctly. She'd lost Emily once; she wouldn't lose her again.

When she'd given all her contact information, Emily giggled. "Mom ... I might call you between now and then, if that's okay."

"Emily." She felt her heart bursting within her. "Please do."

"I love you, Mom."

There it was again. The name she'd never been called before. *Mom. I love you, Mom.*

It was still impossible to believe any of it was true, but there was no denying that the caller was her daughter. She swallowed hard. "I love you too, sweetheart. I've loved you and missed you every day of your life." She drew her first full breath in an hour. "I still can't believe you found me."

"I didn't." Certainty filled her tone. "God did." She paused. "But we can talk about that later."

When the call ended, Lauren snapped her cell phone shut. She turned to her friend, so full she thought she might burst.

"Oh, Scanlon." She searched his eyes. Whatever happened from here, her life would never be the same. "My daughter is alive!"

"I gathered." He smiled at her. "You're going back to the States?"

"Yes." She pulled away and looked around her room. "As soon as they'll let me go. My father's sick. He ... he doesn't have long."

"Will you get there in time?"

"I don't know. Maybe."

"Amazing, huh? You go eighteen years without seeing him, and your daughter finds you just in time?"

Lauren felt herself being drawn back to the conversation she'd just had with her daughter. Emily said God had found her. She blinked and looked at her friend again. "Definitely amazing."

A hint of sadness flashed in his eyes, but he smiled. "I'm glad for you, Lauren. Really."

Though it meant she was leaving, and though there was now a sudden possibility that she might never come back, she believed Scanlon really was glad. That was the sort of friend he was. Even so, the uppermost thought in her mind right now wasn't leaving him or the Middle East or the job she so loved. Not even close.

All that was on her mind was the miracle. She had a daughter. A living, breathing young woman with a voice like sunshine. And in just over a week, she was going to meet her. See her face. Hold her in her arms.

And her parents. She would see them again. Feel her mother's arms around her, see her father's face glow with love — a love that had been misguided for a season when she was a teenager — but a love fiercely strong all the same. Yes, she had a daughter to meet and parents to reunite with.

And eighteen lonely years to make up for.

☙

Emily hung up the phone. She was shaking, trembling from her fingertips to her feet. Finding her mother's picture, her identity, had been one thing. But actually *talking* with her? It was more than Emily could've dreamed. Her mom sounded shocked and fearful, disbelieving and overjoyed. But there was something else in her voice. A deep, abiding sorrow. For all the years they'd lost.

Emily stood and stared at the picture next to her bed, the one of her parents when they were teenagers. "God—" she lifted her eyes to the window, the blue sky beyond—"a miracle is underway, and already it's more than I can take in."

She remembered the pain in her mother's voice when she talked about Shane. Emily still needed to find him, find a way to connect him with her mother. She sucked on the inside of her cheek and remembered something else. The hurt in her mom's voice when she realized Papa was sick. They still had so much healing to work through, so much forgiveness to find if they were going to have peace.

A long sigh eased from her lips. She needed to get downstairs and tell her grandparents about her phone call with her mother. But first she needed more time to talk to God. Because yes, the miracle they all needed was finally underway, but it was hardly finished.

Rather, it was only just beginning.

Twenty-Two

Shane wasn't sure how to break it to her.

After a week of praying and searching his Bible and hitting the gym twice as long as usual, he had the answer he'd been looking for. It jumped out at him just that morning, shouted at him from the book of Proverbs, the third chapter. There in verses five and six it said, *Trust in the Lord with all your heart and lean not on your own understanding; in all your ways acknowledge him, and he will make your paths straight.*

He read the words three more times through, and suddenly the answer was clear. His own understanding had led him into a relationship with Ellen Randolph. His own understanding had allowed Ellen to design a plan for his life, a winding path that would take him where she wanted him to go. And yes, he'd gone along with it, because by his own understanding the plan made sense.

But it wasn't God's understanding.

Shane clenched his fists and looked at his watch. He moved onto the patio, restless. Ellen would be there in ten minutes, and the two of them were supposed to go to dinner. He'd thought all day about whether he should cancel and talk to her before the meal, or wait until afterward. He decided to wait. The least he could do was share one last meal with her before telling her it was over.

He sat down on a chaise lounge and stared up into the palm trees that lined his backyard. Long ago he had put his trust in God. Though his parents moved him to California, and he had felt his heart rip out a little more with every mile that came between him and Lauren, he gave everything over in faith. He trusted the Lord to lead him through the rest of his days. Of course, his parents had their own plans. Plans they'd made clear before the first month of his senior year in high school.

His father came into his room before bedtime one school night that year. "About time to apply for colleges, hey, son? I've talked to my friends at Harvard and Yale, even a few at USC." He winked. "Looks like you're a shoo-in for any of the three."

Not until that moment did Shane fully understand what his parents had done. The move wasn't about investments in California. It was about investing in him, about protecting the plans they had for him, the plans to have him finish high school as an all-American football player with a future as golden as the sun.

That night he told his dad news that shocked him. "I don't want to go to business school, Dad. I don't want an MBA or ownership in a bank or the chance to run a mortgage company. I want to fly a fighter jet."

It took most of the next six months for his wishes to sink in. Even then it was clear his parents were frustrated. They moved him away from Lauren, but nothing they could do would move him away from the plans God had for him. That spring, a few months before he graduated, he ran into a navy recruiter with a booth set up in the lunch area. Shane could almost feel God directing him over, making him pick up a brochure and ask questions.

From there, the pieces fell into place. He went to college at UCLA and then enlisted for officer's training school and naval flight training. By the time the Gulf War came around, he was one of the top fighter pilots in the navy.

His parents learned to accept his decision. In time, they were proud of him for flying jets for the U.S. military, bragging to their friends about his awards and medals. Shane was glad, but it wasn't what motivated him. He was born to fly; that's what the Lord had shown him.

Every time he flew he felt God leading him home at the end of a mission. He was serving his country, serving his fellow man, and following the life God had given him all at the same time. His only sorrow was missing Lauren. For more than a decade that void hit him at the end of every day and between shifts and in noncombat situations when he was forty thousand feet up behind the controls of a jet.

He would gaze into the endless blue and remember the note she'd scribbled for him back when they were kids: *You're gonna fly one day. When you go, take me with you.* Only he never found her, so she never knew. Never knew that he'd done what he wanted to do, what God had created him to do. He breathed in the cool Reno air. And now ... here he was. On the wrong path again.

How did it happen? How did he let Ellen convince him that a position in politics would be better than working at Top Gun, better than driving out to the naval training base every day and living his dream? There was something else too. Since he'd been seeing Ellen, he'd come to believe that he didn't want children, that with all the plans ahead of him, there wasn't time for raising a family. All because for a short while, his own understanding seemed better than God's.

But not anymore.

The doorbell rang, and then he heard the sound of her in the entryway. "Hello?"

"Ellen. I'm back here." He stood and met her. "You look pretty." He kissed her cheek and led her back into the house. "I'll get my keys."

"Shane." Her tone was a mix of no-nonsense strength with a hint of vulnerability.

He turned around. "Yes?"

She exhaled slow and tired. "It's over, isn't it?"

For an instant, he almost denied it. How could she have known? All he'd told her was that he wanted to talk. Nothing more. He slipped his hands in his pockets and took a few steps closer. Her eyes told him that she wasn't guessing. She knew. Somehow she'd figured it out.

He stopped and looked to the deepest places of her heart. "How did you know?"

"This." She pulled something that looked like a small photograph from her purse and handed it to him. "I found this on the front seat of my car this morning. It must've fallen out of your pocket."

Only when it was in his hands did he look at it. As he did, his heart sank. It was his picture of Lauren. She was right. He'd been looking at it the night before, when she pulled up to take him to dinner. In the rush of the moment, he slid it into his pocket and hurried out to meet her.

Ellen lifted her chin, her pride clearly intact. "I thought you'd let her go, Shane."

"I have—" No. He stopped himself. Anything he said about letting go of Lauren Anderson was a lie. He promised Lauren long ago that he would love her until the day he died. Wasn't that what he'd engraved in the ring he bought her? *Even now.* Even now, when it made no sense to hang onto her memory, his promise was good. He put the photo on the closest bookshelf and took Ellen's hands in his. "I'm sorry." He worked the muscles in his jaw. "I thought I had."

She smiled, and the brilliance of it almost hid the pain in her eyes. "I thought so too." She wriggled the ring from her finger. It contained a total of two carats, nothing like the small ring he'd bought Lauren a lifetime ago. "Here." Her eyes glistened. "I can't be second best, Shane."

"I know." He took the ring and tried to see past her pretense. "I think we would've made a good team."

"Me too." She gave his fingers a heartfelt squeeze. "But I don't want a teammate, Shane. I want someone who adores me."

"I understand." He pulled her to himself and folded her in his arms. "I'm the problem, Ellen. Not you. You're perfect."

She nodded, and when she drew back he noticed her makeup was still intact, her eyes dry. "I've spent the day working through this, so, if you don't mind, I think I'll get going."

"Okay." He released her and she took a step.

Holding her purse close to her side, she nodded at him. "Good-bye, Shane."

"Good-bye." He held up his hand and waited as she turned and headed back to the door.

When she reached it, she looked at him once more over her shoulder. "You didn't want to be governor anyway, did you?"

The sadness in his heart was genuine. She had offered him the kind of life most guys in his place would've jumped at. He felt God's words shouting from the foundation of his heart. *Lean not on your own understanding; in all your ways acknowledge him, and he will make your paths straight.*

Ellen was waiting, watching him. He took a few steps closer one last time and shook his head, his eyes never leaving hers. "No, Ellen. God made me to be a pilot. I love politics, and I'd vote for your father and everyone on the party ticket as long as the issues are what they are today." He brushed his knuckles against her cheek. *God, let her move on quickly from here. She deserves so much more.* "But the truth is, I only thought I'd like politics because I liked you. Your father was a politician, and I thought it made sense if I became one too."

She covered his hand with her own, and after a few seconds she took hold of the door handle and backed up another step. "You know something?"

"What?"

"I'm glad you figured it out." Her smile was more genuine now, as was her sorrow.

"Me too."

She opened the door and stepped out onto the porch. "And I'm flattered that you liked me that much." She nodded at him and held his eyes another few seconds. Then she turned and walked down his sidewalk to her car waiting along the curb. When she was gone, he grabbed his phone and went back outside on his patio. His chest ached, and he knew why. She wasn't right for him, but he cared about her. He was going to miss her, and once again he was going to be alone.

Now it was time to break the news to his parents.

Sheila Galanter hung up the phone and barely made it into the living room where her husband Samuel was reading the newspaper.

"It's over." She leaned against the doorway. Moving any further into the room wasn't an option. All her energy was taken with trying to sort through the news.

Samuel lowered the newspaper to his lap. "What is?"

"Shane and Ellen. They called it off."

"Hmm." He looked up at the ceiling for a few seconds. "Can't say I blame him."

"Samuel! Listen to you." She was catching her breath now. "Ellen was a lovely girl."

"She was that." He looked at her. "But she had Shane's life planned out for him."

"We did the same once, remember?" She walked into the room and sat on the edge of the chair opposite him.

He groaned and released the footrest in the recliner. It snapped down into place, and he sat straighter than before. "Sheila, it was only a few weeks ago that you were chock-full of doubts about this impending marriage."

"*I* didn't have doubts." Her tone changed. "I was worried he did."

"Well— " Samuel leaned forward and gave her knee a quick squeeze—"looks like you were right." He studied her. He knew her so well. "Shane's still young, Sheila. He'll find someone else."

It was exactly what she was thinking. But Shane's age wasn't the problem. The awful reality was that their son hadn't truly loved someone since—"What if this is all our fault, Samuel?" Her voice slipped to a whisper. "Have you ever thought of that?"

A shadow fell over her husband's eyes, and he folded his hands on his lap. For more than a minute he said nothing, as if he was being sucked back to that awful time when they'd felt forced to start a new life in order to protect their son.

A long sigh escaped him. "I haven't wanted to."

"But you have, right?" All those years, two decades since they'd left Chicago, and never once had Sheila gotten up the courage to talk to her husband about this. They made their decision and never looked back. But now the past had limped into the room with them, torn up and bleeding, impossible to ignore. Not that they were crushed about the breakup between Shane and Ellen. But the fact that their son had never let go of Lauren Anderson. She watched her own feelings play out across his face, and she already had her answer. "Samuel, talk to me."

He drew in a deep breath. "When we moved that boy here, I knew with everything I was that it was the right decision." He spoke through clenched teeth, allowing a rare show of emotion. "He was seventeen, Sheila. What were we supposed to do?"

"I don't know." A crack formed in her heart and she hung her head. Samuel was right. They'd wanted only the best for him. The move had been Samuel's idea, but she had supported it. To the point of losing her best friend, she'd supported it.

"He wanted to marry her and … and be a father all before he finished high school. I couldn't stand by and let that happen." Samuel spread his fingers over his chest. "Please … tell me you don't blame me, Sheila."

"How can I?" She lifted her hands and let them drop in her lap again. "I was the one meeting with Angela, telling her we needed a plan." The crack widened. "I talked about Lauren like she was— " She looked at the floor, the memories so close she could touch them. "I talked about Lauren like she was completely to blame." She twisted her expression and looked at Samuel again. "I lost my friend because I couldn't, not for one minute, think Shane was anything but a victim."

Samuel took her hands in his. For a long time he ran his thumbs along hers. Then he shook his head. "We were wrong. I've known it for a long time."

"He's looked for Lauren all his life." She felt her eyes grow distant. "Sometimes when I'm on the Internet, I type in her name, just to see what comes up."

He studied her, eyes wide. "I've done that, too."

"We should've looked for Angela and Bill. They would know where to find her."

A strange look came over him and he gave a single shake of his head. "No. They have no idea. At least they didn't five years ago."

What was he saying? She held tighter to his hands so she wouldn't fall off her chair. "You called them?"

"I called Bill one day at work. The conversation was short. No apologies, no accusations. We didn't talk about the baby." He shrugged. "I asked him if he could tell me how to get in touch with Lauren."

"You did that?" She'd been married to him for thirty-eight years. How could they not have talked about something this important?

"Shane was gutsy and strong and a military hero, but he was dying inside for missing that girl." His expression grew soft. "I asked myself how I could show Shane I loved him. How much I really love him." He blinked twice, but his eyes remained damp. "Finding Lauren was the best thing I could think of."

"Sam ..." She slid to the floor and crawled the few steps that separated them. She had never loved him more. "You were exactly right."

"Only Bill told me he didn't know where she was. She ran away after she had the baby. That was the end of the conversation." He eased his fingers along the back of her hand. "I guess we all paid for what we did to those kids."

A small cry came from her. "If I'd known that was going to be my only grandchild ..." She hugged his legs and rested her head on his knees. "Oh, Sam. We're *still* paying for what we did."

"Yes." Sadness choked his voice. "Sometimes I lie awake at night wondering if the baby was a boy or a girl, and where that eighteen-year-old child might be now."

In that moment, Sheila felt the crack give way, felt her heart tear in half. She knew with utter certainty that she would never be the same. Because here was the truth. She wasn't the only one who dreamed about the grandchild they'd walked away from, or who agonized at her son's loneliness. She and Samuel had lived their lives in a sort of quiet denial, never talking about their biggest decision, never facing how it had forever changed them all.

And what about the Andersons? How could Lauren run away and never look back? Where had she gone? A tingling started at Sheila's forehead and worked its way down her face. Lauren would've only run to one place—Southern California. Because she would've been as driven to find Shane as he had been to find her.

This new realization added yet another layer to the hidden tragedy that was their lives. The only thing that could save them was if the broken pieces all found their way together again. Healing *could* happen if Shane found Lauren, if she and Samuel made things right with the Andersons. But how? How was that even possible?

Guilt and regret smothered her, made her wish with all her being that somehow that might really take place. But it was impossible. Miracles like that simply didn't happen.

At least not to horrible people like them.

Twenty-Three

It was the right decision, but that Monday morning Shane could still feel the ache in his heart. He missed Ellen, missed the way she made him laugh and the animated way she entertained him with stories from her father's world. Without her, the weekend had been quiet and uneventful. Shane didn't need anyone to tell him how the next season of his life would go. It would be a lonely one, maybe the loneliest yet.

He pulled into the parking lot at Top Gun, killed the engine, and climbed out. The day was chilly, but the sky was a brilliant blue. He leaned against his car, crossed his ankles, and stared toward heaven.

"Okay, God, I'm trusting you." He smiled, but it didn't erase his sadness. "Show me what's next." He gave a salute toward the sky. "I'll be on standby until then."

He breathed in and headed toward the back door of the building. He needed speed, needed to buckle into a cockpit and fly like the wind through the forever sky. Maybe that would help him feel better.

It was 8:50 in the morning when he reported at the desk. He picked up a stack of mail and was on his way toward the instructors' lounge when one of the guys behind the counter motioned to him. "Captain Galanter?"

"Yes?" He kept his eyes on the mail. There was a familiar envelope in the bundle, something from the office of Ellen's father. The young man a few feet from him said something, but Shane missed it. He tucked the mail under his arm and frowned. "Sorry. What'd you say?"

"You have a message, sir." He held it out. "She says it's urgent."

Shane walked back to the counter and took a small slip of paper. "Thanks." He nodded at the guy, turned, and headed down the hall. As he did, he looked at the message. It was handwritten, taken early that morning. He read it: "Please call Emily Anderson in Wheaton, Illinois."

Anderson? Shane came to a slow stop. Emily Anderson in Wheaton? He stared at the number and wondered ... Emily? Emily Anderson? He leaned against the wall, dizzy with the thoughts racing through his head. Was it possible? The wild hope bursting within him wasn't so much because of her last name, or even because she was from Wheaton. But because her name was Emily.

The name that—

He blinked hard and shook his head. Maybe his thoughts were fuzzy because of Ellen, or because it was a beautiful Monday morning and he couldn't wait to get up in the sky. Either way he needed a clear head. Thinking about Lauren or the baby or anything from the past would only hold him back.

Her name had to be some sort of coincidence. Anderson was a common name and so was Emily. Still, he needed to call the woman. Probably a teacher, someone bringing a group of kids to Lake Tahoe and looking for an educational side trip. Happened all the time. He stepped into his small, boxy office and eased himself into his chair, all while reading the message one more time. It had to be about a tour group, he was convinced.

He dialed the number and waited. He would take care of the call, set up a tour date for the lady, and get into his flight suit.

All before nine o'clock.

☙

Emily was typing another e-mail to her mother.

The e-mails and phone calls had given them a wonderful chance to connect, even before a face-to-face meeting. This time the topic was journalism, how badly she wanted to write for a newspaper the way her mother did. She was just finishing it when the phone on the desk next to her rang. She answered it, her eyes still on the computer screen. "Hello?"

"Yes, Emily Anderson, please. This is Captain Shane Galanter returning her call."

She gasped, and then covered her mouth so he wouldn't hear her reaction. There was still no way of knowing if she had the right man. Even so, her heart was in her throat, and she was on her feet. She paced out of the room and to the end of the hallway. "This is Emily." A knot tugged at her stomach. "I'm looking for a Mr. Galanter. I'm just not sure I have the right one."

"Okay." The man sounded at a loss. "There's only one of us at Top Gun, if that helps."

"Well ..." She stifled a nervous bit of laughter. What if this *was* him? What if she was actually talking to her father—her very own father!—for the first time in her life? "Actually, I'm not sure that the Shane Galanter I'm looking for is an instructor at Top Gun."

He chuckled. "Why don't you tell me about the one you're missing."

"Good idea." She liked him. He had a kind voice and a sense of humor. "My Shane Galanter has dark hair and dark eyes and he's pretty tall. He grew up in Chicago and dated a girl named Lauren Anderson. Then the summer before his senior—"

"Emily." The teasing lightness in his voice was gone. In its place was a sense of quiet shock. "You have the right Shane Galanter. Now it's my turn." He hesitated. "Who are you?"

She stopped pacing and leaned against the wall. It was him! She'd found him! A smile pushed its way up her cheeks, just as the first tears filled her eyes. After all these years had it really been that easy? A matter of spelling his name right and finding him through the Internet? The story began spilling from her at record speed. "I'm your daughter." A sound came from her, part laugh part sob. "I've looked for you all my life, only I was looking on the Internet and I was spelling your name wrong, until last week when I found my mother's journals and I realized your name had two *a*'s and that's how I—"

"Emily?" He sounded breathless, almost doubtful. "Your mother's name is—"

"Lauren. Lauren Anderson." She giggled out loud. "I found *her* five days ago, the same day I called you."

"I just got the message. I ... I can't believe this." His voice was thick, choked with what must've been almost overwhelming emotions. "So she did it, she gave you up for adoption."

"No, not at all." Emily exhaled hard. There were so many pieces to pull together. "It's a long story. I'm not sure where to start."

"I don't know anything, Emily." He laughed, his tone soaked in disbelief. "Why don't you start at the beginning."

"Okay." She slid down the wall until she was sitting on the floor. "When you and your family left for California, my mom was desperate to find you ..."

The story poured out in all its detail. All the while Emily was overcome by a joy that made her feel like she was floating. She'd found her dad! They were actually talking on the phone. It was more than she could imagine. She'd found both her parents in the same week. And now it was up to her to get the information to her dad so he could join them. He would come, she had no doubts. She'd asked for a miracle.

And God was making it happen.

Twenty-Four

Lauren felt like she knew her daughter, and it had only been a week.

During that time over the phone, they'd filled each other in on much of what they'd missed, the facts they hadn't known about each other. Lauren told Emily about her first trip out west, and how sick Emily had gotten.

"I thought it was my fault." Lauren willed her voice to convey the depth of her regret. "When they told me you were gone, I knew I only had one hope left—to find Shane."

She told Emily about coming to Los Angeles and finding an apartment and getting a job. How she'd been determined to finish college and start a writing career, and how every day along the way she never stopped looking for Shane.

Other times the conversation would be about Emily. Lauren learned that her daughter had a deep faith, one that colored everything she did, everything she felt. Emily shared the highlights of her childhood, the special moments at home and in school, and her decision to play soccer.

"I still play now, at Wheaton College." There was pride in the girl's voice. "Grandma says my dad was an athlete."

"Yes." Lauren's heart felt scraped bare. Not only because of all she'd missed, but because Shane's memory was alive and standing next to her all the time now. "He was a baseball player."

They talked about Lauren's parents and how anxious they were to see her, and about Emily's place on the school newspaper. But no matter how many times they talked or how often they exchanged e-mails, Lauren couldn't really believe her daughter was alive—not until she saw her in person.

Finally, on a Saturday afternoon, after five hours of air travel, Lauren grabbed her things from the overhead compartment of a 737 and headed through the plane and down the Jetway into Chicago's O'Hare Airport. Even then she couldn't believe she was home again. Back where it all started, all those years ago. Eighteen years. A lifetime.

Emily's lifetime.

She exited out the gate and followed the signs to baggage claim. Emily was going to meet her near the entrance. Lauren wore a conservative skirt and a jacket with low pumps, the sort of outfit she might wear to the *Time* magazine office. Her hair was freshly trimmed, as long and blonde as it was when she left home. As she walked down the concourse, her heart kept time with her heels. All her life she'd cradled other people's children, wondered what Emily might've looked like if she'd lived. Now, in a few minutes, she would know.

The reunion would be beyond anything she could've dreamed, but it would be marked by sorrow. Emily told her the day before that her dad's cancer was much worse. The doctors were giving him a few weeks at best. Lauren picked up her pace, seeing in her mind's eye her father the way he looked when she left home. Her heart hurt because they had so little time now. But it was impossible to feel only sorrow. After all, whatever time they had was a gift she'd never dreamed of having.

The crowds were heavy, and Lauren dodged around a large group of teenagers dressed in basketball uniforms. Emily probably traveled with her soccer team. Maybe the two of them had passed just like this in an airport sometime and had never known it. She darted toward the escalator, steadying her carry-on bag in front of her and gripping the rubber handrail.

Live combat didn't make her feel this nervous.

The escalator carried her down, slowly, slowly. Lauren peered into the clearing and she saw a hallway and a pair of double doors. Just beyond them was a pretty girl with dark hair, pacing a few steps one way and then the other, her eyes never leaving the doorway. Was that her? Lauren had about five seconds to study the girl, but in the end she didn't need even that long to know. The girl had Shane's dark hair, his striking features. And at the same time she was a brunette replica of herself at that age. Lauren stepped off the escalator and rushed through the doors, out of the way of the flood of people behind her. She stood there, staring at the girl, her heart in her throat.

The reality hit her just as their eyes met, as they held, and as they spoke volumes without saying a word. This was her daughter, her Emily! Her baby girl really was *alive!*

Emily spoke first. "Mom?" She came to her. "It's you, right?"

"Yes, Emily." Lauren dropped her bag and held out her arms. Her daughter came to her then, rushed into her embrace, and stayed there. Lauren rocked her back and forth as tears streamed down her cheeks. Their hug was warm and sure, and it took Lauren back to the last time she'd held Emily. She'd missed a lifetime of rocking her, but she wouldn't miss one second more. "You're so beautiful." She breathed the words into her daughter's hair. "I can't believe you're really here."

"Me neither." Emily drew back. Her eyes were bright as the sun, even though her cheeks were tearstained. "I looked for you all my life."

"I missed you every day." She pressed the side of her face against her daughter's. "If I'd only known."

Emily sniffed, and a bit of laughter came from her. "But you're here! You're really here. Now we'll never be apart again, okay?"

"Okay." She studied her daughter, reveled in the sight of her. They'd missed so much together, that maybe Emily was right. Maybe they would find their way to the same city and never be apart again. It was a piece of the story that hadn't yet been written. Lauren's life had been in the Middle East, but that was before finding Emily. Now the future held more questions than answers.

"Hey." Emily stepped back and picked up Lauren's bag. "Can we get something to eat? I brought a photo album we can look at."

It was past one o'clock, but until then she hadn't realized how hungry she was. "Here? At the airport?"

"Why not?" Emily linked arms with her. "We're here, right?"

"Right." Lauren couldn't remember feeling this happy, not since her daughter's birth. They collected her two checked bags and headed back through the double doors up the escalator to a small Mexican restaurant.

Emily kept checking her watch and finally Lauren gave her a curious look. "Are we late?"

"No." She laughed, but it sounded nervous. "I told Grandma and Papa we'd take our time."

"Okay, then." They ordered, and Lauren found a table. When they were seated she leaned closer. She couldn't get enough of Emily, the way she looked so much like Shane and so much like herself all at the same time. She covered her daughter's hand with her own. "Why don't you show me your photo album?"

"All right." Emily grinned. "Let's start at the beginning."

The first photos showed her as a toddler, taking her first steps, and sitting in front of a white-and-pink frosted birthday cake with one lit candle in the middle. Each picture was like a precious, painful window to all Lauren missed, all she'd lost out on. Why hadn't she gone back? Even one phone call and all the lonely years could've been avoided. By the second page she felt overcome with sorrow.

"Wait, Emily." She leaned her elbow on the table and shaded her eyes with the back of her hands. "I'm sorry."

"Mom." Emily took tender hold of her wrist and peered in at her. "Hey, don't be sad."

"I am." She sniffed. "I should've been there, and now ..." A sob slipped free, and she willed herself to find control. "There's no way to get that time back."

"Yes, there is." Emily leaned in and kissed her cheek. "That's what pictures are for. They give you a way back."

"But it hurts so much." She wanted to be strong. This was her first chance in nearly two decades to actually be a mother to her daughter. She shouldn't be the one leaning on Emily. "I'd give anything to go back and do it all over again."

"I know."

"Really?" She lowered her hand and looked into her daughter's eyes. "Really, do you know how much I wish I'd been there?"

"Yes, Mom. I know. I could tell from the first time we talked." She closed the photo album. "We can look at this later."

Lauren sat up a little and stared at the blue leather cover on the book of photos. She could do this, especially with Emily at her side. She could go back to a missed lifetime and watch her little girl grow up in pictures, and somehow she would get through it. Without question she would be stronger for having done so. "No, I want to see them now." She put her arm around her daughter and smiled. "Just don't be embarrassed if I cry, okay?"

"Okay." Emily's eyes shone with compassion.

The next photos showed a preschool Emily riding a shiny red tricycle, then Emily dressed as a fairy princess for Halloween. Before they could turn the page, two of Lauren's teardrops hit the plastic covering. Lauren grinned at Emily. "See? Told you."

They both began to giggle, and then—for the first time in their lives—Lauren and Emily fell into a side-splitting round of laughter, the cleansing, complete sort of laughter only a mother and daughter can share.

❧

Emily couldn't get over it.

She and her mother had been together less than an hour, and already she felt a bond that would last a lifetime. Neither of them liked refried beans, but they were both crazy for spicy guacamole and black olives. They both broke their chips in half before dipping them into the salsa. When they noticed, they laughed again.

The photos and the food, the little habits they had in common, all of it was a wonderful distraction. And it helped Emily keep from telling her mother what was coming next: that she was about to see Shane Galanter.

Because she couldn't tell her. Not yet.

The phone call with her father had been amazing, and they too had talked a few times since.

He had the same strong faith as Emily, which was not the case with her mother. And only a week before Emily found him, he had broken off an engagement. Emily couldn't help but believe that was somehow part of the miracle God was pulling together.

"So, Mom ..." They were done eating. Emily planted her elbows on the table and rested her chin in her hands. "Tell me about Dad."

Her mother's eyes grew dreamy and faraway, but defeated at the same time. "He was amazing." She crooked her finger and pressed it first beneath one eye, then the other. "He wanted so much to be your daddy." She hesitated, directing her gaze across the concourse and out the full-length glass windows toward the runway. "He asked me to marry him." Her eyes found Emily again. "Did you know that?"

Joy filled Emily's soul. "No. I didn't." Her grandparents hadn't said anything about an engagement. She felt angry for the briefest instant, but then she let it pass. She could talk to them later about why they hadn't shared that information. The important thing was that long ago her parents had wanted to be married. It was all she could do to stay seated when she wanted to dance around the table and shout out the news. She settled herself down. "Tell me."

"It was before his family moved away." She narrowed her eyes and looked off to the distance again. "He gave me a ring engraved with the words *Even now.* He told me he would always love me, even now when things seemed so impossible." Her eyes glistened. "I wrote a story back then about the two of us in one of my notebooks and that's what I called it. *Even Now.*" She took a slow breath, the memories clouding her eyes.

"I found it." She took a quick breath, not wanting to break up the memory. "I haven't read the whole thing. But the message on your ring ... that's so romantic."

"Yes." A resignation filled her tone. "Shane was always that way."

"So what happened?"

"Nothing, really. Shane thought if we were engaged that our parents would work with us. He tried everything to find a place where he could live while we finished our last year of high school."

"Nothing worked out?" It was all so sad, so tragic. And though she knew what was coming in a half hour, Emily found herself getting teary eyed.

"Our parents just wanted us apart." There was no condemnation in her mother's eyes, no animosity. Just resignation. "Shane's parents owned his car and everything else. After he bought me the ring, he didn't have ten dollars left." She gave a sad laugh. "So they took him to California, promising that he'd have a way back to Chicago as soon as he graduated."

"They lied." The possibility hadn't occurred to Emily before. She might've grown up with her mother and father if these grandparents she didn't know had done something to help their son stay in Illinois. "That's so sad."

"It is." Her nod was firm. "But I forgave them. I had to." She smiled. "Otherwise I would've shriveled up and died from hating them."

Emily watched her mother. Being with her was like opening a chest with layers of treasure that would take a lifetime to experience. She leaned back and squeezed her mother's hand. "You know what I hope?"

"What?"

"I hope I'm loved that way someday."

A bittersweet longing knit her mother's brow together. "Me too, Emily. Me too."

The conversation shifted then. They talked about life in the Middle East and her mother's friend, Scanlon.

It was the first time her mother mentioned him, and Emily felt a ripple of alarm. "Are you two ... you know, are you dating?"

Her mother gave her a pensive smile. "No—" she raised an eyebrow—"though Scanlon might think we are." She grew more serious. "He's a wonderful man. I think he'd like a future with me, but ..." She lifted her shoulder. "I know what love is, Emily. I might not have had it for very long, but I had it. Unless I feel that way again, I don't see myself getting too serious with anyone."

They talked more about Scanlon and the recent tragedy at the orphanage. Her mother got tears in her eyes again when she talked about a little girl she'd met there—Senia, a seven-year-old with a missing front tooth.

"I'm sorry." Emily kept her tone low. "How's your arm?"

"It's healing. It still hurts, but even that's fading."

Emily didn't want to think about how different the attack might've played out. How awful it would've been to find her mother and learn that she'd been killed all within a few days. Her mother changed the subject again, telling Emily about the stories she'd covered while in Iraq and Afghanistan. They realized that one of them—a cover story about the veil being removed from the women in the Middle East—was a story Emily had written a report about for her English class.

"Wow." Emily took a sip of her pop. The moment was approaching, and she was getting more excited by the minute. "Who'd have thought my mother would be famous?"

Again they laughed, and her mom went into another tale of danger and a story she'd written early in the Iraqi war. This time Emily was only catching half the details. She was about to burst from keeping the truth in.

Her dad's plane was landing in fifteen minutes!

"Emily?" Her mother angled her head. "Are you okay?"

She jumped to attention. "Of course. I was just thinking how much I'd like writing for a magazine someday." Silently she congratulated herself on the good cover. "Want more chips?"

Her mother looked puzzled. "We stopped eating chips awhile ago, honey." She laughed and gave Emily a silly look. "Let's get home." A ribbon of pain flashed in her eyes. "I want to see Mom and Dad."

"Now?" Emily's toes tapped out a panicky rhythm beneath the table. "I was going to tell you about the soccer season. We almost went to the playoffs, did I mention that?"

"You drove here, right?" Her mother was already pushing back from the table, wiping her mouth and gathering her dishes on the tray.

"Right." Emily grabbed her fork and stuck it into the lukewarm mix of chicken and lettuce that covered her plate. "But I'm still working on my burrito."

She made a pleading look. "Could you maybe bring it with you? I really want to get home."

"Okay. When you put it like that." She grinned and went back to the counter for a carryout box. She took her time scraping the contents of her plate into the container, and then clearing her dishes from the table. She could feel her mother getting antsy, but she had to get the timing perfect.

They'd arranged it all. Her dad would walk off the plane and head down the concourse to the baggage area. When he reached the bottom of the escalator, he would call her cell phone, letting it ring once. She had her phone in her jeans pocket, set on vibrate. His call would cue her to take her mother and meet him.

Without drawing attention, she checked her watch. Five more minutes. Suddenly she had an idea. She swiped her hand over the table, making it look like she was trying to clean off the crumbs. But as she did, she knocked over her pop, splashing it onto the floor and under the table. "Oh!" She jumped back. "I'm so clumsy."

Her mother darted across the café and grabbed a stack of napkins. "Here." She gasped. "Yikes. Emily, look out. It's coming off the table onto your shoe."

"Oops." She sidestepped the stream of pop. "I think I need more napkins."

They worked together to clean the mess, and then Emily stood and tossed the wet garbage into the trash can. "The trouble is, I'm more thirsty than ever."

"Well— " her mother pointed to the pop dispenser— "your cup's okay. Why don't you fill it before we go?" Her eyes danced in a way that was only half teasing. "Maybe you'd better get a lid too."

Emily pointed her finger in the air as if her mother's suggestion was a good one. She was filling her cup with Dr Pepper when the phone in her back pocket vibrated. She gasped and nearly spilled her drink again. But instead she slipped a lid on it and hurried back to her mother. "Okay. I'm ready."

"You sure?" She grabbed her carry-on bag and headed toward the café entrance. They were halfway out the door when her mother pointed back at the table. "Your leftover burrito!"

Emily turned and brushed her hand at it. "I'm not that hungry after all."

Her mother shrugged and gave her a crooked grin. "It's hard to keep up with you, Emily."

"I know it." She looped her arm through her mother's and held her chin high. "Everyone on the soccer team always tells me that."

Her mother hesitated, looking at the signs over the concourse. "Which way do we go?"

"This way." Emily's heart pounded hard within her. She hoped she wouldn't drop from anticipation before they reached him. "We have to go back through the baggage area."

"Isn't there a quicker way to—"

Emily dragged her toward the escalator. "Nope, this is the best way." She cast her mother a quick grin. "Trust me."

❧

Shane Galanter had lived a lifetime for this moment.

He was standing next to his suitcases, at the center of the baggage area, just off the main path leading to the escalator. Even now it felt like he might be dreaming. How many times had he seen a blonde with her build, her graceful mannerisms, and followed her only to realize he'd been wrong again? That initial conversation with Emily was still fresh in his mind. From the first few lines it was clear that he was the man she was looking for and that she wasn't part of any school tour group. But when she explained that she was his daughter ... It had been more than he could take.

All along he'd wondered about what had happened to his child. Sometimes—as with the woman at the hotel the night of his engagement party—he would see a blonde with older kids and wonder for a minute if maybe one of them was his. But there were so many missing pieces. He wasn't sure if Lauren had kept the baby or not, and if she had, he didn't even know if his baby was a boy or a girl.

When he realized who Emily was, he couldn't make plans fast enough to come out to see her. That was when she told him that Lauren was coming too.

Lauren ...

How long had he looked for her, wondering if he'd ever find her again? The photo he had of her was getting worn around the edges. He looked at it all the time, dreaming of this day, praying it might happen. What would it be like, seeing her after so many years? His heart pounded and he tried to dismiss his fears. What if she'd changed and her feelings for him were long dead? It would almost be easier never to see her again than to look in her eyes and know she'd left her love for him somewhere in the past.

No. As hard as it might be, he wouldn't trade what was coming. He loved Lauren still, there was no way around the fact. Whatever the coming hour held, he would let his heart ride it out.

He wore jeans and a white button-down shirt. Civilian clothes. Emily hadn't told him much, but she'd mentioned that Lauren was a reporter for *Time* magazine, a correspondent in the Middle East. That meant that they might have far less in common now than they once had. It was something he didn't want to think about, not yet. A wave of people filed off the escalator and out the double doors, but none of them was Lauren. Three more people, an older couple carrying a boxed up poodle, and then ...

They were walking arm in arm, two women with the same look, one blonde, one brunette. He straightened, willing himself to hold up. He wasn't sure about the girl, but the woman was Lauren. He'd seen her in his dreams every night since he moved to California. She was older, but the years had only made her more beautiful.

The younger of the two—Emily, it had to be—stopped and looked first one way, then the other, and then straight at him. Her eyes lit up, and he could hear her gasp from twenty feet away. For a second she turned to Lauren, but then she looked back at him again, as if she didn't know what to do first.

She tugged Lauren a few feet in his direction, and then she let go and ran the rest of the way. "Dad!" Her arms were around him, and she was crying.

"Emily ..."

Here she was, the child he'd longed for, the one he'd never forgotten. His daughter, his very own! This was the girl who kicked at his hand as an unborn baby. That was their last contact until now.

They hugged arms tight around each other, before his daughter leaned back and looked him up and down. "Look at you! No wonder Mom was crazy about you."

He laughed and framed her face with his hands. The face that was so like his own. "I never thought I'd see this day, Emily." He wanted to look at Lauren, see if she'd followed their daughter closer. But he needed to have this moment first. "I promise you I'll spend the rest of my life making up for the years we've lost."

Emily gave him a quick hug, then—as if she suddenly remembered—she jumped back and both of them looked at Lauren. Her bags had fallen over, and she stood there, frozen in place, her mouth open.

The minute their eyes met he felt it, the connection. How had he thought for a minute that what they shared might've changed over the years? He had always known nothing could change it, and he was right. For a long moment they stood there, trying to believe what they were seeing. Tears ran down Lauren's cheeks, and finally he couldn't wait another second. He went to her at the moment she started toward him, and they met in the middle. If it were a movie scene, he would've swept her up, twirled her around in a circle, and kissed her the way a soldier kisses his girl after a long tour of duty.

But this moment held as much sorrow as it did triumph. As wonderful as it was to see each other, Shane couldn't help feeling desperately sad. They'd lost two decades. And the privilege of raising their child together. That loss would always be with them. They stopped in front of each other, and slowly, with all the tenderness he had to give, he drew her into his arms. The lost years slipped away like so many seconds, and he soaked in the feel of her. They fit perfectly together, the way they always had.

"Lauren … I can't believe it's you." He could feel her heart pounding against his chest.

She held him tighter. "I looked for you … for so long …" She drew back and searched his eyes. "Where've you been, Shane?" Her crying grew harder, her voice the barest whisper. "I couldn't find you."

People were milling past, casting curious glances at them. Not far away Emily had righted her mother's luggage and now she was watching them, her face taken by a smile that stretched from ear to ear. Shane tucked Lauren's head in close to his chest and swayed with her, feeling himself responding to her presence. "I thought I'd lost you forever." He kissed the top of her head.

"Me too." Her voice was a mumble against his shirt. After a few seconds she took a step back and studied him. "In my dreams you looked just like this, Shane."

"You too." They had so much to catch up on. He wanted to ask her why she changed her name, and what life had done to her way of thinking now that she was a *Time* magazine correspondent. He needed to tell her that he was in the navy, a fighter pilot, but all that could wait. He smiled at her. "Emily found me a few days ago." He leaned sideways and flashed their daughter a grin.

She gave him a cute little wave, and he did the same.

"I asked her not to tell you." He put his hands on her shoulders and searched her eyes. Looking into them was like getting his first drink after years in the desert. "I wanted you to be surprised."

"Surprised?" She took a few steps back and bent at the waist, bracing herself on her knees. When she looked up her expression was still filled with disbelief. "I'm surprised my heart's still beating."

He laughed and took her hands. They stood there, not quite able to get enough of each other. Finally he felt his smile fade. "You know about your parents?"

She nodded. "Daddy's sick. He might only have a few weeks to live."

"Emily told me." He motioned for their daughter to join them. When she did, he put one arm around her and one arm around Lauren. He felt a rush of joy at the way they felt against him. Lauren and Emily, both of them. The feeling was amazing, like he'd found a missing part of himself and now—finally—he was whole again. He blinked back the wetness in his eyes and gave them each a light squeeze. "Let's get back to the house."

Emily nodded. Fresh tears filled her eyes, but she smiled at both of them. They were halfway to the parking lot when Emily said, "This is it, exactly."

"This moment, you mean?" Lauren looked around him and smiled at their daughter. Shane's throat tightened. Their daughter. Their little girl. A part of each of them …

"Yes. When I asked God for a miracle, a picture came to my mind." Emily skipped a few steps in front of them and turned around, her arms spread wide. "This picture. Exactly this."

Twenty-Five

It was the first day Bill hadn't felt like getting out of bed. Angela asked him a few times, suggesting that he join her at the kitchen table for hot oatmeal or later that he sit on the sofa with her and watch a movie. The kids would be there by four o'clock. It was important that he stay awake and alert.

But he had only taken her hand and looked straight to the part of her that belonged to him alone. "Everything hurts, Angie. I'm sorry."

His answer dropped her to the edge of the bed. She sat there shaking. It took awhile until she said anything. "You never told me."

"I didn't want to." He smiled and laced his fingers between hers. "I have pills if I need them. It's just that I want to be alert when the kids come." His shoulders slid up and down against the pillow. "I figured if I rested all day I could fake it a little tonight."

That was at noon. He slept most of the day and now he was up and sitting in his recliner in the family room. She studied him from the kitchen and wondered how he would look to Lauren and Shane. Older, of course. But he was thin now, much thinner than before. His face was gaunt and the cancer had left his complexion ashy gray. He was cold too. No matter how high she kept the thermostat, he needed a blanket across his legs. Tonight he was using two—both of them extra thick.

Still, with all the changes and the pain he was in, his eyes glowed as he looked at her. "Any minute!"

"Yes." All their searching and praying and wanting their daughter had come to this. Lauren and Shane together again in the same room. With their daughter. And with them.

Part of her was so excited she could barely put the apple pie in the oven. But another part of her was terrified because she and Bill were at least partly responsible for separating them. If only Bill had asked the phone company to leave forwarding information on the recording connected to their old number. It was something he regretted every day. She wasn't about to bring it up now.

Once the pie was set, she poured the two of them coffee and joined him in the family room. She took the chair she liked best—the one closest to him. Just as she sat down, she heard a car, and after a few minutes, the sound of Emily's voice. Angela closed her eyes and reached for her husband's foot. "Father God, be here tonight."

She expected them to ring the doorbell, then realized Emily would never do such a thing. So she wasn't surprised when she heard the group come into the entryway, and after a bit of hushed conversation, she heard Emily's voice heading up the stairs with what must've been Shane. Angela stood and waited, her heart barely beating. Were Emily and Shane giving them this time alone with Lauren? It was something she had wanted, but never voiced. There was silence in the entryway for a few seconds, and then the sound of heels on the tile floor.

And suddenly—there she was. Standing before them, like something from a dream.

"Lauren ..." Tears blurred Angela's vision and a sob caught in her throat. She was afraid to move or cry or say the wrong thing.

Lauren blinked and tears slid down her cheeks. Their eyes locked and she massaged her throat. "Mom ..." Her eyes shifted to Bill. "Dad ..."

Angela couldn't wait. She crossed the room, and carefully, as if her daughter might break, she took Lauren into her arms. With one hand on the back of Lauren's head and the other pressed to the small of her daughter's waist, Angela cradled her the way she'd done when Lauren was little, when she'd come home from kindergarten with a skinned knee.

Only this time she and Bill had caused her daughter's pain. And it went far deeper than any childhood scrape. "I'm so sorry, honey." She muttered the words against the side of Lauren's face. "I've spent my life being sorry."

Lauren felt stiff at first, as if the awkwardness of the moment kept her from giving in to her emotions. But as they embraced, Angela felt her daughter letting go, felt the sobs shaking her slight frame. "I'm ... I'm sorry too."

When their tears slowed some, Lauren took a step back and turned toward Bill. Angela watched them. *God ... You did this. You brought her home while we still had a chance to be together. All of us, the way we should've been from the beginning.*

"Daddy, how are you?" She reached the edge of his chair and he held his hand out to her. She took it and leaned closer, hugging him for what seemed like a minute. She eased onto her knees, bringing them face-to-face. "Does it hurt?"

He shook his head and brought his hand up along her face. "Not anymore." With his other hand, he brought her fingers to his lips and kissed them. "We were wrong, Lauren. I'm so, so sorry, baby."

Angela felt her composure slipping. He was a strong man, Bill Anderson. Strong and intelligent and not given easily to shows of emotion. At least, not before Lauren left. When she didn't come back and they couldn't find her, she'd watched him change. What he'd done by leaving their forwarding information off the recording, he'd done in love. He loved Lauren and would've gone to any lengths to protect her. It was that protective instinct of his that longed for Lauren with every passing hour. She was his little girl, and in some ways he hadn't been complete until just this minute. With her safely in his arms again.

Lauren looked weak as she struggled to her feet. The day had been an emotional one for all of them. She wiped her cheeks with her knuckles and looked at Angela and then Bill. Her eyes settled on Bill. "I'm the one who left." She lifted her chin a few inches. "I thought Emily was dead and I panicked. I never ..." Her voice cracked and she held on to the back of Bill's chair for support. "I never should've gone without saying good-bye." Her expression was a twisted mass of sorrow and regret. "Forgive me ... please?"

She dropped to the arm of Bill's chair and put her arm around him, leaning close and letting her head rest against his. "I missed you, Daddy." She looked up and turned the other way. "You too, Mom. How did so many years get away from us?"

Angela came to them, and the three formed a hug full of hope and promise and second chances. There was no talk about Shane, but Angela knew that would come. They couldn't move too far ahead without first letting go of the past.

Lauren lifted her head and looked at Bill again. "I'm sorry ... about the cancer."

"I didn't ask God to make me better." His voice was hoarse, barely understandable. He framed her face with his fingers again. "I only asked him to bring you home."

ൿ

The three of them talked in whispered tones before Angela found a box of tissues and passed them out. Lauren took one and stood. "Can Shane come in now? He wants to see you."

Angela felt like the worst person in the world. He was really there, the charming young man who had loved her daughter with such devotion, the kid who had purchased a wedding ring and asked Lauren to marry him so they wouldn't be torn apart. He had come, even though she and Bill had acted to keep them separate from each other.

"Yes, Lauren. Bring him in."

She left the room, and Angela turned to Bill. "Can you believe it? She's really home."

"She's beautiful." He sat up a little and pulled the blankets higher on his lap. "But her eyes aren't what they were. Do you see it?"

Angela hadn't wanted to admit that. To do so meant taking blame for even more damage. But Bill was right. "I see it. I think it has to do with her faith."

"Does she ... have faith?" He winced, as if the pain of thinking such a thing was worse than anything the cancer was doing to him.

"I don't know." She took hold of his shoulder. "I can only believe that with the miracles God has brought about in the last few weeks, He won't stop short of that one."

Bill nodded, and as he did, they heard footsteps in the entry again. This time all three of them filed into the family room, with Shane leading the way.

He smiled and came to them, giving Bill a firm handshake. "Mr. Anderson, it's good to see you." Then he turned to her. "Mrs. Anderson." He released Bill's hand and hugged her. It wasn't the hug they'd received from Lauren, but it was one that spoke forgiveness. Whatever Shane Galanter had once held against them, those feelings were no longer a part of him.

"Shane." Bill coughed and held his hand out to Shane once more.

"Yes, sir?" The handshake held.

"My wife and I owe you an apology." Bill's eyes had been dry until now. But here, with Lauren and Emily standing a few feet away arm in arm, and all of them gathered together for the first time, tears welled up and trickled down his leathery cheeks.

"It's over with, sir." Shane kept hold of Bill's hand. "God made it clear to me a long time ago that we can't go back." He looked over his shoulder at Lauren and Emily, and then at Bill once more. "We can only be glad for today."

"Something else." He rubbed at his throat, his voice raspy. "I understand you're a captain in the navy, a fighter pilot, is that right?"

Angela watched Lauren's expression change. She looked down at the floor, but only for a minute.

"Yes, sir. I train fighter pilots at the Top Gun facility in Reno, Nevada."

"Well, then, I have to tell you—" Bill gripped Shane's hand harder than before—"I couldn't be prouder of you if you were my own son."

Again a shadow passed over Lauren's eyes, and Angela felt a strong prompting to pray. *What is it, God? Does she disapprove of Shane's job?* With Shane and Bill discussing the navy, and Emily grinning, talking about how her dad was going to take her up in an F–16, it hit Angela. Of course Lauren had a problem with Shane's job.

She'd been covering the war for *Time* magazine for the past two years. Her political views and Shane's would be at polar ends of the spectrum by now. What if Lauren found all of them too conservative, their faith too upfront? What if she stayed for only a few days and then ran away again, certain she could never belong? Fear wanted a place in the midst of their group, but Angela wouldn't allow it.

God, this is Your territory. The years might've changed Lauren, but that's okay. She's entitled to her opinion—whatever that opinion is. She settled her gaze on Lauren, aching to go to her and hold her again, her only daughter. Instead she finished her prayer. *Father, let her feel Your love this week. I know I'm asking for a lot, God, but please use this time to stir in her the faith we share with Emily and Shane. Please . . .*

Even as her prayer ended, she felt a deep uneasiness, a sorrow that their decisions twenty years ago had pushed Lauren far away, not only from them, but from God. The Lord had been so good to them in the years since Lauren left. The tragedy of losing her, of raising Emily without her parents had turned them to a deep, life-sustaining faith. From what Emily told them, in his pain and loneliness, Shane had found a relationship with Christ also.

Now she would pray with every breath that one day soon the same would be true for Lauren.

Twenty-Six

Lauren had been waiting for this moment all day. Waiting for it and dreading it all at the same time. She and Shane were about to be alone for the first time in two decades.

The night had been amazing. All five of them had talked and cried and told funny stories about the years they'd missed until finally her dad was too tired to last another minute. Her mother walked him to their room, and Emily stayed up talking with Lauren and Shane until just a few minutes ago. After so many years, none of them could get enough of each other.

Now it was after midnight, and she and Shane and Emily were heading upstairs to tell Emily good night.

"Can I ask you something?" A smile played on Emily's lips, as they reached the top of the stairs and she looked at the two of them standing together. "I always used to wonder what it would be like to have my parents tuck me in. You know, like other kids." Her eyes were dry, but her tone rang with sincerity. "Would you do that? Please?"

Lauren's heart sang. She felt honored her daughter would even ask. Emily was no longer a child, after all. How wonderful that she didn't feel too old to still be a kid around them. She tugged on Emily's sweater sleeve. "You lead the way."

And so the three of them trucked down the hall to Emily's room, Lauren and Shane a few steps behind. Shane held her hand, and the sensation stirred countless emotions in her. How often had she dreamed of this, the normalcy of such a moment? That she and Shane might be heading upstairs to bid their daughter good night, the way real families did.

Emily slipped into her bathroom to put on her pajamas, leaving Lauren and Shane standing near the doorway. He slid his arms around her waist, and she let him draw her close. No matter how long she looked at him, she couldn't get enough. It was as though they'd never been apart. All evening they'd sat close together, and she could hardly think for the way Shane's fingers felt linked with hers.

It was the same way now, in his arms. She came to him willingly. Time had done nothing to dim the desire between them, that much was certain. "Can you believe we're here?" His voice was low, his breath soft against her cheek. He nuzzled his face against hers. "You feel so good, Lauren."

"I used to fall asleep each night wishing ..." She traced her finger along his collarbone. "Wishing I'd wake up in the morning and you'd be there beside me. That we were married and together." She dragged her hand through the air beside them. "Like all this would just be a terrible nightmare."

"Mmm." He breathed in near the nape of her neck and then drew back enough to meet her eyes again. "We should've had a lifetime of that by now." He lifted his hands to her face and worked his fingers into her hairline. A low groan came from him. "It kills me to think of all we missed."

The bathroom door opened, and Shane pulled back. He took hold of Lauren's hand, but he hit the light switch and Lauren could see him grinning at both of them in the dark. "Okay, young lady, time for bed."

Emily giggled and padded past them in her socks. Then she climbed in between the covers and pulled them up near her chin. "Can you pray with me? That's part of tucking in."

Lauren shifted, but tried not to show her discomfort. She'd considered God an enemy since she got the news that Emily was dead, since she'd driven away from Chicago that terrible day. Faith belonged to the rest of them, not her. It wasn't something she wanted, either. If there *was* a God, He had let them lose a lifetime together. Why Emily and Shane cared for such a God, she didn't understand.

Still she wasn't about to resist. This wasn't a debate on theology. She let Shane lead her to the side of Emily's bed. Suddenly the full extent of what was happening hit her square in the heart. She was saying good night to her daughter—the baby girl she'd thought was dead! She was sitting next to her in a dark room, getting one of her first chances to be Emily's mom. She sat on the edge of the mattress and ran her fingers through Emily's bangs. Next to her Shane's quiet voice rang out clear and confident, full of a faith Lauren had stopped believing in years ago.

"Dear God, we're here tonight because You allowed it." He drew a deep breath. "I thought I'd live my life never finding either of these two, but You—You brought us together. We pray Emily will sleep well, and that tomorrow we'll all wake up and find that it's really happening, that it's not just a wonderful dream." He hesitated, and his tone grew heavier. "Help us not to be angry or sad over all we've lost. But help us celebrate what You've given us today. In Jesus' name, amen."

Shane leaned down and kissed Emily on the cheek. "Good night, Emily." He tapped the tip of her nose. "Thank you."

She smiled, and the little girl she must've been shone in her eyes. "For what?"

"For letting God use you." He stood and headed for the doorway.

It was Lauren's turn. She looked down at Emily and once more brushed her thumb across her daughter's forehead. "I remember the last time I did this."

"At the hospital?" Emily rolled onto her side so they could see each other better.

"Mmm-hmm. You were so sick, so hot. I sat there next to your bed and I did this. I touched your forehead, begging God to let you live, to bring you back to me."

Emily searched her eyes. "Don't you see, Mom?"

"See what?"

"He answered your prayers." She gave a little shrug. "Here we are, just like you asked."

A lump lodged in her throat, but her words found their way around it. "I like your attitude, Miss Emily. I'm proud to be your mother." She leaned in and kissed her on the forehead. Then she whispered, "Good night, sweet daughter. I love you." The words felt wonderful on her lips. "I can't say it enough."

"Love you too."

Shane was waiting for her out in the hallway. Without saying a word he eased his fingers between hers again and led her back down the stairs to the living room. Gentle flames danced in the fireplace, and through the oversized picture window it was snowing.

He turned out the lights, and when they reached a spot near the fireplace, he stopped and tugged her into his arms again. "Hi." He brushed his cheek against hers, holding her with a gentle firmness.

"Hi." Panic tried to interrupt the moment. Were they going to talk or was it just assumed that they would start up again where they'd left off?

"Here we are." He searched her eyes ... Was he going to kiss her? Did she want him to? She swallowed. Her knees were weak and her heart was racing hard. Of course she wanted him to kiss her. But was it right, when they hadn't talked yet?

Before she could answer her own questions, he began humming a James Taylor song, one that had been their favorite the year she got pregnant. Slowly, and with his eyes still locked on hers, he swayed her in a dance that made her head spin. She felt herself being sucked in, pulled to a place where she wouldn't ever want anything but the feeling of his arms around her.

What little resistance she'd brought with her to Chicago melted like the snowflakes hitting the window outside. Maybe they didn't have to talk, not yet. This was what she'd wanted all those years, wasn't it? A chance to be in Shane Galanter's arms again, alone in a dark room with just the sound of a fire crackling in the background.

Their swaying slowed and he brought his hands to her face. In an unhurried, barely controlled way, he worked his fingers into her hair again and brushed his lips against her cheek. "I never stopped loving you."

"Me neither." She breathed in the scent of him—his warm breath, his fresh shampoo and cologne. He smelled wonderful. The day had already been so emotional, and now this. Their eyes held, and she knew. It was going to happen.

His lips found hers first, and he left the lightest kiss there. "Lauren ... don't ever let go."

"I won't." Her heart was talking now. This time she found his lips and kissed him the way she was dying to. Full and slow and with a lifetime of bottled-up passion. His arms tightened around her, and they swayed every now and then, and after a few minutes they made their way up against the wall closest to the window.

The air between them changed, and she felt the same trembling in his body that was moving over her. Shane pulled back first, pursing his lips and exhaling hard. His eyes blazed with desire, mirroring the feelings that had to show in her face as well.

"Okay." He chuckled and rubbed the back of his neck. He let her go and crossed the living room where he sat at one end of the sofa. "Looks like some things haven't changed."

She let her arms hang at her sides and she shook them. No one made her feel the way Shane did. She grinned at him through the dim light of the fire. "No, some things definitely haven't changed." He was waiting for her, so she crossed the room and sat a foot away from him. A little space would be good right now.

Something he'd said made her wonder. Maybe she wasn't the only one afraid of sorting through the years and taking a harder look at who they'd become. She ran her finger down his forearm. "Did you mean—" her voice was kind—"that some things *have* changed?"

His expression gave him away. He looked down but only for an instant. When his eyes found hers again, he gave her a sad smile. "I know who you are, Lauren Gibbs."

"Lauren Gibbs?" She lowered her chin. How much did he know? She kept her tone light, not wanting to lose what they'd found in the past hour. "Does my fighter pilot read *Time* magazine?"

The sorrow in his face deepened. "He does."

An awful feeling crept into the moment. A year ago she'd written an article stating that Iraqi residents had no respect for American fighter pilots. She'd quoted one man saying, "They are the epitome of the ugly American. Cowards afraid to face their enemies. Flying overhead and destroying our towns and villages, our homes and neighborhoods with the push of a button."

The article included a brief paragraph detailing a response from the air force and another from the navy, rhetoric about how air strikes were actually more humane because the targets could be pinpointed within a few feet. Had he seen that story? She had the awful feeling that he had. She sighed. "You saw my piece on fighter pilots?"

He brushed his knuckles against her cheek, the love in his eyes still strong. "It was posted at the base for six months." He chuckled. "Just about every fighter pilot wrote a rebuttal. Last time I checked, your story was pretty well surrounded."

She groaned and let her head fall back against the sofa. "Shane ..." She sat straight again searching his eyes. "How did you wind up on the wrong side of this war?"

He took her hand and in the smoothest sensation he brought it to his lips and kissed it. "The question is—" his voice held no accusation; only the same love from earlier that night—"how did you?"

His words placed a thin line between them. "Shane, just for a minute forget all your naval air training." She was careful not to sound hard or sarcastic. "You're a Christian."

"I am." His kindness didn't waver.

"So Jesus taught about peace, right? He came to bring us peace."

"Actually, He came to bring us life." Shane's words were slow, easy. His eyes still held hers and his tone was relaxed. "Life to the fullest measure."

"Okay, good." She bit her lip. "If He came to bring us *life*, then how can you be part of a war that kills people?"

"Lauren." He ran his fingers along her forearm. "Conflict has been around since Cain and Abel. For most of time people have fought wars, lots of them with God's approval."

She could feel her blood pressure rising. "Okay." She breathed out, "How can you support a God who would want war? Innocent people killed?" She sat straighter, putting another few inches between her and Shane. "Isn't the goal supposed to be peace?"

"Yes." His voice was a little more intense. "Do you think I don't want peace in Iraq? Peace in Afghanistan?" He pulled one knee up on the sofa and turned to face her. "Because I fly fighter jets?"

The question threw her. She'd had these talks with conservatives before. Even military conservatives. They always trotted out the causes for war: weapons of mass destruction, vicious dictators, torture among civilians. But no matter how long and fast they talked, she felt the same. How did two wrongs make a right? How could the U.S. take a stand against dangerous weapons in Iraq, and then drop dangerous weapons to make its point?

But never, in all her days of reporting in the Middle East, had she heard a military captain say that he wanted peace. She searched his eyes. "Peace, Shane?" Her voice held question marks, nothing more. "You spend your days training fighter pilots how to find and destroy enemy targets, and you want peace?"

He was quiet for a minute. The slight rise in his intensity faded. "Where were you on September 11, 2001?"

She didn't want to talk about the terrorist attacks. It was the same story with half the war supporters she'd interviewed. It made the U.S. military sound like a bunch of whiny kids. *They hit us first* ... Still, this was Shane. Regardless of their differences this side of yesterday, she owed him a thoughtful answer. She crossed her arms and pressed her good shoulder into the back of the sofa. "I was in Los Angeles at the office." The memory came sidling up like a smelly drunk at a bar. "I watched it, horrified like everyone else."

"Did you know anyone in those buildings?"

"I didn't." She drew her feet up in front of her and hugged her knees. "But I was one of the reporters on it. I interviewed people in Los Angeles who'd lost friends or family." The sick feeling she'd known all that week came back. "It was awful." She studied his face. Maybe he had other reasons for asking about it. She reached out and touched his hand. "What about you?"

He stared at the fire, his eyes full of something she couldn't make out. "I was in Reno, at the Top Gun facility. Got a call the night before from a buddy of mine, went through navy fighter pilot training with him. Only Benny didn't want to be a career fighter pilot. He wanted to be a firefighter. FDNY." Shane squinted at what must've been the garish glare of the past. "We talked about his wife and kids, the great weather they were having." Shane smiled at Lauren. "I told him he should come out to Top Gun and take a ride in an F–16 with me."

Lauren knew what was coming. She looped her fingers around his. "He was on duty the next morning?"

"He was." Shane looked at the fire again. "His wife told me he made it to the sixty-first floor before the South Tower fell." He met her eyes again. "They never found his body."

She waited a minute, giving the story time to fill her heart. "I'm sorry."

"Thanks." He gave her fingers a light squeeze. "I've thought a lot about peace. I studied it in school, believe it or not."

"Really?" Her tone told him she was teasing in a gentle sort of way. She tried to picture him hanging out with the people she knew in college, the journalism students. "You wore tie-dye and sandals in college, did you?"

"Close." He chuckled. "The sandals, anyway." He rested his arm along the sofa back and ran his fingers over her shoulder. "I didn't want what my parents had. Materialism and business investments and a life of plastic facades. I knew that much." He gave her a serious frown. "College was interesting for me. I asked a lot of questions, studied the history of civilizations and what exactly constituted peace."

She was impressed. A large number of her liberal friends hadn't done that. Yes, she agreed with them, but that didn't mean their opinions were based on fact. Hers were. She interviewed people all day long. If anyone should have the facts on why war wasn't worth fighting, she should.

He must have seen she was interested, because he continued. "Time and again I saw the same thing, Lauren." His eyes implored her to hear him. Really hear him. "I saw that we could have peace only through strength."

Another military motto, one she'd heard bantered about far too often. Still, she stopped herself from reacting. "What does that *mean*, Shane? Peace through strength?"

He gave her question some thought. "I guess it's like this. We've lost an awful lot of men in this war, and that's a tragedy. One life lost is a tragedy. But when we look at the plans the terrorists had for this country, I see the benefit of strength. The peaceful benefit." He ran his thumb over the top of her hand. "They had very detailed plans, Lauren. I saw them. They thought they'd make September 11 look like a minor incident."

Even after a lifetime of standing on the other side of this fence, she wanted to understand him. If things had been different, they wouldn't be having this talk. No doubt she would've been on his side, searching for a way to justify the things she inherently believed. "So ..."

He held his hands out to the sides, face up. "They haven't struck again, Lauren. Their plans fell to rubble. Their rubble."

"They messed with the wrong people, right?" Again she was careful to sound open, interested. Not condemning. "That's what you're saying?"

"Sort of. I mean you're over there, Lauren. You walk down the streets and shop in the villages and see the people." He paused. "When's the last time you saw an air raid, an air attack by a U.S. fighter pilot?" A partial smile played on his lips. "The only reason we're still there is to help the new government get set up. And that's peaceful, right? We pull out and, well, you know what'll break loose over there."

She thought about the attack on the orphanage. "It's already loose. I didn't make the article up, Shane." She sighed. "The people I talk to live in fear and stay indoors most of the time."

"Yes." A hint of frustration crept into his tone. "Because those are the people your magazine *wants* you to talk to."

"Okay." She eased her feet back to the floor, her eyes never leaving his. "You think we have peace through strength because we flexed our muscle, right? We showed them. If they thought they could mess with us, they had another think coming. Something like that?" Her opinions were coming through a little too loudly. She drew a slow breath to bring down her tone. "But maybe that only makes us bullies."

"Lauren." He took hold of both her hands. "Do you really want to talk about this tonight?"

"Do you really want to avoid it?" Her answer was quick, and regret filled her. She ached to go to him, lose herself in his arms, and kiss him all night long. "I'm sorry."

He reached for her and she slid closer to him. "You see things your way, and I see them mine. Can't we be okay with that for now?"

"Yes." She looked at him. Their faces were close again. "For now."

"Meaning what?" He angled his body toward her, tracing her jaw with his finger.

"Meaning we don't have to talk about it this week, Shane. We can figure it out later, when it's time to go home."

He kissed her then, and in the time it took her to respond, all the passion from earlier was back. He eased himself from her and took a breath. That's when she noticed his eyes — they were eyes that belonged to a seventeen-year-old boy she'd promised to love forever.

"You're forgetting one thing."

"What?" She didn't want to talk. She wanted to be lost in his arms, searching desperately for a way back to what they'd shared before.

"You forgot that this *is* home. Here." He kissed her again and another time. "Right here, with me."

She wanted to believe him. Oh, how she wanted to. But she couldn't. He was wrong. Home was her apartment in Afghanistan, where she wrote stories that shed light on the reasons war could never bring about peace. Home was hitting the dusty roads with Scanlon beside her, his big canvas camera bag sitting on the seat between them. But she couldn't say so.

Not when she planned to spend the next week pretending he was right.

TWENTY-SEVEN

Emily woke to the clipped sound of a single siren.

She sat straight up and looked at her dresser alarm clock. Six a.m. Lights were flashing outside the window and suddenly she was awake enough to understand what was going on. Her heart felt like it was turning somersaults inside her chest. Something must've happened with Papa.

Her mom was sleeping in the office; her dad on the living room sofa. Now she and her mother met in the hallway and hurried down the stairs. They were halfway down when they saw her grandpa on a stretcher, being taken out through the front door. Her grandma was saying, "I'll be right out. I want to ride with him." She shot them a quick glance. "He had a seizure. They want to admit him, just in case there's something they can do."

Near the side entrance to the living room, Emily's dad walked up and gave his head a quick shake. "Mrs. Anderson, can I do anything?"

"Bring the others." Her grandma ran into the entryway with Papa's two blankets. Then she took quick hold of Shane's wrist and looked at the rest of them. "He's stable. He'll be okay for now. Come later this morning, okay?"

Emily padded down the stairs the rest of the way and darted over to her grandmother, giving her a fast hug. She had never been more afraid in all her life. "Tell him we're praying for him."

"I will." She paused, and Emily thought she looked about to collapse. "The doctor told me seizures would mean he was close to the end." She took another step toward the door. "I thought you should know." She bid them good-bye and then she left.

The three of them stood in the entryway, listening to the ambulance pull away. Every few seconds the sirens gave a short blast—probably so they wouldn't disturb the neighborhood any more than necessary.

Emily's throat was tight. "I can't go back to sleep."

"No." Her mother took slow steps the rest of the way down. She wore a white T-shirt and what looked like black running pants. "Let's go sit on the couch."

Emily couldn't help but notice the way her mom went to her dad and slid one arm under his and up along his back. Emily had wondered what their time alone would bring about, and now she had her answer. They were happy and in love and probably making plans to get married. Just like she'd always dreamed. But there was one problem. In her dream, Papa wasn't on the verge of dying just when everything was coming together.

They sat on the sofa, her dad in the middle, and for the next two hours they took turns talking and dozing off, leaning their heads on each others' shoulders. At eight o'clock her dad stood and stretched. "I'm going to take a shower." He looked at the clock near the front door. "Let's try to leave in an hour."

When he was gone, Emily slid closer to her mother. She was terrified about her grandpa, but she couldn't let that stop her from enjoying this time with her mom. For a few moments she leaned into her, resting her head on her mother's good shoulder. Then she sat up and gave her mom a hopeful look. "So, is he just like you remembered?"

"Shane?"

Her mother's reaction wasn't quite right. She smiled, but she didn't light up like she should've.

"He's very handsome, if that's what you mean."

"He is." Emily giggled. "But I meant the other stuff." She scrunched her shoulders up a few inches. "Do you think you'll be back together after this?"

Her mom looked at her, and then let out a sad, frustrated sigh. "Honey, seeing him again ... this time together is wonderful." Her tone softened. "But don't get your hopes up." She sighed and took hold of Emily's hand. "We've grown up a lot in eighteen years."

Emily tried not to gulp. She'd wondered but been afraid to ask. With their opposing occupations, her mom and dad had to be in opposite corners, for sure. "It's about the war, right?"

"That's one area." Her answer was quick and it shook Emily's confidence. "We've become very different people."

"It doesn't seem that way. Not when I look at you."

She smiled. "I like being with him. That part's easy."

"Well ... then maybe it'll work out after all."

"Emily." Her mom lowered her chin, and in a nice way her look said the conversation was over. "Let's just enjoy this week." Her smile faded. "We have Papa to think about. That's most important right now, okay?"

Her answer didn't come easily. "Okay."

She wanted to scream or run or keep them together in this same house until the end of time. But none of that would bring her parents together the way they'd been before, in a way where their politics and differences wouldn't matter.

Only God could do that.

❧

Emily's questions had Lauren off balance all day. But she couldn't spend much time thinking about Shane or how they'd changed or whether they could find something again when this week was over. Her father was far too sick to think of anything but him and her mother and how quickly the end was coming.

She and Shane and Emily arrived at the hospital just after nine. Her mother met them in the hall outside his room. Lauren took the lead, meeting her mom halfway and taking her hands. "How is he?"

"It's moving so fast. It could be anytime." She looked down and their foreheads came together.

Lauren gripped her mother's arm at the news. "No ..."

It was too soon. She hadn't had time to talk to him or find out what she'd missed for all those years. On the hardest days in the Middle East, she always believed she could go back home if she wanted to. Her daddy would always take her back. But now he would be gone, and a place in her heart would never be the same again.

Her mother was trembling, probably tired and scared and trying not to break down. A moment later Emily and Shane came up and circled their arms around the two of them.

"Is he awake?" Shane's voice rang with compassion. "I'd like to see him. Maybe pray with him."

"He is." Her mom sniffed and straightened a little. "We should all go in. He's been asking for you."

Why did she run when she did? Why didn't she at least call? Just one call and she would've found Emily and her parents. Together they might even have found Shane. Maybe she'd be writing for the *Tribune* and covering features or entertainment—something less life shattering than war.

She trailed the others into the room. Her heart felt like it was being dragged behind her on a chain. Had she done this to her father? Had his grief and longing and missing her all those years given him a deadly disease?

No. She couldn't think that way, not now when he needed her smiling face at his bedside. He was greeting Emily, and she watched her daughter lay her head on her grandpa's chest. "Papa, we're gonna stay here all day, okay?"

"I'm ... sorry I'm sick." He gave her a weak smile and then looked around the room at the rest of them. "Not much of a party, huh?"

Emily nuzzled her face against his. "We don't need a party, Papa. We just need you."

Shane looked back at Lauren and motioned for her to come closer. She did so without hesitation, but her attention was still on her father and Emily, the relationship they had. Emily had told her that her dad had changed, that he wasn't the way he'd been, wasn't the man who'd hurt her so. Watching the two of them, the way her dad held Emily's hand and spoke softly to her, she knew the truth. Her daughter was right.

In some ways, it was another loss. Had she come home sooner, she would've had time to share that same sort of tender relationship with him. Emily gave him one more hug and then she stepped back. Next, Shane put his hand on Lauren's father's shoulder. "God has a plan in all this." Shane's voice was strong and compassionate, a tone that showed how much he cared and that he held no hard feelings toward the man. "Don't forget that, okay?"

Her dad looked intently at Shane. "My girls are going to need you."

"Yes." His chin trembled, but he clenched his jaw and nodded. "I know."

"Don't leave them, okay?" He glanced at the others. His eyes settled on Lauren, and she wasn't sure who his next words were directed at. "They need you ... even if they don't think they do."

Shane reached back and took Lauren's hand. "I know, sir. I'm not going anywhere." He eased back against the wall and gave Lauren a look that melted her.

It was her turn. She came to her father's side. "Hi, Daddy."

"Hi, little girl."

Her eyes were dry, but a sob caught in her throat. She remembered a thousand times when she'd greeted him that way, back before she'd taken up with Shane, when he thought of her as the girl who couldn't do anything wrong. In some ways this was better. Because he certainly knew the truth. She was miles from perfect, yet his eyes told her he loved her no less. In fact he cared for her more than ever. His hand was rough against hers. Rough and dry and cold, as if death was already staking its claim on him. She leaned close and kissed his fingers. "We need more time."

"Yes." His voice was gravelly, so low it was impossible to hear him without leaning closer. "You know ... what I'm going to tell you."

She wrinkled her nose, confused. "No, Dad." Her heart skipped a beat. Was this when he'd remind her that the whole tragedy of their lives was her fault, that she never should've slept with Shane in the first place? He wouldn't do that now, would he? She swallowed her fears. "What do you want to tell me?"

"About Shane." The words were an effort for him. "That young man has loved you forever." He took a rest and for a moment he did nothing but breathe. "He still loves you." His look grew more intense. "And you love him too, I ... know you do."

She felt the sting of tears. She'd spent all these years forcing herself not to cry. But now, crying was as familiar as breathing. "Yes." She didn't turn around or look at Shane. She wasn't even sure he could hear them. "Shane loves me."

"Don't ... don't let him go again. Love doesn't mean ... seeing eye to eye on everything."

Was her father that aware of what was happening around him? Had he really known that who they'd become as adults could make her and Shane walk away from this week and close the door on their past for good? Even thinking about it hurt her, but what choice did they have? She drew a steadying breath. "Dad, I—"

"Shh." He held her hand to his cheek and winked at her. His eyes danced as they hadn't since the group of them walked into his hospital room. "Don't analyze. I'm right about this." His lungs sounded raspier than before. "You've lost so much, Lauren. Don't lose what God wants to give you now."

Lauren felt her own wisdom dissolving. He was right, wasn't he? She had lost so very much. They all had. Losing Shane now would be tragic, even if she still couldn't see a way for it to work between them. She leaned over and put her cheek against his. "Daddy!" She hugged him, wishing she still had a thousand more times to do this. "How do you still know me so well?"

"Because—" he brushed his scruffy unshaven face against hers, the way he'd done when she was little—"daddies never forget their little girls." He looked at her, leaving just enough space between them so he could search her eyes. "When I get to heaven ... I won't forget you even then. I'll be waiting ... for you there, believing you'll be along one day. Just like I ... believed you'd be along one day ... for the last eighteen years."

She couldn't talk, couldn't squeeze a single word past the emotions stuck in her throat. Instead she held him and willed life into him. He was kind and wise and gentle, and he loved her—he always had. Even when he hadn't used the best judgment in showing her, still he loved her. Now she wanted another thirty years with him. At least.

Please ... please ...

She didn't know who she was pleading with, but it didn't matter. She had to try. Snuggling against him, her knees ached from the awkward position, but she didn't move until there was a sound at the door. Only then did she straighten and look past the years to his tender soul. "I love you, Daddy."

He gave her hand another squeeze. "I love you, sweetheart."

At that moment, a familiar-looking couple in their late fifties or early sixties walked through the door. Lauren looked at them and frowned. She knew them from somewhere. Their eyes held the haunting look of guilt and trepidation, as if maybe they were entering a place where they weren't welcome. In a rush, Shane went to them—and in a sudden flash she understood.

Sheila and Samuel Galanter. Shane's parents. The people who had once been her parents' closest friends. The people who took Shane from her. Lauren felt her knees start to shake and she braced herself against the hospital bed. Why had they come, and what could they possibly say now? For a moment she couldn't decide whether to excuse herself from the room or stay and hear what they had to say. She looked at the floor, her heart racing, and she made up her mind. She would stay.

Whatever was about to take place, she wanted a front-row seat to see it.

⁂

Angela was trying to keep from falling to the floor.

She was standing on the other side of Bill, opposite Lauren, when first Samuel, then Sheila walked through the door. At first Angela couldn't make herself believe what she was seeing. The stress of Bill's illness, the wonder at having Shane and Lauren back, all of it was maybe making her a little loopy.

But then Shane went to them. "Mom, Dad." He hugged them one at a time and then stepped back.

Angela couldn't see Shane's face, but she had the sense he wasn't surprised. Had he called them, asked them to come? Across the room, Emily moved close to Lauren and whispered something. Lauren nodded, her face pale.

Next to Angela, Bill slid a little higher on his pillow. "I can't believe it." He looked up at her, his voice hushed. The Galanters were still talking to Shane near the door, so they couldn't hear him. Bill covered her hand with his. "Did you know about this?"

Angela shook her head. Fear and trepidation filled her. What would the four of them say after so many years, so many hurts? She kept her eyes on Bill, her whispered words shaky. "I thought I was seeing things."

The Galanters made the first move. Sheila took a few steps into the room, her eyes vulnerable and heavy with ... could it be? Was it remorse? The beginnings of hope stirred in Angela's soul. Ten feet away now, Sheila looked at Bill, and then, after a long beat, she shifted her gaze. Angela swallowed hard as her eyes met that of her long-ago friend.

Sheila's voice broke as the first words left her lips. "I'm sorry, Angela. I was ... so wrong."

Angela couldn't speak or move. She didn't dare draw a breath or blink until the words found her heart. Sheila was here and she was sorry? Was it really true?

"Bill, Sheila's right." Samuel took a step closer and put his hand on the foot of Bill's bed. "We—" His eyes fell, and Sheila reached for his hand. When he looked up, his eyes shone with emotion. "We were wrong. We owe you an apology."

The entire scene played out in a handful of seconds, but still, so far she and Bill hadn't said a word. Angela's eyes were full, blurring her vision. What could she say after such a long time? Shane backed up and stood next to Emily and Lauren, the three of them doing their best to blend into the background.

Samuel cleared his throat and continued. "We were wrong, how we handled the situation with our kids." He narrowed his eyes and worked the muscles in his jaw. Then he gave a solid shake of his head. "We were wrong in too many ways to count."

"We knew Shane was here." Sheila took another step toward them. She looked at Bill. "We knew you were sick. And we had to come. We've let so much time pass."

Angela hung her head for a moment. Her knees were steady, but her whole body shook. There had been years and years when she believed she'd see Lauren again, and maybe even Shane. But she never once thought she'd see this—these old friends finding a way back to the same place. She looked up and her eyes met Sheila's. "I ... can't believe you came."

"We're so sorry." Samuel put his arm around Sheila's waist. He had been an intimidating businessman in his day, a man who neither smiled nor laughed easily. But now—if the sincerity in his eyes was any indication—he was a changed man.

Sheila held her hand out. “Forgive me, Angela … please.”

Angela felt herself break, felt Sheila’s words finally connect in her heart. Her tears fell hot and quick onto her cheeks as she held her hands out to her lost friend. “Sheila … of course. It wasn’t just you. We were all … all of us were at fault.” She embraced Sheila, overcome. There was no going back, no way to regain the years they’d lost, no way to undo the damage they’d done to their kids. But here now, forgiveness was happening, and it was the most wonderful feeling in the world.

She drew back and made a sad sound. “Why were we so stubborn?”

“I don’t know.” Sheila sniffed and smiled through her tears. A smile that showed how deeply she meant the apology, how sorry she was for everything that had happened between them.

Angela’s heart soared as the moment played out. The four of them had made a plan that separated their friendship, yes. But it had done more than that. Their actions had cost Lauren and Shane every hope of a future, of being a family with Emily. The cost was too high to measure.

Samuel worked his way toward Bill’s bed. With both hands he clasped his outstretched fingers. “It’s been too long, Bill.”

“Yes.” Bill kept his hands locked with Samuel’s for a long time. Long enough to erase the differences that had brought them to this point. Bill’s chin quivered as he looked up. “All that matters is you’re here now. And that you understand something.”

“What?” Samuel’s voice was thick with feeling.

“We’re every bit as sorry as you. What we did …” he looked the other direction at Lauren and Shane and Emily. Then he turned back to Samuel. “What we did to those kids was wrong.”

“It was.” Samuel looked at Lauren. “Forgive me. We … we didn’t know what we were doing.”

Angela studied Lauren, saw the doubt in her eyes and the small hesitancy in her expression. Apologies were well and good, but the things done to Lauren and Shane had changed their lives. Forgiveness would take time.

Lauren gave Samuel a stiff nod. "I know." She gave Emily a slight hug and reached out to rest her hand on Shane's shoulder. "We all would do things differently if we had another chance."

Lauren couldn't believe her eyes. She was still processing the scene playing out in the hospital room, and now Shane's father had apologized. Next to her, Emily leaned closer. "Another miracle," she whispered. "I prayed for this too."

But Lauren wasn't sure. How was it a miracle that the people who had separated her and Shane were here now? This was a private moment, her last few hours with her dad. She wanted to tell the Galanters to leave and come back in a year or so. When she'd had time to process everything that was happening.

All around her the apologies continued, and after a few minutes the two older couples found their way again, the way long lost friends do. Even when their differences had cost them half a lifetime, even when Lauren wasn't sure she liked the idea.

Throughout the day she and Emily and Shane stayed close, walking down to the cafeteria together at lunchtime and giving the friends time to catch up. For two days they stayed almost constantly around her father's bed, the sweet, tender moments with him marred only by the occasional update from the doctors that there was nothing they could do. He didn't have long. There was talk about him going home, but the decision was made that it would be too painful to move him.

He was comfortable in the hospital, the pain medication flowing through his IV at just the right rate to allow him conversations with her and Shane and Emily, with the Galanters, and especially with her mother. Once, sometime Monday afternoon, Lauren and Shane spent an hour in the cafeteria alone. Their conversations had been so consumed with her father that they hadn't talked much about each other.

"So ..." Shane sat across from her and covered her hands with his.

She knew what he meant, the way she'd always known. Their flights were scheduled to leave later that week, and they still hadn't found any answers. None that made sense, anyway. Her eyes held his. "Us, you mean?"

He wrapped his fingers around her hands. "I heard what your dad told you yesterday morning."

"I wondered." Her heart ached just looking at him. His eyes held a depth that took her breath away. He was conservative, a military guy with a fierce support for the war, but he didn't seem like any warmonger she'd ever written about. And how was that? Navy captains weren't supposed to have feelings like this, were they? Still, what was she supposed to say? That she'd move to Reno, Nevada, of all places? Settle down somewhere outside Fallon Naval Base and get excited about the fact that he was training the next generation of fighter pilots? She looked down at the place where their fingers came together. Maybe if she said nothing, they could sit like this forever, holding hands and pretending things were exactly the way they'd been when they were kids.

He tried again. "Can I go on record saying I agree with him?" His voice was light, but his eyes gave him away.

She didn't know what to say, so she fell back on her most familiar ally: teasing. "About what? About heaven?"

"Okay." He gave a thoughtful nod. "That too." His gaze held hers and wouldn't let go. "But mostly that love doesn't mean seeing eye to eye on everything."

She tilted her head, willing him to comprehend what they were up against. "Shane, I'm a senior reporter at one of the top magazines in the country, and I'm in that position because of my stories on the war in the Middle East." Sadness crept between every word. Sadness and longing and resignation. "There isn't a reader in the nation who doesn't know where I stand." She lowered her chin and kept her tone light. "And then there's you, over on the other side of the table."

"Navy captain, supporter of the Republican Party, fan of the president." His eyes melted into hers. He brushed his thumb along the top of her hand.

The move kicked out the foundation of her resolve. "Right."

"So ..." The people at other tables in the dining room seemed to fade from view, the conversation too deep for any distractions. "We'd have interesting dinner conversations, right?" He gave her the boyish grin that had haunted her dreams for a decade after he left. "Is that so bad?"

"Shane." She felt herself melting. "Really, I mean, think about it. What do we do? Get married and live at the Top Gun facility? So I can write articles condemning the war straight from command central?"

He shrugged. "You'd get quicker feedback."

"Anyway." She couldn't resist him another minute. Her salad was gone, so she pushed her tray back and slipped around the table to his side. "How was your lunch?"

"You changing subjects?" He crooked his finger beneath her chin and eased closer to her.

"You're quick, Shane." She breathed the words against his chin, moving her lips closer to his. "I always liked that about you."

"Really." His mouth found hers, and he slid his fingers up along her cheekbone. The kiss didn't last long, but it made her dizzy all the same. He drew back. "I thought you liked this." He kissed her again, his eyes full of light and love and humor. The way she remembered them being. "Besides, we wouldn't be the first couple separated by our politics. You've got Schwarzenegger and Shriver ... Mary Matalin and James Carville."

"I know." She exhaled hard. He wasn't making this easy. If she sat here much longer he might even start making sense. A slight thrill swirled in her heart at the thought, but she looked past it. "Those couples didn't live in different countries, though."

He looked like he wanted to volley back, but he didn't. Instead he brought his lips together and looked deeper into her heart, to the long ago places where memories of him once ruled. "There's always a way, Lauren."

Thoughts of her father drifted through her mind, followed by the fact that in a week or so this time together with Shane would probably be nothing more than a wonderful coda on a lifetime of wondering. Even though they hadn't solved anything, she was grateful to him, glad that he'd kept the discussion silly and lighthearted, and even hopeful. Now, when time was so desperately short, that's what they needed most.

On their way back up to her father's room, Shane eased her into a doorway. "Hi." The word was a breathy whisper as he brushed his face against hers. He kissed her once more and when he pulled away he said, "Just working on military public relations."

She had a serious answer, something about sensibilities and their obvious differences. But it wouldn't come to the surface. Without the words, she returned his kiss, breathless with the way he made her feel. When she took a breath she could do nothing but grin at him. "You know what?"

He brought his lips to hers once more and then found her eyes, his voice full of desire. "What?"

"You're good at it."

☙

Her daddy was going downhill fast.

By the next day he was too weak to do anything more than look at them through tired eyes. Close friends from her parents' church came by the hospital twice that morning to circle his bed, hold hands, and pray. The first few times Lauren didn't join in.

"I'll wait in the hall." She gave a polite smile, using the moment to visit the restroom or grab a water from the vending machine. But as she left that first time, the pastor's voice stopped her. She hesitated, standing in the hall, listening ... amazed. She'd prayed that way once, hadn't she? Back when she and Shane were so sorry for sleeping together?

In the course of the day, a dozen different prayers came back to her. She'd begged God to let Emily live and she'd begged him to help her find Shane. It was noon when it hit her. Emily was right.

God had done both. Maybe not in her timing, but then hadn't they always been taught that God had His ways, that His ways were better than their ways, even when it didn't feel like it? Another prayer was happening inside her father's room, so she leaned against the wall outside and tried to remember ...

How had it happened? How had she and God moved so far away from each other? The answer was easy. She pictured herself standing over the small hospital bed, Emily lying there gasping for breath, burning up. The doctor told her Emily had almost no chance of living, and so God was the only answer left. Lauren had begged Him to let her live.

She remembered what it felt like hours later to have the nurse tell her Emily was gone, the shakiness in her chest, the terror streaming through her veins. Okay, yes, God had let her daughter live. But hadn't He robbed her of the chance to see Emily grow up, to be a part of her life?

And what about Shane? God knew how badly she wanted to find him. If she'd come across him, then she would've felt compelled to go home again, and there she would've found Emily. A decade sooner or even more. Wasn't that God's fault too?

After starting her new life in Los Angeles, God became just one more part of her past, one more person she'd walked away from. Then, as she got into political reporting and moved her way up on the *Time* magazine staff, she began believing the same thing so many of her peers believed. That Christians were hypocrites.

She had only to check her e-mail to see that much. The meanest, most negative letters often came from readers who called themselves believers. But it wasn't just that. Lauren couldn't understand how a person with faith in Christ could also support the war. She hung her head and listened to the prayer taking place in her dad's room. Prayer wouldn't resolve anything. It wouldn't save her dad. And it wouldn't answer the questions building inside her.

Right on the heels of that thought, a voice raised, the words coming to Lauren as clearly as if she were inside the room rather than in the hallway.

"Lord, we know that all things happen for a reason, but that doesn't mean we understand this. We pray You'll be with our friend, Bill, and that You'll lead him gently from this world to the next. I know You'll be waiting for Him in that beautiful place, the place You've prepared for him. And so we thank You for Bill's life, for every day he's had with us and with his family. Please give them the ..."

Lauren hugged herself. It took all her strength to stand there and not go into the room, to not join that circle of people. But why? She shook her head. Guilt. Of course. What must her dad think, looking around and seeing her mom and Shane and Emily, special church friends, and even Shane's parents.

But not her.

Dad had been so certain in their talk the day before. When she got to heaven, he'd be waiting for her, just the way he'd waited for her all these years since she'd gone away. And if he was right, if there was a heaven, then her mother would be there, and Shane and Emily. All of them, everyone she loved. But what about her?

What about me, God? She pressed her lips together. Did God strike people dead for being sarcastic? But then, why should He?

He hadn't exactly delivered answers to her prayers. The same integrity that drove her to verify sources for her work hit her now like a sledgehammer.

God had *delivered the answers. Just not the way I wanted. So I walked away.* Something she was good at.

Drawing in a steady breath she peeked into the room. They were still praying, and with their eyes closed, heads bowed. Everyone except Shane. He must've heard her, and now he had one eye open and he gave a short nod for her to join him. She skirted silently around the outside of the circle, then slipped in between him and Emily.

Someone was saying, "We thank You most of all for the peace You've given this family. Your peace goes beyond our understanding because it happens on the inside of us, where our hearts are. Not on the outside where life can be so difficult. It's that internal peace You've given them. Restoration and healing, divine redemption, all of it has come to the Andersons in recent days, and we thank You. Your peace should be the goal of every believer, and today, well, we could take a lesson from Bill and Angela and their family."

Lauren felt her sinuses swelling again. Who *were* these people? They sounded so different. They certainly weren't like the Christians she'd known. But that didn't matter. Because something from the man's prayer caught at her. He mentioned peace, but not the peace she spent her days thinking about—not the kind that would bring an end to the war in Iraq and Afghanistan. What had he said? God's peace happens on the inside, where the heart is, right? Not on the outside where life was hard.

She pressed her hands more tightly into Emily's and Shane's. This was the peace she'd searched for all her life, wasn't it? And though she still wasn't sure how to find it or make it happen on the inside, suddenly, in that moment, standing there beside those she loved most in the world, it seemed possible. As she stayed in the circle of prayer she felt love and acceptance raining down on her, showering her with a feeling she hadn't ever known before. It was a feeling that lasted even after the moment ended and the church friends left.

And it had everything to do with prayer.

The hours passed slowly, with little response from her father, and late that night he slipped into a coma. The loss was enormous. Even with Shane and Emily and her mother huddled close around her, Lauren felt like she was falling from an airplane without a chute. All these years, she'd convinced herself her parents had been wrong, that their actions had cost her a lifetime with Shane and Emily. But she'd forgotten the people they really were. The father who had run along beside her when she learned to ride a bike, the one who went running with her on weekend mornings when she was in junior high, and who once in a while stopped to pick her a bouquet of wildflowers on the way home. He loved her as sure as summer followed spring. Love had indeed driven him to do the things he'd done when she was pregnant with Emily.

A pure, misguided sort of love.

Now that she was home, the good times were clear again. Her dad was a kindhearted, gentle man whose humor and compassion was like balm to a gaping wound that had never come close to healing. This time when the four of them gathered around to pray, Lauren did something she hadn't done since she left home—she silently joined her voice with theirs.

"It won't be long," the doctor told them. "He won't last through the night."

The man was right.

By one o'clock in the morning, her father's breathing slowed. Lauren watched the monitors, counting down as the numbers showing how much oxygen her father was getting fell. 80 ... 70 ... 55 ... 40 ...

Half an hour later, it was over. Her father's breathing stopped. Lauren stared, disbelieving, at the still form on the bed, then turned to cling to Shane and Emily. She clutched them close, burying her face against them, not sure if the sobs echoing around were hers or theirs. She let them go and turned to her mother, opening her arms and folding them around her as they grieved his loss.

The Galanters were there too, holding onto each other and quietly crying.

How could this be real? How could he be gone? Mere days ago he'd been well enough to sit with them, to visit and hold hands. It had been terrifyingly fast, not at all the way Lauren had thought cancer progressed. But at the same time it was merciful, because there had been little pain, no surgery, no horrendous chemotherapy or radiation. If only she could find some comfort in that. But there was none. Because all she knew was that her daddy was gone, and she'd missed way too many years with him.

Before they left the hospital, her mother looked at each of them, tears still on her cheeks. "For weeks I've been praying for your father to be healed." She folded her arms, hugging herself tightly. "I couldn't understand why God didn't answer me, why the cancer wasn't taken from him. God is the Healer, and we needed His help." She looked intently at Lauren and Shane and Emily, one at a time. "Today while we were praying, God made it clear that my prayers had been heard. Your father, your papa, was healed of something far worse than cancer." She smiled through her tears. "When we found you, Lauren, and you, Shane ... watching the two of you discover Emily ... well, Bill was healed of a broken heart."

Sorrow and peace wrapped around her grief, and Lauren held tight to Shane's arm. If only she could have another few weeks with him, another day. Maybe they could've talked about this healing her mother was talking about. She squeezed her eyes shut and leaned her head on Shane's shoulder. *Daddy ... I can't believe you're gone ... just when we found each other again.* The pain was so consuming it threatened to bring her to her knees. But if her mother was right, then it wasn't all sad. It couldn't be.

Daddy had been healed in a way that still seemed unbelievable. And that brought about a sort of hope that held her up, kept her from falling. Next to her, Emily had her arm around both of them. Her daughter's tears came harder now, but something was different. Now her sobs were almost joyful. She looked up at her mother and the connection Lauren felt between the two of them was stronger than ever. And suddenly Lauren understood the joy in Emily's tears. She smiled at her daughter and felt the mix of sorrow and triumph in her own expression. Because her father wasn't the only one healed of a broken heart that week.

They all were.

Twenty-Eight

For all they'd lost and all they'd found, in the end they came full circle.

Shane couldn't get past that fact, not through Bill Anderson's touching funeral or in the days that followed. Now it was Saturday, and as he stood near the ticket counter at Chicago O'Hare, Emily and Lauren at his side, Lauren's mother and his parents next to them, the sad truth was glaring. They were right back where they'd left off nearly nineteen years ago—standing on the brink of good-bye.

Shane's parents' plane would be the first one out. Lauren's was next, and his was a few hours later. They walked as far as they could toward the security line, and then his mother turned to Angela. The two hugged and held on for a long while. When they pulled apart, his mother said, "Think about it, will you, Angela? I can't believe God would give us another chance to be neighbors."

"Definitely." Lauren's mother had dark circles under her swollen eyes, and she looked gaunt from the grief. But for all of that, her expression held a supernatural peace. "We'll have to get things in order and sell the house." She looked at Emily, and the two shared a sad smile. "We're ready to move. Emily wants to finish college on the West Coast, anyway. We don't have anything keeping us in Illinois now."

Emily looked at Lauren, and Shane's heart broke for her. His daughter looked like a lost little girl, caught up in more emotions and changes than anyone should have to go through in a week's time. Emily gave Lauren a sad smile. "You can put in a good word for me at USC, right?"

"Of course." So far Lauren had made no promises to any of them, other than the obvious: she would keep in regular contact with Emily. Now she looked weary, buried beneath the weight of the good-byes that lay ahead. She put her arm around Emily and pulled her close. "They'll be lucky to have you."

Shane stood on Emily's other side, and he smiled at her. "Once you move out west, we'll see each other all the time. LA is a day's drive from Reno, and only an hour in the air." He stroked the back of her head, her silky dark hair. Losing Bill had been terribly hard on her. Shane could feel how much she needed her dad now that the most important man in her life was gone.

His parents added their approval. "We've missed so many years with you." His dad held out his arms, and Emily went to him. "All we can do now is catch up."

"Yep." Emily put her arms around Shane's mother too, and a sad sort of quiet fell over them. His dad looked at his watch. "We better get going."

Shane stepped up and gave them each a hug. Though the mistakes his parents made hadn't severed his relationship with them, as it had Lauren and her parents, there still was a sense of loss there, beneath the surface. It was something they never talked about. But that was going to change. Shane knew it. He could feel a new depth to their relationship. One more bit of proof that healing had, indeed, come to all of them. He stepped back beside Emily and held up his hand. "See you next week sometime."

Another round of good-byes was spoken and the four of them watched his parents head through a door and file into the security line. When they were out of sight, an ache settled in Shane's gut. The hardest part lay just ahead.

Emily was still clinging to Lauren, but she was looking down, as if she couldn't face the moment just yet. Lauren held out her hand to her mother. Angela didn't hesitate. She came and the three generations of Anderson women formed a tight knot of tears. Shane wanted to join them, but they needed this time—just the three of them, a picture of what a mother-daughter bond should be. He could hear their voices, and he let their words soak into his soul.

"Do you forgive me?" Angela rested her head on Lauren's. "I'm so sorry, honey. You'll never know—"

"Of course I forgive you, but it was me too." Lauren's voice was raspy. Her shoulders trembled as she spoke. "I only wish I'd come home sooner."

"I'll always see us the way we were in the family room that night." Emily smiled through her tears. "Papa sitting there with his big smile, and all of us together for the first time." She made a sound that was mostly laugh. "I have parents and grandparents, and a legacy of love someone should write a book about! I even have my special papa in heaven waiting for me. What could be better than that?"

Only one thing, of course, but Emily seemed determined not to bring that up. Last night she had found Shane and Lauren seated on the living room sofa, talking. She plopped down between them and announced, "I think you two should get married."

"Is that right?" Lauren looked surprised, but she kept her deeper feelings to herself.

"Yeah, I mean—" she looked at him—"you already asked her."

Shane's eyes widened. "I did?"

Emily poked him with her elbow. "Eighteen years ago, silly."

"Oh." Shane gave Lauren a quick grin. "She has a point."

Emily's eyes found Lauren next. "And you already said yes."

Shane had barely restrained a grin as he held up his finger. "Another point."

But Lauren only gave them both a wistful look. "If only it were that easy."

Emily hadn't pushed the issue, but before she turned in for bed she pulled Shane aside. "I'll never stop praying about it."

He winked at her. "Me neither."

So it was no wonder Emily was being quiet on the matter here, in the midst of good-byes. She'd done what she could. Now it was up to Lauren and God. Most of all, God.

The group hug among the three women ended, and they pulled apart. Lauren looked over her shoulder at him and held out her hand. Shane took it, savoring the feel of her skin against his.

Angela was asking, "Will you stay in Afghanistan?"

"For now." Lauren's answer was quick, but it cut Shane deep. He tried to catch Lauren's eye, but she kept from looking at either him or Emily. "I love what I do there." She finally looked at Emily, her expression tender. "I can come back often."

Shane wanted to shout, "What about me? What about *us?*" But that would wait until they were alone. Instead he took a deep breath and looked at the faces around him. "I need to get going."

"Me too." Lauren picked up her bag and swung it over her shoulder.

"All right, then," Angela held out her arms and hugged first Shane, then Lauren. She let herself linger with her daughter. "Be careful, Lauren. Please."

"I will." Lauren rubbed her left shoulder, the one that was still healing. "Especially now."

It was Shane's turn. He hugged Lauren's mother, and then Emily. For a moment, he kept his hand along the side of his daughter's face. He looked down into those dark eyes, marveling.

"I'm so proud of the young woman you are." Time would never come between them again, not the way it had before. The moment he'd seen her, held her in his arms, she'd become part of him. So much so that it was tearing at his composure to leave her. "I'm sorry I wasn't there for you when you were growing up."

She covered his hand with hers and clung tight. "You didn't know."

"But I do now." He kissed her cheek and let his hand slip to her shoulder. "We've got a lot of good times ahead, sweetheart."

"Yep." She hugged him again and their eyes held as he stepped back. She looked at Lauren next. "Mom ..."

They came together in a last embrace that made Shane's throat thick. There would be phone calls and e-mail and visits, God willing. But with Lauren in the Middle East, any good-bye could be their last.

He watched the two of them, knowing they were too torn up to say anything more. Finally Angela put her arm around Emily, and the two of them waved. Then they turned and headed for the exit. Shane and Lauren watched them until they were gone. Then, without saying a word, Lauren fell into his arms.

"I didn't want the week to end." She mumbled the words against his chest.

"It doesn't have to." He kissed the top of her head.

She said nothing, and after a few seconds he picked up his bag and the two of them walked through the door and got into the security line. They held hands as they walked to her gate. Lauren's plane was already boarding.

He faced her and lifted her chin with his fingers. "Did you hear what I said earlier? What I've been saying all week?"

Her eyes held a sort of torment he hadn't seen before, as if the battle inside her was far more frightening than the one she was going back to write about. She took a step closer, so their legs were touching. "Yes." The word sounded strained. "Yes. I heard."

"So then ..." He kept his tone easy, his words slow. Even if it killed him to tell her good-bye after finding her again, there would be no last-minute sales pitch to convince her to stay with him. His heart hurt and he wanted to weep, but now wasn't the time. Instead, he dug deep down and found a trace of humor. "Does this mean you're breaking our engagement?"

A single laugh burst from her throat, and she let her forehead fall against his chest. "Shane." She lifted her eyes to his again. "Be serious."

He hesitated. "Why, Lauren?" He felt the smile fade from his face. With his eyes holding hers, he traced her jaw, her neck. "Would that convince you to stay with me?"

She brought her hands up along the sides of his face, and with fresh tears brimming in her eyes, she kissed him. It was a kiss filled with finality, and when she drew back she was breathless, her emotions giving way. "I'll think about it, Shane." She shook her head. "I just don't see how it can work."

He understood. As he searched her eyes, he prayed the way he'd been praying since their first conversation that week. *Please God ... show us how to make this come together.* And in that instant he realized something. It wasn't only their politics that were different. It was their faith. Without that in common, Lauren might be right. *God we need You ... she needs You.*

"What are you thinking?" Her voice was low, her eyes locked on his.

He worked his fingers through her hair and kissed her once more. "I'm trying not to."

"Attention passengers—" a tinny voice came over the loud speaker system—"this is the final boarding call for Flight 92 to New York. All ticketed passengers please proceed directly to Gate C20 for immediate boarding."

He took a step back and pain cut through him, as though his heart were being ripped in half. He caught his breath, forced himself to smile, to speak. "You better go."

She nodded, too choked up to talk. She mouthed the words, "Bye, Shane." And then, with a last look at him, she turned and headed for the Jetway.

There were no desperate statements, no promises that she'd call or write or stay in touch. She just turned ... and was gone.

Swallowing hard, he stared at the terminal around him without seeing anything. Hoards of people pushed past, but he barely noticed. He just stood there, unable to take a step away from the gate, to be the one to put more space between them.

Finally, his feet took over. He drifted toward the window and watched the plane back away, shift gears, and begin positioning on the runway. He could still see her face, her blonde hair and blue eyes. Could she see him too? Did she feel what he felt? That even though she was leaving, their hearts were still connected? Would always be connected?

Father God ... help.

Things had worked out for everyone that week. Emily had her parents, and Bill had a place in heaven. His parents and Lauren's had found friendship and healing, and none of them would ever be the same again because of it. Yes, things had worked out for everyone.

Everyone except Lauren and him.

He kept his eyes on the aircraft, watching the same window, the one where he was sure he could see her, no matter how far away the plane was. Finally the craft circled into place, and after a brief pause, barreled down the runway, lifting up through a hole in the sky.

Taking Lauren with it.

Only then, did Shane drop to the nearest chair, cover his face with his hands and let the tears come.

Twenty-Nine

Lauren was one of the first to exit the plane. She collected her things and headed out onto the concourse, not really aware of anything around her. Her mind was consumed with Shane, with their time together, with all she'd turned her back on. How had she let things go so terribly wrong?

For the past six hours she'd done nothing but relive every wonderful moment with him, weighing it against the reality of the life she had in Afghanistan. From Chicago to New York where she had to change planes, she'd asked herself the same question over and over again: it couldn't work, could it?

No. How could it? How could she believe the way she believed or cover the war the way she had always covered it, and spend her nonworking hours sharing a life with a navy flight instructor at the Top Gun facility. And what about their beliefs? He spoke about God at every turn, and she ... well, she was still trying to forgive Him.

She and Shane together? The idea was ludicrous. But by the time she reached New York she could no longer deny one very obvious truth. Letting Shane go now was even more so.

When the plane taxied to the gate, she hurried off and talked with the woman at the counter. Yes, the woman told her. She could do this, and yes, they could see that her bags followed her. But she had just thirty minutes if she wanted to make the flight.

Lauren paid the price, then pulled her cell phone from her pocket and dialed the Los Angeles office of *Time* magazine. When she had her editor on the line she had to stifle a bout of giggles. "Listen, I have a favor to ask."

"Whatever you want, Gibbs." She'd worked with this editor for three years. "We just hope you're ready to get back to work. The magazine needs you."

"I'm ready." She swallowed, not quite believing that she was doing this. "But I need time away from Afghanistan. I want a temporary new assignment, if that's all right."

"Sure." Her editor didn't hesitate. "You've earned that much." He hesitated. "Where do you want to go?"

She closed her eyes and lifted her face. "Reno, Nevada."

"Reno?" A pause. "Are you crazy?"

She smiled. "Yes." Another giggle. "You know what? It's wonderful!"

With her editor's promise to make the arrangements, Lauren ran from one concourse to the next, barely making her flight. Now, if the schedules had held up, her plane would land fifteen minutes before his.

Her flight was quick, and before she knew it, she was walking out the door, into the Reno Airport. With each step, she picked up her pace, and with five minutes to spare she found a seat at the gate, his gate. One with a direct view of the Jetway. When she was sure she had enough time, she dug through her bag until she found it. The small cardboard box that was never more than a few yards from her.

The whole week, every time she and Shane were together, she'd wanted to pull it from her bag and share it with him. Because the moment she did so, he'd know. She'd never forgotten, not through the years of college, no matter where her reporting took her. But the moment had never seemed right.

Now she looked at the faded, creased photographs and-—careful not to damage the pictures in any way, she took out the ring. It still stirred emotions in her, memories of a love that nothing in all her life had equaled. With deliberate care, she slipped the ring on her baby finger, closed the small box, and placed the box back into her bag. No, she couldn't have brought out these things earlier. This way she'd had time to think it through. It was true, they wouldn't have everything in common. But they shared what mattered most for now, and in time they would figure out if the rest would work or not.

Emily's face danced in her mind, and tears stung Lauren's eyes. They had a daughter—their precious baby girl, all grown up and longing to be loved—and they shared a past and a romance that knew nothing of struggles with faith or political differences. She was pretty sure she believed in God, after all. And if He was real, well then, she and God had some mountains to scale. But mountains were meant to be climbed, right? And the politics thing, well, Shane had been right. If others could pull off a bipartisan marriage, maybe they could do the same thing.

There was a rustling of activity behind the gate counter, and an aircraft pulled into view. Lauren's heart beat so hard she thought it might burst through her chest. But at least it wasn't broken anymore.

She stood, her bag high on her shoulder, and watched the people file through the door. A mother with two babies; a group of businessmen; two couples, tanned and laughing, moving slowly and talking with their hands ...

And then he was there. At the doorway.

Lauren started to shake. Emotion flooded her, coursing through her veins and making her hands and feet tingle. She felt hot and cold at the same time. Would she fall to her knees, faint from all she was feeling? *Lord, if You're real ... I can't believe this. What is this feeling?* She wasn't sure what startled her more: her reaction to seeing Shane, or that she'd spoken to God about it.

Sucking in air, she took a step closer, and then another. Shane followed those in front of him through the door, staring at the ground as he walked. He looked so ... grief stricken. Defeated.

Oh, God, I did that to him. I'm so sorry ... I love him so much!

As though he heard her broken inner cry, Shane hesitated—-and looked up. Their gazes locked, and she saw the reality hit him like a physical force, saw the emotions flash in his eyes. Disbelief and shock and amazement. And then, shining out with such intensity that it engulfed her, love. A love that made Lauren feel like she could fly.

He moved, slowly at first and then in a rush that closed the distance between them. Before she had time to take a breath, his arms were around her, clutching her, and they were rocking, holding on to each other the way she'd ached to hold him every hour that they'd been apart. Lauren wasn't sure how long they stood there, but finally they shuffled to the side, out of the way of the other passengers. Shane searched her eyes. "What ... how ... ?"

She grinned. "I called my editor." Her eyes danced, and the feel of his joy flowed down to her soul. "I told him maybe I better be stationed at Reno for awhile."

"You did?" He clasped his hands at the small of her back, holding tight to her. The familiar teasing filled his voice. "How come?"

She lifted one shoulder. "I figured you had a point." A giggle slipped from her overjoyed heart.

"A point?"

"Yes." She leaned up and kissed him, kissed him in a way that left no doubts about her feelings. "Magazine reporters are supposed to be unbiased, right?"

"Right." He brought his lips to hers again, cradling her face in his hands. "So?"

"So, maybe it's time I spend a little time on military public relations."

He chuckled, and it became a full-blown bout of laughter. The whole time he held on to her, his head tipped back, delighting in the moment.

When his laughter died down, she pulled the ring from her little finger. "Here." She handed it to him, waiting as he recognized what it was. "Do you still mean it?"

He looked at her, lost in her eyes. Then he took her left hand and with heartbreaking tenderness placed it on her ring finger. "I love you, Lauren Anderson."

"I love you too." She held her breath. He'd stopped short of asking her to marry him, but that was okay. Maybe, if the next season in their lives went the way she wanted it to go, the question would come. For now, though, they could at least give it a try because they had time. Sweet precious time.

He still had her hand in his. "God brought us together, and now nothing can ever take us apart. I'll never love anyone like I love you, the way I love you. Even now."

She hugged him, and suddenly he lifted her off her feet and swung her around in a circle. When he set her down, he raised his fist in the air and shouted out loud. "Thank You, God!"

People passing by looked at them, and a few smiled. In that moment Lauren recognized the feeling inside her, the one that was still flooding her with warmth. Peace. Again not the peace she'd spent so much time thinking about all these years, but a peace that was deeper, more lasting. A peace she wanted to feel all the rest of her days.

Shane was pulling his cell phone from his pocket, opening it and grinning at her.

"What are you doing?" She held onto his elbow, watching him, smiling so big it hurt.

"The thing I've been dying to do since I saw you standing here." He tapped a series of numbers into the phone. "I'm calling our daughter."

☙

Emily hung up the phone with her dad and darted through the house to tell her grandma the news. Her mother and father were together again! Yes, they had a lot to work through, her dad had told her, but they were together. That was all that mattered.

Her mom was as thrilled as she was, but Emily couldn't talk about it for long. She had something important to do first. She went back to the kitchen, grabbed the phone book, and looked up the number for Wheaton College. It was time to make good on a very special promise.

God gave her the miracle she'd prayed for—every last detail of it. They would always miss Papa, but suddenly the future looked like it might be everything she'd ever dreamed of. She'd asked God to make her an instrument of peace. Her birth had torn everyone apart, but in the past few weeks God had used her to bring her family together again. No, the final chapter hadn't been written. But she believed it would be, that the God who had seen to every last detail of this miracle would see her parents through the next season of their lives, as well.

Now she would follow through on what she'd promised Him.

She found the phone number to the university, dialed it, and asked for the journalism instructor. The receptionist put her on hold for a moment, but then a familiar voice picked up the line.

"Hello?"

Emily's heart soared. "Ms. Parker?"

"Yes?"

"This is Emily Anderson. I've, well, I've had some personal issues to deal with at home, but I wanted you to know I'll be back when school starts."

"I heard that your grandpa died." Her voice was warm, sympathetic. "Your grandma called and left a message." She hesitated. "I'm very sorry, Emily."

"Yes." She swallowed. "Me too." A robin landed on a patch of grass where the snow had melted. It hopped around, found a worm, and flew off again. New life was like that, always just beneath the icy surface. Emily blinked and held the phone tighter. "Can I ask you a favor?"

"Of course. Anything."

"Could you save me a spot for a short story in the creative magazine? I know you're assigning articles this week, and I have a special one. It's a story I want the whole world to know."

"Really?" She sounded interested. "What's it about?"

"It's about life and love. And miracles." She grinned and the joy inside her felt absolutely wonderful. "I'm calling it *Even Now*."

From the Author

Dear Reader Friends,

Some time ago I felt the Lord bringing together in my heart a story about peace. Obviously, at this time in our nation's history, peace is a volatile topic, something bantered about in casual conversations and debated by pundits across the country. Where the line between parties once was a picket fence, in many cases now it's solid brick and razor wire.

The war in the Middle East has contributed to this, and so has the strength of both support and animosity toward our current leader, President George Bush. In the news not so long ago, a woman was chased and threatened with her life for having a bumper sticker supporting the president.

The issues surrounding Operation Enduring Freedom are complex. One of the benefits of writing about a character like Lauren Anderson was that I felt sympathy for people on her side of the fence. Lauren had nothing against American soldiers. She simply believed that peace would only be found with peaceful behavior. Shane also was sympathetic. He wasn't a person crazy for war, and he certainly had no blood thirst. Rather he believed peace came through strength. He didn't want to see children orphaned or soldiers killed. He only wanted to help protect and defend.

Because of these two characters, I learned something while writing *Even Now.* I learned that once in a while the two sides are closer than they think. Especially when faith is a common factor. The issues are complex, and so I think sometimes the best way to work things out is, well, not to work them out. If you and someone you love have a difference of opinion on something, maybe it's best to let it stay that way. Respect each other's right to believe what you believe. Respect each other. Agree to disagree, my dad used to say.

When people do that, I've seen the most amazing result: love happens. People start finding the things they do have in common and they start loving the person for simply being a brother or a father or an aunt or a cousin. Obviously there are some differences of opinion that happen because one person is standing by Scripture and another person isn't. In this case, please go ahead and take a stand for the truth. That's what Jesus wants us to do. But at the same time, take your stand in love.

Sometimes we need to say, "I don't agree with that and here are the reasons why. But I love you so much. Let's go to lunch."

Conversations like that will build bridges between you and the people with whom you're at odds. And often, when we love people despite our disagreements with them, we give them a chance to cross that very same bridge. In the process, we may find more common ground than ever before.

Ultimately, I loved writing about Lauren and Shane, because real peace isn't found by either of their methods. It's not found at antiwar protests, and it's not found by dropping bombs—although there are times when both events might be appropriate, so long as our troops are always supported. Here's the point that Emily understood so well: real, lasting peace is only found through a lifesaving relationship with Jesus Christ.

Period.

Knowing Christ means that all the world might be falling apart just outside your front door—maybe just inside it—yet that inner peace, that inner knowing, remains unshaken. A quick formula for all of us would be this: Does your world feel out of control? Are you lacking peace in your marriage, your finances, your health, or your relationships?

Add Christ.

Add prayer and Bible study and conversations with other people who share your faith.

Your mind is only so big. To the degree that it is occupied with Christ, you simply won't have anything left for unrest and worry, frustration or hopelessness.

If you're reading about Jesus for the first time, then please take a few minutes and quietly—in your own words—ask Him to come into your life and clean house. Ask Him to be in charge of you from now on, and let Him be not only your Savior, but your Lord, your Master.

If you make that decision for the first time, here and now, contact a Bible-believing church in your area. Talk to a pastor, get involved in a newcomers' group, and start the greatest journey of your life. If you aren't able to do that, then send me an e-mail and write, "NEW LIFE" in the subject line. My e-mail address is *rtnbykk@aol.com*.

I love receiving letters from so many of you, and recently I received a very sad letter. A woman was alone after her husband had left her, and now she wanted to kill herself. She envied people who had died, because at least they had peace. I was grateful for the chance to tell her that life is always worth living. No matter what your situation, God has a plan in it, a purpose, a reason why your life can make a difference. Many times people who feel this way need professional help and medical advice. But many other people who struggle with such thoughts need to add a whole lot more God to their schedules. Volunteer time, Sunday school, various church ministries. Most churches are crying out for God in prayer, God in Bible study, and God in service. Remember, more God equals more peace. Or as many people say: No God, no peace. Know God, know peace.

Things are going very well—if very busy—in our happy household. My husband is considering staying home from his teaching job next year and homeschooling our boys. It's a funny situation, because we love our local public schools. They're truly wonderful, with many of the old-fashioned benefits that too many schools have let slip away. But we are excited to see what "A Year with Dad" will bring about. Also, it will give us much more time together as a family—since I can write the books God gives me while they're having lessons.

Please continue to pray for us. We greatly appreciate your love and concern, and we feel your prayers time and time again. If you're already receiving my e-mail newsletter, look for the next one soon! If you'd like to receive it, stop by my website at *www.KarenKingsbury.com* and fill in your e-mail address.

As always, I love hearing from you. I pray that you are enjoying the Christmas season, and remembering through it all the call to love one another—even the people sitting opposite the fence from you.

Until next time ... in His light and love, Karen Kingsbury.

Book Club Questions

Explain how Shane's parents reacted to the news that their son's girlfriend was pregnant. Why do you think they reacted that way?

How about Lauren's parents? How did they react to the news, and why?

"What would Jesus do?" is a common question these days. Analyze both of the above situations and discuss them in light of that question: What *would* Jesus have done in the situation with Shane's parents? What about Lauren's parents?

What were the first signs that the friendship between the two couples was in trouble? Why did the friendship between the two couples fall apart so quickly?

Tell about a time when you were tempted to manipulate a situation to your advantage.

How did the two couples manipulate their children, and what danger signs did they ignore along the way?

Explain how deception played a role in the falling-out that happened between Lauren and her parents.

Tell about a situation where you or a person in your life has come out well-adjusted after a difficult start or a difficult set of circumstances.

What were the signs that Shane wasn't ready to marry the politician's daughter?

Lauren liked to think of herself as a gutsy reporter. What were the signs that she also had a tender heart?

What do you think is important for a marriage to work? Is it important to share political beliefs?

Emily prayed for a miracle and God granted it. How have you seen Him work miracles in your life?

For many years Emily longed for her parents. How is God the parent to those without parents?

God always answers prayers, but not always in our timing or the way we had hoped. Explain how this truth played out in the book, and how has it played out in your life?

Discuss God's provision in the lives of Emily and her family members. How has God provided for you in difficult times?

EVER AFTER

In Memory of Joshua Dingler

I bring you this book in honor of the memory of Joshua Dingler, age nineteen.

At the final stages of editing *Ever After*, I received a letter from one of my readers—Karen Dingler. She said God had used one of my books to help her understand that her son, Joshua Dingler of the First Battalion, the 108th Armor Regiment of the U.S. Army in Calhoun, Georgia, had not died in vain.

What defined Joshua was his life, how he lived. Joshua was the son of a pastor, Tommy Dingler. His mother had just taken on the role of his army unit's family support group leader when his family learned of his death. Joshua left behind a younger brother, Samuel.

When he was a young boy, Joshua played Little League baseball. He was a Boy Scout who earned the rank Life Scout, and in middle school, he went to Australia and New Zealand as a student ambassador for People 2 People. He helped out at church and volunteered at the sound booth. He was in JROTC at East Paulding High School in Hiram, Georgia, where he was known and loved by everyone he came in contact with. He would defend NASCAR to anyone who questioned it as a sport. Joshua planned to come home and marry his high school love and wanted to be a history teacher.

In honor of Joshua, I am starting two new links on my website, *www.KarenKingsbury.com.* The first is for Active Military

Heroes. The second is for Fallen Military Heroes. If you have a friend or loved one serving our country, please send me a photo and a brief description of that person—name, rank, where they are serving, and how we can pray for them. The Active Military Heroes page will honor these men and women. It will be a place where readers can see the face on the fight for freedom, a place where readers can visit to pray for each other. If you've lost a loved one or a friend in military action, please send that photo and a brief description also. This will be posted on my Fallen Military Heroes page. Joshua Dingler's photo will be at the top of that page. If you are sending a photo and information, please put the word "SOLDIER" in the subject line and send it to *Kingsburydesk@aol.com*.

As you read the pages of *Ever After*, think about Joshua Dingler. The sacrifice for freedom is a real one. And please pray for and support the families and members of the U.S. Military. Pray every day.

In His light and love,
Karen Kingsbury

Joshua Dingler, 1986–2005

Acknowledgments

As always, this book couldn't have come together without the help of many people. First, a special thanks to my great friends at Zondervan, who believe in this sequel and have enormous dreams and prayers for the way it will touch people and change lives. Thank you!

Also, thanks to my amazing agent, Rick Christian, president of Alive Communications. I am amazed more as every day passes at your integrity, your brilliant talent, and your commitment to the Lord and to getting my Life-Changing Fiction™ out to readers all over the world. You are a strong man of God, Rick. You care for my career as if you were personally responsible for the souls God touches through these books. Thank you for looking out for my personal time—the hours I have with my husband and kids. I couldn't do this without you.

As always, this book wouldn't be possible without the help of my husband and kids, who will eat just about anything when I'm on deadline and who understand and love me anyway. I thank God I'm still able to spend more time with you than with my pretend people—as Austin calls them. Thanks for understanding the sometimes crazy life I lead and for always being my greatest support.

Also, thanks to my mother and assistant, Anne Kingsbury, for her great sensitivity and love for my readers. You are a reflection of my own heart, Mom, or maybe I'm a reflection of yours. Either way, we are a great team, and I appreciate you more than you know. I'm grateful, also, for my dad, Ted Kingsbury, who is and always has been my greatest encourager. I remember when I was a little girl, Dad, and you would say, "One day, honey, everyone will read your books and know what a wonderful writer you are." Thank you for believing in me long before anyone else ever did. Thanks also to my sisters, Tricia and Susan and Lynne, who help out with my business when the workload is too large to see around. I appreciate you!

And a thanks to Katie Johnson, who runs a large part of my business life—everything from my accounting to my calendar. God brought you to me, Katie, and I'll be grateful as long as I'm writing for Him. Don't ever leave, okay? And to Olga Kalachik, whose hard work helping me prepare for events allows me to operate a significant part of my business from my home. The personal touch you both bring to my ministry is precious to me, priceless to me ... thank you with all my heart.

And thanks to my friends and family who continue to surround me with love and prayer and support. I could list you by name, but you know who you are. Thank you for believing in me and for seeing who I really am. A true friend stands by through the changing seasons of life and cheers you on, not for your successes, but for staying true to what matters most. You are the ones who know me that way, and I'm grateful for every one of you. Please keep praying for me, since I can't do a page of this, not even a word, without God's strength and gift.

Of course, the greatest thanks goes to God Almighty, the most wonderful Author of all—the Author of life (Hebrews 12:2). The gift is Yours. I pray I might have the incredible opportunity and responsibility to use it for You all the days of my life.

Dedicated To ...

Donald, my prince charming. In this season of life, with you working as full-time teacher here at home for our boys, I am maybe more proud of you than ever. I'm amazed at the way you blend love and laughter, tenderness and tough standards, to bring out the best in our boys. A second season of homeschooling? Wow! Don't for a minute think that your role in all this is somehow smaller. You have the greatest responsibility of all. Not only with our children, but in praying for me as I write and speak and go about this crazy, fun job God has given me. I couldn't do it without you. Thanks for loving me, for being my best friend, and for finding "date moments" amidst even the most maniacal or mundane times. My favorite times are with you by my side. I love you always, forever.

Kelsey, my precious daughter. You are just newly seventeen, and somehow that sounds more serious than the other ages. As if we jumped four years over the past twelve months. Seventeen brings with it the screeching of brakes on a childhood that has gone along full speed until now. Seventeen? Seventeen years since I held you in the nursery, feeling a sort of love I'd never felt before? Seventeen sounds like bunches of lasts all lined up ready to take the stage—and college counselors making plans to take my little girl from home into a brand-new big world. Seventeen tells me it won't be much longer. Sometimes I find myself barely able to exhale. The ride is so fast, I can only try not to blink so I won't miss a minute. Like the most beautiful springtime flower, I see you growing and unfolding, becoming interested in current events and formulating godly viewpoints that are yours alone. The same is true in dance, where you are simply breathtaking on stage. I believe in you, honey. Keep your eyes on Jesus and the path will be easy to follow. Don't ever stop dancing. I love you.

Tyler, my beautiful song. Can it be that you are fourteen and helping me bring down the dishes from the top shelf? Just yesterday, people who called confused you with Kelsey. Now they confuse you with your dad—in more ways than one. You are on the bridge, dear son, making the transition between Neverland and Tomorrowland, and becoming a strong, godly young man in the process. Keep giving Jesus your very best and always remember that you're in a battle. In today's world, Ty, you need His armor every day, every minute. Don't forget ... when you're up there on stage, no matter how bright the lights, I'll be watching from the front row, cheering you on. I love you.

Sean, my wonder boy. Your sweet nature continues to be a bright light in our home. It seems a lifetime ago that we first brought you—our precious son—home from Haiti. It's been my great joy to watch you grow and develop this past year, learning more about reading and writing and, of course, animals. You're a walking encyclopedia of animal facts, and that too brings a smile to my face. Recently a cold passed through the family, and you handled it better than any of us. Smiling through your fever, eyes shining even when you felt your worst. Sometimes I try to imagine if everyone, everywhere had your outlook—what a sunny place the world would be. Your hugs are something I look forward to, Sean. Keep close to Jesus. I love you.

Josh, my tender tough guy. You continue to excel at everything you do, but my favorite time is late at night when I poke my head into your room and see that—once again—your nose is buried in your Bible. You really get it, Josh. I loved hearing you talk about baptism the other day, how you feel ready to make that decision, that commitment to Jesus. At almost twelve, I can only say that every choice you make for Christ will take you closer to the plans He has for your life. By being strong in the Lord, first and foremost, you'll be strong at everything else. Keep winning for Him, dear son. You make me so proud. I love you.

EJ, my chosen one. You amaze me, Emmanuel Jean! The other day you told me you pray often, and I asked you what about. "I thank God a lot," you told me. "I thank Him for my health and my life and my home." Your normally dancing eyes grew serious. "And for letting me be adopted into the right family." Well. I still feel the sting of tears when I imagine you praying that way. I'm glad God let you be adopted into the right family too. One of my secret pleasures is watching you and Daddy becoming so close. I'll glance over at the family room during a playoff basketball game on TV, and there you'll be, snuggled up close to him, his arm around your shoulders. As long as Daddy's your hero, you have nothing to worry about. You couldn't have a better role model. I know that Jesus is leading the way, and that you are excited to learn the plans He has for you. But for you, this year will always stand out as a turning point. Congratulations, honey! I love you.

Austin, my miracle child. Can my little boy really be nine years old? Even when you're twenty-nine, you'll be my youngest, my baby. I guess that's how it is with the last child, but there's no denying what my eyes tell me. You're not little anymore. Even so, I love that—once in a while—you wake up and scurry down the hall to our room so you can sleep in the middle. I still see the blond-haired infant who lay in intensive care, barely breathing, awaiting emergency heart surgery. I'm grateful for your health, precious son; grateful God gave you back to us at the end of that long ago day. Your heart remains the most amazing part of you, not only physically, miraculously, but because you have such kindness and compassion for people. One minute, tough boy hunting frogs and snakes out back, pretending you're an Army Ranger, and then getting teary-eyed when Horton the Elephant nearly loses his dust speck full of little Who people. Be safe, baby boy. I love you.

And to God Almighty, the Author of life, who has, for now, blessed me with these.

EVER AFTER

One

Two blue and gray fighter jets raced low over the neighborhood and looped toward the barren mountains in the west. Lauren Gibbs heard the vibration in the subtle rattle of picture frames on the mantel, sensed it in the wood floor of the old house, felt it all the way to her soul. Training drills, same as most days. She froze long enough to watch them, long enough to catch her fiancé's attention.

"They still bug you."

It wasn't a question. Shane Galanter doled out the stack of plates in his hand one at a time onto the white linen tablecloth.

"Not really." Lauren grabbed the napkins and followed behind him, setting one at each place. She caught his eye and hesitated. No fooling him, not when he knew all the back roads of her heart. She released a slow breath. "Okay, yes." She set a napkin down on the next plate. "They bother me."

Shane didn't ask if her frustration was with the noise of the jets, or with the fact that they flew training maneuvers over the neighborhood where he lived, a few blocks from the navy's Top Gun facility in Fallon, Nevada. Or if it was something bigger. Like the fact that these were the very jets and pilots that would be used in battle if necessary.

He didn't have to ask. He already knew.

Because long ago he'd learned to know her mind, back when they first fell in love as kids. Yes, time and circumstances had separated them for nearly two decades, and now that they were in their midthirties, they'd both changed. But even so, ever since they'd found each other again, Shane could still look into her eyes and know what she was thinking.

"Sometimes, Lauren." He crooked his finger and placed it gently beneath her chin. His eyes looked more tired than usual. "Sometimes I wonder about us."

Panic stirred and she felt her world tilt. She shouldn't have hesitated at the noise, shouldn't have looked out the window. "It's no big deal." An anxious laugh sounded in her throat. "This is your life. I can handle it."

He didn't look away. "It's about to be your life too." His tone was kind, careful. "Remember?"

"I know." She put her hand alongside his cheek and kissed him. "By then I'll be used to it."

He searched her eyes. "It's been six months, Lauren."

She refused to give fear a foothold. Instead she kissed him again, slower this time. "I'm trying." She breathed the words against his lips. "Give me that, at least."

The wedding was set for Christmas Eve—not by her choosing. She would've had them married by now. Every conflict resolved and nothing but a bright future ahead of them. Their nineteen-year-old daughter Emily felt the same, especially since her fall figured to be crazy-busy. She had accepted a soccer scholarship to Pacific Lutheran University in Tacoma, Washington, and she was about to start work in the public information office of the army base at nearby Fort Lewis. Following in her father's footsteps. "Make it a summer wedding," Emily had pleaded with them. "Before school starts."

But Lauren figured Emily wasn't worried about her schedule as much as she was worried about her parents working things out. Even so, Shane wouldn't budge. He wanted to wait and work through some of the issues that stood in their way. Faith, his career choice, their politics, and nearly twenty years between the first time they fell in love and this second chance …

That was fine. Lauren would wait. She'd do whatever it took to prove to Shane that she could deal with all this. The smallness of Fallon, Nevada; the hour's drive west to the Fallon Airport every time her editors at *Time* magazine sent her on an assignment. And the incessant sound of fighter jets overhead. She could learn to deal with all of it, right? Even if there were days when being so close to a military base threatened her sanity.

Shane set the plates down and turned into her arms. "So you're saying—" he wove his fingers through her straight blonde hair—"I have nothing to wonder about."

At his touch, the warm tone in his voice, Lauren's world righted itself. She relaxed in his embrace. "Nothing."

"Alright, then." He kissed the tip of her nose. "I'll get the lasagna."

As long as Shane responded to her this way, as long as it took only her kiss to send him into her arms, then she could find a way to live here. She had to find a way. Yes, she was still writing military features for the magazine and flying around the country for interviews several times each month. Most of the time that was enough. So what if some days she wanted to jump on a plane and head back to Afghanistan, to her work as a *Time* magazine war correspondent. Never mind that she still mistrusted the government and the military and their roles in the Iraqi war. Never mind that her fiancé's political views were on the other end of the hemisphere from hers …

As long as she had Shane, she could look past all of it.

The doorbell rang, and Lauren took a step back from the table. Their company had arrived. Three couples, none of whom she knew. Not really. Two of the guys worked with Shane in the training department, and the third was a pilot they were considering as an addition to the instruction staff. Each was bringing his wife.

Lauren took a deep breath. The conversation would be predictable, but she would smile through every minute. She headed for the door, glancing over her shoulder. "I'll get it."

"Thanks." Shane didn't sound at all concerned. His opinionated fiancée was about to share an evening with three couples whose viewpoints didn't line up with hers, but he wasn't uptight. He trusted her.

The thought eased her tension. She smiled, opened the door, and found all three couples waiting. One of the guys was small and compact, with bright, laughing eyes. His exaggerated shrug was full of good humor. "We all showed up at the same time." He looked at the others. "Imagine that."

The others laughed, and a beat later, Lauren did too. "Yes. Imagine that." When everyone was inside, she shut the door and introduced herself. One of the guys—the heavyset one—she'd seen before. But she hadn't met the smaller guy, nor the pilot, nor any of their wives. Lauren felt better once they were past the introductions. The wives—Becky, a redhead; Sally, a blonde; and Ann, a petite brunette—seemed friendly enough. Becky noticed Lauren's colorful beaded necklace.

"I haven't seen anything like it." The woman looked a little too well put together. She moved in closer and studied the beads. "Macy's?"

"No." Lauren kept her tone even. She paused. "Afghanistan." She measured their reaction. "A local woman made it for me."

"Oh—" Becky smiled—"How interesting."

"Yes." Ann, the brunette wife of the shorter pilot nodded. "When we've spent time overseas I always buy from the locals." She looked at the others. "Very vogue."

"The economy in Afghanistan is in a shambles." Lauren touched her necklace. "I try to support the people as much as possible." As soon as she said the words, she chided herself. The explanation wasn't necessary. The redhead was only trying to be kind, trying to find common ground by giving her the compliment.

A silence fell over the group, an awkward silence. Buying a necklace overseas was one thing, but from Afghanistan? As a way of supporting the country's economy? Suddenly it was as if all of them were remembering that Lauren was different. Certainly one or another of them had heard about her, Shane Galanter's liberal fiancée. The one person in their midst who didn't feel a sense of pride and purpose every time she passed a military base, who made her living writing for *Time* magazine.

Finally Ann smiled. "Those Afghani women must cherish the freedom to make and sell their wares."

Touché. Lauren gritted her teeth and kept herself from responding. The brunette was right. If Afghanistan hadn't been liberated, the women couldn't have presented themselves or their jewelry in public. But there were other problems, life-threatening issues that faced the Afghani people and the Iraqis. What was the United States doing about that?

Shane found them in the entryway. He seemed to sense that things were a bit tense. "Well—" he clapped his hands—"Lauren and I made our best lasagna." He gestured down the hall toward the dining room and kitchen. "Let's move in and we can get started."

The others were happy to follow him. As he walked down the hall, Shane grinned at the guys and nodded at their wives. "I'll tell you what," he shook the pilot's hand, "that was some fancy flying you did the other day."

"No doubt." The heavier guy took the spot on the other side of Shane. "Best flying I've seen in years."

The women formed a small cluster as they headed into the dining room. "Speaking of Macy's," Becky tossed her red hair, "It's their big sale this week."

"I *thought* it was coming up." Ann eased her designer purse onto her shoulder and laughed. "Sounds like a date night, ladies."

They rounded the corner and spilled into the dining room. Country music played from the living room, something slow and crooning. Shane took the pitcher of iced tea and held it up. "Anyone thirsty?"

The guys each reached for a glass, but the women kept talking. Lauren hung back in the hallway, pretending to arrange the vase of flowers Shane had bought for the evening.

"Any night but Wednesday." Sally pulled a face that made the other women smile. "Youth group meets at our house on Wednesdays."

"And Chad wouldn't miss that." Ann poked her finger in the air. "The kid hated church until high school. Now you can't keep him away from youth group."

"I think maybe Chad's noticing the girls more than the gospel." Becky raised an eyebrow.

"Whatever." Ann moved toward the guys and the iced tea. "As long as he's going."

"Okay, so Macy's any night but Wednesday." Becky pretended to jot a note. "Let's aim for Tuesday."

Nods of approval followed, and the plan seemed set.

Lauren was still in the hallway, staring at the women. Was this what Shane wanted her to be? Someone whose greatest challenge in a given week was whether Tuesday or Wednesday would be better for shopping at Macy's? Whether the kids liked youth group because of the gospel or the girls?

Then, as if a switch had been flipped, she caught herself. What was she doing, being silently critical of these women? Critical and judgmental and mean-spirited? Were her views against the war so entrenched that she would dislike a group of military wives simply for who they married? Regret and sorrow came over her in a rush. She had no right to judge these women or challenge them. They played both father and mother to their kids much of the time, and during wartime, they faced losses other people couldn't understand.

She drew a slow breath. She would change her mood now, before they thought she was a terrible person. Before Shane saw how she was acting. She could hardly be a supporter of peace and then hurry into conflict right here in Shane's living room. At that moment, Sally tucked a piece of her blonde hair behind her ears, turned toward Lauren, and came a few steps closer. Her slim shoulders lifted in a dainty shrug. "Anything I can do to help?"

Lauren looked across the room. Ann and Becky were lost in another conversation. In addition to everything else they thought about her, now they would think she was rude. She'd have to make it up to them later. She turned her attention to Sally. The woman had compassionate eyes. Lauren gave her a sheepish smile and nodded toward the kitchen. "Help me slice the bread?"

"Sure." When they reached the counter where two hot loaves were sitting on separate cutting boards, Sally tilted her head. "Ann and Becky don't mean any harm."

"I know." Lauren reached into the nearest drawer for a couple knives and handed one to Sally. "I need to remember that everyone isn't an enemy. Just because my views are different from everyone else's in Fallon."

"I know you think so, but you're not that different." Sally shrugged. "War's complicated." Sally washed her hands and dried them on a nearby towel. "We might be married to military guys, but we wonder, we question." She reached for one of the loaves of bread and began slicing it. "We believe in the cause of the war in the Middle East, and we support our troops and the president. But we wouldn't be breathing if we didn't have concerns." Something deep and sad filled her eyes. "Our husbands' lives are at stake."

Lauren washed and dried her hands too and reached for one of the loaves of bread. She hadn't thought about that. Even military people might not see things in entirely black and white. Something stirred in her heart, an unsettling thought that if she'd been wrong about the women she was sharing dinner with, maybe she'd been wrong about other aspects of the war. Maybe some of the things military information officers had told her hadn't been so exaggerated or distorted after all. She ran the knife through her loaf and banished the thought. She could be wrong on some things. Tonight she was, and she was sorry. But she wasn't wrong in her passion to see the war ended, to have the president admit that the loss of life and resources was all for naught and that nothing had been gained in the process.

Sally finished slicing her loaf. She lifted her eyes to Lauren. "I'm a Christian." She looked across the room at Becky and Ann. "We moved here from the Northwest. Most of the women I've met here, navy or married to navy, are Christians too. That defines them more than their politics." She was quiet for a minute. "Seems that peace is a lot more about kindness and sacrifice than any kind of international political paradise."

Peace. There it was again. The idea that peace could come through more than one course of action. Shane had tried to convince her of that since they reunited just before Christmas, back in Illinois. Peace comes from the inside, he would tell her. Lauren wanted to believe it was true, but she couldn't. Not yet, anyway. Sally was waiting for a response. Lauren moved the sliced bread from the cutting board to a wooden bowl. "Peace is complicated, I guess." She kept her eyes on the bread. "Just like war."

"Hmm." Sally added in her bread. "I guess."

Lauren wanted to let the subject go. Talking to Sally—to someone who didn't see her as a freak of nature—was nice. If she stopped now, they could at least have the beginning of a friendship. But she couldn't let it go. "What I want is a peace that'll send our kids home where they belong." Her tone was gentle, with a subtle pleading. Maybe if she explained herself well enough, they could be friends despite their fundamental differences. She sighed. "I keep thinking of all those young people who've lost their lives. That's why I'm against the war." Lauren looked over her shoulder at the chatty women in the dining room. "If any of you lost a husband or brother or daughter, you'd switch sides in a heartbeat, don't you think, Sally?"

"No." The blonde woman covered Lauren's hand with her own. She exuded patience and her eyes shone in a way that Lauren had seen before — with Shane and their daughter Emily. "That's not how it works."

Something tightened in Lauren's gut. She didn't want to hear about patriotism and courage. Patriotic, why? Courageous over what? Sacrifice for whom? Dying for the sake of dying? Wasn't that all any of them could say about a convoy of American kids being killed by a roadside bomb? Or being struck down by an insurgent sniper?

Lauren sighed. "I'm sorry, Sally. I sort of have my mind made up on all that." She smiled. "But tell me about the Northwest. Our daughter's moving to Tacoma to play soccer for Pacific Lutheran University. I've always wanted to visit."

A sad smile tugged at the corners of Sally's lips. "We lived in the Portland area." She breathed in. "It's beautiful. Water runs through much of the city, and the trees are ..."

Lauren felt herself drift. In her mind's eye, she was no longer in her kitchen, but standing among the orphans in a dusty, hot little structure where forty kids lived. She could almost feel herself handing out lollipops and then being called out into the courtyard. Hear someone say her name and then the sound of children running out behind her, following her ...

Hear the scream of bullets spraying from snipers' guns a dozen yards behind the building ... hear the little girl crying out as she hit the ground ...

No!

Heart pounding, Lauren tried to focus on Sally's words, to let her description of Portland push the ugly images from her mind.

She succeeded for a while, but during dinner, when the guys discussed the Fallon base and upkeep of older fighter jets, her mind drifted again. Back to the orphanage, the attack. The little boy and girl who lost their lives. The women wailing as they knelt over their bodies, crying out for an answer, a reason.

Midway through dinner, Dan, the heavier guy, set down his fork and looked at her. "You and Shane grew up together, is that right?"

Lauren was caught off guard, but she smiled. Maybe this was when she could show them she was capable of compassion. "Yes. Our families were friends."

Dan pointed at her and then at Shane. "You were apart for twenty years, Shane told me."

"Right." Shane wiped his mouth with a napkin. He had a take-charge tone, as if he wanted to protect her from whatever direction the conversation might go. "Our daughter Emily brought us back together."

Lauren's heart warmed. She loved that Shane was quick to come to her defense. Even before there was any actual need. "I decided to move from Afghanistan to Fallon." She looked at Shane, and for a moment there seemed to be no differences between them whatsoever. Just her and Shane and a love that would stay between them until they died.

"So you're not covering the war anymore?" Becky adjusted her chair so that she could see to the far end of the table where Lauren was sitting.

"Not as much." Lauren fought the uneasiness that rose within her. *Come on. Just because they're asking about my writing doesn't mean they're ready to attack.* She forced herself to relax. "Most of my stories still involve some aspect of the war, but usually with interviews of politicians in Washington, D.C., or some other major city."

"I wanted to be a writer when I was in college," Sally took a sip of her water. "I still do sometimes. The travel must be hard for you and Shane."

"It is." She thought about her last trip, how she had dreaded coming home to Fallon but missed Shane all at the same time.

"Bet you were surprised when you heard about Shane studying world issues and peace in college." Dan leaned back and pushed his empty plate aside. "If anyone understands this war, it's Shane Galanter."

Shane straightened and reached for the salad bowl. "Lauren understands it too." He smiled, his tone a little strained. "Just from a different angle."

The conversation switched gears, but Lauren's heart was dizzy with wonder. No matter what their struggles privately, Shane would defend her to the ground in public. Just the way he'd done here. Dan had tried to make a point that Shane's opinions were based on years of education. But Shane was more concerned with how people saw Lauren.

With that kind of love, how could they have any problems at all?

Later, when dinner was over and the guests had gone home, Shane found her on the back patio. He came up behind her, eased his hands beneath her arms and slipped them around her waist. "Tonight was hard?"

"No." The stars shone from every corner of the sky — the one thing she loved about Fallon. She leaned her head back against his chest. "Not after I stopped being a jerk."

"You mean that was the *nice* you?" He took hold of her shoulders and gently turned her around so she was facing him. His voice held a hint of humor, but his eyes showed his frustration. "It was hard. For both of us. For everyone at the table. We're talking about renovating the naval fleet, and you ask if anyone has any idea how many homeless people could find housing for that kind of taxpayer money?"

"I was curious." She searched his eyes, willing him to see her sincerity. "I smiled, I was pleasant. I'm not trying to be difficult, Shane. Really."

"Okay, but Lauren, have you ever considered how you sound to these people? These women's husbands ... their lives are on the line." His voice was low and so sad. Sadder than she'd heard him in a long time.

"Yes. I've thought about it." She winced and brushed her knuckles against his cheeks. "Shane ..." She groaned. "I'm sorry. I don't want to be mean or critical. Sometimes I just can't help what I say."

He studied her. "Yes, you can. You meant everything you said tonight. It drove you crazy to sit at the same table with those women."

"I liked Sally." She bit her lip. "But the other two treated me like I was from a different planet."

"Because you act like you are." He linked fingers with hers. "Because you want to be different."

"Shane ..."

"No, it's true." Again his tone was kind, but his eyes told her he was serious. "One of the guys pulled me aside in the kitchen after dinner." Shane sighed, and the sound seemed to come from deep in his heart. "He said you were very interesting, intelligent, but he wondered how we'd ever work out together." Shane's tone grew resigned. "He was worried for me, Lauren."

"So ..." Her heart pounded. She hated when their conversations went this way—which they did more and more often. "I love you." She took a step closer and brought her lips to his. "Did you tell him that?"

"He knows." Shane looked like he wanted to kiss her longer, but he resisted. "I told him the whole story a few weeks ago. About our early years and how we just found each other again."

"Exactly. And that's enough, Shane. We found each other again for a reason. We both believe that. We don't need to agree about everything." She looped her arms up around his neck. "Every couple has differences."

"But ours define us. Not just our politics, but our faith."

Lauren stiffened. He was more than a little troubled if he was bringing up faith again. "I said I'm trying." Her words were small and quiet, but they were the truth. Their daughter Emily was doing everything she could to help Lauren understand the faith she and her father shared. But something deep inside held Lauren back. *What's wrong with me? Why can't I think like everyone else? Why do I have to make everything so hard?*

She turned and walked out into the yard, her back to Shane. He didn't follow.

Lauren sank into a lawn chair. She and Emily talked at least twice a week. At nineteen, with her second year of college on the horizon, there was so much for Emily to talk about. Still, the conversation always turned to faith. Lauren agreed with everything her daughter said—in theory anyway. Since reconnecting with Shane and with her family, it only felt right to reconnect with the beliefs she'd held as a child.

But believing in God and having a relationship with Him were two different things. When her thoughts turned to her Creator, she couldn't bring herself to ask the questions Emily wanted her to ask. *What is my purpose, God, what are the plans You have for me? What do You want from me?* No, instead she found herself asking more practical questions. *Why do You allow wars? And how could so many Christians support the U.S. involvement in the Middle East? Didn't fighting go against the very principles of the Christian faith? And why did so many soldiers have to die?*

So far she wasn't hearing much response from God, but that was understandable. The questions were hard, and Emily had said that some things won't make sense this side of heaven.

Period. No, what Lauren really hated was when anyone questioned her faith. When they wanted some kind of simplistic capitulation from her, as though the entire issue weren't painfully complicated. She sighed. Like everything else about her new life.

Footsteps sounded from behind her, and Shane came up by her side. "I'm sorry." He leaned close and kissed her cheek. "I love you, Lauren."

Her anger dissipated. She stood and turned into his arms, exhaling long and slow. "I spent all my growing up years looking for you, Shane." Her voice was a desperate whisper. "You're the only one I've ever loved."

"So—" he brushed aside a stray lock of her hair—"why does it seem so hard, right?"

"Right." They held each other for a long time, swaying as the high desert breeze whistled through the nearby canyons. The temperature had dropped into the fifties, and Lauren would've been cold if not for Shane's arms. She eased back and kissed him. "I have to go."

"I know." He took her hand and led her inside, his steps slow and measured. "We don't need all the answers today."

She hugged him once more before she left, but the moment she climbed into her car and started the engine, fury assaulted her. Not at Shane, but at herself. She was the one making their relationship so difficult. Why couldn't she look the other way or just put her questions aside? Did every discussion have to be a platform for her politics? And what was the point, anyway? She wasn't going to change anything with her attitude.

She kept the radio off, rolled down the window, and let the cool air wash across her face. Her thoughts blew around the car in the breeze. She tried to picture Him—the God Emily talked about, the One who wanted a friendship with her. But all she could sense as she turned onto the main highway was His enormity.

God the Creator. Too big to be involved in the trivialities of her life. *God … are You there?* She waited. Emily talked about hearing from God, sensing His voice and His response deep within her. Lauren stared straight out the windshield and tried again. *God, I need to know … are You there?* She hesitated, but again, nothing. No, as she set out toward her apartment, she couldn't tell whether God was with her or not. But that only figured.

Just one more question He wasn't answering.

TWO

Shane listened as Lauren's car drove away, but he didn't go back inside.

Watching her leave stirred a memory. Once, when he was twelve years old, he and a friend were playing catch in the house. His mother was at the store, and the last thing she'd told him was to keep the baseball outside. "Too many things to break indoors," she'd said.

But it was hot and humid outside that day, so Shane chose to do things his way. He was a good catcher, and so was his friend. They spread out on opposite sides of the living room and tossed the ball carefully. At first. But after a few minutes, they were whizzing it at each other. He was just about to tell his friend to cool it, slow it down, when the ball came firing at him and tipped his glove.

Shane willed it to hit the wall, but instead it smacked with a thud against a decorative vase, something his mother had gotten from one of her trips to Europe. Both boys fell silent, and Shane took slow steps toward the three-foot-high vase. It still looked intact, still stood right where it had always stood.

But as he went to take hold of it, the glass container fell apart in his hands. He remembered trying to hold it in place, to keep the pieces together as if he could somehow will it whole again.

He squinted at the night sky.

That's how it feels now, Lord. About Lauren. Things *looked* whole and good. They were together, after all. Engaged to be married on Christmas Eve. But he had the feeling, if he didn't hold onto her just right, everything would fall apart. He gripped the railing and tried to remember when he'd first noticed the cracks.

That was obvious, wasn't it? From the beginning.

Emily worked so hard to bring them together last winter, but it had only taken him and Lauren one evening to figure out that they stood on opposite sides of a political chasm. Only God could bridge such an abyss.

They began by talking about the article she'd written for *Time*, the one slamming fighter pilots. He could still hear her voice that night in her parents' house, after everyone was asleep. Snow fell outside and bright flames crackled in the fireplace.

She'd let her head fall back against the sofa. "Shane … how did you wind up on the wrong side of this war?"

He took her hand, worked his fingers between hers. "The question is …" his voice held no accusation, "how did you?"

Talk of the war seemed to place a wall between them, one they volleyed over the rest of the night. She asked him to consider the fact that Jesus came to bring peace, and that no one could call himself a Christian without also wanting peace.

"I want peace, Lauren. We all do. The question is how we find it." Passion filled Shane's words. Passion and an anger that she hadn't seen in him before. "And just so you know, Jesus didn't come to bring peace, He came to bring us life. Life to the fullest measure."

"Okay, good." She kept her intensity. "If He came to bring us life, then how can you be part of a war that kills people?"

The debate raged the rest of the evening. She used arguments in favor of pacifism, and he tried to explain peace through strength. But at the end of the night, they were no closer to bridging the distance between them. They might never even have tried, except that week, they watched her father die.

After his death, Shane asked Lauren not to leave, not to return to her post as a war correspondent in Afghanistan. Their differences could be worked out, especially if she could find the faith she'd been raised with. When her father died, his loss struck a nerve deep inside her. She'd missed her father's last two decades because of her anger and stubborn pride. The thought of leaving Shane, of missing a life with him, was enough to shake her convictions.

Even so, it wasn't until she was on the plane, flying away from him, that Lauren finally changed her mind. At her connecting destination, she called her editor, asked for a stateside job in Fallon, and flew to meet Shane. He smiled at the memory. No matter how long he lived, he would always see her the way she looked that day. As she walked up, he lost his breath and his heart all in the same instant. She'd come back to him! She cared enough to come! And for a while, everything was sunshine and laughter. She rented an apartment and they spent hours together every available evening.

The first cracks came about eight weeks later, in early spring.

Lauren attended a series of parties on the base with Shane, and each time she seemed to slip a notch backward, back to the person she'd been when they talked near the fireplace that first night. Instead of being patient and understanding toward the military and its efforts, she was uptight and sarcastic, her thoughts running in direct contrast to his.

Several times he'd reminded her that he too had studied the topic of peace, that he'd researched past civilizations and wars in order to form his conclusion. And what he'd learned was that peace could only come through strength. They talked again about September 11, and the plans the terrorists had, to make the events of that day seem minimal in contrast.

"Yes, we're at war," Shane said one night, "but terrorists haven't taken the life of one single U.S. citizen on American soil since we began fighting back."

Sometimes Lauren listened more intently, as if maybe she was finally seeing his way of thinking. But always she came back to one of her own sticking points. How could the U.S. send young men—boys, really—into battle? Did they understand what was at stake, and the risk they were taking? Wasn't there another way to protect the United States through diplomacy and international peace treaties—without sacrificing lives?

Lauren's ideas sounded so wonderful, so idealistic. Peace conferences, discussions with leaders of terrorist groups, diversity and tolerance training for children, an antihate program designed to help cultures learn to accept and respect each other.

"Educating the next generation *has* to be better than putting their lives in danger." Every time she said this, she searched his eyes, desperate for him to understand.

Those were the most frustrating moments of all. Times when he wanted to take her by the shoulders and shake her. Education? *Tolerance* training? Anyone who understood the terrorist mindset knew such an approach was utterly ludicrous.

They'd gotten into it again a week ago, and finally he'd had enough. "Terrorists have one goal, Lauren. One goal. To kill people who don't agree with them. And more often than not, that means people who live in or agree with the thinking of Western civilization. Terrorists are honored to die for the cause, so there's no reasoning with them, no educating them." He gathered his emotions and found a level of control. "The only option is to protect ourselves by weeding them out, arresting them or eliminating them."

"And now that we're fighting back, the attacks have stopped, right?" She could be so cutting at times, so sarcastic.

He fixed her with a hard stare. "On American soil, yes."

She turned away. "It's just a matter of time, and you know it. We're more vulnerable than anyone likes to think. And we just keep getting in deeper over there."

"Lauren, everyone wants a quick and easy war, but passing the reigns of freedom on to a region formerly run by dictators and terrorists is not a quick and easy job."

Shane rubbed his hand over his face, as though to erase the memories of their struggles. The entire topic made him feel sick and tired. His shoulders slumped a little and he turned back toward the house. Normally he'd put on some music, something to keep him company while he cleared the table and loaded the dishwasher. But this time he worked in silence. Even his thoughts weren't allowed to make noise. Not now. He'd done all the thinking he could for the moment.

Even though the thoughts didn't surface then, he wrestled with them all night and went to work the next day feeling unsettled and anxious. Dan Barber, one of the guys who'd been over for dinner, spotted him in the lunch room and moved to his table.

Dan was always laughing, and today was no exception. He plopped his burger down and rested his forearms on the table. "I was sitting across the room, and I see my best buddy over here eating a spinach salad by himself and looking like he maybe has a few days left to live, and I ask myself, 'Self, what could be eating my buddy that way?'" He rapped his knuckles a few times on the table. "So I told myself it could only be one thing." His smile faded. "Lauren Gibbs."

Shane sighed. He dragged his fork through his salad and tried to sort through the feelings pounding his heart. Anger and sorrow, and frustration and defeat. "What am I going to do with her?"

Dan crossed his arms and looked down at the table for a moment. "Girl's more liberal than Ted Kennedy. Thank goodness she's a lot better looking." When he looked up, all traces of the teasing were gone. "You love her, don't you?"

Shane pushed his salad plate back and stared at his friend. "Since I was a boy."

"Man." He shook his head. "I'm not sure you'll ever see eye-to-eye with her."

"Me either." The words jabbed at Shane's heart. But the truth remained. "And maybe we don't have to. Maybe we can at least learn to respect each other. Couples don't have to have the same political views, right?"

"Right." He didn't sound convinced. "But most couples don't make a living defending their politics." Dan straightened and found his familiar chuckle. "Or maybe one of those surgeries, a partial lobotomy. Remove that part of her brain that's been so conditioned it can't think for itself."

"Hey—" Shane could hear a mix of anger and hurt in his voice. Dan didn't mean harm, but his flip comment hurt. "Lauren's entitled to her way of thinking. She cares deeply for people." He pushed back from the table. "Maybe I need to work harder to see her point of view." The idea felt freeing. After all, he couldn't change Lauren's opinions, but he could certainly work on his own so that she would feel more of his support. He felt his anger fade. "You're a praying man."

"I am." Again the laughter was missing from Dan's voice. "You don't have to ask, buddy. Becky and I are praying for the two of you every night. Even got the little ones in on the action." He paused and looked as if he might wrap up his bit of dialogue there. But instead, he pushed on, his tone more tentative. "Ever thought that maybe, just maybe, the two of you aren't right for each other? That maybe you'll never find happily ever after?"

Shane shifted his gaze toward the wall of windows overlooking the airfield. He breathed in sharply through his nose and steeled himself. For a long while he said nothing, memories of another day, another decade playing again in his mind. "Life's been hard on her, Dan." He looked at his friend, but his mind was filled with images of Lauren. He loved her so much, but was love enough? He sighed. "Life changed us both."

"Then maybe it's time to let go."

His frustration crowded his throat, coming out in a choked growl. "I keep thinking that if life could change her once, it could change her again, expand her views so she could see more than her own. The same way maybe I need to broaden mine." His eyes found the window once more. "And then we'd be okay again, the way we were back when we were kids."

"Maybe that's all you were meant to be together. Just kids. Finding out about love. Maybe you were never meant to be together as adults." Dan shrugged. "Just a thought."

They fell silent, and though Dan didn't say anything else, his concern was clear. Shane's mouth felt dry. Could Dan be right? Were his and Lauren's good days behind them? If they hadn't been separated, they might have had a chance. Might have grown up seeing things the same way. But now ...

Shane looked at his food, dragged his napkin across his mouth, and tossed it on the plate.

Dan dug into his burger and motioned to Shane's spinach salad. "Better hurry and eat before it wilts."

"That's okay—" he picked up his plate and threw it into a trash can a few feet away—"I'm not hungry." He saluted his friend. "Catch you later."

As he walked out of the cafeteria, he passed a table of young pilots. All of them nodded toward him, but he was almost certain he heard one of them say something about Lauren. Shane picked up his pace. Of course they were talking about Lauren. She was one of the most well-known war correspondents, and while her reporting was intelligent and deep, it was also overtly critical of the war. Of course everyone was talking about them. They probably thought Shane had experienced one too many g-forces.

Outside, he slowed his pace and, as he'd done every day since finding Lauren, he lifted his eyes to the endless Nevada sky and wondered what she was doing, what she was thinking. *Lord, is everyone else right? Are we too different to share love and a life together?* His questions lined up like so many sections of a barbed wire fence, separating him and the woman he loved.

At that moment, in the distance, a fighter plane roared down the runway and lifted off the ground. In seconds it was rushing toward the heavens, blazing fast and unstoppable.

Just like Lauren.

No matter what he wanted for the two of them, she was determined to go her own way, do her own thing. She continued to write for *Time*, surrounding herself with a way of thinking that left her suspicious of the U.S. military, and often downright antagonistic. He sighed and looked at the nearby mountains. *God . . . only You can help us now. With You, something could soften her views, help her become less suspicious. Or maybe soften mine. Whatever it takes to help us find our way together. Make it a miraculous change. Help us both see the truth.*

His prayer ended, and he felt a blanket of peace settle around his shoulders. He wasn't going to give up yet, not when he'd asked God for a miraculous change. Because with the Lord working in their lives, anything could happen. She could finally understand why he believed so strongly in peace through strength, and he could find compassion toward the articles she wrote.

Yes, with God, all things were possible. Wasn't that what the Bible said in the book of Matthew? And if all things were possible with God, then a relationship with Lauren could still be real and right and good. The changes could happen a little more every day. Or all at once, if God willed it. Then they might discover the happiness and love they both wanted. A life together was possible, it had to be. God wouldn't have brought them back together only to have everything end in misery and frustration. Shane smiled to himself and began walking once more toward his office. He would keep praying, and one day they would find common ground.

Why, with God they might even find happily ever after.

THREE

Emily couldn't believe so much could happen in a single week. She finished classes and finals at Wheaton College, confirmed her scholarship and housing at Pacific Lutheran University, packed her things into two suitcases and four boxes, and finally set off for the Northwest. Now she was at her new university in Tacoma, about thirty miles south of Seattle, unpacking her box of photos in a new residence hall on a new campus, and wondering if she was crazy for agreeing to the change.

The photograph at the top of the box was surrounded by two layers of bubble wrap, and Emily eased it open. She looked down at the image of her grandparents, the two people who had raised her and loved her and encouraged every dream she ever had—whether it was excelling on the soccer field or finding her parents. Because of her grandparents' support, she'd seen all her dreams become realities—even this one. The goal of spreading her wings and trying life on her own.

She studied the picture for a moment. No surprise that so much had taken place in a week, not when she remembered all that had gone on in the past six months. Her papa was diagnosed with cancer, and at almost the same time, she'd done the impossible: found her parents. Her dad had been working as an instructor at the Top Gun facility in Fallon, and her mother was a writer for *Time* magazine. Their reunion had taken place in December, the same week Papa lost his battle to cancer.

Emily sat the photograph on the small nightstand near her narrow bed. The residence halls at PLU were not much bigger than her walk-in closet back at her grandparents' home. She removed the next picture from the box—a more recent shot of her parents taken at the airport after her grandfather's funeral.

"I still can't believe it, God." She dusted the frame and set it on the nightstand next to the other. "You amaze me."

Her roommate already had her things set up. Pam King was one of the best goalies in collegiate soccer, a transfer student, same as Emily. The two had been assigned the same residence hall, but they hadn't met until yesterday at the soccer orientation meeting. They sat next to each other and snickered at the same bits of sarcasm from the coach. By the time they realized they were in the same "res," as the others called the residence halls, they were on their way to becoming fast friends.

Emily finished unpacking and sat back on her bed. The summer would be a full one. She had chosen PLU for two reasons. First, the scholarship included tuition, room, and board—entirely based on her soccer ability. Second, it put her on the West Coast, closer to her parents and her grandmother—who was selling the house she'd grown up in and moving to Southern California to be near Emily's dad's parents—people who had been best friends with her grandparents until twenty years earlier.

A cool breeze drifted through a small window screen, bent and dirty from age. Between the gentle wind and the photographs she was unpacking, Emily's thoughts drifted back in time. Twenty years earlier, her parents were teenagers, juniors in high school in Illinois. When they came to *their* parents and told them they were expecting a baby, life as they'd known it completely fell apart. The adults—Emily's two sets of grandparents—grew angry and distrustful, pointing fingers of blame for the scandal. Her dad's parents thought they solved the problem by moving to Southern California.

Of course, the move solved nothing. Emily's mother tried every day to locate her boyfriend, and days after Emily was born, her mother set off for California. Only after Emily came down with a dangerous case of pneumonia did her mother turn around and head back to Illinois. The next day, after holding vigil at her bedside all night and finally going home for a few hours of sleep, her mother called the hospital to check on her. But something went terribly wrong. Emily's mother was connected to another patient's nurse, who informed her that her infant daughter was already gone. Her mother figured that meant Emily was dead.

Overtired, riddled with guilt, her mother determined never to forgive either set of parents for separating her from the boy she loved. So once again—this time alone—she set out for California and never looked back. Not until Emily finally tracked Lauren down and contacted her in Afghanistan last winter, did she know her baby girl hadn't died from pneumonia that day, but rather had lived.

The reunion took place last December in the days before Emily's papa's death. The Galanters came to Illinois, and they and Emily's other grandparents finally made peace with each other.

The scent of lavender mixed with the breeze and filled the room. Emily smiled. The fact that her grandparents' friendships had been restored was one more part of the miracle. And now, in what could've been her grandmother's most lonely days, she was living just down the street from the friends she'd spent two decades missing.

Everyone was back together, and in just a few short months, Emily would stand up at her parents' wedding. The event would be the culmination of a lifelong dream, something Emily had prayed and wished for all her life. Ever since the wedding plans were in order, her schoolwork had come easier and her soccer playing was better than it had ever been.

She took hold of her foot and stretched the muscles along the front of her leg. It was as if now that her life was whole, now that her parents and grandparents were at peace, she could finally focus all her energy on her own life, on the gifts God gave her.

Emily checked the clock on her dresser. Nine-thirty already. Practice was in half an hour. Though the season wouldn't officially start until fall, they had six weekend tournaments scheduled between now and then. Practices were from 10 a.m. to 1 p.m. every day. Then, when she'd cleaned up, this afternoon was her first shift as an assistant public information officer at nearby Fort Lewis.

She'd seen the army base a few times from the freeway, but today would be her first time through the gates. She hadn't gotten the job the usual way—by walking in and applying. Instead, she mentioned to her father that she'd like to work there. The base was only a short drive from PLU, and working there would give her a better understanding of the military and whether she'd like that sort of career one day.

Her dad wasted no time making calls on her behalf to one of his friends—a high-up official at the base. As it turned out, the public affairs office needed an assistant, and the details were worked out in a single day. Emily was a journalism major, about to start her sophomore year. Working as a public information officer so early in her college career would look fantastic on her résumé.

She could hardly wait to start.

With a final glance at the photos of her parents and grandparents, she dressed in her practice clothes, clipped her iPod to her shorts, and stuck in her earbuds. The soccer field wasn't far from the residence hall, so it made for a good jog. By the time practice started, Emily was already warmed up.

Pam had gone to breakfast with another teammate, and she was already at the field when Emily arrived. The two waved to each other, but over the next three hours, Emily didn't think about anything but what was being asked of her by the coach.

He was a demanding man, a person whose sarcasm was his only comic relief. Otherwise, he ran practice like a drill sergeant.

Emily didn't mind. She needed someone to push her, to help her find the limits of her abilities.

When practice was over, she jogged back to the room, showered, ate a grilled chicken salad at the cafeteria, then set out for the school parking lot. She arrived at Fort Lewis twenty minutes before her scheduled shift.

The base was bigger than it looked from the road, taking up acres of land on both sides of the I-5 freeway. Emily liked the feel of it, the American flags that flew proudly from a number of the buildings, and the armored tank on display near the main entrance. Never mind that the area was known for its rainy gray skies; in the few days she'd been there, the weather had been nothing but sunshine. Now as she studied the complex and the blue sky that framed it, the picture was almost surreal.

She'd lived most of her life not knowing that her father was involved in the military, and still she'd always felt a sense of pride when she'd seen an officer or a convoy of army vehicles. After September 11, though she'd only been fourteen, she made a beaded flag pin and wore it every day for a year. When the announcements came in that the U.S. had launched a retaliatory attack on Afghanistan, and then on Iraq, she was one of the few kids she knew who rushed home from school to watch the footage.

Papa used to tease her that her blood wasn't red. It was red, white, and blue. Patriotic Polly, he'd called her. "That's my girl, giving us old folks hope for the next generation."

Her pride in America, in its military strength, was almost instinctive. War was a tough subject, and she had as many friends in support of it as against it. Emily didn't like war, but on her own she could see some benefits. For instance, the way the country seemed so much safer since the military took action against countries harboring terrorists.

But the war aside, there was something admirable about people who devoted their lives to serving their country. Emily might not work for the military after she earned her degree, but then again, she might make it a career — the way her dad had done. She would never know unless she tried.

She straightened her shoulders and headed toward the front doors of the main building on the base.

She'd had a conversation with a nice woman the day before, and now she knew that her first stop was the personnel office. She found it, no trouble, and smiled at the older man working behind the counter.

"I'm Emily Anderson. I start work here today."

"Ah, yes. Emily." The man looked beneath the counter for a moment and brought up a packet with her name on it. "Your father is Shane Galanter, isn't that right?"

"Yes, sir." Pride warmed her chest. "He arranged the job for me."

"Well — " he tapped the packet — "you let him know we're all happy to have his daughter here. Shane Galanter is a fine instructor, one of this country's best."

"Thank you, sir. I'll tell him."

She was going to like this job, she could already tell. If only her mom hadn't taken the news so hard.

"The military, Emily?" She hadn't exactly sighed, but her tone hinted at her frustration. "Isn't it enough that your father works for the navy without you bringing another branch into the picture?"

"Mom ..." Emily tried to conceal her surprise. "I thought you and Dad were more on the same page about all that now."

Her mom's hesitation had been enough to stir a flicker of concern in Emily, but then her mother's voice relaxed. "We are, it's just ... I pictured you working for a newspaper, not the military."

Those words were the only grains of sand in an otherwise smooth transition to Tacoma and PLU—and now here, to the job at Fort Lewis. Emily dismissed the memory. Her mother's questions and concerns about the military would only lead her to a deeper understanding of the man she loved: Emily's father.

Emily took the packet of paperwork and moved to a nearby table. Ten minutes later she had filled out the necessary forms and signed all the documents. When she returned it to the man, he directed her to a place against a partition. He took her picture and after a few minutes, gave her an ID badge.

She was on her way down the hall to the public affairs office when two young uniformed soldiers turned into the same hallway and headed toward her. A smile played on her lips and she nodded at them in passing. Both were nice looking, but the tall one closest to her held her gaze longer than necessary.

A rush of warmth moved across her cheeks. *Get a grip, Emily.* She kept walking, but a sudden realization hit her. Until now, she hadn't considered that the base would be swarming with guys her age. Though she'd dated back at Wheaton, she'd always been too busy with school and soccer and the search for her parents for any kind of serious relationship. Besides, she'd learned something from her parents. Relationships were better when they happened later in life—certainly not a few months shy of her twentieth birthday.

No, she wasn't looking for a boyfriend. Not when she owed it to the soccer team and to her boss at Fort Lewis to give them everything she had.

Boys could come later. It was that simple.

Still ... there *was* something about a guy in a uniform.

The public information office was just ahead on her right, and as she opened the door and went inside, she had the instant feeling she was home. A staff of people in cubicle spaces tapped away at keyboards. Two of them were sharing an easy conversation as they worked.

"Here's one the papers haven't pounced on." The comment came from a woman in her mid-thirties or so. "The number of guys enlisting is up — not just here, but across the country."

"Of course they haven't run that story." The man sitting across from her leaned back in his chair and grinned. "Doesn't support their notion of disillusionment."

"I guess."

Emily chuckled under her breath and made her way to the counter. A pretty, slender black woman was typing and staring at her computer screen. "Be with you in a minute." Her voice was pleasant. She finished whatever she was working on, then stood and held out her hand. "You must be Emily Anderson."

"Yes, ma'am. Reporting for duty."

"Good." The woman smiled. "I'm Vonda. I've got about three dozen press releases that need copyediting. Ten need to be twice as long, and twenty need to be cut in half. I think I'll start you on that."

She was upbeat and energetic, and between her and the few other people, the office had a wonderful feel to it. The woman showed her to a seat in front of another computer. "This will be your station for now. Let's go over a few things."

Emily tucked her purse beneath the desk and listened while the woman went over the operating system and how to access the press release files. She was fifteen minutes into the training when the door to the office opened and a soldier walked in.

Emily's eyes widened as heat tickled her cheeks again. It was the tall soldier from the hallway.

"Justin, thank goodness." The black woman threw her hands in the air. "This is our new girl, Emily Anderson." She put her hand on Emily's shoulder. "I need you to get her up to speed on the process of editing releases." She looked down at Emily. "And this is Justin Baker. He puts in three shifts a week here because he's got *big dreams*." She raised her eyebrows at Emily. "Hotshot officer. Wants to run the place one day."

"Not for a few years, Vonda." Justin grinned and looked at Emily. His eyes were a shade of green that almost looked airbrushed in. "And sure, I'd be happy to help."

"Thanks." Emily forced the word and tried to exhale.

Justin had short light-brown hair. He was so handsome that her heart stumbled into double time. Even so, this wasn't the time to act weak at the knees. This was a job, her role here a professional one. She needed to act accordingly.

She gave him the same smile she'd given Vonda a few minutes earlier. "It shouldn't take much." She looked at the computer screen. "I think I've just about got it."

A phone rang on Vonda's desk, and she made an exaggerated wipe across her forehead, as if Justin had rescued her in the nick of time. As Vonda went to answer her phone, Justin pulled a chair next to Emily's. "Okay, the press releases are always in that file," he pointed to a folder on the computer desktop. "That way they're easy to access."

He walked her through the steps and even switched chairs with her so he could show her how to cut a release from the bottom while still keeping transitions and important details, and then how to lengthen a release. "You need to call up the interview file. Usually you can find enough quotes and details in the reporter's notes to double the size of any release. The reporter has to okay it afterwards."

She was listening, she really was. But her mind just couldn't seem to stay on task when everything about the guy next to her filled her senses. His cologne ... the subtle scent of soap and laundry detergent on his freshly starched uniform. And that wasn't all. His voice was kind and soothing, and she found herself wondering what it would be like to sit next to him at the movies or at a concert.

"Emily?"

She jumped and turned. He was looking at her, his expression blank.

"Did you hear me?"

Again her heart pounded. What was *wrong* with her? She almost never had this reaction around a guy. She straightened herself. "Sorry. I have a lot on my mind."

"I was just explaining that Mr. Williams makes the decisions on the length of releases. They're written at sort of a standard word length, and then the editing can cut that in half or double it—depending on where the release is being sent."

"Right." Good. She was recovering well. She would stay focused the rest of the afternoon.

Justin finished training her, then he sat back and smiled. "How's your dad?"

"My dad?" Emily hesitated, fingers poised over the keyboard. She lowered her brow. "You know him?"

"He and my dad spent time together in the Gulf War. I guess they were pretty good friends."

"We don't ..." She shook her head. "We don't have the same last name. So how did you figure it out?"

Justin laughed, and the sound was easy and genuine. "Your dad remembered that mine was stationed out here in the Northwest. Once you had the job here, the two of them talked." He shrugged. "My dad called me the next day and told me you were coming." He grinned at her. "Said you'd be brand-new and to look out for you. That sort of thing."

"Is that right?" She allowed a bit of teasing into her tone.

"Yeah." Justin crossed his ankle over his other knee. "But he didn't tell me you'd be gorgeous."

Again the air seemed to leave the room, as if some giant human vacuum was controlling the oxygen level, laughing at her and daring her to try and take a breath. She swallowed and willed her trembling heart to find its normal rhythm again. "Well, thanks." She looked at the computer. "And thanks for the training."

From the front counter, Vonda gave them both a look and brushed her hand in their direction. "Looks like we got us a pair of smitten youngsters." She shook her head. "Don't fight it, Emily. Once Justin sets his sights on a girl, it's all over." She smacked her lips together. "Mmmhmm. 'Mr. Smooth,' that's what we call him around the office."

Justin held his finger up and started to say something in response, but instead he let his hand fall to his side and gave Emily a lopsided smile. "Vonda doesn't hold back much."

She giggled. "I can see that." Ignoring the strange way she felt, she turned once more to the computer screen. "I better get to work."

The afternoon passed in a blur, and Emily did her best to stay wrapped up in the press releases. But every now and then, she'd look up and catch Justin watching her. To hear Vonda talk about him, he was a player. Someone who had the same smooth lines for every girl he met.

But his eyes told a different story. By the time Emily left the fort that day, she wondered if she'd ever get to hear that story. Either way, she was sure of one thing.

She would never step foot on the base without looking for the tall, green-eyed soldier with the honest smile that made her heart jump the way no other guy's ever had.

FOUR

Lauren was checking her email, reading a letter from her editor when the phone rang. Even after living in her Fallon apartment for half a year, the place was sparsely furnished. Just a kitchen table and two chairs, a sofa, a television, and a computer balanced on top of an old stand she'd picked up at a garage sale. Her bedroom held a simple double bed.

The phone sat on the edge of her computer stand, and she answered it on the second ring. "Hello?"

"Mom?" It was Emily. She sounded energetic and hopeful—the way Lauren figured she must've sounded before running away to California all those years ago. "How are you?"

Lauren glanced at the email from her editor. It started out the same as the others he'd been sending every few days:

> Lauren, we understand your need for a stateside time of respite. But it's time to take your rightful place in the Middle East. No one can report the war like you can, Lauren. Your successors haven't been …

She closed her eyes and focused on her daughter. "Good, honey. I'm good." The email shouted at her, calling her a liar. She turned her back to the computer. "Working on another feature."

"Really? That's so cool." Emily was always easily impressed. She was a writer, after all, so every time Lauren talked about her job with *Time*, Emily seemed to hang on every word. "What's it about?"

"iPods and MP3 players, how they're causing a generation of kids to suffer early hearing loss." She chuckled. "Nothing too exciting."

"Oooh." There was worry in Emily's voice. "I listen to mine all the time."

"Just keep the volume down."

"Okay." Emily seemed in a hurry, as if she'd called for something other than just to chat. "So how's Dad?"

The question was rhetorical; Lauren could tell by their daughter's voice. She made regular attempts to help her parents find common ground, but she didn't really expect there to be trouble between the two of them—especially not troubles that loomed like a tidal wave over them and their plans for a future. Lauren tried to dismiss the memory of Shane's face from the night before, when once again they'd fought. She cleared her voice. "He's great."

"Good." Emily laughed. "Mom, you won't believe this."

"What?" It felt good to hear her daughter's enthusiasm. Maybe some of it would rub off, and Lauren could take a fresh look at the way her new life was falling apart. "You scored three goals in your scrimmage yesterday?"

"Well—" her laugh became a giggle, the way she must've sounded as a little girl—"okay, that too."

"Really?" Lauren stood and wandered across her apartment to the front door. "Seriously, Em? Three goals?"

"Four, but one was called back."

"The coach must be glad he signed you."

"I think I'm a little gladder than him, even." Her words danced with a new sort of joy. "'Cause guess what?"

Lauren chuckled. "I give up."

"Well," there was a definite smile in her voice, "you know I'm working at Fort Lewis, at the army base just outside of Tacoma?"

"Yes, I know." Lauren opened the door and stepped out onto her small porch. She sat in the webbed folding chair there and trained her eyes on the mountains. "Is it working out?"

"Definitely. I'm editing press releases and running errands and answering phones. It's great experience." She hesitated. "And I met a guy, Mom."

A guy... so that was it. Lauren felt herself smile. "Well, well. My busy Emily wasn't supposed to have time for guys, remember?"

"I still don't." She laughed in a shy sort of way. "But it's the weirdest thing, Mom. I can't get him out of my head. I mean, every day I go to work and I'm like, you know, looking for him. But I don't really look for him because then he'd think I like him, and Vonda says he's Mr. Smooth to every girl he meets."

Lauren felt a rush of familiar feelings. What her daughter was describing was exactly how she'd felt about Shane once upon a yesterday. "Who's Vonda?"

"She runs the front desk at the public information office, remember?"

"That's right." Lauren wished she were with Emily in person. It'd be nice to hug her daughter and celebrate with her, but she needed to be a mother first. Especially after going so long without being one. "Vonda thinks the guy's a little too smooth, is that it?"

"He's not really." Emily giggled again. "I mean, I don't think so. I haven't seen a string of girls coming by to visit him at the office." She grabbed a quick breath. "And guess what else? His father is Dad's friend. They were together in the Gulf War."

So... the boy was from a military family. Lauren tried to hide her concern. Emily sounded so smitten—something Lauren hadn't heard from her in the six months they'd been getting to know each other. She didn't want to dampen her daughter's excitement, even if she could feel herself being outnumbered.

In the distance, two fighter jets roared into the sky and circled wide over the tops of the mountains. She closed her eyes. "How interesting."

"It is interesting." Emily's voice lost some of its enthusiasm. "We haven't gone out or anything. But still ... I don't know, Mom. I'm tearing it up on the soccer field and I love my job, but at night when I talk to God, it's like I can't stop thinking about Justin."

"Be careful, Em. The smooth types can be the worst of all."

"I know." She was the sensible Emily again. "I just thought I'd tell you. And hey, I almost forgot. Can you and Dad come for a visit the first week of August?"

"A soccer game?" Lauren's heart soared. No matter what conflicts needed addressing in her own life, being reunited with her daughter was enough to make her smile.

"Yes. A tournament. Coach thinks we could win it."

Lauren did the math. The tournament was six weeks away. Truth was, there were times when she didn't think she'd survive that long before calling for a peaceful surrender with Shane and hightailing it back to the Middle East. But maybe a visit to see Emily would give them something to plan for, a reason to stay together and work things out. If that was possible.

"Mom ... how's that sound?" Emily's tone was slightly impatient. "Sorry, but I have to run. Soccer practice is in twenty minutes."

"Okay, well ... sure. I mean, yes, I'll definitely ask your dad. If he can get some time, I can too."

"Great. Okay, I gotta run, Mom. I'll call you in a few days. Love you."

"Love you too." Lauren hung up, then stared at the phone. It still didn't seem possible, that her daughter had been alive all these years—that she'd become such an accomplished, responsible, intelligent young woman—all while Lauren was busy trying to forget she'd ever given birth to a daughter—a daughter she thought long dead.

And now ... as if there was no harm done, Emily accepted her, welcoming her into every aspect of her life, inviting her to soccer tournaments and talking about her hopes and dreams. Even talking to her about this—her feelings for the young soldier.

It was more than Lauren dared hope for.

The sound of the fighter jets faded, and Lauren stood and moved back into the apartment, to her place at the computer. The email was still on the screen, and this time she read it through.

> Lauren, we understand your need for a stateside time of respite. But it's time to take your rightful place in the Middle East. No one can report the war like you can, Lauren. Your successors haven't been hard-hitting enough, questioning enough. It's like they're buying into the notion that somehow good is going to come from the money and resources and people we're losing over in Iraq and Afghanistan. Anyway, we've arranged for you to step right back into your same position and carry on the way you were before. We have a ten percent pay hike waiting for you, and for Scanlon, of course. He's still shooting pictures for us, still waiting for his partner to join him. Won't you think about it, Lauren? The offer's open-ended. We'll be waiting for you. Just say the word. Bob Maine.

"Bob, Bob, Bob ..." Lauren sighed and read the letter over one more time. It was the same message he'd given her twice that month already. "What am I going to do with you?"

She tried to picture it, saying good-bye to Shane again, packing her things, and returning to the Middle East. She'd be put up in the media headquarters in Afghanistan at first, the same place Jeff Scanlon still lived. The two of them would reconnect, falling into the easy camaraderie they'd always shared. He was a good friend, and she missed him. Missed the work they did together.

Only Scanlon understood how the war had changed her, how reporting the casualties and destruction every day made an impression on one's mind that never went away—no matter how many stories a person might write on the dangers of MP3 players.

Everything about the offer sounded fantastic. She'd be out of Fallon, rid of the well-meaning military men and women who couldn't see past the flag, and she'd be doing something worthwhile with her life. All of it sounded wonderful, except one part. The part where she'd have to say good-bye to Shane.

He was the love of her life, wasn't he? How long had she looked for him, dreamed about him, pined for him after she left Illinois and headed to Los Angeles? She'd wept every mile of the way, broken over the loss of their daughter and angry at their parents for separating them.

Why hadn't someone—anyone—shown the sense to let them stay together? There was no telling what might've happened. The two of them would have stayed on the same page, certainly. They would've struggled financially, but they would've raised Emily in the faith they'd been brought up in. No taking opposite trails on the journey of life, because they would've walked every step together.

Lauren closed down her email program, stood, and wandered to her bedroom. If she were honest, she had to admit her apartment didn't look like it belonged to someone trying to put down roots in Nevada. Even her clothes were still in stacks on the floor against the wall. The only thing that gave the room any distinction was a framed photograph on the windowsill. A picture of her and Shane, not from this past year, but from her other life. Back when she was just seventeen and believed with all her heart that she and Shane would be together forever.

She went to the photograph, picked it up, and studied the people in the picture. Sometimes, when she was frustrated with the sound of fighter jets and idle military chat, she would look at the photo and convince herself that she'd been too young back then, too naïve to understand love.

Or she'd tell herself that Shane wasn't the same person, that the kindness in the young man's eyes was no longer there. He was a steely navy Veteran, an instructor with a bark that caused young pilots to stand a little straighter, fly a little sharper.

But as she stood there, she knew the truth. Shane hadn't changed. He'd always stood for what was right. No, he wasn't perfect, but he wanted so badly to be on the good side. And what he lacked, he made up for with a faith that knew no bounds.

No, Shane hadn't changed.

She dusted her finger over the glass, bringing their faces into clearer focus. They hadn't been too young to understand love. Their eyes told a story even she couldn't rewrite. The love they shared back then was pure and raw, uncomplicated by politics or differing viewpoints. It was enough to make her drive away from home and never look back. Enough to keep her searching for him years after it no longer made sense.

So ... what now?

She looked out the window and tried to picture Shane, dressed in his decorated white uniform, sitting at a desk that overlooked the entire Top Gun airfield. She would tell him about Emily's offer, about taking a trip to Tacoma and seeing where their daughter lived and played and worked. But she was kidding herself if she thought that was going to solve anything.

She'd been asking God what chance they had, and how she could ever become the sort of military wife Shane needed. She'd tried swallowing her opinions, muffling them, and banishing them altogether. But always they came back, and always she and Shane argued because of them.

She set the photograph back on the windowsill. She'd been looking for an answer to her prayers, searching her heart and Shane's eyes, and examining their relationship every time they'd been together lately. God's answer *had* to be somewhere—His will as clear as the love that once shone from their faces.

When she was around Shane, she still felt weak in the knees, her heart still responded the way it had when she was a girl. She loved him as she would never love another man. But their differences loomed larger every time they were together.

She looked out the window at the streets of Fallon, and slowly, gradually, it hit her. Maybe God had been trying to answer her prayers all along. Maybe he'd tried once, twice, three times. Nine times. But this time—finally—she was able to hear what He was telling her. The message hurt her heart even to consider it. It wasn't spoken with the voice of God, of course. But with one that was even more familiar.

The voice of her editor, Bob Maine.

FIVE

The breakthrough happened that same afternoon, the day Emily shared her feelings with her mother. She'd been determined not to make the first move with Justin. There were countless reasons why. She was busy, she had to be dedicated to her team, she was still getting used to the Tacoma area, she didn't know him well enough.

The list was long.

But that didn't change the way she felt every time he walked into the room. He was broad shouldered with a rugged face and a quick sense of humor. Just like her dad. Already she knew that Justin's faith, his beliefs, mattered as much to him as hers did. Even so, she wouldn't make her feelings obvious. Especially after the Mr. Smooth comments from Vonda. If Justin Baker *was* a smooth talker, let some other girl fall for him. She was certainly too busy to be taken on a meaningless ride.

That afternoon, she was editing releases when he pulled a chair up beside her and waited for her to look at him. When she did, she couldn't stop her breath from catching in her throat. She kept her tone light. "More training?"

"If you need it." He gave her a look that made her laugh.

"Not really." She raised one eyebrow. "See, I had this teacher, and, well ... he was so talented, I don't have a single question."

"That's good." He ran his tongue along his lower lip and shifted in his seat. It was the first time he'd looked nervous. "Hey, Emily, I want to clear something up."

"Okay." She turned to face him.

"I hear you over there, Justin Baker, all flirty and everything." Vonda was a relentless teaser. She stood at her desk and winked in their direction. "Just go on ahead and get over yourself, Mr. Smooth. Ask the poor girl out, already. She's dying for you to do it." She made a loud exasperated sound and sat down hard on her seat. "Love is wasted on the youth, I tell you. Wasted!"

Justin looked at Emily for a beat, and then leaned his head back and groaned. "Thanks, Vonda."

"Anytime." Vonda picked up the phone, her attention mercifully off the two of them.

Emily gave him a sympathetic smile. "You were saying?"

"Right." He looked at her, and she noticed his cheeks were darker than before. He couldn't be any more irresistible. "About the Mr. Smooth part." He shook his head. "It isn't true."

"It isn't? How's that?"

"Well ..." He craned his neck and cast a quick look in Vonda's direction. His voice dropped a notch. "The thing is, if I were Mr. Smooth, I would've already done it."

"Done what?" Emily enjoyed the exchange, wherever it was leading.

His eyes found hers, and he looked beyond the surface to someplace deep inside her. "Asked you out."

And just like that, his feelings were on the table. She felt herself lifting off the floor, floating around the room. But when she looked down, she could see herself still in the computer chair, her feet still on the ground. She remembered first to smile, and second to breathe. "Really?"

"Yeah." He exhaled as if he'd been holding his breath. "Emily, you don't know how hard that was."

"Your turn, Miss Emily." Vonda was off the phone again. She smacked her hand down in a mock show of disgust. "Do I have to come over there and teach the two of you how to do this?"

Emily laughed. "That's okay." She looked at Justin and her insides felt all jumbled together. "I think we can figure it out."

Justin shielded his eyes with his hand and shook his head. "Thanks again, Vonda."

"Like I said, anytime."

"So?" Justin lowered his hand and winced. "Can I take you out to dinner? After work tonight?"

"Sure." Emily kept her tone light. She looked over her shoulder once more. "But I'm not sure how we'll get by without Vonda."

"Me either." He shrugged, and the gesture made him look adorable. "I guess we'll never know if we don't try."

They both laughed, and Justin snuck back to his work station—thankfully under Vonda's radar so they avoided any comments about how it went or whether Emily had made the boy's day by saying yes. The rest of the shift passed in a blur, and every few minutes Emily had to remind herself to focus.

What could it mean, Justin asking her out? Had he been feeling about her the way she'd been feeling about him? Like even the most beautiful summer day couldn't compare to the way it felt simply to sit in the same room together, working on press releases and breathing the same air?

When their shift finally ended, they decided he would follow her back to her residence hall, and they'd both ride in his car—a Jeep Cherokee his dad had given him. He opened the sunroof as they set out, and she settled into the spot beside him. The leather seats felt soft and inviting. "I like it."

"I had no idea Dad was giving it to me." Justin kept his eyes on the road. Now that Vonda wasn't around, he seemed relaxed, at ease. As if the two of them had known each other forever. "I came home from my first tour in Iraq and my parents met me at the airport. They drove me to the base, and there it was in the parking lot. Covered with yellow ribbons." He smiled. "My first car."

Emily studied him for a moment. So, he'd been to Iraq. The detail was proof that the two of them didn't know each other nearly as well as it might seem. She pressed her shoulder into the seat and faced him. "How long were you there?"

"A year, about the same as most guys." Something changed in his eyes.

"I thought ..." She remembered the first time she met him, "I thought you wanted to *run* the base."

"Vonda exaggerates." He grinned at her. The evening was still sunny and would be for another three hours, but the temperature had cooled. He looked up at the sunroof and back at her. "You cold?"

"No." She brushed her fingers over her long sleeves. "It feels good."

"It does." He pulled onto the freeway and merged into a heavy flow of traffic. "I wanna be career military. Like my dad." He shot her a quick smile. "Like yours." He shrugged. "If they let me run the base, I'll take it."

"So ..." She didn't want to ask, didn't even want to picture him in danger—this golden young man who had so easily taken up residence in her heart. "So what did you do in Iraq?"

"I'm trained for medic work, but that's not where I spent my time. I did the frontline stuff, kicking in doors, looking for insurgents." He made a face that suggested it was no big deal. "Traveling in convoys, that sort of thing."

Each bit of description hit her like a blow. He'd been in the most dangerous positions, she knew that much from her conversations with her father. Army guys who went looking for insurgents were the ones in the greatest danger. Certainly with his family's pull, he could've been worked off the front line, still serving without putting his life in imminent danger.

When she didn't say anything, he gave her another quick look. "Hey, it wasn't so bad. The people love us over there."

Emily was fascinated and frightened all at once. "Tell me about it."

"The truth isn't something you'll read in a newspaper article—" he winced—"or in a magazine piece your mother might write."

So he knew about her mother. Emily's expression must've changed, because he hurried to cover himself.

"My dad says your parents' story is complicated. I mean—" he changed lanes—"people are entitled to their opinions, Emily. Don't get me wrong."

"I'm not." They were already in Seattle, and ahead she could see the Sound and a hundred sailboats dotting the water. "I think ... I think a lot of people helped shape my mother's viewpoints."

He nodded toward the water. "Pike Place Market okay? They have some great seafood restaurants."

"Seriously?" She'd heard about the place from some of the girls on the soccer team, but she'd never been anywhere other than school and Fort Lewis. "I'd love it."

He took the next exit. Ten minutes later, he had a parking space near the water, and they climbed out and began walking toward the closest pier. Seattle had an eclectic feel about it, a mix of fast-paced business people in their suits and nice dresses, and urban earthy types with baggy clothes, long hair, backpacks, and sandals. Over all of it towered the Seattle Space Needle.

The sun was still high in the sky, and the smell of exhaust fumes and seawater mixed in the cool breezy air. When they'd settled into a comfortable pace, Justin took a slow breath. "Like I was saying, it's so different over there. I went expecting a battle, and I found one. The war is a long ways from over."

"That's what I hear." She kept her pace even with his, and every now and then, the smell of his cologne mixed with the evening wind.

"But the best part was the people." He smiled and his eyes took on an added depth. "They're so glad to be free, Emily. Men, women, and children—all of them so grateful. To most of them, we're the heroes." He gave a single laugh. "My mom made a scrapbook with all the pictures I took. Pictures of me and the people of Iraq. Especially the kids."

"So ... so you weren't in a lot of danger?" They were walking down a hill now, along a cobblestone road, and just ahead, the sun cast a blanket of diamonds over the water of Elliott Bay and the distant Puget Sound.

"There was danger." His smile faded. He was quiet for a moment, and then he looked at her. "I lost two buddies, guys who were hit by a roadside bomb on a day when I stayed back to do weapons inventory."

She felt her heart sink. "I'm sorry." And she was. But at the same time, she breathed a prayer of thanks to God for sparing Justin, for allowing the soldier beside her the chance to live the life ahead of him.

"The majority of people here and over there support us, and that's a good thing." His words were slower now, thoughtful. "It's not like it was for the Vietnam guys. Not hardly. But still—" he looked up at the sky and squinted at the setting sun—"I wish more people knew the truth. We're getting a lot done over there, Emily. It's a good thing, even with our losses."

The conversation shifted to her and her role on the soccer team. "I've played midfield since I was a little girl, and it's more fun now than ever."

"Because you can see the light at the end of the tunnel?" His comment wasn't rude or flip, just an honest observation.

And an accurate one. "Yes." She felt her arm brush against his, and the sensation sent a shiver all the way to her feet. "I'm good, but I won't be on an Olympic team or trying out for the pros." She gave him a sad smile. "This is it, so I'm giving it everything I have."

"I'd love to see you play." They came to an intersection and crossed, stepping up onto a sidewalk that ran along the water's edge. "I played, back in high school."

"Really?" Again Emily had the sense that she'd always known him. If they'd been at the same high school, they would've been the best of friends. Or maybe they would've found the sort of teenage love her parents had shared. She blinked away her thoughts. "What position?"

"Midfielder. Same as you." They stopped and he looked out at the water. "I miss it sometimes. But it wasn't my passion." He cocked his head and met her eyes again. "Not like being in the army."

Emily's admiration grew. "When did you get back ... from Iraq?"

"In October. Right before the holidays." He leaned his forearms on the metal railing that separated the sidewalk from the embankment down to the water. "Made my parents happy."

"So now ... you're done?" She kept her tone light. The question dangling in her heart wasn't one she wanted to ask, but she had to know. She rested her arms on the same metal railing and turned her head so she could see him. "Now you work on other training and, you know, learning how to run the base, that sort of thing, right?"

He chuckled and—intentionally or not—slid his right arm over so that it was touching hers. "I have one more tour, if that's what you're asking."

Fear tightened her airways, and she stared out at the farthest bit of ocean she could find. No, he wasn't going back to Iraq, that couldn't be what he'd said. "But ... but you already did the dangerous stuff, right?"

"They're looking for guys to go twice." He stood a little straighter. There was no worry or concern in his voice. "I can't very well lead guys if I'm not willing to make sacrifices myself."

His answer was exactly what she would've expected him to say. "So you'll be back on the front lines?"

"Probably." He smiled at her and nudged her arm with his. "But that's where the people are, Emily. It's what makes me sure we're supposed to be there. Besides, God's got my back. I felt Him with me every minute last time I was there."

She had the sudden urge to run. What point was there in getting to know this wonderful guy beside her if he was going to leave for another year in Iraq, if nothing about his future was even a little bit sure? But before those feelings could take root, she stopped herself.

God knew the plans He had for Justin, same as He knew the plans He had for her. Neither of them was guaranteed their next breath. So why borrow worry from tomorrow? She breathed out and felt herself relax. "When, Justin?" She didn't move her arm, didn't break the connection between them. "When do you go?"

"End of September." He smiled and eased his fingers between hers. "Come on. Let's find some dinner."

They walked slower than before, and with her hand tucked in his, Emily had to keep telling herself she really was here, he really was beside her, walking with her hand in hand along the edge of Seattle's Puget Sound. And no, she wasn't floating ten feet off the ground, no matter how she felt.

For the rest of the evening, they avoided talk of his return to Iraq. Instead they found a restaurant and were seated near a window that overlooked the water. He took the spot across from her and told her about his younger sister.

"She's eighteen now, four years younger than I am." He unfolded his napkin across his lap, clearly at ease in the upscale dining room. "The whole family has a list of stories about her."

"Like what?"

He grinned. "Like the time she bought a new cell phone. She was all excited because it had a speed dial feature for up to thirty phone numbers." He planted his elbows on the table and rested his chin on his fist, his eyes on Emily. "So we're at dinner that night and she's going on about which numbers she's programmed in, and how one of them is 9-1-1." He changed his voice to sound like a ditzy girl. "'That way, if I have an emergency, I can just dial star-two-seven instead. Or was it star-two-eight?'" Justin's laugh was full of warmth and affection. "The rest of us rolled. Only my sister would think it could save time to dial star-two-seven instead of 9-1-1."

They ordered salmon and vegetables and a couple of lattes. When the waiter left, Justin asked her about her parents. "I know they were apart for a long time, but I don't know the whole story."

So she told him, told him how they'd been so in love, and how the things her mother had written about her father could still make any of the three of them teary eyed. She told him about the struggle of her mother's pregnancy, and how none of her grandparents had supported the young couple.

"The amazing thing is that I found them." She folded her hands in her lap and searched his face. "It was my dream, my daily prayer that God would bring them back to me and to each other." She took a sip of her coffee. "He did both. I can't ask for more than that."

The hour was relaxed and full of more stories. They finished eating and popped peppermint candies into their mouths as Justin paid the bill. When they were outside, he took her hand and led her once more to a spot along the railing. The sun was just dropping below the horizon. Nearly ten o'clock. Right on time for a Northwest summer night.

Pink and orange streaks mixed with deep blues as the sunset began leaving its mark on the sky. Again Justin stood close to her, his arm touching hers a little more than before. A smile tugged at the corners of his lips, and in the glow of the setting sun she could hardly take her eyes off him. "Why the smile?"

"Because—" he looked down and chuckled, soft and low—"I was thinking about Vonda."

"Crazy Vonda?" Emily felt a shiver run along her spine again, and she wasn't sure if it was from Justin's nearness or the cooling air.

"Yeah. I can almost hear what she'd say if she were standing behind us."

"What?" She angled herself to face him more than the water.

"She'd say, 'Enough already, Mr. Smooth. Do I have to come over there and tell you how to do it?'" He turned too, his shoulders squared to hers. Only a few inches separated them. His tone changed, and there was a pull between them that Emily couldn't resist. He swallowed, still imitating the office manager. "'Or will you just go ahead and ... kiss the girl.'"

Emily had been kissed once before. After a prom date with a guy she had a crush on for most of her junior year. But here, now, she knew what was coming and she wanted it more than she wanted her next breath. She moved closer, so close she could smell the peppermint on his breath. "You know what I think?"

He brushed his cheek against hers and drew back enough to see her eyes. "What?"

"I'd hate to frustrate Vonda." Her words came out slow, breathy. The foot traffic on the sidewalk had tapered way off, but she wouldn't have cared if they'd been standing in a crowd of people.

"Yeah." He moved in, slowly, tenderly, and touched his lips to hers. "Me too." His hand moved to her waist and drew her close as he kissed her again, slower this time, longer. The tentative sweetness of his kiss told her more clearly than words that they stood together on the edge of a canyon of emotions and feelings. All they needed to do was find the courage to jump.

Emily could've stood there all night being kissed by Justin Baker, kissing him back. But after a few minutes, he touched his knuckles to her cheek and gave her a final kiss. "I need to get you back."

"Okay." At the seemingly abrupt end to their closeness, she suddenly felt unsure of herself. What was she doing, standing here letting a guy she didn't really know kiss her? Maybe he really *was* the smooth talker Vonda declared him to be, and now that she'd kissed him, maybe he wouldn't ask her out again. After all, this was new to her — so new she wasn't sure what to do next, how to transition from head over heels back to a sane conversation.

But before she could worry anymore, he took her hand and brought it to his lips. With the most tender care, he kissed it, his eyes on hers. "Can I say something without scaring you?"

She could hear her heart pounding, feel it as far down as her knees. "Yes." What could he want to tell her? That he was sorry? That he regretted kissing her when they hadn't known each other that long? She held her breath.

"I have the strangest feeling, Emily." He studied her face, and this time he placed both his hands around her narrow waist.

"What?" She was frozen, waiting.

"Like all my life has been leading up to this one … single moment."

She wanted to tell him she felt the same thing. But all she could do was breathe and nod her head. For a moment, it seemed he might kiss her again, but instead he tucked her arm in his and walked her back up the hill toward his car. This time the conversation turned to relationships.

"I figured you had a boyfriend." Justin smiled at her, and in the fading light his eyes sparkled. "A girl as beautiful as you. With a heart like yours."

She laughed. "No wonder Vonda called you Mr. Smooth." The air was colder now and she began to shiver.

Justin slipped his arm around her shoulders, and as they walked, they fell into a rhythm that seemed as old as time. "I'm serious. I would've asked you out a week ago, except I figured you had someone."

"Okay." She looked up at him, not sure she wanted to know. "What about you? There must be a line of girls waiting for you somewhere."

"Nah." He laughed and shook his head. "I went to college on a running-start program. Focused on ROTC and graduated at twenty. Never really fit into any group. You know, not a jock, not a druggie, not a musical type, not a whiz-kid. I dated here and there, but I sort of stayed to myself."

When they reached the car again, he hesitated. "I *so* don't want to take you home yet."

"I know." Would he lean against his car and pull her into his arms? The way she sort of hoped he would?

No. He was too much of a gentleman for that. Instead he led her around to the passenger door, opened it, and held it for her. When he slipped into the driver's seat, he smiled at her. "You think Vonda'll be able to tell? Tomorrow when we're at work?"

She giggled. "Probably."

The drive home went too fast, and when they reached her residence hall, he walked her up to the door. "Tonight was amazing."

"Yeah." She wasn't sure what to make of her feelings. A sudden shyness mixed with a longing she'd never known. She wanted so badly to kiss him again, but the timing seemed wrong. She took a step toward the door. "Thanks, Justin."

"See you tomorrow." He hesitated, then turned and jogged down the steps.

When he was gone, she hurried inside, and there in the entryway were three girls from the soccer team. Pam was one of them.

"My goodness, Emily, who was the hunk?"

She looked back at the driveway and the Jeep Cherokee just pulling away. "Justin." She let her eyes find Pam again. "Justin Baker. He's a soldier from Fort Lewis."

"He's hot." Pam whistled.

"He's beyond hot." One of the other girls shaded her eyes and looked out toward the fading taillights. "He's the hottest guy I've seen on campus all summer." She took hold of Emily's shoulder. "Tell me he has a brother, please, Emily."

"He doesn't." She laughed and waved them off. She didn't want to stand there in the entryway making small talk with her teammates. She wanted to get to her room, wash her face, and crawl into bed, where she could relive every moment of the last six hours. While she could still feel his breath on her skin, his kiss on her lips.

While the memory was still so alive she could be absolutely certain she'd spend the rest of the night dreaming about it.

Her last thought before going to sleep made her smile. Vonda was wrong. Love wasn't wasted on the youth. It had found her when she least expected it, and wherever her new relationship with Justin went from here, she had a feeling the journey would be magical.

And that however long the ride, the two of them would enjoy every minute.

SIX

Shane felt the tension between him and Lauren long before they took their seats on the plane. She was quieter than usual, and once in a while he'd catch her dabbing at her eyes, maybe trying not to cry.

He looked out the window as the plane took off. How had they grown so distant? He still loved her, still wanted to share his life with her. The feelings he had for her, he'd never have for anyone else. After a lifetime of missing her, he knew that. Knew it as certainly as he knew his name and rank.

She hadn't said anything about running, but he had the feeling she was thinking about it. Twice in the past few weeks she'd mentioned emails from her editor, invitations—no, not invitations, but downright pleas—for her to return to the Middle East.

"Is that what you want?" He asked her yesterday, the last time she'd mentioned the emails.

"No." She came to him, looped her arms around his neck, and leaned her head on his chest. "I want you, Shane. I've always only wanted you."

So why did their differences feel more pronounced every time they were together? He wanted to talk about wedding locations and honeymoons, but the conversation always took a different direction.

"Don't you feel bad," she'd said the last time he mentioned a honeymoon, "taking a trip to some luxurious beach when the people in Afghanistan are struggling just to survive?"

"Okay." He took hold of her shoulders and looked into her eyes. "Does it help the people in Afghanistan if we stay home?"

She shook her head and turned away, more upset than was fitting for the moment. "You don't understand me, Shane. I'm not saying we can't go, just that it makes me sad, thinking about the people over there." She hung her head, her voice a million miles away. "I'm sorry. I guess I'm being a real drag."

Through the last part of June and all of July, Lauren spent most of her time on the road gathering information for one story or another. When they talked—in person or on the phone—they discussed the coming trip to see Emily's new school, her new residence, and her new guy, Justin Baker.

Shane had hoped this trip would give them a chance to remember why they were together in the first place. But now here they were, and though Lauren was beside him, she might as well have been back in Afghanistan for how close she felt.

He stared at the city below, watched it get smaller and smaller as the aircraft found its cruising altitude.

He drew a deep breath. *Lord, I can feel You up here. So close it's like I could reach out and touch You. But what about Lauren?* His eyes stung and his throat felt thick. *Father, I've looked for her all my life and now she's here. But her heart seems half a world away. What can I do, Lord? How can I stir inside her the feelings she once had? The feelings she had last winter when she followed me to Fallon?*

Remember, my son, love never fails. Not ever.

The answer resonated in his heart and seemed to come from someplace right behind him. He knew better than to turn around and look. But when God's answers were this clear, they always left him with a sense of awe. The Lord, the Creator of the universe, cared enough to answer his simple prayers. And this time, the answer was especially strong, because it came straight from Scripture. First Corinthians, chapter thirteen.

Love never fails.

He breathed out and relaxed his jaw. Then he turned his head and leaned in close to her. "Hi."

She was reading a magazine. Without hesitating, she slid it back into the seat pocket in front of her and shifted so she was facing him. "Hi."

He framed her face with his hand and worked his fingers into her hair. His eyes met hers, and the confusion he saw there only made his heart hurt more. "Lauren, don't leave me. Please."

"Shane ..." She covered his hand with her own. "Why do you say that?"

"Because." He swallowed, searching her eyes, desperate to see the love and certainty he longed to find there. "I can feel you pulling away." His voice was a whisper, one that was barely louder than the roar of the jet engines. "A little more every day."

Tears filled her eyes, and her chin quivered. For a while she didn't speak, then she managed to force tight words free. "I don't want to leave."

"Okay, then." He could feel the tears in his own eyes. "Stay. Please, Lauren. Stay."

The impossibilities lay dark and flat in her eyes, her expression. "We need a bridge. Only ..." She gulped, and two tears slid down her cheeks. "Only I'm not sure there's a bridge that big."

"Love is the bridge, Lauren." He ran his fingertips along the side of her face. "I'll never love anyone like I love you."

She nodded. "Okay." Her answer told him only this much: they couldn't talk about forever, couldn't figure things out here, surrounded by the other passengers. She closed the gap between them and touched her lips softly to his. "I love you that much too."

They didn't speak again the rest of the short flight. Their discussion had pulled back the shades and revealed a terror too dark and horrible to imagine, too great even to consider. Later, after they'd had a chance to see Emily, they'd talk about it again. Because whatever was making things worse, whatever was placing this barrier between them, wasn't going to go away on its own.

In the half hour before the plane landed, Lauren rested her head on his shoulder and fell asleep. Shane savored the feel of her body against his, reveled in the sensation of her nearness without her angry opinions, his frustrated comebacks. He stroked her hair, and when it came time to get off the plane, she woke and smiled at him.

"I can't wait to see Emily."

"Me either."

Just like that, they made a silent pact to put all talk about themselves on hold. At least for now. They rented a car and headed straight for the university. The sky was blue with temperatures in the mideighties. Emily had been telling them that the weather was wonderful in Tacoma.

"That or the company you're keeping?" Shane teased her the last time they talked.

"Well—" Emily sounded wonderful, full of life and love and purpose—"let's just say it could be raining every day and neither of us would notice."

On the drive from the airport to PLU, Shane thought about how strange life was. Gary Baker had been one of his closest friends in the Gulf War. They were in different branches of the military, but they were together for planning meetings and strategic multibranch cooperative assignments.

When their stint in the Gulf ended, they remained friends. Over the years, their visits and conversations happened less frequently, but that never mattered. They had the sort of friendship that withstood time.

When Emily chose to take the PLU scholarship, and then when she asked Shane about getting a job at Fort Lewis, he remembered. That was the base where Gary had been stationed before he retired. Now he lived ninety minutes south in a small town called Kelso, the place where he'd grown up and where he and his wife Carol raised their two kids. But still he might know who to talk to at the army base. Shane was on the phone to his old friend that afternoon.

"The timing couldn't be better," Gary had told him. "They're looking for someone part-time. My boy's working at that office a few days a week. I know exactly who you should talk to."

By the end of the week, Emily had a job. But never, not once, had Shane given a second thought to the idea that Gary's son would work with Emily. Not until she called toward the end of June, giddier than he'd ever heard her.

"How do you know, Dad? When it's really love?"

"Well ..." His feelings were mixed at her question. All those years he'd ached because he'd missed out on her life, hadn't known where she was or even *if* she was. Now that she'd found him, it felt strange to hear her so excited about a boy. Strange to have to share any part of his little girl. He cleared his throat and tried to sound paternal. "For one thing, it usually takes longer than three weeks."

"I don't know." Her voice had a dreamy quality to it. "We've gone out almost every night. I think it took us about three hours to figure it out."

By the end of the phone call, just for something to say, Shane asked the boy's name. That's when Emily giggled. "You know him, Dad. I wasn't going to tell you until you met him in person, but you might as well hear it now. His name's Justin Baker."

"What?" Shane about slid out of his seat. Several times Gary and Carol had sent pictures of Justin. He was a handsome kid, but he was a kid, right? Way too young to be talking love with Shane's little girl. "Isn't he still in high school?"

Again Emily laughed. "No. Justin's dad said the same thing. He thought I was like seventeen or something."

"Yeah, because nineteen is so old, right?"

"Almost twenty." She paused. "You and mom were ready to get married a whole lot younger than this."

Married? Shane's heart skipped a beat. The statement must've been for effect. Certainly Emily hadn't met a boy and fallen so hard the two of them were talking marriage. "Marriage, Emily? Are you trying to tell me something?"

This time Emily laughed. "Dad, of course not. I'm just saying … Justin's twenty-two. He finished college at twenty."

"Well, I wouldn't expect anything less from the son of a man like Gary Baker."

"Good." She made a clapping sound that carried over the phone lines. "His parents are coming up for my tournament, so you and Mom will get a chance to connect with them."

The weeks had flown by since then, and now here they were. He and Lauren, on their way to the first game of the tournament.

They had just enough time to check into their hotel on the way to the field. When they got there, Shane could see a set of bleachers already full of people.

"What if they don't like me?" Lauren was holding his hand, but she lagged a step behind. "And why does it seem like we spend our entire lives around a military base?"

Shane smiled at her. "Practice, Lauren." He tickled the corners of her mouth. "People will like you a lot more if you're smiling."

"I'm sorry." She did, but he could feel her resistance. They drew closer, and Lauren stopped twenty yards short of the bleachers. "I want to look for Emily." She shaded her eyes. "Wait … there she is! Number seven!"

Suddenly Shane realized what he was watching. Their daughter had spent a lifetime kicking around a soccer ball. Game after game, practice after practice, the people cheering in the stands for her were her grandparents. Never her parents. Until today. Now, for the first time, he and Lauren were together doing what they should've done all of Emily's life.

Watching her play soccer.

Shane linked his arm through Lauren's. "Look at that." They watched their daughter dart around two defenders, dribbling the ball like it was attached to her ankle by a string. Then, at just the right moment, she sent it across the field to a teammate streaking toward the goal.

The defender running just ahead of Emily's teammate didn't have time to adjust her footing, and before even the goalie could react, Emily's teammate shot the ball back to her, and she fired it into the goal. The entire team raised their hands, jumping and running out to meet Emily.

A shiver passed over Shane's arms. "She's amazing."

"She is." Lauren was just about to say something else, when people approaching caught her attention. She looked off to the side and smiled. "Hello."

Shane followed her gaze and there was his friend, Gary Baker. And next to him was a strapping boy four inches taller than Gary. Justin, no doubt. "Hey! I can't believe this!" Shane took a few long strides and wrapped Gary in a big bear hug. "It's been too long, friend. Way too long."

They pulled apart and Gary pointed out at the soccer field. "Your girl's good."

"Thanks." Shane grinned toward Emily, still getting congratulatory hugs from her teammates. Then he turned his attention to the tall soldier standing beside Gary. "And who's this young man? Don't tell me it's your little Justin all grown up?" Shane felt Lauren come up alongside him. He put his arm around her shoulders and stuck his hand out toward the young man. "I'm Officer Shane Galanter. Your dad's buddy."

"Sir." He saluted. "Lieutenant Justin Baker, sir."

"At ease, lieutenant. The question is, when did you get to be taller than your daddy?"

Justin laughed. "He asks me that all the time."

The play on the field resumed, and Lauren stuck out her hand first to Justin, then to Gary. "I'm Lauren, Emily's mother."

"Nice to meet you, ma'am." Justin wore his casual dress: camouflaged pants and a buttoned-down shirt. His manners were impeccable.

Gary smiled at Lauren. "Come meet Carol. I think you'll like her."

They moved to the bleachers, and after ten minutes, Carol and Lauren were talking about the plight of third-world countries and the work humanitarian and Christian groups were doing to alleviate the AIDS epidemic.

Shane leaned in close to his friend. "Did you tell her to talk about that stuff?"

"Who, Carol?" Gary looked at the two women. "No, she's always been interested. Tells me we're going to take a year off and do mission work in Africa someday."

Shane felt the tension in his soul ease. Lauren had found a friend, something neither of them expected. He was about to ask Gary how things had been in Kelso, when the action on the field came to a sudden stop. A girl from the opposing team was on the ground, and instantly a group of coaches surrounded her.

"Paramedic!" one of the coaches shouted. "Someone call a paramedic!"

Shane whipped out his cell phone and dialed 9-1-1. He wasn't sure of the emergency, but in a calm voice he told the operator that a soccer player was down and seriously injured at PLU's soccer field. "I'm not sure of the address."

"That's okay, sir. Your cell phone has a GPS locator."

Shane was relieved. Before he could get off the phone, Justin bolted down the bleachers and out onto the field. "He has medic training," Gary was on his feet, squinting, trying to make out the scene.

Shane finished his call and watched as the young soldier took control. He must've identified himself, because the coaches cleared away. Even from their view in the bleachers, it was clear the player had been cut across her calf. She must've been kicked, the cleats from another player's shoe slicing into her.

Justin didn't hesitate. He took off his shirt and pressed it over the wound. Then he raised the girl's leg and propped her foot up on his shoulder. He was talking to her, still applying pressure on the wounded leg as the paramedics arrived.

Once they'd wrapped her leg with sterile bandages, Justin took his bloodied shirt and returned to his place in the bleachers. Everyone in the stands applauded, and as Shane looked, he saw Lauren. Her mouth was slightly open, her eyes full of awe for the young man.

"That looked serious ..."

"It was. The slice was pretty deep, nicked an artery for sure."

"I wondered." Lauren touched his shoulder. "You might've saved her life."

He shrugged and wadded his shirt in a ball near his feet. "I guess the team trainer was in the locker room helping another player, someone injured earlier." An easy grin played on his lips. "I knew what to do. Anyone would've done the same thing."

Shane gave Gary a look, one that said he too was impressed by Gary's son. When the game was over, when PLU had won, 4–2, one of the coaches from the opposing team came over and thanked Justin. "Thanks for what you did. She was losing a lot of blood." He looked sickened by the thought. "I don't think the rest of us realized how serious it was, that an artery was involved."

Again Justin brushed off the comments. He shook hands with the coach, but his eyes were already searching the field. Shane followed the boy's gaze and spotted Emily jogging across the field toward them. Justin met her partway, and the two hugged for a long time.

Shane wasn't sure where to focus his attention. On the way Justin Baker looked at his daughter, on the beauty of what the two of them obviously shared, or at Lauren. Gary and Carol were making their way down the bleachers, heading for Emily and Justin, but Lauren still sat there, watching from her place on the top row of the stands.

"He's so ... compassionate." She didn't blink, didn't look away from the place where the two young people were talking and laughing. "Did you see that, Shane?" She finally shifted her gaze to him. "Did you see how he responded?"

Whatever was going on in Lauren's head, he wanted to understand it. "Of course he reacted that way." Shane looked from her to Justin, and back again. "He's a trained medic, Lauren."

"But I ..." She bit her lip, and emotion welled in her eyes. "You're kind that way, Shane. But that's because I know you. Soldiers — the soldiers I've written about — are more concerned with taking a life than saving it."

Shane couldn't believe she'd said such a thing. Was that really what she thought? That Shane and his peers were nothing more than well-trained killing machines? "Lauren, that's a terrible thing to say."

Almost as soon as he uttered her name, her expression changed. She put her fingers to her mouth and shook her head. "Listen to me. How could I have thought such a thing? It's like ... it's like I can hear myself for the first time." She looked at Justin again. "Like that young man is the first soldier I've actually seen for myself. Without looking at him through the lens of my training, my experiences."

Shane didn't know what to say. He was still stunned that somewhere in her heart, Lauren had harbored such a warped view of soldiers. But saying so would be overkill, especially when she looked so shocked, almost angry at herself.

Whatever was happening inside her, Shane was sure God had used the actions of a very special young man to open Lauren's eyes a bit. He took his fiancée's hand. "Come on. Let's go congratulate our daughter."

"Yes." They reached the bottom of the bleachers when Lauren turned and looked at him. She hadn't ever looked more serious. "I'm sorry, Shane. For ever thinking that."

"It's okay." He gave her a tender kiss. "Come on. Emily needs us."

They met up with the others in time to see Emily pluck at Justin's white T-shirt. "Good thing you had this on." She stood on her tiptoes and kissed his cheek. "Otherwise the team would've been too distracted to play the rest of the game."

Shane smiled, savoring the feel of Lauren's hand in his. They made small talk, congratulating Emily on her game and her goal, and listening while Emily updated them on the condition of the injured player. "The other coaches heard word near the end of the game. She lost a lot of blood, but she's been stitched up. She'll be fine in a few weeks." Emily held out her hands, her brow raised. "Whoever heard of slicing open an artery in a soccer game? I'm so glad she's okay."

Carol Baker put her arm around her son. "Thanks to Justin's quick thinking."

"Yeah—" Emily grinned at him—"my hero."

"And don't you forget it." Justin laughed and looked around the group. "Emily's next game isn't for a few hours. Let's get lunch."

Shane reveled in the feel of the group, the way his friend and he had so easily reconnected, how Carol and Lauren had found common interests. And now that he saw them together, he couldn't help but be thrilled for Emily. Justin was the sort of young man he could only hope to see his daughter marry one day. The fact that the soldier was his friend's son only made things better.

But none of that compared to what he'd seen in Lauren's eyes as she sat on the top rung of the bleachers. Lauren presented such a strong front, an impenetrable fortress that refused any viewpoint but her own. She was absolutely convinced she knew the truth about issues involving politics or the war, and apparently about soldiers. Today, though, there was a break in that wall.

Shane could only pray that it was a beginning, and that one day very soon, the tender, passionate Lauren he had known and loved would find her way out from behind the wall. At the very least, he had something that day that he hadn't had in months. He had hope.

And for now, that would have to be enough.

Seven

Something was changing in Lauren's heart, and though she didn't want to dwell on it, she was horrified at the realization she'd stumbled onto that morning. That she'd harbored ill thoughts toward all soldiers. Her attitude had been inexcusable.

But what did the experience mean? Would this change of heart go deeper, into the far reaches of her opinions? She wasn't sure.

Not until talk at the pizza place turned to the war.

Back at the soccer field, Carol seemed like such a wonderful, rational person. But now ... she was passionate about the United States' commitment to finish the task in Iraq. "The thing people don't understand is the good our troops are doing." She looked from her husband to Shane, and then to Lauren. "Iraq is a different place today, a better place because of the sacrifice our military is making."

Almost against her will, Lauren felt her defenses rising again. She opened her mouth and then closed it, casting her eyes down at the laminated menu. *What's wrong with you, Lauren? It's one conversation, let it go.* She gritted her teeth and tried to find a diversion. The license plates that hung on the wall. That could distract her, right? She studied them, forcing herself to steer clear of the talk around the table. Fifteen seconds, twenty, and the license plates weren't doing it. Instead she made lists in her mind of the interviews she needed to conduct for her next *Time* piece. But it was no use. The conversation drew her like gravity until she couldn't hold back a minute longer. Carol was still waxing on about the benefits brought to the people of Iraq because of the war.

Lauren sat up straighter and found a tight smile. "But the insurgents will only take over again as soon as the U.S. pulls out. So what's the point?" She bit her tongue, but it was too late. Her words had escaped before she could run them by the filter in her mind, the one that was supposed to help her act with more social graces.

Shane shot her a look across the table. She softened her tone and managed a smile. "I mean, how much longer will it take?"

"There's two ways to tell that we're winning this war." Justin took a sip of his root beer and set his cup down. "First, U.S. citizens have been safe on our own soil. And second, we're building an infrastructure of freedom through trade and government that has never been known in the Middle East."

Lauren nodded and turned her attention to her ice water. Why couldn't she be more like them? And how could the young man across from her be so compassionate one minute, and so committed to what basically amounted to killing the next? It was one of those times when she felt like a fish flopping around on dry ground, crazy in need of a place where she might fit in.

She said little throughout the rest of lunch, but in the car on the way back to the soccer field, she looked at Shane and frowned. "I'm sorry. Again."

"Whatever." He smiled at her, but his eyes held frustration. "I thought maybe today, after your reaction to Justin's rescue ..." His voice trailed off. "I don't know. I guess I thought you might see everything else differently too."

"I sort of wondered about that." If she could take back her comments at lunch, she would. Or she'd say it more carefully. But that didn't change how she felt. "I'll try harder the rest of the trip, okay?"

Shane sighed. He worked the muscles in his jaw. "That's just it. I don't want you to have to try, Lauren." He looked at her. "Don't you see?"

She did, and there was nothing more she could say. Instead she reached out and took his hand. Because as long as he was there beside her, as long as his fingers were woven between hers, she had proof that they were still together.

Even if good-bye was feeling closer every day.

Something was wrong with her parents.

Emily said good-night to Justin earlier than usual and stood at the window of her room, tears in her eyes. *God … they're not getting along. I can feel it. Show me what to do.*

She pressed her forehead against the cool glass and remembered the conversation at the pizza parlor. Her parents' politics were still coming between them. Which was crazy because they were supposed to have all that stuff worked out. A small circle of fog built up on the window, and she rubbed it with her fist.

Her mother needed to be more careful with what she said, that's for sure. But her dad too. The couple of glances he gave Mom must've hurt her feelings. Emily turned away from the window and plopped down on her bed. Pam was out, probably studying with a few of their teammates down the hall. The solitude felt good; she needed to think.

If her parents didn't start trying to understand each other a little more, then something tragic could happen. She let herself fall back on the bed and stared at the ceiling. All this time … all this time she'd been thinking everything was okay, that they'd agreed to disagree on the war, and that they'd found a peaceful way to handle their differences.

But if what she'd seen today was any indication, things between them were far from worked out. In fact, as they all left the pizza parlor, she could feel the tension between her parents. Emily let out a slow, painful breath. *God, they can't fall apart now, not when they're supposed to be planning a wedding. Please, God ... whatever it takes, please help them work through their differences.*

The war was a complicated issue. Emily might work at an army base and understand her father's opinions, but she understood her mother's too. Her mother had seen the harsh reality of war firsthand. Of *course* she hated war. Anyone who'd been through what she had would hate it.

Emily sat up and hunched over her knees. Her body ached from the soccer games that day, and there were more to come tomorrow. She needed to get to sleep so she'd be ready to play. But after she washed her face and climbed into bed, it was still another half hour before she fell asleep. When she did, it was with images of her parents filling her heart and mind.

And the certain belief that somehow God would close the gap between them.

❧

For the next three days, Lauren alternated between cheering for Emily—whose team made it to the final game—and studying Shane and his friends. Gary and Carol were some of the nicest people she'd met. Much nicer than anyone she'd connected with in Fallon.

Even so, their views and hers were worlds apart.

The night before the tournament championship, Emily pulled Lauren aside at the soccer field and searched her eyes. "Are you okay? You and Dad?"

A few seconds passed while Lauren caught her breath. "The two of us?" She made a silly face. "Of course, honey."

Doubt remained in Emily's eyes. "I've been watching you. It's not like it was at Grandma and Papa's house. Something ... I don't know, something's different."

Lauren thought for a moment and then decided. She needed to be at least partially honest with her daughter. Otherwise, if things didn't work out, the girl would be blindsided. Lauren took hold of her hands and looked to the worried places in Emily's soul. "We have a lot of differences, your father and I. Things we're still trying to work out."

Fear threw itself into the mix of emotions playing out in Emily's expression. "But you love him, right?"

"Of course." She soothed her thumbs over the tops of her daughter's hands. Her tone changed. "But you need more than love, Em. Sometimes you need common ground." She hesitated, and the familiar sting of tears poked at the corners of her eyes. "Your dad and I are still working on that."

"So ... how can I pray for you?"

Of course this was Emily's answer. She'd spent a lifetime praying that she'd find them, and that if she did, they'd find love again together.

"Seeing Justin, getting to know him, that's helped a little." She gave her daughter a sad smile. "Just pray that God'll give us a bridge, a way to understand each other better."

Emily studied her. "You understand, right, Mom? That none of us want this war."

"That's what I keep hearing." She refused to get into a debate with her daughter minutes after a soccer game.

"Well, it's true. We don't want war." She pressed her hand against her heart. "We want a safe country, and we want the people of Iraq to be free. If it takes a war to make that happen, then we'll fight to win." She paused, seeming so sure of herself. "Can't you see how that makes sense?"

Lauren wanted to dig a hole and hide from all of them. Shane and the Bakers, even Emily. How could she be so different from the rest of them? How could they not see that fighting was never the answer? A safer America? That could be accomplished through peace talks and treaties. Wasn't that what parents always taught their kids—talk things out, don't resort to violence?

So why couldn't the people she cared most about in the whole world see the situation in that light? Or why couldn't she see it in theirs?

Emily was waiting, so Lauren pulled her close and hugged her, stroking her back. "You know what makes sense?"

"What?" There was such angst in Emily's voice. She inched away, clearly still wanting answers.

"Why PLU gave you a soccer scholarship." Lauren grasped at the upbeat tone, the one that felt more familiar, easier when it came to Emily. "Honey, you're wonderful! It makes me so sad to think how many games I missed."

Gradually, Emily's expression changed until it was clear she'd made a conscious decision to let go of the previous topic. A smile replaced her concerned look and her eyes began to dance. "It doesn't matter how many you missed. It matters that you're here now."

"And tomorrow's the championship!"

"Exactly." Emily leaned in and held her mother for a long while. "It'll all work out, right, Mom?"

Her daughter's simple words were like swords pricking the surface of her heart, allowing a pain that knew no bounds to slip free. "I hope so, sweetheart. I truly hope so."

The topic didn't come up again that night or the next day as they wished Emily luck before the championship. Again Lauren sat with Shane and the Bakers at the top of the bleachers. This time they didn't talk about war or politics or the Middle East. They simply cheered Emily on.

Just after halftime, Lauren's cell phone rang. She checked the caller ID and felt her breath catch in her throat. Bob Maine, her editor. She stepped down from the bleachers and took the call several feet away. "Hello?"

"Lauren, tell me you're at the airport." The man's gruff voice belied a heart as big as the magazine's towering offices in New York City. "You haven't answered my emails."

"Because I've been busy working, Bob. Remember that? This is the first week I haven't turned in a story."

"But they're stories anyone could write."

"Thanks." She kept her tone from getting too serious. This wasn't the time to make a decision about returning to the Middle East.

"Lauren ..." He gave a frustrated groan. "Okay, not *anyone*. You're doing a great job reporting stateside. But we don't have anyone like you over there, baby. We need you. Even just for six months."

Six months. The thought bounced around her mind like an errant pinball. She could do that, couldn't she? Make a six-month commitment, go overseas, report on the war, and maybe while she was there, try to look at things the way Shane and his peers saw them.

She turned and saw her group in the bleachers. Shane caught her eye, his smile as genuine as the summer sky. "Bob." She pinched the bridge of her nose and shook her head. "I can't make that decision now. I need ... I need time."

"How much time?"

"A month, at least."

He sighed. "I'd like you there first of September. I'm serious, Lauren. Do what you have to do, but make it happen. That's where you belong, and you know it."

The conversation ended, and Lauren returned to her place next to Shane.

"Who was that?"

She kept her answer matter-of-fact. "Bob Maine."

Shane rested his elbows on his knees. "Still bugging you about getting back to the Middle East?"

"He won't let up." She looked away and turned her attention to the soccer field. For the rest of the game, while Emily's team won the championship and then on into the evening during the celebration at a nearby restaurant, she didn't dare look too long into Shane's eyes. Or Emily's.

She'd told Bob the truth, she would think about it. Soon. But right now she couldn't do anything of the sort. Shane knew her too well. And if she let herself think about leaving, and then looked too long into his eyes, she'd break down there in front of everyone. Because Bob Maine's offer gave her more than just the chance to see things the way Shane did.

It gave her an escape. Back to the familiar danger of reporting war firsthand. And that thought stirred a longing deep inside Lauren. If she gave in, then sometime in the next few weeks she'd have to do the impossible. Look into the eyes of the only man she'd ever loved and tell him good-bye. Yes, just for six months. But if she fell into her routine the way she expected she would, the good-bye might last a whole lot longer.

Maybe even forever.

Emily couldn't shake the terrible feeling.

Yes, the tournament had gone perfectly. She'd played some of her best soccer ever, even scoring the winning goal for the tournament championship. She'd been giddy after the game. Then, when she saw her family and Justin's together, it gave her a kind of premonition. As though, just maybe, the two families would be together again this way—not for soccer games, but for life.

The terrible feeling had nothing to do with her game or her guy. She was in love, and everything about Justin Baker was more wonderful than she'd ever imagined. Rather her fear came every time she looked at her mother. The feelings she'd had that night in her room and the conversation with her mother the next day only served to worsen her fears. Something *was* off between her parents—and she was worried. Maybe their troubles were why they'd avoided a summer wedding.

Ever since they found their way back to Fallon together, Emily believed without a doubt that her parents had worked out their differences, that the wedding plans were in full force, and that the toughest conversations between them were probably about where they'd honeymoon. Something like that.

But now, all her certainty about her parents had changed.

Her mother was quieter than usual and less affectionate around her father. She seemed distant, and no matter what Emily's dad did to include her in the conversation, her mom acted out of sorts. As if she couldn't quite connect with anyone.

Not even Emily.

As her parents left after the last game was over, she hugged them both, and when she was in her mother's arms, she whispered near her ear. "Be happy, okay?"

Her mom looked into her eyes, longer than usual. "I will, Emily." She paused. "The important thing is for you to be happy, okay?"

Now that her parents were gone, now that Emily and Justin were heading back to her residence hall in his car, she was struck by a thought. Her mother must've meant something by her comment. Like maybe the important thing was for Emily to be happy because she, herself, wasn't. Was that it? And what about the other part?

I will, Emily . . .

Did that mean she was about to find her happiness somewhere other than with Dad? Some other way than being Dad's wife? By the time they reached the PLU parking lot and the place where Justin always dropped her off, Emily was so tense she was sick to her stomach.

"Hey—" he took her hand—"what's on your mind?"

"My mom." She looked out the window at the shadowy branches in the trees that lined the lot. "I get the feeling she and my dad aren't happy."

"Hmmm." He released her hand and gently moved his to the base of her neck. He massaged her tight muscles, slow and easy. "I sort of saw that."

"But Justin—" she looked at him—"you don't understand. My parents love each other so much."

"That's what you've said. You were going to share some of your mom's journal pages about how much she loved him, remember?" His voice had a calming effect on her heart. He kept working at the knots in her neck. "I still want to see them."

"Okay." The thought of her mother's journal entries restored some sense of calm to her world. Her mother might be confused, even conflicted about how her viewpoints didn't line up with the rest of her family's. But Emily's parents loved each other. There was never any question about that.

Justin leaned in and kissed her. "One day, when we're a whole lot older, we'll be dancing at their ten-year anniversary dinner and we'll remember this night. Because I'm going to pray every day that God works a miracle for your parents." He kissed her again. "The way He's worked a miracle for us."

Emily's fears dissolved like the tension in her muscles. "When we're a whole lot older, huh?"

"Yep." He pulled back and searched her eyes. "The timing's a little unclear right now, but just for the record—" he grinned and the sparkle in his eyes shone even in the dark—"I'm never letting you go, Miss Emily. Not ever." He held up his pinky finger. "Pinky swear."

She giggled. He could always make her laugh. That was one of the things she loved most about him. Before Justin, she'd been a little too serious. Now she laughed so much more easily. Even times like now, when she was worried about her parents. She clasped his little finger with hers. "Pinky swear."

"I mean it." He laughed as he let his head fall back against the seat. "It's not exactly a diamond ring." His eyes held hers. "But that'll come in time."

Sure, she'd just met him and they'd only been together a matter of weeks. And yes, when they talked like this, it was more silliness and flirting than anything. But somehow deep inside, Emily had no doubts. Even knowing he would return to Iraq in a month or so, she was certain Justin was right. That one day she'd wear his ring and they would dance together at her parents' tenth wedding anniversary. God had brought her parents back together for a reason, and one day soon they'd have the answers to the questions that never quite went away.

"You know what I love about you, Emily?" Justin smoothed his hand over her dark hair and brushed his thumb along her bangs.

"What?" She wished it weren't so late. They could hang out in the commons room, watch television, and snuggle together the way she loved. But the coach had called a meeting for the morning, and she needed to be at her best. Even if coach cancelled practice, which most of the players assumed he would do after such a sound tournament win.

Justin slipped his hand around to the back of her head and kissed her once more. "I love that it's enough for you that we live happily right now. And the whole ever-after stuff can come later."

Emily grinned. This time she shifted so she was closer to him, and the kiss came from her. "There's plenty of time for ever after." She was breathless. She needed to get inside. Otherwise the feelings he stirred in her would keep her awake all night. "And right now, nothing makes me happier than you."

He drew her close, and she let him. But finally she pulled away. "Good-night, Justin."

"Good-night."

She was halfway up the outside steps when he rolled down the car window and yelled as loud as he could, "I'm crazy about you, Emily Anderson."

At first those words had been hard for her. Love, the way she thought of love, was something her parents defined, not something she'd ever really considered for herself. But now there was no stopping her feelings, no lying to herself. Justin Baker was the most amazing guy she'd ever met. She cupped her hands around her mouth. "I'm crazy about you too!"

He stretched over to the passenger seat so she could see him better. Then he held his little finger out the window. "Pinky swear?"

She laughed but held hers out toward him in return. "Pinky swear!"

By the time she got inside and climbed into bed, her thoughts had nothing to do with her parents or her fears about their relationship. All she could think about was Justin and the way he made her laugh and love. And how, with him in her life, every day felt better than the last.

Happily, indeed.

She didn't need a ring or a promise or a date to convince her that Justin was right for her. Neither one of them was going to walk away, not after what they'd found. They could survive however long it took.

Even if they had to wait years for the ever after.

EIGHT

Word came on a cloudy Saturday morning, the third week of August, as Justin was heading out to meet Emily. PLU's soccer practice had been early that day, and Justin had planned a surprise for the two of them — a hike in the foothills of the Cascade Mountains east of the city.

His commanding officer saw him heading out and pulled him aside. "Lieutenant Baker, I need to speak with you." He ushered Justin into his office and handed him a slip of paper. "You leave for Iraq Monday, September 24. You've been assigned to a six-month tour, shorter than before." The man's tone was matter-of-fact. After all, this sort of news went out every day around the base. "I just received notice." He paused. "I wanted you to have as much time as possible to prepare."

"Sir, thank you, sir." He felt the familiar thrill, the rush that in just a month or so, he'd be back on the front lines doing what he loved — wearing the army uniform and taking a stand for justice. Helping people who had no help and safeguarding American soil. He stood a little straighter. "I'll be ready, sir."

The man nodded. "Dismissed, soldier."

Justin saluted as he left the office, but not until he reached his Jeep did the news actually sink in. Facts swirled in his head and made him dizzy. The most obvious was this: He and Emily would say good-bye in just one month. Four weeks to continue the crazy, wonderful, magical whirlwind that had been their lives ever since their first date. He wanted to take her to the Space Needle and Blake Island and Issaquah. He planned to walk with her along the trails of the Washington Park Arboretum and kiss her halfway down Azalea Way, the path that wound through the grounds.

All of that in just a month.

But there were other bits of information filling his mind as well. He had to be ready physically and mentally, emotionally and spiritually. There was no other way to take on a task like this. Iraq was a tough place, and he wouldn't do the United States Army justice if he wasn't prepared.

Then there was the fact that this tour was going to be shorter than the first. Six months instead of a year. Before meeting Emily, he would've wondered about that, even complained. If he wanted to be a leader one day, then he needed to spend his share of time on the front lines. That was only right.

But six months would count just fine. That, plus the year he'd already done. He'd have plenty of experience by the time he finished this next tour. Besides, he'd signed up for a year, and if that's what they wanted, they would've assigned him to a full twelve months. The shorter tour could only mean one thing. God was smiling down on him, knowing that every day without Emily would feel like a month, and that half a year was probably all either one of them could take.

Justin did the math.

Six months in Iraq meant staying through the holidays and into the spring, but by the end of March he should be on his way home. With no more tours ahead of him, he could do the thing he'd wanted to do since the first time he'd taken Emily on a date.

He could ask her to marry him. It didn't matter how fast things had moved. He was more than crazy for her; he loved her. He had no doubts. He would ask her to marry him and then maybe a year later, the summer before her senior year, they could plan on a wedding. That would give him time to get additional training and take a paid position. They could get a nice apartment and start their future together, living and loving, waking up in each other's arms.

But the proposal would have to wait. Because though he knew how to survive with the danger, nothing was really certain until he came home. Even six months was a long time—long enough that Emily's feelings for him could change, or he could get assigned to permanent duty overseas.

Still, the odds of either one of those things happening were slim. The possibilities came to life like so many summer wildflowers, dotting and coloring the hillside of his future in ways that took his breath. The news—knowing his departure date—would be sad for her at first. But they could stand anything for six months. He climbed into his Jeep and drove to PLU. Never mind the clouds. The future was so bright, he had to squint to look at it.

He only hoped that after hearing his news, Emily would feel the same way.

Hiking the nearby hills was the best idea Justin had come up with that week. He was never at a loss for ideas. They'd been dating steadily for more than two months, and he'd treated her to the sort of memory-making summer that seemed like something from a dream. Every day was more magical than the one before.

Justin was amazing.

Emily had known it from the beginning, when his cheeks turned red beneath Vonda's relentless teasing. She'd known it when he took her to the small church just off the base, when she watched him hanging on every word of a message on sacrifice, and when he'd lifted his chin and closed his eyes during the praise music. And she knew it when he made a point of asking her to go every Sunday morning after that.

He'd opened up his heart and shown her the picture of a man who was as gentle as he was strong. She knew more about his background now. He and his sister were very close — though, according to Justin, they were known to have drawn-out arguments. And his entire family saw him as a hero. Not just because of his time in Iraq either.

That wasn't all she found out. A few days after the soccer tournament, the two of them were editing news briefs in the public information office when Vonda set down her telephone receiver.

"Justin Baker, how many things are you involved with, anyway?" Her voice boomed across the office.

Emily looked up from her computer.

He made a silly face and shrugged. "Take a message, Vonda. I'll call them back at my break."

"The senior center, the teen center, the city-subsidized daycare center, the local grade school ..." She shook her head and returned to the phone call. After she'd taken a message, she hung up the phone and did an exaggerated sigh. "Boy, you make Mother Teresa look lazy. How'll you find time for that pretty girl of yours if you stay so busy?"

"It's nothing." He winked at her and then looked at Emily. His expression told her that there were things about his life she didn't yet know. Things he wanted to share with her.

"It's something, all right. And anyway, you don't need involvement to keep yourself on your toes. That's what you've got me for!"

Justin laughed and Emily did the same thing. But a strange and wonderful feeling spread from her heart outward. Justin volunteered his time? And how come he hadn't talked about that before? She'd known guys in her past who bragged about the least little bit of charity or community work. Anything to look good.

Justin had done the opposite.

"Why?" she asked him later. They had taken their lunch outside to a picnic table. "Why didn't you tell me?"

"Come on, Emily." His easy laugh filled the air between them. "How would that sound? We're just getting to know each other, and I bore you with a list of things I'm involved in?" He grinned. "Besides, the Bible says don't let your left hand know what your right hand is doing." His shrug seemed to dismiss whatever praise was due him. "It's not like I'm saving the world. Just spending time with people."

She was awed, intrigued. Over the course of lunch she found out that he spent a few hours every week or so at the Veteran's center. If he didn't admit to fighting with his sister every now and then, Emily would've been tempted to search his back for wings.

"I love Veterans." She studied him, still trying to figure him out.

"People forget about those old folks." His tone was nonchalant, as if every guy his age took time to visit with Veterans. He swallowed a bite of his sandwich and looked at her. "They served our country with everything they had. The World War II Vets and the Vietnam guys." His eyes grew deeper, more serious. "The stories they tell would make you cry, Emily. How they watched friends fall and die in battle, and how they wept over having to kill the enemy."

He was quiet for a moment, and the silence felt comfortable. Then he looked at the blue sky beyond the trees and his voice grew more intense. "The sacrifice they paid, they paid for all of us. So we can go to church and choose our careers and," he smiled, "even so we can sit here and eat lunch together." He looked at her. "Freedom is as basic to us as breathing." He shrugged. "It's easy to take for granted. I don't know." The sunlight caught his eyes. "I guess the least I can do is spend a little time getting to know them, letting them know that their sacrifice wasn't in vain. That people haven't forgotten."

Emily could barely eat. She hadn't thought guys like this existed. When her surprise let up a little, she pushed harder, asked more questions, and learned that he spent an hour every Saturday after lunch at the city's teen center. Justin had played soccer and basketball in high school. Even though he hadn't run with the popular jock crowd, he still knew sports and was athletic enough to jump in and play with the kids who came to the center.

"Most of them don't have dads." He narrowed his eyes and looked up for a minute, toward the branches of one of the big evergreens that lined the picnic area. "I can't imagine growing up without a dad." His eyes grew watery. "When I was in grade school, a buddy of mine had a father in prison. A real bad guy, into drugs and gang stuff." Justin's voice grew softer, and his expression changed as he drifted back.

"One day when my friend was twelve, he climbed on his bicycle and headed out to the prison. He wanted to talk to his dad, whatever it took. His mother wouldn't take him, didn't want the guy having an influence over her son. So my buddy rode off to find him on his own. Only he never made it. Got his bicycle tires stuck in a rut along some rural road and flipped his bike right in front of an oncoming bus."

Emily gasped and put her fingers to her mouth. "That's terrible." When she looked up, she saw tears in Justin's eyes.

"He never knew what hit him." He sniffed and his voice grew more determined. "I couldn't get over that. The boy just wanted his daddy. Wanted him so badly he would've done anything to get to him." He exhaled. "A lot of the kids who enlist in the armed services were raised in single-family homes, did you know that? Either their dad was gone all the time or in prison, or divorce took him away and off to another family."

"I didn't know."

"It's true. Lots of the kids who come here have a brilliant future ahead of them. But a good number are looking for a way out, any way but the way they were raised." He set his sandwich down on his plate and pulled a few sesame seeds from the bun. "Those kids are so hungry for an older guy in their life, it's unbelievable.

I think about my dad, what a great guy he's been for me." He angled his head. "So what if I show up and play hoops with them once in a while. No big deal. But maybe when they hit the pillow that night, they miss their dad just a little bit less because someone took time to hang out with them."

"Do they ever give you a hard time about the war?"

Justin considered her question. "You know, for now these kids think the world of soldiers." He smiled, slightly embarrassed. "I guess by going out and meeting with the kids, I'm helping that generation have the right understanding of the military. The world will tell them soon enough that we're the bad guys, that we're warmongers. I want them to know the truth—that we're willing to give our lives so that they'll have a safe place to go to school, a safe neighborhood where they can live and play and grow up."

When Emily returned to her room that evening, she was dumbfounded. Justin truly cared for the people he helped. The Veterans and the lost teens and the innocent youth. It all came back to his understanding of what constituted a leader: "Being a leader means making sacrifices, Emily, and what've I really sacrificed? The things I do are fun. I'm a people person. What can I say?"

She wanted to pick up the phone and call her father, brag to him about how wonderful her new boyfriend really was. But that day as she reached for the phone, she changed her mind before she punched in the first number. Justin hadn't shared the information with her to impress her, but to help her understand him. And he'd only done so after she found out about it through Vonda. That made it all the more special. She made a decision that day that she would keep the details about Justin quiet and close to her heart.

The recent memories faded, and she looked at her watch. Justin would be there any minute. She grabbed her backpack and headed for the foyer of her residence hall, where she always waited for him. Yes, if she and God were the only two who knew how special he was, then so be it.

She reached her spot and anchored herself against the wall. Again, images of the past few weeks came rushing back. She'd gone with him to the teen center a few times, once to visit with the schoolkids, and twice to play basketball. She had Saturday afternoons off, and basketball was a great cardio workout. But more than that, her times to go to the center with Justin gave her a chance to see him in action.

He was a natural leader, no doubt.

Both times she'd joined in the pick-up games, and he would make sure she was on his team.

"Come on, Baker," one of the teens said the first time she went. He thumped his chest. "She's too pretty for you, man. Put her on the sidelines where she can cheer nice and proper."

"Not all pretty girls are cheerleaders." Justin chuckled. He was completely at ease around the tougher kids. "Here's how it is. She's on my team, and even though she's pretty, we'll still beat you."

The guys laughed and shoved each other, talking smack. But once the game got underway, Emily worked beautifully with Justin. His passes were right to her, giving her one easy layup after another. The final score had them on top by four points. Justin took his camera with him everywhere, and as they finished, he took it from his backpack and handed it to one of the teens. "Get our picture, okay?"

The guy shook his head. "Girls."

"I know, I know." He took her hand but kept his distance as he raised a brow at her. "Don't stand too close. I need a shower."

She laughed and took her place beside him.

"Ready?"

They smiled and the boy took the picture. Another memory made. But it wasn't so much the game that Emily remembered from that afternoon. It was the way Justin hung around with the guys afterward. He brought a twelve-pack of Coke and gave everyone a can, and for more than an hour, he sat on a set of steps listening while the guys talked about school and sports and girls. Whatever was on their minds.

Her thoughts shifted, and Emily looked at her watch. He was ten minutes late. She checked her cell phone, but no text messages, no missed calls. Strange. Justin was late once in a while, but usually he'd call. She leaned forward and scanned the parking lot. Then she let herself fall back against the wall again. He would have a good reason, whatever it was.

She smiled and remembered the ride home from the teen center that first time they'd gone together. She had studied him. "Don't you have any faults, Justin Baker?"

"Me?" He pointed to himself and gave her a mock look of surprise. "How can you even ask?"

She giggled. "Come on, I'm serious. I've never known anyone like you."

"Truth? The list is too long to go into."

"Like what? You don't wash your car once a week?"

"That too." He loosened his grip on the wheel and looked at the road ahead of him. "Let's see. Okay, I have this dog, Buster. He was my best friend until I enlisted, and now I almost never make it home to take him on walks. That's a big one." He held up two fingers. "Second has to be my room. It's been a mess since I was old enough to walk. No matter what my mom tried, I couldn't keep it clean." He gave her a wry look. "I guess that's sort of a warning. If you wanna break up with me, I'll understand."

"Confession." She winced. "My room's probably worse than yours."

"Yikes. We'll have to hire a housekeeper for sure." His laughter faded. "But that's only the beginning of the list."

She felt her heart opening to him. "What's at the top?"

He stared at the road for a handful of seconds. "Fear." He gave her a side glance, and for the first time she could see cracks in her soldier's armor.

"Fear of what?"

"I don't know." Clouds had gathered and it gave the moment a quiet depth. "Of being in battle and doing the wrong thing, of letting my squad down." He looked at her again. "Of dying before I ever have the chance to live."

She sat back and absorbed this revelation. After a while she put her hand on his knee. "I didn't know."

He grinned, trying to lighten the mood again. "I don't think about it much, because, well ... you know. I'm never gonna die, right?"

"Oh, you mean that big *S* on your chest, Superman?" She giggled.

"How'd you know?" He chuckled. "No, seriously. Most of the time I can convince myself I'm not afraid of that stuff. The risk is my choice, you know?"

"Yes."

"But if I'm honest—" he drew a long breath—"if I'm really honest, I sometimes struggle with it. Way down where no one can see."

"Except me." She moved her hand to his.

"Except you. Because you and I share that X-ray vision."

They laughed, and that night after dinner they drove south to his parents' house. Buster was an English springer spaniel, black and white with gray around his whiskers. "Buster—" Justin hooked the leash onto the dog's collar—"I'd like you to meet a special girl." He went through with formal introductions, but Buster couldn't have cared less.

He only had eyes for Justin.

Clearly the dog hadn't forgotten the days of his youth, when Justin was young and had all sorts of time on his hands. The dog stayed close by his master's side throughout the walk, glancing up every few minutes with a look of admiration that said it didn't matter if Justin came to walk him only once a year. The dog's love for his boy was undying.

When they were finished, Justin crouched down and nuzzled his face against the dog's. "Atta boy, Buster. It's a good thing Dad takes you for walks when I'm not around, huh?"

The dog licked Justin's cheek and then whined as they walked away and headed into the house.

"See?" he told her later. "That dog deserves better. Definitely a big-time fault."

There were others, but not many that Emily could see. Once in a while he'd be late picking her up because he'd tried to squeeze too many events into a single day. But overall, it had been perfect. The weeks had flown by like a wonderful movie heading all too fast toward the ending.

And today would be one more amazing experience. Hiking the foothills east of the city. She exhaled and moved to the door. Where *was* he? He'd never been this late before. At eleven forty, when he was a full fifteen minutes late and she was about to call his cell phone, his Cherokee pulled into the lot and zipped around to the driveway just outside. She smiled and skipped down the stairs. As she climbed in, she grinned at him. "I was beginning to think the clouds had scared you off. But I checked the forecast. No rain for days." She squinted out the windshield. "I guess this is more of a marine layer, and according to the paper, it should burn off in an hour or so, as long as ..."

Suddenly she felt it.

He wasn't smiling, wasn't saying anything in response. She'd been rambling about the weather without even stopping to ask how he was or whether there was a reason he was late. She stopped midsentence and looked at him. "Justin?"

"My commander pulled me aside on my way out." He didn't look afraid or upset. Just very serious. He put his hand on her shoulder. "I ship out September 24."

The news knocked the wind from her. She pressed her fists to her stomach and hunched over a little. *Come on, Emily, breathe.*

You knew this was coming. And she had known. But for the past six weeks she'd lied to herself, convinced herself that maybe Justin was wrong, maybe the army wouldn't need him back in Iraq for another tour. Maybe the summer they were sharing really would go on forever, endless and perfect.

But now ... now there was a date, a time when she would have to say good-bye and trust God that somehow Justin would return to her, that He hadn't brought a boy like Justin Baker into her life only to take him away forever. She swallowed hard and lifted her eyes to him. "For sure?"

"For sure." He massaged her shoulder. "But there's good news, Em. It won't be for a year like I thought. Only six months."

"On the front lines?"

He smiled. "That's where they need medics most."

She was still barely catching her breath. Six months on the front lines in a war where there were casualties every day. She had no idea how she'd survive a single week, let alone six months. "Have you ... have you told your dad?"

"Not yet." He bit his lip. "I wanted you to know first." He brushed her hair back from her face. "Now listen, no sad eyes, okay? Six months is nothing, Emily. I'll come back and we can do what I've wanted to do since the first time we went out."

She felt the dark cloud lift just a little. "What's that?"

"Well—" he came closer and kissed her, longer than usual and with a passion that left them both breathless—"I guess you'll have to wait and see."

She kissed him again and gave him a pretend pout. "What if I don't want to wait."

He rubbed his nose against hers. "Ever after's worth waiting for. Don't you think?"

Ever after. Emily put her arms around his neck and held him close. He was right. He'd come back in six months and they could talk about forever, about how God had made them for each other, and how once he was back they would have an entire future to plan.

They continued on with their hike that day, lost in a world all their own, laughing about how Justin's dad had found an old sweatshirt of Justin's and given it to Buster, and how the dog wouldn't sleep without it now. "Talk about a guilt trip." Justin stayed right behind her as they hiked, and halfway up the trail, when she slid on some loose rocks, he caught her in his arms.

"Well, that settles it." She steadied herself and grinned at him. "You definitely have a talent for saving lives."

Justin glanced at the hillside. The drop-off was maybe ten feet. "You would've skinned your knee, but I don't think that fall would've killed you. Just to be honest."

They laughed and she started out again. "Just stay behind me, okay? You never know when I might fall."

"You got it."

The day was full, and Justin took pictures left and right, even finding a passerby to snap one of the two of them near the top of the trail.

When they finished their hike, they drove to the teen center for basketball. Later, after the games, Justin told them about his leave date.

"Man!" One of the teens, Bo, the one who seemed to be the group's leader, had a sweaty T-shirt in his hands. He wadded it up and tossed it on the ground. "That stinks."

"Yeah, how come Uncle Sam gets you two times around?" Another teen crossed his arms, doing his best to look tough. But there was no hiding the tears that had sprung to his eyes. His chin quivered. "Stupid war, anyway."

Justin took a slow breath and looked at each of the kids. "It's not a stupid war, guys. Really." He picked up a pebble, turned it around in his hands, and tossed it out onto the basketball court. "The stuff I've seen over there would amaze you. The war's helping more than you'll ever hear about."

"Still—" Bo cocked his head back—"you already been there once."

"I wanted to go back." Justin rested his elbows on his knees and looked from Bo to the others. "When you believe in something, you put your whole heart into it." He looked at Emily. "Whether that's a girl, or fighting for your country."

Emily studied the guys. A lump formed in her throat. She tried to swallow, but she couldn't. The teens looked like the most lost group ever, devastated and not sure how to react to the fact that Justin would be leaving them.

One of the teens, a smaller kid who hadn't said much, looked up and nodded. "I'm proud of you, man. When I'm eighteen, I'm enlisting too. My mama says it'll set my whole life straight, being in the service."

"Yeah." Another boy, one who'd hung his head at Justin's announcement, looked up at his friends. "Me too. I'm enlisting soon as I graduate high school."

"But man!" Bo shook his head. "What about all that danger?"

"Okay, well, that's why I'm telling you." Justin's voice was kind, but stern. "Not so you can hang your head and be mad at the military." His expression softened. "So you can pray. Pray for me every day, and pray for the other guys out there. We're doing a good thing. Pray that we'll make progress and that God'll use us while we're there."

"Pray you'll come back in one piece, you mean." Bo smiled, but as he did, a single tear rolled down his cheek. He cussed under his breath. "I mean it, man. Come back safe."

"Hey, now." Justin gave him a friendly punch in the arm. "I'm not leaving for a month. You have lots of time to take me in hoops between now and then."

"Yeah." Bo returned the punch. "Just come back."

Emily wiped at her own tears, and on the way to her residence hall later, she and Justin were quieter than usual. Finally she reached for his hand. "Did you ever think that maybe you don't need a second tour? Maybe ... maybe you're doing enough over here to get all the leadership skills you could ever use."

"The way I see it, the good leaders all go twice, Emily." His voice held something she hadn't heard before. Not the fear he'd confessed, exactly. But a sense of duty, obligation. Every other time he'd talked about his second tour, it was with a tone that suggested he almost looked forward to it. But this time was different.

"So you've thought about it at least?" Her voice was soft.

"A second tour is expected of any committed soldier. Most of us don't have a choice, and just because I'm a lieutenant, because I have more training, more education, doesn't mean it's not expected of me." His eyes held a longing. "It's the right thing, Emily. But that doesn't mean I wouldn't rather be here with you."

Those words made her feel more loved than anything he'd told her so far. Yes, he was going back to Iraq and yes, it was the right decision for him. But he'd given her a glimpse through a chink in his heroic armor.

In a perfect world, he would never leave her side. But that was just it.

The world wasn't perfect.

When they arrived at the parking lot, he turned off the engine and reached into the backseat. "I brought my Bible." He opened it. "I want to show you something." He turned to Genesis. "Listen to this. It's from chapter 29." He began to read.

The story was about Jacob and Rachel, how Jacob had loved Rachel from the beginning, and how working seven years for her seemed like only a few days because of his love for her. When Justin reached that part, he stopped. He looked at her, his eyes full of questions. "Do you know what I'm trying to tell you, Em?"

She felt hesitant and unsure. Her eyes fell to the open Bible, but she shook her head. "Not really."

He pressed his hand to the page. "That's how I feel about you." He took her hand and looked long at her. "At the end of summer I'll have to go away, but time can't separate us, Emily. Not six months or six years. Because that's how much I love you."

Her heart melted. "Justin—"

"I mean it." He leaned close and kissed her. "Go on in. But remember that, okay."

"You're amazing."

He smiled. "Go."

As she headed up the steps that evening, she remembered how she'd slipped during their hike, and how he'd been right there to catch her. It was how the teens felt, how the Veterans probably felt too. Justin was their fallback guy. The one they could count on when no one else was around.

She could only do what he'd asked the teens to do. Pray for him, for his effectiveness in the Middle East and for his safe return. So that whenever life gave her a reason to trip up, he would always be there, ready to catch her.

Justin Baker, her fallback guy. Her hero.

NINE

The weeks of summer disappeared, and finally Lauren had to face the facts.

There had been no improvement between her and Shane, nothing to convince her she should stay. He'd been busy at work, training a new group of pilots and preparing for a series of raids that would take place from naval aircraft carriers located in the waters off the Middle East.

They were covert operations, plans to bomb headquarters where new terrorist cells were gathering and making plans for attack. All Shane could tell her was that the U.S. government had discovered more terrorist activity, that they knew the whereabouts of the terrorists and which compounds they were using, and that they intended to eliminate them without civilian casualty before they could formulate a strike against the United States.

He was taken up with the plans while she'd given herself over to stories that seemed empty and meaningless. A feature on the college dropout rate, the difficulty college grads had getting jobs that paid enough, the success of a reading program in inner-city D.C., and the humanitarian work being done in New Orleans more than a year after Hurricane Katrina.

Okay, so those stories were important to a segment of people. But the war affected every citizen in the U.S. and the Middle East. When she wrote from Afghanistan, she could help sway public opinion, help people know how wrong and ineffective the war was, and what hardships it created for the Afghani and Iraqi citizens. She could tell the truth about civilian casualties and show that the U.S. had been overzealous in declaring war in the first place.

Maybe her stories would be strong enough to help voters know that it was time to bring in a president who would put an end to the horrors being committed in Afghanistan and Iraq. Those countries would figure out their own way to freedom. If they wanted it badly enough, they'd find a way. But American boys needed to be back home. No matter what Shane thought.

The longer she pictured Justin Baker bent down using his own shirt to stave off the soccer player's bleeding, a girl he'd never met, the more she'd changed her thinking. It wasn't the soldiers' fault they were in Iraq. They'd been taught that what they were doing was right.

If Justin was what U.S. soldiers really were like, then all the more reason to pull out of the war. America couldn't stand to lose a generation of young people like that. Kids who might grow up to be police officers or firefighters or judges, doctors, or lawyers. The very ones who would bring about change in a society that desperately needed it. No, the cost was too great if it meant losing a single kid like the one Emily was in love with.

She'd tried to talk about it with Shane one night, but the conversation hadn't gone well. They shared dinner at his house, and afterward they took a walk to the nearby park.

"Remember when we were freshmen?" Shane held her hand. He stopped and looked at the swings. "We'd walk home together every day past the grade school."

"And if classes were out, we'd stop and swing together." She smiled. The memory was as clear as if it had happened last week. "We'd see who could get the highest."

"You won almost every time." He grinned at her, released her hand, and took a few running steps toward the swings. "Bet I can beat you now."

They both laughed, and the feeling was wonderful—so much better than the tension that seemed to always settle between them. She jumped on the nearest swing. "Race you to the moon."

"And back again."

The same words they'd said every time they'd done this as kids. And as they stretched their legs to the sky, Lauren could almost believe it was possible, that they could look past their differences if only they could spend more time doing this, playing and laughing together.

Shane won easily that evening. When they slowed their swings, out of breath from laughing and the exertion, Shane held up his finger. "Winner. Definitely the winner."

"Okay." She set her swing into gentle motion and waited until her breathing was normal again. "Hey ... guess what?"

"What?"

She narrowed her eyes, still holding onto the swing chain. "I've changed my mind about soldiers."

He looked nervous, as if he was having too much fun to talk about war. "After you got to know Justin, right?"

"More than that." She looked into the deep blue sky. "I used to think they were the bad guys, sort of. The people who were in favor of war—" she gave him a quick look—"which could never be a good thing."

Shane moved his swing ever so slightly. He let out a heavy sigh and stared at the ground. "Lauren ..."

"No, really. I have a point here." She kept her tone light, so she wouldn't shut him off from listening. "I know differently now. The soldiers, the kids like Justin, they're the good guys, aren't they?"

"Yes." Shane looked at her, but his expression was wary, as if he knew better than to agree to anything she might say about the war or the military. "They're definitely the good guys."

She twisted her swing from side to side, her eyes never leaving his. "So that's all the more reason why war's wrong. Because we can't afford to lose the Justin Bakers of this country." She tried to smile, but it didn't come easily. "Does that make sense?"

He stood slowly and held his hand out to her. "We better get back. I have an early day tomorrow."

Lauren had noticed a trend.

When they shared an evening together, if she didn't talk about the war or his job or the Middle East, then they'd find their way to the cozy sofa in his living room. They'd whisper about the past and share kisses—sometimes far later than they meant to. Shane had made it clear that he wouldn't sleep with her, and she agreed that it was best not to. She'd gotten pregnant once. It could happen again. Besides, no matter how liberal her views, she believed sex outside marriage was wrong. The Bible said so, and she truly wanted to do things God's way.

But if the taboo topics came up, their kissing would be quick and marked with strain and distrust, as if both of them knew it was only a matter of time before she'd leave again, and that would be that.

Now it was the first of September and she'd made up her mind.

She couldn't leave Shane, not on her own. Couldn't tell him she didn't love him and care for him when she still did, when her feelings for him had never been deeper. But she couldn't stay either. Shane deserved a wife who would praise him every day for his commitment to national security, who would celebrate covert air strikes as one more sign that America was in safe hands.

Men needed compliments. Her mother had taught her that when she was a teenager. But how could she build Shane up when she disagreed with what he was doing? And since she didn't have the strength to break things off, she'd made a different sort of decision.

To tell Bob Maine yes. Yes, she would go back to Afghanistan, and yes, she would work alongside Scanlon. She would report on the war the way she'd always done, and she would look harder this time—in case she was wrong. She would commit to a full year, and when it was over—if Shane was still interested—they could talk, see if they'd come any closer to finding the common ground she'd prayed about. See if they'd figured out a bridge long enough to span the distance between them.

They were meeting at the park again that night. Lauren didn't want dinner—she wasn't hungry, and after she told him her news, he wouldn't be either. She arrived ten minutes before Shane and took a spot at their usual picnic table. She had just long enough to study the endless expanse of mesquite bushes that covered the dusty, dry hills surrounding Fallon, just enough time to watch a pair of fighter jets zooming out of sight in the distance. Why had she ever thought it could work?

Lord... I don't understand how we got into this mess. Why did You let us find each other? And how come I ever thought I could survive here in Fallon?

She listened, and after a minute she began to see a Scripture verse forming in her mind. *My ways are not your ways.*

The verse was one she and Shane had talked about before. God's ways were different than man's, right? Wasn't that what it meant? But why would the Lord place that verse in her mind now? She sat still, observing the world around her. Not too far away, an older couple held hands as they walked along the paved perimeter of the park. Closer still, a family with two young boys was having fun on the play structure.

My ways are not your ways...

Did God want her to see that maybe her way of thinking wasn't right? Was that it? If so, she was willing. *Lord, if I'm wrong, show me. I only want what's best for this country, for the soldiers and the people of the Middle East. If my ways aren't Your ways, then please, Lord ... show me Your ways.*

She realized then that her prayer was one of the most common ones uttered throughout the Bible. Not a prayer for her will to be done, or for her way of thinking to be right. But a cry for wisdom.

What did the Bible say? Wisdom was more precious than gold or silver, better than honey, and worth any amount of searching, right? Wisdom was seeing things as closely as possible to the way God saw them, understanding them the way He understood them.

And it was admitting that maybe she was wrong—or maybe she and Shane both were—and being open to whatever God wanted to teach her. That was wisdom. *Fine, Lord ... I'm here, I'm open. I never wanted to hurt Shane this way, never wanted to hurt myself. So please, God ... give me wisdom.*

As she finished the prayer, she spotted Shane pulling into the parking lot. He got out of his car and walked over, his steps slower than usual. *He knows*, she told herself. *He has to see what's coming.*

He took the seat opposite her and folded his hands on the table. "You know something?" His expression was open and vulnerable, and it reminded her of the cold winter night when he drove to her house, the day before his family moved him to California. He had come as a last-ditch effort, desperate for a way to avoid saying good-bye.

"What?" She felt like a schoolgirl again, lost in his eyes. This was her Shane, the man she'd looked for all her young adult life.

"My heart still beats faster every time I see you." He reached across the table and she did the same. Their fingertips touched, and the sensation was warm and intimate. "I'm here because you want to talk." A sad smile played on his lips. "And knowing you, that can't be good. But even so," he looked deep into her eyes, "I see you and I want to shout to the heavens. You're here. You really are here after all those years apart."

"Shane..." She couldn't be doing this, could she? Meeting with Shane to tell him good-bye? She swallowed hard and searched his eyes. She was right; he knew what was coming. But even so, he wasn't angry or distant. Instead he held his whole heart out for her. "I'll never regret coming here, following you here to Fallon."

"Hmmm." His eyes never lost contact with hers. "Why don't I like that opening?"

"Because—" She hung her head and made a sound that was more cry than laugh. When she lifted her chin, she could already feel tears in her eyes. "I admire you, Shane. I don't tell you enough." She brushed her fingertips against his again. "You've committed your life to doing what you think is right, to living the way you believe is best." She let her voice drop a notch. "Most people could go their entire lives and not be able to say that."

"You admire me, Lauren?" His words were a caress. The longer they sat there, the harder this was going to be. "Is that what you came to tell me?"

"No." Her answer was quick and bathed in compassion. "But it's true. And I don't think I've told you enough. I might not—" she waved her hand around, frustrated at herself—"I might not agree with you, but I admire you for taking a stand. Really, I do."

"Okay." He looked like he didn't want to ask the next question. But he had no choice. "So why are we here?"

She brought her hand back to his. "Because—" she held her breath—"I'm leaving in the morning." There was no way around the obvious, not anymore. She had to tell him, because if she didn't say the truth soon, she'd run around the table and fall into his arms and make promises to him that she could never keep.

"Leaving? For an assignment?"

"Yes ... no." She breathed out and let the explanation come. "My editor wants me back in Afghanistan, Shane." Her emotions caught her off guard. This was the only sane choice, the only answer. The only way even to find out if God's wisdom went against her own, or if compromise was something she was supposed to work on. She pressed her finger to her upper lip and fought for control. "I've told you before. He's been asking me all summer."

Whether he had expected this or not, Shane's face grew a shade paler. "You're going back to the Middle East?" He tightened the hold he had on her hands. "Tomorrow morning?"

"Yes." She felt terrible, and she wondered at her sanity. If she hadn't run off to California looking for him, if she hadn't turned her back on her family twenty years ago, then everything would be different. Back then she would've driven to the moon to find Shane, to reconnect with him. Now, here they were, together again, and she was choosing to walk away.

"So that's it, huh?" He sat a little straighter, and for the first time since he arrived, there was anger in his eyes, in his tone. "That's all the warning you're giving me?"

"Shane, if I'd told you any sooner, I wouldn't go. I'd change my mind, because that's what being with you does to me. It makes me think impossible thoughts, like we could work things out, when nothing that's happened between us since I moved here makes that look even close to plausible."

He released her hand, stood, and turned his back to her. When they were teens, Shane had been willing to live with friends or with a teacher so he could stay in Illinois and marry her the way he wanted to. He would've worked three jobs so that after graduation they could live on their own and raise their child.

But the choice hadn't been his. That summer, when Lauren was weeks away from delivering, Shane's parents moved their family across the country. Oh, they promised he and Lauren would stay in touch, but that was a lie, same as the lie her parents had told her—that they'd connect with the Galanters as soon as they settled in California.

Now it was like the same thing was happening all over again. Shane had been willing to make things work, willing to listen to Lauren's arguments, willing to go to counseling or take longer trips away from Fallon.

But like before, the choice wasn't his.

He crossed his arms, his shoulders stiff and unmoving. If his heart was breaking, he wasn't showing it. She sat there, helpless. "This is all my fault, Shane." A couple of young moms walked by. Lauren waited until they had passed before finishing her thought. "I don't expect you to understand."

"Understand?" He spun around and put one foot on the bench where he'd been sitting a few moments ago. He leaned closer. "Lauren, you give me no time even to breathe, let alone understand."

"That's because I just made up my mind last night." She wanted to go to him, fall into his arms, and stay there. But it wasn't the time. "I've thought about it all summer, Shane. Wondered if I was crazy to want to leave, or crazier still to think I could stay."

"I *love* you, Lauren." He clenched his jaw and shook off the emotions that seemed to battle in his eyes. "What do our views on the *war*—" he spat the word like it was poison—"what do they matter? Certainly there must be more we can talk about than that." He waved his hand over his head. "Like the years we lost … and our role in Emily's life and the stories you're writing and what plans we have for the future. We can talk about our faith, and how important it is to find a church where we'll both fit in." He did a single laugh, one that held no humor whatsoever. "See, Lauren? Have you thought about those things?"

While he was talking, another pair of fighter jets soared into the sky overhead. The sound shook the park, and the little boys with their parents looked up, staring and smiling. Lauren waited until the sound died off. Her shoulders slumped and she shook her head. "I live in Fighter Town, U.S.A., Shane. Sometimes I can't think at all for the constant sound of the jets overhead."

"So that's it?" He tossed his hands and put his foot back down on the ground. "We meet here and say good-bye, we go our separate ways like we never found each other again?"

"No." She was on her feet now. She moved around the table and stood before him. "I'm not leaving you, Shane. I'm taking a job in the Middle East. One year, that's what I've promised. And something else." She waited until he met her eyes. "I've asked God to show me if my beliefs are wrong or too strong. If I should compromise somehow. I've asked Him for wisdom." Tears clouded her eyes. "I don't know what else to do."

For a long while, the anger lingered in his expression. But then the fight seemed to leave him. He held out his hands and took her into his arms. "A whole year? What if He shows you before that?"

"Then I'll come home." She met his eyes and touched her fingers to the side of his face. Then she brought her lips to his. Their kiss was borne of desperation and longing and sorrow. When it was over, there were tears on both their cheeks. "I'll come home, and I'll pray with every fiber of my heart that you'll still be here waiting."

"And in the meantime?"

"In the meantime … you'll have a lot less stress at dinner parties."

He smiled, but it faded before it reached his eyes. "Promise me something?"

She wanted to tell him yes, anything he asked. But they both knew that wasn't true. Instead she angled her head and prayed he'd see her heart. "I can try."

"Promise me you'll go back with open eyes." His tone was tender, filled with meaning.

"Okay." It was an easy promise to make. She'd already prayed for wisdom, and though she expected to feel even more strongly against the war a year from now, she could promise him to keep her eyes open. At least that. "If I'm wrong, I'll say so."

His eyes grew wet and he blinked twice. "Me too."

She traced his brow and his cheekbone. "I only know that nothing will change if I stay here."

He nodded. "You'll have email?"

"I will." She didn't want to commit to writing. Life in Afghanistan or Iraq, depending on where they stationed her, would plunge her into a different way of living. Besides, it would only hurt worse to keep Shane on the line as a pen pal. "I don't know how often I'll write."

Her words were one more blow, and she watched them hit their mark somewhere inside him. "Don't take risks, Lauren. There's nothing valiant about going places where the military warns you to stay out."

"I know. I'll have my jacket and helmet, my gear. I'll be careful." It was what she had to say, what all reporters told their families and loved ones. But they both knew the truth was something else. If the story meant going to areas of conflict, then she'd go—same as her colleagues. They all lived and worked with the understanding that they were observers, the ones who captured the news, never the ones who made it.

But after being shot at that day at the Afghanistan orphanage, Lauren knew better. Constant danger was a very real part of the job. Many journalists had died covering the war. She could only promise to be as careful as possible, nothing more.

"Hey—" Shane put his hands on either side of her face—"did I ever tell you what I thought that first day, when I came down the airport escalator and walked into the baggage area, and there you were? Standing next to Emily?"

She smiled, even as another layer of tears clouded her vision. "I don't think so."

"I thought I was dreaming." He drew her close. "Because all my life I looked for you, Lauren. The month before Emily called, I was supposed to get married."

"I know."

"But I never told you why I broke up with her."

Lauren waited, savoring the feel of his arms around her, knowing this would be the last time they held each other for a long time. Maybe forever. "She wanted you to be a politician, right?"

"Yes, but that wasn't why we broke up." He looked past her, as if he were seeing those days again. "I kept a picture of you in my top drawer, the way you looked when you were seventeen. And at night, in my dreams, I would imagine how you must look now, nearly twenty years later." He paused. "I'd be walking downtown or at the mall or at the gym, and I'd see a blonde woman with your profile, and I'd chase her down."

"What?" Lauren couldn't keep from giggling. "Are you serious?"

"Yes." He smiled, but again his expression held more sorrow than laughter. "I'd get just close enough to call out your name, and the woman would turn around and I'd know. It wasn't you." He narrowed his eyes. "The last time I did that was the night Ellen and I announced our engagement."

"Shane, that's terrible." She tried not to sound jealous. She hadn't heard the details of the story before, but her heart hurt even imagining him that close to another woman. "What happened?"

"I was heading up in the elevator and the door opened a few floors shy of where the party was about to start. Through the doors I saw a blonde woman who looked like you. At least, I thought she did." He brushed his thumb against her cheek. "I slipped out and chased after her, ran down the hall and into the indoor pool area. I must've looked like some sort of crazy man, running in there dressed in a three-piece suit."

"What did she say?" She was flattered and sad all at the same time. He cared so much for her. How could she leave him? "Did she know you were following her?"

"I stopped just inside the pool deck area. She had two teenage boys with her, and an older guy with gray hair came up and kissed her. That was the first time I saw a clear view of her face, and I knew two things. First, that it wasn't you."

"And second?"

"I couldn't get married. Not when my heart had never let go of the dream, the hope of finding you."

The story filled her heart. She pressed her head against his chest, and for a long while she listened to his heartbeat. "I didn't know."

"So when I saw you that day in the airport, at first you were just one more blonde woman who looked like my Lauren. I was about to rush up to you and ask if you were her, when I spotted Emily. Emily who looks so much like you and so much like me. And that's when I knew. Every prayer I'd ever uttered on your behalf had been answered."

She closed her eyes. Every prayer but one. Because his prayers had been like hers, like Emily's. That if they ever found each other again, they would find the same love they'd shared before. That they would never say good-bye again.

Only here they were.

She was about to tell him they should get going, she had to pack before she caught her flight in the morning. But he beat her to it. "I guess we better get it over with."

Already something in his voice had changed, something that told her he was steeling himself to the pain that lay ahead for both of them. The beginning of letting her go. She stared into his eyes and tried to memorize the look there, tried because there would be dark days ahead when the only way she might hear God's voice, understand His wisdom, was by remembering this moment.

They kissed, and when they came up for air, they were both quietly crying. "I love you, Lauren. Take that with you, okay?"

"I love you too, even if—" she sobbed twice—"even if I'm the most stupid woman on the planet for letting you go."

His lips touched hers one last time, and when he pulled back, he wore the look of a broken man. He mouthed the word, "Good-bye," and for a long time held her gaze. Then he turned and made his way back to his car.

She watched him go, and with every bit of distance that came between them, she felt herself grow weaker, until finally she dropped to her knees and sat back on her heels. *Don't go, Shane . . . tell me I'm wrong! Make me stay!* She wanted to shout at him that it wasn't too late. He could still talk some sense into her. But the words wouldn't come. Almost as if her mind knew better than her heart what needed to happen next.

He looked at her one final time before he drove away, and even from her place on the ground, she could see he was crying. Not just teary-eyed or choked up, but weeping. And she knew then that this was the hardest thing either of them had ever done.

It was one thing to say good-bye back when they were teen-agers, when the decisions were being made for them. But they were adults now who had found their way back together. And this good-bye was of their own choosing. Or of her own choos-ing. And in that moment, as a torrent of tears filled her heart and overflowed onto her face, she wondered if maybe Shane was right after all. Maybe everything about the last season of her life had been nothing more than a wonderful, terrible dream, from which it was inevitable that one day they would both awake. And they'd be right back where they started.

Alone in the world and wondering what would've happened if they'd never had to say good-bye in the first place.

TEN

Justin had their final day together all planned out.

Neither of them had any commitments, nothing to do but spend the time together. He was going to miss celebrating Christmas with Emily, so he took some money he'd been saving and stopped by a jeweler at Tiffany's in downtown Seattle's Pacific Place, a store they'd visited a few times on their dates there. What he found was perfect for Emily, and maybe—just maybe—wearing it would help the time go by faster.

Fall was in the air, but the days were still long and sunny. Emily had asked where they were going, but he kept it a surprise. "Trust me, it'll be perfect."

"I know." Emily had told him that the night before. "I just wish it wasn't happening so soon."

He made some joke to lighten the mood, and they both laughed. Because laughing felt so much better than crying. But now the day was here, and he was minutes away from leaving to pick her up. Everything was all set and loaded in his Jeep. The last thing he grabbed before he left his barracks was his camera. All summer he'd been good about taking pictures. It was part of what was going to make this day special.

He had just enough time to do one more thing. He sat down at his desk and pulled out a piece of lined paper. His words would come easily. With her, they always did.

Dear Emily…

He stopped there and remembered how this rollercoaster had all started. At the office of public information.

Nothing had changed about Vonda. Back at the beginning of August, she looked at them one day, clucked her tongue against the roof of her mouth, and shook her head. "Now listen here." She aimed her eyes at Emily. "Don't go acting like you're not in love. The whole office knows about it."

"But this is work." Emily grinned at her. "There can't be fraternizing at work, right?"

She brushed her hand like she was swatting at a pesky fly. "Fraternizing? You two wouldn't know how to fraternize if it meant a pay raise." She pounded her fist on the counter. "I say life's too short. If two people are in love, then don't hide it. In fact—" she stormed over and jerked her thumb in Justin's direction—"get up, young man."

Justin did as she said, chuckling under his breath. She made a big show of sliding his chair to an open computer next to Emily's. "This is your new work space." She took Justin's hand and led him to his chair. "Go on, take it." She rolled her eyes at Emily. "I have to tell you two everything." She waited until Justin was sitting down. "Good. This way you two lovebirds don't have to keep puttin' on a show, and you can hold hands when you want to."

She gave a firm nod of her head.

From that point on, Justin sat next to Emily. It was better that way, because Vonda was right. Being with her at work and pretending she wasn't sitting on the other side of the room was by then almost impossible. Love had caught him off guard and now it consumed him, especially at work when they'd tried so hard to keep their feelings hidden, to separate their jobs from life outside the office.

Justin looked out the window, the memories still playing in his mind. He'd had his last day at the office on Friday, and Emily and Vonda threw him a surprise farewell party. Afterward, when it was time for him to go, Vonda gave him a kiss on the cheek. Then she waved her hand at him. "Go on, get out of here." She drew back and froze, her eyes never leaving his. Suddenly her expression changed. Her chin began to quiver and her eyes welled up. Then she brought her hand to her mouth, and two trails of tears overflowed onto her cheeks. "Now look at me! All blubbery and everything." She wiped at her eyes, took hold of his shoulders, and looked straight at him. "Justin Baker ... you come back now, you hear? That's an order."

His throat thick, he saluted her. "Yes, ma'am."

She gave Emily a hug. "I'm the one who told you about him, so you make sure you do your praying, got it? We all gotta do our praying."

Before he left, she pressed a tissue first to one eye, then the other. "You're a good boy, Justin. I've seen my fair share of kids go off to war and never come back. But that ain't you, understand? This old world needs the likes of you, and I mean it. So don't do anything to get yourself killed."

He wasn't sure how to react. Vonda was always the strong one, the most blunt woman he knew. But now she was showing a side he hadn't seen. He hugged her, and when he and Emily were out in the hall, he realized Vonda wasn't the only one crying. Emily was too.

"Hey." He pulled her into a hug. "What's all this?"

"I don't know." She pressed her head against his chest. "I just want it to be March."

"It will be, sweetie. Soon enough."

But no matter how strong he acted around Vonda or Emily or the teens at the center or even his parents, deep inside he was waging a different kind of war. The one against fear. Before when he'd gone to Iraq, he had nothing to lose. He only wanted to do his part, fight for the United States, and make the war effort that much stronger. But when he left back then, he left with his whole heart and soul and mind.

Not so this time.

He looked at the paper before him and tried again.

Dear Emily,

I can't believe the worlds you've opened up to me this past summer. Things I never would've dreamed have come true and ...

The words flowed as if she were standing before him and he was getting one last chance to tell her everything he felt. When he finished writing, he folded the page and tucked it in an envelope. There. Now he was ready to go. He hadn't overlooked a single thing.

So he was a little afraid. That was something he'd have to live with. Because Emily was worth longing for, and that's exactly what he would do. Every day while he was in the desert, no matter how important the work, he would long for her.

And one day very soon, he would come back home, and if he had his way, never—as long as he lived—leave her side again.

Eleven

Emily had steeled herself for this day, prepared for it by praying and journaling and taking long walks across campus just so she could think. With her mother back in the Middle East, her entire world felt like it was spinning out of control. And now this—her last day with Justin. When she woke that morning, she had tears on her cheeks even before she stepped out of bed.

Her parents had failed. Sure, they told her they might have another shot at a relationship someday. Sometime. But the dream of seeing them married was over. Even still, today was harder. Justin was leaving. There could be nothing sadder than that.

He picked her up a little after noon, and from the moment she joined him inside his Jeep, she felt something different between them, a sorrow that neither of them had allowed until this day.

"I have a few surprises for you." He grinned at her as he drove off the campus and entered the freeway. He wore his dress uniform, and he'd never looked more handsome.

"Me too. For you." She turned her eyes to the road because it hurt too much to look at him, to imagine him with grime on his face and mud on his boots, working the front line and kicking in doors. Her heart felt heavy inside her, and it remained that way until they pulled into a parking spot near Seattle's waterfront. She laughed, because if she didn't, the tears were bound to come. "The same place?" She slipped her bag onto her arm. "You're taking me to the same place we went for our first date?"

"Sort of." He swung a backpack over his shoulder and held her hand.

Even the air felt the same as it had the first time they were there. They walked past tourists and burly fishermen lugging buckets and poles over their shoulders. A chorus of seagulls filled the air, and every once in a while, Justin's eyes met hers as they strolled along. She savored the sights and smells, breathing them in. She would remember this day forever. When they reached the water, instead of going to the restaurant where they'd shared their first meal, he took her out onto Pier 55, to the place where a three-level white cruise ship was loading.

"Justin, are you serious?" She stopped and stared at the ship. "You're taking me on a cruise?"

"Yeah, well." He rubbed his knuckles on his shoulder. "The Bahamas seemed a little far for an afternoon ride, so, you know—" he grinned—"I settled for this."

She'd heard from a few of the kids on campus that the lunch and dinner cruises that made their way around Elliott Bay and Puget Sound were worth every penny. The perfect place for a romantic date. But she and Justin had been forced to catch their moments between their other commitments. Though some of the cruises lasted only an hour, most were longer, and besides that, they were expensive.

Before they boarded, Justin snagged an older couple strolling past on the pier. "Please ... could you take our picture?"

Both of them lit up. The man held out his hand. "Absolutely, young man." He gave Justin a handshake before taking the camera from him. "And thank you for the fine job you and your guys are doing for our country."

Emily's heart swelled with pride. He *was* doing a fine job, even going to Iraq showed what sort of man Justin was, what sort of man he was going to become in later years.

"Thank you, sir." Justin took Emily's hand and moved her back a few steps so they were standing with the cruise ship behind them. "Okay, whenever you're ready."

Before the man snapped the picture, his gray-haired wife leaned in and smiled. "Oh, dear, aren't they the most adorable couple? Just like you and me at that age."

"The way we looked an hour ago." The man grinned and then looked at them. "Okay, one ... two ... three." He snapped the picture and handed the camera back to Justin. "Someday, when you're old and gray like us, you'll look back on that picture and understand about the passing of time. Don't blink, young people!" He jabbed his finger in the salty air and smiled. "Enjoy every minute."

"Thank you. We will, sir." Justin waved to them and then turned to her. "Good advice."

Emily could only nod. Could the man possibly have known how accurate he was or how timely his message? They boarded the ship and spent the first hour eating a lunch of grilled chicken. After that, they went up on deck and found a secluded bench on one side, a spot where the view was breathtaking. The ocean air felt wonderful, and with the design of the ship, the wind wasn't too strong.

"I can't wait another minute." He set his backpack down and went to unzip it.

"Wait." She put her hand on his. "Let me go first. Please."

He grinned at her, and the sun on the water made his eyes look greener than ever before. He sat up straight again. "Okay. You go."

Her heart beat hard. Gifts weren't always her thing, but she'd thought long and hard about this one. She pulled the wrapped item from her bag and handed it to him. "Here."

He looked puzzled. "Hey ... I didn't know you were doing this." He slid his fingers beneath the paper, and in a matter of seconds he could see what it was. "A scrapbook? Are you serious, Em?"

She'd been working on it every night, long after she would normally be in bed. Even her coach had noticed that she wasn't as peppy as usual on the practice field. A few weeks before, she'd asked him for a copy of all their photos, the ones he'd been so careful to take ever since the summer began.

He burned the entire file onto a CD, and she'd made two sets of prints. One for herself, and one for him. Now every hour of effort felt more than worth the time. "Your mother told me you like scrapbooks."

"You talked to my mother?" He ran his fingers over the red linen cover and the photo at the center, one someone had taken of the two of them after her championship soccer game.

"Yeah. That day we went there to walk Buster." She giggled. "I'm good at secrets."

"I guess." He looked at her. "Actually, I've never made a scrapbook. I just take the pictures. I sent my mom a ton from my last tour in Iraq, and she put them into a book. Gave it to me that Christmas." His smile faded. "It was the best gift she's ever given me."

"That's what she said."

"I can't believe this ..." He opened the book and looked through it, taking time to read the captions she'd written beneath each picture, to admire the time she'd put into decorating each page and creating a theme around each layout. There were pictures of their strolls along Puget Sound, and the one Bo had taken after their basketball game that first time at the teen center. Photos from walking Buster, and of them working side by side at the public information office.

Beneath those, she'd written: *Smooth Talker, indeed.*

Another photo showed where Vonda had slipped in behind them, and Emily had written, *Vonda knew before either one of us. And Vonda's never wrong.*

There were pictures of them with their parents taken the weekend of her soccer tournament, and one of him with the teens at the center, and another of him playing cards at a table full of Veterans.

Justin, she'd written. *You'll always be my hero. But you'll always be theirs too.*

Slowly, page by page, he worked his way through the book. On the last page, was a picture of the two of them at the end of their hike that day in the foothills of the Cascade Mountains, east of Tacoma. *One thing I ask of you, Justin Baker*, she'd written beneath it. *That whenever I fall, you'll always be there to catch me.*

When he finished, he looked at her, his eyes glistening. "I'll keep it with me wherever I go."

"Okay." She'd created it on lightweight paper, careful to keep the size small enough that it would fit in his backpack. "Every time you look at it, just know that I'm thinking of you, praying for you." She pointed to the last page and an envelope she'd taped there. "Inside is a letter. You can't read it until you're in Iraq."

"How ..." He swallowed hard, and a tear slipped onto his cheek. "How am I ever going to walk away from you at the end of the day?"

"I don't know." She pressed her palms to her eyes and tried to stop her own tears from forming. "If you figure it out, tell me, okay?"

They both laughed, and the sound lightened the moment. It was a beautiful day, and but for a six-month stint in Iraq, they had no reason to be sad. Justin wrapped the paper around his scrapbook and tucked it into his backpack. Then his eyes met hers. "My turn."

She hadn't given any thought to what he might be doing for her. She'd spent all her energy creating the scrapbook, putting it together and believing that somehow—another world away—it would bring him the strength and determination he needed to keep going, to keep being careful, and to come home again, safe and whole.

Now she wondered what he'd planned for her. She took hold of the bench on either side of her and watched while he lifted a small wrapped rectangular box from his backpack. "Start with this."

"Justin ..." She couldn't still her racing heart and wondered if maybe she would faint from the mix of joy and impending sorrow. She opened the paper carefully and then lifted the velvet lid of the box beneath it. There, nestled on a piece of satin, was a white gold bracelet with a single heart charm at the center. Her breath caught and she had to work to make herself heard. "It's ... it's beautiful."

"Read it." He pointed to the heart.

She took the bracelet from the box and held it close. On one side of the heart, in delicate engraving, it read, *Justin and Emily.* On the other side, it said only, *Genesis 29.*

The memory came back in a rush. The Bible verse he'd read to her the day he got news of his deployment date. He'd written it at the end of several notes since then, *Genesis 29.* She looked at the engraved words now and tried to see them through her tears.

"I meant what I said the first time I read that to you." He leaned his head against hers, his voice so soft she could barely hear it over the sound of the cruise ship. "I might be going away for six months, Em, but I'll work my tail off every hour, knowing that nightfall will bring me one day closer to coming home to you."

She couldn't speak. She was trembling, overwhelmed by feelings she'd never known before. She handed him the bracelet and held out her wrist so he could place it on her. When it was secure, she looked at it, admiring how it glistened against her tanned skin. "I'll never take it off."

"Good." He sat up straighter and dug back into his backpack. This time the box was longer, but it was wrapped the same way. He handed it to her. "This one means even more."

She removed the paper and opened it, and inside lay the most delicate white gold necklace, one that matched the bracelet, and at the center, another tiny heart.

He took it gently from her and fastened it around her neck. "It's belonged to you for a long time now." He hooked it and then adjusted it so the heart was in the middle. "But this way you know for sure." His eyes found hers. "My heart belongs to you, Emily. It'll belong to you forever."

Joy and sorrow and longing and disbelief all mixed together and swirled inside her. Justin Baker's heart belonged to her and her alone. She touched the tiny piece of jewelry and then brought her fingers to his face. "It's perfect."

"Like you." He kissed her, and when he pulled away, his eyes danced. "Just one more thing."

"Justin, you're spoiling me." His thoughtfulness was more than she'd ever imagined.

"I figure this is our Christmas." He reached into the backpack once more and pulled out a bulky, round package. "Here. This one's a little more practical."

She laughed and felt the heart on her bracelet jingle as she opened this last gift. Inside was a Starbucks travel mug, one big enough for even a large drink. The outside was a collage of their pictures, the same ones she'd used for his scrapbook. He'd sized them onto a single piece of paper, some large, some small, and he'd printed it off and slipped it inside the plastic casing.

"I know how you like your coffee." He gave her a quick kiss. "This way you can know that wherever you are when you're drinking one, I'll be over there in Iraq drinking something a whole lot more like mud than coffee. And wishing I was here with you instead."

She studied the pictures, basking in the array of memories they represented. "I love it."

"And I love you." He worked his hand around her waist and slid closer to her, kissing her the way she longed to be kissed. Only a few seconds had passed when he pulled back and snapped his fingers. "I almost forgot." He reached into his backpack one more time and pulled out an envelope. "I wrote this for you. But you can't read it until I'm gone."

She took the envelope and pressed it close to her heart. "This might mean more than all the other gifts put together." She slipped it into her bag, next to the travel mug.

And then, suddenly, they had nothing left ahead of them but good-bye. He took her hands and searched her face. "How's your dad?"

"Sad."

"I'll bet." He looked out at the water. "And your mom?"

"Busy back at her job. They're moving the whole *Time* magazine team to a building in Iraq." She frowned. "Maybe you'll see her there."

It was a topic they'd already spent hours talking about. Her mother had called from the airport the day she was leaving for the Middle East. "Honey, I had to tell you before I left. I'm going back to Afghanistan, back to my job writing about the war."

Emily couldn't have been more shocked if her mother had said she was moving to the North Pole. "But … you and Dad … you're getting married in December."

"No, Emily. We're not. Not this year, anyway." Her mother had sighed, and Emily wasn't sure, but it sounded like she was crying. "I need to see the war again for myself, be there and experience it. Write about it." She made a little coughing sound. "Maybe I'll find out that I've been wrong about our involvement over there. Or maybe …" She hesitated, her voice tight. "Maybe I'll find out I've been wrong about thinking I could ever make things work with your dad."

Emily had begged her to change her mind. "Mom, no. Go home and think it through. Remember your journal? All the things you felt for Dad, remember that? You can't give up now. So what if you don't agree with him?"

But it was too late. Her mother had made up her mind. The phone call was only her way of being courteous enough to tell Emily herself, rather than waiting for her father to tell her the news.

She'd called her dad the moment she hung up from her mother. By then she was crying, unable to grasp what had happened and at a loss to do anything about it. "Dad ... tell me it isn't true."

He waited until she had control of herself, and then he told her that yes, it was true. "Your mother has a lot of searching to do, Emily. Maybe we both do. Pray for us. This isn't what either of us really wants."

Later she'd shared every detail with Justin, how frustrated she'd been and how helpless she'd felt. She peered out across the water. The subtle vibration of the cruise ship engine vibrated against her back. "Before, I always knew there was something I could do. Like it was up to me to find my parents and reunite them." She looked at him. "But now ... now this is their decision. Her decision. It doesn't matter what I want, they have to work things out for themselves."

Justin took her in his arms and stroked her back. "It's something they need to figure out. Especially your mom." He released her but kept his hand around her shoulders. "God has a plan for them, just like He has a plan for us. If that means the two of them should be together, then they'll figure it out." He kissed her. "I'll pray for that, okay?"

A trio of seagulls swooped low along the side of the ship and then lifted out over the Sound. Emily watched them fly away, and she remembered something. She'd never shown Justin the pages from her mother's journal, the way her parents had been so in love with each other. A week ago, she'd made copies of the writings and tucked them in her purse, intent on showing him. But she'd forgotten about them until now.

"Hey—" she picked her purse up and dug around in one of the side pockets—"I almost forgot."

"What?" His voice held a desperate knowing. They had only hours left, after all.

"My mother's journal. I was going to show you, remember?" She pulled out the folded pages. "I only have to look at this to know they belong together."

He leaned his shoulder into the side of the ship. "Read it."

She smiled. This was something else she liked about being with Justin. The easy way they had together. She scanned down the page and found her favorite spot. "This was what she wrote their junior year of high school. Spring of 1985." She hesitated, then with a steady voice, she began. "'Shane and I talked about love. Real love. We both think it's weird that our parents don't understand how we feel about each other.'" She smiled at Justin.

"Parents never change."

"Nope." She found her spot and kept reading. "'They act like we're a couple of kids who have no clue what love is. But here's what I've learned when I'm with Shane.'" She bit the inside of her lip, staving off the surge of emotions in her heart. "'Real love waits in the snow on your front porch so you can walk to school together in the fifth grade. It brings you a chocolate bar when you fall and finish last in the seventh grade Olympics.

"'Real love whispers something in the middle of algebra about your pink fingernail polish so that you don't forget how to smile when you're doing math, and it saves a seat for you in the lunchroom every Friday through high school. Even when the other baseball players think you're stupid.'" Emily laughed and caught Justin's eyes.

"Your mom was quite the writer, even back then."

"Yes." She ignored the tear rolling down her right cheek. "'Real love has time to listen to your hopes and dreams when your parents are too busy with the PTA or the auxiliary club or the business they run at the local bank.

"'Real love stays up late on a Saturday making chocolate chip cookies together, flicking flour at you and getting eggshells in the batter and making sure you'll remember that night the rest of your life. And real love thinks you're pretty even when your hair is pulled back in a ponytail and you don't stand perfectly straight.'" Emily's voice cracked and she had to stop for a moment. When she regained her composure, she finished. "'Real love is what I have with Shane. I just wanted to say so.'"

"Hmmm." Justin put his arm around her again. "That's beautiful."

"Exactly." She dabbed at her tears, folded the note, and put it back in her purse. "Sometimes I wonder how long it's been since my mom read her own words."

"You could send that to her." He stroked her shoulder. "Make a copy and mail it to her."

"True." She hadn't thought of that. When she found her mother last winter, she gave her an entire box of her short stories and journals. But she doubted her mother had read through them, the way Emily had—line for line—when she wasn't sure she'd ever even find her mother. She looked up at Justin. "I might do that. Maybe it would help."

"Right." He stood and moved to the railing. Then he held out his hand to her.

She took it and found her place beside him. "The water's so dark."

"It's like that off Kelso too." He lifted his chin, and the ocean breeze washed over his face. "Growing up, my dad used to take me fishing along the waterfront and he'd always tell me the same thing. 'Don't go out past your ankles, son. The water's deep along the Northwest coast.'"

"I love how you and your parents are, how close you are." They rested their elbows on the railing, and she noticed her new bracelet. She'd told him the truth. She wouldn't take it off, not as long as he was away and she was praying for his return.

"I'll miss them. And my sister." He turned his head and looked at her. "But not like I'll miss you."

She didn't want to talk about that yet. "Tell me about Kelso. What was it like growing up there?"

"Very different than Wheaton." He grinned and turned his attention back to the water. "At least that's my guess."

"Wheaton was nice, but it'll always be a suburb of Chicago. The big city feeling's never very far away."

"I used to long for a place like that." He chuckled. "But by the time I was in high school, I began to appreciate what I had in my own little town. The fact that my teachers had students who were the *kids* of students they'd had twenty years before." He was quiet for a moment. "There were parades and community picnics, and after spending a lifetime there, you couldn't go to the grocery store without running into ten people you knew."

"Really?" Emily liked the idea. "They probably gave you a big send-off when you enlisted."

"They did. My family held my going-away party at the American Legion hall, and half the town showed up." He looked like he was picturing the event. "Kelso's a blue-collar town, really. Lots of folks in shipping and construction. And they fly the flag higher than any people I know."

"I love that. How America's working class is so patriotic. They're the heartbeat of this country, for sure. The soul and strength." The wind was making her cold. She moved closer to him, so their sides were touching. "You could see it at the last election, the way the heartland, the country's backbone, was so supportive of family values and military strength."

"Yep. My hometown'll be supporting me this time, same as last. Tying yellow ribbons around trees and flying flags. That sort of thing."

The captain came over the loudspeaker then and announced that they'd be returning to the pier in five minutes. Emily looked at Justin as the message ended. It was one more reminder that their time together was borrowed.

"Someday, I want to take you on a real cruise." He turned so he was facing her. They were still alone on the deck, trying hard to be lost in the moment as if they had forever and not just five minutes. "We'll go somewhere warm where the water is shallow and clear and pale blue green."

"Sounds wonderful." She faced him and slid her feet between his. "But this was wonderful too." She gave him a shy smile. "Thank you. For everything."

He slid his arms around her waist and held her tighter than before. "I wish I had another week. Even another day."

Her hands came up along the back of his neck. "Not me. I want the six months to be over. The sooner the better."

Fifty yards away, a small speedboat whizzed by, and a group of guys on board howled in their direction. "Hey!" one of them shouted. "Go for it, man!"

Justin grinned and nuzzled his nose against hers. "Yep." He let out a soft moan. "I wish that too sometimes."

She felt her face grow hot. She understood what he meant, what the guys on the speedboat meant. The feelings she had for him took her places she knew better than to hang around. "Someday."

"I know." He kissed her, moved his lips over hers in a way she would remember long after he left in the morning. When he drew back, there was no denying the passion in his eyes. "Someday."

They felt a gentle thud as the ship reached the dock, and again the captain came on, thanking the passengers for joining them on the cruise and asking everyone to drive safely as they left. Justin laughed and took a step back. "I think that's our cue."

Her body ached to be near him, to stay near him. But God had provided a way to protect them from making bad choices before, and today was no different. They joined hands and left the ship. It was still only four o'clock, and for the next two hours they walked through Pike Place Market, checking out the shops and smiling at the strange people they saw along the way, the man juggling raw fish, and the girl in flowing gauze playing her harp blindfolded.

"You wouldn't see that in Wheaton!" She laughed and linked her arm through his. The hours flew, and before they left, he took her to the same restaurant where they ate on their first night out together. He even requested the same window table.

After dinner, he took her back to PLU and parked. Both of them knew the hour that lay ahead would be neither quick nor easy. They walked to their favorite spot, the bench just down the path from her residence hall. It was sheltered by a hedge of bushes on one side and a grassy field and evergreens on the other. Every time they sat there, they felt completely alone.

They looked at his scrapbook again, and she admired once more the travel mug he'd given her. The sun set before nine o'clock, and for the next half hour they sat there sharing kisses and sweet memories of every happy time they'd spent together that summer.

Finally, it was time for him to go. His flight was set for six in the morning, which meant he needed to leave the barracks by four. His commanding officers wanted the group that was deploying in bed by ten-thirty. His family would pick him up and take him to the airport, saving their good-byes for his final hours in Tacoma. But tonight belonged to her.

He walked her to the steps, and then—in a spot where no one in the building could see them—he eased her into his arms. "What a summer, huh?"

Her heart raced. She felt like they were on the Titanic, sliding off the deck with no way to stop, no way to keep from falling into the icy waters below. "Justin." She held onto him, needing the feel of his arms around her. And suddenly she could see him, crouched down behind a broken wall, gunfire zipping through the air overhead. "Please!" Her voice was a desperate cry. "Don't go. Don't leave me."

"Baby ..." He ran his hands down her back, along her arms, then he eased back and searched her face. "I'll come back. I promise. Everything's going to be okay."

"Don't." She shook her head, terrified of the feelings that stood like crumbling mountains all around her. "You can't promise that."

"But I believe it." He touched her face, and the feel of his hands was like velvet. "I've done this before, remember?"

She clung to him, and every heartbeat felt like the clock ticking, counting down the time they had left together. Tears filled her eyes and spilled onto her cheeks. "Take ... take me with you. Wherever you go ... I wanna be there too."

"I wish I could." He kissed her tears, kissed them as they fell from her eyes. "You have my heart." He held her necklace, the tiny heart that hung there. "Don't forget that."

Sobs came over her then. She hadn't wanted to do this, hadn't wanted to break down until she was safe in her room. But if she never let go, if she held him this way and never said good-bye, then he would miss his plane and maybe he'd change his mind. Maybe Iraq didn't need him, after all. Not when the Veterans and the schoolkids and the teens at the center all needed him. Not when Buster needed him.

Not when she needed him.

"Hey." He kissed another tear. "Every now and then, when you have a day off, maybe you could drive down to Kelso and take old Buster for a walk. Tell him I'm thinking of him."

She hung her head against his chest and grabbed three quick breaths. "O-o-okay."

"And stop by the teen center. Give 'em updates for me, alright?"

She couldn't bring herself to respond. She held onto him; he felt so whole and good and right. Justin Baker, the greatest guy she'd ever known. *Bring him home, God … please. Don't let anything happen to him.*

"Emily?" He eased back a bit and lifted her chin. "Will you do that, will you go there for me?"

She nodded. There was a question she wanted to ask, and now seemed like the time. "Are you afraid?"

He waited, searching her eyes. "Yes."

She sniffed. "You hide it well."

"Thanks." He breathed in slowly. "Soldiers aren't supposed to be afraid."

"Justin …" Never mind that she looked like a mess, that her tears were coming in buckets. She wanted to stand in the middle of Fort Lewis and make an announcement. *You can have any soldier you want, but not this one. Because this is the one I love! He's too good to work the front lines, too good to lose.* But the time for announcements, for changing his mind, had passed.

He was going, and she was only making it harder by losing control.

She steeled herself against the pain and stood straighter than before. "Have you figured it out yet?"

"What?" He had tears in his eyes too, but he was keeping his composure.

"How we're supposed to say good-bye?" She allowed a handful of quick sobs, and then she held her breath. *Enough. Get a grip, Emily. Come on.* She pursed her lips and blew out. "Okay, wow." She tried to smile, because otherwise she would fall to the ground and weep for a month. "Sorry."

His expression sobered. "No." He kissed her, the sort of kiss like he'd given her before, the kind that left them both dizzy. When it ended, he moved his thumb tenderly over her lips, his voice a whisper. "No, I haven't figured it out."

"Me either." She looked at him as long as she could, and then she flung her arms around his neck. "Be careful, Justin. Please. And when it's all over, come back to me."

He kissed her once more, and this time he held onto her the way she'd held onto him a moment earlier. Like he was terrified to walk away. But finally, he did. He took her hand and held it until his feet moved him far enough away that they had no choice but to let go. "I'll write."

She nodded, angry with herself for her tears. Not because they gave away how she was feeling, but because they blurred her eyes. And she wanted to remember every second of this good-bye, every detail of his face and his eyes, his strong shoulders and the crispness of his dress uniform.

"Good-bye, Emily." He was ten feet from her. He blew her a kiss, his eyes never leaving hers. "I love you."

"I love you." She mouthed the words, and it took every ounce of her resolve not to run after him, not to insist that he find a way to take her with him. So she could be sure he wouldn't place himself in danger, because she would never let him. Not for a minute. She held onto the stairway railing to keep herself in place. "Write."

"I will." With one long, last look, he turned away and jogged to his Jeep. He slid into the driver's seat and drove away. She watched him go, and already she could feel the distance between them. *Hold me up, God … don't let me fall apart.* When his taillights disappeared, she clutched the stairway railing and bent over it. *God … no. How can he be leaving?*

Daughter, I am with you. Even now, I am with you.

The words spoke peace to her soul, life-giving, life-saving peace. And they reminded her that with Christ, she wouldn't fall, because He would give her the strength to stand. She would stand as the days passed, stand every time she heard news of an American casualty, and she would stand even as her heart broke for missing him.

She would visit his parents and Buster and the teens at the center, because that's what Justin wanted her to do. Besides, for the next six months she didn't dare fall. Not when Justin Baker would be too far away to catch her. She would stand, and she would do it all in God's strength.

All for the love of a boy who had stolen her heart in one unbelievable summer. A guy whose heart she would wear on a chain close to her own. A soldier who was everything good and pure and strong and right about the U.S. military, and who had already given her a summer of happily.

Now all she had to do was wait six months for him to come home, so that one day that spring he could promise her the rest. A lifetime of ever after.

Twelve

The compound in Iraq was more primitive than the one in Afghanistan, but it suited Lauren's mood. She and Scanlon had connected again; they'd gone out and shared dinner and talked about everything that had gone on since their last time together.

"So—" Scanlon looked at her over the rim of his glass of red wine—"did you come to any conclusions?"

"About Shane?" This was the discussion they'd had before she left for the States, before she made her decision to move to Fallon. Scanlon understood the situation, and he'd let her go easily, the way a friend would let another friend move on to a better place. But still he was curious, and she didn't blame him. She was drinking green tea. She picked up her small cup and took a sip. "Yes."

"And?"

"I love him." This was the tough thing about Scanlon. They'd kissed once, a lifetime ago, and she knew his feelings for her. If he had things his way, they'd fall in love and get married, a sensible relationship built on all the things they shared in common—their work, their views, their passion for seeing the war come to an end. But her heart could never quite agree. She shrugged one shoulder. "I love him more than ever."

"Then why are you here?"

"I love him ..." She looked down at what was left of her tea. "But I'm not sure I can live with him." She shook her head and found Scanlon's eyes again. "We're so different."

He didn't look glad, and his tone held nothing in the way of celebration. He only reached out and squeezed her hand. "I'm sorry, Lauren."

"Me too." She pictured Shane, the way he'd looked the last time she saw him. "So sorry, sometimes I think I might get on the next plane and toss every view I've ever held."

"Only you can't do that." Scanlon's voice was simply matter-of-fact. "Because the views you hold run to the very core of your being, Lauren. You know that."

Yes, she did. She considered Scanlon's words throughout those first weeks while she grew reacquainted with the people of Afghanistan. But then word came from the main office in New York City. Bob Maine wanted them in Iraq. The action was there now, and no story about war in the Middle East would ring completely true unless it was being written there, from the middle of the battle.

She and Scanlon celebrated the decision. The closer the better, that's the way Lauren saw it. She'd given up Shane for this, after all. And she'd prayed for wisdom. There could be no place like Iraq for God to show her the answers she was looking for.

The move took place at the end of September, just after Justin Baker and his division arrived in one of the war's hot spots outside Baghdad. Lauren had spoken with Emily about their goodbye, but her daughter had been brief, almost short. "I keep trying to find something in my life that's going right."

"Emily!" The comment stung Lauren and gave her a chance to see just how hurt her daughter was by her return to the Middle East. "Your whole life is right. You're intelligent and beautiful. You have your whole future ahead of you."

"I know." She sighed. "It's just … a few months ago the whole world seemed perfect, and now …"

Again Emily's words hurt. She remembered herself kneeling on the ground, too heartbroken to stand. "Leaving your father was the hardest thing I've ever done." Her words were clear, certain. "It's complicated, but I had to come back here, Emily. So that I'd know if there's any way your dad and I can ever have a future together."

Emily's tone eased some. "I'm sorry. It's just … sometimes I feel like the timing is pretty lousy. First you leave. Then I barely have time to breathe and Justin's gone. I keep thinking you could've worked it out if you wanted to."

Of everything Emily had said in that conversation, that last part was the most painful. She'd wondered if sometimes her viewpoints gave those she loved the impression that she was the enemy. They hadn't talked again since then, though they'd exchanged a few emails. Phone service was spotty in the new compound, and once they got situated, two weeks ago, the story assignments came at them in bunches. Everything from the coverage of roadside bombings, to the progress of rebuilding the infrastructure in Baghdad.

In Iraq, she was visible enough that she no longer wore the khaki shorts and tops she could get away with in the journalists' compound in Afghanistan. Now she wore long skirts and blouses over her protective gear, and a handkerchief around her blonde hair—her way of showing respect for the cultural mandates that still existed in Iraq. So far her stories all had the feel of those she'd done from Afghanistan. Futile fighting, frequent failures, and the stories of fallen men who died for reasons that seemed as dusty as the desert.

Still, she would drop into her bed each night with the same prayer: *Show me, Lord. If there's something I'm missing, show me. Give me Your wisdom.*

Now it was mid-October, early Wednesday morning, and she and Scanlon were heading out to the heart of the city, to the place where protests were taking place over the upcoming election. Lauren was tempted to have her story all but written. The protestors were obviously citizens who didn't want a puppet government, the leaders assigned by U.S. influence. They wanted their own people.

She could already imagine the quotes she'd get.

"Could be dangerous today." Scanlon was working with one of his cameras. They'd been given an SUV to use while in Iraq, and this time she was driving.

"Definitely." The people loved reporters, at least that was her experience. Other than the time at the Afghanistan orphanage when she and Scanlon became targets, for the most part locals relished the chance to have their voices heard. Still, Scanlon was right. Anytime there were protests, there were bound to be crazy people, insurgents or radicals intent on making a statement, suicide bombers who would proudly drive into a crowd of protestors.

She steered the SUV around a pothole and wondered if Justin was working nearby. Were he and his company stationed in the area? If so, he might be working the same protest. According to the military party line, soldiers made their presence felt whenever an agitated crowd gathered, especially when the protest centered around an election.

The reporters she associated with felt differently. With the U.S. military flexing its muscle around Iraq's election time, the only voice that would be heard was one the United States approved of. Lauren made a right turn onto the main highway through Baghdad. The U.S. involvement, that's probably what the protest was dealing with. Either way, she was about to find out.

A few miles down the road, she spotted a crowd. *Stay away from crowds*, Bob Maine told them. *Park at a distance and walk in. You'll have a better sense of danger that way.*

Good counsel. She pulled the SUV over and parked it along the roadway. Then she turned to Scanlon. "Ready?"

He stuck his camera into his bag, latched it, and took a deep breath. "Ready."

The temperatures had started to drop around Iraq, and that day was cooler than any that week. Even still, the surroundings never changed. Everything—sky, ground, buildings—all the color of desert dirt. She swished her skirt out from the car door and swung her bag over her shoulder. "Let's go."

As they came closer to the crowd, Lauren stopped. She'd been a journalist long enough to know better than to rush into a situation, even when she was stateside. Sometimes more could be learned by observing than by any interview she might get.

Scanlon took his camera from his bag and began shooting. The scene was one of chaos—vendors selling wares from dilapidated card tables, protestors waving signs and shouting, and U.S. soldiers dotting both sides of the road, armed and ready. Like their leaders said, in case violence broke out.

She took a notepad from her bag and grabbed two pencils. She slid one beneath the scarf that hid her hair, and with the other she wrote down her observations. *Protestors angry ... soldiers stiff, stonelike.*

"Let's get closer." Scanlon led the way, and they moved to within thirty yards of the action.

That's when she spotted something.

In a vacant lot, amidst the rubble of what must at one time have been a building, a group of U.S. soldiers was holding what looked like a picnic. Children played all around them, and two of the uniformed Americans stood near the back of a U.S. Army vehicle, handing out bags. A strange feeling stirred in Lauren's heart.

All during her time in Afghanistan, she'd heard about the good U.S. soldiers were doing in the Middle East, but she'd never seen proof. Until now.

Scanlon lowered his camera. "Are you seeing what I'm seeing?" He took slow steps into the street and looked both ways. "Come on."

She followed him, and that's when she saw something else. One of the young soldiers—one of those playing with the Iraqi children—had a familiar build, a familiar way about him. Could it be Justin Baker? She and Scanlon found a spot on the sidewalk, right on the edge of the action taking place in the vacant lot.

"Okay, catch!" The soldier and three others were tossing a football with fifteen or twenty street kids. The children were laughing and jumping and waving their hands, each of them wanting the ball. When one of the kids snagged it from the air, the soldier grinned. "Good job!" And then he said something else, something that sounded similar, only it was in Arabic.

Lauren could hardly believe her eyes. The lot was filled with at least thirty soldiers, and all of them were helping the kids in one way or another. The bags being handed to the children contained a sandwich, a water bottle, and some sort of toy. Lauren could see that now, because as the kids walked away, they tore into their bags, chattering in happy exclamations about what was inside.

Scanlon held up his camera and then lowered it again. He looked the other direction, toward the angry mob of protestors. "Looks like we have a choice."

"Looks like two stories." As soon as she heard herself say the words, she was struck by the notion. Two stories. Two sides of the same assignment. There were the gruff soldiers, the ones making their presence known to the protestors. But there were these men too. Americans, giving to the Iraqi children out of their own time and resources. No, not out of their own resources. Out of the resources of the U.S. military.

She shaded her eyes and squinted. Maybe it was Justin. Could she possibly have run into him this quickly, this easily? She could've gone an entire year and not seen him. The soldier took out a camera and snapped a picture of three little boys, each of them holding onto a part of the same football. That's when he turned and spotted her, and she knew.

It was Justin, Emily's guy. Hadn't he told them over pizza that day that the U.S. was doing good in Iraq? Hadn't he said that no one stateside would believe the changes taking place or the goodwill being spread to the people?

Of course, she hadn't believed him. Not a word of it. Because she'd based all her information on what she'd seen herself, on what she read in her own magazine, and on what she heard from the other news sources. CNN and the *New York Times* and *Newsweek*. They all said the same thing: no one wanted the war, people were tired of the losses, nothing good was coming of it.

So where were the stories on this sort of event, this chance for the soldiers to interact with the Iraqi kids? She caught Justin's attention and nodded her hello. He looked surprised, but then he smiled and waved. Lauren nudged Scanlon. "Start shooting. I want this feature in the next issue."

"But ..." He looked at the protestors. "That's not what we came for."

She studied him. Of course he was hesitant. They'd been told what to cover, and this certainly wasn't it. But this was part of the story. She was starting to understand that. "Scanlon." She kept her tone level. "We were sent here to cover the war." She looked at Justin once more. He was catching the ball and flinging it back to the group of young boys. "This piece hasn't gotten a whole lot of coverage."

They spent an hour, Scanlon taking pictures and Lauren talking to the kids and taking notes. The soldiers she spoke to seemed wary, and small wonder. What had she told herself on the way here? That the story was really already written, right? A chill passed down her arms and legs. What if she hadn't been sent to get the news, but only to verify it? The story had been chosen long before she and Scanlon arrived on the scene. *Cover the protest*, Bob told them. *Find out why they're angry at the U.S.* She was still in the middle of the soldiers and kids, but she peered down the street to the protestors. She would find out. She turned her attention back to her notepad. But first she would get this story.

Finally she worked her way to Justin. She wasn't sure what to make of the feelings inside her ... betrayal and anger and remorse and uncertainty. This was just one story. No matter how unexpected, it wasn't enough to change her views. But it certainly had her attention. For the first time, she even felt a little awkward, uncertain about her role as a reporter. She lifted her eyes to those of the young soldier's.

"Ma'am." He nodded at her. "I wondered if I'd see you out here."

"Me too." It was easy to see why Emily was so crazy about this boy. "I've never …" She glanced around at the merriment taking place. "I haven't been to Iraq. I … I didn't think things like this really happened."

He grinned. "I tried to tell you."

"I know." She held his gaze. "I'm sorry, Justin. I've asked God to show me where I'm wrong, to help me find balance." She looked at the dusty ground, and then back at him. "I guess this is one of those times."

"Yes, ma'am." He winged the ball back to the kids. "You talk to Emily much?"

"No. We're writing."

"Us too." He wiped the grime from his forehead. "I miss her like crazy."

"She feels the same way."

He nodded and grabbed the ball from the air again. Once more he grinned and shouted words of praise at the children in their language.

"How did you learn that?"

"Our job is twofold, ma'am." Justin looked slightly confused, as if she should already know the information he was sharing. "We need to hunt down the insurgents, the terrorists, and we need to help Iraq become a free country. We couldn't really do that without knowing some of their language."

English was fairly common in the Middle East, but Justin was right. If they were going to reach out to the children and help introduce democracy to a nation that hadn't known it before, they'd need to know the language. At least enough to play a little football with the kids.

Lauren didn't want to take up more of his time. "I'll tell Emily we saw each other."

"Okay." He jogged back a few steps and threw the ball again. "Tell her I love her." His eyes shone. "Tell her I'm counting the days."

"I will." Lauren's throat hurt. If she could whisk this young man to safety, to a plane that would take him home to Emily, she would.

She and Scanlon had all the information and photos they needed. It was time to move down the street toward the protestors. As they drew closer, Lauren stopped to survey the crowd. Some of them were hopping and waving fists, grouped in a tight circle and chanting something she didn't understand. Something anti-American, no doubt.

As she watched, a man ambled up and studied her. "You from U.S.?"

She felt suddenly vulnerable. Yes, she had her protective Kevlar, but that didn't matter. Cameramen and reporters could be blown to pieces same as soldiers — even with their safety gear. Lauren took a step closer to Scanlon. Scenes like this protest were rare in Afghanistan, though flare-ups continued. She held up her press badge, the one she wore around her neck. "Reporter."

The man nodded and pointed at the protestors. "You hear what they say?"

"No ..."

Scanlon moved in close beside her. He had his camera, but he also had a can of mace. Just in case.

Lauren squinted at the mob. "What are they saying?"

"They say no more violence against voters, against leaders." The man's weathered eyes grew watery. His English was difficult to understand. "Every time good man try take office, insurgents kill him, kill supporters. Kill voters."

"What?" Lauren hesitated, but slowly, like the first few pebbles in an avalanche, the meaning of his words hit her. As they did, she felt her world turn upside down. She lowered her brow and looked at the man. "You mean … they want the U.S. out of Iraq?"

The man's mouth went slack and his eyes widened. He held up his hand and bowed his head, shaking it as hard as he could. "No … never! Not yet, no." He said the same thing until finally Lauren interrupted him.

"Sir, please. I need to understand."

"My people—" the man lifted his eyes to hers—"so grateful to Americans. So grateful. We have hope now, a chance to work and grow and live with our families." Anger twisted his expression. "But some want old ways, old terror ways." He shifted his attention to the protestors. "Now we say, enough. Time to stop the violence." He pointed at a few of the soldiers. "Americans try to stop violence." He bowed twice. "We glad for Americans."

"Okay." Lauren looked at Scanlon, then back at the man. "Can we take your picture?"

"Yes." He pointed at her notepad. "You write down what Yusef say. We glad for Americans!"

Lauren wasn't sure which way was up. She began scribbling, capturing the things Yusef wanted to tell her. Then she looked at the protestors again, but this time through new eyes. These weren't the insurgents, the terrorists opposed to the United States. If they were, then where were the flag burners? The men who would gleefully burn an image of the U.S. president?

They weren't around, because these people wanted the same thing the U.S. wanted for Iraq. Democracy and peace, a safe place to live and work and raise their families. Suddenly a connection became clear. Lauren looked at the empty lot, where the children and the soldiers played together. She aimed her question at Yusef. "Whose children?"

"Those men." He pointed at the protestors. "Most people want free election and personal rights." Tears filled his eyes again. He nodded at the children. "They are our future. They want live in world without terror."

"Yes." Lauren could almost feel her beliefs being ripped to shreds, the foundation she'd stood on crumbling as fast as the words falling from the old man's mouth.

He jabbed her notepad, more intense than ever. "You tell them Yusef says so."

She looked at him a moment longer. Did he know? Was he aware of the news that came across the televisions and daily papers in America? Did his compatriots know that the reality playing out here in the streets was not the story being told to the citizens of the United States?

Suddenly, the weight of her responsibility hit hard. All along she'd seen herself as a Pied Piper, a solitary voice with the ability to make people fall in line with her way of thinking. Never once until now had she felt guilty about how she'd used that power, about how maybe she hadn't told the full story.

She felt sick to her stomach. What if she'd been wrong? What if, even half the time, she'd missed the story in her zeal to uphold her beliefs? She accused the U.S. military of using unnecessary strength, but what had she done? What about her colleagues? To come into a situation like the war in Iraq with a predetermined mind-set was to do the entire world a disservice, wasn't it?

Yusef ambled off to join the other protestors, and Lauren realized she was shaking. "Did I just hear what I thought I heard?"

Scanlon filled his cheeks with air and let it out slowly. He removed his baseball cap and raked his fingers through his short hair. "If I didn't know better, I'd think the whole thing was staged, something set up by the army."

Her question and his answer sent another wave of alarm through her conscience. Were they that conditioned, that even witnessing the truth, they doubted what they were seeing? All because it didn't line up with their viewpoint? "I feel sick." She rummaged through her bag and pulled out a bottle of water. Without stopping for a breath, she downed it.

At that instant, before she could put the empty bottle back into her dusty canvas bag, an explosion of gunfire rang out from what looked like a deserted brick building across the street from the protestors.

Screams filled the air, and Scanlon grabbed her, slammed her to the ground. "Lauren, don't move!" He whispered a string of obscenities. "We gotta out get of here!"

From her place on the ground, she saw three protestors fall, squirming, twisting in pain, their blood spilling into the street. Lauren sat up, too horrified to look away. One of the men was Yusef. Kind, passionate Yusef. Who wanted so badly for the children in the empty lot to get a chance to grow up in a free society. Now everything he believed in was draining away on the streets of Baghdad, where the truth screamed as loud as the wailing protestors. The life Yusef spoke of would never be. Not for him.

Yusef was dead.

Thirteen

Lauren tore her gaze from Yusef's fallen body. Scanlon hovered over her, both of them low to the ground. Her breathing came fast and hard, and she stared at the dirty road inches from her face. *Focus, Lauren. Come on, focus.* She wanted to run to Yusef, see if there was something she could do to help. But that would be too dangerous. Besides, he was gone. She had seen enough death to know. Sweat broke out on her forehead, and her heart pounded so loud it was deafening. *Watch, Lauren. Observe. And tell the story. The true story . . .*

She eased herself free from Scanlon's protection and lifted her eyes to the horrible scene. "I want to *do* something," she hissed.

"We can't." His voice was breathless, thick with fear. "Stay low until it's safe. Then we run for it."

He was right. Here, low to the ground, they weren't a target. The streets were full of people cowering low. She looked at Yusef again, what she could see of his body. Other protestors surrounded the victims, wailing and waving their fists at the place where the shots had rung out. At the same time, a dozen U.S. soldiers—the ones who had been standing stiff-faced along the edge of the protest—sprinted toward the building, weapons drawn. They broke down the door and raced inside.

Lauren looked at the empty lot in time to see Justin and his fellow soldiers round up the children, hiding them behind the army vehicles. Several of the little boys, who moments earlier had been tossing a football, were weeping and screaming, clinging to the Americans.

More gunfire exploded from inside the building, and Lauren had just one thought: *Please, God ... let those be American guns.* Because that would mean the assailants were dead, the way Yusef and his friends were dead.

The protestors only wanted what most people wanted—-freedom and hope and a chance for a future. Yusef had believed with every syllable that the election could be held in peace, and that the Americans would help make it happen. But now ... she watched, aching for them as the protestors fell to their knees beside the fallen, rocking back and forth, wailing over their loss.

Next to her, Scanlon aimed his camera at the empty building, at the grieving protestors—and finally at the American soldiers protecting the children—shooting a few dozen quick pictures.

Then, in the time it took for Scanlon to grab her arm and pull her to her feet, a whole new array of thoughts hit her. If there had been more support for the war, more aggression on the part of the U.S. troops, maybe the men who fired those shots would've been hunted down long ago. Maybe they'd be in jails or eliminated. But so many Americans had helped spread a mind-set that made any support of the war taboo.

Americans like her.

She took one last look at the place where Yusef's body lay. As Scanlon led her from the scene, she couldn't keep herself from looking. "I'm sorry, Yusef." She whispered the words at first. Then she shouted them, so loud that across the street she was sure Justin Baker could hear her. "Yusef ... I'm sorry!"

"Come on!" Scanlon sounded terrified. "We have to get out of here."

She turned and ran along behind him, leaving the battle to play out as it would. And now what? She was supposed to go back to her compound and open her laptop and pound out a story undermining the U.S. military and its role in the war in Iraq? After she'd seen U.S. soldiers handing out food and water to kids? After she'd watched with her own eyes as they played football, and even as they rounded up the kids and protected them with their lives? As they ran into a building full of insurgents in an attempt to protect the Iraqi protestors?

She was supposed to look the other way about the things Yusef had told her? Write a story that made the protestors into something they weren't? Anti-Americans anxious for the U.S. to leave them alone?

Scanlon took the driver's seat as they headed back. Lauren was glad. It allowed her time to cover her face and let the tears come. Was this how Justin Baker and his company spent their time? Lending as much safety and hope as they could to the people who wanted what Yusef wanted?

How could she ever look in the mirror again, ever write another story the way her editor expected her to write it? Her stomach rumbled and her heart lay in a heap, just like the gunned-down protestors.

Oh God ... God ... have I been wrong all this time?

Daughter ... I am with you.

The answer sounded so loud, she wondered if the Lord was in the backseat, guarding her, helping her, answering her constant cry for wisdom. She let her tears come.

"Lauren ... it was one day, one scene." Scanlon seemed to know what she was thinking. "You can't throw out everything you believe because of that."

"Maybe I can." She dragged her hand across her cheek and glared at him. It wasn't his fault, the turmoil twisting within her, but it felt good to take it out on someone. "Maybe we've all been wrong."

"War's more complicated than that. Than one side completely right, one side completely wrong." He kept his eyes on the road, his voice calm. "You're a journalist, you should know that."

"Yes, I should." She made a sound that didn't come close to releasing her frustration. "So how come I've been so one-sided? How come so many of us have been?" She covered her face again. War *was* complicated. Valid debate might exist over the way a war was carried out or whether one target was more dangerous than another in the battle. But the core of *why* it was happening and its purpose?

She'd never allowed the possibility that the stories she'd heard from soldiers and commanders might be true, that the U.S. really *was* doing a good thing for the people of Iraq, or that by dismantling terror cells, they really *were* protecting the interests of the United States.

It had sounded like so much military rhetoric, and sometimes at the end of the day, she would join Scanlon and other U.S. reporters and practically mock the news being handed them by the military's public information officers.

"Do you realize what happened out there?" Lauren lifted her head and looked at her friend. "We discovered a lie, Scanlon. One that too many of us have believed for way too long. That nothing good could come from war, that nothing could ever justify it." She pointed over her shoulder at the scene they were leaving behind. "But that ... what we just saw. That at least makes this war understandable, doesn't it?"

What was wrong with the insurgents, that they'd fill a building, hiding like cowards, and shoot into a crowd of people whose sole intention was to help build a better Iraq? The factions that tore apart the country were so different it was frightening. Were these the people she had wanted the president to reason with?

She leaned back against the passenger seat and tried to get a grip on her emotions. It was one day, one incident. Her beliefs hadn't been formed in a day, and neither could she release them that quickly. Scanlon was right. Maybe she was overreacting. Witnessing a killing could do that to a person.

The road was bumpy beneath them, and Lauren still couldn't catch her breath. *God ... what did I just see? That was just one flash of a moment in this terrible war, right? What am I supposed to feel?*

Daughter, I have given you wisdom. You would do well to listen.

Lauren shut her eyes. The response was so clear, Scanlon might as well have said it. But it wasn't Scanlon speaking. The voice—the still, small voice—was God's. And what was He telling her? He'd given her wisdom? When? In the events that day?

No ...

Her eyes widened. Not the events, but the heart of the matter—the passion behind the events of war. Maybe that's what He had shown her today. Suddenly she remembered something. Months ago Shane had tried to tell her everything Yusef had said. Shane had reminded Lauren of September 11, of the terrorists who in cold-blooded exactness would take control of jetliners and fly them into buildings.

"Reason with someone like that, Lauren?" He gave her a sad look. "No one wants war, but how are we supposed to protect the U.S. from that sort of killer without going after them?"

Today's images flashed in Lauren's mind like a horror film. She closed her eyes but they wouldn't go away. Justin and his buddies playing with the Iraqi children, the protestors shouting and ranting, Yusef jabbing her notebook. *You write down what Yusef say. We glad for Americans!*

She gritted her teeth and opened her eyes. God's answer was clear. There *was* wisdom to be learned from today, and the best thing she could do was look for it, listen to it.

If she'd been wrong in her views, her staunch beliefs, then she needed to say so. Even if it meant losing her job. She leaned back against the headrest and stared at the desolate roadway ahead. She had begged God for wisdom, and in a single morning He had nearly drowned her in it.

Yes, war was complicated.

But what she'd seen that day was as simple as breathing. And every word of her story would reflect the truth about it.

She willed herself to relax. If she was going to write the stories in her heart, she needed to be calm, at her absolute best as a journalist. Otherwise her editors would think she'd gone soft, that her time in Fallon hanging around military types had tainted her thinking.

Shane's face came to mind.

Nothing could've been further from reality. She had left Shane —knowing she could be leaving for good—all so she could defend her way of thinking, her absolute belief in the inherent evil of the war and its perpetrators.

God, I want to see Your wisdom from today. Give me the words as I write. Please. Is this just one day, one instance? Are there really people swarming the streets of Baghdad, wishing Americans would stay and help? She pictured Justin, the look on his face as he played catch with the kids.

Last year she'd written a story about how violent soldiers were teaching a generation of Iraqi kids to be fighters. She had based her story on the same sort of rhetoric she accused the army's public information office of spilling. Her research was covert, interviews with people in a clandestine setting. The contact usually showed her something small-scale. In the case of the story about soldiers teaching violence, the contact had introduced her to three young boys, all of whom had rifles.

"We fight Americans," the chosen young spokesman for the group said. "We fight them until they leave."

Lauren wanted to kick herself. Looking back on it, she had to admit it was just as likely the kids had been young terrorists. Because only the terrorists would want U.S. soldiers removed from a scene like the one she'd just witnessed. Still, she'd written an entire piece on the notion, leaving millions of Americans who read the story with a sense that the army was somehow bringing harm to the people of Iraq.

God … I feel faint, sick inside. Please … if I've been wrong, if I've written stories that furthered the cause of people like those in that building, then please … use me to change that thinking, to balance it. Please, God.

She wasn't ready to call Shane and tell him she was wrong about much of what she'd believed … but she was close. When she returned to the journalists' compound, she said very little to Scanlon. There was no time to waste. She hurried to her room, opened her laptop, and started a new document. Then, as though her next breath depended on it, she began to write a story.

A story different from any she'd written in all her life.

FOURTEEN

Justin saw it.

As clearly as he saw the protestors fall in the hail of bullets, he saw the change in Emily's mother. It was in her eyes. The widely read, famous journalist Lauren Gibbs hadn't been to Iraq before. In Afghanistan, according to Emily, the few times she'd witnessed anything like the soldiers and the kids, the events had seemed staged to her. But today was different. It had been spontaneous-—there was no way she couldn't see that truth. And in the time it took for their eyes to meet, he knew what was happening.

Justin sucked in air, trying to catch his breath, very aware of the danger around him. He hovered over a group of kids, most of them crying or whimpering. "It's okay." He soothed his hand along the shoulders of two of them. "It's okay." He looked over his shoulder, but Lauren Gibbs was gone. Even in the midst of the chaos, he couldn't help but smile. God was answering their prayers. His and Emily's and Emily's father's. Probably even the prayers of Lauren Gibbs, herself. Emily said her mother had asked God for wisdom. At the same time, she didn't believe her mother was open to God's answers. Not really, anyway.

But Emily, at least she's praying, Justin wrote in a recent email to her. *Wherever people are praying, there's always hope. Don't forget that.*

Another round of gunfire rang out across the street, and the children pressed in more closely to him and the other soldiers. Justin was torn by what to do next. The kids needed protecting, certainly. As long as he and the guys from his company stayed, they could keep the kids from running into the streets and getting killed.

But from the gunfire echoing all around them, there was a battle raging in the building. What if the guys needed help? One more soldier could make the difference in taking the insurgents out. He looked at the terrified faces of the kids, felt the way they clung to him, tugging on his shirt, begging him with their eyes not to leave. Not to ever leave.

He had no choice, of course. He would stay with the kids. But still his eyes found the building and he uttered a constant prayer for the safety of the soldiers.

"Help." One of the boys looked up at him, pleading with him in Arabic. The child couldn't have been more than five years old. He held out his arms to Justin. "Please."

The sound of bullets, the screams, the wailing coming from the men that were the kids' fathers—all of it was more than this little boy could take.

Justin picked the child up and swung him on his hip. He pressed the boy's head to his shoulder and motioned to the other soldiers. They needed to get the kids behind the convoy of military vehicles. "Make a wall!"

His buddy Joe Greenwald nodded at the others down the line. "You heard him, make a wall!"

Good ol' Joe. The two had served side by side during their first tour and now they were rarely apart. Joe shared his faith and his passion. They bunked next to each other, and now that they were back in the theater of action again, they were as close as brothers. Already he'd shown Joe his scrapbook from Emily, and Joe had whistled long and low.

"Lucky guy, Baker."

"I know." He ran his finger over the picture of the two of them on the front cover. "Lucky and blessed, all at once."

Joe was stationed at Fort Lewis too. He looked a little harder at her face. "Isn't she the girl we saw in the hall that day?"

That first day, when Emily started working at the base, Joe had been the one walking with him in the hall. She smiled at both of them, and when she was gone, Justin had elbowed his buddy. "Bet she's the new girl in my office."

"Bet you're not that lucky."

A few weeks later, Joe shipped out for Iraq, anxious to get back to the action. They hadn't met up again until Justin arrived at the end of September. That day when Justin showed him Emily's scrapbook, he pointed at the picture. "It's her, isn't it?" He gave Justin a playful shove. "You *dog.* You were right. She wound up working with you, didn't she?"

Justin let his eyes linger on her photo. "Yeah, she certainly did."

Joe didn't have a girl. He was a big guy with an even bigger heart, but he was too shy for most girls. "Know why I like hanging out with you?" he'd ask Justin every now and then.

"Why?"

"Cause—" Joe smiled—"you have a reason to get back home. That makes you the safest soldier out here."

Now Justin watched Joe come alongside him, helping him get the guys in line. Joe positioned himself at the other side of the group of kids and directed the soldiers near him until the entire company had done what Justin ordered. In a few seconds, they placed themselves between the building and the horde of frightened children.

The little boy in his arms snuggled close against his shoulder. Was his father one of those who lay dead? Justin hoped not. He held the child for almost an hour, until the U.S. soldiers spilled out of the building carrying four covered bodies on four makeshift stretchers. A small American flag lay across the first one.

Justin looked away. Another one down. He prayed it wasn't one of the men from his company. He clung to the child in his arms and waited while a few of the soldiers crossed the street and reported on the situation. The snipers had been insurgents, of course. Members of a new terrorist cell. Like cancer, the cells took root wherever they could, and these few had been operating in the abandoned building, probably no more than a few days.

The good news: all three terrorists were taken down. But not before an American lost his life. The soldiers gave them the name of the casualty, and Justin felt the slightest sense of relief. He was from the East Coast, a soldier from another company. But even so, he was a life lost, someone's son and someone's friend. Someone's high school love. He was here for the same reason they were all here, because it was the most right thing he could think to do with his life.

Joe circled the guys around the kids and nodded at Justin. "Pray for us, will you?"

Justin bowed his head, and around him, several of the Iraqi children did the same thing. His throat was tight, but he found his voice anyway. "Father, we are sad and broken by what's happened here today, by the loss of life for freedom's sake." Justin opened his eyes enough to see a little boy watching him. His eyes were wide and he was still shaking. Justin gave him a look that said it was okay, he was in good hands. "Lord, give us strength. Help us look to You, who went to the cross for freedom's sake. You know all about sacrifice, God. Thank You for our fallen comrade ..." He hesitated, steeling himself against his emotions. "Thank You for his sacrifice."

He coughed and his voice grew stronger. "Be with his family, and let them know that their soldier ... didn't die in vain."

"In Christ's name," Joe said, his voice strong. "Amen."

The kids lifted their heads and looked around, not sure what to do next.

A gust of wind and sand blew across the empty lot. Justin shielded his face and held the boy in his arms a little tighter. The child and his friends would never fall to the bullets of the terrorists who had taken up residence across the street. Not if he had anything to do with it. He set the little boy back on the ground and pictured Lauren, the change in her eyes. If he'd seen right, she would never be the same after what she witnessed today on the streets of Baghdad.

None of them would be.

That night they turned in to their barracks earlier than usual. They weren't in tents anymore, but old buildings. This was one the U.S. military had taken over just outside the city. Justin pulled out the scrapbook. He stretched out on his cot and positioned his light overhead so he could see better.

"Her again?" Joe was already lying on his bed, his hands beneath his head. He grinned at Justin. "I mean, not that I blame you."

"Yeah." Justin opened the cover and stared at the first page. "You spend enough time out there, and life back home starts to feel like a dream, like it never even happened."

"It happened, alright." Joe gestured toward the scrapbook. "Pictures don't lie, Baker."

Justin sighed. "I know." He kept the book open and reached for the printout of Emily's latest letter. He kept a stack of them inside the makeshift nightstand that stood between his bed and Joe's. "Neither do emails."

"At least you got someone writing to you." Joe smiled. He didn't feel sorry for himself, Justin could tell. Being around the guys, around the other soldiers in the company, had changed Joe actually. Made him funnier, more social.

"There's a girl waiting for you too." Justin felt his mood lifting. He tossed his friend an easy grin.

"I know, I know. I just haven't met her yet."

"Exactly."

They were quiet for a while, and Justin fiddled with the paper in his hand. He wanted to read it again, but not until he looked at their pictures, not until he let himself hang around the sunny halls of yesterday. He turned the page and studied himself, the way he looked sitting on the steps of the teen center, talking smack with the guys.

Had Emily found time to visit them? If she had, she hadn't said so. But from the sound of it, Buster was in good shape. She spoiled him every time she had an afternoon off. Justin felt the note in his hand, and again he resisted the urge to read it. Notes from Emily had to be savored, like everything else about her.

"Oh, Baker, come on." Joe turned onto his side and propped his head in his hand. "Go ahead and read it. You're killing me with the suspense."

"What?" Justin gave him a teasing look. "I thought my emails from Emily bored you."

Joe rolled his eyes. "Not much else going on for entertainment." He motioned with his hand. "Get on with it, already."

Justin laughed and moved the scrapbook aside. He liked nights like this, when he and Joe bantered back and forth. It helped wipe out memories from the day—especially days like that one, when the violence had come so close it was unnerving. He and Emily wrote to each other about once a week, since it took almost that long for the letters to come through. Like the other soldiers, he had only limited access to the computer, and so they'd earmarked Mondays as the day to check for letters from each other.

As he'd done with several of her previous emails, Justin opened this one and began reading it out loud. "'Hey, Justin, it's me …'"

"As if it could be anyone else." Joe rolled over onto his back again and grinned at the ceiling. "Go on."

"I was trying." Justin kicked his buddy's cot. He could feel his smile growing, and it felt great. A reminder that he was still alive, no matter how much death happened around him.

"Okay, okay."

Justin looked back at the paper. "'I visited Buster again today. Your family is sort of feeling like the one I always wanted to have. Hope you don't mind, but you know—you being so generous and all—I didn't think you would.'" Justin chuckled and shook his head. He loved when her letters had this humorous tone. It was better than the times when he could practically hear her crying between the lines of her emails.

"Don't skip parts."

"I'm not." He found his place. "'Anyway, Buster's missing you bad. I thought you should know. He's still sleeping with your sweatshirt, but now—I guess he sort of associates me with you. Because, I'm serious, he looks at me for half a second and then he looks right past me. As if he expects you to walk around the corner. Only it doesn't stop there. I hook him up to his leash and we start walking, and about every few steps he stops and cranes his neck around my ankles and stares—just stares at the empty place behind me.'"

Justin laughed out loud. "I wish I could see that."

"Me too." Joe smiled. He kept his eyes on the ceiling as if he was picturing everything Emily had described.

Outside the wind had picked up. It howled through the cracks in the doorjamb. Justin held up the paper and started in again. "'Anyway, I admit it. I think your dog's a little loony. But he's growing on me. Lately I've been bringing him chicken scraps from the cafeteria. I'm pretty sure by the time you get back, he'll be looking around your ankles trying to find me! Ha! Just kidding. The dog would sit at the window waiting all day for you if he didn't get hungry once in a while.'"

She painted a funny picture, but it touched him at the same time. Buster mattered to him, and she knew it. She was spending time with the dog for him, because the time he'd missed with the dog grated on him. And she was taking it upon herself to right that wrong the only way she knew how. By being Buster's friend.

"Is that it?" Joe looked disappointed.

"There's a little more." He took a quick breath. "'Anyway, you said you wanted scores, so here goes. We won both games last week, 5–1 and 3–2. I know, someone on defense must be slipping if we allowed two goals. But you'll smile at this. I scored two of the three goals and had another assist. The coach says giving me a scholarship was the best decision he ever made. I figure you'd have to agree. Imagine if I'd gone to San Diego State, like I thought about doing? Well, Justin ...'" He skimmed the next few lines. "'Missing you like crazy. Love you, Emily.'"

"Hey!" Joe sat up. "You skipped a part."

"That's the deal." Justin chuckled and leaned back against one elbow. "I have the right to censor."

"Shoot. I miss all the good parts." He made an exasperated sound. "You still walking around with her picture in your boot?"

"Yep. Every day."

"Man, I can't relate." He shook his head. "I'm hittin' the hay. You can read over the lovey-dovey parts in peace."

Justin smiled. "'Night, Joe."

"'Night." His buddy flipped off his light switch and rolled onto his other side.

"Don't forget your prayers."

"Ah, man!" He craned a look over his shoulder. "You interrupted me. I was already past the *Dear God* part."

A bit of laughter shook Justin. How great it was having Joe's friendship. These Baghdad nights would be too lonely without his buddy. Some nights they didn't talk about Emily at all, but pulled out their Bibles and went over the book of James or Colossians or Hebrews. Anything that might give them peace and hope to fight another day.

He opened the letter again and found the part he'd skipped.

Justin, I can't believe you've been gone nearly three weeks. It feels like three years. Whoever said absence makes the heart grow fonder was right. Only I'm not sure how much fonder my heart can get without bursting through my chest. If you come back and find a hole where my heart used to be, you'll know why.

It made him smile, Emily that crazy over him. *Let her know, God, let her understand that I feel the same way.*

He sighed, careful to keep quiet so Joe could get some sleep. He found his place and kept reading.

I'm drinking coffee out of the mug you gave me. That means I'm thinking of the mud you're getting over in the desert and yes, I know. You wish you were here with me, drinking a latte instead ... just for the record, I wish the same thing. Thinking of you, Justin. Missing you like crazy. I love you, Emily.

Justin folded the letter and placed it in the drawer with the others. Then he reached for the scrapbook. Slowly, he worked his way through the photographs. By the time he finished, Joe was out to the world, snoring louder than usual. He put the book away. It was late. Tomorrow he'd need to be as sharp as he'd been today. Careful to keep his head low when the bullets started to fly.

He turned off the light and lay in bed, his eyes open. A lot had happened today, a lot that filled his head with images he'd have for a lifetime. But the one that stayed with him as he fell asleep wasn't the protestors lying in a pool of blood or even the Iraqi children—before and after the attacks. It wasn't the little boy who'd clung to him for so long. It was a different image.

The one of Lauren Gibbs, her eyes truly opened for what Justin guessed might've been the first time in her entire life. And as he fell asleep, he wondered what she must've been thinking as she drove away. And he wondered something else.

What she would write for *Time* magazine as a result.

FIFTEEN

Bob Maine reached the end of the story on his computer screen and leaned back in his chair. He cussed under his breath. "Gibbs ... what'd you go and do?"

He'd known it was coming. Half a year in the shadows of Top Gun could change a person. Still ... Lauren's first stories hadn't seemed different. Same cutting-edge reporting, same skepticism. He stared at the screen. But this? He shook his head. Children clamoring after U.S. soldiers, protestors trying to thank the United States? It sounded like something the military public information office would cough up on its own behalf.

Whatever was going on, he had to get to the bottom of it. He'd placed an urgent call to the compound and left a message for her. He knew her schedule; he was expecting her call any minute. If this was what she was going to produce from Iraq, she'd be better off stateside.

"Hurry up and call, Gibbs." He tapped his finger on the desk and scrolled to the top of the story. He'd already read it twice. He was partway through the first paragraph for the third time when the phone rang. He grabbed it. "Bob Maine."

"Bob?" The connection wasn't great, but the static couldn't hide her defensive tone. "This is Lauren. You read my report?"

"Gibbs!" Across the room, a line of reporters looked his way. He lowered his voice. "Are you *kidding* me? This PR babble you sent me is your coverage of the protest?"

"I was there, Bob. I saw every bit of it." Her tone was passionate. "No, it isn't what I usually find when I go out to cover a story. But I'm a reporter, and a very good one. You said so yourself." She took a breath. "You sent me over to Iraq to get the news, right? Isn't that right?"

Bob wasn't sure what to say. He hadn't expected this. A sheepish promise to edit her story, yes. But a fierce defense of it? "What are you trying to say, Gibbs? That the report you gave me is fair and accurate?"

"Yes." She didn't hesitate. "More fair than anything I've ever written."

"Meaning what?"

"That's exactly what I'm going to tell you." And for the next thirty minutes, his star war correspondent not only explained the events she'd covered in the report, she explained her personal biases and how they'd affected her reporting. She sounded sharp and intelligent—and troubled.

When she finished, Bob was still frustrated. But she'd made her point. "You should've been a lawyer. They get paid more."

"But this—" her tone held vindication—"this means more."

"Fair and accurate?" He was still skeptical, but now his doubts seemed unfounded.

"Fair and accurate."

At the end of the day, when Bob sent the story on to copyediting, he could only hope one thing. That the readers of *Time* magazine would agree.

Shane had heard very little from Lauren.

Not that he expected to hear much. She'd left with her mind pretty well made up, her viewpoints firmly in place. Which was why he couldn't wait to get his hands on a copy of *Time* magazine, the issue that was circulating through the offices at Top Gun. Something's happened to Lauren Gibbs, he kept hearing.

Pilots had stopped him in the halls twice that morning. "Sir, your fiancée ... what happened to her?"

At first Shane had been terrified. Had she been kidnapped or killed? But the pilot must've seen from his expression what he was thinking. "She's not hurt or anything. She's just ... I don't know, changed. Read the articles in the latest *Time*. You'll see what I mean."

Shane's heart pounded and he turned around, headed back to the lobby where the latest issues of a dozen magazines would be sitting on a table. He was halfway there when another pilot stopped him. "Did you read Lauren's recent stuff?" The guy grinned. "What'd you do, brainwash her?"

Something about the guy's tone bugged him. "Haven't read it." He kept walking. He wasn't trying to brainwash Lauren. She was entitled to her views. He only wanted her to find balance, to see where he was coming from. He found a copy on the table. The cover showed a scientist holding a test tube, but one of the smaller headlines read, "Democracy Suffers a Blow in Iraq."

Okay, so how was that headline different from anything Lauren had written in the past? The headlines were nearly all negative, intent on showing the ineptitude of the war effort. He took the magazine, stepped outside, and found a bench a few feet away. If something had changed in Lauren, he would know it. As surely as he knew her voice, he would know by her words if God had helped her see the war in a new light.

He flipped to a layout near the middle of the magazine. The pictures were graphic, as they often were in *Time*. One small photo showed three bodies, broken and bleeding, with what looked like protestors gathered around, obviously grieving the loss of the men.

But it was the center photo that caught Shane's attention. Lauren never would've chosen to have her photographer get that shot. Not the old Lauren, anyway. Then he realized not only what was happening in the photo, but who it was. The photo showed a grinning U.S. soldier tossing a football to a cluster of

Iraqi children. But not just any U.S. soldier. This was Justin Baker. His friend's son.

Shane stared at the photo, studying it.

Beneath the picture, the caption read:

> Lieutenant Justin Baker and a company of soldiers from Fort Lewis spend an afternoon playing with Iraqi children and handing out food and water. The children's fathers were protesting insurgent violence a hundred yards down the street when gunfire broke out, killing three of the protestors.

What? The emotions assaulting Shane were too deep, too many to identify all at once. First there was pride. Good for Justin — stationed in the middle of Baghdad near some of the worst violence, and still finding a way to bring joy to the kids. Shane closed his eyes for a moment, and he could hear the boy talking about the war at the pizza parlor that night.

We're doing good over there, really. The kids need to know that we're their friends. We want democracy and freedom for them, so that they'll know a different life than the one their parents were forced to live.

Shane blinked his eyes open and stared at Justin's face. That night, Lauren had looked away, played with the straw in her drink and acted like she hadn't heard him.

But here he was, he and his buddies, and no amount of political discussion could change the simple fact. Good was being done. Period. The picture proved it. Shane let his eyes wander over the rest of the photo. In the background a convoy of military vehicles seemed to hold bags, and a group of soldiers could be seen passing them out to the children. A small box near the picture provided statistics about how many humanitarian bags had been given to children in the past year, and a list of some of the things the children had been given. Water, food, candy, paper, pens, and toys.

Shane looked to the top of the layout and there it was: *Story by Lauren Gibbs.* And the photos—he scanned the bottom of the first page. Yes, *Photos by Jeff Scanlon*, Lauren's closest friend from *Time.*

Confusion came at him then. Photographers took hundreds of photos in a given afternoon, so why use this one when it told a story the media typically chose to ignore? Wouldn't Lauren have had a say in which photos were used? Especially on a spread like this one?

The answer was obvious. Of course she'd had a say. She and Scanlon and their editor.

Hope and disbelief fought for position in his heart. He'd looked at the photos. Now he needed to read what she'd written. There were two stories. The first bore a headline that said, "U.S. Soldiers Come to the Aid of Protestors, One Soldier Dead."

A slow breath leaked from between his lips. Another death, another loss. He read from the top of the story.

> A U.S. soldier was killed Wednesday in Baghdad while defending a group of peaceful protestors. Violence erupted when insurgent terrorists rained down bullets from a vacant building at the Iraqi protestors, killing three Iraqi citizens. U.S. soldiers stormed the building where the terrorists were hiding, fatally wounding all three insurgents. The single U.S. casualty was a nineteen-year-old soldier, the first to enter the building in pursuit of the terrorists.
>
> Minutes before the attack, one of the protestors, a man named Yusef, explained that his people were protesting violence by terrorists.
>
> "We protest violence against voters, against leaders," Yusef explained. "Every time good man try take office, insurgents kill him, kill supporters. Kill voters." Yusef said he was passionate about the need for a protest, especially

in the days before the upcoming elections. "My people so grateful to Americans. So grateful. We have hope now, a chance to work and grow and live with our families. We glad for Americans."

Glad for Americans? Had Lauren really heard those words? And then chosen to use them? He kept reading.

> Tragically, Yusef was one of the protestors killed in the violence.
>
> "The Iraqi people, for the most part, are in favor of the war, because eventually it will buy them the freedom they want," said one military commander at the scene. "When this war is over, we will have severely restricted terrorists' ability to work and operate from this part of the world, and we will have secured a democracy for the Iraqi citizens."
>
> Debate rages over whether the cost for such a victory is too high, in taxpayer dollars and in human life. "We believe in freedom and a safe place to live—both in the United States and in the Middle East. It's not something we take lightly," the commander said. "Yes, the cost is high. But it's a cost we must be willing to pay if we're going to see change."

The article went on, but Shane couldn't see the words, couldn't absorb another sentence without stopping to think through what he'd just read. Countless times, he and Lauren had debated the power of the press. "You go to cover a story and you see what you want to see," he'd told her. "A million things happen at a newsworthy event. You take the hundred pieces you want to use and place them in the order you want. And you tell me that's fair reporting. There's no such thing, Lauren."

"The facts rise to the top, Shane. I get assigned to a story, and I talk to the people in charge, and I report the facts."

"*All* the facts?"

"Of course." She resented his insinuation that somehow the news ran through a filter in her mind.

But here, in the article in his hands, Lauren had presented the facts in a way that could've been totally different. If she'd written the story a year ago, she would've pointed out that U.S. soldiers carelessly engaged in a gun battle with Iraqis while children played nearby—something that would've given the picture that American soldiers were heartless killing machines.

This ... this story was nothing of the sort.

As he kept reading, the picture was very clear. Not only because of the way Lauren had written it, but because it was one he'd heard described to him tens of times before. He kept apprised of military briefings and updates on the war, and the scene that had played out in Baghdad the day before was a sadly common one.

The citizens of Iraq, with their first taste of freedom, were anxious to have a new way of life, passionate about capitalizing on the democracy that had been shown to them so that their families and their children's families would never know the terror of an evil dictator. Having taken reams of bad print, the U.S. soldiers rarely went on the offensive during a peaceful protest, rarely searched buildings or alleyways looking for terrorists.

Instead they stood guard, giving the citizens their chance to protest, to make a plea to their fellow Iraqis to take a stand for freedom. Then, when something went awry as it often did, the soldiers stepped in and came to the defense of the Iraqi people. Too often, such a rescue involved the loss of American life.

Always, when he spoke about the war with other military leaders, the consensus was the same. The president needed more support, morally, politically, and financially. The U.S. had the ability to hunt down terror cells, dismantling them and putting insurgents in prison, or destroying them along with their plans for destruction.

But the military had been forced to work with one hand tied behind its back—largely because the media had convinced the masses that funding and manpower for the war in Iraq was no longer necessary. Worse, that it was a waste of American life and money to fight the war even one more day.

Shane looked back at the page. A sidebar story ran with it, explaining the work Justin and other soldiers in his company were doing, how they felt the need to befriend the children of Iraq.

Lauren … are you trying to tell me something? Has God worked on you this quickly? A shiver passed down his back and along his legs. *What's happening in your heart that you'd show this side of the war?* He could hardly wait to talk to her, but he wouldn't make the first call. If she'd turned in a story like this, then she was in a great amount of inner turmoil. The facts—a balanced view of the facts—had come smack against her longtime beliefs.

Yes, he'd definitely be better off waiting until she'd had time to think things through. One day soon, Lauren would call him. In the meantime, he would keep praying for her. He read a little further into the sidebar.

> "If these kids' parents wanted us out of their country, they'd never be allowed to spend a morning playing with us, receiving handouts from us," Baker, 22, said. "Spending time with the kids here helps them see life is going to change. Democracy will win in the end."

Shane smiled. *Good for you, Justin. Good for you.*

He pulled out his cell phone and looked at the time. Emily would be on her way to her first class, but he couldn't wait. He dialed her number. As it began to ring, he scanned the article once more.

"Hello?"

"Honey, it's Dad." The joy inside him came out as a quiet laugh. "Have you seen the new *Time* magazine?"

"No." She sounded breathless. "My roommate and I jogged this morning, and now I have five minutes to get to class." Her voice held concern. "Does Mom have something in it?"

"She does." He wasn't sure where to begin. "But nothing like we've seen before. First of all, the main picture is of Justin. Right there in the middle of *Time* magazine."

"Really?" He could tell by her voice that she'd stopped cold, no longer concerned about her class schedule. "Are you serious?"

"Yes. Your mother must've seen him in Baghdad the other day." His tone changed. "A soldier died, Emily. It was a hard day at war, but your mom ... I don't know what's happening to her, but the story is so much more balanced than anything I've seen her write."

"I'll get a copy in the library." She hesitated. "Dad, are you sure? You really see something different this time?"

"You've been praying, right?"

"Right."

"Mom tells me even she's been talking to God." Shane smiled. "Read her stories. The pictures alone are something most Americans have rarely seen." He remembered that she was in a hurry. "I'll call you later. I want to hear what you think about it."

"Okay."

"Hey, and also ... I want to fly out to see you one of these weekends so I can catch a game."

"We're still undefeated."

"That's my girl." He ran his fingers over the still open magazine. "Talk to you later, sweetie. I love you."

"Love you too."

They said a quick good-bye and Shane slipped his cell phone back in his pocket. Once more he read the article, and this time he could almost hear Lauren talking to him through the lines of the story. Yes, war was tragic, yes, it was complicated. No one wanted war, least of all the members and families of the military.

But some things were worth defending. Freedom and democracy and a way of life that Americans had become accustomed to, a way of life the people of Iraq were only now getting to taste. He could hear her saying all that, and something else.

Not yet, maybe, not so soon, but if these were the types of stories she might find in the middle of Iraq, then one day not so far off, the two of them might figure out that they weren't that different after all.

The article might be the bridge they'd spent most of the past year looking for. Because only a change of heart would've allowed Lauren to present the story the way she'd done here. And in the quiet of that morning, he had to wonder. Maybe events like these, stories like this, would become a regular part of her war reporting. If they did, then her time in the Middle East just might give them the thing they'd never been able to find.

Common ground.

SIXTEEN

Emily couldn't get to the library fast enough.

She believed her dad, that something in her mother's article was proof that God was opening her eyes, changing her heart. But even more, she wanted to see the photo of Justin. She carried her books in her backpack and jogged down the paved path to the old brick library, the place where she'd spent countless hours studying.

She'd chosen a minor in sociology, something she'd fallen into because of Justin. The impact he had on the Veterans and schoolkids — and especially on the teens — was impressive. She'd always pictured herself as a writer, even a reporter. Only she would present the facts without bias, at least as much as possible.

But now she wasn't sure she could be a responsible journalist without also being involved in the community around her — -volunteering the way Justin did. Her writing courses had always been easy, and she wasn't far enough in her studies to work for the campus newspaper yet. So her fall schedule had three sociology classes. But social studies required hours of homework and reading. After the soccer field and the little campus chapel, the library was where she spent much of her time.

She came to the stairs and took them two at a time. The image she had of Justin, the one she carried in her heart, was the one of him in his dress uniform, standing beside her along the railing of the cruise boat. He was tanned and at ease, his eyes shining with love. Twice so far, he'd sent her digital photos of himself in Iraq. He and a buddy named Joe, standing in front of their barracks, or him and a group of Iraqi children, where it was impossible to tell who was enjoying the moment more—Justin or the kids. She hurried through the double doors and over to the counter where the library kept its periodicals. She found it almost immediately, several copies of the newest edition of *Time*. *Okay, God … show me what my dad saw. Let me know if she's starting to see things differently. Please …*

She grabbed the top copy and plopped down in the closest chair. It took her seconds to find the layout. And suddenly there he was. She brought the magazine closer and studied him. Somehow seeing him in *Time* magazine made his situation terrifyingly real.

It was one thing to look at a digital photo attached to an email. But here … there was no denying the obvious. Justin was a world away, smack in the middle of one of the most dangerous parts of Iraq. She inhaled sharply, refusing to give in to the tears building in her throat. Her feelings were a mix of sorrow and longing and the very deepest pride.

Because there was Justin, doing what he did best. Helping people, leading by example. War was raging a hundred yards down the street, but Justin was watching over the children of the protestors. If he and his company hadn't been there, then what? Then the little boys and girls in the picture would've been gathered around their protesting fathers.

And when bullets rang out, the children would've likely been among those killed. She studied the faces of the children. No doubt some of them had lost dads that day, but they hadn't lost hope. Because the American soldiers in their midst gave them and their parents and their city a reason to believe that no matter how great the losses along the way, freedom would win. Democracy would rule.

But even as her heart swelled with pride, a sick feeling spread through her. *Justin … what are you doing so close to snipers, on the same streets as terrorists?* As she looked at his smiling face, at the strength in his arm as he cocked the ball back, ready to release it, the magazine in her hands began to tremble.

Not even one month had passed, and every day, every hour, placed him in danger. She tried to exhale, but only a tiny bit of air eased through her lips. Panic surged inside her. What if he didn't have the right safety gear, the right weapons? What if on that same street, that very day, terrorists in another building took aim—in his direction?

Her lungs wouldn't work, and she felt a layer of perspiration building on her forehead. Her legs shook—and suddenly she realized what was happening. She was having a panic attack, something she hadn't felt since the days before she found her parents. Sometimes she got so caught up in worry—that she'd never find her parents, that they might already be dead, or that they wouldn't want to meet her even if she found them—that her body simply tried to shut down.

That's what was happening now.

The what-ifs loomed larger than life, towering over her, suffocating her. Her eyes darted around the room, searching for someone who might help her, but the only one she could see was the librarian—far in the other corner of the library.

God! I can't breathe! She set the magazine on the table and bent over, resting her arms and her forehead on the hard surface. What if Justin never came home? How would she ever survive the loss? How would—

Daughter, I am with you ... my peace I give You.

Like a punctured tire, the air slowly released from her too-tight lungs. *Lord ... is that you?*

Be still and know that I am God.

Every cell in her body felt the command, heard the words. Her muscles responded, relaxing, and finally her lungs filled with air. The Lord was with her. He was here watching over her as she looked at the magazine, here listening to her thoughts as panic began to take hold of her.

He wasn't going to let her fall apart, and He wasn't going to abandon Justin or her mother. She exhaled again. *Thank You, God.* She straightened slowly and leaned back against the hard, cold chair. She could do nothing to change the facts. Justin was in Iraq because he believed in being there. He was doing what he felt born to do—defending the cause of freedom, no matter the cost.

She mustn't do this again, let her thoughts and fears run away with her. Okay, Justin's picture was in *Time* magazine. That didn't make his being there more real. He was there. For another five months he'd be there, and she would have to find a way to deal with her feelings, her fears.

The way was obvious. *God … I forgot You were with me, but You are. You're right here.* She closed her eyes and felt herself beginning to cool down, felt the panic leaving her body. *You spoke to me even before I called out.* She took another breath, a cleansing, slow drink of oxygen.

Then she turned her eyes to the story, her mother's story. Fifteen minutes later, when she'd read every word, she knew two things for sure. Her father was right—something was changing in her mother; otherwise she never would've presented the day's events in this light.

And second, God wasn't only with her, helping her through the panic. He was with her mother and with Justin and with every child smiling in the picture. For a long moment, she considered the loss of the U.S. soldier, the nineteen-year-old who had been first into the building, shot down by insurgents. Somewhere on the East Coast, the boy's family was getting the news, being dealt the worst blow of their lives.

The cost was high, and too often the cost had a face, a name, a history. But the young soldier had gone into battle knowing the risks, aware of the costs. Same as Justin. She could only hope that in the days to come, as the boy's family and friends gathered to pay him tribute, they would thank God this generation included young men and women willing to sacrifice everything—the way military people had been willing to do since the country's inception.

All so that Americans could go on living a life they'd come to expect, one they so easily took for granted.

She no longer felt sick, and the panic that had threatened to dominate her minutes ago subsided entirely. The Bible had much to say about peace. But almost always the picture Scripture presented wasn't one of God calming the storm. Rather He calmed the person caught in the storm. John 16:33 told the truth about life on earth: "'In this world you will have trouble. But take heart! I have overcome the world.'"

It was that last part that made all the difference. And after she checked out the magazine, as she headed off for class, Emily could feel God's peace the way it was described in Philippians, chapter four. A peace that passed all understanding.

Her classes lasted until after lunch that day, and soccer practice kept her on the field in the pouring rain until three. When it was over, she did something she'd been doing at least once a week. She went to the teen center. This time she took her copy of *Time* magazine, tucked safely in her backpack. It was too rainy to play basketball, but inside the center was a ping-pong table, and the guys were just as competitive about that as they were about hoops.

The teens seemed to look forward to her visits, and though at first they intimidated her with their tough exterior and baggy pants, now she saw them the way Justin saw them—as boys without dads, kids lost in a world that often moved too fast to notice them.

"Hey, pretty mama! You came back!" It was Bo, the teen who'd been most affected by Justin's absence.

Emily grinned at the group. "Today's the day, Bo. You and me at the ping-pong table. You're going down."

He made a sound that told everyone in the room she was as wrong as she could possibly be. "I'm ready, girl. Say the word."

"Okay." She came closer. "But first I have to show you something." She set her backpack down and pulled the magazine from inside.

"You brought us something to read." Dexter, another of the guys who'd been close to Justin, made a teasing sort of frown. "Come on! I thought this was a teen center, not a library."

The others laughed, but Emily held up her hand. "Justin made the magazine."

It took a few seconds for the information to sink in. Bo was the first to her side. "My main man, Baker?" He peered over her shoulder. "Show me."

The guys gathered around, and she turned the pages to the spread in the middle. "See?"

Bo took the magazine from her and scrutinized the photo. As he did, as his buddies pressed in behind him getting a closer look, something in Bo's face changed. His eyes softened, and the tough-guy exterior fell away. He smiled and a quiet chuckle came from his throat. "That's my homeboy ... out there saving the world."

Dexter took hold of the left page, and for a moment Emily thought about warning them. She still needed to buy her own copy. This one had to be returned to the library intact. But Dexter didn't damage the pages. Like the others, he was transfixed by what he saw.

"See, man?" One of them shook his head. He tapped the article with his finger. "That's what I'm talking about. That's why I'm enlisting." Marcus—the shortest in the group—jabbed his finger in the air for emphasis. "That's what Justin's always telling us, how the war's getting things done over there."

"Over here too." Another teen bobbed his head, pride written in the lines on his forehead. "When's the last time you saw a plane crash into a building, huh? That's what I want to know."

Bo was silent, his attention still fixed to the picture of Justin. Emily had stepped back. They needed their space, needed to have their moment, proud of their friend, awed by the sight of his face in *Time*. Absently, she touched the small heart that hung around her neck. Justin's heart. She turned her attention to Bo again, and that's when she saw it. Two teardrops fell from his face and splashed onto the page. He wiped at them, clearly embarrassed. Then he sniffed hard and lifted his eyes to Emily. "Can you give him a message?"

"Of course." Her throat was thick, her heart heavy for Bo.

"Tell him ..." Bo's eyes fell to the picture again. He touched Justin's face with his fingertips. "Tell him that he's doing a good thing, okay?" He looked at her again. "But tell him to hurry himself on back here, because we—" His voice was strained with tears. He made an angry face that hid his sorrow. He pinched the shoulder of his T-shirt between his thumb and forefinger and plucked it, the way kids sometimes did. He sniffed again. "Because we need him more than they do."

"Yeah." Dexter nodded and slung his arm around Bo's shoulders. "Tell him that for me too."

Later, when the magazine was put away and a dozen ping-pong games had been played, Emily was headed back to her car when Bo stopped her. "Could you do me a favor?" He looked over his shoulder, as if he didn't want the rest of his group to hear him. "Could you bring me a copy of that magazine? Maybe we can, you know, put it up on the wall here. So we don't forget to keep watching the door for him."

Emily reached out and squeezed the teen's hand. "Of course."

Back at her residence hall, Emily hurried to the bank of computers on the second floor. This was what she'd been waiting for all day, the chance to hear Justin's voice through the lines of his email. She signed on, feeling the jangle of her bracelet against her wrist. While the computer worked, she glanced at the engraved heart. *Emily and Justin. Genesis 29.* Suddenly her mailbox appeared. Sure enough, there was his email address and a subject line that said only, "Missing you."

Her heart skipped around, the way it always did when she was about to read his letters. God's peace kept her going, but Justin's letters gave her something to look forward to, one way of counting down the days until he returned.

Her eyes raced to the first line, ready to drink in his words like a person dying of thirst. She pictured him, the way he'd felt that last day, hugging her, whispering good-byes. With his voice alive inside her once again, she started to read.

Dear Emily,

The violence is heating up. We can feel it. It's always this way before elections, and it underlines the reasons we're here. These people want democracy, and we won't win this war until they have it, until they're capable of hunting down and capturing terrorists on their own, so that nothing could threaten their freedom ever again.

Okay, enough of that.

I have to tell you, you're spoiling Buster. Scraps from the cafeteria? By the time I get back home, he won't remember me.

She smiled. They both knew that was hardly true. Buster's loyalty ran straight through him. She kept reading.

The days are getting cooler here, which is a good thing. But nothing seems to make the time pass fast enough. I guess you probably know I saw your mom. Maybe when you get this, you'll already have the next magazine. I'm anxious to see what she writes. That day was pretty intense. I think it touched her, Emily. Really. I guess time will tell.

Oh, Joe says to tell you he's jealous. I get all the email and he gets none. But don't feel too bad for him. I read him your letters and that makes him feel a little better. Entertained, he says. And don't worry. I reserve the right to censor as I'm reading. Some things need to be just between the two of us.

Hey, help me out on something, okay? Don't let Buster kiss you. He can't if I can't, that's the way I see it. And how about the guys at the teen center? Have you been back to play ping-pong with them? Oh, and ask Bo about his grades. He's a junior this year, and he promised me nothing less than a C. Especially in science and math. Tell him I'm talking to God about him—every day. The other guys too.

You won't believe this. Joe says I'm a slob. Even when I only have a duffle bag full of stuff to take care of, I still can't keep things clean. Oh well. There's not much around here that's really all that clean, anyway. And something else. I haven't made much time for my morning workouts. We get up and eat and hit the road almost immediately. You'll blow me away in a race when I get back, that's for sure.

But give me time. I'll be ready by summer, for sure.

Emily's eyes clouded, but she smiled anyway. As if Justin could ever really be out of shape. He cared too much about giving his best to let that happen. She scrolled down.

So, yeah. This is the part I hate, the end part. I sit here and all I can see is you, the way your eyes looked on the boat that day and at your dorm afterwards. I don't hear the wind howling outside, or the sound of gunfire and explosions, but your voice, asking me to take you with me, begging me not to go. I feel your face beneath my fingers, your lips against mine.

I miss you, Emily. A little more with every breath. Keep praying. All my love, all the time … Justin.

She read the letter through again, and when she reached the end, there was nothing she could do to stop the tears from burning two hot little trails down her cheeks. She printed the letter and then hit the reply button.

Dear Justin …

You're famous! I'm attaching a link to the story in Time *magazine, and I'm saving you a copy. But I have to warn you. You'll be signing autographs by the time you get back here. Your picture's bigger than life. And obviously I know about you running into my mom. Wait till you read her story.*

Emily kept typing. She told him about the magazine piece and her conversation with her father. She told him about her time at the teen center and the reaction of the kids when they saw the article.

At first, Bo couldn't stop smiling. He said something about you being his homeboy, out there saving the world. But the longer he looked, the more his expression changed. Bo didn't want me to see, but he got tears in his eyes, you know? He told me to tell you that he's proud of you, that you're doing the right thing. But he and the guys need you more.

There, I told you.

She went on, giving the details of her soccer games and the weather and her plans to go to Kelso on Sunday to visit Buster.

Don't worry, Justin. I won't let him kiss me. My lips are off-limits until you come back. And then … well, let's just say we better keep away from private places, okay?

She told him about her panic attack at the library, how she almost let fear swallow her whole.

I get like that sometimes, when I think of you out there on the streets of Baghdad. But God grabbed hold of me before I stopped breathing altogether. He sort of tapped me on the shoulder and was like, "Uh, Emily ... I think you're forgetting about My peace." And I was like, "Right. How could I forget?"

Anyway, I can't wait for you to read the article. It's a pretty good picture of you. I can't wait to hear what the rest of the team says when they see it. They keep asking if you've got a friend or a brother—someone they could meet. I'll have to tell them about Joe. Maybe he could get some email, after all.

I know what you mean about remembering that last day. Sometimes I'm walking across campus, looking at the changing leaves, and I feel your breath on my skin, as close as if you were walking beside me. I'm hanging on, Justin. But only barely. So be safe. I'll be praying, and when I'm not praying, I'll be missing you. I love you, Emily.

She hit the send button and sat back, watching her letter disappear from the screen. As they often did, her fingers found the heart around her neck and she rubbed her thumb across it. All she could think as she signed out, collected the printed email, and headed back to her room, was that Bo was right. They were all proud of Justin and the work he was doing. After today, all of America couldn't help but be proud. But no matter what he accomplished in Iraq, he was needed more back home. By his family and Buster and the Veterans and the schoolkids. By Bo and the guys at the teen center.

And most of all, by her.

Seventeen

Angela Anderson closed the cover of *Time* magazine and moved to the front window of her new town house. She wouldn't call it a premonition, but her heart felt unsettled, the way it had so long ago when she and Bill and the Galanters made the decision to separate Lauren and Shane.

Now here she was, widowed and living near the Galanters. Everything had worked out for everyone—except the two kids who had loved each other more than life. At first, after their reunion, she had been certain that Lauren's decision to live in Fallon meant everything would end happily for her daughter and Shane. Lauren had been touched by her father's death, softened by the restoration of friendship between them and the Galanters.

But every time Angela talked to Lauren, she felt it coming, felt her daughter pulling away. Lauren wouldn't be boxed in, not now anymore than when she was a girl. Back then all four of the adults in her life had figured it was best for her and Shane to be apart.

Lauren had shown them.

She had done such a great job of disappearing that none of their attempts to locate her had amounted to more than disappointment. Until Emily stepped in.

Angela held the magazine to her chest and studied the street below. Children played in a grassy field across the way, a game that looked like kickball. Two of the kids—a boy and girl, maybe twelve or thirteen—seemed particularly close, the way Lauren and Shane had been back when they were kids.

Maybe that's all this feeling was, the sense of guilt and shame over what she and her husband and the Galanters had done. They'd manipulated Lauren and Shane, and in the process denied them of a life together. At least last winter, when Emily found her parents and brought them together for a final week with Bill, it had looked like their future could still be salvaged.

But there was no way to get back the years they'd lost, no way to relive the decades that should've belonged to them alone, decades that might've been golden if the parents in their lives had trusted that Shane and Lauren could actually know real love when they held it in their hands.

Angela sighed.

She missed Bill more on days like this, days when it would've been good to talk through her feelings. He would have told her they couldn't waste today regretting yesterday. Their energy would be better spent making tomorrow so good, the glow of it cast bright light even on the dark shadows of the past.

Something poetic like that.

She could call Sheila Galanter, and she would. Later. But for now she needed to talk to God more than anyone else. Because she didn't fully understand why she was feeling this way. The article should've brought smiles for the rest of the day. Lauren's viewpoints seemed to be softening, and Justin Baker was perfect for Emily, a shining example of young patriotism, the sort of boy who gave the older generation hope for the future.

So what was the problem?

The longer she dwelt on her unease, the more it seemed like a sense of impending doom. Maybe it was because Lauren had placed herself in such a dangerous place. Journalists were not immune to the violence in a war-torn place like Baghdad. The news told the stories every month or so of how a journalist was captured and tortured or held for a few weeks and then beheaded.

Angela shuddered. If that happened to Lauren, then how could she live another day out from under the cloud of guilt? That very minute, Lauren should've been living with Shane, happily married for twenty years, parents to a houseful of kids, with Emily the oldest.

None of that had happened. But now—if the article was any indication—Lauren's heart was changing. Her viewpoints were broadening. Which meant everything was going to be okay—hopefully sooner than later. Lauren could ask her editor if she could work from Fallon once again.

War was no place for her daughter, not when she'd spent two decades unable to find true happiness. Angela turned and set the magazine down on a lace doily that covered a small round end table. She was tired, more than usual. Fear was probably eating away her energy.

She sat down in the upholstered chair near the window, leaned back, and closed her eyes. *God ... what is it I'm feeling? Is it guilt? Is it Bill, another day of missing him?* She waited, but there was no response, nothing but the sound of the children playing outside.

Lord, I beg You. Bring Lauren home to Shane, where she belongs. Please ... use the stories and events in Iraq to turn her heart around, and once that's happened, make her feet turn around too. Bring her home safely. And please, God—keep using Justin Baker.

When she finished praying, she sat for a while, savoring the sound of the children across the street. Where had the years gone, the ones where Shane and Lauren would play out back for hours and hours? Hadn't it seemed like life would go on that way forever? And maybe it would have, if only she and the others had been more forgiving.

The way the Lord had so graciously forgiven her.

By the time she went to the kitchen and put a chicken in the oven for dinner, she had a much better outlook. There was no need to worry. Lauren was going to come home, she and Shane were finally going to marry and find happiness, and Justin Baker was going to keep winning the war in Iraq. They'd had enough sorrow in their lives. Surely God wouldn't allow more. The unsettled feeling was just left over from all that had come before. But here, today, life was going to be just fine. Even more than the nagging sense of dread, Angela could feel it with everything in her being.

EIGHTEEN

They were halfway through November, and Justin was more homesick than ever. The stretch between Thanksgiving and Christmas loomed like a terrible period of exile. It was late at night, and the task that lay ahead the next morning was a considerable one.

Justin rolled onto his side. He needed his sleep. But he needed to hear Emily's voice more.

For a crazy minute, he thought about finding his commander and asking to make an emergency call. Only there wasn't an emergency, not really. Just the fact that his heart hurt from missing her. He flopped onto his back and stared at the dark ceiling.

Next to him, Joe was snoring. Rumbling like a slow freight train. Justin closed his eyes and tried to find that calm place in his mind. The one he needed to find every night before he could fall asleep. He and Joe had read the Bible that night, the book of John, chapter sixteen. In it was the verse Justin thought about often when they were out in Baghdad: "In this world you will have trouble. But take heart! I have overcome the world." Indeed. God's peace and grace and strength were all that got him through.

Two more U.S. soldiers had died that week. Two guys Justin knew from holding operations around the city's polling centers. They'd been traveling in a caravan from one location to another, when a car loaded with explosives and traveling the opposite direction crossed the middle line and drove straight into them.

Justin and his company had seen the fireball from a mile away. Suicide bombers. More terrorists. More insurgents.

A long sigh pressed through his lips. They should have twice as many troops in Baghdad and around every hot spot in Iraq.

Additional surveillance equipment should be brought in, and the army and marines should be given the green light to do whatever it took to get the insurgents. He hated that they seemed so often to be sitting ducks, always on the defensive and never making the first move.

But how could they increase their efforts unless the people of the United States got behind them fully, completely?

He flicked on the light overhead. Sleep was useless. Maybe he'd find some peace if he spent time with the scrapbook, the place where Emily lived. Her letters had been like air to him lately. Everything she had to say gave him hope and brought him another reason to count down the days, to long for home.

Not that he minded serving in Iraq. If he had it to do again, he'd still choose a second tour. But he hadn't thought the holiday season would hit him with such a longing for home.

He studied the photo of Emily and him, the one on the front cover of the scrapbook. She was so beautiful. On the outside, yes. But that wasn't what he saw when he looked into her eyes. He saw the person she was on the inside, her soul. She was taking sociology courses, she'd told him, so she could "be like him when she grew up."

He smiled at the thought. *Emily* ... He ran his thumb over the image of her face. *You don't need to be like anyone but yourself.* The schedule she'd been keeping was enough to make him tired. Soccer and schoolwork and weekly visits to his parents in Kelso. He teased her about Buster, but secretly Justin was thrilled. How great that she was taking time with his dog. That, and the fact that his parents and his sister looked forward to her visits. They all mentioned her when they wrote.

But the thing that made him most grateful was that she'd been dropping by the teen center. Guys like Bo and Dexter were easy prey for the corner drug dealer, boys without fathers, kids whose culture centered around narcotics and violence. Teens like that needed a reason to come to the center, a regular face they looked forward to.

Emily had become that face.

One time, Bo wrote him an email. *Look out, homeboy. When you come home, your pretty mama might belong to me.* Justin chuckled softly. Bo's letter was cocky and brash, but no question the kid expressed a sense of security in hanging out with Emily each week. Almost as if by seeing her, they were assured that one day, when his six months were up, Justin would walk through the door of the center with her.

He yawned and turned the pages slowly, taking in the light that came from Emily's eyes, her smile. She thought he was a hero, a guy who had no faults. But that wasn't true. Every day it was an effort to head out to the streets of Baghdad knowing that something could happen to him, something that would keep him from ever seeing her again.

That was his secret, the little fear that never quite went away. The secret only she knew about. He smiled at the final photo, the one he'd added into the book their last night together, after he'd gotten back to the fort. It was the picture the old man had taken on the pier, the one with the ship in the background. What had the guy said? *Someday, when you're old and gray like us, you'll look back on that picture and understand about the passing of time. Don't blink, young people. Enjoy every minute.*

The first time Joe looked at the scrapbook, he stopped at that picture and shook his head. "You'd never know you were hours from saying good-bye. The two of you look about as happy as any couple I've ever known."

It was true. That's what being with Emily did to him. Her presence, her happy heart that day, made him forget the hard times just ahead. And that's what looking at her pictures did for him now.

He yawned again. The elusive calm filled his mind. *Okay, that's all I needed, God. Thanks for reminding me how lucky I am.*

He put the scrapbook away, turned off his light, and in what felt like five minutes, he heard Joe's voice in his ear.

"Come on, you bum. Get up!" Joe was in his boxers, one leg in his fatigues, one foot trying to find the other leg hole. "We're late."

"Late?" Justin shot up in bed. "What about the alarm?"

"Didn't go off. A few guys from down the hall pounded on the door." He jumped a few times in place and pulled his fatigues all the way up. "All I know is we have ten minutes before the caravan takes off."

Ten minutes? Justin groaned. He was up and dressed in seconds, and he rummaged through the bottom drawer of his dresser for one of the protein bars he'd brought from home. Instant energy for moments like this.

"You sharing?" Joe had his shirt buttoned, and he was perched at the edge of his bed, tugging his boot onto his right foot.

Justin grabbed another one and tossed it. "You owe me."

"Always."

With a minute to spare, they hurried outside and jumped into their spots in their military vehicle. Ace, the driver, turned around and raised a brow. "Cuttin' it kind of close today, hey guys?"

"Yeah, well—" Joe was still tucking his pant legs into his boots—"lover boy here kept the lights on all night."

"Not all night." Justin fastened his chest gear.

"Girl trouble, huh?" Ace waited until the car in front of him pulled out, and then he gave a burst of gas and their vehicle fell into line. "Forget about her, Baker. Distractions are never good."

"She's not a distraction." He mouthed a sarcastic thank-you in Joe's direction. "Things are great between us."

"Right. He can't fall asleep until he's hung out in the pages of his scrapbook for half an hour." Joe elbowed him, his eyes dancing.

"How sweet." Ace steered the vehicle with one hand. "Did you get briefed on the mission today?"

"Last night, same as everyone else." Justin settled back against the seat, ignoring the way the bumpy road jarred his back.

"We're checking out another abandoned building, right?" Joe leaned his head against the doorframe and closed his eyes. "If we can stay awake."

"You better stay awake. These are the big dogs, pal." Ace kept his eyes on the road. Ahead of them the caravan of cars was hard to see through the cloud of dust coming up off the road.

The big dogs. Justin let the words roll around in his mind, his soul. How many times had they done this? Gotten a tip that gunfire or bombs had come from a specific location, and then gone in, kicking down doors and breaking up another bunch of bad guys? Too many times to count. Medics willing to work the front lines were always needed.

God … give us Your eyes, Your ears.

He heard no response, but he could feel the Lord with him. The way he always felt it. He stifled another yawn and slid his fingers down the back of his boot. He pulled up her photograph.

Even on a hurried day like today, he'd remembered. Her picture was part of his uniform now. When he printed the photos from their lunch cruise that last day, he made a copy of one particularly good shot of Emily. Then he found someone with keys to the public information office, and he laminated it. That way he could keep it with him, and no amount of dirt or sweat would hurt it.

Most of the time out in the field, he didn't have time to look at it, to pull it up from the back of his boot and feel the strength it gave him. But today they were traveling from one end of Baghdad to the other, and a half hour in the car meant plenty of time to think about Emily. Sometimes, he liked to picture his homecoming, and how the spring and summer would play out.

He knew where he would ask her the question, the one he could hardly wait to ask. He closed his eyes and imagined it all taking place. He would get the ring, the solitaire she'd admired once when they went to Pacific Place.

I like simple rings, he could hear her saying. *A simple band and a simple diamond.*

"You're too easy." He had poked her in the ribs, laughing with her.

"Not really." She raised her brow, her eyes dancing. "Only when it comes to rings."

Anyway, he'd get the ring. Then he'd take her down to the waterfront and he'd find the same cruise ship, the lunch cruise. And they'd go to their private spot on the top deck, and there—out on the water—he'd ask her to marry him.

He could see her eyes, feel the wind against his face. He cupped the laminated photo tight in his palm. She would hug his neck and tell him yes, over and over and over again. And they'd talk about churches and flowers and colors and bridesmaids. And the months would pass and they'd hold the wedding somewhere with walls of windows and light coming in from every possible angle.

She would look like an angel in her wedding dress, and he would stand there trying to breathe as she made her way down the aisle and—

The explosion happened so fast he didn't have time to react. One second he was standing in a church somewhere in Tacoma, dressed to the nines, watching his bride walk down the aisle toward him, and the next …

Nothing had been louder in all his life. It shook him and mixed with the sound of breaking glass and disintegrating metal. The pain hit then, ripping through him with a heat and intensity that left him dazed. He couldn't draw a breath, couldn't feel his legs, couldn't see anything but deep wet red and muddy brown, and fire and smoke.

"*Emily!*"

He screamed her name because maybe this was part of the dream. Maybe he'd fallen asleep and the sliver of fear, the one that never quite went away, had magnified a thousand times over and created a hellish nightmare. Yes, that had to be it. "*Emily?*"

He was shouting her name, but he couldn't hear himself, couldn't make the words loud enough to actually be heard. And then, in a rush, the explosion faded, the noise stopped, and he felt himself land hard against the road.

That's when he realized what was happening. He wasn't dreaming. Ace must've hit a roadside bomb. Somehow the cars in front of them missed it, and theirs ...

Theirs had taken the hit.

The hot feeling grew worse with every attempt he made at breathing. And what about his legs? Why couldn't he feel them? He opened his eyes, struggled to see even a sliver of light. *God ... no, not now. Please ... don't let me die here. I need to talk to Emily.*

Emily! Again the sound of his own voice wouldn't quite clear his throat. *Emily, baby, I'm sorry ... I never meant for this to happen ...*

There were feet shuffling near his head, feet and the shouts of voices. "Justin!" It was Joe; he'd know his voice anywhere.

"Joe?" He blinked hard, once, twice, and finally ... finally opened his eyes. His buddy was kneeling over him, his uniform and his face were splattered with blood and dirt. And something else. Tears. "Joe ... what ..." He coughed. Couldn't catch his breath. "What happened?"

Joe clenched his fists and leaned his head back. "Help! Someone get us help over here! Now!"

"Joe ..." His strength was leaving him. The burning feeling was worse, but now it felt like his lungs were filling up, like he was drowning, only there wasn't any water and his mouth was parched. He held out his hand. "Talk to me, Joe."

"Justin, hang on, buddy." Joe dropped to his knees and took his hand. "They're coming, okay?"

"What ... about my legs?"

"Don't look, man. Keep your eyes on me, okay?" He looked over his shoulder, and the intensity in his scream was frightening. "*Hurry!* We need help, now!"

Justin turned his head just a little and there was Ace, his body ripped to shreds. A roadside bomb. That must've been it. Ace was gone. No one was hovering over him, no one looking to help him.

So that meant he still had a chance, right? He was alive ... Joe was calling for help. But what about his legs? He and Ace had been sitting on the same side of the car. And Joe ... what about Joe?

"Joe, man ... you okay?" Justin's eyes were closed again, and he fought to open them. Was that blood trickling down the right side of Joe's face? "You're cut, buddy ... put ... put pressure on that thing."

"No!" Joe sounded panicked. He shook his head hard and lay his entire body across Justin's, across the upper part of his legs just above his knees. "We gotta stop the bleeding." He shouted again. "We gotta stop the bleeding. Someone ... someone, help!"

Justin wanted to say something, but he felt drugged, like he was in the middle of an intense sleep and nothing—nothing at all—could wake him. He was getting married, wasn't he? Watching Emily walk down the aisle toward him?

"Hang in there, Justin!" Joe was crying now. Joe, the big oaf who never took anything very seriously, was crying. "Don't leave me! Please, Justin, don't leave me!"

"Okay ..." He ran his tongue over his lower lip. "Joe ... buddy ... pray."

Joe nodded, his motions quick and jerky, frantic. "God!" He stared up at the sky. "God ... help us! Please!"

Justin gave the slightest nod. He wanted to say something, but his mouth wouldn't work. Maybe he just needed to rest a bit, work up the strength to get the words out. But wait. There was something in his hand. Not the hand Joe was holding, the other hand. He ran his fingertips over it and then he remembered. Emily's picture. He still had Emily's picture in his hand. With all his might he tried to lift it, and finally, barely, he did.

He couldn't draw a full breath. The heaviness, the heat pulsing through him was too great. *God ... let me see her. Please ...* He tried once more, and this time he squinted against the bright blue sky. *Ah ... there. Thank You, God ...*

He could see. He turned his head—and there she was.

His Emily. Smiling at him, willing him to be strong, to fight hard even now. *Emily, baby ... I'm sorry.*

"Justin!" Joe was crying harder. "Here, give it to me." He took the photograph and held it up close. "She's waiting for you, man. Don't quit on me."

Running feet came up from a couple directions and he could hear other voices.

"Too much blood loss ..."

"There's nothing to save ..."

"Get him on a stretcher ..."

"He's still breathing ... we have to try."

The words and sentences blended together, but they told Justin what he already suspected. His legs were gone. Joe was lying across him, and that's all that had kept him from bleeding to death. Just like Ace.

They were trying to move him now, but he didn't want to go. Not until he could talk to Joe. He squinted, and black circles rolled around in his vision. "Joe ..."

"I'm here, buddy." His friend was kneeling beside him, Emily's picture still upright in his hand, still stretched out close so Justin could see it. So he could savor it.

"Joe … tell her … I love her."

"*You* tell her, Baker." Joe dragged his free hand across his cheeks. His nose was runny, and his tears mixed with the blood on his face. "She's your girl."

Justin was out of air, out of strength. His life was draining away, so the only reason he could talk now was because God was giving him this time, this moment. He looked at the picture of Emily and then at Joe. "Be her friend … for me." He winced, because the pain was worse, exploding through his body the way the bomb had exploded through their vehicle.

"Don't!" Anger flashed in Joe's eyes. "Don't talk that way."

At that moment, one of the medics came up and put his hand on Joe's shoulder. He shook his head and gave Joe a couple hard pats. Joe seemed to understand what the guy meant, same as Justin did. There was no point. Justin had a minute left, maybe less. Too much damage, too much blood loss.

He felt dizzy, desperate to close his eyes and get back to the dream, the one where Emily was walking toward him, his beautiful bride. But he needed something from Joe. He forced himself to think, to concentrate. What was it?

Then it hit him. He needed Joe's word. "Promise me … promise you'll be her friend." Because when this day was done, she'd need a friend in the worst way. He was sure of it.

Joe hung his head and sobbed. He still held out the picture of Emily, kept it positioned so Justin could see it. "No, God! Please!" Joe tightened the hold he had on Justin's hand, and he lifted his chin. Lifted it just enough so their eyes could meet. Then he said the words that looked almost impossible for him to say. "I promise. Whatever you want."

Relief flooded through Justin and his eyelids closed. The pain was unbearable, the heaviness and burning and heat that filled his body. But now there was a peace … a peace from God, one that passed all understanding. Joe would tell her. He'd be her friend, because he'd given his word.

Justin could feel himself falling, falling fast and far, away from the streets of Baghdad, away from the carnage of bodies and broken car pieces that lay strewn around him. *Once more, God ... let me see her one more time. Please ...*

And then, with no strength left at all, he opened his eyes. He looked at Joe and felt the corners of his mouth lift ever so slightly. "Thanks, man. Keep ... keep praying." What else? There was something else he wanted to say. He concentrated with all that remained in him. "Tell them I ... I wanted to be here. Tell them to win ... this thing."

"I will." Tears streamed down Joe's face, but he wasn't shouting, wasn't screaming for help. "I love you, man. Save me a spot up there, okay?"

Justin felt himself smile. "I will. You ... and my family ... and my guys at the center. And Emily." His eyes found her picture. "I'll save ... a spot for her—"

Deep inside him, he felt his heart struggle. *Beat ... beat.* Long pause. Another beat. His pulse was slowing down, fading. *Emily ... don't be mad at me, baby.*

Her face, her deep blue eyes, were the last thing he saw.

His thoughts blurred and his eyes closed, and in the flash of an instant, the darkness was filled with a million shining moments. He and Emily meeting for the first time at the public information office, and Vonda saying, *He wants to run the place one day*, and he was grinning at Emily and telling her, *Not yet. Not just yet.* And Vonda was shaking her head and clucking her tongue. *Looks like we got us a pair of smitten youngsters. Don't fight it, Emily ... don't fight it.*

And Emily was raising an eyebrow at him and asking, *Mr. Smooth, huh?* And they were walking along Puget Sound and their arms were touching and he was thinking he'd never felt like this in all his life. And suddenly he was on a soccer field, jerking his shirt from his body and bandaging up the girl's leg, and Emily was looking in his eyes and saying, *You're my hero, Justin. You'll always be my hero.*

The scene changed and they were hiking in the hills east of Tacoma, and she was a few feet ahead of him and she tripped and fell into his arms, and she was begging him, *Just stay behind me, okay? You never know when I might need you to catch me.* And they were walking but the path became a pier and there was a cruise ship in the distance and a little old couple and the woman was saying, *Oh, dear, aren't they the most adorable couple? Just like you and me at that age.*

And he was standing at the foot of the steps of her residence hall and Emily was crying. She was crying and he couldn't make her stop, no matter what he said. And she was whispering, *Please ... don't go. Don't leave me.* And he was running his hands down her back, her arms. *Baby ... I'll come back. I promise. Everything's going to be okay.*

And suddenly her arms were around his neck and he could feel her body against his, taste her tears in his lips, and through her tears she was saying, *Take me with you. Wherever you go ... I wanna be there too.*

And he was reminding her that he would take her if he could, but in the meantime ... in the meantime she would have his heart. She would always have his heart. And the picture changed again. He was sitting in his bunk at the barracks, looking at the scrapbook and being jolted awake and rushing to the car, to the caravan. And he was resting his head and picturing her, the way she would look when she walked down the aisle, his cherished bride ...

Finally, the images faded, and all that remained was warmth. Warmth and light and a sense of hope and peace and perfection. And one lingering thought. He hadn't kept his promise. Because he wasn't going back at all, and so what was she going to think? *Don't be mad, Emily ... I love you ... I'll always love you.*

The sadness faded along with her image as the reality set in. *I'll save a place for you ... save a place for you ...* The light was golden now and beyond it a great city, shining and perfect. And he knew—he absolutely knew—that there would be no more tears, no more dying, no more destruction or devastation.

The pain was gone.

He could feel his legs again, strong and healthy, moving beneath him. He wasn't going back, he was going somewhere better. The place he was created for, the place where he belonged. Where his family and Joe and the teens, where the Veterans and the schoolkids, and where Emily one day would join him.

He was going home.

NINETEEN

Carol Baker knew before she opened the door.

She heard the car outside and came to the entryway. And through the window in the door she watched the pair of uniformed soldiers get out and stop, their eyes fixed on her house. She saw them start up the walkway. Her mind raced. When was the last time they'd talked, the last time they'd heard from Justin? And what was the news yesterday?

Three soldiers killed in a roadside bomb.

Same as always, the story stopped her in her tracks. The soldiers remained unnamed pending notification of family—

There was a knock at the door, and she shook her head. No ... not her family. The notification belonged somewhere else.

"Gary!" She shouted her husband's name. He was in the back den, watching football highlights from the weekend games. How stupid they were! They should have been trying to call Justin. Because that was where he was stationed. Right there, where the roadside bomb struck. "Gary, please!"

She heard footsteps in the hall. "Honey, what—" His voice dropped off. Through the window in the door he must've seen what she'd seen. The army green, the shadowy figures of soldiers. His eyes met hers, but he didn't say a word. She could see the blood draining from his face, but he was silent as he came to her, one slow step after another.

Her heart pounded so hard she expected it to give out on the spot. Because if her Justin was gone, then she would be gone.

Even if her heart continued to beat for another forty years. "Not Justin ..." She whispered the words and moved aside.

A second knock sounded, so loud it seemed to shake the house, shake her foundation, her core. *God ... not Justin.*

Gary swallowed—swallowed so hard she could hear him. Then he did what people do in a situation like this. He opened the door. And all she could think was that this was how it happened, how people were notified. This scene played out all the time, as long as war had been going on.

But she'd never pictured it happening to her. Imagining such a thing would've been to live in constant fear, hounded by it, hunted by it, suffocated by it. She never could've let Justin go if she'd thought for a minute that this was how it would end.

Everything seemed to happen in slow motion. Gary opened the door, and the soldiers on the front step hung their heads. Hung them for what seemed like forever.

She wanted to scream ... *What? Why are you here? And why so down? My Justin is the toughest soldier in Iraq. He isn't dead. There's no way he's dead.*

"Can ... can we help you?" Gary sounded frozen, like he hadn't had time to catch his breath. He held the door handle so tight his knuckles turned white.

The soldiers looked up, and one of them had tears in his eyes. She could hear Justin, five or six years old, running inside with a skinned knee ... and she was getting a cloth, something to wash away the blood, and he was saying, *It's okay, Mommy ... soldiers don't cry ... soldiers don't cry ...*

But they do. They did. Because he had cried at the airport when he said good-bye. Not hard or long, but the tears were there for both of them. All of them. That's when she remembered Jill, their daughter. She was at an all-day dance camp. She wouldn't be home until late that night. How were they going to tell her that her brother was gone?

Finally, one of the soldiers handed Gary a letter. "I'm sorry, sir. Your son ... he was killed yesterday in Iraq. Victim of a roadside bomb." He nodded to the letter. "The details are all there."

With every hateful word, she felt her knees giving way. As they apologized one more time and turned around, she spun to Gary and collapsed in his arms. "No!" Her voice wasn't the slightest bit familiar. It was a guttural scream, high-pitched and desperate. The sobs hit her, and she wailed like a crazy woman. "No, Gary! Not Justin! Never Justin!"

Gary held her, clung to her, almost as if he needed her support as much as she needed his. "God ... we can't do this. We beg You to hold us." He sounded on the verge of collapse. "We have no ability to get through what lies ahead for us." Desperate, cavernous sorrow overflowed his words. "Please, God ... hold us."

Carol wanted to shout that it was too late. God had already taken their son. But she couldn't because she didn't believe it. She exhaled and slowly, sadly, her world began to right itself. Screaming and yelling wouldn't do anything now. Justin was gone, dead. Struck down doing what he felt so strongly about.

"We need ... to read the letter." Gary cradled the back of her head in his hand and kissed her forehead. Then he led her to the couch. He opened the envelope and read the first line out loud, the line every military family member dreaded reading. "We regret to inform you that your son, Lieutenant Justin Baker, was killed in action ..."

He read the whole thing, the part about Justin's courage and great attitude, the fact that he would be remembered as a role model for other soldiers, for all U.S. citizens, and then the details of that day. The caravan had been heading to the far side of Baghdad, intent on finding insurgents, when the car Justin was riding in hit a roadside bomb. One soldier in the car in front of them was killed. In Justin's car, he and the driver had died.

His body would be shipped home within the week.

There were no real facts, nothing that gave them a glimpse of Justin's final moments. When Gary finished reading, he folded the letter and set it on the sofa beside him. Then he pulled Carol into his arms and together, locked in the saddest embrace, they wept. The anger and shock were still there, but they had grown dim, overshadowed by a vast consuming sorrow that would never go away.

Not as long as either of them lived.

Minutes became an hour, and still they sat there, weeping for the son they would never hold again, never laugh with or share a meal with. Finally, as the numbness and panic faded, memories mixed with Carol's tears. Because Justin had been born to be a soldier. When other kindergarten boys played baseball or ran cement trucks through the dirt, Justin wanted nothing more than a child-sized army uniform.

Carol leaned back against the sofa. Her sobs were quieter now, but they were constant. So many tears, more than she knew she could cry. And a million memories. "Remember ... that Christmas when he was six?" she looked straight ahead, seeing the room as it had been at Christmastime sixteen years earlier. "He opened that uniform and he couldn't wait to put it on."

"'I'm gonna be a Ranger one day, Daddy!' That's what he told me." Gary's voice held a smile leftover from that day. "'I'm gonna fight the bad guys.'"

When his playmates came over, Justin would give them one of his green plastic guns and they'd play war games. His fascination never waned, not through junior high or high school. Not as he kept his commitment to ROTC through college, and not after he enlisted.

She turned and looked at her husband. "There was never any life for him other than the military."

"No." Gary squeezed his eyes shut.

Carol put her hand on his shoulder. Her husband, the man who had been Justin's closest friend. What was he thinking? That Justin had just written to them the other day, or that he'd sounded so upbeat, so alive? How could they even consider planning a funeral for their sunshine boy, the son who had been everything to them?

Gary looked at her, and the tears came harder. "He would've been … the best commander." He tightened his hands into fists and pressed them hard against his knees. "God knows he would've been the best."

Her husband was right. How could God need Justin more in heaven than the world needed him right here? Than *they* needed him. And suddenly she gasped. Because only then did it hit her. "Emily."

Gary hung his head, and his tears became sobs, sobs that came from a bottomless ocean of grief that would never, ever go away. When he finally regained control, he looked up. "We have to tell her. In person, Carol. Today."

She tried to speak, but she couldn't. Suddenly twenty-two years fell away and Justin was minutes old, cradled in Gary's arms. And her husband was looking at her with those same teary eyes. Where had the years gone? Each one dropping off like so many summer days. Through it all, nothing could've prepared them for this.

He was right. Emily needed to know. She closed her eyes, but the tears came anyway. Streams of them. Poor Emily. Carol let the sobs come, let them wash over her reminding her that the nightmare was real. Way too real. She brought her hand to her face. How would she find the strength even to move? Once a long time ago, she'd heard a talk by Elisabeth Elliot, the famous wife of Jim Elliot, the murdered missionary. One thing she'd said had stuck all these years. *Sometimes, life is so hard you can only do the next thing. Whatever that is, just do the next thing. God will meet you there.*

No matter how hard it would be, telling Emily was the next thing. Carol stood, and it took every bit of her energy to walk across the room and into the kitchen. She needed her purse. Gary followed, but before she found the bag, she spotted Buster at the back door. At his feet, crumpled in a ball, was Justin's sweatshirt. She stared at the dog, just stared at him. Because the longer she looked, the more she didn't see the sweatshirt, but Justin. Age fifteen, and sixteen, and seventeen—sitting outside on the patio petting Buster or brushing him or hooking up his leash for a walk.

As if the dog somehow knew, he began to whine, whimpering and pawing at the door. Gary exchanged a look with her. A look that said every step, everything they had to do that day and the next and the day after that, would be all but impossible.

He went to the door, opened it, and crouched down. "It's okay, Buster. It's okay."

But it wasn't, because Buster would never see his master walk through the door again. Carol ached for the sadness inside her. The tears would never stop, because it would take forever to cry the river of sorrow raging inside her. Gary led Buster back to his doghouse and tucked Justin's sweatshirt in close beside him. "There, Buster. Go to sleep."

Carol watched, unable to move, unable to do anything but breathe and cry and wish with every breath that she had one more chance, one more time to hug her child and look at him and marvel over the boy she'd raised. The soldier, the friend, the son. The hero.

Gary grabbed his car keys and his wallet. "Let's go."

She nodded. It was time to do the next thing. Now she could only pray that Elisabeth Elliot was right, that somehow they'd survive the coming hours.

Because God Himself would meet them there.

TWENTY

Emily had finished her last class of the day and was heading back to her room when her cell phone rang. It was email day, time to get her weekly letter from Justin. That alone had made it a good morning — that and the fact that the recent rains had let up just enough to allow a few glimpses of blue on the PLU campus. The air was colder than it had been all fall, and snow was forecast for Thanksgiving.

She grabbed her phone from the side pocket of her backpack and checked the Caller ID. Strange. She didn't recognize the number.

"Hello?" She kicked at a loose pile of fallen leaves and smiled at a passing student, a girl whose room was down the hall from her own.

On the other end, the caller wasn't saying anything.

"Hello? Is anyone there?"

"Emily?" The man's voice was familiar, but he sounded upset, his words thick and muffled so she couldn't quite pinpoint it.

Her heart hesitated. Who could be calling her so upset he could barely talk? "Yes? Who's this?"

"Gary Baker."

Emily stopped cold in the middle of the walkway. "Mr. Baker? What's wrong?"

"Honey, we're here at your campus. Carol and I. In the parking lot. Can we meet you somewhere?"

What was this? Justin's parents were in the parking lot? And his father sounded like he'd been crying? Her entire world rocked hard to one side. She looked for a place to sit down, but there was none. The bench. They could meet at the bench, the same one where she and Justin had spent so many late hours talking before he said good-night and headed back to his base. "By the stairs," she managed to say. "Meet me at the bench."

She snapped her phone shut without saying good-bye, without asking any of the questions that shook her mind, her senses. What had happened? What terrible thing would cause Justin's parents to drive an hour north without calling first? She ordered her feet to start moving, and they obeyed. But her head was spinning, even as she walked.

One of the kids in her sociology class had the paper out that morning, but what had it said? Three soldiers dead ... another roadside bomb. At the time, Emily had chided herself. Usually she checked the news—either at night or before heading off for class. But she'd had a game the day before and spent a few hours at the teen center. Between her busy schedule and her homework and daydreaming about Justin, she hadn't had time to think about anything else.

Not even the war.

Justin had been gone nearly two months. Four more and he'd be home. She'd stopped getting sick over every report of a casualty. There were thousands and thousands of soldiers in Iraq; Justin would be fine. He'd promised. Her feet moved faster. She was imagining things. All she needed to do was meet the Bakers at the bench and look in their eyes, and then she'd know that his promise was still good.

He was fine.

So why are they here, sounding so upset?

Okay, maybe he was hurt. Maybe he was coming home early. But so what? She'd be there to meet him, and whatever help he needed getting better, getting back on his feet, she'd be there for him. Whatever he needed.

Once she saw the Bakers, she'd know.

Or maybe something had happened to Buster. He was an old dog, after all. If Buster died while Justin was away fighting, he'd never forgive himself. Yes, that made sense. If something had happened to Buster, the Bakers wouldn't want to tell her over the phone. They'd need to talk about it in person, so that they could come up with the right words, the right way to tell Justin.

She walked faster, and there, up ahead, she could see them. Mr. and Mrs. Baker, standing near the bench, the one that belonged to her and Justin. From far away, it seemed strange seeing Justin's father there. The two looked so alike, and if she didn't know better, she'd think it was Justin himself. The way he might look in a few decades, when they were looking back at the picture they'd taken that day on the pier, knowing that what the old couple had said about the passing of time was all too true.

But it wasn't Justin.

It was his father and his mother, and they were watching for her, staring at her. She took shallow breaths, all that her lungs would allow. Her heart banged against her chest. She wanted to stop, turn around, and run the other direction. But she couldn't. Whatever this was about, she had to know. Now, before another minute passed. She began to jog—and then to run.

She reached them breathless, and that's when she saw the tear stains on their faces. The red in their swollen eyes. "What ..." She leaned over her knees and waited until she could breathe again. Then she straightened. "What's going on?"

Justin's mother held out her arms. "Emily ... I'm so sorry, honey."

Emily shook her head. She didn't want to be hugged. She was a competitor, not a meek person who would fall apart when the game momentum turned on her. She took the woman's hand, but she held her ground. "Tell me."

His father took a step forward. "He's gone, Emily. He was killed in battle yesterday."

The moment his words were out, a wall threw itself up between the person standing in her shoes and the person who so loved Justin Baker. A wall made of thick cement and razor wire. The sort of wall no emotions were ever going to get around.

She shook her head and took a step backward. "No." She held up her hand. "No, it's not true."

"Emily ..." His mother began to cry. "We just found out. We had to tell you in person."

Justin's father crossed his arms, and tears forged two trails down his cheeks. "He was on his way across Baghdad, and his car ... the car hit a roadside bomb."

A roadside bomb? The one mentioned on the front page? Were they trying to tell her that Justin had been one of the three soldiers killed? She began to tremble. Her coat was too thin for winter weather. She pulled it tightly around her waist and shook her hair free from the collar. Why were they standing here like this, crying? Justin wasn't dead.

She needed to tell them. "I heard from him ... just the other day. I probably have an email—" she pointed toward the residence hall and her hand shook hard—"right up there. His letter is right up there waiting f-f-for me."

"Honey." Justin's mother put her hand on Emily's shoulder. "Please ... I know this is hard for you. Our daughter's at a dance camp, but we got her a message to leave early. She'll be home later tonight. We tried to call your father, but he was out." Her voice cracked. "It's hard for all of us."

They tried to call her father? Emily stood a little straighter. Whatever bad information Justin's parents had gotten, they didn't need to all stand outside in the cold. She wasn't being the least bit hospitable. She tried to smile, but her lips wouldn't lift. "Mrs. Baker, Mr. Baker ... you've come a long way." Her voice was calm, because they were wrong. Of course they were wrong. "Why don't you come in and wait in my room. That'll give me time to check my email."

Gary Baker nodded and put his arm around his wife's shoulders. "We'll follow you."

"Good." She led the way up the stairs. "How's Buster?"

Justin's mother exchanged a look with her husband. Then Mr. Baker said, "We can talk about him later. Let's get inside."

She moved through the entryway and down the hall to her room. Pam was gone for the afternoon, so she used her key and opened it. "You can sit there." Emily motioned to a single sofa that sat against the wall between the two beds. Again she'd forgotten her manners. "Can I get you water, anything to eat?" She moved past them and opened a small cupboard. "We have fruit leather."

Justin's parents wore looks of astonishment, and his mother seemed on the verge of a breakdown. They took their places on the sofa and Mr. Baker shook his head. "No. We'll ... we'll wait here, Emily."

Good. She didn't want to hear anything else about Justin, not when they were completely wrong. He was fine. His letters told her that he knew what he was doing, defending the various ethnic groups in Iraq, the ones in favor of freedom and democracy. He'd done this before, that's what he told her. He knew his way out of the battlefield. Just four months. Sixteen weeks and he'd be home again.

She ran up the stairs to the computer station and signed on. *God ... help the Bakers. They're so upset.* She felt arms behind her, arms that were holding her up. But even that was strange, because she wasn't about to fall. She only needed to check her email and find the letter from Justin.

The screen came to life and there it was. A brand-new letter. Hah! Just like she'd known it would be there. The subject said the same thing it always said, "Missing you." She opened it, but she refused to read it. Not here. Not with his parents sitting in her room certain that Justin was dead.

Dead, of all things! The idea was ludicrous! While his letter was printing, she stared at the Internet Explorer button and warned herself not to look. It wasn't possible. The wall was firmly in place. No matter what the Bakers believed, they were wrong. She could run a check on the Internet and then she'd know.

Don't do it! A voice deep in her heart warned her. *Don't look. You're right; his email is enough.*

But she had to look, because if she could find the story, if she could find the names, then she could make a printout of that too and take it to his parents. Then they could hug each other and smile and thank God that they were wrong.

And they could talk about Buster and how sixteen weeks wasn't really all that long, and they could go home where they belonged. Yes, that was a good idea. The letter was still printing, so she'd run the search real quick. The Internet was always helping her find things.

That was how she'd found her parents, how she'd first made contact with them and brought them back together. Yes, the Internet would know, and then she could tell Justin's parents. Everything was fine. Justin was fine. Her heart thudded harder, her breaths quick and raspy.

She called up Explorer, and then opened Google. With her fingers shaking so hard she could barely type, she went to the search box and typed in the words, "roadside bomb, three soldiers." Despite the part of her heart that was desperate for her to stop the search, she hit enter. Then she waited.

The first story was one dated that day. The source was CNN. Fine, CNN would have the facts. Especially if the story was dated that day. She called it up, and as she did, she told herself she wouldn't actually read it. She would print it out, and she and the

Bakers could read it together. She hit print, but as she did, her eyes betrayed her.

They scanned the story, and that's when she saw it.

A blur of names, and there in the middle of them …

"Justin Baker, 22, from Fort Lewis."

"No." She slid back her chair and jerked to her feet, staring at the screen. "You're wrong. You're all wrong!" The wall was crumbling, but Emily wouldn't let it. Not all the way. She was in a match for her life, down 3–0 with the championship on the line. *Be tough, Emily*, she could hear her coach shouting at her. *Be tough!*

And she would be.

She grabbed the pieces of paper from the printer, ran back to her room, and snatched up her purse and car keys.

"Emily …" Mr. Baker was on his feet. "Where are you—?"

She held up her hand, stopping him. "I can't … I'll be back." Then she ran as fast as her feet would take her, out into the hall, down the stairs, and into the parking lot. Her car was parked in the back row, and that was good. The running felt right, something she could do to get her head back in the game.

God … guide my hands. I can't think, can't breathe, so guide my hands. She climbed into her car and took off, out of the parking lot and onto the freeway. Not until she took the exit did she really understand where she was going, where her car was taking her.

The Sound, of course. Puget Sound, the place where she'd come so many times with Justin. She folded the printouts. Then she stuffed them into her jacket pocket and put her keys in the other. Overhead, the clouds were gathering again, threatening to break open just like her heart. But not yet, not until she reached the water's edge.

She kept running, ignoring the way her ribs ached, the way her lungs burned from the effort. And finally, finally she reached the metal railing. She tilted her head back, gasping for her next breath. The boardwalk was empty, deserted on this cloudy mid-November afternoon. Her sides heaved, and she leaned on the railing, leaned on it the same way she and Justin always did whenever they came here.

But this time she didn't look out at the water; she bent almost all the way over. *Fill up, lungs, come on.* And after a minute, they did what she asked of them. She straightened and tried to remember what she was doing. The Bakers had come up from Kelso and they'd been crying.

Be tough, Emily ... be tough.

She needed to read the papers in her pocket, but which one first? She knew before she took another breath. The letter of course. The letter that would fill her heart and mind and soul with Justin's voice, his laughter and wisdom, his compassion and love. She was still shaking, even harder than before. She took the papers from her jacket and figured out which was which.

In a rush, she thrust the CNN article back in her pocket. Then she opened the other page, slowly, reverently. And suddenly her hands weren't shaking anymore, and the breeze felt like his breath, his touch. *Talk to me, Justin ... talk to me ...*

She scanned the top of the email. It was dated three days ago. She swallowed hard and tried to ignore that single detail. The date didn't matter; this was Justin, alive and talking to her. Her eyes found the place where the letter began.

Dear Emily,

I can't believe it! I read the article finally, and, well ... I mean, I believed you, of course. But wow! Your mom! Are you sure she wrote that story? Just kidding, but still ... you and your dad are right. Something's happening in her heart, no doubt.

Emily closed her eyes. She clutched the letter with both hands, picturing him. This was something new—he'd read the article. She opened her eyes and kept reading.

> *I'll never forget that day. Talk lately is that the Iraqi people are afraid to come out of their houses. I don't know. I guess that might be true in some regions, but around here they come out. Even the kids. Obviously. And you know why?*
>
> *Because we're here. Maybe your mom is seeing that too.*

Emily smiled. *Yes, Justin, you're right.*

She was halfway through the letter, so she slowed down. As long as the letter was in her hands, as long as Justin's words were echoing through her mind and her heart, then he wasn't gone. No matter what the next piece of paper told her. She found her place.

> *Anyway, enough about that.*
>
> *Did I tell you I carry your picture with me? Because I do. I know, it's a little sappy, but how else can I survive another four months without you? Joe thinks I'm going soft, but I told him the same thing I told him before. He's just jealous.*
>
> *So yeah, I took one of the pictures from the cruise and I laminated it. I keep it in my boot so that if there's ever enough time, I can take it out and look at it. I figure there you are back in Tacoma drinking lattes out of my mug and looking at our pictures. I need something to look at too. Even if I'm thousands of miles away from my next cup of Starbucks.*
>
> *Something else has been helping me lately.*

Emily closed her eyes. *Slow down … you have to slow down.* What would she do if by some crazy chance the Bakers were right, or if her eyes really had seen Justin's name in the CNN article?

Then this would be her last time to hear him, the last time she would feel his arm next to hers leaning against the railing overlooking Puget Sound. *Okay*. She drew a steady breath. *Slower.*

Something else has been helping me lately. Whenever I get tired of all the dust and grime and desert, when the violence seems like it's never going to end, I let myself do a little dreaming. Even in the middle of the day. I can picture myself coming home and finding you that ring. The simple one.

You're smiling, I know it.

Okay, so then I take it a step further, and I can see the wedding, Emily. The tux and the dress and the people filling the pews, and I can hear the doors of the church open, and there you are. Stunning. My precious bride. I can feel you in my arms, dancing that first dance and knowing that if I have my way, I'll never leave you again. Not ever. And there it is. One more way I can stay sane until I see you again.

You know how I thought last summer was amazing? Well … it'll be nothing compared to this one. I can't wait, Emily. To see you, to touch you, to hold you. You're with me always. You have my heart. I love you, Justin.

Emily refused to take her eyes from the page. She could read that last part a thousand times and it would never be enough. *You're with me always … you have my heart … I love you.*

And then, somewhere deep inside her heart, the wall began to fall. It didn't happen slowly, but all at once. Like the Twin Towers.

She lifted her head and looked out at the Sound, as far out as she could see. And suddenly, as surely as she knew her name, she knew it was true. She didn't need to read the CNN article. It was there all along.

Justin was gone.

Rain started to fall, and it mixed with her tears, as if God Himself were there beside her, weeping over Justin the way He'd wept over Lazarus. She didn't want Justin's letter getting wet, so she slid it back into her pocket.

Sobs didn't come, not right away, and she wasn't surprised. They would come later, but for now she couldn't picture him lying on a street in Baghdad, couldn't picture him torn apart. Because that wasn't the Justin she knew, the one she would keep forever alive in her heart.

The ocean breeze sent the rain sideways and it washed against her face, against her silent stream of tears. What was it? Had he been too good to be true, was that it? She wasn't sure, but she couldn't consider the depth and breadth of his loss. Not fully. He was gone, and that was enough for now. As if she was only being given a small peek into the pain and sorrow that lay ahead.

If only she hadn't finished reading the letter. She would've pulled it out and read it again, but she didn't want it to get wet. Instead she had everything else about him alive and within her. His voice and his smile, the smell of his cologne. It hit her then, why she wasn't falling apart. Because in every possible way, Justin was still alive, real and good and whole and strong.

There was too much good about Justin Baker to feel only sadness, even with the knowledge that he was gone. Before she could mourn his loss, or even imagine it, she had to celebrate him. Her eyes lifted, beyond the water to the sky. The rain was still falling, but there in the distance, was a break in the clouds and a section of the purest blue.

He was there. Somewhere beyond the clouds.

God … You're so lucky. She smiled and the slightest laugh sounded on her lips. She could imagine a heavenly version of Vonda, introducing Justin to the rest of the gang and shaking her head. *You know Justin. Wants to run the whole place someday.*

Her smile faded. *God ... You must have big plans for him. Because if he can do more up there for You than he could down here, well ... that would be something. And I know he will. Because ...* Her eyes filled with another layer of tears. *Because You wouldn't have taken him otherwise.*

Countless questions lined up around the perimeter of her heart, peering in at her, making themselves known. What would happen to Buster, and who would talk to the Veterans, and how would a generation of schoolkids learn about the good things soldiers were doing in Iraq?

And what about the teens?

But she couldn't face any of the questions. Not yet.

She could see her coach's face again. *Be tough, Emily. Be tough.* But this wasn't the time to be tough. By loving a soldier, this was the risk she'd taken. That one day, this moment might come and his name would join the thousands of others on a military tombstone. No matter what she told herself, she'd always known this could happen.

She wiped her nose, wiped the rain from her cheeks and her chin. Never mind the end, she would've fallen for him all over again if she had the chance, spent the summer dreaming with him and playing with him and figuring out for herself everything her mother had ever said about love.

But still ...

She hugged herself and watched the patch of blue, watched it until the clouds swallowed it up and the sky became all cloudy gray once more. She needed to go, needed to get back to her room and fall into Justin's mother's arms. But she couldn't pull herself away. As long as she was here, as long as she had his last letter in her pocket, then she didn't have to think about the questions storming the edges of her heart. Here she could look at Pier 55 and at the cruise ship. The very same cruise ship where he'd promised her his heart. And she could feel the rain on her skin the way she'd felt his touch that day.

She looked out at the water again. *Talk to me, Justin ... talk to me.*

And his words were there, as close as her next heartbeat. *I can't wait, Emily. To see you, to touch you, to hold you. You're with me always. You have my heart. I love you.*

There was much she had to do, and she would do it proudly, with strength. The way Justin would've wanted her to do it. She'd take care of everything he would've taken care of, and when the tears became sobs and she couldn't breathe for the pain, she would know it was okay to fall apart.

Because God would do what Justin had done for her that summer.

He would walk beside her, and when she fell, He would be there to catch her.

With that knowledge, she pulled away from the metal railing and walked back to her car, her feet moving slowly along the cobblestone roads, remembering every time she'd walked them with Justin. Somehow she made it to her car and shut the door. She held the steering wheel with both hands, but it was an effort even to start the engine. As she pulled away, she could barely see the road for her tears, but it wasn't until she walked into her room, until her eyes met Mrs. Baker's, and then Mr. Baker's, that she felt the full force of Justin's loss.

"Justin ..." That was all she could say. She stumbled across the room and collapsed into his father's arms.

"It's okay, honey." The man stroked her back, rocked her as if she were his daughter. "We're going to get through this."

"I can't ..." she sobbed against his chest, her body reeling from the loss. Justin was dead? How could it be? His email was still in her pocket. "I don't ... I don't think I can ..."

She felt his mother come up alongside her, and the three of them stayed that way for a long time, hugging, holding onto each other, and doing what they could to convince each other that Justin's dad was right.

Somehow they were going to survive without him.

And deep inside, Emily knew they would. They would survive, but without Justin, how were they ever going to *live*? And that was the question that shouted at her the loudest, more than any of the others.

The question only God could answer.

TWENTY-ONE

Lauren hadn't left her cramped quarters at the journalists' compound for two days. Fighting had picked up, and her editors had asked her and Scanlon to stay put. Better to do the wrap-up story, the what-happened story, than to wind up in the middle of the action.

That sort of coverage was for dailies and television news, not *Time* magazine. And so she'd used her time to work on an opinion piece and catch up on her email. That, and sit by her window looking out at the desert and wondering about the stories she'd seen play out since she'd come to Iraq.

Apparently Scanlon could sense the change in her. He was in her room now, sitting in the chair across from her bed. There was no escaping the suspicion in his eyes. He drummed his fingers on his knees. "Okay, look." His hands went still. "I know what you're thinking."

"What?" She had her laptop open, but she set it down beside her. "I'm not turning soft, if that's what this is about."

"No, not soft. Just ..." Scanlon took hold of the arms of the chair and surveyed her. "Different."

"Okay, so sue me. I'm different." Lauren hated her tone. Clear proof she hadn't taken the time she needed to actually process the things she'd seen. Sure, she'd had fleeting thoughts of regret or remorse. Doubts about her opinions of the past, whether she'd led Americans to the wrong conclusion about the war. But she and Scanlon had been too busy to really think things through.

Scanlon looked hurt by her response. He leaned over his knees. "I'm your friend, remember? I'm out there with you. I see the same things you see, hear the same stories. I have my doubts too, okay?" He sighed. "I just wanted to hear it from you, what you're thinking. What you're feeling."

What was she feeling? Antsy. Ready to get on the next flight home, that's how she felt. Crazy for how badly she missed Shane. That everything she'd thought was written on her heart in ink was now only sketched in fading pencil. But how could she say that? "I don't know, Scanlon." She reached into her dresser drawer. "Emily sent me this." She held out a folded piece of paper.

Scanlon stood, crossed the room, and took it. "What's it say?"

"Read it." Lauren swung her feet over the edge of the bed and walked to the window. She could hear Scanlon opening the paper. She remembered the way she felt when she first read the email a few weeks ago. Emily had copied a section of Lauren's long-ago journal right into her letter.

Here, Mom, the email said, *read it and see if you remember loving Dad like this.* And then it began. A whole section Lauren wrote on love, back when Shane was everything to her. Some of the lines were profound, much deeper than she remembered feeling. But since reading those long-ago words, she couldn't shake them. Couldn't get them out of her head, even if she wanted to.

The letter was all she needed for a whole parade of memories to return. Even the memory of making chocolate chip cookies. Shane was her best friend back then, and she lost him. The loss had changed her, darkened her entire existence. She vowed to find him, to love him, no matter how long she had to search.

Behind her, she heard Scanlon lower the paper. "Profound."

"Yes." She turned around and folded her arms. "I miss him."

"You knew you would. That was never the question." Scanlon lowered himself to the chair again. "The question was whether you could *agree* with him."

Scanlon was right. Missing him was never the question. And yes, they'd been busy, but she knew the answer, didn't she? It wasn't an easy one, wasn't one she even knew how to live with yet, but slowly, assuredly, she nodded. "Yes." Her voice held a fear she hadn't known before. The fear that possibly she'd been wrong. "Yes, Scanlon. I think I can agree with him now. About some very big things."

Frustration flashed in Scanlon's face, but only for an instant. He stood and brought the letter back to her. "I wish you would've said so."

Now it was her turn to feel frustrated. She tossed the letter on her bed. "I wasn't sure. I'm *still* not sure." She looked out the window again. "I watch people falling in the streets and write about soldiers being ripped apart by roadside bombs, and I hate this war more than anyone ever could hate it."

Scanlon was quiet for a moment. "You hate it ... but you understand it." His voice dropped a notch. "Is that it?"

"I think so." She faced him again and leaned on the windowsill. "What if we'd never declared war on Afghanistan or Iraq?" She made a sound that was part laugh, part dawning realization. "Can you imagine? I mean, I never thought about it that way. War is wrong. Period. That was my mantra."

A mantra Shane had responded to that first night when they were together at her parents' house in Wheaton. She remembered his words and repeated them now. Not because Shane had said them, but because she was starting to understand them. And believe them. "What happened on September 11, Scanlon, that was only the beginning. Everyone knows that now. The terrorists' plans were beyond anything we can begin to fathom, even now."

Scanlon exhaled hard.

"Don't dismiss me." She stood, angry. "You said you're my friend. Then listen to me. I'm not talking rhetoric here, I'm talking firsthand observation."

He frowned. "Meaning what?"

"How can we think anything but the obvious? It's been five years, and the terrorists haven't harmed a single American on U.S. soil. So the war must be working, right? Is there any other conclusion?"

"Maybe it worked at first, when we made the air attacks, but what about now?" He waved his hand toward the window. "All that violence out there can't be doing any good."

"So what's the answer?" The debate had raged inside her ever since she spotted Justin Baker playing with the Iraqi children. It felt wonderful to finally put words to her feelings. She waved her hands in the air. "Just walk away and hope things work out for the people here? 'Cause you and I both know what would happen if we did that. The terrorists would recruit another generation of kids, and new cells would start up, and a dictator would rise to power. And before you know, we'd be staring into the rubble of another catastrophe, wondering what went wrong."

He stuck his hands in his pockets and his shoulders fell an inch or so. "I don't want to fight with you, Lauren." His eyes told her he was astonished, amazed at the things she was saying. "Is this really how you feel?"

His question hit straight at her soul. "I'm not sure. But it's starting to make sense, starting to make me wonder if maybe Shane and Justin Baker are right."

Scanlon looked skeptical. "About what?"

"That what this war needs is more support, more financing. So we can finish the job right and *then* get home."

He was about to respond when the phone on her desk rang. Lauren looked at it, startled. The line was for incoming and local calls only, something her editors at *Time* had established for her. Cell phone reception was spotty, so the landline was the best way to keep open communication. She hesitated. Maybe it was

Bob Maine giving them the all clear to hit the streets and find the stories in the recent wave of violence.

She crossed the room and lifted the receiver. "Hello?" Her eyes were on Scanlon. She didn't want to offend him or scare him off, but what was she supposed to do with her feelings?

"Lauren ... it's Bob."

"Hey, let me guess. It's okay to step outdoors again."

"No." He was a serious man, but his tone was heavier than usual, sad almost. "That's not why I'm calling."

She dropped to the edge of the bed. "Talk to me, Bob. What's going on?" Had something big happened in the U.S., some event she'd missed by being there in Iraq?

"I'm calling with a special request from Shane Galanter."

Shane ...? Her heart skipped a beat and slammed into double time. "What ... what request?" Scanlon was still watching her, but now she looked away, found a spot on the floor so she could concentrate.

"Lauren, the three soldiers who were killed?"

"Yes." Her mind raced. How did the violence in the streets of Baghdad affect Shane? Was he that worried about her, that he'd called her editor? "I'm aware of that."

Bob sighed, and the sound rattled over the phone lines. "One of the soldiers was Justin Baker." He paused. "I'm sorry."

The news hit her like a physical blow. She closed her eyes and turned her head from the receiver. *No, not Justin. No, God ...*

"Lauren ... are you there?" Gruff old Bob sounded worried about her, brokenhearted for her.

She gripped the phone and forced herself to speak. "Yes." She looked up and motioned for Scanlon to leave. Her eyes begged him to understand that she needed to be alone. Needed to process whether the conversation with Bob was even taking place.

Scanlon mouthed the words, "Everything okay?"

She shook her head and closed her eyes again. She waited until she heard him leave, heard the door close behind him. Then she found her voice once more. "Are you sure, Bob? Justin Baker?"

"Yes." Her editor hesitated. "Officer Galanter would like you to contact the army headquarters there and accompany the soldier's body back to the United States." He exhaled hard. "Oh, man ... I hate this, Lauren. I really hate this." He sounded like he was fighting tears. "Shane and your daughter will be waiting for you."

Lauren felt a flood of tears gathering in her heart. She was a reporter, a veteran of war correspondence. Tears didn't come often or easily. But all she could picture were those Iraqi kids, grinning and laughing and playing catch with a soldier who would lay down his life for them. *No, God ... not Justin.*

"Lauren, what should I tell Officer Galanter?"

She steeled herself. This was part of her job, wasn't it? Reporting the casualties, surrounding herself with the reality of war? She would get through this, and she would do it for Emily and Shane, for the Bakers. She would fly home with their son's body, and she wouldn't leave his side for a moment. "Yes. Tell Shane yes. I'll contact headquarters as soon as I get off the phone."

"Okay." Bob's tone was quieter, defeated. "I'm sorry, Lauren."

"Me too." She thanked him for calling and then, before her emotions overtook her, she made the next call. For the purpose of her stories, she was often in touch with officials at the army headquarters. She had the number written on a card beside her phone.

In a matter of minutes the plans came together. They'd be shipping Justin's body stateside in the morning. By special request, they'd agreed to allow her to accompany the body home. Justin's friend, a soldier named Joe Greenwald, who was injured by the same bomb, would make the trip with her.

Blindly, like a person in a trance, she hung up the phone and walked down the hall to tell Scanlon. He listened, then came to hug her. "I'm sorry."

As she stepped back, she knew what he was thinking. She gritted her teeth, anger rising within her, taking place of the shock. "Everything I said a minute ago?" She searched his eyes. "I was wrong." Justin's face came into view again, and she shook her head. "There can never, *ever* be a reason for losing a kid like Justin Baker. Not ever."

The tears didn't come until she was back in her room.

How in the world was Emily taking the news? The guy had been everything to her, her first taste of real love—the way Shane had been Lauren's first taste. Lauren had watched them together and known as Shane had known. What Emily and Justin shared was strong and real. Neither Lauren nor Shane had any doubts that one day, when Justin returned from Iraq, he would pledge his life to their daughter.

Emily had already started talking about the wedding.

Lauren put her head in her hands. Her mind was racing. What about what she'd just told Scanlon? Was that really how she felt? Now that one of the victims was someone she knew, she couldn't possibly find it in herself to support the war effort? Was that right?

She curled up on her bed, closed her eyes, and buried her face in her pillow. She had come here asking God for wisdom, that she might see things the way He saw them, think about them the way He thought about them. So what was she supposed to make of *this*? That there were no easy answers, no right sides and wrong sides, was that it?

She didn't know, and her heart hurt too badly to try to figure it out. *God ... Lord ... if there's wisdom to be gained in the next week, let me find it. Because I don't understand. It's my job to have educated opinions, to know the facts. But I don't understand this.*

The prayer swirled in her head over and over as she laid there. She wept for the family whose son was gone forever, and for the Iraqi children who looked up to him, and for her precious daughter who would never again kiss him or hold him. Never marry him.

No, she didn't understand any of it.

And the most terrifying thought was the one she fell asleep with.

Maybe she never would.

Twenty-Two

As it turned out, Justin's parents didn't know even half of what he was involved in. Emily traveled back to Kelso with them that night, the night she learned of his death, and when his sister Jill came home, Emily sat in the other room so her parents could break the news to her in private.

Later, when the wailing had died down, they all sat in the living room, and Emily told them she would take care of letting everyone know, all the groups he was involved with.

"Groups?" His mother's cheeks had been wet all evening. She clung to her husband's arm, barely strong enough to be curious.

"Yes." She looked at Justin's father and then at Jill. Their faces were blank also. "He volunteers a lot of his time." She realized she was still using present tense, but that was okay. It was too soon to talk about Justin in anything but present tense.

His mother raised her chin and sniffed. "He ... he used to do volunteer work here. When he was in high school. But I didn't know ..."

"He didn't like talking about the things he did for other people." Justin's dad sat up a little straighter. "What all did he do?"

That was one of the few highlights of the day. When Emily had the chance to tell them about Justin's work. She told them about the Veterans, and how Justin believed it was no big deal. "He used to tell me someone needs to hear their stories, to keep their legacy alive." She held a damp tissue in her hand and caught her tears as they fell. But her voice remained clear as she continued. She told them how he visited local classrooms, telling school children about the good the U.S. soldiers were doing over in Iraq.

And she told them about the teen center.

"My goodness ..." His mother looked at her husband and then back at Emily. There was a catch in her voice. "Someone has to tell those boys."

Emily nodded. "I will. Justin would've wanted me to do it."

She stayed at the Bakers' house that night, and she heard from her dad. Her mom was going to fly home with Justin's body. And after the connecting flight through the air base in Germany, they were scheduled to arrive in two days. Plans for Justin's memorial service came together sometime around midnight, and by one in the morning they were all drained. Sleep was restless that night, and several times she woke up, sobbing, her pillow soaked. But as morning dawned—as she gradually faced the day, and as the reality of Justin's death hit her again—Emily knew it was time. She would drive back to Tacoma and break the news to the teens and the Veterans. Everyone he spent time with.

When she reached her residence hall again, when she was controlled enough to speak, she sat at a table and picked up the phone. The person at the school district would be the easiest of all. She took a deep breath, begged God for strength, and dialed the number. When she was connected to the right person, she explained she was a friend of Lieutenant Justin Baker.

"Yes, we know Justin." The woman sounded all sunshine and smiles. "Several of our classes are writing cards and letters for him. They've taken up a collection of Jelly Bellies." She laughed. "Every time Justin ever came to talk to a class, he brought Jelly Bellies."

Emily exhaled. *God ... what am I supposed to say?* She pinched the bridge of her nose and searched for the words. "Yes, well, I'm afraid I don't have good news, ma'am."

"No?" Gradual alarm filled the woman's tone. "Did something ... is he okay?"

"No ... he isn't. He was killed this week in Iraq."

The woman on the other end gasped. It was a long time before she said anything. "I'm so sorry."

"We all are." She had promised herself, promised God, that she wouldn't break down today. The people who knew Justin needed her to be strong. But there was no getting around the sorrow. It seeped from every pore, grew with every breath.

"When ... when is the service?"

Emily gave her the details and asked her to pass on the news to the teachers and kids who knew him. She hung up the phone, then hesitated.

Her next task wouldn't be as easy.

The rain hadn't let up since the day before, so she wore her jacket. The one Justin liked best because it made her blue eyes stand out.

The Veterans met every day after lunch at the American Legion hall. They played bingo and poker or just sat around the table telling stories of the old days. War stories, mostly. Emily had only been with Justin once when he visited them. She thought it would be good for her writing someday to watch Justin interact with the old guys.

But their time that day had given her an even greater appreciation of the man she loved. He sat there in their midst, every bit a part of the group, and there was no getting around the pride that filled the room.

Justin wasn't like other kids his age. He was a throwback. Hope existed for the entire generation if there could be one young soldier like Justin Baker, that's what the Veterans thought of him. And they loved him for taking the time to remember them.

When Emily and Justin left that day, one of the men, an old guy in a baseball cap covered with military patches and hunched over in a wheelchair, his jacket not quite straight on his shoulders, pointed a finger in Justin's direction. "I know you're shipping out, but you be careful now, young man." He patted the place on the table beside him. "We'll keep your spot open."

Emily tried not to think about the image as she drove to the hall that day. The old guy couldn't have been serious about saving Justin a spot. Not with all the Veterans looking to get in on a conversation or a game of cards. Table space seemed to be at a premium. She drove without ever really seeing the roads or the stoplights, her body moving in a sort of automatic motion so that her heart and mind were free to think about Justin.

She pulled into the parking lot, walked up the flower-lined sidewalk, and peered into the window. The place was packed, but there at the table …

The old guy with the jacket was there, and beside him was an empty space. The place set aside for the young soldier, the one who had brought them hours of joy. *Okay, God … hold me up.*

When the lump in her throat subsided, she pushed her way to the door and went inside. The action around the table and in chairs and sofas along the walls all stopped.

"Hey!" A big jovial guy waved at her, beckoning her to come closer. "You're Justin Baker's girl!"

What was she supposed to do? How could she say it, when every time … every time she heard the words cross her lips, they felt more shocking than the last? Justin Baker … dead? Even now she had his email in her pocket.

The men were smiling at her, waiting for her to join them. The guy in the jacket patted the empty spot beside him. "I'm Vern. You tell that young soldier of yours we're keeping his spot open. Just like we said we would."

"I'm …" Her tears cut her off midsentence. She hung her head for a moment, willing herself to find even a sliver of control. When she looked up, the expressions on all their faces had changed.

The jovial guy stood and came to her. He put his hand on her shoulder. "What is it, darling? Tell us."

She dabbed at her tears and looked at him. Maybe if she said the words in a hurry, all at once ... She took a breath. "Justin was killed in Iraq this week. A ... a roadside bomb."

The reaction hit them in slow motion. Beside her, the old guy took his hand from her shoulder—then removed his hat and held it over his heart. Around the room, the others did the same thing, taking off embroidered military baseball caps and holding them over their chests.

One of the men asked about the service, and Emily pulled out a few cards with the information. A muffled round of condolences came from the group, and she realized that their reaction was different than most. They'd been there, witnessed the destruction of war firsthand.

For the most part, the men's eyes were dry. But before she left, Vern straightened his jacket and looked at her. His eyes brimmed with tears. "As long as I'm here, I'll save him a spot. Just so you know."

Emily nodded. She looked around the room, hoping they could see that she couldn't speak or she'd break down, collapse right there on the floor. She left, and for a long time she sat in her car, her head on her steering wheel. *Why, God ... why?* She'd asked the question over and over, but she never sensed an answer. She didn't need one. It was enough to know that God held the number of their days, and that if He'd taken Justin, then it was Justin's time.

But still she asked.

And she tried to convince herself that it was really true, that when he came home in the morning it wouldn't be with a running embrace and whispers of love. It would be in a pine box, with an American flag draped across the top.

Now she had one more stop. The hardest of all.

The teen center wasn't far from Puget Sound, located in the tougher part of downtown Tacoma. This was their afternoon, the one day a week when she showed up and mixed with Bo and Dexter and the guys, playing ping-pong and telling them the latest news from Justin.

They'd be expecting her.

As she made her way there, her eyes grew dry. Fear masked the sorrow, because how in the world was she going to walk into that teen center and tell them Justin was gone? And how would they react once she told them? What was she supposed to do with eight teenage boys being dealt one more blow, one more harsh bit of reality?

When she found a parking spot, she pursed her lips and forced the air from her lungs. Justin had been reading Philippians, chapter four. That's what he told her. That meant he'd been focusing on the very thing she desperately needed if she was going to have the strength to leave her car, the strength to walk through the doors of the center.

Peace.

Please, God … breathe Your peace into me now. I can't do this otherwise …

With her very next heartbeat, she felt God's presence surround her. She could almost hear Him saying, *My daughter, ask and you shall receive.* His peace permeated her fear and sorrow, filling her with the promise of new life. One day the dark clouds of this time would lift, because morning always came. No matter how long and dark the night.

That was God's promise.

She braced herself and forced her feet from the car and on in through the front doors. Bo and Dexter were playing a hot game of ping-pong when she walked in. They must've sensed something different about her, something in her eyes or on her face, because the smile that flashed on Bo's face faded almost as soon as she took a step forward. He caught the little white ball in his hand and leaned his fists on the table. "Why you looking like that, pretty mama?"

Fear rang through every word, undermining the machismo he tried to put off. The others picked up on it, because they stepped away from the foosball table and the pop machine in the corner and drew close. Slowly, they gathered around Bo, their eyes on her.

She could feel God moving her forward, taking her closer to them. But all she could see was Bo taking his sweaty T-shirt off, wadding it up and throwing it on the ground that far-off summer day when Justin told them he was leaving. That, and the tears in the boy's eyes when he looked at Justin's picture in *Time* magazine. *Tell him we need him more ... tell him we need him more.*

Bo tucked the ball in his pocket and took quick steps around the table, his eyes never leaving hers. "Emily ..."

Her name sounded strange on his lips. He'd never called her that. Justin's girl, pretty girl, hot mama, yes. But not Emily. He came to her and put his hands on her shoulders. He searched her eyes, his lips slightly open. "Talk to me ... why you lookin' like that?"

Dexter came up, and then the guys who were planning to enlist, followed by the others. She covered Bo's hand with her own and shook her head. "He's dead, Bo. He's dead."

"*What?*" Bo swore under his breath and jerked away from her. "Don't *say* that stuff, girl. Don't say that about my homeboy."

This was what she was afraid of. That the emotions these kids had bottled up would explode in a burst of anger once they knew about Justin's death. She needed to be strong for them, but now—from nowhere—a wave of sorrow knocked her to her knees. She covered her face with her hands and began to weep.

Because Bo was right.

These guys needed Justin more than anyone in Iraq needed him. And now he was never coming back, never going to play another game of hoops with them again, never sit on the steps of the center and shoot the breeze about girls and school and the reason he believed in God.

She didn't dare look. Didn't open her eyes to see how the guys were reacting. She heard someone slam their fist on the table, and another boy kick a trash can. At least that's what it sounded like. And that's when she knew she had to look, because she was doing this for Justin. He wouldn't have run from the raw pain that filled the room.

He would've embraced it.

She opened her eyes and looked around. They'd all scattered. Bo stood, face to the wall, his hands behind his head. Softly, he hit his forehead against the brick again and again and again. She could hear him saying, "No way ... not my homeboy."

In the other corner, two guys had dropped to a pair of chairs, their heads all the way back, eyes focused on the ceiling. No tears, no anger, no emotion. Nothing. She shifted her attention. Dexter was gripping the trash can. He picked it up with both hands and slammed it against the cement floor. Other guys were responding like Bo, their faces to the brick wall, shutting out the world.

She knew where to start. She went to Bo, and when she was close enough, she put her hand on his shoulder. She had no idea how he would respond, whether he would spin around and shout at her or knock her hand off him and run from the building. *God ... the peace You've given me, give it to Bo. Let me show it to him. Please, God ...*

She dropped her voice so only he could hear her. "Bo?"

Slowly, she felt the tension leave his shoulder, and then the rest of his body. He turned around, and she saw that he'd skinned his forehead on the bricks. But that wasn't all. He was crying, weeping like a little boy who'd lost his best friend. Or the only dad figure he'd ever known. Anger twisted his features again, and he thumped his chest, ignoring the tears streaming down his face. "I *told* him not to go."

"I'm so sorry." She didn't give him a chance to push her away. He was a tall kid, almost a foot taller than her, but she didn't hesitate. She put her arms around his waist and embraced him.

At first she thought he might pull back, but then what was left of his hard exterior fell away. He hung his head on her shoulder and wept. "Why? Why him?"

Emily couldn't turn around and see how the others were handling this, the sight of their leader breaking down. But she didn't have to. She heard footsteps behind her, and first Dexter, then the two future enlistees, came up and put their arms around her and Bo. A minute passed and the others joined them, so that she was surrounded by a group of crying tough guys whose whole world had come undone in as much time as it took her to tell them Justin was dead.

When the crying subsided, when she was sure they were at least stable, she took a step back and pulled a handful of cards from her coat pocket. "The service is Saturday."

Bo took a card and fresh tears spilled from his eyes, angry tears. He shoved the piece of paper back at her, his words so many rocks. "I ain't got no car, pretty girl."

"Yeah. How we supposed to get there?" Dexter let his card hang limp in his hand.

Emily hadn't thought about that. She looked over her shoulder at the office. Through a window, she could see a man working there, but apparently he was only filling in — someone displaced from a desk job at the city. Not someone passionate about the kids. Never had she heard about him interacting with the teens. Justin had told her the guy was there more for security than anything else, at least until they could find a full-time counselor. Still, he was in charge. Maybe he would have an answer.

"Can you all be here that day, meet here three hours before the service? Say at about ten o'clock?" She hoped so. The idea that they wanted to come meant more than they could know. Further proof of Justin's impact on their lives.

The guys looked at each other and a few of them shrugged. "Yeah ... of course."

"Okay, just a minute." She hurried to the office door, knocked, and then entered before being asked. She explained the situation and asked if the man could provide a city van or a bus, some way for the kids to get to Justin's service.

The man behind the desk looked at her, his face blank. "For a funeral?" He set his pencil down and gave a sad laugh. He pointed out his office window at the kids huddled together near the ping-pong table. "Those kids see more death than you want to know about. Drug wars and gang fights. One more day, one more funeral." He shook his head. "I wish I could help, but my hands are tied. They cut the budget again this year. Cut the pay for counselors—-which is why we can't get someone in here to work with the kids." He frowned. "No way I can get a van or a bus." He looked back at whatever he'd been working on. "Sorry 'bout that."

She ground her teeth together and stared at the man. That was it? No offer to make a phone call or see if there was money somewhere to help the guys? How did people get so calloused? And no wonder the teens looked forward to Justin's visits. At first she'd figured he was probably one of lots of volunteers, another great role model for the teens. But she was beginning to understand. He was probably the only role model they had. And now he was dead.

Without saying another word, she whipped around and shut the door behind her. The guys were watching, waiting for an answer. The sketchy hope in their eyes broke her heart. She locked eyes with Bo. "A van will be here at ten o'clock." She looked at each tear-stained face, one at a time. "For sure."

Before she left, she took one more risk. "Justin's death has left a lot of hurt behind. I wonder—" she held her hands out to either side—"I wonder if all of us could just take a minute and pray."

Dexter smiled, even though his eyes were swimming in tears. "Justin was always trying to get us to pray, man."

"Yeah." Another stepped forward and took Emily's hand. "Too bad it took this to make it happen."

With only the hint of reluctance, the others stepped forward. Bo took one hand, and the rest fell in and formed a circle. He squeezed her fingers. "Can I say it … can I try, I mean?"

Emily could almost picture Justin, somewhere in heaven, getting a front-row seat for this. She couldn't talk, so she did what she could. She squeezed Bo's fingers and nodded.

He closed his eyes and hung his head, and around the circle the others did the same thing. Emily kept her eyes open. She wanted to savor this, the way Justin would've done if he were here.

Bo cleared his throat. "Okay, God, so like … we're all here and we're really ticked off. Ticked don't even cut it." He sounded like he was talking through a clenched jaw. "I just have to ask if You'd please let people know what a good guy Justin was. He was our homeboy, and, I don't know." He sniffed. "Like a brother, I guess. I know he never shoulda gone, but he did. And now he's with You." His voice broke, and for a moment there was only the sound of his muffled sobs. "Take good care of him. Give him a hoops game like we used to play. With some good comp. And be with his girl. Because she's being strong for us guys, but inside I know her heart's breaking in half." Another sob stopped him, and he struggled to find control. "Heck, all our hearts is breaking in half."

He released Emily's hand and wiped his cheeks. Then he took hold of her fingers once more. "Thanks for helping him find his way here in the first place. None of us'll ever be the same. You know, gangstas and stuff. Justin wanted better for us than that." He paused, as if he wasn't sure how to end the prayer. "That's all. Amen."

Emily had attended church all her life. She'd grown up active in Sunday services and Sunday school and midweek Bible studies. In her twenty years she'd heard hundreds of beautiful, eloquent prayers.

But none had ever made her feel as close to God as this one.

The prayer of a grieving teenager whose first words to God came from a heart that was broken in half.

TWENTY-THREE

Lauren had never covered the sending-off of a dead soldier back to the States before. She'd seen the pictures, of course. Her magazine once ran a special about how bodies were lined up unceremoniously in the bellies of planes and brought back to the States in what amounted to covert operations. As if the commanding officers were trying to keep the picture of human loss from the public eye.

As she stood on the tarmac, with Justin's company lined up on either side of the walkway, she had no choice but to admit the obvious. If this was a typical send-off, they'd gotten that story wrong. The reason the military hadn't paraded reporters in for a closer look at flag-covered coffins wasn't because there was something to hide.

It was out of respect.

Every fallen soldier, every body that left the Middle East in the cargo compartment of a plane, in a box with a flag over the top, mattered deeply to the military. She could see that much simply by watching the proceedings taking place.

A color guard made the presentation of the flag, and every eye in the company was on the red, white, and blue. Then, when the flag had been properly presented, a group of Justin's closest friends carried the coffin to the far end of the aisle. On either side, soldiers moved in unison, their fingers lifting to their brows and staying that way. In a frozen salute.

Lauren studied them, the look in their eyes as they bid their comrade farewell. How could the United States be anything but supportive of these young men? If they needed more supplies or more manpower, then someone better get on the ball and get it to them. She caught herself. If she meant that, then what about the comment she'd made to Scanlon?

An ache spread through her chest.

Why did everything about the war have to be so complicated? All along she'd thought it was either her way or Shane's. A person could either be for the war or against it. But now neither answer seemed right. The only thing she'd really decided was that every U.S. citizen should support the young men fighting for freedom in the Middle East.

Every single citizen.

And if even a single American felt disdain for soldiers because of a story she'd written, then shame on her.

The procession started to move, and Lauren could barely watch.

Joe Greenwald, Justin's bunk mate, held the front end of the coffin. Lauren had met him earlier, when she first arrived. Joe was a big teddy bear of a guy, but there was no denying the wetness on his cheeks. When the coffin had passed by, when the men had carried it up the stairs and into the plane, they went for the next one, and finally the third. Each body was going back to a different base, but the first leg of the journey started here.

Finally, Joe was given his release orders, papers stating that because of his injury, a gash in his head that had taken nearly thirty stitches, he wasn't required to return to Iraq. Lauren found out that this was Joe's second tour. Same as Justin. Now he would go back to the base and decide whether he wanted to enlist for another four years—make the military a career choice, the way Justin had decided to do.

Not until they were on the plane and the doors were shut, did Lauren take her seat next to Joe and say the words that had been building in her heart ever since she arrived at the base. She turned and studied the young man's face, the pain in his eyes. "I'm sorry, Joe. About Justin."

"Yeah." The soldier's lower lip quivered. "Me too."

"You and he were good friends?"

Joe nodded. He looked across to the window on the other side of the plane, and for a single instant, he glanced over his shoulder at the flag-draped casket a few feet away. "Best friend I ever had."

"I wish I'd known him better." She turned to face him. "You were with him that day, with all the Iraqi kids, weren't you?"

Joe managed the hint of a smile. "Which day?" He chuckled and soothed his finger and thumb along his brow. "Oh, that Justin. There were never enough hours."

"My daughter says he was like that at home too."

"The volunteer work." Joe shook his head. "If I wasn't his roomie, I would've thought he was an angel or something."

"Messy?" Lauren winced.

"The worst. Dirty shirts hanging from his bed, stuffed in the drawers." He shifted positions and looked straight ahead, seeing into the past. "I'd tell him, come on, man. Isn't it easier just to wash the clothes rather than work so hard to hide 'em?"

They were quiet for a while as the plane gathered altitude and settled in. Lauren wouldn't talk to him the whole time. He needed rest, no doubt. Time to think and grieve. But she wanted him to know her thoughts — in case he had any preconceived ideas. "My daughter, Emily ... she loved him very much."

"I know." He leaned back, his eyes distant. "He'd read me her emails. I'm not sure I can face her."

"She's hurting, but she's strong. She's had a lot of loss in her life already. Things that happened when she was just a baby, when her father and I were separated."

"Right." He looked straight ahead again. "Emily talked about some of that in her letters."

"Really?"

"All about you and her dad and stuff." Joe looked at her. "Justin was happy for you, Ms. Gibbs. He thought maybe God was changing you, softening you. Something like that."

"He has been." Lauren still didn't have all the answers, but her response was an honest one. "It started that day when I saw the two of you handing out bags and tossing a ball with those kids. I kept thinking, 'Why isn't that the picture I have in my head when I think about soldiers?'

He gave a sad nod. "Lots of people have the wrong picture."

"My stories lately … I hope they're helping some readers see things more clearly." She fell quiet. Then she remembered something Joe had said a few minutes ago. "What you said earlier, about facing Emily … I'm not sure she knows you're coming. We never talked about it."

"Good." He made a tight line with his lips, and his eyes grew watery. "That'll give me more time to figure out what to say."

Lauren tilted her head. "What to say?"

Joe opened his mouth to speak, but no words came. He shaded his face with his hand and looked down at his lap. When he finally lifted his eyes, the pain there was so strong, she could feel it.

"Joe?" She didn't know if he needed a hug or a touch, but neither one seemed right.

"Justin … he was lying there … dying." He twisted his face up, fighting the tears, angry. "He made me promise to talk to her, to … to be her friend." He swallowed hard. "Only … how am I supposed to do that when every time I look at her, I'm going to see the other part of the picture?"

Again Lauren wasn't sure what he meant.

In light of her confused look, Joe reached down and pulled a red book from his bag. "This." He handed it to her. "Emily made him a scrapbook." His emotions took the upper hand for a few seconds. "Every night … Justin would look at it. I mean every night. He musta showed it to me a dozen times, until finally I opted out."

Lauren looked at the book in her lap and stared at the picture on the front page. It had dirt smudges and worn areas. Joe wasn't exaggerating. Justin must've spent hours in the book for it to look this way.

"See?" He pointed to the photo on the front. "Every time I look at her, I'll just see the other half of the picture. Justin. Because he's supposed to be the one coming home to her."

Lauren tried to absorb it all. Her heart was heavy for the young man beside her. He'd been through so much in the last few days. Riding along beside his best friend, a routine trip across the city, and suddenly being cast into the street, his vehicle ripped apart, bodies lying all around. He'd knelt there and watched Justin's life drain away and then he'd made a promise. A promise he had no idea how to keep.

"Something else." Joe reached into his bag again and pulled out a smaller object, a photograph. He held it out so she could see it. "He had this thing laminated, crazy guy." He laughed, but it came out more like a sob. "Carried it with him in his boot. And wouldn't you know … he was holding it when we hit the bomb." Joe pulled the photo closer and looked at it. "Had it in his hand the whole time he was dying, only …" He hung his head, too distraught to speak.

This time Lauren didn't hold back. She took gentle hold of his arm, fighting the sadness in her own heart. The scene the young soldier was describing was gut wrenching, but more than that, it gave her a window to how much Justin Baker had loved Emily.

Joe's shoulders shook for a time, and then he exhaled hard and looked up. "Sorry. I think I'm getting past it and then … I don't know." He looked dazed, his eyes numb. "So Justin was losing strength fast and … I took the picture from him, held it up so he could see it." Joe looked at the photo once more. "It was the last thing he saw before he died." He brushed his knuckles rough and hard beneath his eyes. "Right after I promised to talk to her, to be her friend."

Lauren took the picture from Joe and studied it. The lamination had kept it intact, but even so, it was slightly bent and smudged. The single thing Justin had kept with him to give him hope about the future, about a time when he would be back in Tacoma, taking Emily on dates to Puget Sound and living the life of any other twenty-two-year-old kid.

But that was just it. She ran her thumb over the photo. Justin wasn't any other kid—or any other soldier. And nothing she could say would ease the pain of his loss. She returned the picture to Joe and settled back in her seat to look through the scrapbook.

In the brief year that she'd known her daughter, Emily had always seemed mature for her age. Almost more like the adult than either she or Shane or their parents. It was Emily who doggedly hunted down information about Lauren and Shane, determined never to give up until she found them. It was Emily standing strong beside the two of them in the hospital room when her grandpa—Lauren's father—was dying of cancer last December. Emily was a planner, an organizer, a peacemaker.

But she was a girl too. A girl so in love with Justin that she'd taken time to add paper flowers and cutout hearts to the pages of the scrapbook. And silly things, bits of jokes and memories that only the two of them could understand. *Just call me klutz*, near the picture of the two of them hiking, and *I'm not that simple*, and *Tell me about ever after*.

It all spoke of laughter and frivolity, the kind that was perfectly fitting for a girl her age. And now ...

Lauren breathed in hard through her nose. Now Joe would have to find a way to give the scrapbook back, and Emily ... all Emily would have to remind her of that beautiful summer with Justin Baker were a handful of photographs and paper memories.

Lauren gave the book back to Joe and turned toward the window.

The rest of the flight she said little. Every now and then she could feel Joe crying beside her, and she didn't want to intrude. Didn't want to turn and look at the casket either. For a while she actually slept, but as she did, she dreamed about Shane. The two of them running in the seventh-grade Olympics and she tripping over her shoelace and falling flat on her face.

She missed him so much, and even that made her feel bad. Because Shane was meeting up with Emily and Justin's family, and she'd see all of them at the end of the trip. In less than a day, she'd be safe in Shane Galanter's arms one more time.

But Emily would have no one.

That's when she remembered Joe. Poor, dear Joe sitting beside her. *God ... maybe You could help him keep the promise to Justin ... Please, let them find a friendship in each other.*

The flight continued and they made a change of planes in Germany. They slept most of the next leg, and in what felt like only a few hours, they were landing, and suddenly Lauren's stomach hurt. How could she face them? She'd been wrong to report the war as she had, that much was clear. Where the lines between right and wrong lay, she still wasn't sure. Maybe there wasn't a line.

But one thing was certain. What she'd seen in the past few months had changed her heart. Wonderful things—and terrible things too. But nothing was going to hurt as much as stepping off this plane and seeing the devastation in her daughter's eyes. Emily was so young. How could she even begin to survive the days ahead?

Slowly, a realization struck. For all that Emily was mature for her age, for all the ways she seemed more together than Lauren, losing Justin had probably brought her to her knees. Emily needed love and support and someone to hold her, someone to stroke her hair and convince her that somehow everything was going to be alright. Someone to hold her even if she needed to cry all day long. Yes, it was time for Lauren to be more than an item on her daughter's prayer list.

It was time for her to be a mother.

Twenty-Four

Shane was dressed in uniform, his back straight as he stood between his daughter and his friend, Gary Baker. The rain had let up, but the air was damp and the sky over Tacoma was a lifeless gray. Shane had his arm around Emily, though neither of them spoke. Other than the rumble of planes landing and taking off, the only sound was the quiet muffle of tears.

Constant tears.

The return of a dead soldier was handled different ways. But in this case, they'd been given access to meet the plane on the tarmac. Justin's body would be carried from the plane to a waiting hearse while a color guard stood by. The transfer would be brief, after which time the hearse would take his body to the funeral home in Kelso, where it would stay until the funeral two days from now.

Shane watched the plane come into view, probably the one they were looking for. Right on time. He willed himself to stand strong, to stay strong. The people on either side of him needed his strength. But inside—in the place a soldier always kept but rarely showed—Shane had no idea how he was going to survive what was coming.

He kept his eyes on the plane, because that's what military men did when a fallen soldier returned home. But his mind drifted back to the moment when he first found out. He'd been at his desk, minutes away from observing a pilot on a testing mission, when the phone rang.

It was Gary, and for the first few seconds he said nothing. Finally, Carol took the phone. She sounded terrible, like she was fighting the flu. But somehow she managed to tell him the news. Justin was dead. One of the three soldiers killed in the most recent roadside bombing.

Death was part of life for the military. Shane had known that ever since he shied away from his father's push toward banking and business and instead enlisted in the navy. The Gulf War brought news like this, as had the wars in Afghanistan and Iraq. But no matter how often it happened, the news never came easily.

The phone call was short. Shane managed only to say he was sorry, and that he'd fly out in the morning, that he'd be there for them and take care of what they needed. When he hung up, he stood, shut his office door, and walked to the bank of windows behind his desk.

Of all the enemies a soldier faced, only one could ever truly threaten him: Futility. Soldiers were men of faith and family and conviction. They took the risks willingly, believing with every breath in the cause they defended. But futility could cut a soldier's legs out from under him, take away his purpose and his passion all at the same time.

Shane looked to the distant sky, the clear blue over the mountains of Fallon. That was the problem in Vietnam. Young men who signed up to defend their country wound up in a war without support from the government or the nation. Futility. That terrible sense of waking up in a war-torn village, looking around at the broken men and thinking of the missing men—and having just one question.

What's the point?

There had to be a purpose to military strength, and as long as Shane had been in the navy, he'd had one. Defending U.S. soil had never seemed more necessary than it had in the past decade.

Especially for fighter pilots. The ones who swept in and eliminated an enemy in a twelve-hour campaign, the ones who left news anchors shrugging their shoulders and reporting to Americans that all the fear and worry about the men on the front lines was for naught.

Sometimes, fighter pilots finished the job before the ground battle even got started.

That's the way it was with the Gulf War, and that's the way the United States citizens expected it to go with the wars in Afghanistan and Iraq. Quick and easy, a bombardment by U.S. fighter pilots, a dusting off of the hands, and everyone could notch another victory.

But the problem in the Middle East was more complicated than that. The enemy didn't wave a flag or stay in one place. They were insidious and cowardly, hiding in clusters and striking in ways that were almost impossible to stop. It was like trying to eliminate fire ants in Texas or Oklahoma. They went underground, and when they surfaced—with a roadside bomb or a suicide attack—it was too late.

Even so, the war in Iraq did have a purpose, and with purpose came passion. The passion he took to work with him every day. The passion Justin Baker lived by.

But that day, standing there with trembling knees trying to absorb the news, looking out onto the airfield at the naval training academy, Shane pictured Justin—the photograph in *Time* magazine of the young soldier playing with the Iraqi children, pictured him playing hoops with the guys at the teen center and holding his daughter's hand. Justin was everything good about the U.S. military, and now he was gone. And in that moment, Shane felt futility like he'd never felt before.

What *was* the point? Maybe Lauren had been right all along. They were spending millions of dollars and losing lives every day, and for what? If so many Iraqi people were still bent on fighting against freedom, then fine. Let them live in their mess, and let's get the American boys home. Safe where they belonged. So that not another Justin Baker would ever return to his family and loved ones in a coffin.

And so he stood there, futility breathing its ugly, putrid breath down the back of his neck. During the Gulf War, Shane was in terrible firefights, times when he and his wingman barely made it out alive. He'd taken part in wicked combat, dodging tracer missiles and ground-to-air rockets. But no battle ever felt more fierce than the one he fought in that moment.

The one taking place inside him.

Lord ... He hung his head, the claws of futility sharp around his neck. *Give me my purpose back. Give me a reason to wear this uniform, please ... Everything I've done, everything Justin fought for, it can't all be for nothing, can it?*

Then—slowly at first, but then fast like a music video—-images ran through his mind. God's people fighting for righteousness time and time and time again. Joshua and the battle of Jericho, Moses leading his people from captivity in Egypt, David and Goliath ... Every time men took a stand for what was right, God had given them the strength to prevail.

He stood straighter, held his head higher.

It was wrong to hijack a plane and fly it into a building full of people. Wrong for any possible reason. It was wrong to strap on explosives and walk into a crowd of people, and wrong to plant roadside bombs along the streets of Baghdad in a cowardly attempt at killing U.S. soldiers.

The war against Iraq wasn't a battle of wills, wasn't a matter of differing opinions. It was the United States stepping up to the plate and taking on a form of evil that threatened to destroy anything in its way. He felt God's presence around him, inside him, and futility slouched its way to the corner of his office.

There was a purpose in what they were doing. If the United States didn't take action against countries of terror, the whole world would pay the price. And if along the way it cost the life of someone good and golden, someone like Justin Baker, then the fight would become all the more dear, all the more full of purpose.

Because the cost was so high.

Shane felt the victory that day, minutes after Gary's phone call, felt all sense of futility leave him and his office and the job all of them were doing on behalf of the United States. He drew in a full breath and pushed his shoulders back. He would wear his uniform proudly, standing strong for the Bakers and his daughter, and for everyone who would attend the funeral. Everyone who would feel the loss of the young soldier.

He would be strong, but he would carry Justin's loss with him until the day he died. Because in Justin's loss, there was purpose all by itself. To accomplish what the boy had set out to accomplish. Victory and freedom and a world without terror.

Shane blinked, and the memory of that day faded. The jet plane came to a stop a safe distance away, and airport security officers motioned for the small group to come forward. He was right; it was the plane they were waiting for.

"Dad ..." Emily clutched his arm. "I can't do this ..."

He braced her, held her up and pressed her to his side. "We'll do it together."

Gary and Carol huddled around their daughter Jill, the three of them taking slow steps toward the place where the hearse had pulled up and the color guard now stood. Justin's family reached their places, and Shane and Emily stood beside them. After a minute, the door to the plane opened. For what felt like an eternity, there was no movement.

Then, a lone figure appeared near the door, and then a second. Both were soldiers, and they exited the plane holding the front end of a coffin. The soldiers saluted the color guard, the flag, and then moved the coffin through the door and onto the plank.

Tears poured down Emily's cheeks and her body shook, racked by sobs. She didn't cry out or wail, but in her whimpers Shane could hear what she was saying. "Justin … No, God … not Justin."

The loudest one in their midst was Jill Baker. She was a senior that year and busy at school. Gary had told Shane that Jill had deep regrets for not taking time to drive up to Fort Lewis more often. For not making a habit that year of sharing lunch or a conversation with Justin.

"My brother!" She wailed and held out her hand toward the coffin. "Just one more day, God … why can't I have one more day?"

Shane fought tears, stiffening his back until he saw the person trailing the coffin, holding up the far right corner.

Lauren, his only love, her eyes downcast.

Everything about her looked different. She was broken. He could see it in the way she held herself, the way she hung her head. And even from where he stood, Shane could see that she was weeping.

His eyes clouded over and he tightened his hold on Emily. Somehow in that moment, he knew Lauren truly had changed. It wasn't just the way she'd been reporting on the war lately. The change must have been in her heart—and he had the strongest sense that sometime that week he would know his prayers had been answered.

Lauren lifted her head and looked around, and then their eyes met. She hesitated, but only for an instant. Her cheeks were red and tear stained, but she focused on the task ahead, staying with the coffin, walking behind it. When the procession was halfway to the hearse, the soldiers stopped. The color guard approached the casket, performed a salute, and then retreated to a spot near the hearse again.

Shane could almost feel Emily straining against his arm, wanting to break free and go to him, to the young soldier she loved. But that wasn't protocol, and Emily knew it. Instead she pressed her head against Shane's shoulder, and between low sobs she whispered, "This ... this wasn't how it was supposed to be."

Shane turned his focus to the coffin, to the flag draped across the top. If futility was going to have something else to say, this would be the moment. The moment when reality stood before him, looming as large as the pine box. Instead Shane felt his heart swell with pride. The red, white, and blue had been what prompted a kid like Justin Baker to enlist in the first place. Shane had heard the stories from his buddy, knew about the patriotism that ran deep in Justin from the time he was a young boy.

And Justin was right to believe in the meaning of the flag, same as Shane was right and every American who held pride for the red, white, and blue was right. Because with all its flaws and differing opinions, the United States really was the greatest country on earth—the birthplace of freedom.

The flag would always evoke a sense of purpose and passion and pride in Shane, whether it was flown in front of a school or government building, waved at a high school football game, tattered in battle, or planted on a heap of rubble where once a towering office building stood.

Or whether it was draped across a coffin.

He watched as they reached the hearse, and Shane noticed that one of the soldiers, the one at the front right corner of the casket, was crying. A big guy with a bandaged forehead. Then Shane remembered. Gary had said something about a kid named Joe, a soldier who had been Justin's best friend, a guy who had been riding with him and survived the bombing.

The soldier at the front of the casket had to be Joe.

When they slid the coffin into the hearse, the color guard retired the flag and the hearse pulled away. Beside him, Emily's sobs shook her body, and finally, when she could no longer see the funeral car, she turned and buried her face against his chest. Shane stroked her back and watched as Lauren and Joe said something to the other three soldiers. The three nodded, shook hands with Joe, and headed for a waiting car.

Lauren and the wounded soldier walked slowly, reverently toward Shane and the others.

As he watched her, he felt a surge in his heart. The body in the coffin could just as easily have been hers, she'd been in that much danger. He wanted to run to her, take her in his arms, and breathe in the nearness of her, the reality of her. She was here, and she was home!

But Emily needed him, so he waited. Lauren came closer and her eyes held his. When she reached them, she put her hand on Emily's shoulder. "Honey ..."

Emily eased away from him and turned around. For a few seconds she looked at her mother, her eyes flooded with tears. A mix of emotions played on her face, and Shane understood. There was hurt and grief and even a little anger. Maybe because of the way Lauren had viewed the war last time they were all together.

Whatever her hesitation, it fell away and she melted into Lauren's arms. "Mom ..."

Shane folded his arms, his feet shoulder-width apart, the stance of a soldier. But he couldn't tear his eyes off them, mother and daughter, grieving together. He had been there for Emily, no doubt. After she'd broken the news to the people in Tacoma, they'd had almost a full day to talk about Justin and for her to cry in his arms.

But she needed her mother.

After a long time, Lauren released Emily and put her hand on the shoulder of the soldier, the boy standing awkwardly a few feet away. "Emily ... this is Joe Greenwald."

Apparently no other introduction was needed. Emily's face twisted in a fresh wave of grief, and she moved from Lauren's embrace into the wounded soldier's open arms. "He … he loved you, Joe."

Joe squeezed his eyes shut, and his body shook. Before he released her, he said, "He loved you too."

Gary and Carol and Jill came closer, moving as one unit. "Let's go back to the house." Gary looked shaken, but there was a strength in him that couldn't be denied. The retired soldier, the police officer. He would draw his strength from God, even as his family drew their strength from him.

Shane turned to Lauren and Emily, and only then did Lauren reach out to him. With one arm still securely around their daughter, she drew him close, and in her eyes Shane saw what he hadn't seen since they reunited a year ago.

Faith and love and forever, and something else.

Common ground.

Twenty-Five

Emily borrowed the twelve-passenger van from her soccer coach. It wasn't registered to the school, but rather to the team, so there was no legal reason why she couldn't drive it. At nine-thirty that morning, under skies that had cleared overnight to a surreal blue, she drove the van onto the freeway and headed north, toward the teen center.

Strange how the planning and preparations for this day felt something like a wedding. The wedding she and Justin would never have. There was the church and the white roses and the special music and the close friends and family who would share from the pulpit. People would wear nice dresses and dark suits, and afterward there would be a reception in the church hall. There was a guest book and even several hundred printed programs, small booklets that had kept Justin's mother and her working late into the night, folding and stapling each one.

Everything but Justin.

The memory of the casket, of the soldiers carrying his body down the ramp, and of Joe—straight and stoic, tears coursing down his face—would never leave her. She couldn't go five minutes without seeing it play again in her mind. From the moment Justin picked her up that day at her residence hall and told her the news—that he had a deployment date—she'd pictured his homecoming.

Pictured, as clear as day, flags and confetti and people cheering. And Justin—back straight and proud, walking off a plane and into her arms.

That was the homecoming he should have had. Not this.

Never this.

She checked her features in the rearview mirror. Her eyes had been dry all day so far, but fear ran in the small lines near the corners of her eyes. From the moment she climbed out of the guest-room bed in the Bakers' house until now, every minute, every step, every heartbeat took her closer to one o'clock. The hour Justin's funeral would begin.

The drive north from Kelso had been filled with song. She'd made several CDs in the days since hearing about Justin. One was all praise music—songs like "I Still Believe" and "Walk by Faith," by Jeremy Camp; and "Dare You to Move" by Switchfoot. On it she had written in permanent ink just one word: "Help." Because singing to God, praising Him in the midst of this, her darkest hour, was sometimes the only way she could get through.

Last night, after the funeral programs were made and stacked in a box, she lay in bed reading her Bible. She read 2 Chronicles, chapter 20—the scene where God's people had come under attack. In it the Lord promised that He would fight the battle. But not until the people joined hearts and voices in praise to Him did victory come.

And so she sang.

Another CD held songs that were special to her and Justin, and songs about losing someone. She played it when the only way to let the sadness out was to weep. Today, when she still had so much ahead of her, she didn't dare play that one.

Now she was minutes from the teen center. The guys didn't know she was coming to get them, and from their reactions the day she told them the news, they probably thought she'd arranged some sort of public transportation. And at the time, Emily wasn't sure how she was going to pull this off. Just that she was.

Because God would make sure those kids had a way to Justin's funeral.

The minutes passed, and she reached the center exactly at ten. She took a parking spot on the street adjacent to the small building, and that's when she saw them. Emily uttered a small gasp. The scene waiting for her brought with it the first tears of the day. Clustered just outside the front door of the center were the boys, the tough teenagers, who but for Justin, might've been running with a gang that day. Bo and Dexter and the rest, all dressed in what had to be their nicest clothes. Baggy belted jeans and dress shirts, their hair neatly combed. They looked sad and scared and out of sorts, their hands deep in their pockets.

Before they had time to notice that she was driving the van, and that the van was for them, something caught her eye. One of the boys who had been missing from the group darted out of a secondhand store with a bag in his hand. As he reached the others, he pulled a buttoned-down from the bag, jerked off his T-shirt, and slipped into the new shirt.

Emily bit her lip. So that was it. The boys—most of them anyway—must've scraped together a few dollars and gone to the secondhand store. So they would look appropriate at Justin's service. She pressed her fingers to her eyes. "No. No crying. Not now."

Bo noticed her then. He led the others, sulking closer, his eyes confused, suspicious. She rolled down the window that separated them, and he pointed to the van. "What'd you do? Steal it?"

"No." She laughed, and the release felt wonderful. "Crazy kid, get in before I leave without you."

They piled in, admiring the van's paint job and the upholstery on the inside. She could imagine that in normal circumstances, a two-hour drive with these boys might be a bit wild. They'd ask for loud rap music and wave at pretty girls along the way. But not this time.

Each of them found a seat, and what little conversation there was died down before she hit the freeway. She played her "Help" CD and the guys were quiet the rest of the way. Along the drive,

Emily wondered if any of them had even been out of the city. They were a mixed group, some black, some Hispanic, some white—but all of them had that tough inner-city look, and all of them were bound to feel out of place in a small town like Kelso.

But they'd come anyway. They'd come in their secondhand dress shirts, trusting that somehow a ride would show up for them at ten o'clock. All for the love of Justin. Emily tried not to dwell on it. Otherwise, her eyes would be swollen shut before the funeral.

The church the Bakers attended was on the south side of town, and Cowlitz View Memorial Gardens, on the north. She reached the church just after twelve noon, and already a crowd of people stood outside, waiting for the doors to open. Emily parked the van and stared wide-eyed at the people gathered there.

They were all ages, older couples and young children, families and groups of high school kids. Many of them held flags, and some held signs. *Justin, We'll Miss You!* and *Stay Strong America* and *Justin Believed in the U.S.A.*

Emily blinked back tears.

"Wow." Bo's voice held a level of awe that hadn't been there before. "Looks like he was their homeboy too."

Uniforms dotted the crowd, some worn by white-haired men and others by young Boy Scouts. That's when she saw them. A group of uniformed Veterans near the back of the crowd, one of them in a wheelchair with a jacket that wasn't quite straight on his shoulders.

They'd come. The Veterans Justin had befriended had traveled south for his service. Emily caught two tears and brushed them off her cheeks. Not yet, she couldn't cry yet. She turned around and sized up her group of teens. "We're early."

Dexter pointed at the crowd. "Or not."

"We are." She nodded. "I want you to follow me. We'll go in through the back, and you can find seats."

"The front row." Bo lifted his chin. "I wanna be in the front row." His chin shook a little. "As close as I can be."

"Well ..." Emily wanted to hug him. She held her breath and tried to find her voice. "The ... the first row is usually for family."

Bo plucked at his shirt and nodded at his friends. "*We're* family." His face twisted and it looked like he might cry. "Look—" he sat up straighter, his eyes flashing anger. "I ain't never met my dad, and my mama's in prison. When I was eight I tried to knock off a liquor store jus' so I could be with her." He clenched his jaw. "My grandma died when I was ten, and my aunt ... she's gonna kick me out when I turn eighteen." The anger left as quickly as it had come, and something in his eyes made him look like the child he still was. He pressed his lips together. "Justin's all the family I got."

"Bo ..." The heartbreak all around her was more than she could take. "You can sit where you want. Whatever you think's best."

Dexter looked from Bo to her, and back again. "What she means is, the first row's for his mom and dad and stuff." He gave Emily a sad but understanding smile. "I get it."

"Fine." Bo wasn't backing down. "Second row, then."

They filed out of the van, an unlikely procession, and went around the crowd to the back of the church. Bo led the way, but he stopped when they walked inside. The casket was already there, positioned at the front of the church, the flag draped over it like before.

Emily knew it would be there, but the teens ...

Bo shook his head and buried his face in the crook of his arm. He stifled a sob while the others stood behind him, not sure what to do next. Those with baseball caps removed them, and after a while, Bo lowered his arm. He looked at the casket. "Man ... why'd you have to get yourself killed? I told you we needed you more."

He walked down the aisle, his eyes never leaving the coffin. When he reached the second row, he kept walking. Emily followed behind with the others, glad they were early. She was a little worried about what Bo might do next. But Justin would've wanted the guys to have this time, this chance to express their feelings.

Bo reached the casket, stopped, and crossed himself. Then he took a tightly folded piece of lined notebook paper from his pocket, and put it on the casket. He kept his hand there, leaning on the coffin, and he hung his head. "I shoulda been there too, man. I shoulda had your back, the way you always … always had mine."

Dexter joined him, and then, one at a time, the others did the same. They surrounded the casket, placing their hands on the flag and uttering quiet, heartbreaking good-byes. After several minutes, Bo left the note, took a step back, and saluted. He didn't use two fingers, he used all five, and it wasn't the crisp military salute that would mark the rest of the day. But it was the one Emily would remember long after the service was over.

Bo moved into the second row, first spot near the aisle, and the others filled up the seats beside him. They were set, so Emily excused herself—and that's when she saw the lone soldier on the other side of the church, sitting in the back, his hat in his hands.

Joe Greenwald.

Emily steadied herself and headed in his direction. When she reached the pew where he was sitting, she took the seat next to him. "How you doing?"

"Not so good." His eyes were bloodshot, and he looked dazed, as if he hadn't quite figured out how a few days ago he and Justin were teasing each other about dirty clothes stuck beneath the bed and now he was at a church in Kelso about to tell him good-bye.

Emily covered his hand with her own. "At Justin's parents' house … the other night. You said you needed to talk to me?"

"Yes." He opened his mouth but no words came out, and he made an exasperated sound as he hung his head.

She wouldn't push him, not now. Joe had been with Justin when the bomb went off, he had knelt by him in his final moments. When the time was right, she wanted to hear the details, what Justin had said, his last thoughts. She patted Joe's hand and eased back. "Maybe later, okay?"

"Okay." He didn't look up, didn't make eye contact.

She stood quietly, giving him his space, and went to find her parents and the Bakers. After a round of hugs and quiet words, she opened the church doors so the crowd could file in. Then she worked her way through the people until she reached the old Veterans.

She bent down and gave the white-haired man in the wheelchair a hug. "Sir ... Justin would've been honored that you came."

The man sat tall and straight in his chair. "We would've driven all day to be here." He straightened his jacket. "We loved that boy."

"Yes." Emily nodded. "Me too."

She stayed with the group of Vets, and by the time they were inside, the church was almost full. A military contingency in dress uniform filled the front of the church, standing guard near the casket and on both sides of the pulpit area. Joe Greenwald was one of them.

For a single moment, Emily stopped. Until she blinked, until she took a closer look, any one of the soldiers might've been Justin. And she realized he would have been standing there if the fallen soldier had been someone else. An ache greater than she'd ever known filled her heart. The soldiers up front were so real, so alive. If only she could've had one more chance to be with Justin, even just in the same room the way she was in the same room with these soldiers. To hug him and hold him and hear his voice close beside her.

Just one more time.

That's when Emily saw what was happening. People were placing things near the casket. Everyone seemed to have something for Justin, a card or a letter, a flower or a teddy bear. Joining Bo's simple folded note now were so many items, it was impossible to see the flag.

Emily hurried to find Justin's mother, and the two of them found a stack of wicker baskets in one of the church closets. They returned to the sanctuary and set them on the floor around the casket. Then, carefully, they placed every item into one of the baskets.

"Thank you." Carol took her hand as they finished the job. "I want to take these home."

Just then a group of parents entered the church with thirty-some schoolkids between them. The children all wore shirts that said Elmwood Elementary. The school where Justin volunteered his time talking to the students. Emily whispered an explanation to Justin's mother, and then together they went to meet them.

"I'm Emily. I spoke with your principal." She shook the adults' hands.

One of the men stepped forward. In his arms was a box. "The kids made cards and letters for Justin a few weeks ago." The man wasn't crying, but his eyes were damp. "We were getting a package together to send him for Christmas. The kids ... the kids collected twenty-three pounds of Jelly Bellies for him and his buddies." He held it out. "Is there some place we can put it?"

Justin's mother covered her mouth, too shocked to speak. Emily slipped her arm around the woman, hugged her, and then motioned for the man to follow them. The box was placed next to the last of the baskets. Emily looked inside it. Dozens and dozens of letters and cards and Jelly Bellies.

Further proof of the lives Justin had touched.

That's the way it went as the church filled and overflowed out into the courtyard, everyone coming with a different gift, a different reason why Justin had mattered in his or her life. There was a group of Kelso football players, guys who knew about Justin and planned to be career military men because of him, and a cluster of teachers who had taught Justin when he was in high school.

Neighbors and church members and a hundred soldiers from Fort Lewis. One of the last people to file in was Vonda. She wore a dress and held an embroidered handkerchief. Emily went to her and the two embraced.

Vonda didn't hold back her tears any more than she had held back her opinions. She looked at Emily straight on. "That boy was crazy in love the moment he laid eyes on you."

Emily couldn't fight off the tears another moment. They came like constant reminders of all she had lost, all she would never have again. "I know."

"Now don't go tellin' yourself that things didn't work out." Vonda's tone was strained, her words hard to understand through her muffled weeping. "They worked out, you hear? Because one day with a boy like Justin Baker woulda been worth all this sadness." She took two quick breaths. "Mr. Smooth Talker."

Emily couldn't speak, so she nodded, never breaking eye contact with Vonda.

Her voice fell to a painful whisper. "He was gonna run the place, remember?"

"I know." She held onto the woman again. "I know."

Vonda touched her handkerchief to her eyes and gave a single shake of her head. "I'm gonna miss that boy something fierce."

"Me too."

Vonda turned away and found her seat, and just like that it was time for the service to begin. Emily took her place in the front row between her parents; on the other side of the aisle, the Bakers huddled together. Only then did Emily realize that her grandparents were there also. All three of them. Emily gave each of them a sad smile and then turned her attention to the front of the church.

The service passed in a blur. Most of the time Emily couldn't take her eyes off the coffin and the large portrait of Justin his father had set there. The eyes, the smile, the charisma coming from the picture almost made it feel like Justin was there, looking over all of them, urging them to believe that he was fine, happy and whole and anxious to see them again one day.

A pianist started the ceremony by playing and singing a song from MercyMe, "I Can Only Imagine." The song moved the entire room, and by the time it was over, after the final refrain built to the place of wondering whether upon his death a person would fall to his knees or dance before Jesus, everyone was weeping.

Now it was time for sharing. The first person to speak was Joe Greenwald.

Emily had heard him and Justin's dad talking about the funeral the other night at the Bakers' house, but she wasn't sure if Joe was actually going to get up. The way he'd looked before the service, she was pretty sure he'd declined. But now, walking stiffly in his uniform, Joe moved up the few stairs and took his place behind the podium.

"I'm Lieutenant Joe Greenwald." He leaned into the microphone, and a squawk sounded from the PA system. He eased back, his discomfort as plain as his army dress greens. He pulled a piece of paper from his pocket, unfolded it, and looked at it. Ten painful seconds passed, and then he exhaled hard and slid the paper back into his pocket.

He looked at the crowd, and his eyes welled up. "I'm here for Justin." He blinked twice and steadied himself. "He ... he asked me to tell you something."

Emily's heart went out to the guy, the one Justin had considered a comrade and brother, a believer and friend. He seemed quieter than Justin, but the compassion in his expression, the honesty in his eyes, was hauntingly familiar. No question the two shared a kindred spirit. Emily closed her eyes for a brief moment. *God, give him the words. Hold him up the way You've been holding me.*

Joe swallowed hard. "He wanted to be in Iraq; he believed in what we're doing over there—no matter how complicated."

Silently Emily cheered on Justin's friend. He was standing straighter now, conviction taking over where fear and sadness had reigned only an instant ago.

"He didn't want to die." Pride rang in his voice. He pressed his lips hard together, struggling. "He didn't want anyone to die. But he believed that ... that all men have the right to be free. To live without fear." He gripped the podium and took a half step back, hanging his head, overcome for the moment. When he looked up, there were tears on his cheeks. "I love Justin. And I know you love him too. There is ... no way to measure his loss."

Emily rested her head on her dad's shoulder and took a tissue from her mother. She pressed it against one cheek and then the other, her eyes never leaving the gripping scene playing out at the front of the church.

Joe inhaled and seemed to hold his breath. He looked slowly at every one of the Fort Lewis soldiers standing at attention around the front of the room. "He told me to tell you to win this thing!" He nodded at one group of soldiers and then the other. "Win this thing for Justin Baker."

One soldier in the middle, a clean-cut black guy, slowly brought his right hand to his brow, and with an intensity that matched the tears in his eyes, he saluted Joe. And all around him, down the line on either side, the other soldiers did the same. Ignoring his wet cheeks or the way his eyes filled with fresh sorrow, Joe returned the salute.

Emily could feel something happening behind her. She turned and looked, and around the room, first one soldier, then two more, then dozens from each side of the church, stood and saluted Joe in silent compliance with Justin's dying request. And before Emily could absorb the show of support, others began to stand—retired military and current military, no doubt.

Then from a row near the back, Justin's Veteran friends stood. It took them longer. Three used their canes for support, one had a walker. The white-haired man in the crooked jacket sat a little straighter in his wheelchair, and each of them also saluted.

Joe held his salute, his mouth tight, stoic in the face of the dramatic show of support. Finally, he raised his hand toward the heavens and said, "They heard you, buddy. They heard you." Then he leaned toward the microphone and gave a last look at the crowd. "Thank you."

Emily wasn't sure who made the first move. It was quiet at first, and then it built in intensity. Applause from people in the room. Again Emily turned around. First on his feet was Bo, and with a look, the other teens joined him. Then, all over the church, people rose from their seats, hands clapping. Not the way they'd applaud if this gathering were to welcome home the troops, but loud and long in a show of support that couldn't have been stronger.

Across the aisle, Emily caught a look at the Bakers. Justin's parents sat on either side of Jill. All three clung to each other, weeping, clearly touched by the outpouring. Justin's dad stood, turned, and gave a single wave to each side of the congregation, silently thanking them for caring, for understanding the sacrifice their son had made on behalf of his country.

On behalf of them.

Joe joined the applause, and when after a minute it died down, he returned to his place in line with the other soldiers.

After that, Pastor Kirby did most of the talking. Speaking with a smile and a sparkle in his eyes, he told about a freckle-faced kid who one time brought a water gun to Sunday school along with a wadded up pair of socks. Quiet laughter sounded around the church.

"You see—" the pastor motioned toward the mourners—"those of you who knew Justin best are nodding." More laughter. "And some of you probably know the story. Mrs. Ellis, the Sunday school teacher, pulled him aside and asked him what he'd brought." The pastor paused, his eyes smiling. "'A gun and a hand grenade,' Justin told her."

The pastor raised his brow, and a few more ripples of laughter came from the congregation. "'Why in the world would you need a gun and a hand grenade at Sunday school?' Mrs. Ellis asked. Well, you know that way Justin had of grinning and making you forget he'd done anything wrong? That's what he did. Just grinned at Mrs. Ellis and said, 'If the bad guys attack our class, I'll keep it safe.'"

Emily hadn't heard the story before. There were more. Stories from Justin's days as a Boy Scout, and how he'd earned his Eagle award a year ahead of schedule. "It wasn't that long ago we gathered right here in this building as Justin accepted his Eagle badge—something only a few young men ever accomplish."

Surprise filled Emily's heart, and she looked across the aisle at Justin's parents. She had known he was a Scout, but an Eagle Scout? He hadn't told her, same way he hadn't told her at first about his volunteer work.

Pastor Kirby was going on. "Justin stood right here—" he pointed to the spot next to the pulpit—"and promised to uphold the Scouting tradition, to be a person of principle and integrity and virtue." He gave a confident nod. "Justin was that young man everywhere he went, right until his very last moments."

As the pastor finished talking about Justin, he commented on the lives Justin had touched. "I'll bet we could spend a week in this room, letting each of you come up and tell what Justin meant to you."

Emily glanced across the aisle to the second row. Bo and Dexter were nodding.

"And so we must do the thing Justin would want us to do. We look to the flag and believe in its worth." A few "amens" rose up from the crowd. "And we must look to the cross, to the ultimate sacrifice, the true source of our hope. Where Justin's hope came from." Pastor Kirby smiled, but he hesitated. His face twisted up just enough for all of them to know. He too was struggling that day. "He would not want us to walk away from this room weeping and mourning. There is a time for that, yes." He sniffed. "But today Justin would want us to walk away celebrating his life, happy for all that he brought to us, and he would want us to be determined. Determined to live our lives the way he lived. With passion and purpose, with his eyes on the flag, and his arms outstretched to the cross."

Pride filled Emily's heart, and she linked hands with her parents. Justin was everything people said about him. And none of them — none of them — would ever be the same now that he was gone. But the pastor was right. Justin's was a life worth celebrating. And in that instant, Emily made a decision. She would cry when the tears came, and she would mourn. But she would not rest there, not stay there. Justin would not have wanted her to live in a dark place, grieving the days his death had taken from her. He would've wanted her to smile at his memory. Celebrating every single day they'd been given.

She had lost much, so much. But with Justin, she could never look at his loss without also looking at the incredible gift she'd been given, the gift of knowing him, of loving him.

No matter how short the time.

TWENTY-SIX

Lauren survived most of the service with only a few tears. Not that she wasn't grieving Justin's loss same as everyone else. But her heart and mind and soul couldn't seem to land on the same page. Every moment of the memorial was a reminder that Justin was no longer with them, that the nation had lost someone golden, one of its very best.

And for what?

She had seen the good things American soldiers were doing, and for the most part she'd come to trust the military public information office press releases—whereas before she'd disregarded them out-of-hand. Despite warring ethnic groups and the threat of civil war throughout Iraq, she'd also seen the desperate desire on the part of most of the people for freedom without violence, the need for democracy for themselves and their children.

In addition, she'd been privy in recent months to details of terrorist plans that truly would've made the events of September 11 seem small in comparison. The war efforts in the Middle East and the covert operations taking place on U.S. soil had prevented those, no doubt.

But was anything worth losing a young man like Justin? Could America really support a war where thousands of soldiers had lost their lives? She was just one reporter, after all. Without support from the media and the masses, the war in Iraq really might be pointless, right?

And everything she read—even from reporters she knew well and trusted—said that support for the war was at an all-time low. So where did that leave guys like Justin? Lauren wasn't sure, but she couldn't clear her head of the thoughts, couldn't feel quite right about any part of the funeral service.

The only certainty was the sadness, because it filled every heart, every pair of eyes in the room. None of them, of course, sadder than her precious daughter's. Emily had wept through the service, taking a fresh tissue every few minutes. Lauren felt a mix of heartbreak and protection, responsibility and sacrifice as she and Shane sheltered their daughter, feeling the way the sobs shook her slim frame.

What if Emily hadn't found Shane and her? How could she have gotten through this morning without them? She would've had her grandmother, of course. Lauren's mother. But still, Lauren found herself thanking God throughout the memorial, grateful that though she'd missed Emily's first steps and first smile, first words and first day at kindergarten, she was here for this: to hold her up as she walked through a season of grief that would no doubt change her forever. Emily would always have a special relationship with her grandma. But here, on a day when she was being forced to say good-bye to the only boy she'd ever loved, she needed her mom and dad.

When the service was over, Gary Baker asked them to be second in line in the motorcade procession to the cemetery. When they filed out of the church, Emily looked at Shane and then at her. "Let's get to the car, okay?"

Lauren understood. With all the emotion of the afternoon so far, she didn't want to talk to mourners, not yet. She wanted to take her place in the procession—the hearse, the Bakers, and then the three of them. As close to Justin's body as possible. Behind their car, Joe Greenwald had agreed to drive the van with the teens from the center.

"We're family," Bo had said. "We go after you."

There were no arguments.

Shane took Lauren's hand and led the way. She melted a little more each time he looked back at her and Emily. Shane Galanter, who knew her better than anyone and loved her anyway. The love in his eyes was something no other man had ever shown her, even after she'd left him again. He would've laid down his life for her, he loved her that much. A love she had spent a lifetime searching for. A love that would resonate in her heart as long as she lived.

But would he want her now? After all the grief she'd caused him?

Lauren held Emily's hand as they followed Shane through the milling crowd. This wasn't the time to think about Shane. That would come later.

They were driving a rental SUV, and the three of them climbed in, Lauren in the passenger seat and Emily in the back. As soon as they were situated, Shane reached over and wove his fingers between hers. The feeling reminded Lauren that she was still alive. They both were. She breathed in and felt new life stir inside her soul. After this dark day—if God would give them a miracle—they might finally find the life together they'd always dreamed of sharing.

Shane pulled up behind the Bakers' car, and in the side mirror, Lauren watched Joe steer the van into place, and after that, a convoy of military vehicles fell in behind them. Lauren wasn't sure what to say, and she decided on nothing. The moment seemed to demand quiet—a deep, honoring silence. She stared out the window and replayed yesterday evening, the hours they spent at the Bakers' house.

Carol had brought out Justin's keepsake book from his first tour in Iraq. "I think I'll set it up at the service. In the back." She angled her head and studied the book in her hands, then held it out toward Lauren. "Here. Emily's already seen it."

Panic tried to bury her, but Lauren resisted. Looking at the book would remind her of the cost of war, but it would also remind her that in some ways she'd contributed to that cost.

She took the keepsake book from Carol Baker and drew a slow breath. Then she took the book to the Bakers' sofa. Carol followed and sat on one side, Emily on the other.

The cover was adorned with fancy stick-on letters spelling out *Lieutenant Justin Baker — One Soldier's Journey*.

Lauren studied Justin's picture, his striking face and the grin that lit up his eyes. But all she could see was the young soldier playing catch with Iraqi children in an empty lot fifty yards down the street from a mob of protestors. A young soldier whose love and care for those kids had stopped her cold.

"He always wanted to be a soldier." Carol leaned in so she could see the pages better. "I remember," her eyes grew distant, "he was seven years old, and once in a while he'd still wake up frightened in the middle of the night. He was such a sweet little guy." The corners of her lips came up in a sad smile. "Anyway, one night we woke up with him in the middle, and as he opened his eyes, fresh from sleep, he looked at me and said, 'I had a dream, Mommy.'" She looked at her son's photo again. "I asked him what he dreamt about and he said, 'I got to try out for the army.'" A tender laugh rippled from her throat. "He told me, 'I did drills and pushups and running!'"

Lauren and Emily listened, imagining the scene.

"His older cousin had just been in a play, and the night before we'd talked about how they staged tryouts and picked the best actors to be on stage. And I told him that — " she looked up — "you know, you don't have to really *try out* for the army. They take every healthy, law-abiding guy who signs up."

Carol's voice grew soft, and she looked off. "And I'll never forget. He said, 'But you *should* have to try out, Mommy, because only the very best boys should get to fight for America.'" Her voice broke. "Only the very best."

Emily reached across the book and took hold of Carol's hand for a moment. Her daughter wasn't shaking or sobbing like at other times in the days since Lauren had been back, but her face was wet, her eyes never leaving the photograph. Then she linked her arm through Lauren's and laid her head on her shoulder.

Pictures danced to life in Lauren's mind, the little boy, blond back then, tanned and green-eyed, waking up with his bed-head and telling his mom about his dream. And that same boy running out to the soccer field, ready to help the fallen player. "Carol ..." Lauren could barely eke out the words. "If there were tryouts, he would've been first picked."

"Thanks." She nodded. "I know. He was born to wear the uniform."

They spent the next hour looking through the keepsake book. With every page, every layout, Lauren felt her views leaning hard in the other direction again. Justin had sent home photos of him and Joe and a few other soldiers from his company surrounded by Iraqi men. Men grinning and cheering and waving Iraqi flags and American flags all at the same time.

Several photos, with different groups taken on different days.

Beneath, his mother had included emails Justin sent home. One of them read, *It's an amazing feeling, Mom. Helping these people find a freedom they've only dreamed about. It makes every minute here worth it.*

There was a photo of Justin and a teary-eyed Iraqi man, their arms around each other's necks. Below the picture, Justin's letter said:

> *This is Ali-Abdul. He's a young father here in Baghdad, a guy with four kids. We were protecting the market where he gets his food, and he came up and gave me his change. I don't know, a bunch of coins worth maybe a dollar or so. But I got the feeling it was all the guy had. He wouldn't take it back either. Wouldn't hear of it. I mean, Mom, I really tried to give the guy his money. But he started crying, then he shook his head and started to walk away. You know*

me with my camera. I had to get his picture. He told me he would die a thankful man for what Americans have done for his country. Wow. I mean, I know there's lots of bad over here, because war is always bad. Always. The sacrifice is unspeakable. But this is what I see time and time and time again. People like Ali-Abdul. No matter what you read in the papers, this is what's going on over here.

Taped to the page next to that layout were six Iraqi coins. The change from Ali-Abdul.

Lauren played Justin's last line over in her heart. *No matter what you read in the papers . . .* Or in a magazine, right? The sorts of stories she had churned out every week without ever thinking about the repercussions. Because repercussions weren't her problem. War was wrong for any reason, and she had a right to say so. That's how she'd always felt.

Until the last few months.

She turned the page to photos of children waving and people working in makeshift marketplaces, all signs of a new sort of freedom. Only a few letters talked about Justin's fear, his realization that he wasn't merely on some kind of humanitarian expedition.

There is an insurgent group here in Baghdad that hates us, Mom. I studied this stuff in college; and I understand. At the root of this war is a spiritual battle that has been waged against mankind and against God's people since the beginning of time. But still . . . it's weird, you know? Being here and knowing that hiding just about everywhere are people who hate me enough to kill me.

Just because I'm an American.

A couple of the photos showed a more playful side to Justin, and it reminded Lauren that he really wasn't much older than a kid. A picture of him and Joe sitting on the dirt outside a tent, a small basin of water between them. They each had a toy sailboat, and like a couple of little boys, they were sailing them across the surface of the water. Under the photo, his email read in part, *I won the sailboat race, in case you have to ask. I mean, look at my tricked out boat. And yes, the water was wonderful.*

Emily laughed, but it mixed with the sound of a stifled sob. "He loved being on the water. We sailed on the Puget Sound before he left." Her smile faded. "We were ... going to take a cruise to the Bahamas."

What impressed Lauren most about the keepsake wasn't any one picture, but the preponderance of them. The message—from Justin's emails and from Ali-Abdul's coins and especially from the photographs—was loud and clear. The war in Iraq was more complicated than she'd ever wanted to see.

When they finished looking at the book, they moved to the kitchen table and Carol showed them that day's newspaper, the one with a front-page tribute to Justin. The headline read, "Kelso to Honor Local Fallen Hero." The article started on the front and moved inside with an entire page dedicated to the story and photos of Justin and his days growing up in Kelso.

One photo showed him at school—second grade, maybe third—dressed in a child's mock army uniform, saluting a teacher. Another was a close-up of him and his sister Jill a few years later, freckle-faced and suntanned, each of them holding a string of fish. There were photos of Justin in his Kelso High basketball uniform, and a photo of him the day he graduated from college, proud and tall in his cap and gown.

The pictures told the story. The sweet, sometimes mischievous, little guy he'd been, and the genuine young man he'd become. Lauren put her arm around Emily's waist as they stood side by side and looked at the photos Carol had chosen for the article. They studied the newspaper tribute quietly, each lost in their own memories of the young man. Carol finally ran her fingers over the photo of him in uniform. The rest of the night Lauren caught Carol looking at the picture a number of times.

There was a knock at Shane's window, and the memories lifted. Lauren turned to find a soldier—one of those who had stood near the front of the church.

"Sir, we're asking everyone in the procession to keep their headlights on. We'll have a police escort, so we should be able to stay together."

Again the thought had hit her. Was it unpatriotic to disagree with a war that had taken a kid like Justin? Could a person support the troops without supporting the government's decision to stay in a war? Or had Shane been right when he'd said that while no one wanted war, sometimes it was unavoidable—for the defense of the nation or the support of a people struggling for freedom? In that case, it was a matter of fighting for what was right and making a commitment to sacrifice, whatever the cost, for the sake of victory.

But could the people truly continue to support a war that had gone on so long? Even one that was netting positive results for the U.S. and Iraq? Lauren looked at Shane, at his strong jaw and the way he kept his eyes straight ahead, not on the Bakers' car, but on the hearse in front of it. He had been shaken by Justin's death. They'd talked about his battle with futility, and his realization that as long as the United States was free, there would always be a purpose in defending her.

Shane was as good and golden as Justin. And she'd been willing to walk away from him. Suddenly, as she looked at him, her heart filled with love, and a dawning happened in her. When the sadness of this day had dimmed, before they made a decision about what came next, she would talk to Shane. She would tell him that life was too short to live without the sort of love they felt for each other. The love they'd always felt toward each other.

The cars in front of them began to move, and Shane set their vehicle into motion. A wave of cold fear and sorrow hit Lauren, dissolving her thoughts. How could they be here, part of a procession to lay Justin Baker to rest? He was just standing there, a few feet in front of her, tossing a football with those kids, right? Just the other day. A part of her still refused to believe that he was in the flag-covered box in the hearse ahead of them.

Eight miles of two-lane roadway separated Kelso Community Church from the cemetery on the far end of town. They headed out of the church parking lot and turned right. The sight of the hearse put a lump in her throat, and she looked down. How would the Bakers possibly get through this day? She leaned on Shane's shoulder, drawing strength from him, relying on him.

He kissed her forehead. "I'm praying for Gary and Carol." His voice was soft, a caress against her battered conscience.

"Yes." She could do that too. Talk to God about the Bakers.

She was just getting started when Emily let out a soft gasp from the backseat. "Look!"

Lauren sat up. "What?" She turned her attention to the roadway and then saw for herself.

As the procession slowly moved forward, they saw people lined along the sidewalks on either side of the road—all of them holding American flags. These were not mourners, but Kelso citizens who had turned out to pay final respects to one of their own. Lauren watched, mesmerized as they passed a gray-haired couple. The frail, bent-over woman held a small flag, and the man, his hat over his heart, saluted. Next they came upon a pickup truck with ten teenage guys standing in the bed, hands on their hearts. A full-size flag flew from a pole planted in the ground beside them.

Shane said nothing, but his eyes looked wetter than before and the muscles in his jaw flexed as he drove. Lauren and Emily were silent, stunned. Lauren studied the people, saw the pride in their eyes. The line of them didn't seem to have an end.

They passed a group of handicapped adults, flags flying from their wheelchairs and walkers. Auto mechanics still in their uniforms, office workers in ties and suits. An entire Girl Scout troop came next, and even from the car, Lauren could see that several had tears on their cheeks.

Next was a group of medical workers in scrubs, together holding a single flag; and then what looked like most of the Kelso football team, all in uniform, their helmets tucked beneath their arms. There were entire families, some with babies in strollers, some with kids on bikes. And a Little League team standing wide-eyed along the curb.

Lauren looked back as block after block, mile after mile, the show of support continued, unlike anything she'd ever seen. She'd witnessed her share of parade routes and people gathered three deep along a stretch of road. But this was different. A parade route had people laughing and moving about.

These people stood motionless. Even the children had their attention entirely turned to the procession. Lauren wouldn't have believed if she hadn't seen it, this deep respect for Justin — for all soldiers.

Suddenly she realized she was crying, and it occurred to her what was happening.

God was giving her one final bit of wisdom on the topic she'd wrestled with for nearly a year.

He'd taught her to temper her views, shown her another side to the war — just as she'd asked. And now He was dealing with her final question. Could Americans still support a war effort that had gone on so long? That had cost so dearly?

The answer lined the streets all the way from the church to the cemetery. It was hard to imagine Kelso even had so many citizens, and yet they'd found a way to come, to support Justin and his family and his country for eight solid miles. Lauren took a tissue from her purse and pressed it to her cheeks. They pulled into the cemetery, and she felt overwhelmed with the desire to let Shane and Emily know how she was feeling.

She sniffed and turned so she could see them both at the same time. "Before we get out, I want to … to tell you something."

Shane had her hand. His eyes met hers, and she felt his compassion all the way to the center of her soul. She made her living as a writer, but now she had to search for the words. "When I left Fallon, I prayed for understanding, for wisdom. But … I didn't really expect to learn anything, because, well, I knew I was right." She sniffed. Her confession released a landslide of emotion she hadn't known was there. Because this was the first time she'd shared any of her new feelings with the two people she loved most.

"It's okay." Shane's tone was kind beyond understanding. "We don't have to talk about it now."

"I want to." Lauren searched his eyes. "Please."

Shane looked hesitant. Clearly he had no idea where she was going with this.

"Today … now … I can't go another minute without telling you that God has changed me." Her eyes blurred, but she stayed strong, as if by telling them, she could lend some sort of purpose to the sadness. "He's shown me time and again that my one-sided views were wrong. Shane—" she looked at him—"you were right. War is complicated and no one wants it. No one wants a young man like Justin to die." She pressed her fingers to her upper lip, fighting for control. "Yes, it's okay to question, and all of us wish there was a better way. But in the end—" she looked out the windshield at the hearse—"it comes down to supporting the troops. Even if you don't agree with everything about the war."

Emily looked down.

"So I want to apologize." She waited until she had Emily's attention again. "I'm sorry, Emily. And I'm sorry, Shane." The grief and regret caught up to her. It blanketed her and made it hard to breathe. She covered her eyes with one hand and fought her emotions.

"Mom ..."

Lauren looked up.

Emily touched her shoulder, rested her hand there. "I wrestle with all this too." Her eyes were dry. "I think of what the world just lost." Her voice grew tight. "What *I* lost." She looked at the soldiers filing along either side of the line of cars, ready to take the casket to its final resting place.

Emily shook her head. "I can't think of a single cause that would've been worth losing Justin. But here's the thing." The look in her eyes grew intense and she searched Lauren's face, then Shane's. "Justin believed in it. He was over there, he understood what this war's about more than any of us." She looked at Lauren. "Even you, Mom." Peace filled her features again. "He believed in it. That's enough."

"I know." Lauren held her daughter's eyes for a long moment. They filed out of the car then, and Lauren was last out.

She looked ahead to the white tent, the burial site where the procession would wind up. As they started walking, Shane took her hand. Nothing had ever felt so right in all her life. She watched Emily fall in among the teens Justin had visited with every week. Without talking, Joe walked along one side of Emily, and the boy who had declared himself family, on the other.

As they moved toward the tent, Lauren studied her daughter. Controlled and composed, Emily was the picture of strength. It was amazing, really, the maturity she was showing. Where did she get her wisdom? First in finding her parents and playing the diplomat time and time again. And now this. The answer came as soon as she breathed the silent question. Emily's wisdom came from God. Same as the wisdom she, herself, had prayed for.

Lauren replayed her daughter's explanation. Justin was the soldier, the one risking his life in Iraq every day, the one briefed on the missions and the purpose of the battle. He had believed in the war enough to sacrifice his life for it. In that assessment—more than any Lauren had ever done—there was wisdom.

And that was enough.

Twenty-Seven

Carol Baker couldn't take her eyes off the casket.

These were her final minutes, the last moments she'd ever have with her son. She clutched something in her right hand, something she'd saved for this time. No telling how many people filed in around the small white tent, the place where the coffin would be lowered to the ground. Carol appreciated every one of them, but she didn't look. Couldn't look.

There was only her and Gary and Jill and Justin. The way they'd always been for as long as she could remember. Only now, Justin would never smile at them or joke about Carol's cooking or ask about Buster or offer to run Jill to Starbucks. Now all they had was this, their final moments together.

And even then, Carol knew she was wrong. Justin wasn't in the box. He was free, whole and well, enjoying life the way it was meant to be enjoyed. Without war or conflict or anything but constant love. Pure love. Carol liked to think that heaven had a window, a way for people to look in on the ones they loved still on earth. But now ... now that seemed impossible.

Because heaven had no tears. And there could be no way for Justin to look down at his family in this moment without crying.

The graveside service was more formal, shorter than the memorial at the church. When it ended, seven soldiers from Fort Lewis lined up a short distance away and performed a twenty-one-gun salute. Emily and her family and the teens sat in the row behind them. In the front row, Gary sat between her and

Jill. When the first shot rang through the sky, Carol clutched her husband's arm and buried her face in his shoulder.

No, they couldn't be here. The salute couldn't be for Justin.

As the second shot echoed across the cemetery, suddenly she wasn't sitting next to Justin's casket. She was drinking iced tea on the back deck of their house on one of Kelso's endless summer days, and Justin was a nine-year-old towhead running around the corner into the yard, waving a cap-style rifle in the air.

"Take cover, Mom, the bad guys are right behind me."

And she was ducking behind the picnic table until Justin popped out from the bushes. "We won!" And he was coming to her, tossing his gun on the table and throwing his arms around her neck. "I'll always protect you. Okay? Cause I'm gonna be the best soldier in the whole world."

The third shot split the air.

Carol held tighter to the object in her hand. *God, I'll never survive it without You. Never.*

Gary was whispering in her ear, "It's okay ... we'll get through this."

But there was more sadness still ahead. The haunting refrains of taps filled the air, and when the song finished, the American flag was removed from the top of the casket. Two soldiers folded it and handed it to Joe Greenwald. Joe looked at Justin's parents, and never breaking eye contact, he carried the flag over and laid it in Carol Baker's arms.

She looked at it tenderly, longingly—remembering the long ago infant son she'd held in her arms. Then she cradled the flag against her chest, stood, and hugged Joe. Held him for a long time. When she finally let him go, Joe nodded to Justin's sister, exchanged another salute with his friend's father, and then moved a few feet away toward Emily. He stopped at her father, nodded, and then the two of them exchanged a salute. Next he shook hands with Emily's mother, and finally he looked at her.

He took both her hands in his, and she stood and hugged him. As she did, he spoke the words that broke Carol's heart. "He loved you very much, Emily. He ... he told me to tell you." Emily couldn't say anything. None of them could.

Joe drew back, took her hands again, holding them so tight his knuckles turned white. He locked eyes with her. "I'm sorry." Joe returned to his place in line with the other soldiers.

After a few minutes, the ceremony was over. Soldiers and commanders came by to pay their respects, and Carol gave the appropriate handshakes and hugs. But all the while, she never strayed more than a few feet from the box, from his body.

Finally, all that remained were a handful of people. Emily and her parents, the teens, and a few old Veterans—the ones Justin would talk to on Tacoma's rainy afternoons. Emily broke away from the group and approached the casket, opposite where Carol and Gary and Jill now stood.

She was a beautiful girl, Emily. Justin wanted to marry her, and he would have. He'd told her so in one of his letters home from Iraq. *I've made my decision*, he'd told them. *She's the one. Now if I can only survive between now and the day I can finally see her again ...*

Emily would've made a wonderful wife for Justin. They would've had children and raised them to care about people, to do the right thing. Carol felt another wave of sorrow wash over her. Poor Emily. She loved her son as much as anyone. She had been his first love, and from the beginning, Carol and Gary and Jill had embraced her.

Carol realized the precious girl standing across from her was young. Surely Emily would find love again one day and raise the babies she might've had with Justin. Which meant that the relationship she and Gary had built with her was—for the most part—over.

Emily came another step closer to the grave. Throughout the service, Carol had watched her show deep concern for everyone else. The teens, the Vets, even Justin's friend Joe. Every time Carol looked at Emily during the service, her eyes were on the speaker or the soldiers or the baskets of gifts that stood around the front of the church.

Never on the casket that held the boy she loved.

But now ... the cemetery service was over, and she found her way to the edge of the grave. Finally, without interruption, she stared at the casket. Her hands and knees shook, and after a minute she leaned close and placed her hand on the cool top. Her tears came then, streams of them. She closed her eyes and ran her thumb along the smooth wood.

After a while, she straightened. She kissed her pinky finger and pressed it to the box for a long moment. Then she turned and went to her parents, moving into an embrace from both of them. Off to the side, the rough-looking group of teens stood in a cluster, hands in their pockets, looking unsure about what to do next. The outspoken one came closer. Bo, Carol had heard Emily call him, the one who considered himself family.

He clutched the tent pole as if it might kill him if he took a step closer. But somehow he found the strength, and as he reached the box, he leaned on it with both fists. A single sob ripped at him, grabbed him. "Justin, man ... why?" The words were a whispered cry, desperate and haunting.

Emily pulled herself from her parents' arms when she saw him, this teenage man-child, crying his heart out for the loss of his friend. She went to him and waited three feet away. After a few seconds, the teen pressed his forearm to the casket twice, and then held it out in the air and did a one-sided handshake, maybe the one he and Justin used to do. Finally he pressed his fist to his heart and then pointed heavenward.

Only then did he turn around, notice Emily, and fall into her arms, a big kid looking for someone to love away all the hurt and pain. Carol watched the two of them move toward the others, giving the Bakers their space. Jill and Gary walked the few steps together, and Jill laid a flower on the casket.

Gary hesitated, even after Jill returned to their places near the first row of chairs. He was a strong man, a man much like Justin would've been if he'd had the chance to grow up. But this was a good-bye he'd never intended to make. He laid his hand on the casket, fingers slightly spread. The picture of it reminded Carol of the way her husband's hand had looked a thousand times on their son's shoulder, when the two of them would stand side by side at the end of a church service, or fishing on the edge of a lake.

"Justin—" His voice broke. He squinted and pressed his other fist to his eyes. "I'm so proud of you, son." He waited a minute and then returned to his seat.

And like that it was Carol's turn. She'd been waiting for this moment all day, her chance to be alone with her son. Only now it took everything she had left to make the walk, because she didn't want to say good-bye, couldn't imagine saying good-bye. She reached the edge, and suddenly she could see him lying there, the way he looked stretched out on his bed at night, his green eyes closed, muscled arms flung up onto the pillow.

Picturing him that way made her heart seize up into her throat. She couldn't take a breath or exhale or do anything but stare at the box. They had to get him out of there. He needed air! They both did. The cemetery people couldn't put him into the ground, couldn't leave him here. Because just a minute ago, he was running up and hugging her, telling her all the crazy, dangerous, tender things that had happened in Iraq. He had never been more alive in all his life, and so how could he be here at all?

She jerked her gaze away from the casket and looked up through the towering evergreens that lined the cemetery at a slice of blue. No. He wasn't sleeping in the box. Slowly she exhaled. That was the only way she could do this, by telling herself the truth. He was climbing mountains outside the city of heaven. Strong and more alive and whole.

A small bit of air filled her lungs, and she reached out and touched the casket. She still had the flag in her arms, and she looked at it. Anything to delay the moment. She ran her fingers over the silky blue and the sewn-on stars. Because blue stood for courage, and no one had ever tackled war more courageously than her son. "You got your wish, Justin." She whispered, so no one—not even Gary and Jill—could hear her. "You were the best, honey. The very best."

Then she took the object, the one she'd been holding in her hand since the graveside service began, and placed it on the casket, a few inches from the flower. The small plastic figurine had been one of Justin's favorites as a boy. He would fall asleep with a handful of them lined up along the side of his bed. They had all known back then which direction his future would go. The only thing Justin ever wanted to do was defend his country.

As she walked away, as she felt the physical force of separation, of leaving her son's body behind, she pulled her eyes away from the casket. The last thing she saw before she turned back to her family was that one small green toy that Justin had given her for Mother's Day a lifetime ago. She still had one on her dresser, where it would stay until the day she died, because it would remind her not of his death, but of his childhood, his boyhood, his teenage years. His life.

A much-loved, well-worn, army green, plastic toy soldier.

❧

The reception would be back at the Bakers' house, but first Emily needed to comfort Bo and Dexter and the other teens. They had held up well through both services, but now it seemed Bo might collapse to the ground. And so she held him until finally his sobs subsided.

"Bo … we need to get going." She looped her arm through his. Joe was standing with the other guys, though none of them were saying much.

The boy sniffed and nodded. "Okay." He looked over his shoulder at the coffin. "He's not there, right? That's what he always told us. Believe in Jesus, and at the end a guy goes to heaven, right?"

Emily smiled. Her eyes were swollen, but she was tired of crying. Justin was gone. Now it was time to celebrate his life—this afternoon and every day she had left to live. "That's right. He's not there."

Bo straightened. "Alright, then." The tough guy image was back, but not like he'd worn it before. Something in his eyes was different, softer and gentler.

Emily prayed it always would be. They met up with Joe and the others, and she and Joe exchanged a look. They still needed to talk, maybe later at the Bakers' house. For now, she appreciated his presence, the fact that having him nearby was—in some strange way—like having Justin there.

In the distance, she saw the Veterans making their way to their cars. Several of them walked with canes, their jackets decorated with dozens of colorful badges and pins, proud to be a part of the brotherhood that Justin belonged to, the brotherhood of soldiers. The man in the wheelchair held up his hand in her direction before his buddies wheeled him toward a cluster of cars—most with handicapped placards.

Emily waved back. This was not the last time she would see the old men. She would go to them, check in on them once in a while and keep them posted about life at Fort Lewis. Because that was one way she could keep Justin's memory alive.

They were almost to the van when Dexter shoved his hands deep in his jeans pockets. "What are we supposed to do now?" His tone was angry, defeated. "What's the point?"

Emily was about to answer him, about to tell him that Justin never would've wanted him to think that way, when Joe cleared his throat. "Hey, man, Justin talked about you guys all the time." Joe kept walking, his steps slow, eyes downcast. "He believed in you." He stopped and looked Dexter straight in the eyes. "And he believed in serving his country."

Two of the guys—the ones with plans to enlist—nodded, silent.

"Listen," Dexter did an exaggerated shrug, "you ain't got no idea what it's like livin' in my shoes, trapped on the streets. No way out." He stuck his chest out and crossed his arms. "Justin ... he knew, man. He knew like nobody." He threw his hands up. "So now what?"

Joe wasn't backing down. He'd never met the guys until today, but clearly he wasn't going to let this moment pass. "Now?" He put his hand firm and hard on Dexter's shoulder. "Now you get your education and you make something of yourself." Joe's lip quivered. "You make Justin proud, because that's what he wanted for you. It's what he believed for you."

Bo took a step forward. His eyes moved around the group to each of the guys, and finally, to Dexter. "The man's right." He looked more composed than he had all day. "Justin believed in us. Maybe ... maybe it's time we believed in us too."

For the first time, the idea seemed to sink in for Dexter. For the others also. Justin had believed in them. Dexter eased his stance. He bit the inside of his lip and gave the slightest nod. "Okay." Then he motioned for the others, and they all started walking toward the van again.

Emily wanted to raise her fist in the air. Here it was, the victory she'd been looking for all day. Justin *wasn't* gone. He wasn't in the casket, about to be lowered into a dark hole in the ground. He was here. He was in the warm smile of a teary-eyed World War II Veteran, and in the innocent eyes of a busload of grade school kids. He was in the firm grip of a soldier named Joe Greenwald, and he was standing beside her, gazing out at Puget Sound. Where he'd always be. But in this moment, maybe most of all, he lived on in the words of a troubled young teenager.

A guy who would forever believe in himself, in his future, in his reason for being alive. And one day—no matter how long or sad the good-bye—they would see him again and know the impact he'd made, the legacy he'd left behind, the lives that had been changed.

All because Justin Baker had lived.

Twenty-Eight

Lauren was standing off by herself, watching Carol Baker grieve, when she saw her mother approaching. She looked older, more tired. Coming to the service was important to Lauren's mom. She'd told them after hearing the news about Justin that she would've come even if she'd had to drive up. Instead she'd flown in yesterday afternoon and shared an early dinner with Emily and Lauren and Shane.

She'd raised Emily, after all. Of course she had come.

"This is the hardest thing my granddaughter's been through," she told Lauren after dinner. "I had to be here."

During the service, she'd given them space, understanding that Emily was struggling in more than one way. She had lost Justin, yes. But unless a miracle happened, she was about to lose any hope of her parents ever reuniting. Lauren took her eyes off her mother and looked at Shane, across the green spread of grass, several rows of tombstones away. He was talking to Gary Baker.

There wasn't much time; Lauren's mother seemed to understand that too. Her return flight was set for tomorrow, and now, as she drew near, Lauren had a feeling she may have come to Tacoma for more than a chance to support Emily.

She stopped a foot away, close enough that Lauren could hear her ragged breathing. "Something in the air here." She gazed at the trees that surrounded the cemetery. "Never had so much trouble drawing a breath."

"You're not sick?" Lauren wasn't used to worrying about her. They'd been out of touch for nearly two decades, long enough that most of the time she forgot she even had a mother. But now that Emily had brought them all back together, Lauren expected to have her mom around for a long time. Especially after losing her father to cancer a week after finding him. Lauren lowered her brow, worried. "You've been getting checkups?"

"I'm fine." Her mother waved her hand, as if she were swatting a fly. "Probably just allergies."

"Could be." She looked at her daughter, climbing into the van full of teens fifty yards away. "Emily says they're bad up here."

Her mother was quiet. When Lauren turned to look at her, she had no doubt. Her mother hadn't walked over to talk about allergies. Lauren turned her back to the rented SUV and tilted her head. "You're coming to the Bakers' house?"

"I am. Haven't had a chance to talk to Emily yet, not the way I want to." Her mother narrowed her eyes, thoughtful. "She's doing well. God's carrying her. I can see it."

Lauren gave a few slow nods. "He is. No way to get through a day like today without faith."

"No." Her mother drew a slow breath. She looked away, but only for a moment. "Lauren, there's something I have to say."

The words reminded her of the semi-speech she'd given Emily and Shane as they arrived at the cemetery. As if death had a way of making people get around to the point, a way of highlighting everything anyone ever said about life being too short. She studied her mom, the woman she'd spent so many years hating. All she could see in the older woman's eyes was love. Lauren gave her a sad smile. "I thought maybe you did."

"Yes." She held Lauren's eyes. "It's about Shane."

Lauren found him again, still talking to his friend. "Shane?"

Her mother looked over her shoulder at the two men, then back. "Don't let him go, Lauren." Her voice sounded suddenly scratchy. "It's ... it's my fault you ever let him go in the first place." She spread her fingers across her chest. "I take full blame. But now ..." She looked at Shane again. "I see the way he looks at you, how he still watches you when you cross the room. The way he used to do all those years ago."

Lauren's heart fluttered. "Really?"

"Honey—" her mother gave her a look that said she knew—-"I'm not wrong about this. Shane loves you as much today as he ever did."

The surprise of her observation was wearing off, and her heart fell back to a normal rhythm. But the thought stirred something deep in Lauren's soul. Shane watched her when she crossed a room? The years fell away and she stared at him, Shane, the only one who could make her feel seventeen again.

"What I want to tell you, Lauren—" her mother took hold of her hand and searched her face—"is that he loves you. He's crazy about you. He'll never love anyone the way he loves you."

"I've been thinking that."

Her mother made a relieved sound. "Good." The familiar guilt and regret cast shadows on her mother's face. "I couldn't bear to see the two of you throw away what you had ... what you still can have ... all because of differing opinions."

"Well ..." Lauren looked at the flag flying near the corner of the cemetery, the way it unfurled in the breeze. The red, white, and blue and all it stood for. "Our opinions are closer than they used to be."

Her mother's brows lifted. She hesitated, absorbing that bit of information, then shifted her gaze to the van just pulling away. "I think of Emily, all she's lost." She had Lauren's hand. "You and Shane still have a chance, honey. Don't ... please don't let him go. Not again."

Lauren was struck by the intensity in her mother's tone. But at the same time, another sort of realization hit hard. Her mother was right. If she didn't do something to stop it, in a few days, she and Shane would both board flights headed for two entirely different locations.

They'd already told Emily they'd stay another week, through Thanksgiving. Long enough to spend time with her, talk to her, and give her space to cry and laugh and remember the crazy, happy months since she'd met Justin. Emily wanted the three of them to visit the Space Needle and Issaquah, Blake Island and Pike Place Market, the spots Justin had taken her.

"If I go back now," she'd told them, "I'll still feel him with me. Before I forget how."

There was no arguing with that, because there was no arguing with grief. A person simply did what her heart led her to do. If that's where Emily wanted to go, how she wanted to spend her days after the funeral, Lauren and Shane would go with her. But at the end of the week, next Saturday, maybe they could spend an hour at the small church Emily had found.

Fallon wasn't so bad now that Lauren understood the military a little better. An entire town full of men and women with the same mind-set as Justin Baker? That wouldn't be such a horrible existence, would it? She and the others could disagree on politics, but some things finally made sense. The idea that a country like Iraq deserved freedom, and the notion that terror—the sort that would fly a plane into a building, or fire a bullet into a sign-waving man named Yusef, or detonate a bomb beneath a vehicle containing a kid who wanted everything good and right—that sort of thinking had to be eradicated. No questions.

Yes, she could live in Fallon now, because it was like an optical illusion. The people who lived and worked around the Top Gun facility used to seem like criminals to her, bullies looking for a fight, wanting to flex their collective muscle. But now she saw them more as police officers, people with the heart and courage to defend and protect.

A strange thing had happened since she wrote that first story about Justin and his fellow soldiers, since she dared to report the war the way so many people in Fallon had talked about it. Other reporters had started doing the same thing. One network correspondent who was interviewed the week before declared her admiration for the men and women of the military, and how it was an honor to risk her life beside them if that's what it took to tell their story. Their real story.

Lauren smiled when she saw the interview.

The press was starting to get it, starting to understand that complicated matters were never entirely one-sided — no matter what a reporter's personal views might be. She could leave the war reporting to the many other capable journalists in the Middle East, and *Time* would find another reporter to pal around with Scanlon.

She was finished, ready to move on with her life.

Shane's face came to mind — his voice and his touch. They'd have their differences, of course. But what couple didn't? And if Lauren returned to the sort of stories she'd been doing before — conducting interviews around the country — she would still have her independence, her time outside of Fallon. Most of all, she would have Shane and she would have peace — not the sort that she had spent her adult years writing about, searching for. But the type of peace that passed all understanding. A peace that could only come from God and His wisdom, and a knowing that she was finally where she belonged.

With Shane, where she had always belonged.

The thought that had hit her a moment ago returned. What about it? An hour in the small church where Emily and Justin had gone, a moment in time to promise forever to the man who had gently taken hold of her heart when he was only a kid. Would he have her? Would he believe that she could share a house with him in Fallon, entertain with him, and understand the people who made up his world?

Or was it too late?

Lauren took her mother's other hand. Patience shone from her mom's eyes, a patience and a persistence that said she wasn't going to leave this conversation without an answer. Lauren looked at her for a long time. "I won't let him go, Mom." Conviction rose within her, a conviction she hadn't fully acknowledged until now. "I know what I want." The words sounded foreign coming from her mouth. She hadn't voiced them to anyone yet, even herself. "Shane and I, well, we had this date all planned, something big set for Christmas Eve in Fallon." Her heart beat harder at the thought. "But I'd do it this week. On Saturday after Thanksgiving … if Shane'll have me." She felt a tentative smile on her lips. "He might say no, because, well … I've been—" she wrinkled her nose—"a little difficult."

"Are you saying—" her mother's face lost a shade of color—-"are you saying you'd marry him this week if he'd take you?"

Only then did she realize the significance of her words. The great and lasting significance. "Yes." No hint of doubt remained. She wanted to marry Shane and grow old with him, love him the way she'd never been able to love him before. "Yes!" She let loose a quiet laugh. "I want to marry him, Mom. That's what I'm saying." Her forehead grew damp, even in the late afternoon breeze. She would marry him that Saturday if he would take her, if he would trust that she was ready to commit her life to him, if he would forego all the fancy planning and flowers and simply hold her hand at the front of the small church and promise her forever.

The way she was suddenly desperate to promise it to him.

Her mother's eyes grew watery. "Well, then that settles it."

"What?" Lauren's heart was still racing within her, the future bright with possibilities that had eluded her all her life.

"I need to change my plane ticket." Her mother squeezed her hands, her eyes glistening. The look on her face said that the wedding was already a done deal, as if she—even better than Lauren—knew without a doubt what Shane would say.

She grinned. "Because I wouldn't miss this for the world."

Twenty-Nine

Funerals were strange.

Emily was amazed how, as the day wore on, the group of family and friends who had known Justin best rode a wave of emotions that seemed to change with every passing hour. What had started at the beginning of the day as resolve had given way to gut-wrenching grief and unending sorrow.

But now that she'd made the round trip to Tacoma to drop off the teens, she joined the others at the Bakers' house. The joy she found there surprised her, but after an hour she was laughing too. A laughter that would've made Justin proud to be a part of them. people told stories about him — the time he rode his bike through the neighbor's freshly paved driveway and denied the charge to his mother.

"I only had to take him outside to see the black tire track leading all the way from Mrs. Johnson's house to ours." Justin's father chuckled. He was sitting in one of the chairs at the kitchen table, his wife and daughter on either side, and Buster sleeping at their feet. Justin's sweatshirt was tucked beneath the dog's paws.

Also sitting around the table with her were her parents and grandmother, and Joe Greenwald along with a few other relatives. The stories kept them there, spellbound, celebrating Justin and every time he'd ever made them smile. Emily savored each one, learning a little more about him with each telling, each round of laughter.

Around seven o'clock, a lull fell over the table. The men moved into the family room, and the women headed to the kitchen to make coffee. Again the atmosphere was familiar. Trays of food on the counter, the smell of barbecued chicken and potato casserole and baked apples, all brought to the house by friends. Flames danced in the fireplace in the next room, and country music played, a soft backdrop for the conversations and occasional rounds of laughter that filled the place.

Emily closed her eyes and breathed in. This could've been any other gathering, a Saturday afternoon when their families had come together for a holiday party. She could picture him beside her, laughing with Joe and teasing his mother for breaking down and letting Buster in the house.

She blinked and the truth was glaringly obvious. Justin *wasn't* there. He never would be again. With the others off to different rooms, she and Joe were the only ones at the table, and she studied him—for the first time since they'd spoken at the church earlier that day. He was staring at his hands, his shoulders stiff, uncomfortable.

Emily's heart hurt for him. How must he feel? Today should've been another attempt at bringing order to the streets of Iraq. Justin should've been beside him in their Humvee, riding through Baghdad and taking care of business, counting the days until their tour was up.

"Joe?" Her voice was soft. "Wanna take a walk?"

He looked up and something crossed his expression, a sense of obligation and inevitability. He didn't break eye contact. "I think we need to."

She stood and found her coat near the front door. He did the same, but he also grabbed his backpack from the floor. Neither of them said anything as they went out the front door and closed it behind them. Darkness had already set, and with the clouds overhead, the only light came from the tall lamps that lined Justin's street.

Emily pulled her coat more tightly around her and stuck her hands in her pockets. Winter was in the air, and rain in the forecast. The breeze was biting, but it made her feel alive, helped lift the stifling sense of death she had carried all day. They hadn't walked too far when Joe stopped and leaned against a tree.

"It should've been me." He breathed in sharply and stared into the darkness. "Justin … he had everything to live for." Joe looked at her, to the part of her heart that was barely holding on. His eyes pooled with sympathy, empathy. "He loved you, Emily. So much."

This was the moment they'd both put off, and Emily steeled herself against it, willed herself to hear what Joe had to say without falling apart again. "You were with him. When …"

There was no need to finish her sentence. Joe understood. He slid one foot up against the tree trunk and stared at the ground. "He was sleeping when it hit, dreaming I think. Because an instant after the explosion, he was calling for you."

Tears gathered in her eyes and she held her breath. She didn't want to cry, not now. This was the only chance she'd ever have to hear the details of that terrible hour. But she hadn't expected this. He'd called for her? A moment after the explosion she had been there in his mind? The news filled her with a gratitude and sorrow greater than anything she'd known.

Joe sniffed. "It was like … like he was talking to you." He lifted his fist to his mouth and waited. "He told you he was sorry, he … never meant for it to happen."

The story unfolded, how Joe was cut, but alright, and how he crawled out of the mangled vehicle and found Justin on the ground. "His legs … they were torn up." Joe raked his fingers through his short hair. "I knew he was in trouble. I started calling for help. Justin … he was pretty dazed. Didn't know what had happened. But right away he started asking about his legs."

Emily didn't want to picture how Justin looked, how bad the scene must've been for Joe. She exhaled. *God ... please get me through this.* She didn't want the details, but she'd wondered about something ever since she got the news. Justin was a medic, and he would've helped a soldier in trouble. But had there been medics on hand in *his* hour of need? Or had he bled to death without any help? A cold bit of wind slipped in through her coat and she hugged herself to ward off the chill. "Were there medics? Nearby?"

"Not at first." Joe narrowed his eyes, which again grew distant, as if the tragedy was playing out again in his mind. "I leaned across him, using my body to stop ..." He shook his head, and anger crept into his tone. "It didn't help. He was bleeding pretty bad."

Emily felt sick, faint. There was a street sign a foot from her, and she leaned against it so she wouldn't fall.

"He didn't ask about his legs after that." The anger faded from his tone. A sad sort of laugh came from him. "He was more worried about me, told me I had a cut over my eye and I needed to get pressure on it. I told him I was fine. I kept ..." His shoulders hunched forward. "I told him to hang on, and he ... told me to pray. So I did, I prayed out loud." His eyes lifted to hers. "I kept telling him you were waiting for him, that he had to hold on for you."

Sadness filled every part of her. She had questions, not for Joe Greenwald. For God. But they would have to wait. She kept her eyes on Joe, willing him to finish.

"The medics came then, and they tried." His face twisted, and he suddenly looked like a young kid, crying because he'd lost his best friend. "It was too much. Too much blood loss, his injuries too bad. There was nothing—" He stopped a sob midway and shook his head hard.

Emily had watched Justin's friend suffer long enough. She took the backpack he was holding and set it on the ground beside him. Then she pulled him into her arms, hugged him the way she'd hug a brother. He clung to her, held on so tight, she could barely breathe. "Emily … I'm sorry."

"It's okay." She stroked his back, willing him to survive the loss, same as she was willing herself to survive it. "If it's too hard, Joe, you don't have to tell me."

He released her and leaned against the tree once more. "No. I … I have to. I promised him."

A car drove by on the street a few feet from them. As it passed, Emily lifted her words to God. *Please … help him through this. Help us both, Lord.* As she silently spoke the words, the chill inside her eased. God was with them, even now, even with her questions and confusion. Emily anchored herself against the street sign and waited.

"That's when I noticed this." He lifted the backpack and held it with one hand. With the other he reached inside, rifled through the contents, and pulled out what looked like a small picture. He handed it to her.

It was a laminated photograph of Emily, one that Justin had taken at the pier that day, just before their cruise. The picture was bent and splattered with dirt. The one he'd written to her about. Emily studied it, remembering that afternoon. Their future had seemed so real and bright. She turned her eyes to Joe. "He told me about this. He kept it in his boot."

"He was holding it when … when the bomb went off."

Emily stared at the photograph, tried to make out the image of her face through the cloud of fresh tears. If she'd had any doubt about his feelings for her, any doubt about whether she was on his mind in his final moments, this erased them all. He'd been thinking of her, looking at her picture even as his life drained away.

Joe held the backpack to his chest. "He told me to tell you he loved you, but …" He was more composed now, the sobs having retreated to a place where—like hers—they would never be far away. He squinted. "I told him to tell you himself. You were *his* girl."

A sad smile lifted the corners of Emily's mouth. She appreciated Joe, his heart and his spunk, his willingness to carry out the message for Justin, his determination in those final moments to spur Justin to hold on and fight for every breath.

"I think he knew he didn't have long. He kept his eyes on your picture and—" Joe's expression changed and he swallowed hard. Whatever was coming next, his discomfort was evident. He searched her eyes. "He asked me to be your friend, Emily. That's what he wanted."

Emily folded her fingers around the bent piece of plastic and hung her head. As he lay there dying, Justin's thoughts hadn't only been about her, they'd been *for* her. That she might have a friend to help her survive his loss. She tucked the photo into her pocket and held her coat tighter around her body. *Justin ... how can you be gone?*

Then she remembered Joe, the soldier who had just bared his heart by passing on a request from Justin—a request that clearly made him uneasy. Her silence was bound to feel like rejection. Sure enough, as she lifted her eyes, he was looking at the ground.

"We don't even know each other, Emily. It's okay ... you don't have to ... I mean, I only told you because—"

"Joe." Her tone was tender, but firm. She took hold of his arm and searched his face. This was what Justin wanted, and she was glad. Being friends with Joe would help ease the loneliness, give her someone to listen when all she wanted to do was talk about the love she'd lost. "I want to be your friend."

The awkwardness in his eyes lifted a bit. "Yeah?"

"Yeah." She let go of him and hugged herself again. "I think that'd be nice. You aren't going back to Iraq, right?"

He absently touched the bandage on his forehead. "No. I'll have to do my part from here now."

"Okay, then." They didn't need a plan or a date. They could exchange cell phone numbers and make arrangements to meet for lunch or dinner or for a walk around campus. They would be friends because Justin asked them to be, and because it made sense. Overnight, Justin's loss gave them more in common than they might've found in a year.

Joe reached into his backpack again. "I brought you a few other things." He pulled out the red scrapbook, the one she'd given Justin before he left. With great care he dusted it off and looked at it. "He read the thing every night." His eyes found hers. "I mean, really. He knew every page, knew it by heart." Joe did a sad laugh as he handed it to her. "I think even I memorized it."

Emily's hands shook. She took hold of the book and brought it close. Somehow it smelled like Justin, and she felt her heart breaking again. She had never planned to get it back, never imagined a scene like this one. Joe's words played again in her mind. *He read the thing every night … knew it by heart.* She held the book tighter. She would look at it later, study each page for signs that Justin had camped there, finger smudges or bits of dirt. She found Joe's eyes. "Thank you. For bringing it to me."

He nodded. "There's more." He pulled out a manila envelope. "All the letters you sent, and a few notebook pages, things he wrote when he couldn't sleep." He handed her the envelope.

Emily tucked it inside the cover of the scrapbook. The night was getting colder, and they needed to get back. Her cheeks were dry now, because the things Joe had told her had eased some of the pain. Almost as if she too had been there beside Justin when he died. "Did he … say anything else?"

Joe thought for a few seconds. Then his eyes shone with a sweet sadness. "Yes." He looked at the dark sky beyond the trees. "He said he'd save a place for us. For his family and the guys at the teen center, for me—" his eyes found hers again—"and for you. Those were his last words. He was looking at your picture, and he told me he'd save a spot for you."

Another chilly breeze came over them, but a strange warmth made its way through her. She imagined the moment, Justin looking at her picture, wanting to save her a place in heaven. "Did he talk much about the boys, the teens at the center?"

"Mmmhm." Joe eased the backpack onto his right shoulder. "All the time. After missing you, his next concern was for those kids." Joe uttered a soft laugh. "And Buster, of course."

Emily smiled. "Of course." That was Justin, serving in one of the hottest spots in the war and worried more about his dog than his life.

Joe motioned toward the Bakers' house. "We should get back."

"Yes." They began walking, their steps slow, pensive. How strange it was having this mountain of a guy beside her, a new friend she wouldn't have found if it wasn't for a promise between two buddies. "Thanks, Joe. For everything."

He brushed off the thanks and slipped his hands into his coat pockets. Like before, he looked nervous, not quite sure about whatever was coming next. "About those guys at the teen center … maybe we could head out there and hang with 'em once in a while. The way Justin used to do."

This time Emily's smile started deep inside her soul. "I think they'd like that."

As they made the rest of the walk in silence, Emily felt a connection with Joe she hadn't imagined ever feeling. Because Joe wanted to be like Justin, same way Bo and Dexter and all the young guys wanted to be like him. So maybe that would become Justin's legacy, another part of himself he would leave behind. His loss would always be a terrible thing. Emily could live a hundred years and she would never quite heal, never quite get through a day without missing the young soldier who had captured her heart that perfect summer on the shores of Seattle.

But the world would be a different place because of him, a better place. No matter how brief, his life had counted. It had mattered in a deep and lasting way. *This is the bus stop*, she could hear him saying as she took the steps up to his parents' front door. *The great journey is on the other side.* Indeed. Her soul stirred and a new kind of calm came over her. Justin was gone, but he had left behind his wisdom and laughter and a thousand precious memories. And something else. She smiled at Joe as they reached the front door.

He had left her a friend.

THIRTY

Shane didn't want to think about saying good-bye. But it was coming. There was no way around the fact. The day after Justin's funeral, Lauren took him up to Seattle's Space Needle. The rest of the week belonged to Emily, she told him. But today it needed to be just the two of them. They rode five hundred feet up to the *O* Deck and stood against the railing, looking out at the city. After a long while, Lauren turned to him. "Shane ... we need to talk."

The look on her face told him she had something serious to say, and a part of him wanted to stop her. She couldn't give him a farewell speech. Not after all they'd been through that past week. Time and again things between them had seemed better than ever. So why weren't they talking about staying together? Shane steeled himself. "Why do I feel like we've done this before?"

"This is different." She took his hands, and the look in her eyes softened. "In the last few months I've learned a lot. I prayed for wisdom and God gave it to me." Her voice held none of its usual skepticism. "It's easy to step back and see something through the lens of personal bias." She stared at the breathtaking view. "I can stand here and see a harbor or a city or the mountains, and I can think that's what makes up Seattle." She looked at him. "But it's not until I get down from the Space Needle and walk the streets, not until I climb the mountains or find my way to the waterfront, that I can actually know something about the city."

He listened, wanting to draw her into his arms. Hope shone a flashlight on the dark places of his heart. This was the Lauren he had fallen in love with, the one who was levelheaded and careful with her opinions. He let her finish.

"That's what happened to me in Iraq these last few months." She exhaled and looked through the wall of glass again. "I had a chance to walk the streets and talk to the people and watch the soldiers—guys like Justin—and see for myself why this war is important."

He hadn't been sure where she was going with her thoughts, but he was touched. This wasn't the good-bye he'd expected. Not yet, anyway. She'd brought him to the Space Needle so she could tell him how she'd changed, how her eyes had in some ways been opened. But before he could ask her what else was on her mind, what might lay ahead for the two of them, she turned to him and kissed him. Kissed him the way she hadn't done since their first night back together at her parents' house in Chicago a year ago.

"Twice you've asked me to marry you, and twice it hasn't worked out." Her eyes were soft, full of light and love. "Now it's my turn."

For half a second, Shane wondered if he'd slipped into some sort of dream. Then it dawned on him. Maybe this was her way of reacting to Justin's death. If so, he wanted to stop her before she said anything else. "Lauren … we don't have to decide this now. Last time we rushed the decision and look what hap—"

"Shane." She put her finger to his lips. "I haven't rushed this. I've missed you with every breath, every heartbeat. Almost worse than I missed you the first time we were apart." She slipped her arms around his waist, and her eyes found the way to the most private part of his soul. The place no one else had ever found. "I want to marry you and move to Fallon with you. I want to sleep with you and wake up next to you and share your passion for freedom and safety and for doing what's right—even if that sometimes looks a little different to each of us."

Doubt must've flashed in his eyes because she giggled. "A *little* different, Shane. Not so different that I see white where you see black. Not anymore. I told you … I've changed. God changed me."

He put his hand alongside her face and searched her eyes. This was the scene he'd only dreamed about. "I thought you brought me here to tell me good-bye."

"No. Never again." She moved her arms from his waist to his neck. "I'm done saying good-bye." Her voice trembled. "If … if you'll still have me, then marry me. Marry me this Saturday at Emily's church and let's get started."

He laughed. She was always ready for a project, a purpose. "Get started?"

"Yes." She kissed him again. "On forever."

And that had been that.

The plans came together quickly—almost everyone they wanted to attend was already in town, and his parents were able to catch a last-minute flight. His mother had pulled him aside last night, her eyes teary.

"I've prayed for this for two decades, son." She took his hand. "We were wrong, what we did. But God's ways are better than man's, and now here you are. Here we all are."

Morning took forever to come, and when it did, Shane still couldn't believe it was happening. He wore his dress uniform and stood next to a preacher at the front of a church, the one Emily and Justin had attended just off the base at Fort Lewis. Organ music filled the air, and the faces in the first few rows of the church grinned their approval. And of course, in a few minutes he would do what he'd dreamed of doing since he was a junior in high school.

He would marry Lauren Gibbs Anderson.

The church held everyone who mattered most to them. Emily, who was in the back room with her mother, would be Lauren's maid of honor; and Gary Baker, standing on his other side, sharp in his dark three-piece suit, would act as best man. His parents, who had flown up from California the day before, sat in the second row next to Angela Anderson—Lauren's mother. Carol and Jill Baker were there, as was Joe.

And that was all.

He looked at his parents and then at Lauren's mother. Twenty years ago, the three of them had fought this moment with everything in them. They were wrong back then, and they'd admitted so time and again in the past year. But only this moment—this marriage—could truly free them of the guilt and regret they carried.

Shane smiled. There was no anger now, no residual bitterness. Never mind the years he and Lauren had lost. They had a lifetime ahead of them. Shane caught Gary Baker's eyes, and he gave him a look that said he still couldn't believe this was happening. That a family could survive such terrible, unfathomable grief, and such limitless joy—all in one week.

He stared at the back doors of the church and waited. He and Emily had talked that morning. "Justin's life mattered in a lot of ways, too many to count," she'd told him. "But Daddy, you know what?" Her eyes were soft, full of emotion. "I think his life counted for this too. God used Justin's life to change Mom's heart." Her eyes glistened. "And He used Justin's death to show her that love never has enough time."

Shane smiled. Love never has enough time. Leave it to Emily to sum up the entire situation with one sentence. She was right too.

He heard the music change, heard the beginning refrains of the traditional wedding march begin. Love never had enough time, but what time was left, he would savor. Every single second.

The double doors opened, and there she was, his bride. She wore a striking white dress, her blonde hair swept up in loose curls. But what made her beauty absolutely breathtaking was the look in her eyes. Reporting on the war, spending time with cynical people, being angry much of the time—all of it had taken its toll on Lauren. The entire time she lived in Fallon, he rarely saw her eyes soften, rarely saw her intensity let up.

But now ... she looked seventeen again. She had no chip on her shoulder, nothing to prove. She was simply the tender girl he'd always loved, the girl with a heart bigger than the ocean and a soul full of kindness and love. Finally taking the walk they had both dreamed about.

The walk down the aisle.

Since her father had died the year before, she had explained that she wanted Emily to walk her down the aisle. "She spent a lifetime praying and dreaming about this moment," Lauren had told him. "She's the one who brought us back together. Long after we gave up. I can't imagine anyone else walking with me."

Neither could he.

Emily wore an elegant lavender dress, her dark hair styled much like Lauren's. As she walked next to her mother, Shane caught Joe Greenwald watching her. The two had been together every day since the funeral, and Shane was glad. Emily needed a friend, and because of Justin, she had one.

Lauren was closer now, and their eyes held. Shane had expected to be choked up at this part of the ceremony, watching Lauren walk to him, knowing that finally they had found their way to this moment. But instead he wanted to laugh, wanted to raise his fist in the air and shout for all the world to hear. After searching and longing and praying and crying, here they were.

And nothing would ever separate them again.

⚜

Lauren had never felt more certain in all her life.

She walked, unblinking, her eyes on Shane's, and inside she celebrated like never before. She was marrying Shane Galanter! They'd agreed to write their own vows, but Lauren didn't have to. She'd written them long ago, when she was a teenager, and she'd been reminded of them just a few months ago by Emily. Always Emily.

Her daughter stood tall, proud beside her. But there was no denying the way she trembled as they walked, arm in arm. Emily had waited for this morning all her life, and now it was here. Even in the darkness of the valley of the shadow of death, this day would cast a light. A brilliant light.

She reached the end of the aisle and the music stopped. The pastor smiled. He had talked with them yesterday morning, asked them and encouraged them about their faith and their determination to keep Christ at the center of their marriage. It was a reminder. They had gotten here by God's grace, and they would stay together the same way. In Christ alone. Even if Lauren was still figuring some of that out.

"Who gives this woman to be married?" The preacher's voice rang clear and strong.

Emily smiled up at her. "I do." She kissed Lauren on the cheek and then took her place to the side.

Lauren turned her eyes to Shane. He looked like a dream, and she felt herself react to his presence. How long had she searched for him? Longed for this day? He walked down the steps, his eyes never leaving hers. Then he took her hand and led her back up the stairs to face the preacher.

"I had a chance to meet with the bride and groom yesterday." The man smiled at the handful of people in attendance and raised his brow. "I must say, normally when a couple wants a wedding to come together quickly, my advice is to wait. But in this case—" he grinned at Lauren and then at Shane—"the wedding is way overdue." He opened the Bible and read a passage from Colossians and another from 1 Corinthians 13. He focused his talk on love and sacrifice, and how it was impossible to have one without the other.

Lauren glanced at Shane, and he met her smile. The pastor was right. All their lives had been a picture of that truth. Love and sacrifice, and how one couldn't exist without the other.

Finally it was time for the vows. Shane went first. He and Lauren faced each other, and he took her hands in his. "Lauren, I don't know about love except what I've felt for you. I refuse to think about the years we lost, but only about the ones that will begin here, now." He paused, and for a moment they both seemed to forget where they were. There was so much between them, so many memories that only the two of them shared.

Shane took a slow breath. "I promise to be with you, stay with you, love you, and laugh with you. I promise to listen and always look for new ways to show you how much I care." The corners of his lips lifted. "Most of all, I promise to lean on God through life's trials and tragedies and triumphs. Because if I lean on Him, you can always lean on me."

It was her turn. Her throat was thick, and she didn't want to take her eyes off Shane for a single instant. "Shane ... you taught me about love a long time ago. And though I searched, though I became someone even I didn't recognize at times, I never stopped believing in that definition. The one I've held onto since I was seventeen. This is what you taught me." She opened the piece of paper that had been folded tightly in the palm of her hand.

"Real love is this." Her voice rang clear through the church, "Real love waits in the snow on your front porch so you can walk to school together in the fifth grade. It brings you a chocolate bar when you fall and finish last in the seventh grade Olympics." She smiled at him, seeing the way he looked that long ago day. "Real love whispers something in the middle of algebra about your pink fingernail polish so that you don't forget how to smile when you're doing math, and it saves a seat for you in the lunchroom every Friday through high school. Even when the other baseball players think you're stupid."

A few quiet laughs came from the front of the church.

Lauren's chin quivered, but she kept on, looking from the page to Shane and back again. "Real love stays up late on a Saturday making chocolate chip cookies together, flicking flour at you and getting eggshells in the batter and making sure you'll remember that night the rest of your life. And real love thinks you're pretty even when your hair is pulled back in a ponytail and you don't stand perfectly straight."

She folded the paper and handed it to him. His eyes were damp, but he mouthed the words, "I remember."

She smiled and looked to the most tender place in his heart, the place where the teenage Shane still lived. "And this year, you taught me something else. Real love lets you figure out the answers by yourself. It says good-bye for a season and prays for your return. Real love understands about love and sacrifice and is willing to live accordingly." She held onto his hands tighter than before. "Shane, you've spent your life showing me what real love is. I understand now, and I promise to spend the rest of my life loving you like that." She blinked back tears. "As long as we both shall live."

From a few feet away, they both heard Emily stifle a squeal, and again there was laughter.

The pastor stepped closer and took the rings from Emily and Gary. He explained the significance of the unbroken circles, and the promise they would represent for all time. As Shane slipped the band of white gold onto her finger, she felt the greatest sense of rightness. Yes, her life was full before she found Shane again. She had a career and a purpose. But her life wasn't complete until now.

The rings in place, the pastor nodded to Shane. "You may kiss your bride."

He did so in a way that took her breath and made her anxious for every tomorrow they'd share together. Before they parted, before the pastor could present them as husband and wife, out of the corner of her eye, Lauren saw Emily close her eyes and lift her face skyward.

Their daughter was praying, no doubt. Thanking God, because no matter how hard the journey, they were here. Where they had always belonged. And this time no one and nothing would separate them until death intervened. The bridge to this place had been built with wisdom and prayer and love and sacrifice.

But most of all, it had been built by God.

As Shane drew back, as they shared a smile of sweet expectation and oneness, Lauren was reminded. The miracle God had given them was greater than either of them had imagined possible. Because they had found something they never really believed they'd find, something only God could've given them. A place to start and stand and build upon. A place to love and laugh and live.

Precious, priceless common ground.

Thirty-One

Eighteen Months Later

The haunting sound of taps rang out across the base as the Memorial Day service came to an end. Rain had fallen relentlessly all day, but it stopped an hour earlier, and now only the gray clouds remained.

Emily took the hand of the soldier beside her, and silently they walked to his pickup truck. When they were inside, as Joe Greenwald started the engine and pulled out of the parking lot, Emily turned to him. He still held her hand. "It feels like yesterday."

"I know." He smiled at her, no longer the tentative smile of a young man uncertain about how to proceed. Rather, a smile born of friendship forged in the flames of grief. Friendship … and something else.

Something deeper.

They had planned this day for a month, knowing what they would do, where they would wind up, and now Joe drove his truck onto the southbound I-5 freeway and settled into a steady pace. They were headed for Kelso, for the place where Justin was buried.

There had been no way to foresee how the past year and a half would unfold, no way of knowing how pain would bring the two of them so close. Emily leaned her head back and closed her eyes. They had been determined to be friends because Justin asked them to be.

But from there, the bond between them took on a life of its own.

It started with the teen center. A month after Justin's death, Joe picked her up at her residence hall and drove her downtown. She had worried that the familiarity of the afternoon would wear her out, leave her emotionally drained. But instead, the time together that day had breathed new life into her. Justin's work, being carried out the way he would've wanted it to be.

Snow fell lightly as they made their way into the center that day, and there they were. The guys who had loved Justin so much. Bo seemed to notice them first. He gave Emily a questioning look, and then he turned to Joe.

"What's up?" The question was loaded, fully defensive and almost threatening.

Joe separated himself from Emily and approached him. "Thought we'd play a little ping-pong." He shrugged. "You know, since there's snow on the court."

Bo crossed his arms and stuck out his chest. He looked at Emily and back to Joe. He began to shake his head, slowly at first and then faster. "Oh, no you don't." He jabbed a finger at Joe. "I know what you're doing."

"Bo ..." Emily took a step forward.

Joe held out his hand, stopping her. "It's okay." He looked at Bo. "I've got this."

"No, you ain't *got* this, man." Bo raised his voice. He gestured hard toward Joe. "You think you can walk in here and take his *place*? Is that it?" He waved off Joe, turned, and paced three steps. Then he stopped, his voice louder than before. "You can't take his place, man. No one can." He pointed to the door. "Get out. We don't want you."

Dexter lifted his chin. The others looked like they felt the same way.

Emily felt tears on her cheeks even before she knew she was crying. Of course they didn't want Joe, they wanted Justin. They all wanted Justin. But he was gone, and Joe was determined to help these kids, to pick up where his buddy had left off. She reminded herself to breathe as she watched Joe.

He laughed, as if Bo's attitude hadn't affected him at all. "Man, I didn't come to babysit you." He crossed his arms. "I came to whip your tail in ping-pong." He held up his hand. "But hey, if you're afraid, that's cool." He looked at Dexter, and then at the others. "Someone's gotta be up for the challenge, right?"

A gradual shift happened among the teens. They glanced at each other and then at Bo, as if to question whether he would really back down from someone calling him afraid. Bo looked angry; he'd been tricked. He gritted his teeth and hissed in Joe's direction. "Someone wants me to beat 'em at pong—" he flicked his shirt, all macho and tough guy again—"then I say bring it."

He walked to the table and picked up a paddle and a ball. "Come on, white boy, bring it."

Joe rolled up his sleeves. "Yeah, that's the Bo I heard about all those nights in Iraq. All talk, no action."

"What?" Bo let his mouth hang open. "I could take Justin any day."

"Fine." Joe practically spat the word. "Let's see what you got."

That first game was one of the fiercest, most intense competitions Emily had ever seen. When it was over, Joe had won more than the game. He had won the respect of every boy at the center. Once a week they began coming, and over time Joe forged a relationship with the guys, a friendship. And at the end of that semester, Bo showed them his report card. Nothing less than a *C*, even in math and science.

Joe would never be Justin.

But he brought his own brand of loving and learning, and that was more than enough. Emily liked watching him, liked seeing how he was quieter than Justin in some ways, and yet maybe more able to connect with the teens individually. And he was funny. Humor gave Joe a connection the guys hadn't expected.

Half the time Joe was teasing them, and the other half he was telling them how God was the only way off the streets.

Joe's parents lived in Ohio, the Akron area. He was the youngest of six kids, the sometimes quiet one in a loud and fiercely loyal family. Three of them had already decided on military careers. Emily liked hearing stories from Joe's childhood, the growing-up years, how Joe and his brothers would wrestle and chase after each other and stage contests for everything, from eating hot dogs to swimming across the river that ran through town.

His parents thought Joe was headed for a military career too, but he was only serving for a season, getting money for college. Joe wanted to be a doctor. "There's a lot of ways to help people," he had told Emily. "Serving your country in war, or serving your fellow man in a doctor's office."

She agreed with him and found their discussions more fascinating all the time—whether they centered around Iraq, and Joe's thought that the country should be divided into three states—one for the Kurds, one for the Shiites, and one for the Sunnis. Or whether they were talking about the application process for med school. Joe was twenty-one back then, a year older than her, and already he'd taken enough classes between tours in Iraq that he was midway through his sophomore year at the University of Washington.

That same month, when Joe first made contact with the teens at the center, they took the first of several trips down to Kelso. Buster was getting slower. Maybe because he missed Justin, or maybe because he was getting older. Either way, he needed to be walked, and Emily had developed a fondness for him.

Justin's parents welcomed them like long lost friends, though Emily caught his mother looking at her, watching the easy way she had with Joe. That first time, the two of them went outside and hooked Buster to his leash. Justin's old matted sweatshirt was in his doghouse where he had been sleeping.

"Hey, boy ... remember me?" Emily petted him behind his ears, the way Justin had always done.

Buster wagged his tail.

"See that?" She smiled at Joe. "He likes me."

Joe stooped down and patted the dog. "Justin was crazy about him."

Buster hid behind Emily's leg, fearful and maybe a little puzzled over the young man who had some of Justin's mannerisms, but yet wasn't Justin.

They walked Buster through the Bakers' neighborhood, and after an hour, the dog warmed up to Joe. Before they left, Justin's mother pulled Emily aside. "I'm glad you and Joe are ... you know, becoming better friends." She smiled, but tears filled her eyes at the same time. "Justin would've wanted that."

Suddenly Emily understood the haunting looks she'd been giving them since they arrived. She must've thought Emily was developing deeper feelings for Joe, feelings that went beyond friendship. And only one month after Justin's death. Emily shook her head, her voice low so she couldn't be heard by the men in the other room. "Mrs. Baker, there's nothing between us." She shrugged and felt her own eyes tear up. "We have Justin in common, that's all."

Mrs. Baker gave her a sad smile, and she nodded as if to say she understood more than Emily on this matter. "It's okay, Emily. You're young." She put her hand on Emily's shoulder. "No one would expect you to stop living. Especially not Justin."

The conversation stayed with Emily and troubled her. For another three months she worried about what people might think, what they might say. When she talked to her parents — who were happier than ever — she downplayed the time she was spending with Joe.

Meanwhile, she and Joe continued to spend all their free time together. They met with the teens once a week, and every now and then they visited the Vets at the American Legion hall.

"I love this," he told her once, "carrying on in Justin's place." The look in his eyes was deep and sincere. "But there's something I've always wanted to do. Those roadside bombs maim as many guys as they kill. If you'll go with me, I think I'd like to start visiting the VA Hospital."

And so they did that too, spending an afternoon every few weeks hanging out with soldiers who had lost an arm or a leg, or who were recovering from some other sort of war injury. Emily enjoyed the conversations they had with the soldiers, but even more, she liked watching Joe. She was struck by the easy way he had with people, his sense of humor and how it created an almost instant bond with anyone he met.

On the six-month anniversary of Justin's death, they spent a day at Blake Island State Park, a tiny oasis in the middle of Puget Sound, eight miles out from Seattle's waterfront. They hiked the trails and explored Tillicum Village and spotted a pair of bald eagles diving for fish near the shore.

But not until after lunch, when they were sitting on a fallen log staring at the ocean, did Joe turn to her. And suddenly, there it was. The one thing they'd never discussed, never dared to imagine. At first he said nothing, but he didn't have to. His eyes told her that he was feeling the same way she was.

Somewhere along the path of healing and holding onto Justin's memory, a special sort of love had taken root. And now it was deep enough that they could no longer ignore it, no longer spend an afternoon together without somehow acknowledging the feeling.

He took a long breath. "Can you feel it, Emily?" His voice was so soft, it mixed with the ocean breeze and resonated deep in her soul.

She didn't have to ask what he meant. Her eyes held his. "Yes ... I feel it."

A consuming guilt gathered around them, staring them down, daring them to state the obvious. Emily couldn't look at Joe. She let her eyes find a place in the sand near her tennis shoes. How had it happened? Having feelings for Justin's friend was wrong. She'd known when she lost Justin that she would never love the same way again, that no one could ever take his place. So how had they come to this place, to these feelings? And worse, how could they deny their strength, when quietly, beneath the surface, their hearts had already started something too strong to walk away from?

Joe reached for her hand. "We can take it slow, Emily."

The touch of his fingers against hers sent shivers down her spine. She could barely breathe, had to will herself to stay there beside him. What would Justin think? How could they live with themselves for letting this happen? Justin had asked them to be friends, nothing more.

But even so, she didn't let go of his hand. What had he said? They could take it slow? She nodded. "Yes. We ... we have to."

"Look at me, Emily." Again his voice was tender, resigned.

She lifted her eyes and realized that her knees were shaking. It was May, and the weather was still cool. But the chill inside her came from their conversation and not the temperature.

He looked long at her, studying her eyes. "Justin wouldn't be angry with us. He ..." Joe's chin quivered. "He asked us to spend time together. Deep inside—in those last minutes—he had to know."

Emily thought that through. He had to know? Was it possible, that as he lay there dying he had asked Joe to be her friend so that one day she could find a love with him, the love Justin could no longer give her? She swallowed hard. "I don't know." She felt sick, ashamed of herself for being attracted to Joe, for having feelings for him. "It'll take time."

And it had. Their first kiss came seven months later, on Christmas Eve. By then there was no denying the obvious. Through a trail of grief and sorrow, God had forged in them a friendship that would never be broken. Could never be broken.

The bond they shared was deep and anchored in a faith that had survived the most difficult test. Her parents celebrated with her when she told them the news—that she and Joe had moved into a dating relationship. And Justin's parents had rejoiced as well, telling the two of them that it was right and fitting that they find their way together.

"Justin would've wanted this," his mother said. "I saw it coming, Emily. We're happy for you both."

Emily appreciated their support, though she suspected they had shared tears over the situation as well. Same as she and Joe. This wasn't how things were supposed to work out, but they had. Now everyone involved needed to find a way to understand and move on.

Some nights, before she returned to her room, they would sit on the bench—the one she and Justin once sat on—and they would hold hands in silence. Simply missing Justin and all he'd meant to them. But by the time they reached the one-year anniversary of his death, after they took a week over Christmas break and visited her parents in their Fallon home, this much was clear: Justin had brought them together.

There was nothing guilty or shameful about that, and they agreed to let the New Year define a change, an end to the constant grief and sadness, and a tender new beginning for the two of them.

Emily opened her eyes and let the memories of the past eighteen months fade. She had Joe now, and she loved him with everything inside her. No, he would never be Justin, but that was okay. What she and Joe shared would always—in some ways—be deeper, stronger, because of the painful journey they'd traveled together.

It was fitting, really. That the trail of tears they'd walked would end and begin here on this day, Memorial Day, the day when Justin would always be first in their minds. As long as she lived she would remember their summer together. He had given her happily, but he had promised her more.

And now, because of him, she and Joe had found that elusive something, that thing that for a while seemed lost for all time.

And maybe somewhere down the road, they would even find ever after.

From the Author

Dear Friends,

Thanks so much for journeying with me through the pages of *Ever After*. I learned much about myself and about love as I wrote this book. I learned about sacrifice and patriotism. Without a doubt, I learned that I have a deep-seated respect and gratitude toward the men and women who serve our country through the armed forces, and for their families—all who sacrifice some, and some who sacrifice all.

My family often teases me when I write a novel. They sneak into my writing room with a cup of tea or a bowl of grapes or a sandwich, and they wonder at the tears in my eyes. "They're make-believe people," my husband tells me.

But not to me.

In my heart, they live and breathe and move, and when I write, I feel like a reader. The story is always entirely a gift from God, and me, the humbly grateful soul who gets a first peak at it. But this story was different. I wept more than ever before while writing *Ever After.* For the first time since I started writing books, I had to keep a box of tissues on the table beside me. One morning Kelsey walked in.

"Hi, Mom. Do you need anything?"

"Hi." I turned to her, a tissue in one hand, tears streaming down my face.

"Oh. Sorry for interrupting." She gave me a strange look. "But ... uh, can I get you anything?"

"Yes." I looked at her through clouded eyes. "Counseling."

And that's how I felt through the writing of this book. I was happy and joyful with my kids and family one minute, and then five minutes later I'd be at my laptop weeping over the loss of Justin Baker and the complexities of war. My emotions were so strong, and the story so vivid, that one day after breaking my personal record for words written in a given day, I found my husband and told him, "I love writing more than breathing. I just have to tell you. I absolutely believe this is where God wants me, and I love what I'm doing more today than ever in all my life."

Which is a good thing, since I've got lots more books ahead, God willing.

But the depth of my emotions made me sit back and ask myself where the feelings were coming from. And that's when I realized that they came from my gratitude for the men and women who fight for and defend our country. The story of Justin and Emily is all too real for thousands of people across our great land. Sacrifice is very much a part of living life as an American—and a story like *Ever After* lets us take time to remember that, to acknowledge it.

This book so completely filled my heart that I wrote it faster than any other. Like a living picture, it poured out of me in just five days. Five days. I was gripped by the story, and all I could picture was that in many ways, there was nothing fictional about Justin Baker's story. Like all of you, we know young men and women serving our country, people who need our utmost respect and support. People who lay down everything out of devotion to America.

If there was a point, a message I pray you received from *Ever After*, it was this: Love is not possible without sacrifice, and sacrifice is not possible without love. Isn't that what Jesus taught? He died on the cross as the greatest sacrifice, the greatest gift of love, and it's through His grace and salvation that we can do anything good and lasting.

Regardless of our differing political views, we must—as Americans—agree to pray and be grateful for the people who put their lives on the line so the United States can remain a free nation. I found myself loving Justin for who he was and for all the tens of thousands of young people he represented. These people are the heartbeat of America.

The cost of freedom is great.

Our family heard that message on Memorial Day this year, just as I was finishing the story of *Ever After*. At a quiet military cemetery in our town, I stood in dark sunglasses next to my husband and kids, crying silently through the entire ceremony. I was struck by the pride in the hunched over World War II Veterans, and the deep pain still in the eyes of the Vietnam Vets. I watched the flag being raised over the cemetery at the end of the service, and I clutched tightly to my family, thanking God for the privilege of living in America.

I pray that you might understand love and sacrifice a little better for having read *Ever After*. If you aren't familiar with Jesus Christ and His sacrifice on the cross, or if you'd like to know more about how you could receive His gift of salvation, please contact your local Bible-believing church. You could also write to me and put the words, "NEW LIFE" in the subject line. I'll be happy to send you a Bible and pray for you, that you'll find salvation in the only One who can give it.

The gift is free to you, but it was never really free. Jesus paid the price.

In the same way, living in the U.S. is free to all of us, but freedom is never really free either. A cost is being paid every day by the military men and women and families in our midst. Let's not forget that.

If you are among those serving our country, I thank you. With all that I am, I pray you will know how grateful I am, how grateful our family is, and how often we pray for your safety and success. Likewise, if you are among the hundreds of thousands of family and friends of those serving, my heart goes out to you. Thank you for allowing your loved one to serve and to sacrifice.

The price you are paying has not gone unnoticed.

You see, my little Austin—eight years old—is a kid like Justin Baker was. He plays army games and talks about "trying out" for the army one day—so that he can be among the best soldiers fighting for the United States. "I wanna keep America safe," he'll tell me.

He's just a kid, and I'm sure his interests could change over the coming years. But today, I see his tender heart and his great conviction, and I know—already I know—the great sacrifice it would be to take him to a recruiting office and let him begin a soldier's journey.

So for now I hold on a little longer to all my kids, and I remain grateful. Grateful to a God who would give us a land called America where we can live and serve Him and exist in freedom. And grateful to this country's military families. I pray for God's hand of protection and blessing on you all.

One more thing. You might remember at the front of this book, I dedicated *Ever After* to the memory of soldier Joshua Dingler. I learned about Joshua long after I finished writing this book. But the more I found out about Joshua, the more I discovered that his life had an uncanny resemblance to my fictional character, Justin Baker.

Like Justin, Joshua left behind a girl he planned to marry. He went into battle proud to help a nation find freedom, and in his brief life he was known for the way he helped other people. Like Justin Baker, the real-life Joshua Dingler was remembered by an entire city at his funeral. The day of his memorial service, thousands of people lined Highway 92 from the Pickett's Mill Baptist Church to the cemetery. People holding flags, men saluting from the bed of a truck, and endless rows of men and women with their hands over their hearts.

But Joshua Dingler is not a fictional character. He is real, and I pray that this book brings honor to his memory. What defined Joshua was not his death in Al Mahmudiyah, Iraq, south of Baghdad, August 15, 2005. For that reason, please visit my website at *www.KarenKingsbury.com* and pray for the military members represented there. Also, please send in your photos and bios of your loved ones serving our country. Check my website for details.

Finally, as always, I'd love to hear from you. My website is growing constantly and has become a community of readers and people like yourself. There is a link where you can post a prayer request or pray for others in need, and there are links for book clubs and readers looking to connect with each other. I've also included a blog with constant journal updates and a look into the writer's life, as well as my life as a wife and mother. It's my way of helping us all feel like friends.

There are also contests all the time. One ongoing contest is this: When you finish reading this book, lend it to someone who hasn't read one of my novels. Then email me and write, "SHARED A BOOK" in the subject line. In the message, tell me the first name of the person you shared with and why you shared the book. You will be automatically entered into a drawing that will take place each spring. The winner will bring a friend and spend a day in the Northwest with me and my family. Check my website for details, updates, or changes to this or any contest.

In the meantime, know that I am praying for you and yours. May God's face shine upon you. Until next time,

In His light and love,
Karen Kingsbury

Book Club Questions

Explain Lauren Gibbs's feelings toward the war at the beginning of *Ever After*. What had shaped her viewpoints?

Do you think it would've been possible for Lauren to continue living in Fallon without spending additional time in the Middle East? Why or why not?

Discuss Shane Galanter's feelings toward war and the military at the beginning of *Ever After*. What had led to his viewpoints?

What are some of the differing opinions in the United States today regarding war in the Middle East or the defense of the country? Discuss.

Share an opinion that is different from yours regarding this issue. What do you think might lead someone to have this opinion? How can you better understand that person?

Explain how it is possible to have differing opinions and still be like-minded on the bigger issues. How did Shane see this as a possibility for him and Lauren early in the book?

Describe the character Justin Baker. What made him such an amazing young man? Why would a young man like Justin want to join the armed services? What characteristics do you see as common in the men and women you know who serve this country?

Give examples of Justin's character, and how Lauren, Shane, and Emily could see that character in action during the summer when he and Emily were dating.

Why did Justin feel strongly about serving in Operation Enduring Freedom, and the war in Iraq?

Why did Lauren feel she had to return to reporting on the war? What did she expect to find when she returned, and what did she pray for?

What was the epiphany for Lauren, the turning point that broadened her viewpoint on the war? Explain that scene and the emotions Lauren felt.

What emotions and feelings did Lauren have when she witnessed Yusef killed by a sniper? How did she feel about the war then, and her prior reporting on it?

Based on Justin's emails, photos, and firsthand accounts, what were his feelings toward the war? What were his feelings toward the Iraqi people?

How did Emily react to the news that Justin had been killed? Did it change her opinions on the validity of the war? How did Lauren react?

Explain Shane's feelings as he received word about Justin's death. What did he feel was the one enemy that could threaten a soldier? Why?

How did Shane find his way back to having purpose in his position as an officer in the military? Explain his feelings when Justin's body returned home in a flag-covered casket.

Explain the support Justin and his family received during the memorial service and graveside service. When have you seen that sort of outpouring of support for a member of the military? Describe the time.

The lasting message of *Ever After* deals with love and sacrifice. Explain how those two are intertwined, and how they model the greatest sacrifice of all—the one Christ made on the cross.

Tell about a soldier in your family or circle of friends. What price did he or she pay in the fight for freedom?

What can you do to support the troops in your area? How can you involve your family or church, your friends or coworkers?

Read this sample chapter
from Karen Kingsbury's book
***Take One*, from the Above the Line Series.**

One

CHASE RYAN DOUBTED THERE WAS ENOUGH oxygen in the plane to get him from San Jose to Indianapolis. He took his window seat on the Boeing 737, slid his laptop bag onto the floor space in front of him, and closed his eyes. Deep breaths, he told himself. Stay calm. But nothing about the job ahead of him inspired even a single peaceful feeling. On Monday Chase and his best friend Keith Ellison would set up shop in Bloomington, Indiana, and start spending millions of dollars of other people's investment money to make a film they believed would change lives.

Even during the rare moments when that fact didn't terrify him, Chase could hear the quiet anxious voice of his wife, Kelly, splashing him with a cold bucket of reality. "Only two million dollars, Chase? Seriously?" She had brought it up again on the way to the airport. Her knuckles stayed white as she gripped the steering wheel. "What if you run out of money before you finish the film?"

"We won't." Chase had steeled his eyes straight ahead. "Keith and I know the budget."

"What if it doesn't go like you planned?" Her body was tense, her eyes fearful. She gave him quick, nervous glances. "If something happens, we'll spend the rest of our lives paying that off."

She was right, but he didn't want to say so. Not when it was too late to turn back. The actors were arriving on set in two days, and the entire film crew would be in Bloomington by tomorrow. Plans were in motion, and already bills needed to be paid. They had no choice but to move ahead and stick to their budget, trusting God that they could make this film for two million dollars, and illustrate a message of faith better and stronger than anything the industry had ever seen.

Failure wasn't an option.

They reached the airport, but before she dropped Chase off, Kelly turned to him, lines creasing the space between her eyebrows. She was only thirty-one, but lately she looked older. Maybe because she only seemed to smile when she was playing with their two little girls, Macy and Molly. Worry weighted her tone. "Four weeks?"

"Hopefully sooner." He refused to be anything but optimistic.

"You'll call?"

"Of course. Every day." Chase studied her, and the familiar love was there. But her anxiety was something he didn't recognize. The faith she'd shown back when they lived in Indonesia, that's what he needed from her now. "Relax, baby. Please."

"Okay." She let out a sigh and another one seemed right behind it. "Why am I so afraid?"

His heart went out to her. "Kelly ..." His words were softer than before, his tone desperate to convince her. "Believe in me ... believe in this movie. You don't know how much I need that."

"I'm trying." She looked down and it took awhile before she raised her eyes to his again. "It was easier in Indonesia. At least in the jungle the mission was simple."

"Simple?" He chuckled, but the sound lacked any real humor. "Indonesia was never easy. Any of us could've been arrested or killed. We could've caught malaria or a dozen different diseases. Every day held that kind of risk."

The lines on her face eased a little and a smile tugged at her lips. She touched her finger to his face. "At least we had each other." She looked deep into his eyes, to the places that belonged to only the two of them and she kissed him. "Come on, Chase ... you've gotta see why I'm worried. It's not just the money."

He caught a quick look at his watch. "You're afraid we won't finish on time and that'll put us over budget and—"

"No." She didn't raise her voice, but the fear in her eyes cut him short. "Don't you see?" Shame filled in the spaces between her words. "You're young and handsome and talented ..." Her smile was sad now. "You'll be working with beautiful actresses and movie professionals and ... I don't know, the whole thing scares me."

She didn't come out and admit her deeper feelings, those she'd shared with him a week before the trip. The fact that she didn't feel she could measure up to the Hollywood crowd. Chase ached for her, frustrated by her lack of confidence. "This isn't about the movie industry. It's about a bigger mission field than we ever had in Indonesia." He wove his fingers into her thick dark hair, drew her close, and kissed her once more. "Trust me, baby. Please."

This time she didn't refute him, but the worry in her eyes remained as he grabbed his bags and stepped away from the car. He texted her once he got through security, telling her again that he loved her and that she had nothing to worry about. But she didn't answer and now, no matter how badly he needed to sleep, he couldn't shake the look on her face or the tone of her voice. What if her fears were some sort of premonition about the movie? Maybe God was using her to tell Keith and him to pull out now—before they lost everything.

Once on the plane, he tightened his seatbelt and stared out the window. But then, Keith's wife was completely on board with their plans. Her father was one of the investors, after all. Besides that, Keith's daughter, Andi, was a freshman at Indiana University, so the shoot would give Keith a window to Andi's world—something he was grateful for. Andi wanted to be an actress, and apparently her roommate was a theater major. Both college girls would be extras in the film, so Keith's entire family could hardly wait to get started.

Chase bit the inside of his lip. From the beginning, all the worries about the movie came from him and Kelly, but now that he was on his way to Indiana, Chase had to focus not on his fears, but on the film.

He ignored the knots in his stomach as he leaned against the cold hard plastic that framed the airplane window. The movie they were making was called *The Last Letter*, the story of a college kid whose life is interrupted when his father suffers a sudden fatal heart attack. The kid isn't sure how to move on until his mother reveals to him a letter—one last letter from his father. That letter takes Braden on a quest of discovery in faith and family, and finally into a brilliant future Braden had known nothing about.

The story was a parable, an illustration of the verse in Jeremiah 29:11: "'For I know the plans I have for you,' declares the Lord, 'plans to prosper you and not to harm you, plans to give you hope and a future.'" The verse would be their mantra every day of the filming, Chase had no doubt.

He closed his eyes, and in a rush he could hear the music welling in his chest, feel the emotion as it filled a theater full of moviegoers. He could see the images as they danced across the big screen, and he could imagine all of it playing out beyond his wildest expectations.

But the way from here to there could easily be a million miles of rocky back roads and potholes.

They were still at the gate, still waiting for the plane to head out toward the runway. Chase blinked and stared out the window, beyond the airport to the blue sky. Every day this week had been blue, not a cloud in sight, something Chase and Keith both found fitting. Because no matter what Kelly feared, no matter what pressures came with this decision, here was the moment Chase and Keith had dreamed of and planned for, the culmination of a lifetime of believing that God wanted them to take part in saving the world—not on a mission field in Indonesia, but in packed movie houses across America. Oak River Films, they called themselves. The name came from their love of the first Psalm. Chase had long since memorized the first three verses:

> *Blessed is the man who does not walk in the counsel of the wicked or stand in the way of sinners or sit in the seat of mockers. But his delight is in the law of the Lord, and on his law he meditates day and night. He is like a tree planted by streams of water, which yields its fruit in season and whose leaf does not wither. Whatever he does prospers.*

Oak River Films. That everything he and Keith did would be rooted in a delight for the Lord, and a belief that if they planted their projects near the living water of Christ, they would flourish for Him. Chase shifted in his seat. He silently repeated the Scripture again. Why was he worried about what lay ahead? He believed God was sending them to make this movie, right? He pressed his body into the thinly padded seat. *Breathe. Settle down and breathe.*

In every way that mattered, this film would make or break them in the world of Hollywood movie production. Easy enough, he had told himself when they first began this venture. But as the trip to Bloomington, Indiana, neared, the pressure built. They received phone calls from well-meaning investors asking how the casting was going or confirming when the shoot date was. They weren't antsy or doubtful that Chase and Keith could bring a return for their investment, but they were curious.

The same way everyone surrounding the film was curious.

Keith handled these phone calls. He was the calmer of the two, the one whose faith knew no limits. It had been Keith's decision that they would make the film with money from investors rather than selling out too quickly to a studio. Producers who paid for their projects retained complete creative control—and the message of this first film was one Chase and Keith wouldn't let anyone change. No matter how much easy studio money might hang in the balance.

Moments like this Chase worried about all of it. His wife and little girls back home, and whether the production team could stick to the aggressive film schedule they'd set. Chase massaged his thumb into his brow. The concerns made up a long list. He had to manage a cast of egos that included an academy award winner and two household names—both of whom had reputations for being talented but difficult. He had to keep everyone working well together and stick to his four-week schedule—all while staying on budget. He worried about running out of money or running out of time, and whether this was really where God wanted them—working in a world as crazy as Hollywood.

Chase took a long breath and exhaled slowly. The white-haired woman next to him was reading a magazine, but she glanced his way now and then, probably looking for a conversation. Chase wasn't interested. He looked out the window again and a picture filled his mind, the picture of an apartment building surrounded by police tape. The image was from his high school days in the San Fernando Valley, when a major earthquake hit Southern California. The damage was considerable, but the Northridge Meadows apartment symbolized the worst of it. In a matter of seconds, the three-story apartment building collapsed and became one—the weight of the top two floors too great for the shaken foundation.

A shudder ran its way through Chase.

That could be them in a few months if the filming didn't go well, if the foundation of their budget didn't hold the weight of all that was happening on top of it. Chase could already feel the weight pressing in along his shoulders.

"Excuse me." The woman beside him tapped his arm. "Does your seatback have a copy of the *SkyMall* magazine? Mine's missing."

Chase checked and found what the woman wanted. He smiled as he handed it to her. "Helps pass the time."

"Yes." She had kind blue eyes. "Especially during takeoff. I can usually find something for my precious little Max. He's a cockapoo. Cute as a button."

"I'm sure." Chase nodded and looked out the window once more. Pressure came with the job, he'd known that from the beginning. He and Keith were producers; with that came a certain sense of thrill and awe, terror and anxiety, because for every dollar they'd raised toward this movie, for every chance an investor took on their film, there was a coinciding possibility that something could go wrong.

"You ever wonder," Chase had asked Keith a few days ago over a Subway sandwich, "whether we should've just stayed in Indonesia?"

Keith only smiled that slow smile, the one that morphed across his face when his confidence came from someplace otherworldly. "This is where we're supposed to be." He took a bite of his sandwich and waited until he'd swallowed. He looked deep into Chase's eyes. "I feel it in the center of my bones."

Truth and integrity. That's what Keith worried about. The truth of the message when the film was finally wrapped and they brought it to the public, and integrity with the cast and crew, the investors and the studios. For Keith, every day was a test because God was watching.

Chase agreed, but the pressure he felt didn't come from being under the watchful eye of the Lord. That mattered a great deal, but God would accept them whether they returned home having completed their movie mission or not. Rather Chase worried because the whole world was watching to see what sort of movie the two of them could make on such a limited budget. And if they failed, the world would know that too.

Unlocked

A Love Story

Karen Kingsbury, New York Times *Bestselling Author*

Holden Harris, 18, is locked in a prison of autism where he's been since he was a happy, boisterous three-year-old. At school he is bullied by kids who do not understand that despite his quiet ways and quirky behaviors, Holden is very happy and socially normal on the inside, where he lives in a private world all his own.

Then one day the head cheerleader and star of the high school drama production is rehearsing when Holden stops and listens, clearly drawn to the music. Ella Reynolds notices and takes an interest in him, learning about autism and eventually helping Holden win a spot in the school play.

At the same time Ella makes a dramatic discovery. Long ago, her parents and Holden's parents were good friends, and she and Holden played together until his diagnosis of autism, at which time Ella's mother distanced herself from the friendship.

Not until a tragedy takes place at the high school does Ella take a public stand against the way the more popular privileged kids treat those who are different. At the same time, Ella continues to be a friend to Holden and in time their mothers realize that something special is happening. Hurts from the past are dealt with and all around Holden miracles begin to happen in various relationships. The greatest miracle is the change in Holden, himself, and everyone is stunned by the transformation they witness. Ultimately, the community comes to understand that many people walk around in a personal prison and that only by love and faith can the doors become unlocked, the way they dramatically do for Holden Harris.

Available in stores and online!

Shades of Blue

Karen Kingsbury, New York Times *Bestselling Author*

A fairytale future. A Checkered past. A decision awaits.

Brad Cutler, twenty-eight, is a rising star at his New York ad agency, about to marry the girl of his dreams. Anyone would agree he has it all—a great career, a beautiful and loving fiancée, and a fairy tale life ahead of him ... when memories of a high school girlfriend begin to torment him. Lost innocence and one very difficult choice flood his conscience, and he is no longer sure what the future will bring except for this: He must go back to the shores of Holden Beach in search of his first love, and a forgiveness neither of them has ever known.

Three people must work through the repercussions of a decision made long ago before any of them can look toward a new future.

Available in stores and online!

Oceans Apart

Karen Kingsbury,
New York Times *Bestselling Author*

A riveting story of secret sin and the healing power of forgiveness.

Airline pilot Connor Evans and his wife, Michele, seem to be the perfect couple living what looks like a perfect life. Then a plane goes down in the Pacific Ocean. One of the casualties is Kiahna Siefert, a flight attendant Connor knew well. Too well. Kiahna's will is very clear: before her seven-year-old son, Max, can be turned over to the state, he must spend the summer with the father he's never met, the father who doesn't know he exists: Connor Evans.

Now will the presence of one lonely child and the truth he represents destroy Connor's family? Or is it possible that healing and hope might come in the shape of a seven-year-old boy?

Let's Go on a Mommy Date

Karen Kingsbury, New York Times *Bestselling Author*

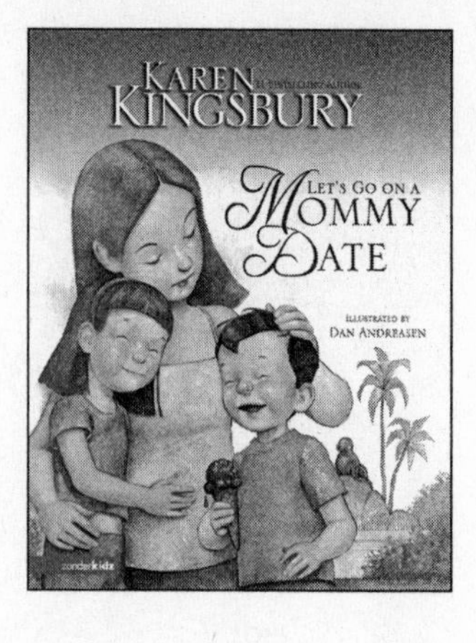

So, what is a mommy date?

This playful, rhyming story describes some of the best – the zoo, circus, park, animal farm, or movie theatre. But in the end, spending time together is what a mommy date is all about—whether it's a fun outing or simply snuggling down to read about such adventures together!

Available in stores and online!

Let's Have a Daddy Day

Karen Kingsbury, New York Times *Bestselling Author*

"When you're all grown up and you look back on this day, you'll know how much I loved you 'cause we took the time to play."

A Daddy day? Why not! What better way for a child to enjoy being with Daddy—and Dad to enjoy being with his little one?

These heartwarming rhymes by bestselling author Karen Kingsbury offer great ideas for children to have simple, fun times with Daddy, and to come up with ideas of their own. Geared for kids and dads alike, this endearingly illustrated book will become a cherished addition to the family library.

Available in stores and online!

Share Your Thoughts

With the Author: Your comments will be forwarded to the author when you send them to *zauthor@zondervan.com*.

With Zondervan: Submit your review of this book by writing to *zreview@zondervan.com*.

Free Online Resources at www.zondervan.com

Zondervan AuthorTracker: Be notified whenever your favorite authors publish new books, go on tour, or post an update about what's happening in their lives at www.zondervan.com/authortracker.

Daily Bible Verses and Devotions: Enrich your life with daily Bible verses or devotions that help you start every morning focused on God. Visit www.zondervan.com/newsletters.

Free Email Publications: Sign up for newsletters on Christian living, academic resources, church ministry, fiction, children's resources, and more. Visit www.zondervan.com/newsletters.

Zondervan Bible Search: Find and compare Bible passages in a variety of translations at www.zondervanbiblesearch.com.

Other Benefits: Register yourself to receive online benefits like coupons and special offers, or to participate in research.